A GENERATION OF LEAVES

A GENERATION OF LEAVES

A NOVEL BY

Robert S. Bloom

BALLANTINE BOOKS · New York

Library of Congress Cataloging-in-Publication Data
Bloom, Robert S.
A generation of leaves / Robert S. Bloom.
p.   cm.
ISBN 0-345-36957-2
1. Morris, Gouverneur, 1752–1816—Fiction.   2. United States—
History—1783–1815—Fiction.   I. Title.
PS3552.L6395G46   1991
813'.54—dc20   90-93533
                                                        CIP

Design by Holly Johnson
Handlettering by Anita Karl

Manufactured in the United States of America

First Edition: July 1991

10 9 8 7 6 5 4 3 2 1

For my father and mother
Abraham and Isabelle Bloom

As is a generation of leaves,

so is that of humanity.

The wind scatters the leaves

upon the ground, but the live forest

burgeons with leaves again

in the season of spring returning.

So of men one generation grows

while another dies.

HOMER
THE ILIAD

CONTENTS

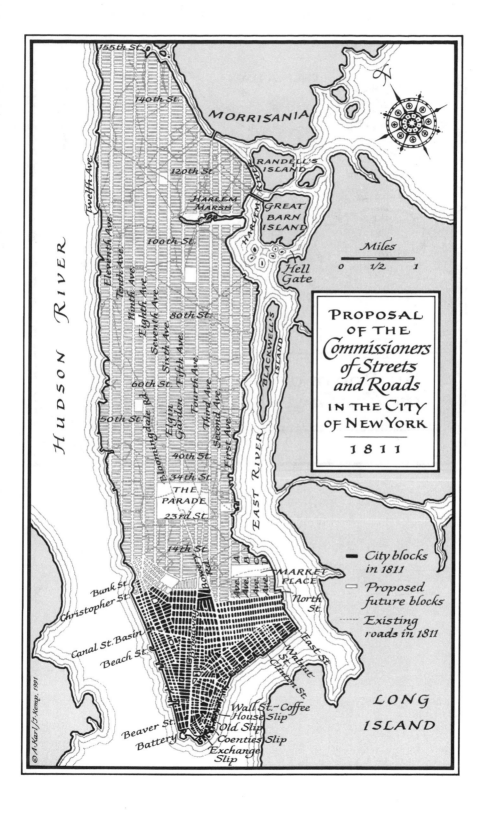

155th St.

140th St.

MORRISANIA

120th St.

RANDELL'S ISLAND

HARLEM MARSH

GREAT BARN ISLAND

100th St.

Twelfth Ave.

Eleventh Ave.

Tenth Ave.

Ninth Ave.

Eighth Ave.

Seventh Ave.

Sixth Ave.

80th St.

Fifth Ave.

Fourth Ave.

Third Ave.

Second Ave.

First Ave.

60th St.

Bloomingdale Rd.

Elgin Garden

50th St.

HUDSON RIVER

HARLEM RIVER

Hell Gate

BLACKWELL'S ISLAND

EAST RIVER

Miles

0   1/2   1

PROPOSAL
OF THE
*Commissioners
of Streets
and Roads*
IN THE CITY
OF NEW YORK

1811

40th St.

34th St.
THE PARADE

23rd St.

14th St.

Bunk St.

Christopher St.

Bowery Rd.

MARKET PLACE

North St.

Canal St. Basin

Beach St.

Broadway

East St.

Walnut St.

Clinton St.

City blocks
in 1811

Proposed
future blocks

Existing
roads in 1811

LONG

ISLAND

Wall St. – Coffee
House Slip

Old Slip

Coenties Slip

Beaver St.

Battery

Exchange
Slip

© A. Karl / J. Kemp. 1991

CANADA

Lake Ontario

N E W

Y O R K

Lockport Rochester Utica Little
Falls

Syracuse

Schenectady

*Lake
Erie* Buffalo Albany

THE ROUTE OF
the Erie Canal

Miles

0 75

©A·Karl/J·Kemp, 1991

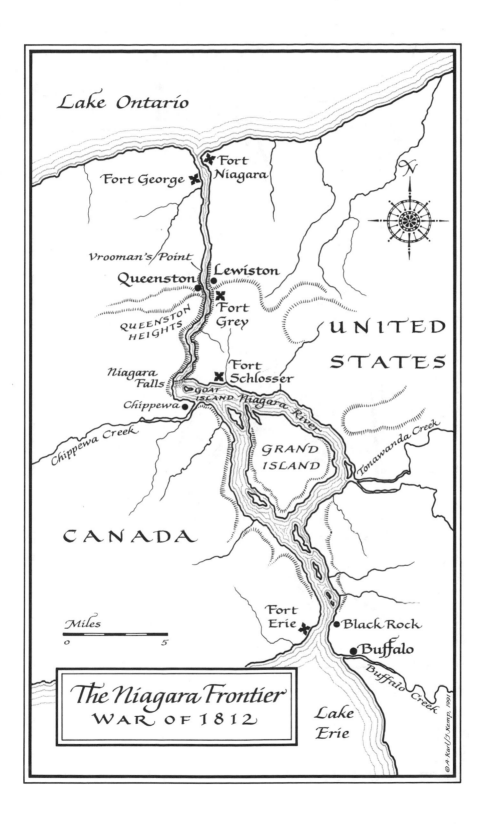

Lake Ontario

Fort George ✗   ✗ Fort Niagara

Vrooman's Point

Queenston • • Lewiston

✗ Fort Grey

QUEENSTON HEIGHTS

UNITED STATES

Niagara Falls

✗ Fort Schlosser

GOAT ISLAND   Niagara River

Chippewa •

Chippewa Creek

GRAND ISLAND

Tonawanda Creek

CANADA

Miles
0   5

Fort Erie ✗   • Black Rock
• Buffalo

Buffalo Creek

Lake Erie

© A. Karl / J. Kemp, 1981

The Niagara Frontier
WAR OF 1812

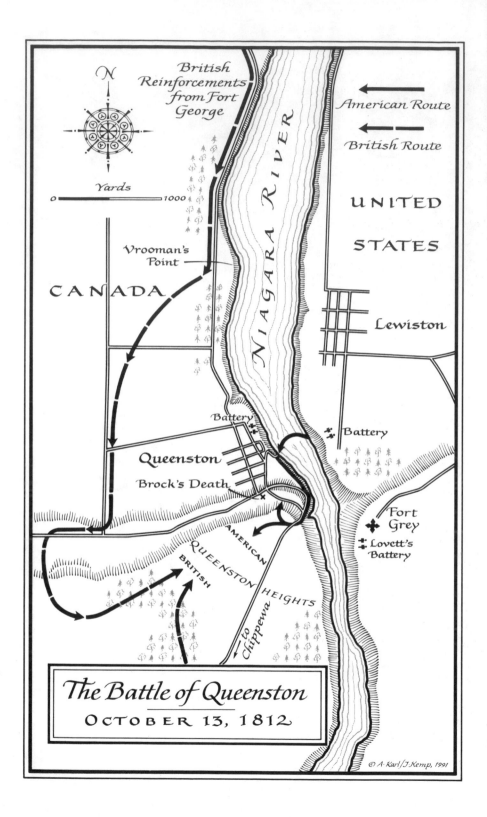

The Battle of Queenston
OCTOBER 13, 1812

© A. Karl/J. Kemp, 1991

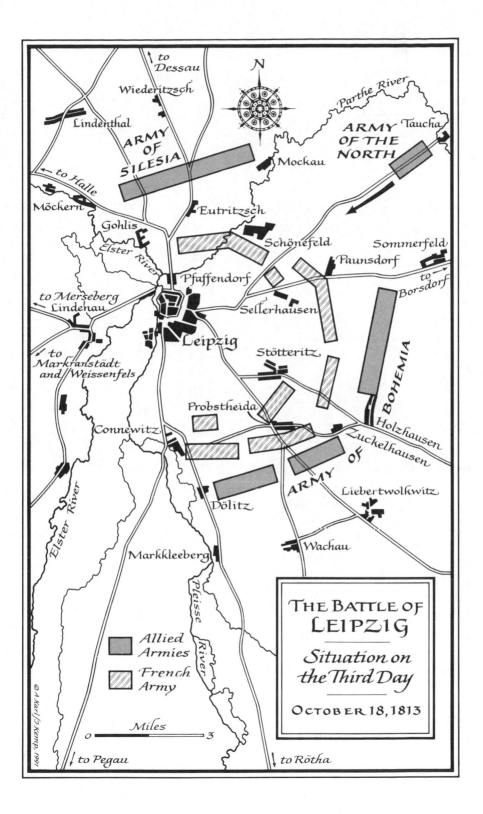

N

to Dessau

Wiederitzsch

Lindenthal

ARMY OF SILESIA

Mockau

ARMY OF THE NORTH

Taucha

Parthe River

to Halle

Möckern

Gohlis

Eutritzsch

Schönefeld

Sommerfeld

Elster River

Pfaffendorf

Paunsdorf

to Borsdorf

to Merseberg
Lindenau

Sellerhausen

Leipzig

Stötteritz

BOHEMIA

to Markranstädt
and Weissenfels

Probstheida

Holzhausen

Connewitz

Zuckelhausen

ARMY OF

Liebertwolkwitz

Dölitz

Elster River

Markkleeberg

Wachau

Pleisse River

Allied Armies

French Army

© A. Karl/J. Kemp, 1991

Miles

0   3

to Pegau

to Rötha

**THE BATTLE OF
LEIPZIG**

*Situation on
the Third Day*

OCTOBER 18, 1813

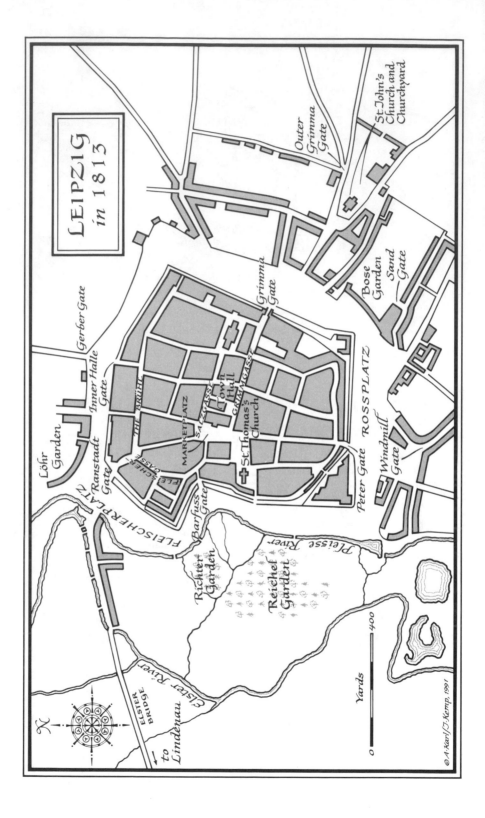

LEIPZIG
in 1813

St John's
Church and
Churchyard

Outer
Grimma
Gate

Bose
Garden
Sand
Gate

Gerber Gate

Grimma
Gate

Inner Halle
Gate

ROSSPLATZ

Löhr
Garden

THE BRÜHL

MARKETPLATZ

SALZGASSE

Town
Hall

GRIMMGASSE

St Thomas's
Church

Peter Gate

Windmill
Gate

Ranstadt
Gate

FLEISCHER
GASSE

Barfuss
Gate

FLEISCHERPLATZ

Richter
Garden

Pleisse River

Reichel
Garden

Yards

0   400

ELSTER
BRIDGE

Elster River

to
Lindenau

N

© A. Karl/J. Kemp, 1991

N

Mount
Vernon

MARYLAND

DEL.

Fredericksburg

Potomac River

VIRGINIA

Rappahannock River

Little
Guinea
Creek
Glenlyvar   Tuckahoe
Horsdumonde   Richmond
Big Guinea
Creek
Green Creek
Bizarre   Williamsburg
Flat Creek
Appomattox
River   Petersburg

York River

Yorktown

James River

Norfolk

Miles
0   50

■ Estates

THE
Bizarre Plantation
AND VIRGINIA

NORTH
CAROLINA

© A. Karl / J. Kemp, 1991

Partial Genealogical Chart

*(The names of prominent persons
in the novel are underscored)*

William Randolph
of
Turkey Island
m
Mary Isham
of
Bermuda Hundred

William II	Thomas	Isham
of	of	of
Chatsworth	Tuckahoe	Dungeness
	m	*m*
	Judith Fleming	Jane Rogers

Mary Randolph	William Randolph	see
m	*m*	DUNGENESS
James Keith	Maria Page	*(page xxii)*
Mary Randolph Keith	Thomas Mann	
m	Randolph, Sr.	
Thomas Marshall	(1741-1793)	
	m	
John Marshall	┌─ 1. Ann Cary	
(1775-1835)	of Ampthill	
Chief Justice	(d. 1789)	
of United States	2. Gabriella Harvie	

see
TUCKAHOE
(page xx)

```
          │              │              │               │
     Richard        Sir John        Edward          Elizabeth
        of              of             of                m
     Curles        Tazewell Hall     Bremo        Richard Bland
        m                                               │
   Jane Bolling                                Theodorick Bland, Sr.
        │                                               m
       see                                      Frances Bolling
     CURLES                                             │
   (page xxiii)                                  Frances Bland
                                                 (1752-1788)
                                                       m
                                              1. John Randolph
                                                 of Matoax
                                                 (1742-1775)
                                                     see
                                                   CURLES
                                                 (page xxiii)
                                              2. St. George Tucker
                                                 (1752-1827)
                                                       │
                                              ┌────────┴────────┐
                                           Henry          Nathaniel
                                        St. George         Beverley
                                           Tucker           Tucker
                                        (1780-1848)       (1784-1851)
```

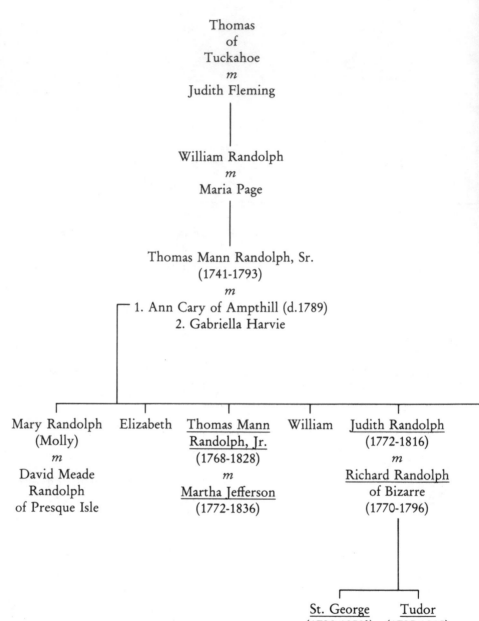

Thomas
of
Tuckahoe
m
Judith Fleming

William Randolph
m
Maria Page

Thomas Mann Randolph, Sr.
(1741-1793)
m
1. Ann Cary of Ampthill (d.1789)
2. Gabriella Harvie

| Mary Randolph (Molly) *m* David Meade Randolph of Presque Isle | Elizabeth | Thomas Mann Randolph, Jr. (1768-1828) *m* Martha Jefferson (1772-1836) | William | Judith Randolph (1772-1816) *m* Richard Randolph of Bizarre (1770-1796) |

St. George   Tudor
(1792-1859?) (1795-1815)

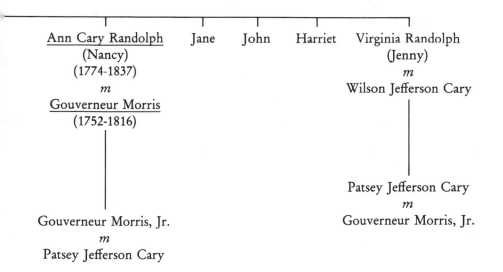

Ann Cary Randolph   Jane   John   Harriet   Virginia Randolph
(Nancy)   (Jenny)
(1774-1837)   *m*
m   Wilson Jefferson Cary
Gouverneur Morris
(1752-1816)

Gouverneur Morris, Jr.   Patsey Jefferson Cary
m   *m*
Patsey Jefferson Cary   Gouverneur Morris, Jr.

DUNGENESS

Isham
of
Dungeness
m
Jane Rogers

|

Jane Randolph
m
Peter Jefferson

|

Thomas Jefferson
(1743-1826)
President of
United States
m
Martha Wayles Skelton

|

<u>Martha Jefferson</u>
(1772-1836)
m
<u>Thomas Mann
Randolph, Jr.</u>
of Tuckahoe
(1768-1828)

CURLES

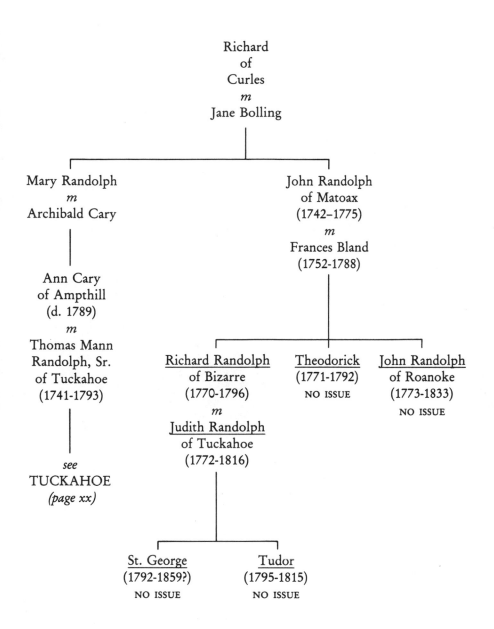

Richard
of
Curles
m
Jane Bolling

Mary Randolph
m
Archibald Cary

John Randolph
of Matoax
(1742–1775)
m
Frances Bland
(1752-1788)

Ann Cary
of Ampthill
(d. 1789)
m
Thomas Mann
Randolph, Sr.
of Tuckahoe
(1741-1793)

see
TUCKAHOE
(page xx)

Richard Randolph
of Bizarre
(1770-1796)
m
Judith Randolph
of Tuckahoe
(1772-1816)

Theodorick
(1771-1792)
NO ISSUE

John Randolph
of Roanoke
(1773-1833)
NO ISSUE

St. George
(1792-1859?)
NO ISSUE

Tudor
(1795-1815)
NO ISSUE

PART I

BETWEEN PAST AND FUTURE

✍

In the middle of the journey of our life

I found myself in a dark wood

where the direct way was lost.

DANTE

THE DIVINE COMEDY

ONE

Each time, the faces are different but the group itself looks familiar. They are all strangers. Why should I crave their affection and respect? Nevertheless, I want them to notice me, to acknowledge my existence in some manner, no matter how slight. Invariably, they look right through me as they walk past on the way to engagements of some importance to themselves. Not a single person in the teeming streets is known to me. My contemporaries sweep by, hundreds of mortals lost in personal reveries. Some slouch in a forlorn manner, immersed in the secret sufferings of their lives; others stride by purposefully, eagerly proceeding with the business of the moment. Speaking and silent, arms akimbo or relaxed, in company or alone, they walk toward and away from me. A crying child holding his mother's hand, two lovers caressing, a poor bedraggled Negro with the look of a runaway slave. A soldier with militant strut, dressed in the uniform of a dragoon, follows a preening young woman. He swiftly passes a wretched old man whose skull has begun to thrust its way into the features of his face. The grim face always evokes the same thought. In a short time, all of these mortals will cease to exist; but the same streets will be crowded by other humans blissfully unaware of those who trod before them.

The curved lanes and alleys of lower Manhattan abruptly give way to straight avenues crossed at right angles by streets in a relentless network of rectangular blocks, an endless chessboard. The city no longer looks familiar. Suddenly the faces are gone; the perpendicular and parallel roadways are deserted. Surprised by the emptiness stretching before me, I turn to look back at the passing multitudes. They have vanished, a tribe of ephemeral phantoms. I yearn to return to the comforting waters of the Battery, but my uneasy steps carry me away from the ocean.

The buildings are gone, but the chessboard continues. At each intersection I pause and choose whether to turn left or right or proceed straight ahead. Each time, the decision is to make no turns. A rural landscape looms ahead. Where one would expect to find horses and cows, there is nothing but pastureland. In the distance I espy a solitary structure of impressive proportions. It is fronted by an estate of enormous area dotted with carefully trimmed shrubs and trees. Crossing the estate on a pitilessly straight road whose parallel lines thrust out to the horizon, I strain to identify the outlines and details of the looming structure. It reminds me of drawings of the great first Duke of Marlborough's Blenheim Palace.

The road leads directly to the forbidding front stairs. Walking up the steps, I pass through massive pillars until the magnificent gilded front doors appear to obstruct my way. They are unlocked and swing open upon the application of slight pressure from my outstretched arms. Another impressive staircase stands before me. Mounting the marble steps slowly, I am surprised to find that I am unafraid, even curious. An exquisite tapestry of a young man being dragged away from a voluptuous temptress dominates the middle of a large vestibule. This entrance hall appears to be the midpoint of a corridor running from one end of the palace to the other. With only a moment of hesitation, I select the corridor on the left-hand side for the commencement of my explorations.

The corridor is so long that it appears to have no end. An infinity of doors extends along each side. Pausing for a moment at the first door, I slowly open it to ascertain that which lurks behind. The room is filled with aristocratic portraits and lavishly ornamental furniture, not at all to my plebeian taste. I quickly become bored with the repetitive procession of extravagant chambers, drawing rooms, and salons. The pounding of my heart begins to throb in my head as it becomes clear that the rooms farther away from my starting point have not been inhabited for many years. They are increasingly latticed with cobwebs. The corridor is a dark abyss of time. There are no more intersections; it is too late to turn back. The remaining doors are locked. I know that I must move forward to the end of the corridor. The journey seems to be without purpose other than to reach that end. Perhaps I am searching for the evanescent and ungraspable phantom of the past. Or is it my own future that awaits me?

When finally faced with an unusual white door at the end of the corridor, I am aware of having lost all sense of the passage of time. Behind the door is a hideously cluttered room. In order to determine its shape, I have to fight my way through one vast lacework of cobwebs after another. The room is shrouded in somber drapes extended in heavy dusty folds to the cold marble floor. Only the fading sunlight creeping through the one uncovered window in the room prevents it from being enveloped in darkness. When a small closet door in a corner of the room reveals itself, I attempt to open it. The door is locked; but it must be opened. Among the musty clutter, I perceive an old-style broadsword beside the dust-covered breastplate of a cuirassier. Manipulating the sword in a manner contrary to its customary usage, I pry open the door. The darkness is almost impenetrable until my squinting eyes become accustomed to it. With the exception of another layer of gossamer webs, the closet appears, at first glance, to be empty. But on a shelf at the top there sits a small casket. With a slight pull, it slides off the shelf. Its weight forces me to drop it to the floor. In order to be able to see the contents, I drag it out of the closet to the gray light of the solitary window and fall to my knees to open it.

There is nothing inside except the dust-covered coils of an old rope. As I reach my hand into the casket to grasp the rope, it begins to move languidly.

The fangs are visible for only an instant before they sink into the palm of my left hand. The indifferent reptilian eyes of the creature stare lifelessly up at me. Aware of my helplessness, I note with resignation the progress of the cold coursing through my veins.

The first night that dream invaded the citadel of my slumber, I awoke screaming. The sweat-drenched palm of my left hand retained the pain of the apparition's twin punctures. For an instant my insubstantial dream castle in the sand refused to be inundated by the inrushing tide of reality. Then it collapsed. With the passage of time the dream has lost its power to prolong the moment of waking. Now I rarely experience sweat and fear. In their place is merely a sense of fatigue accompanying the loss of a night of undisturbed rest. Although in recent years its visitation has become increasingly rare, the dream has distracted me for nearly two decades. Nancy Randolph has never appeared in the phantasmagoria, but I have always linked it to her person. It is as if she had become part of my blood after our initial encounter, when I first dreamed the dream that same night.

Now I am alone, the only living member of my family. The bedroom is cluttered with piles of unread books. The newly-purchased volumes arrive at a rate faster than my poor ability to peruse them. Walter Scott's new history sits threateningly on the table next to my bed. Slips of paper protrude haphazardly from the tops and sides of the older books. Many notes, carelessly scrawled on available copy paper, lie on the floor. Those not of a recent vintage are covered with a thin coating of dust and occasionally are crowned by an abandoned quill pen. A sea of paper has washed up to the edge of my bed. The incoming tide of my vain ambition has submerged my shoes.

For the purposes of this story I shall call myself Daniel Carey. Perhaps out of fear that my great chronicle of the Age of Revolution cannot be completed, I have written this more modest personal history. Because it contains confidential information involving a violation of trust on the part of the author, I have endeavored to assure that it will never be read by any of my contemporaries. They, no doubt, would judge it indecorous and outside the realm of a proper history. Avoidance of personal embarrassment has, I confess, also played a part in my decision to postpone publication. It is my hope that future readers will forgive the author his trespasses and tolerate the inclusion of matters of a private nature. Let posterity be my judge.

That I have spent so many years working on a historical subject as massive as the Age of Revolution is due in no small measure to the influence of my father. With great pride, he informed me at an early age that my birth occurred in the same month and year in which was published the first quarto volume of Edward Gibbon's *The History of the Decline and Fall of the Roman Empire*. Many another father of a child born in that same momentous year must have recited to his offspring the tale of an entrance made into this world concurrent with the Declaration of Independence and the invasion of New York. Yet, to my father, a printer by trade, the chronicler of a great event was often of more interest than the event itself, even one in which he had participated. For it was the American Revolution which took my father away from the bosom of his family for seven long years. In August of 1776 he participated in the Battle of Long Island under the command of Israel Putnam and was among the lucky survivors evacuated to Manhattan Island under the cover of darkness. He fought under General Washington's command at Harlem Heights and retreated with the Continental Army from Manhattan. My mother was left behind in New York City to care for me and my older sister for the entire period of British occupation.

Unfortunately for my future historical endeavors, my infant's mind retained no memories of the first terrible years of British subjugation. Only four days after General Howe's entry into New York City, the great fire destroyed a large part of the western side of the city. Two years later another fire devastated the block south of Pearl Street between Coenties and Old slips. Our house stood within sight of the ravaged block which remained in ruins for the entire dreary period and served as the playing field of my childhood. Because in those years the commerce of the port was almost in total ruin and work was scarce, my mother was forced by necessity to take employment as a servant in a Tory household. My sister and I would stay with my maternal grandmother until my mother came home each evening.

During an earlier conflict, the French and Indian War, my grandparents and my mother, then an infant, were removed by the British with thousands of other French-speaking Acadians from the district of Annapolis in Nova Scotia. Like many others, their house and barn were burned to the ground by British soldiers. Along with numerous Acadian families, they were mercilessly crammed into ships and scattered throughout the colonies. My mother's family was transported to eastern Long Island. My grandmother would regale us with stories of the brutality of the British toward innocent people whose only crime was the suspicion of loyalty to France. Although as a young boy I needed no incentive to throw rocks at the hated redcoats, these stories removed all doubt about the justice of my uncivil activities. When New York was finally evacuated by the British in November of 1783, I was among the young revolutionaries hurling missiles from a safe location at the rearguard columns of troops marching in step to a mournful drum beat to their ships of embarkation at the Battery.

Within weeks my father returned, rebuilt his printing business in the period of great prosperity following the war, and quickly usurped my affections with tales of the ever alluring past. My favorites concerned his experience in the late war, from his departure to his return. Holding me in his arms for the last time before joining the army, he had gazed with awe, like other citizens of New York City, at a sight never before seen in America. New York Harbor had been filled with hundreds of invading ships blackening the sky with forests of masts and rigging. Over thirty thousand trained and fully-armed professional soldiers accompanied the armada, the greatest expeditionary force Great Britain had ever dispatched from its shores. Panic gripped the half of New York's people loyal to the rebellion. Many of them, like my father, found Israel Putnam's troops on Long Island. After the retreat from Manhattan, my father had participated in the battles at White Plains, and Brandywine, where he was wounded for the first time. The next year, 1778, he was bayoneted in the left leg at the Battle of Monmouth, and spent the remainder of the war on garrison duty at various locations. How the stories of his adventures filled my youthful imagination. The names of the battles took on a strange aura that reverberated through my mind like a Kyrie Eleison.

Unlike my mother, who was a devout Catholic, my father had abandoned the Church at an early age and had become an unbeliever. By the time I was twelve years old, he had impressed upon my mind the doctrine that religion was useless superstition and an enemy to reason; Catholicism was not only hocus-pocus, but was also dangerous to the believer. For, it was as hazardous to be a papist in the new world as it was in the old. Numerous times he related the stories of ancient family members who thought it was safe to go to mass after the restoration of Charles II. But two of those family members were murdered in the wave of terror against Catholics following the revelations of Titus Oates concerning the so-called "popish plot." Shortly thereafter our family fled England forever and settled in New York City, which not long before had been New Amsterdam. Six generations must have carefully related the saga of the family victims of the perjuries of Titus Oates. By the time the story was conveyed to me, there was little danger of my being beaten on the way to mass. For, aware of my father's distaste for religious services, I always insisted on staying home with him rather than accompanying my mother to church.

My father proceeded to raise me in the religion of reason. Voltaire, Rousseau, Diderot, D'Alembert, and Tom Paine were my high priests. Liberty and equality sufficed as my liturgy. I too cried out, *"Écrasez l'Infâme!"* His print shop was filled with books. As soon as I finished one, I would receive another from his ink-stained hands. He had me read them in a chronological order from Homer to Swift. The primary enthusiasm of my existence became a quest for knowledge; and it was history, in particular, that captured my attention. Herodotus, Thucydides, Polybius, Livy, and Tacitus were my early gods. They were soon supplanted by modern historians. During a period of prolonged illness which permanently disfigured my face with the sign of the pox, I devoured William Robertson's *History of Scotland* and *History of the Reign of the Emperor Charles V*, David Hume's *History of England*, and Voltaire's *Age of Louis XIV*. The Voltaire I read, with many other works, out of my father's cherished thirty-seven-volume English translation of the complete works of that splendid Frenchman.

After the period of my convalescence I found it more convenient to remain in my world of books inside the house than to venture outside and suffer the cruel taunts and rebuffs of my adolescent contemporaries. My reading continued with Gibbon's *Decline and Fall of the Roman Empire*, the distant mountain it had been my destiny to climb from the month of my birth. That it had taken the first eleven years of my life for its author to complete the work endowed it with a personal significance possessed by no other book. Its brilliance exceeded even my great expectations. His attacks on religion confirmed the teachings of my father. With unequaled learning, he described the role of Christianity in "the triumph of barbarism and religion" over Roman order and reason. He demonstrated that the Christians for centuries had inflicted far greater bloodshed on each other in the course of religious disputes than they experienced from the zeal of infidels. He and Voltaire agreed that the Church had defended by violence the empire she had acquired by fraud. They exposed superstition and rejected supernatural explanations of human events. These were views with which I had inarticulately and timidly trifled. With such strong allies at my side, I openly and belligerently adopted them as my own. But more important than any particular beliefs, Gibbon's work had planted in my mind the fatal seed of ambition to write a history of great scope and significance.

That Gibbon and Voltaire described history as "little more than the register of the crimes, follies and misfortunes of mankind" merely increased my desire to learn the causes and results of centuries of these misdeeds. My *Universal History* of 1779 stated that the world was created in 4004 B.C. in six days and that man first appeared at that time in the Garden of Eden upon the Euphrates. Gibbon certainly would have laughed at such nonsensical history, based on a literal interpretation of a religious tract. It was not a rational calculation of the age of the world, but the only one available. Whenever the world began, whether more or less than six thousand years ago, I wanted to know as much of the story of life on earth as possible. For, along with the stories of the days of Titus Oakes and of the American Revolution, my father told me that we must know the past to understand the present.

"The past is never completely behind us," he would say. "It is always a part of us. Humanity as a whole remains unchanged. The proportion of beggars to men of business or of ascetics to sybarites is approximately the same. Among them there always lurk the religious bigots ready to attack those they deem to be infidels."

Although my fears of being attacked as a popish plotter vanished at an early age, I believe that he was correct. Human nature does not change. Living conditions, language, and knowledge may vary as to time and location, but mankind is animated by the same passions with recurring results. Corruption, cruelty, avarice, belligerence, mendacity, heroism, generosity, and the like are all written into the general nature of the species in substantially the same degree from epoch to epoch. This simple fact permits the historian to attempt to draw conclusions about the present based on the past. While each new chapter of history appears to be completely unique to its participants, one can stand off at a distance and state, with some measure of truth, "There is nothing new under the sun."

The author hopes that the reader will forgive these digressions concerning matters of books and philosophy. But a man's philosophy is the product of his struggle with life. When one has lived an isolated existence like my own, an important part of that struggle has occurred between the pages of books. In fact, it is from a particular book that my story flows, and in this book itself that story continues to exist. Books have been my life. After I left my home, it was from them I earned my daily bread teaching Latin, French, English, and History. Being an unprepossessing pedagogue with little wealth, I probably would have remained a bachelor for the rest of my days. But shortly before she died, my mother arranged a marriage with one of the few Catholic families in the city with a marriageable daughter. It was a marriage of some convenience to me because my wife Emily brought a generous dowry with her. That Emily was a devout Catholic, accompanied by an even more religious mother who later moved in with us, somewhat reduced the commodiousness of the arrangement. Both of them would constantly remind me of my religious duties. *"Extra ecclesiam nulla salus."* There is no salvation outside the church. This is not to indicate that they were both Latin scholars. For beyond the language of church services, they were not interested in books or matters of the intellect. At first, in addition to the delights of Venus, the great differences between Emily and me drew us together. She admired my intelligence and knowledge, and I, her simple religious devotion toward the mundane tasks of daily living. But neither one of us could communicate with any enthusiasm concerning matters of interest to the other. We lived on two parallel levels of existence that could never meet. The initial warmth of the arranged union quickly cooled, and little was left but habit and convenience. We both attempted to make the best of the arrangement and to avoid conflict.

In 1803, two years after the marriage, my father followed my mother to the grave. To my great disappointment, he died a most unphilosophical death. Unlike Voltaire, who turned away battalions of priests, at the hour of death, my father was unable to resist the single priest pleading to reclaim his soul for Holy Mother Church. At the climactic moment before returning to his maker, he consented to extreme unction and recommitted himself to the superstition he had despised. One who spends the early years of life in the rituals of the Catholic faith does not easily abandon them.

His last will and testament left his printing office and accumulated wealth to his wife; in case she predeceased him, his estate was to be divided in equal shares between his son and daughter. Because his will was not changed after the deaths of my sister and mother, all was inherited by me consistent with his intentions. My wife, her mother, and I moved into the spacious quarters above his printing office. For the next four years, with the assistance of my apprentice, I worked as a printer. It is at this point, twenty years ago, that this story begins with an incident of seeming insignificance, the purchase of an old book. Yet, but for this incident, the importance of which I did not realize until years later, the remainder of this story would not have occurred.

Two

In the late afternoon it has often been my custom to engage in a game of chess at a local coffee house. In those days, I won so frequently that it became difficult to find opponents who preferred the joy of playing to the exultation of winning. As an alternative form of amusement, I would wander through the bookstores in and around the vicinity of Broadway. There are enough stores selling books in the city so that visits to particular ones can be spaced by a reasonable amount of time, thereby avoiding the boredom of undue repetition. Even when the selection of books on the shelves has not much changed since a previous visit, the time passes in an agreeable manner. Occasionally a long-sought book or a splendid volume unknown to me will appear on a shelf as if left by some unrecognized benefactor. Because one good book can provide many hours of diversion, such an experience provides just enough incentive to encourage regular return visits. At that time, The Bookworm was my favorite bookstore. The owner, an old curmudgeon named Mr. Van Zandt, seemed to possess knowledge of every book that was ever published. The selection in his establishment was certainly the most diversified of any of the bookstores in the city. It was regularly replenished by Mr. Van Zandt's two energetic sons, who often purchased libraries from the estates of persons recently deceased or from sellers desperate for money. The old man invariably sat on his chair by the door determining the prices of the recent arrivals stacked in piles in front of him. Occasionally his work would be interrupted by a seller seeking an amount for his book beyond that required by the laws of supply and demand. The old bookman would respond to the offer by bellowing in a voice loud enough to be heard by every customer in the spacious store, "That price is not reasonable." The frightened seller would either immediately retreat in shame from the premises or sell the book at Van Zandt's proffered price, usually one-fifth or less of the recompense the seller had originally sought. Sometimes I would note in my mind the newly-purchased book. On my next visit I would laugh to myself upon finding the same book on the shelf at twice the price the seller had first suggested before melting in the blast of the bookman's feigned fury.

One damp, cold afternoon early in 1807, after spending the early part of the day with my apprentice in the printing office, I decided on a whim to walk to The Bookworm. It had been more than a month since my last visit. Mr. Van Zandt was sitting in his customary chair, which had been moved closer to the hearth in order to obtain the benefits of the only warm portion of the premises. As usual, he was busily engaged marking prices on the newly-arrived volumes. Because there were no other customers in the store, he, contrary to his habitual manner, looked up and acknowledged my presence with a nod of his head. As the store was cold, I did not linger over the books but instead hurried to the history section in an attempt to locate any new acquisitions. I hesitated to remove my hands from my pockets even to pull out unfamiliar books. Unless some aspect of the book, such as a word visible on the spine or its binding or color, attracted my attention, my eyes skipped quickly over it. One large old battered quarto did not appear to be worth the price of frosted fingers and bended knees to reach the bottom shelf, so I passed over it and continued my cursory search at the next shelf. Having found nothing of interest, I began to walk toward the front of the store when the same kind of fancy that brought me to the place caused me to turn around and ascertain the contents of the mystery volume. It was dated 1744 and titled *A Journal of the Proceedings in the Detection of the Conspiracy Formed by Some White People, in Conjunction with Negro and Other Slaves, for Burning the City of New York in America and Murdering the Inhabitants*, by the Recorder of the City of New York, Daniel Horsmanden. The ponderous tattered old volume did not appear to merit the two-dollar price written on the inside cover, but the title intrigued me. I carried it to Mr. Van Zandt and handed him the money and the book through an opening in the wall of books in front of him. "An excellent purchase," he exclaimed.

"Why is that?"

"This book has almost completely disappeared. I have not seen a copy for many years." The bookman's warm smile was one he reserved for his most discerning customers.

Because Van Zandt rarely issued such laudatory comments and looks, I knew that the trip had been well worth the risk of chilblains, and triumphantly carried the prize home. If someone had then told me that the book, like a talisman, would magically alter my mundane existence, I would have laughed at the utter preposterousness of the suggestion.

The book was a day-by-day account of the proceedings concerning the infamous New York conspiracy trials of 1741. It had been written three years later by one of the judges who presided at the trials; he was also the City Recorder. Although the book was a totally biased account of the so-called "Negro Plot," it did serve to introduce me to the subject. At the time, I confess, I did not know very much about the history of my own city since most of my reading had been about ancient Greece and Rome and more recent European events.

To understand the "plot" of 1741, one must first look back to the slave insurrection of 1712 in New York City. That revolt was led by heathen African slaves who believed that spells could make them invulnerable to the bullets of white men. No slaves indoctrinated in the passivity of Christian acceptance to one's lot in life participated in the rebellion. The rebels all swore an oath of silence as to their plan to fight to the death rather than remain slaves. Two dozen of them gathered their weapons and hid behind trees near a house they had set afire. When whites arrived to extinguish the flames, the slaves opened fire, killing five people. A number of other whites were wounded. The militia quickly arrived and sealed off the slaves who hid in the woods of northern Manhattan. Eventually the leaders committed suicide. The survivors surrendered. Twenty-one slaves were convicted and executed in a manner designed to discourage future slave insurrections. Negroes were broken on the wheel, gibbeted in chains, and burned alive. After these events, the fearful citizens of New York passed numerous laws to prevent slave rebellions. Thus, restrictions were placed on the manumission of slaves because freed slaves might inspire others toward liberty. If three Negroes gathered together without permission, the penalty was forty lashes on a bare back. Masters became more vigilant about the activities of their slaves lest they be murdered by their own servants. It was out of this atmosphere of mistrust that flowed the bloody events of 1741 a generation later.

The affair of 1741 grew out of the burglary of a tobacconist's shop on February 28 of that year. A tavern owner, John Hughson, and two Negroes, Caesar and Prince, were arrested. When a search of his tavern revealed no incriminating evidence, Hughson was released. Shortly thereafter, a sixteen-year-old indentured servant of Hughson named Mary Burton began to inform the police about her master's activities. She accused Hughson, his wife, his daughter, and Margaret Sorubiero, known as Peggy Kerry or "the Irish beauty," a prostitute living at the tavern, of receiving stolen goods from the two slaves Caesar and Prince. The accused were arrested.

Three weeks after the burglary, while the matter was still being investigated, a number of mysterious fires broke out. The first was in the fort; the Governor's house and the barracks were burned. The authorities announced it had been caused by an accident while some work was being completed within the fort. In the following weeks fires broke out in various other parts of the city. Recalling the events of 1712, some citizens began to suspect that another slave conspiracy was responsible for the fires and related thefts. At that time the city contained ten thousand inhabitants, about one-fifth of whom were African slaves. Fear of the large slave population caused the ready tongues of suspicion to wag throughout the city. Fear induced many citizens to move their valuables outside of the city. On April 11 the Common Council offered a reward of £100 and a full pardon to anyone who would reveal knowledge of the plot. Testifying before the grand jury about the original burglary case, and with knowledge of the offer of the Common Council, Mary Burton coyly announced she would say nothing about the fires. Until then nobody was aware of any connection between the burglary and the fires. Burton then accused the Hughsons, Peggy Kerry, and a number of slaves who congregated at the Hughson Tavern, including two Negroes named Quack and Cuffee, of plotting to burn the entire city. Her testimony caused great excitement in New York.

Peggy Kerry was examined in prison and given hopes of pardon should she incriminate others. She denied knowing anything and stated that if she accused anyone, she would be accusing innocent persons. The slaves Caesar and Prince were hanged based on their confessions that they sold stolen goods; although under sentence of death, they denied any conspiracy to set fires. The slaves Quack and Cuffee were the first to be tried on the basis of Mary Burton's accusations concerning the conspiracy to commit arson. No lawyer in the entire city would represent the defendants. Without any defense attorneys to contend with, the prosecutor procured a convicted thief, Arthur Price, to spy on the defendants in prison. Although he was a convicted felon whose testimony was not legally admissible in court, Price testified that Cuffee had admitted to setting the fires on the command of Hughson. The slaves claimed that the thief was lying. In spite of the fact that their masters testified the slaves were at home when the fires broke out, Quack and Cuffee were found guilty and sentenced to be burned at the stake. The two slaves were offered clemency in exchange of testifying against others; but they continued to insist on their innocence. On May 30 they were dragged to the place of execution. Confronted by the wood piled high around the stakes for their consumption by fire, they finally succumbed to the demands of the authorities and named Hughson as the one who contrived the plot. The bloodthirsty mob that had come to view the executions refused to let the sheriff return the slaves to jail after their confessions. Rather than risk a riot, the sheriff disregarded the promise of clemency and permitted the two slaves to be burned alive.

The Hughsons and Peggy Kerry were also brought to trial. After Mary Burton testified against them, they were confronted by the testimony of Arthur Price that the defendants had confessed to him in prison. There was no defense counsel to challenge the admissibility of Price's testimony on the ground that he was a convicted felon. Several witnesses testified about Quack and Cuffee's accusations at the stake concerning Hughson, even though the law prohibited the use of slave testimony against whites. Again, the defendants did not know enough to object to the improper use of the statements of slaves. On June 12 Hughson and his wife were hanged. John Hughson had admitted deserving death for receiving stolen goods, but denied the existence of a conspiracy to commit arson. His wife denied all. In expectation of receiving money, Peggy Kerry made statements implicating others. When she was brought to the gibbet, she pronounced all her former confessions to be lies. The Irish beauty was then hanged.

On June 19 the Lieutenant Governor issued a pardon to all who would confess and reveal the names of accomplices before July 1. In order to protect themselves, slaves accused other slaves in great numbers. Many incarcerated slaves confessed to escape execution. No doubt enjoying newfound powers she never had as an indentured servant, Mary Burton began accusing scores of whites and Negroes. After the executions of the Hughsons, many were convicted solely on Burton's testimony.

Suddenly and unexpectedly, the range of the trials was broadened. To the despised Negro and poor white defendants, there was added another unpopular group, Catholics. Had my father known the details of this event, he surely would have added it to his list of fabricated popish plots. In 1739 war had commenced between England and Spain as the result of a claim by a British merchant-ship captain, named Jenkins, that his ear had been unjustly cut off by a Spanish official. The conflict, appropriately called the War of Jenkins's Ear, concerned not only the abuse of British seamen, but also prolonged discord concerning the English monopoly of the slave trade with the Spanish colonies and disputes over the boundaries of Florida. General Oglethorpe of Georgia, who had been fighting Spaniards for years along the Florida border, sent letters throughout the colonies warning of Spanish plots to burn all towns of any importance in English North America. One of the letters was sent in May of 1741 to the Lieutenant Governor of New York. The letter warned that many disguised Catholic priests were employed to assist in the project. The letter released the usual flood of religious hatred periodically aimed at Catholics in the colonies.

A number of Spanish Negroes were quickly convicted. The search for Spanish agents caused the arrest of John Ury, a schoolmaster who was unfortunate enough to be familiar with both Latin and theology. Although Ury denied being a priest, it was claimed that his knowledge proved the contrary. By a law enacted in 1700, it was a capital offense for a priest even to enter New York. Mary Burton immediately denounced Ury as a popish priest and the real leader of a conspiracy in the nature of the one suggested in the Oglethorpe letter. This charge contradicted her earlier testimony that Hughson was the chief conspirator. Also, she had previously made no mention of any Spanish religious plots and had testified that the only white persons involved in the conspiracy were the Hughsons and Peggy Kerry. Unable to resist expanding the Negro plot into a Catholic plot, the Attorney General turned to the daughter of the Hughsons, who, since the execution of her parents, had been held in prison under the threat of constantly scheduled and postponed execution dates. Told she would be given a pardon if she confirmed Mary Burton's story and would be executed if she refused, Sarah Hughson agreed to testify against Ury. She, and others threatened with execution, testified about Ury having performed strange Catholic rituals in the Hughson Tavern to bind the conspirators together. Ury supposedly drew a ring with chalk, stood in the middle of it holding a cross, and swore to silence all the Negroes standing around him on the ring. The Oglethorpe letter was read to the jury. The prosecutor then inveighed against the "murderous popish religion" which holds it "not only lawful but meritorious to kill and destroy all that differ in opinion" with it. Ury eloquently denied the charges against him and was even learned enough to challenge Sarah Hughson's statements on the ground that the testimony of a convicted felon was not admissible. In order to permit her to testify, the Attorney General immediately obtained a pardon for Sarah Hughson. Despite his skillful defense, Ury was convicted by the jury after only a few minutes of deliberation. In the moments before his execution on

August 29, Ury swore he never knew the perjured witnesses until his trial. Proclaiming his innocence, he cried out,

> In fine, I depart this waste, this howling wilderness, with a mind serene, free from all malice, with a forgiving spirit so far as the gospel of my dear and only redeemer obliges and enjoins me to ... And now, a word of advice to you, spectators: behold me launching into eternity; seriously, solemnly view me, and ask yourselves severally, how stands the case with me? die I must: am I prepared to meet my Lord when the midnight cry is echoed forth? shall I then have the wedding garment on? Oh, sinners! trifle no longer; consider life hangs on a thread; here to-day and gone to-morrow; forsake your sins ere ye be forsaken forever ...

Exhilarated by her immense power, Mary Burton began to implicate persons of consequence. Her wild charges finally brought the prosecutions to an end. In the Salem witchcraft trials, it was only when the wife of the Governor of Massachusetts was accused of witchcraft that the prosecutions ceased. So it was that the New York conspiracy trials ended only when persons of authority and influence were accused. The fate of Ury was lamented only after he had been hanged. The slaveowners fearful of losing more of their valuable slaves began to protest. The community gradually became convinced that the conspiracy had existed only in the imagination. The passions subsided and reasonable men realized that many innocent men and women had been sent to their deaths.

The authorities, led by judges like Daniel Horsmanden, silenced Mary Burton to protect the validity of the previous proceedings. Despite her obvious perjuries, she received the £100 reward for exposing the plot. She had successfully played the role of Titus Oates for a new generation of gullible souls. September 24 was set apart as a day of general thanksgiving for delivering His Majesty's subjects from destruction. When the madness of the trials finally ended, Daniel Horsmanden began to write his book in an attempt to justify the judicial murders. Of 154 Negroes who had been imprisoned, 13 were burned at the stake, 18 hanged, and 71 transported; the rest were pardoned or discharged. Of 24 whites imprisoned, 4 were hanged and 7 transported.

If the lopping of an ear of an obscure seaman in a distant place could be a cause of the persecution of slaves and Catholics in New York City, it is not surprising that the discovery of a nearly vanished old historical tome could alter the life of a person of little consequence. Perhaps it is the nature of the history of both nations and individuals that events which appear to be insignificant are inextricably linked in a great chain of causation. Sometimes these events are conjoined in such a way as to indicate that the author, if there be one, is a master of dramatic irony. For example, in 1754 an obscure Virginia youth leading a group of American backwoodsmen blundered into a group of French soldiers. In the ensuing skirmish the ensign in command of the French, Coulon de Jumonville, was killed. The French called it an assassination, and as a direct result, a war began that spread across the world to Europe and India. Or as Voltaire described it, "a cannon-shot fired in America gives the signal that sets Europe in a blaze." Shortly after the skirmish, the obscure Virginian was disgraced by being forced to surrender his troops to the French and Indians at Fort Necessity on the fourth of July, 1754. Nine years later the war, known as the Seven Years War in Europe and the French and Indian War in America, ended with a French defeat. The French were driven from the North American continent. So long as their presence threatened the English colonies, there was no chance of a separation between the British and the Americans who required the protection of the mother country. As soon as the French departed, the colonists began to oppose British domination. After twelve years of colonial agitation, a second war began. Because of the military experience gained in the earlier war, which was sparked by his blundering, the obscure Virginian was named commander of the colonial troops. The British were driven out of the thirteen colonies, which became independent. As a result, the Virginian become "the father of his country," a nation which did not exist even in the imagination at the time of his youthful errors. Thereafter, the new country, as fortune would have it, began to celebrate its birthday on the long forgotten day of his humiliating surrender.

Perhaps there is some small irony in the fact that after years of reading histories by brilliant authors, it is a book by a biased author, detested by me, which inspires me to begin to write. Certainly, Daniel Horsmanden's book was one of the first links in the chain of causes leading directly to my ability to relate the story that follows. As I turned each tattered page, the book filled me with a sense of mounting excitement. For years I had yearned to write a book about a historical event or period. At last I had stumbled upon a subject that moved me to action. The "Negro Plot" of 1741 was itself too narrow a topic for my youthful ambitions. My immediate thoughts were to use it as a building stone in an edifice of greater scope. The history of slavery in New York City was the subject that first occurred to me.

Slavery was an institution I had learned to loathe at an early age. When only fifteen years old, I had interfered in a public place with a master who was brutally beating his slave with a heavy cudgel. A number of spectators were watching the event as though it were some form of public entertainment. With the rashness of youth, I stepped between the angry master and the wretched slave, who was lying on the ground trying to deflect the blows with his upraised arms. The wrathful cries of the crowd made it clear that I had disrupted their enjoyment. The master struck me in the face with his cudgel. It all happened so quickly that I was not aware of how many times I had been hit. None of the spectators bothered to assist me. However, my intervention did have the desired effect of causing the master to terminate the beating, at least temporarily. As the actors in the scene vanished, I slowly raised myself from the ground and staggered home. Upon seeing my bloodied face and clothes, my parents were shocked but completely sympathetic to my plight. I could not help but notice with some satisfaction my father's look of pride when he heard the cause of my condition. After the first shock of the beating and the arrival of the pain, I was filled with that sweet sense one feels when attempting to help a fellow mortal, with the additional reward of gaining the approval of others for that merciful act.

There is nothing like the sight of one's own blood to evoke outrage at the injustices of this world. I became interested in the subject of slavery and began to read extensively about it. As a reward for my heroic effort, my father presented me with a copy of the Abbé Raynal's great attack on slavery, *Histoire des deux Indes*. Raynal wrote that if there was a religion which tolerated the horrors of slavery, which condemned the slave who broke his chains and embraced the judges who sentenced him to death, then its ministers deserved to smother under the debris of their altars. The resentment of the Church and State that tolerated slavery had caused the Parlement of Paris to order the book burned. The book, its fate, and my bloody face, all did much to create a youthful detestation of slavery and the institutions supporting it. My anti-slavery views, accompanied by a general disposition to ameliorate the condition of classes least favored by fortune, translated themselves into an early political allegiance to the principles of the French Revolution and Thomas Jefferson's Republican party. Yet, beyond the minimum effort required to vote for favorite political candidates, my strong feelings had little outlet in the sphere of worldly activities. The discovery of the Horsmanden quarto finally moved me to action.

Not for me the fury of the musket, the bustle of political activity, or the fellowship of the New York Manumission Society. In a manner characteristic of my solitary existence, I turned to the quill pen and the painful business of writing. Each day I would spend less time at the printing press. Instead, I would lock myself in my library and read selected books on my chosen subject. Then, waiting for inspiration to set my pen in motion, I would stare for additional hours at the empty sheets of paper. In the winter months the cold in the library was so great that coat, hat, gloves, and boots worn inside were not enough to repulse the chill. The room began to feel like my tomb. My head and eyes were beset with pain and dizziness from reading at night by the flicker of candlelight. The initial exhilaration of conceiving a history was quickly dissipated by the hellish business of writing one. As often happens with one of my melancholy nature, I had descended into a slough of despond from which escape seemed impossible. It was frozen January in my heart with no anticipation of the arrival of spring. Every day was the same, except the loneliness of the previous day was added to my burden, until I began to falter beneath the accumulated misery. Mental flirtation with oblivion became a regular occurrence, although not a serious one. It was perhaps treason against my very existence, except for the absence of the all important overt act.

The light pouring through the window would awaken me at the same time every morning. Even on those gloomy Manhattan mornings when the dismal weather held back the light, some inner clock would mysteriously bring my mind out of the land of shadows. If it were not for the inner compulsion to complete my book and the desire to avoid the blast of coldness attendant upon Emily's awakening, I would surely have remained in bed for hours, until the needs of nature forced me to throw off the protection of the blankets.

A light breakfast would be prepared by Emily's mother, who had moved into our house shortly after becoming a widow, less than three years after our marriage. She was always polite but distant when we were alone. In Emily's presence she frequently referred to me in the third person.

"Where is he going now? I suppose he is going to write again." The tone always indicated disapproval of whatever I happened to be doing. Emily usually would not deign to answer these rhetorical remarks. When Emily was exceptionally discontented with me, she would join in the third person conversation.

"He is leaving us alone as usual. He would rather keep company with his pen."

When she was more annoyed with her mother than with me, she would direct her answer to her mother, leaving me unscathed.

"Mother, must you always criticize? Why don't you just keep quiet?!"

Usually I would only hear the opening lines of this drama before escaping to the solitude of the library. At the period when I began writing, Emily and her mother were more often united against me than divided by their own disagreements. Like my father, I had always refused to attend mass. At the close of the previous year, Emily had pleaded with me at least to attend mass on Christmas eve. I was moved by her desire to save my soul, but I replied, "It would be an act of hypocrisy on my part." She and her mother departed in a state of pique which was increased tenfold by the events at St. Peter's that evening. During the services, a band of anti-Catholic ruffians rioted in front of the church. Although Emily and her mother were terrified by the rioters chanting "papists-papists" outside the church, they were not physically harmed. Nevertheless, when they returned, they aimed their ferocious hostility at me. My defense was a lack of knowledge of the ruffians' plans. "If I had known, I would have come with you." My pleas were rejected, and for weeks neither of them spoke to me. My defense was an honest one. It was true that I disliked religion, which leads men to neglect their duties in this life out of an irrational concern for salvation in the next. Reason, not superstition, is needed to impose order on the chaos of men's lives. But when people insisted on persecuting me or my family because we were Catholics, it became an act of defiance to assert my rights. For that moment I would fervently be a Catholic and challenge those who objected to the religion of my birth. In truth, I regretted missing an opportunity to confront the forces of bigotry. A chance to defend my family had passed irretrievably. Instead of being a hero in my own household, I was an outcast.

After the dreary winter of 1806–1807 the anger in my home subsided slightly and my own mournful state was alleviated by the warmer weather. With the arrival of spring, I would often break the routine of daily labor by taking a Saturday excursion on the public omnibus to a portion of Manhattan Island beyond the limits of the city. Emily loved flowers and plants, so that one of her favorite destinations was the Elgin Botanic Garden, three and one-half miles out of the city and almost one-half of the way up the island. The garden had been established by Dr. David Hosack. Although his prominence in city affairs has increased greatly since 1806, Dr. Hosack was then already an eminent personage in the life of the city. Out of his love of botanical science, he had developed the garden at his own expense and named it after the birthplace of his father in the north of Scotland. Due to the fact that he had been family physician for both Colonel Aaron Burr and General Alexander Hamilton, his name had become widely known. As a result of his unique medical skills, he had been chosen to be the physician present at the infamous duel of 1804.

Since my wife and I had been visiting the garden regularly for years, we would occasionally encounter Dr. Hosack overlooking his vast domain or tending to a needy plant or tree. He was always open and friendly. Whether dealing with the most wretched beggar, the wealthiest patroon, or persons of little consequence like Emily and me, he would treat each person as an equal. This is not to indicate that our conversations had gone beyond the level of the most superficial communications; we usually discussed the weather or the health of his plants. On this occasion we came upon the doctor on his knees tending to a plant. Emily was walking ahead of me; we rarely walked together.

"Good morning, Mrs. Carey . . . and Mr. Carey!" The doctor would have made an excellent politician, as he had the wonderful ability to remember the names of even the most casual acquaintances. Emily acknowledged his salutation with a polite nod as I arrived at her side, presenting to the doctor a somewhat misleading picture of connubial harmony.

"I hope your patients, both human and plant, are flourishing."

"Oh, they are most assuredly," he replied to Emily's opening remarks while standing up and walking toward us.

"Is anything of interest happening at the Historical Society?" My question was intended to move the conversation away from the usual trivial remarks to the subject of history. I was looking for an excuse to inform the doctor about my writing project. After all, he was known to be an active member of the New-York Historical Society, which had been established two years earlier.

"As a matter of fact, at the last meeting the members decided to sponsor a celebration in two years of the two hundredth anniversary of Hudson's discovery of Manhattan Island."

"Well, that gives me a goal for the completion of my history."

Hosack looked surprised, and then exhibited an expression of great interest. "Sir, I did not know you wrote books; I thought you only printed them. What is the subject and how did you come to it?"

I told him that I had been writing a history of New York City, with an emphasis on slavery, from the time of the Dutch to the present. In a few months of writing, my subject had already widened. His response was beyond my most optimistic expectations.

"That's wonderful. I have an extensive library in my house with a great deal of material about New York City. Please come and use it. If I am out, my wife will let you in." He handed me his card.

I was astonished at his unguarded generosity. The wealthy are usually more protective about the use of their property than those with little to lose. I thanked him profusely for his kindness and we resumed our journey. Emily said nothing about my stroke of good fortune and continued walking as if nothing had happened. Since the unfortunate incident on Christmas eve, she consistently displayed a marked lack of interest in my personal affairs. In the past, the frost engendered by our unspoken conflicts lasted only a few days, a week at most. This one appeared to be a permanent change in the weather.

THREE

Sitting in a pew to the side of the church, I watched with a sense of increasing trepidation as people wandered into the chapel. After twenty-six hours without sleep, my exhaustion struggled with mounting panic for domination within me. Never having been gifted with that effortless sociability that appears to be the birthright of so many, I remained alone, detached from the humanity circling about me. Even on one of the few occasions in my life when the focus of attention was to be Daniel Carey, I remained the victim of my inveterate propensity for solitude. For the first time since completing the book, it was my sincere wish that my *History of New York City* had never been written. This regret was momentary and would vanish with the completion of my ordeal; nevertheless, for that moment the wish was a genuine one.

No doubt sensing my anxiety and seclusion, Dr. Hosack approached and patted me on the shoulder. "No need to worry. You will do a splendid job. Reverend Mansfield is to inform everyone that you have had almost no time for preparation." Although the doctor's open, friendly face should have comforted me, it only increased my tension. Perhaps it was because that face was familiar. I would have felt better if there were only strangers in the church; the thought of the anonymity of failure before unfamiliar faces was of some limited comfort to me. A week later nobody would remember the event. But Dr. Hosack's presence meant that my performance could return to haunt me in a glance of his eyes. At least Emily was unable to be present. She was at home caring for her sick mother. Looking up, I saw other familiar faces in the crowd and quickly turned away to escape their notice.

If it had not been for the generous doctor, I would not have found myself in such a predicament. As he had promised, Dr. Hosack opened his splendid library to me. Although many of his books concerned subjects of little interest to me, like medicine and botany, there was an ample history section with a substantial amount of information concerning the development of New York City. So I became a frequent visitor. Dr. Hosack and his attractive wife always made me feel a welcome guest and not an intruder. Occasionally while I worked in the library, Dr. Hosack would introduce me to some of the many important persons who visited his home. A number of them, such as DeWitt Clinton, who was then a State Senator, would relate their own experiences or refer me to valuable sources on the city. When not in my own library or Dr. Hosack's, I would often work in the New York Society Library on Nassau

Street in the same brownstone building where I still spend so many of my days. With the assistance of Dr. Hosack, the then small collection of the New-York Historical Society was also opened for my perusal. Working eight to ten hours each day, usually six and sometimes seven days a week, I finished the book in less than twenty months. The problem of publishing the book then confronted me. This task was to be as troublesome as the hellish job of writing it. I spoke to a number of New York publishers about printing, distributing, and selling the book. The few who would take the time to look at the book made the same sort of negative response. My history of the city was too scholarly to be of any interest to all but a handful of readers. Also, the great emphasis on slavery in the book, which they admitted distinguished it from its predecessors, would not increase sales, because interest in slavery had ended with the enactment of the 1799 New York Emancipation Act. They all agreed there was no public demand for a book like mine. None of the publishers would even consider the usual methods of accepting a subsidy from me or permitting me to attempt to secure an advance subscription sufficient to meet publication costs. Most of them preferred to continue to pirate popular books from England and ignore local writers. In short, their interest was in money and not books. If it were not for my inheritance of a printing business, my book never would have seen the light of day. Unlike many less fortunate authors, I possessed the means to publish my own book and intended to do so. Thus, for the first time in my life, I became a diligent printer. My apprentice, Tom Fowler, and I set the type and acted as partners in operating the wooden hand press. Tom would apply the ink with the foul-smelling ink balls while I laid on the sheets and did the pulling. Never had the tedious work of printing been so exciting to me. That the printed words were my own made the project a labor of love. Even lackadaisical Tom caught some of my enthusiasm. We would work all morning on the book and then devote the afternoon to the regular printing business. Because we had no knowledge of bookbinding, I had to have that work done by another shop at great personal expense.

The first edition of the book numbered two hundred. It was to be the only edition. With no experience in the selling of books, I had great difficulty placing even those few copies with booksellers. In the end, the only arrangement that the sellers would accept was to pocket most of the money from any copies sold and return all the unsold copies to me. It was a miserable and unprofitable business. Certainly the general economic misery created by the embargo did not help sales. I retained twenty copies to give to persons who might be interested in the book. Ten of these copies went to Dr. Hosack, who was asked to parcel them out to appropriate persons. Five copies were piled beneath my chair in the church for distribution after the debate.

In due course a debate on the subject of slavery would have attracted my attention. There had not been one, that I could recall, for many years. If it were not for the books stacked under my seat, I would have been tranquilly sitting in the audience, content to be outside the arena of action. Although a part of me craved visibility and respect, I had become content with my own timid obscurity. But Dr. Hosack read the book within one week of receiving it. When we next met, his response delighted me. He judged it "an extraordinarily brilliant history of our city." With some prodding from me, he did admit that its bulk and scholarship might make it unattractive to the ordinary reader. But his praise did appear to be sincere and not merely for purposes of uplifting my spirits. To my great chagrin, the sincerity of his words was confirmed within days upon the occasion of Dr. Hosack's first visit to my home. When she answered the door and found the distinguished doctor was paying a visit to our humble abode, Emily was dumbfounded. My astonishment equaled hers. After exchanging the usual salutations, Dr. Hosack came directly to the purpose of his visit.

"I have just come from Martin Franklin's bedside. He is terribly ill, has been for the past several days. It will be quite impossible for him to participate in the debate tomorrow." Because I looked puzzled, the doctor added, "You, of course, remember the debate; we discussed it several weeks ago."

"Yes. I had planned to attend. Will it be postponed?" The purpose of Hosack's visit had eluded me. In fact, it was unthinkable to me until he actually proposed it.

"The debate simply cannot be postponed. Reverend Sharp will be leaving the city within the next few days and is unlikely to return for the foreseeable future. You cannot imagine how difficult it was to arrange his participation. Few persons can argue the position in favor of slavery with his eloquence. Someone is needed to take the antislavery side with little time for preparation. Since you have been working with it in your book for so long . . ."

His meaning struck me like a bolt of lightning. In that brief moment a multiplicity of thoughts and feelings coursed through my storm-tossed brain—amazement and flattery that he had thought of me to replace Franklin; terror at the invitation about to be made; mental paralysis as to my ability to conjure an excuse. By admitting my intention to attend the debate, I had obstructed my line of retreat. There appeared to be no other escape route. So I agreed to replace Mr. Franklin out of a paradoxical form of cowardice. Since there was no time to fabricate a credible excuse, I accepted rather than reveal my inner terror to Dr. Hosack. As soon as he left, my only desire was to crawl under the bed and disappear. Alas, no time for terror. There were less than thirteen hours before the debate began in the forenoon of the next day. Emily encouraged me to begin work immediately.

For hours, by the flickering light of candles, I frantically scribbled notes covering every possible argument against slavery. Much of the material came from my book. Unable to sleep during the early morning hours, I continued scrawling until sunrise and then watched the light slowly conquer the darkness covering the city. Although she was exhausted with the care of her mother, Emily took time away from the sickbed to prepare breakfast for me. In my uneasy state, I was unable to eat any of it. "You will be hungry when you return," she assured me. With the most affectionate hug I had received in years, she wished me good fortune.

Thus, in a state of stunned submission to my fate, I sat on the speaker's platform that day in the half-filled Presbyterian Church. The Reverend Nathaniel Mansfield introduced the proceedings. My mind was so intently rehearsing my speech that I was barely aware of the words spoken. He did announce the illness of Martin Franklin to the disappointed groans of Franklin's admirers, and stated that Daniel Carey, author of the newly-published *History of New York City*, would speak in his place. Contrary to Hosack's assurance, there seemed to be no statement to the effect that Mr. Carey had only a few hours to prepare. He reminded the audience that the occasion for this gathering was the abolition of the African slave trade which had become effective on the first day of that year, 1808, fulfilling the twenty-year-old promise of the United States Constitution. For at the Constitutional Convention in 1787, he reminded the audience, the delegates had adopted Section 9 of Article I, which stated that the importation of "persons"—the authors of the Constitution would not use the word "slaves"—shall not be prohibited by the Congress prior to the year 1808.

Because South Carolina was the only state that had not already prohibited the slave trade, the 1808 prohibition created no great public excitement. The year before, the British had abolished the slave trade. At the time of the debate, many thought that the end of the African slave trade meant the end of slavery itself. If it were not for the widespread existence of that sadly mistaken belief, the Presbyterian Church might have been crowded with enthusiastic opponents of slavery. Instead, the pews were only partially filled by a somewhat somnolent crowd.

The order of speakers, the Reverend Mansfield announced, had been determined by lot. The Reverend Matthew Sharp would speak first, in favor of continuing the institution of slavery wherever permitted in these United States. "Mr. Carey" would then speak against continuation. Each speaker would be permitted fifteen minutes for rebuttal. Like two scurvy lawyers arguing extreme points of view, we would attempt to improve the audience's understanding of the truth. What in the deuce lawyers and their pro and con arguments have to do with the truth, I shall never know.

Reverend Sharp walked confidently to the pulpit. He looked to be approximately sixty years of age, a gaunt and austere defender of injustice. He slowly poured himself a cup of water and took one sip. Then he closed his eyes as though he were communing with the Almighty. When the congregation was completely silent, he began to speak. His voice was authoritative and clear. I cringed inwardly at the thought of the comparisons the audience would soon make with the clumsy utterances of my untrained tongue.

"Brethren and fellow citizens: There are those among us who tell you that slavery, which has been accepted for thousands of years, has finally been recognized by the modern world as an unjust and evil institution. Let us not make the common error of supposing that men in one generation are endowed with greater moral insight than those in another. From the commencement of life on this earth, the natural principles of authority and subordination have been an essential part of the structure of human existence. The tyrannical authority of parents over children inevitably flows from the fundamental superiority of the adult to the stripling. Because the female sex cannot compete with the male sex in the pursuit of property and power, women must accept a position in the home dependent on the bounty of men. So it is with slaves. The great Aristotle recognized that slavery emerged from the primitive household or *oikia* and was correspondent to other natural relationships of superior and inferior, the soul to the body, man to wife, father to child, human to animal. Aristotle wrote: 'From the hour of their birth, some are marked out for subjection, others for rule.' And so it shall always be.

"Thomas Aquinas wrote that when a slave had married without his master's permission, the commands of the master should take precedence over the marital duties of the slave. Yes! Even the sacred institution of marriage must give way to the obligations of slavery. Thomas More's Utopia, his imaginary society embodying an ideal of social perfection, permitted slavery. Yes! Slavery is a part of the perfection of civilization. Even John Locke, that great defender of the unalienable rights of man, whose views permeate our own form of government, described slavery as a state of war continued between a lawful conqueror and a captive. For slavery, the obligations of the social contract are suspended, and the slave, like the criminal, forfeits his natural rights. Yes! Even John Locke accepted slavery as part of the natural law governing humanity. Slavery has always been with us and accepted by the greatest of men. To nonphilosophical minds it might appear to be unjust. But the perfection of God's divine plan justifies apparent evils whose broader purposes the limited minds of men are incapable of comprehending. Nature is cruel. Scores of innocent children die each day. Does this mean we can sit in judgment of Almighty God and criticize his creation as wrong? When I was a child, I spoke and thought as a child. I could not understand the good reasons for the conduct forced upon me by parents and teachers. Only as a grown man did I realize the beneficent purposes behind their arbitrary commands. So to the uncomprehending black man it may appear to be an evil act to remove him by force from his home and make him a bondsman in a strange land. It is only when the black is reborn as a Christian that he can understand it was an act of charity and liberation to take him from his dark world of sin and superstition.

"Slavery has been sanctioned by countless nations in all ages. Could such a universally accepted practice be wrong? Governments for millennia have protected it as private property and have created expectations based on those property rights. To deny such expectations causes great harm by destroying the belief in stability, in the security of property which is the essence of civilization. Even property that may have been acquired by illegitimate means, over time becomes protected by the law in order to insure the continuity and permanence of society. Although natural law is little more than the custom of the ages, and that custom has always included slavery, I shall not argue that possible injustice can be defended by an appeal to custom or the tradition of centuries. The only way for men to determine whether slavery is unjust is to judge whether it is contrary to the law of God. Therefore, we must examine that law itself, the Bible. Customs, traditions, and human reasons are all fallible. Only the divine will of the Almighty is infallible. For it contains the divine justice which is beyond our puny human understanding. So let us turn to the Bible and let our decision rely upon it alone. With the word of God there can be no argument."

The direction of Sharp's argument was ominous. He was attempting to transform the entire debate into an argument about the Bible with one who was not a biblical scholar. I frantically searched through my notes for quotes from the Bible. There was only one. Hoping that my internal conflict was not visible to the audience, I struggled to contain the panic rising within me. But the members of the audience appeared to have eyes only for the Reverend Sharp. The scattered, silent congregation seemed already to be firmly in the grasp of his ample powers of persuasion as he plunged into a detailed interpretation of the Old Testament beginning with the first use of the word "slave," when Noah cursed the descendants of Ham, the father of Canaan.

"The words of Noah have remained in effect to this very day. 'Cursed be Canaan, a slave of slaves shall he be to his brethren.' God ordained that race to eternal servitude because he judged slavery to be their proper state. The rule of slavery embodied in that curse is recognized throughout the Old Testament. I will describe to you but a small portion of the numerous passages authorizing slavery as the law approved by the God of Israel."

For what to me seemed an interminable period, he recited a multiplicity of passages governing the buying, selling, and punishing of slaves. With the cumulative effect of these quotations, there could be no doubt in the minds of the listeners as to the Old Testament view of slavery. If this debate had occurred fifteen years earlier, during the early years of the French Revolution, it would have been acceptable for me to ridicule the Bible as a definitive source of law and morality. In those days many from the city, including me, wore red caps and sang *"Ça ira."* But by 1808 most of the members of the audience, I knew, would have considered such an attack as blasphemous. How short are the memories of men, skeptical revolutionaries one year and sanctimonious parishioners the next.

"Who can read these passages from Exodus and Leviticus, of which I have read only a few, and then contend that the Almighty decrees that slavery is immoral? In fact, not a single passage in the Old Testament condemns slavery or even hints that it is wrong. Instead, as we have seen, section after section states that slavery is expressly approved by God and specific rules governing the conduct of slavery are set forth.

"Ah, but you say that we Christians are governed by the laws of the New Testament. What of them? What did our Savior say concerning slavery which existed, at the time of His ministry, throughout Judaea and the Roman Empire? Did he denounce it? No! The simple fact is that He barely mentions it. He did not repeal the laws of the Old Testament unless they were incompatible with the new covenant. 'Think not,' said He, 'that I am come to destroy the law or the prophets. I am not come to destroy but to fulfill.' When he disapproved a rule in the Old Testament, such as Moses's dispensation as to the granting of divorcement, Our Redeemer expressly stated his rejection of that rule in Matthew nineteen. In contrast, on the subject of slavery, Jesus did not so overrule the law of the Old Testament. He said not a word against slavery. But what did his Apostles tell us? To the Ephesians and again to the Colossians, St. Paul delivered the message of the Lord. 'Slaves be obedient to them that are your earthly masters, according to the flesh, with fear and trembling, in singleness of your hearts, as unto Christ . . . Masters, do the same to them, and forbear threatening, knowing that He who is both their Master and yours is in Heaven, and that there is no partiality with him.' "

As with the Old Testament, Sharp continued with a prolix recitation of numerous sections of the New Testament accepting slavery. He was undoubtedly one of those ministers who could torture his congregation with endless sermons on any subject. My thoughts began to wander, and I hoped that the audience was affected in the same way.

"In his Epistle to Philemon, the Apostle St. Paul sends back a fugitive slave to his master after Paul had converted the slave. Does he write to his disciple Philemon and chastise him for the sin of enslaving his fellow man? No. Does he direct Philemon to emancipate the slave? No. He simply asks the master to forgive the slave and receive him back. For the law of God approves slavery. So in Timothy, the Apostle Paul commands, 'Let all who are under the yoke of slavery regard their masters as worthy of all honor, so that the name of God and His doctrine be not blasphemed.' In conclusion, there can be no doubt that the Bible, the word of God, conclusively tells us that slavery is lawful and not a sin in the eyes of the Lord. The reason is simple. As Paul writes in the first letter to the Corinthians, 'Every one should remain in the state in which he was called. Were you a slave when called? Never mind . . . For he who was called in the Lord as a slave is a freedman of the Lord. Likewise he who was free when called is a slave of Christ.' Slavery is not opposed to our religion because God does not regard the condition, but seeks the mind and heart of each man. Liberty does not profit nor slavery harm the eternal soul. In the eyes of the Lord, the slave and the freeman are equal. The both are one."

As the Reverend Sharp was concluding his lengthy speech, the great man entered the church. When Sharp paused to use silence to emphasize a point, as he often did, the sound of Gouverneur Morris's wooden leg and cane could be heard beating a tattoo up the center aisle to the seat reserved for him in a front pew. For the first time the attention of the audience was diverted from Sharp to the imposing figure approaching the platform. Morris wore a powdered wig as though he, unlike the rest of us mere mortals, did not deign to depart the eighteenth century and enter the nineteenth. Every eye seemed to be upon him. Those sitting next to his empty pew rose in deference as he sat down. While he listened to Sharp's closing remarks, his neighbors graciously leaned towards him to extend their greetings and, no doubt, to inform him of that which had passed in his absence. My brief reverie on the person of Gouverneur Morris was shattered by the Reverend Mansfield's soft voice summoning me to the hour of reckoning.

At the pulpit I reached forward to pour a glass of water from the pitcher which Sharp had so confidently wielded. My hand shook so much that I quickly withdrew it and plunged it behind the protective wooden barrier on which rested my notes. My voice cracked and trembled to such an extent that an extended pause was required. The audience seemed to become impatient, so I shakily began to read from my notes in a perfunctory and unspontaneous manner. The fact that the Reverend Sharp had spoken for an hour using only a Bible and without reference to any notes did not increase my confidence or decrease my slavish attachment to my notes. At one point I even began to read from a paragraph that had just been completed a moment earlier. Too overcome by fear to feel any embarrassment, I continued as though no error had occurred. Human beings possess a wondrous ability to become acclimated to any situation no matter how unpleasant; therefore, as the speech continued, my confidence increased. With my spirits rising, I decided to abandon my notes for a moment and refer to the Bible in order to connect my words to those whose ill effect still lingered in the hall.

"The Reverend Sharp would have us believe that slavery is the law of God, stated in both the Old and New Testaments. But I did not hear him mention the Golden Rule. Does not the Old Testament, in Leviticus, state, 'Thou shalt love thy neighbor as thyself'? When the famous Rabbi Hillel, who lived in Jerusalem in the century before Christ, was asked to describe his religion while standing on one foot, he turned to the Golden Rule. His simple answer was, 'What is unpleasant to thyself that do not to thy neighbor; this is the whole law, all else is but its exposition.' Is this rule not also the essence of the New Testament? 'You shall love your neighbor as yourself.' This is described by Christ as one of the commandments on which depends all the law and the prophets. Is it loving your neighbor to seize men and women by force of arms from their homes, to cram them into ships with fettered limbs in a foul floating dungeon where many will die before the long voyage ends? Is it love of neighbor that forces the survivors to be sold like animals without regard to ties of family, husband separated from wife, mother from child, brother from sister, all condemned to perpetual bondage, working under threat of brutal punishment in the most wretched of conditions? Brazilian planters accept it as an axiom that it is prudent economy to work slaves to death and purchase more at the lowest available prices. Is this consistent with the Golden Rule? What would we think if a ship of Negroes kidnapped us from the island of Manhattan? We would ask what right they have to violate the law of nations and enslave innocent men. They would no doubt give an answer similar to that used by our American slaveowners. 'You are white, we are black; that is enough.' Does the Bible support, as the Reverend Sharp would have you believe, such a system based on violence, robbery, selfishness, and greed?

The fact that slavery was accepted in ancient societies does not mean we must continue to tolerate it. Even so-called religious truths or laws are subject to change with the times. In the Middle Ages the Church considered resort to a prostitute to be merely a venial sin. When venereal disease became widespread after Columbus's first voyage in 1492, the Church made it a mortal sin. So slavery could be acceptable in one period and become a sin in another. Morality is not immutable."

Having exhausted all my religious references and sensing that I was entering dangerous territory, I concluded the portion of my speech dealing with religion. "If God made man in His own image, slavery transforms man into a brute. As the Abbé Raynal warned us, 'If the Christian faith did thus sanction the greed of empires, it would be necessary to prescribe for all time to come its bloodthirsty doctrines.' " Believing that Sharp's analysis of the Bible was accurate, but not wanting to criticize the "word of God," I gritted my teeth and disguised my thoughts. "The answer to the Reverend Sharp is simple. Of course the Bible does not sanction slavery. The Reverend's pretense of certitude is a sure testimony of folly."

While speaking, I noticed a young man approach Dr. Hosack and whisper in his ear. The doctor hurriedly maneuvered by the legs of those sitting in his row. He walked over to Gouverneur Morris and shook his hand and then quickly departed. That I regretted Dr. Hosack's departure assured me that my confidence had increased substantially in the course of my speech. This growing confidence was brought to an abrupt halt as I noticed several others follow the doctor's example by leaving the church. With his commanding demeanor, Morris looked up at me as if to demand the continuance of my remarks. Falling back on the material in my book, I described the horrors of slavery in New York City, including, in some detail, the "plot" of 1741. I congratulated my fellow New Yorkers for the emancipation act of 1799. That act had abolished slavery in the State of New York by a system of gradual manumission. All children born to slave women after July 4, 1799, were to be freed over a period of time. The males would become free at the age of twenty-eight and the females at the age of twenty-five. Slaveholders were required to register all children born to their slaves after that date under threat of penalty of a fine for the owner and immediate freedom for the child. Children who were properly registered were to be the indentured servants of the slaveowner until they reached the age of freedom; but the owner could avoid his responsibility for bearing the expense of their support by assigning them to local overseers of the poor.

"Since the Bible recognizes slavery as the law of God, perhaps Reverend Sharp would have us repeal the law of 1799." The audience laughed for the first time. I cautioned against smugness about our own law which forced all slaves born before July 4, 1799, to remain in bondage for the rest of their lives. "We must remember that half measures are not enough. We are saving that part of oppression which is the most valuable to ourselves, our present slaves. We are telling our slaves, we shall not grant you justice, but the next generation of whites will grant justice to the next generation of blacks. This is the justice of the ungenerous. Besides, even the children of slaves are being denied their lawful rights. We know what is happening in New York. Pregnant slave women are being sent out of state to give birth and are returned to New York after their infants are sold. Even children born within the state are being sold illegally for transportation out of the state. Just this year the law has had to be changed to provide that no person can leave New York with a slave purchased within the past ten years. Even so, the illegal traffic in wretched slaves continues. As long as some slavery is tolerated, the liberty of every Negro is endangered. We should free all the slaves of New York at once." The large contingent from the New York Manumission Society applauded loudly. Gouverneur Morris smiled enigmatically. A feeling of power surged through me.

"As the Reverend Sharp has informed you, Aristotle did support slavery; but the great Plato would have abolished it. John Locke did indicate that slavery could be justified as an extension of war. But Locke also stated, 'Slavery is so vile and miserable an Estate of Man, and so directly opposite to the generous Temper and Courage of our Nation, that 'tis hardly to be conceived that an Englishman, much less a Gentleman, should plead for 't.' " The audience laughed a second time. "In *The Wealth of Nations*, Adam Smith wrote that slavery was part of the system of monopoly and special privilege that prevents the forces of self-interest from contributing to the general good. Fifty years ago, Benjamin Franklin calculated the actual cost of American slave labor, including the costs of purchase, maintenance, and lack of interest on capital, and demonstrated that it was far more expensive than free labor in England. This fact, Franklin established, placed the colonies at a disadvantage in trade with England. President Washington freed his slaves when he died; and we all know of President Jefferson's abhorrence of slavery.

"Thirty-five years ago the civilized world did not think that a free people could govern themselves. The United States has proved that a republic can exist even if it is not mentioned in the Bible. Some say that the world cannot exist without slavery. The day will also come when they are proven wrong. Our republic is founded on the principles contained in the Declaration of Independence, which holds it as a self-evident truth 'that all men are created equal; that they are endowed by their Creator with certain unalienable rights; that among these are life, liberty, and the pursuit of happiness . . .' Until we grant the promises contained in the Declaration to all men, not some men, the denial of that equality will poison our lives. For all humanity is interconnected. If we Americans continue to be unfaithful to our promises of liberty and equality, our descendants will face a terrible retribution." Compared to the slight, polite applause following Sharp's speech, the loud applause after mine thrilled me despite the fact that the audience clearly contained few supporters of slavery. I was preaching to the converted.

Before I had completed gathering my notes from the podium, the Reverend Sharp erupted out of his seat, eager to make a reply. He had been squirming uneasily during the course of my speech. He did not even make his usual theatrical pause for a drink of water. "After the many biblical passages I have read to you, my worthy opponent can only cite one biblical command, the Golden Rule, as being contrary to the institution of slavery. Is it conceivable that the Bible would contain hundreds of passages authorizing and governing the relationship between master and slave and then overrule all these specific requirements with one general statement? Of course not. It is deceptive and wrong to construe the word of God in such a manner. If my child desires to play instead of learning his lessons, do I apply the Golden Rule by reasoning that if I were in my child's place I would also prefer to play? That the child should waste his time instead of making himself a productive citizen in the community? It is clear that such an application of the rule is wrong. It makes a mockery of the Golden Rule, which really means do unto others what is just and reasonable for society. Interpreted in this manner, the rule means the father, in his superior wisdom, should require the child to study because that will make him a better person. It does not mean the father should fulfill every infantile whim of the child. So it is with the bondsman who wishes to be free. Applied to the master-slave relationship, the Golden Rule simply means that masters should treat their slaves as they themselves would wish to be treated if they became slaves. It does not mean the slave should be emancipated just because, in his childlike innocence, he wants to be free. Freedom would not be just and reasonable for society nor in the best interests of the slave. As we all know, most slaves could not survive in a state of freedom. Without a loving master to care for him, the slave tends to sink into a state of starvation, misery, and immorality. For the most part, slaves are simply incapable of caring for themselves. They are an indolent people, averse to labor, who, like children, would rather frolic than produce. It is well known that after the war of our Revolution a number of black slaves were carried away by the British from this country to England. Unable to support themselves, they became beggars in the streets of London, where they entreated ship captains to return them to America. They preferred slavery in America to freedom in England. For slaves in our country live in palaces compared to the peasants of Europe. A slave is assured of his daily bread by the interest of his master in preserving his own property. In contrast, the free worker is left to starvation or a life of crime if he cannot find work. If we applied the Golden Rule to slavery in the manner suggested by Mr. Carey, we would no longer redeem black Africans from barbarian, heathen degradation by introducing them to the saving light of the Gospel. Were it not for slavery, the Africans would remain in dark idolatry among savages deprived of any hope for a place in the world to come, condemned to eternal bondage to Satan. If we adopted Mr. Carey's version of the Golden Rule with his suggestion to live by the ideal of equality stated in the Declaration of Independence, we would eliminate any subordination of one man to another. Society would be leveled to a common mob sharing equal portions of misery. Fortunately, this mad idea of equality forms no part of our system of government. It is the Constitution, not the Declaration of Independence, which is the supreme law of our land, and that law adopts the biblical view of the legality of slavery. Slavery exists by the law of God and man. Property rights which must be protected have grown out of the institution. In fact, to emancipate slaves indiscriminately would violate the Old Testament, the New Testament, the Constitution, and the Golden Rule. Emancipation would spread discontent among the slaves of the emancipator's neighbors, threatening public safety and stability. It would violate the command to love thy neighbor."

Sharp then used my own examples against me as proof of the failure of gradual emancipation acts. "As my opponent has conceded, to have the mother a slave and the children free is worse than the situation before 1799, when pregnant slaves were not sent out of the state so their children could be sold and their families separated forever." The "fanciful schemes" to ship slaves out of the country to establish colonies in Africa he denounced as inhumane. "To expel these helpless people from their native soil and banish them from their homes is contrary even to the desires of the slaves." Sharp criticized my description of slaves being barbarously crammed into ships. "The smallness of space allotted to the blacks on slave ships is as much as is allotted to white seamen on ships of war, and less crowded in measurement of cubical air breathed than that of soldiers in a camp of war." As to President Jefferson's views in favor of emancipation, he reminded the audience that the President had recently pardoned the slave trader, Philip Topham, whose release had been approved by the New York Manumission Society, itself the original instigator of the prosecution. Some members of the Society muttered angrily at this reference to a controversial local matter. He also noted Jefferson's statements in *Notes on Virginia* to the effect that the Negroes were an inferior race. "As Mr. Jefferson notes, suffering and love have often produced exalted poetry. Among the white slaves of Rome, several great poets arose though the conditions of slavery were as severe. By contrast, our President wrote, black slaves who have also suffered and loved have produced no such poetry." This statement was too much for Mr. Morris, who stood up. Leaning on his cane, he bellowed, "Sir! Only President Jefferson would expect poor wretches toiling from early morning until sunset under whip and hot sun to return home and write poetry." The largely Federalist crowd roared its approval. It was some minutes before Reverend Mansfield was able to restore order.

Reverend Sharp seemed shaken by the unexpected and overwhelming disapproval of his audience. With an eye to making a quick departure, he rapidly repeated his argument that the law of God, the Bible, is the absolute, final word on whether slavery is immoral. "In our brief existence on this earth, we must be just and humane to our fellow men. It would be injustice and inhumanity itself to free these wretched slaves to murder each other and their Anglo-Saxon superiors or to perish for lack of the necessities of life. Whether slave or master on this earth, we are all the bondservants of the Divine Redeemer whose kingdom is not of this world. In the end of our short lives, we all become equal in the eyes of the Lord." The shaken clergyman quickly sat down. No doubt he was eager to return to his native Maryland, far away from the inhospitable confines of Manhattan.

Seeing that Sharp had failed to win over the audience, I made my rebuttal brief. "The Reverend Sharp talks about Negroes as though they were like sheep or cattle. But we know about Toussaint L'Ouverture and St. Domingo. Sheep do not make revolutions. If we do not remove the injustice of slavery, we also shall meet a black Spartacus." Due to the antislavery fervor exhibited by the audience, my blood was racing. I would have liked to have quoted Dr. Johnson and toasted the next insurrection in the West Indies, but I restrained myself. After describing true religion as the greatest perfection of reason, I called for a reasonable solution to the problem of slavery. Such a solution appeared to me to be the Abbé Raynal's suggestion that each freed slave be given a plot of farmland and a cabin. "The size of our country has recently doubled. We are rich in land and resources. Let us share our wealth with our black brothers, and we can also compensate those slaveowners who lose their property. Although Reverend Sharp denies that we can afford to compensate slaveowners for their freed slaves, that is precisely what we are now doing in New York. Under the law of 1799, masters can abandon Negro children a year after their birth. The children are then considered paupers bound out to service by the overseers of the poor. The state reimburses the towns monthly for support of the children. Many of the overseers are binding out the abandoned children to the same masters who originally cast them out. The towns are then turning the state money back to the original masters. Thus, we have created a disguised scheme to compensate the masters who have lost bondsmen."

After recapitulating the horrors of slavery, I concluded. "All black men who are deprived of their liberty by unjust force may lawfully repel that force in self-defense in order to recover their liberty and destroy their oppressors. It is the moral duty of those who are not slaves to assist those wretches in their attempts to deliver themselves out of the misery of bondage. Whether that deliverance occurs by peaceful means or by an effusion of blood is in our hands. But that day of deliverance will surely come. The glorious prize of freedom for all men will some day be won. Let us hope it can be a victory achieved without the unfurling of bloodstained banners."

The audience applauded politely but without enthusiasm. Although I had attempted to moderate my rhetoric, the rebuttal was too belligerent to suit the views of a largely Federalist audience. One of the only things they liked less than slavery was revolution. Revealing my thoughts in favor of just revolutions had been an error. The Reverend Sharp grasped my hand for the shortest time possible within the bounds of politeness and abruptly made his exit. Other than Reverend Mansfield, the only person who came forward to compliment and congratulate me was the Reverend Peter Williams, who, on the first day of that year, I had heard deliver in the New York African Church an eloquent address hailing the abolition of the African slave trade. Probably because I was one of the few whites in the audience that day, he remembered that I had congratulated him after his speech. It was only as a white face in a room full of blacks that I lost my usual invisibility in society.

"Today, you would have done a far better job," I told him while handing him a copy of my book.

"The Reverend Sharp would never have condescended to debate a black man." He shook my hand and departed. He had not disagreed with my statement. I picked up the four remaining copies of my book and hurried out of the empty church looking for Mr. Morris. He was standing outside in the bright sunshine, surrounded by a crowd of friends and admirers. As I waited patiently for him to finish his discussion, he looked at me as if to say, "You also are waiting to pounce on me." Although somewhat intimidated by this manner of recognition, I continued to wait. At last, when he was alone, I ventured to enter his regal presence. He was a powerful-looking man, well over six feet in height.

Perhaps aware of my hesitancy in approaching him, he smiled at me. "When it comes to slavery, I too have a bit of the Jacobin in me."

I laughed. "Well, it certainly came out when Sharp used *Notes on Virginia.*"

"An old Federalist like me can tolerate all kinds of clerical humbug. But when that malignant old Tartuffe quoted brother Jefferson, even I was driven to insurrection." After briefly chuckling at his words, he suddenly became serious. "In my early years, my own family owned slaves. I learned to detest the nefarious institution then, and I've fought it all my life. It is the curse of heaven on those who tolerate it. But Sharp may have had one point. Social and political stability are values we must consider in its eradication. I fear we shall only rescue our fellow creatures from slavery, proceeding by slow degrees. We may have to content ourselves with planting the tree from which posterity is to gather the fruit."

Like most men of powerful personality, Mr. Morris aroused strong feelings of adulation and hostility. My father had expressed his strong dislike for Morris by calling him "an aristocratic monarchy man." Although suspicious about his conservative politics, I admired his efforts against slavery. Because he was prominently mentioned in my book, I was eager to give him a copy. When I presented it to him, he politely waved it away. "David Hosack has already given me a copy. He spoke quite favorably of both you and your book."

Embarrassed by these complimentary remarks, I changed the subject to my disdain for Sharp's attempt to make religion the sole determinant of political policies. Morris replied that he agreed with me, but only in part. "Yes, the world is filled with charlatans who prey on the gullibility of poor creatures who think they can assure the safety of their souls by some valueless rites. The power of these clerics sometimes makes them think they can control governments. Remember your Livy. *Ut nihil belli domique postea nisi auspicato gereretur.*" Morris could see that I was struggling to translate. "That is, 'In war as in peace, nothing from now on is done without the auspices being taken.' "

Acknowledging my understanding with a nod, I began to reply. "I agree. We must not surrender to religious hocus-pocus. That—"

Morris interrupted. "The consolations of religion do have their place, you know; they struggle with the gloom which constantly threatens the mind. Religion is also probably the best means of habituating naturally wicked mankind to the rule of law. It has persuaded the human animal to morality for centuries. The French overthrew it and went mad for over a decade. It is not for individual minds to sit in judgment of the collective wisdom of the race."

Despite my strong disagreement with Morris's defense of religion, I restrained my tongue, as during the debate, out of fear of losing the sympathy of my distinguished listener. Morris declared that he had to be off to his sailboat at the base of Wall Street before the tides changed. "Young man, I shall read your book." He waved to me and climbed into the carriage his retinue of servants had ready for him. The fact that he had said nothing to me about my performance in the debate indicated to me that he had politely suppressed his negative opinion. Nevertheless, I thought, the man may be an aristocratic monarchy man, but he was utterly charming.

I went home that afternoon and slept for the remainder of the day and well into the next morning.

FOUR

"Well, awake at last." Staggering into the kitchen, I was surprised to be greeted by the inhospitable tones of my mother-in-law. She and Emily were sitting together partaking of apple pie and tea.

"I am not the only one out of bed today," I replied. "You look much improved." In fact, she bore almost no signs of her recent illness, a malady which no doctor could identify. "Do you feel better, Mother?" I always choked on the use of the word "mother" for a person who was not my mother, either by blood or affection. But she insisted on the use of that cherished word.

"My hands are still aching and my legs feel terrible today. No need to worry about me." There could be no doubt. She was her formidable self again.

Emily interrupted. "Tell us about yesterday . . . briefly." Before collapsing into bed the day before, I had mumbled to Emily that the debate went well. In the presence of her mother she knew it was not possible to sustain a coherent conversation, so she was mercifully warning me to save my detailed account for later. As I started to speak, my mother-in-law interrupted.

"Give him a piece of pie." Always the dutiful daughter, Emily placed before me a cup of tea and a plate with a triangular slice of pie.

"Emmy, the point of the pie should always face in. You know that." My mother-in-law had a code of strict rules applicable to every household task. One of these was that a wedge of pie should be served so that the point was the closest portion to the recipient, like a knife pointed at a victim. This permits the diner to work his way from the narrowest part of the pie to the widest part at the circumference.

After surviving the ordeal of the debate, I was in a buoyant enough mood to challenge even one of "mother's" commandments. "Is it not more sensible to serve the pie in the way Emily served it?" The pie was pointed to my left, which I designated as west. "The diner begins with the point and eats his way east." With a full mouth I demonstrated the method while explaining it. "At the halfway point, he can then begin eating from south to north. In this way, he never has to struggle with a portion of the pie that is longer than his fork."

Emily's mother was startled by this revolutionary challenge to a family tradition. Yet she seemed interested in my lecture. Although she knew it was wrong, she was surprised to find her son-in-law speaking about a matter of some use in the material world instead of the usual abstractions about castles and kings which she believed to be of no earthly interest. She began to speak but I boldly continued with the exposition of my Jacobin heresy. "Of course, if the recipient is left-handed, the pie should be served pointing east . . ."

With great seriousness the arbiter of manners brusquely spoke her final words on the subject. "That makes some sense, but it is not the way it's done."

"Who am I to challenge the collective wisdom of generations?" In mock surrender, I shrugged my shoulders.

Emily chuckled through the entire performance. At the conclusion she was laughing uncontrollably. It was one of the only times I saw her laugh in such a manner. That day was also the last time I recall her as being completely happy. In living with a person for a period of years, there are so many moments of contentment, laughter, anger, and tears that with the passage of time they merge into a mass of events without any identifiable chronology. Perhaps she was untroubled at some later time; I doubt it.

In the weeks that followed the debate, I expected my life to be transformed in some miraculous way. Nothing changed. Few copies of my book were sold. Nobody stopped me on the street to praise or criticize the book or my performance at the debate. I remained invisible to the world. Dr. Hosack sent a friendly note apologizing for having to leave the debate to see a patient. He did write that others had praised my performance; I suspected that he was merely being polite. My expectations of hearing from Mr. Morris were also disappointed. At first I thought his silence might have been caused by my failure to give him my card. But Morris could with ease have obtained my address if he truly wanted it. The fact became painfully clear to me that my public performance had not made a favorable impression. The effect was as transitory as yesterday's newspapers.

My timidity in concealing my real views about the Bible as authority on the issue of slavery became a cause for regret, particularly since these views constituted a significant theme in my new project, The Age of Revolution. Wistfully, I pictured myself boldly confronting the audience with my subversive ideas. "The Bible is of no relevance to this debate. In the Second Book of Kings, the Prophet Elisha is jeered by some small boys for being bald. The prophet turns on the boys and curses them in the name of the Lord; two she-bears come out of the woods and kill and maim forty-two of the children. Is this the justice of God, the basis on which we should decide the important issues of this world? For centuries, mankind has suffered under the tyranny of clergymen like Reverend Sharp who claim to speak for God. Why do we seriously listen to their nonsense? Most lawgivers like Moses and Lycurgus have wishfully or dishonestly presented their personal concepts of the law and morality as coming from God in order to force unquestioning acceptance on those they intend to subjugate with their ideas. Only occasionally has a lawgiver appeared, like Solon in ancient Athens, who has been honest enough to admit that he himself has written the laws which are merely the imperfect creations of human reason subject to criticism and improvement.

"It may be conceded that the acquiescence of the gullible makes religion a useful fiction. But must the rest of us be governed by fairy tales? Can we not, like Socrates, engage in a dialogue among men based on reason concerning the issues that control our lives? Or must we accept as the absolute truth the words of charlatans who claim to possess the unique ability to commune with God and even invent personal interviews with the Deity to prove their fraudulent claims? They dangle the hope of an afterlife before us as a substitute for the rational pursuit of happiness and virtue in this life. They attempt to intimidate us into accepting their idea of goodness. They reward us with centuries of religious wars, inquisitions, persecution, censorship, and hypocrisy. Let us admit that religion has been little more than a conspiracy between the Church and the State to frighten people into a docile obedience to absolute rule by corrupt kings and avaricious clergymen. Look into your own minds and hearts for the solution to the problem of slavery; do not expect answers to fall from the empty skies."

No doubt, the hostile audience would have silenced me before the conclusion of such a tirade. The cry of "blasphemy" might have emptied the church. Yet there would have been some pleasure in speaking freely, without concession to public folly. At least I would have been both noticed and remembered. Nevertheless, I hoped that recognition would occur with the completion of my new book, *The Age of Revolution*.

For many years I had dreamed of writing a history to rival Gibbon's masterpiece. While I was completing *The History of New York City*, news of the peace of Tilsit arrived from Europe in the latter part of 1807. The news fixed my intention to embark on a major history of the age. At Tilsit, Napoleon had successfully extended the domain of the French Revolution to the borders of Russia, and from the Baltic to the Adriatic. Although his first three campaigns in Italy and Egypt had established Bonaparte as a great general, it was only with Austerlitz, Jena, and Friedland that it became clear that a colossus had appeared to compare with Alexander or Caesar. It has been many centuries since there has been such a great upheaval in the affairs of mankind accompanied by great historical figures, like Frederick, Franklin, Washington, and Bonaparte, worthy of the importance of these events. What monumental times in which to live. Gibbon had chronicled the decline and fall of an empire built on the Greco-Roman values of reason and concern with this life. This empire ended with the triumph of a new age based on religion united with monarchy. In my view, that age began with the Emperor Diocletian's adoption of oriental despotism, the identification of God and monarch, and the end of even the hollow shell of republican institutions in the ancient world. After almost fifteen hundred years of the insidious collaboration between Church and State, clerical control and monarchy by divine right, a new age began with the American Revolution. The ancient Greco-Roman republican form of government was resurrected. The people appeared to be returning to power as France followed the example of America by throwing off the shackles of kingship and clergy in exchange for government based on the reason of men and not the caprices of the gods. What an epoch for a historian. Surely, I thought, a Thucydides or Tacitus would emerge to be its chronicler. How absurd my optimism about a new age seems two decades later. The chains of the Christian heritage are not so easily broken. The union of a hypocritical clergy and privileged aristocracy is not so swiftly sundered.

In my enthusiasm about the "new age," I immodestly dreamed of becoming its chronicler. The greatness of Gibbon and the immensity of the subject gave pause to my ambitions. Gibbon had originally only intended to cover the three-hundred-year decline of the Empire in the West. Then he added another thousand years for the decline and fall of the Eastern Empire. I consoled myself with the idea that my narrative would extend to little more than one half of a century, beginning with the origins of the American Revolution in the period of the Seven Years War and extending through the adoption of the American Constitution, the French Revolution, and the triumph of Napoleon. In my youthful optimism, I expected to complete *The Age of Revolution* in less than ten years. With the attainment of the biblical three score and ten years, this would leave me with several decades for the completion of other projects. *The Age of Revolution* was never meant to be my life's work. Gradually, it did become an all-consuming project. First, however, an obsession of an entirely different kind was to divert my attention for many years. This diversion was of such magnitude that I have temporarily put aside *The Age of Revolution* to write about it, in this book—to exorcise the demons with my pen.

It was only a few months after the debate that the fateful summons from Gouverneur Morris arrived. Early on a Wednesday afternoon one of Morris's many servants appeared at my door and handed me a note from the great man. The servant, a young man with a French accent, informed me that Mr. Morris had instructed him to await my reply. Eagerly I tore open the envelope. It was an invitation to come to his home, Morrisania, in the morning two days hence. Morris even included sailing directions. These were written in a hand different from that in the invitation and were appended to it. "Up the East River. Stand diagonally across the river so as to get within 300 yards of the York Island shore between 3 and 4 miles above Corlair's Hook. Stand on in the West Narrows. Approach gently the York shore as to be within 10 to 12 yards when you clear the Narrows. On your starboard bow you will see a round rock. Then the tide will shoot you through Hell Gate. My house will be on your right passing my nephew's house." How like an aristocrat, I thought, to assume that everyone owned a sailing vessel for traversing the waters surrounding Manhattan Island. Or perhaps Morris knew, like me, that a place could easily be purchased from one of the boatmen who delivered goods daily along the shores of the East River. Without a moment of hesitation, I informed Morris's man that I would be there on Friday in the forenoon.

Returning to my library, I attempted to continue my work as if nothing extraordinary had occurred. My concentration was shattered. Unlike the purchase of the Horsmanden quarto, I immediately sensed that this invitation was a crucial moment in my life.

For the remainder of the day and the next, I was unable to complete any significant amount of work as I pondered the reason for Morris's summons. It must concern my history of New York City. As always, my mind first leaped to thoughts more consistent with wishes than with reality. Perhaps as a result of the antislavery sentiments stated in the book and at the debate, he wanted me to assist him in an important project for the New York Manumission Society. Or, my thorough knowledge of the geographical history of the city had inspired Morris to seek my assistance in fulfilling his role as President of the Board of Commissioners of Streets and Roads in New York City. He might have need of my writing skills to aid him in writing a history of his own event-filled life. The possibilities were dazzling enough to be the subject of a series of daydreams of my rise to prominence. Knowing that such thoughts would only increase my eventual disappointment, I considered more likely reasons for the invitation. Perhaps he merely wished to inform me of a number of errors in my book. I picked up a copy of the book and began to review all my references to Gouverneur Morris and his family.

Because the Morris family had performed such a major role in New York history, they were prominently featured in my tome. Morris's grandfather, Lewis Morris, had been appointed the first native-born Chief Justice of the Supreme Court of New York. In 1733 he was dismissed by colonial Governor William Cosby due to a legal decision unfavorable to Cosby. The famous trial and acquittal on charges of seditious libel of the printer John Peter Zenger concerned the publication of Lewis Morris's attacks on Cosby. Because of my trade, I could not resist giving great prominence in my book to the heroic printer Zenger, to Lewis Morris, and to the Zenger case, the first great triumph for freedom of the press in the colonies. The grandfather later became Governor of New Jersey. His son, Lewis Morris, Jr., Gouverneur's father, was a prominent member of the New York Council, an assemblyman, and a Judge of the Court of Vice-Admiralty. He had four sons, one of whom was Lewis Morris, the signer of the Declaration of Independence. The greatest member of the family was Gouverneur Morris himself, born in 1752, the youngest of the four sons. A member of the bar of New York, he had been an important supporter of severing links with Great Britain during the early years of the American Revolution. My book quoted at length from a speech he had made before the New York Provincial Congress. In his youth this great lover of Britain had declared, "As a connexion with Great Britain cannot again exist, without enslaving America, an independence is absolutely necessary." Morris would, no doubt, be proud of this. But his service as a member of a committee formed by the New York Provincial Congress to prevent Tory uprisings and to bring to trial suspected loyalists was probably a matter Morris would now wish to be forgotten. Morris is mentioned at length in my book for his role as an investigator, along with John Jay and Philip Livingston, in the Hickey Plot, a Tory conspiracy to raise a force to assist in the British invasion of

New York City in the year of my birth, when Morris was twenty-four years old. Due in part to the efforts of Mr. Morris, Thomas Hickey, one of Washington's guards, was court-martialed and hanged before a crowd of twenty thousand souls on the same day General Howe landed at Sandy Hook. As a result of Morris's strong loyalty to Britain a quarter of a century after the Revolution, I feared that he might have been offended by my dredging up of his youthful crusade against New York Tories. Yet, confidence in the accuracy of my accounts of his activities relieved my anxieties about his possible wrath concerning the matter.

In 1777, the year after the Hickey Plot, Morris had served on a committee to draft a constitution for the State of New York. If Morris had read my book, it was certain that he would be pleased with my account of his role. Despite my abhorrence of his later pro-British Federalist political views, I greatly admired his actions in 1777 and had conspicuously featured them in my book. Although members of his own family were slaveowners, he made a heroic effort to commit the State of New York to the abolition of slavery. His motion to the state constitutional convention recommended that future legislatures of the State of New York "take the most effectual measures consistent with the public safety, and the private property of individuals, for abolishing domestic slavery . . . so that in future ages, every human being who breathes the air of this State, shall enjoy the privileges of a freeman." On this issue Morris was too much of a radical for his peers. The measure was defeated by a vote of 31 to 5.

At the same convention, John Jay, whose Huguenot ancestors had been persecuted by Catholics, introduced into the article on religious toleration a provision which discriminated against followers of the Church of Rome by denying them rights of citizenship unless they swore on oath "that they verily believe in their consciences, that no pope, priest, or foreign authority on earth, has power to absolve the subjects of this State from their allegiance to the same." Morris played an important part in having Jay's vituperative anti-Catholic language replaced by a moderate proviso that toleration granted under the constitution would not be held to "justify practices inconsistent with the peace and safety of this State." Morris's words are now part of the New York Constitution. It was while writing the sections of my book on Morris's struggle against slavery and anti-Catholic bigotry that I first began greatly to admire the man. I was confident that he would approve of my laudatory account of his role in writing the New York Constitution.

Once Morris became a member of the Continental Congress in 1788, his historical importance as a national figure greatly increased. Because my book was limited to New York history, it contains little about his later activities. For *The Age of Revolution*, these activities were of great interest to me. As a result of being appointed one of five members of Congress to investigate the conditions of the army at Valley Forge, he became a confidant of General Washington and an important politician during the American Revolution. In 1780 he came to be a citizen of Pennsylvania and established himself as a lawyer in Philadelphia. Until after the end of the war he was an assistant to Robert Morris, who was not related to him, in superintending the finances of the country. He served as a delegate from Pennsylvania to the great Constitutional Convention of 1787. Because the proceedings of that Convention had remained secret for decades after the adoption of the United States Constitution, I hoped that Morris would be my chief source for divulging the story of that historic conclave. As he had been the United States ambassador in Paris during several of the most important years of the French Revolution, he could provide an invaluable account of events in France and Europe at that time. My only hope for obtaining this crucial information was to gain the confidence of the great man. Thus, it was with some excitement that I departed for Morrisania on a chilly Friday morning.

Since the boatman was delivering assorted goods beyond Hell Gate and up the Harlem River, it only required the payment of one dollar to obtain his agreement to put me ashore at Morrisania, near where the East River runs into the Harlem River on the shore opposite Manhattan Island. He also agreed to provide return passage for me in the late afternoon on his way back to the city. It seemed incredible to me that after thirty-three years as a resident of New York City, I was finally visiting an estate of one of the great landed families. From my humble position the manor houses of these families, the Livingstons, Van Rensselaers, Van Cortlands, Schuylers, and Morrises, were as distant and inaccessible as Versailles might have seemed to a French peasant. As a boy, occasionally I had walked from the city into the countryside along the East River, past Randall's Island and beside the Harlem River to the Manhattan shore opposite Morrisania. It was nearly ten miles from the city. I knew that the great Morris family manor stood hidden behind the trees on the far shore. My childish imagination conjured a vision of a magnificent palace in a remote enchanted land. My boyish dreams of visiting that land had vanished decades earlier. The manorial estates of the patroons had turned out to be even more unapproachable than I had imagined. Now, even as an adult, I experienced a sense of wonder at the reawakening of a childish fancy of crossing to that far shore.

By the time the boat arrived beside the dock at Morrisania, I had decided to tell Morris about *The Age of Revolution* and my hopes that he would provide information for inclusion in the book. It was quite possible that there would be no second opportunity to make such a request. Two young men, more of Morris's innumerable servants, were at the dock to greet me. Together we walked up a long incline to a cluster of fine old elm trees beyond which loomed the solitary tower of the Morris mansion. The great house overlooked a magnificent view of the broad expanse of the river with Manhattan Island on the opposite shore. Before entering the house, I turned to watch the vessels sailing by on the sparkling waters of the Harlem River. The day was perfectly clear, so the jagged coast and islands could be seen for miles, to the East River and back toward the city. In front of the house the lawns were perfectly smooth and the shrubs were all neatly trim-cut. The manor house was not the magnificent palace of my boyhood musings. It rather resembled the style of a French château of ample and splendid proportions. The inside was substantially more imposing than the outside. Upon entering a large hall, I noticed an impressive tapestry of a handsome youth resisting the charms of a voluptuous seductress. It appeared to be a scene from Greek mythology which I was unable to identify. Portraits of the ancestors of Mr. Morris decorated the walls. Below the portraits stood numerous bookcases with glass doors housing a formidable collection of books. Expensive-looking rugs were scattered like small islands dotting the immense ocean of a floor. A feeble old gentleman led me into another large room and offered me a resting place on a generously padded chair. It was directly facing a piano placed near a huge, elaborately decorated fireplace. Other than buildings of state, I had never been inside a structure of such aristocratic splendor. Although one knows such homes exist, there is an astonishment and disbelief on confronting the reality of that which was formerly a mere abstraction. Upon thinking that "people actually live like this," I chuckled at my own naiveté.

"Mr. Morris will see you now." Looking like a footman in livery from a royal coach, a servant guided me into a study surrounded by more bookcases with glass doors, all crammed with volumes. Another generation of lords and ladies looked down from the paneled walls. Gouverneur Morris sat at his desk writing. The servant's announcement of my entrance caused Morris to look up at me. A smile crossed his leonine face as he reached for his cane and raised himself up to greet me. The peg leg attached to Morris's left thigh by two thick leather straps above his knee scraped across the dark polished parquet floor. For a moment I feared that he might begin our meeting by sliding across the slippery surface on his ample aristocratic rump. But before I could move forward to greet him, Morris had crossed the floor with the ease of a young man possessing two good legs. He heartily enveloped my hand in his spacious grasp.

"Delighted you could come," he remarked with what appeared to be genuine hospitality. "We have much to talk about." He escorted me to a sofa and sat in a large upholstered chair facing me. "Fetch us some refreshment, would you, Simon." The servant reacted instantly to Morris's command and departed. I stammered a clumsy greeting of my own, a comment on the weather, and then permitted my host to direct the conversation.

"Your book is excellent. I read it with great pleasure. To my knowledge, there is nothing of its kind available. I shall highly recommend it at the Historical Society. Dr. Hosack will, no doubt, have preceded me." After I thanked him with my usual lack of ease in receiving compliments, we discussed the book and my sources of information, at length. As I had anticipated, Morris commented on the passages about his family and himself. "Did you know that Jay was absent when the antislavery provision for the state constitution was debated?" My shrug indicated my ignorance of this fact. "He left the convention because his mother died. Robert Livingston killed the proposal. With Jay present, we might have had a chance. That failure is one of the great regrets of my career. To think we might have done it over three decades ago."

Morris's man interrupted us to serve wine and cakes. As he poured, he spilled a large amount on the table between us. Some of the liquid stained Morris's light-colored breeches. He displayed no anger at the servant's clumsiness and joked about his own awkwardness to set the flustered man at ease. I was impressed by his kindly manner towards his subordinate. Concern about the feelings of a servant was not what I expected from an aristrocrat. One sure measure of a man's character, I have always believed, is the manner in which he treats his underlings.

"Well, you did succeed with the religious toleration clause. That has been of some direct benefit to me, you know." I was certain that Morris knew my family was Catholic. As soon as the words slipped out, however, I wondered whether an allusion to that fact was unwise. Morris quickly set my mind at ease. His warm manner dispelled any slight fears I maintained of bigotry lurking beneath his genial exterior.

"Yes. I have always opposed the arrant nonsense of religious intolerance. Even in this enlightened new century, we see the success of the same contrivance of ignorance and superstition which duped our forefathers in centuries past. Dr. Hosack told me that your mother was French, from Acadia. My mother's side of the family, the Gouverneurs, was French Huguenot; settled here after the revocation of the Edict of Nantes. Trace the family line back far enough, and we are all refugees from one irrational form of persecution or another." Morris used this opening to launch into a lengthy account of the adventures of his ancestors. His melodious tone of voice was thoroughly captivating. He pointed to a shield on the wall bearing the Morris coat of arms with a crest of a castle in flames and the motto *Tandem vincitur*—at last it is conquered. According to Morris, the crest commemorated the exploits of Colonel Lewis Morris, who served in Cromwell's army and participated in the burning of the castle of Chepstow in Wales in 1648. The colonel and his younger brother Richard emigrated to Barbados. Eventually, Richard came to New York and purchased the immense Morris estate in Westchester County. The land had originally been granted by the Dutch in 1639 to a Jonas Broncks, the first white settler of the county. When Richard died, the Colonel came to New York and later purchased an even larger estate in New Jersey. The orphaned son of Richard was raised by the Colonel and grew up to become Morris's grandfather, later Governor of New Jersey. The plantation of the grandfather in New York became a manor in 1694 called Morrisania. The grandfather, Governor Lewis Morris, was the "First Lord of the Manor." Morris explained to me that the word "manor" came from the French "manoir," meaning a mansion in which the owner of the property dwells permanently. Morrisania, he cautioned, was a freehold manor and not a European feudal manor. He seemed eager to characterize himself as an American rather than an aristocrat of the ancien regime. He admitted, however, that the original "Lord" of Morrisania did possess certain ancient privileges, such as the authority over all waifs, strays, and felons, and patronage over all churches of the manor. Morris's father was the "Second Lord of the Manor." His half brother, Lewis Morris, the signer of the Declaration, who was twenty-six years older than Gouverneur and had died in 1798, was the third and last "Lord of the Manor." Morrisania lost its status as a "manor" during the Revolutionary War. Morris proudly recounted the story of how Lewis had signed the Declaration knowing that the British would confiscate his estate when they invaded New York. At the time, Lewis and his three oldest sons were in the Continental Army. When the British arrived, they burned the manor house and pillaged the grounds. Bodies of the Morris family were taken out of their graves and desecrated. Lewis and his sons took refuge on the family's New Jersey lands and remained in exile for six years. It surprised me to learn that after the war, in 1790, Lewis had petitioned Congress to locate the seat of the Federal government at Morrisania. Congress declined and instead selected the present site on the Potomac River.

"Did you not feel animosity towards the barbaric acts the British inflicted on your family?"

Morris was amused by my question. "Of course. But these brutal actions were the deeds of individual miscreants, not the policy of the British government." Upon hearing his response, I was embarrassed by the simpleminded nature of my question to one accustomed to making subtle distinctions.

Since his brother Lewis had owned Morrisania, I also asked Morris how he had come into possession of the estate. Morris smiled at my inquiry. With great enthusiasm he threw his head back and gestured with his hands as if he had been anticipating the question. He appeared to enjoy relating his account of the family history almost as much as I enjoyed listening to it. "Ah, you see, my father's first wife, Tryntje Staats, had three sons, Lewis, Staats Long, and Richard. She died twenty-one years before I was born. My father remained single for fifteen years. Women are troublesome, but who can live without them? So he married my mother, Sarah Gouverneur. She had four daughters and one son, me. My half brothers never approved of the second marriage and were already adults, so I saw little of them as a child. At the time of the Revolutionary War, my brother Staats Long was a general in the British army, living in England. Rather than fight against his own brothers, he sent his resignation to the King. It was returned and he was told he would not be required to fight in America. The British War Office sent him off to the Mediterranean ports and then to India. When my mother's life estate ended with her death, he inherited her portion of Morrisania. Because he had no intention of ever returning to New York, he sold his remainderman's share of Morrisania to me. I built this house only ten years ago. You see, the old manor is now split in two. My portion is on the east side of the Mill Brook, and Lewis's section is on the west side." He pointed with his cane to the sunlight streaming through the windows. "It is a splendid day today. After lunch, we can ride to the upper farm. I will show you the manor and how it is divided."

Emboldened by the ease of discourse with Morris, I continued to ask him questions about his family. "What happened to your two half brothers? Lewis died, you said, ten years ago."

"Staats Long died in 1800. He was the Governor of Quebec, and more than seventy years old. Richard, the Chief Justice, the youngest of the three, is quite ill these days. He is almost eighty years old. I fear he shall not be with us much longer." Morris became pensive at the thought that he would probably soon be the last of the sons of Lewis Morris. "That generation has almost vanished. I am merely an old bachelor living out his days. By the time one reaches my age, it's too late to change. Children might have made a difference. Life slips by so quickly. But it is in vain we seek perfect happiness. The wise man learns to accept his lot in life." He quickly brightened. "The story of my family is, I think, quite remarkable. If I were not of an indolent disposition, I would write a family history."

As soon as he uttered those words, I thought that he had revealed his purpose. He had summoned me to assist him in writing the Morris family history. But he said no more on the subject. He asked me if I had any children. When I told him that Emily and I had none, he appeared to consider it a major misfortune. I was relieved that he did not dwell on the subject.

After a lunch more sumptuous than any I had ever eaten, he gave me a brief tour of the house, including a stop at the luxurious indoor bathroom. Then he led me outside into the bright sunshine of that crisp, cool day. The servants brought two handsome horses from the stables for our exploration of the wonders of Morrisania. I warned Morris that my riding skills were very slight. He promised to proceed at a leisurely pace; but, being an obviously accomplished horseman, he quickly left me inhaling his dust. I was dazzled by the immensity of Morrisania, which seemed to be much larger than the entire City of New York. As we rode over the endless acres of woods and pastureland, Morris impressed me with his vast knowledge of trees, plants, soil, qualities of grains, everything from the growing of peaches to the breeding of livestock. That I was indifferent to nature and had almost no knowledge of the numerous subjects he discussed only increased my admiration for the breadth and depth of his information and understanding, which seemed to surpass even that of Dr. Hosack.

It was only when we returned to the manor house that Morris finally revealed the purpose of my visit. Leading me back into the library, he withdrew a large scroll from among his papers and placed it on his desk in front of us. He energetically unrolled it, using small, heavy books on the ends to prevent it from rolling into its original shape. At once I recognized a map of Manhattan Island; but it was the island as it had never been. Instead of extending several miles up from the southern tip, the city had expanded fivefold into a megapolis, or as some now would call it, a megalopolis. Above North and Amity, a vast new city had been engrafted composed of endless rectangular streets extending as far north as a street marked "155 St." I knew that it had to be the long-awaited Commissioners' plan for the city.

"Here is the next chapter of your book." Morris referred to the last chapter of my book, which had briefly mentioned the appointment in 1807 of three Commissioners of Streets and Roads for the city. The three appointed

Commissioners were John Rutherford, Simeon De Witt, and Gouverneur Morris. As that last chapter indicated in reference to the future of the city, they had been appointed for a period of four years, with the exclusive power to lay out streets, roads, and public squares which they deemed conducive to the public good, and to shut up any streets or unfinished parts which had previously been laid out north of a specified line extending across Manhattan Island from the Hudson to the East River.

"I expected you might expand the city by one-half or even double it, but not this." My astonishment could not be concealed.

"It is truly an ambitious idea," Morris replied with a trace of pride in his voice. "Also, it is a plan of great simplicity and directness. We divide the island into rectangular lots. Avenues one hundred feet wide extend from the south to the north." Morris traced his finger along the immense avenues running nearly the length of the island. "The avenues are numbered one through twelve beginning with the most easterly. East of First Avenue, the four short avenues above North Street end at the East River and are designated as A, B, C, and D. The cross streets are laid out from First Street as far north as 155th Street. We have reserved ground for a public market between Seventh and Tenth streets and First Avenue and the East River. As you can see, there is a large parade ground, we call it 'The Parade,' and a number of squares ... Bloomingdale, Manhattan, Observatory Place, Harlem Marsh, Harlem Square, and Hamilton Square." As he spoke, he placed his finger on each blank rectangle. "A great deal of the credit for the plan belongs to Simeon De Witt and John Randel, both brilliant surveyors. Do you know them?"

"I know of Mr. De Witt, of course." De Witt had been the Surveyor General of the State of New York for many years. It was well-known that President Washington had nominated him to the Senate as Surveyor General of the United States, but to the surprise of everyone, De Witt had declined the job. "I do not know Mr. Randel."

"He is a brilliant young surveyor. Doing most of the work on this project. He prepared the great map. This first draft was completed last year. Randel is the one I want you to speak to about his work. With your knowledge of the history of the city, I thought that you might be willing to write a critique of the plan for my use. You would, of course, be well-compensated for your time."

Perhaps with excessive eagerness, I replied that I would do the work regardless of the compensation. We quickly agreed on an amount that was generous beyond my expectations. Morris informed me that Randel would not complete the surveying work for the final map for more than one year, so I had ample time to complete my own report. He also asked me to include my comments on the problem of "the Collect." The Fresh Water Pond, known as "the Collect," in those days existed in the middle of the city. For many years it had been one of the city's most picturesque locations. As a child I used to skate on it in the winter and fish in it in the summer. As I later learned, by the late 1790s the Mangin Report stated that the pond had become stagnant and mephitical, a menace to the health of the city's residents. The job of filling the pond had begun in 1803, and in 1809 was continuing. In the area around Canal Street the owners of houses near the Collect began to find their cellars filled with water. Morris explained that the problem had become so serious that aggrieved citizens had recently petitioned the Common Council to appoint special commissioners to resolve the Canal Street problem. Morris feared that this new task was about to be added to the duties of his own commission. He instructed me to consider the matter with John Randel and to include recommendations in my report. He then handed me the map and a draft of a written report.

"Your complete discretion in the matter of this report is essential. Discuss this business with no person other than John Randel." It was clear from Morris's tone of voice that breach of this requirement would not be tolerated.

"You can rely on my discretion," I assured him. "The matter will remain confidential."

Our business seemed to be concluded. As he seemed puzzled that I did not immediately leave, I told him that my boatman would not be returning for an hour or more. Morris was surprised at my reliance on a delivery boat to visit Morrisania. No doubt, he had actually assumed that common folk like me possessed his ample resources for travel. Apologetically, he directed his French valet that I be taken home in his own boat. He assured me that his vessel was always available to transport me to and from Morrisania. I later learned that the delivery boatman never did return to Morrisania to pick me up that day. Because of the abruptness of the conclusion of our business and my expectation of visiting Morris again, I decided to defer asking his assistance on my new book.

On the way back to the city I was filled with exhilaration at entering into an entirely new world that, until then, had been outside the realm of my own mundane existence. It occurred to me that for the first time I possessed a real opportunity to become more than a passive spectator to important events. Dr. Johnson once said, I recalled, that almost every man has some real or imaginary connection with a celebrated character. It appeared that Morris was to be my celebrated character and the connection was to be a real one. He was one of a small quantity of persons who live out their lives in the light of a special grace. Their actions become the stuff of history. Although I knew myself to be one of the faceless millions destined to live and die in obscurity, I still hoped to partake of the light of that special grace, to touch that magic that keeps one's name alive long after it has been carved on a tombstone.

FIVE

With her mother bedridden again, Emily was not amused by my description of Morrisania. At first she seemed to feign a lack of interest in my trip. Preoccupied with caring for her mother, she was sullen and disrespectful in all of her dealings with me. Other than the renewed illness of her mother, I was uncertain as to the reason for this display of anger. For the first time, I was also beginning to lose interest in determining the cause of these repeated incidents of incivility. When I made the mistake of informing her that I would have taken her with me if Morris had invited the both of us, she flew into a rage. After the usual exchange of mutual recriminations, silence again descended upon our unhappy home. The exhilaration of my trip was quickly dissipated by the bitterness of renewed hostilities. The walls of my library failed to protect me from the domestic furies swirling about the house. The reality of my barren household broke through, making my work seem unimportant and returning me to the edge of despair. My hopes of writing a history to rival Gibbon appeared to be ridiculous. In the few short months of working on the new book, it had become increasingly clear that all of the libraries of New York could not furnish sufficient materials for a work of such magnitude. Because much of the period to be covered was recent, in historical terms, I would have to locate and organize materials without the assistance of earlier historical pathfinders. The work to be done appeared to require several lifetimes. I resolved to stop work on the book and to concentrate completely on the report for Morris.

In order to escape the house and gain inspiration for completing the report, I began walking about the city and countryside where the new streets and avenues were to be built. The dismal effects of President Jefferson's Embargo Act were everywhere to be seen, most prominently along the waterfront. Because American vessels were prohibited from sailing to foreign ports, the waterfront was full of shipping; but most of the ships were dismantled and laid up in a useless, rotting state. One looked in vain for the usual mounds of casks, bales, and boxes. Instead, grass was growing on the empty wharves. Many of the sailors who used to be seen in the area had joined the British service or wandered in destitution about the city. The once bustling coffee houses were empty. The scores of carts that used to stand in the street for hire had almost disappeared. The numerous drays and wheelbarrows of former days were no longer to be found. Many of the businesses of merchants and traders had failed for want of commerce. The hum of business and the ceaseless motion of commerce were replaced by a fearful, deadening silence. The unemployed clerks joined the miserable sailors in their aimless wanderings through the city. Sections of the island which used to be safe had become inhabited by cutthroats and cutpurses. It was wise to avoid these areas in the daylight, and suicidal to wander into them at night. The public gallows had become a regular source of entertainment for the mobs of the unemployed. Even in the countryside the farmers had stopped cultivating much of the land, as their produce could be sold only at ruinously low prices. The only thing the embargo had not affected was the scavenger hogs which, as usual, ran wild about all parts of the city.

The miserable state of Manhattan increased my own melancholy. The seizure of war ships and sailors by the British and French had been a source of national annoyance, but still, in all, a tolerable situation. The embargo was not. Our hopes of forcing concessions from the belligerent powers by terminating our commerce with them seemed to have the effect, in little more than one year, of punishing only our own countrymen, particularly those living in the maritime states. Not even faithful Republican supporters of Jefferson, like me, could defend this calamitous policy. Within the prior two years, my support for the party had already begun to wane for other reasons. The most important issue for me had always been slavery. Like my father, I had perceived the Republican party to be the party of democracy and the extension of equal rights to all men. Unlike the Federalists, the Republicans consistently supported the basic principles of the American and French revolutions—liberty and equality with democratic institutions. Yet, in New York, the local Republicans had begun to betray these principles and stoop to the depths of debasement. The ruffian Martling Men were interested only in political power, not principles. In the election of the previous year, 1808, the local Republican campaign song had begun, "Federalists with blacks unite." Because of the strong antislavery position of the Federalists, the few Negroes who voted were supporting Federalist candidates. In order to reduce the Negro vote, Republican poll watchers began to challenge every Negro who could not offer proof of freedom, thereby preventing many lawful voters from exercising their rights. Although I still supported the national Republican party, the New York party was no longer acceptable to me. The patrician Federalists provided no alternative. Yes, they disapproved of slavery, which was already being eliminated in the state, but they opposed democracy and the French Revolution in the name of property and loyalty to perfidious Britain. I had become a man without either a political party or a home.

The one benefit of my political disassociation was that a working relationship with an important Federalist like Gouverneur Morris, which would have been unthinkable in 1800, had, within two presidential terms, become palatable, even attractive to me. The fact that Morris had withdrawn from political life, after his service in the United States Senate, eased my way even further. Therefore, it was with a clear political conscience that I began my work for Mr. Morris. On the Monday after my visit to Morrisania, I set forth to see John Randel, Jr., secretary, surveyor, and chief engineer to the Street Commissioners. Morris had informed me that the office of the Commissioners was in the country, in the village of Greenwich, at the corner of Christopher and Herring streets. In order to get there and view the problems caused by the Collect at the same time, I had to cross a ditch, and cut through Lispenard's salt meadow at Canal Street by means of a wooden plank. After exploring the Canal Street flooding caused by the Collect, I walked through the open fields to Christopher Street. The Commissioners' office was locked. While knocking on the door, I was interrupted by an old man who informed me that Mr. Randel was surveying in the vicinity. He directed me back towards the city. For some time I wandered about asking for John Randel. The mention of his name instantly evoked hostility from several of the persons questioned. One fierce-looking man shouted and made threatening gestures at me before walking away in a rage. Finally, I was attracted by the sounds of a commotion. A young man with surveying instruments was being pelted with cabbages and assorted garbage from the hands of a screaming old virago. Appearing to be unperturbed by the incident, he walked in my direction followed by three robust workmen. When he confirmed that he was indeed John Randel, I informed him of my mission from Mr. Morris. He sent his workmen away to survey another area, and he invited me back to the Commissioners' office. He was businesslike and without the slightest trace of emotion from the recent fracas. As we walked together, he explained that many mechanics and farmers of limited means had purchased plots of land in the area being surveyed. Some had erected dwellings, planted gardens, and otherwise improved their plots of land. They were fearful of the possibility of being disturbed by the plan of the Commissioners. "When they see anyone with maps or instruments, they attack with anything at hand, including dogs, stones, and rotten vegetables. It is a veritable undeclared war between the residents and the surveyors. To complete the job, we may have to call out the militia." Assuming that he was joking, I smiled at Randel's account. He remained steadfastly serious and purposeful. At one point he recited from memory and at length the portion of the law authorizing the Commissioners to estimate the damages that owners would suffer by relinquishing their land, and to report the amount to the Supreme Court for assessment by the Mayor, Aldermen, and Commonality of the city. Although it did seem to me a waste of time to commit such matters to memory, I was impressed by his knowledge and precision. He also explained that he had frequently been arrested by the sheriff due to numerous suits against him, as the agent of the Commissioners, for trespass and damages committed by his workmen, who often were obliged to cut off branches of trees and to cross over property in order to complete their work. "We shall not be able to finish our assigned duties unless we are protected from these constant interruptions," Randel stated without the slightest trace of irritation. Judging from the detached tone of his voice, one might conclude that he had been commenting on the weather.

At the Commissioners' office he showed me a large map similar to the one Morris had used to describe the plan of the Commissioners. He carefully explained it in great detail. He also showed me a number of previous reports concerning the streets of the city. I was pleasantly surprised that he did not view me as an intruder from whom information was to be concealed. Pettiness did not appear to be part of his character. Without reference to any document, he seemed to know the location of every house, hill, rock, and tree affected by the plan. As to the matter of the Collect, he stated that the four-year term allotted to the commission was just long enough to complete the surveying and to prepare a final report. "The Canal Street problem will take years to resolve, probably by the construction of a massive sewer; it would not be advisable or feasible for the Commissioners to undertake that task." Years later I would remember and admire the accuracy of his predictions. After concluding his presentation, he showed me his special instruments. They had been constructed at his own expense, more than $3500 he said, in order to increase the accuracy of his survey. He estimated that they would save one year in the surveying process. Without success, I searched his manner for a trace of pride. Unlike pettiness, I sensed that pride could be found beneath his calm exterior.

As we were talking, I noticed that a chessboard, with pieces arranged as if in the middle of a game, sat on a table in the corner of the room. When we completed our lengthy discussion, I asked Randel if he played. He responded affirmatively and accepted my offer of a game. Before removing the pieces from the board, he wrote down the position of each piece. At my inquiry, he informed me that he had been competing against himself and intended to continue the game later. We commenced our game. He recorded each move on a sheet of paper. "I maintain a record of each game. It allows me to calculate the success of different methods of offense and defense."

Anticipating a difficult struggle, I resolved to control the action by immediately attacking with queen and bishop. Randel made no attempt to take the offensive against my king, but he thwarted each attack by placing my attacking pieces in jeopardy while protecting his own. I pondered each move with great care. My head began to ache with the intensity of the thought required. After each of my moves, Randel would study the board for a minute or less, calmly make his move, and record both my move and his response. After gaining a distinct advantage in bishops and rooks, Randel moved to the offense and abruptly ended the game which had commenced more than two hours earlier. He did not seem at all pleased with the victory. My own exhaustion and failure established a deeper sympathy for my former unsuccessful opponents. Although Randel must have been more challenged by his opponent in solitary games, I offered to play again. He replied, "It is useful to test one's power of reason from time to time against a real opponent. Adds an element of the unexpected." We agreed to play the following week, in the evening at the Tontine Coffee House.

During the course of our first meeting, he mentioned that several times he had seen Tom Paine, who was living in a nearby house. Since Paine had been one of the heroes of my youth, I asked Randel to show me the house. He agreed. After meticulously placing each map, sheet of paper, and surveying instrument in its proper place, he locked the door and we began walking. The ostracized infidel had been living in a small lodging house on Herring Street with a Madame Bonneville and her two sons. In front of the house Randel pointed to a window on the first story. "There he is, in his usual place." He said it as if he were identifying one of his assistants instead of one of the world's great men. Wearing spectacles, with his chin resting on his hand, Paine appeared to be reading a book placed on a small table at which he was sitting. A bottle of liquor stood on the table next to his book. He was the image of loneliness itself. "I have never seen Paine in another place. He is either at the window in that posture or he is not to be seen at all." Randel indicated that he had to return to his office to complete some tasks in preparation for the next day of surveying. Before he departed, he repeated our agreement to meet the next week, carefully reiterating the date and time, as if fearful I might forget.

It was beginning to get dark. While walking back over the open fields, I thought of the melancholy figure of Tom Paine and the abuse he had been subjected to in New York since his return from Europe. The great patriot had not been allowed to vote in New Rochelle. A young psalm singer in the New York Presbyterian Church had been suspended for shaking his hand. He had been beaten by adults and taunted by children. To me, this was a clear indication of the fact that America had changed for the worst since Paine's departure. The great revolutionary ideas of '76 had become little more than empty shibboleths. Paine himself was denounced for clinging to them. In *The Rights of Man* he had quite justly criticized Burke's *Reflections on the French Revolution* by proclaiming that every age and generation must be as free to act for itself as the ages and generations which preceded it. He ridiculed the vanity and presumption of tradition governing beyond the grave as the most insolent of tyrannies. Those were ideas which almost all who supported the American Revolution had once accepted and revered. Now they had become dangerous to the smug and prosperous. In *The Age of Reason*, my favorite of his works, he stated that he believed in one God and a happiness beyond this life. But then he had the temerity to reveal that systems of morality similar to the teachings of Jesus had been preached by Confucius and the Greek philosophers centuries before Christ. Worse than that, he denounced all organized religions, Jewish, Christian, or Turkish, as human inventions established to terrify and enslave mankind and monopolize power and profit. "My own mind," he said, "is my own church." For this, every religious denomination joined to attack him as a "vile Satan," an atheist and a drunkard. In the adopted land he had helped to deliver from tyranny, the savior of the American Revolution was a pariah. I remember feeling great anger and sorrow thinking about Paine at the moment I reached the wooden plank crossing the ditch at Canal Street. A man was standing at the other end. After hesitating for only a moment, I began to cross. There was something terrifying about the figure shrouded in darkness awaiting my arrival on the other side. Immediately, I decided to retrace my steps. My fear increased as I realized that another man was standing behind me at the starting point. There was no turning back. Perhaps they are not working together; maybe they have arrived at both ends of the plank by coincidence, I told myself while moving forward to my destination. The specter on the other side did not move. He is politely waiting for me to cross the plank before he begins, I thought, which did not comfort me as I approached him. He did not move. I considered jumping into the black pit below me, whose bottom was not visible. If they were cutthroats, they would follow me into the darkness. If not, I would simply be a fool. I decided to complete the crossing. Upon stepping down from the plank, I could see the muddy boots and covered face of the man awaiting my arrival. With a swift motion, his right arm swung up toward me. There was a knife in it.

"Deliver," he said in a menacing tone. My knife pierced the skin beneath my chin. I could feel the blood dribbling down my neck. The knife plunged deeper into my flesh, causing me to stand on my toes. The second man stood on the plank directly behind me. As I fumbled in my pocket, a blow struck me on the back of the head.

It must have been only for a period of a few seconds that I lay on the cold ground. When my senses returned, it was apparent that both men had vanished along with my purse. The walk home in the dark seemed endless compared to my journey out to Greenwich Village in the daylight. In order to contain the bleeding, I held a dirty handkerchief to my throat beneath the chin. The cut was superficial. With the realization that I had survived what had appeared for an instant to be the long anticipated moment of my death, relief and joy filled my bosom.

As soon as she realized I was not seriously injured, Emily withdrew the sympathy she had extended when I first entered the house. "It's your own fault. You shouldn't be wandering about the city in the dark." For the next few days my throbbing head prevented me from doing any work. Emily ministered to my wounds only to the extent required to maintain her honor as a dutiful wife. There is no love left here, I repeatedly thought to myself.

Within the week, my research began on the draft report of the Commissioners. At the end of the week, I met with John Randel at the Tontine Coffee House, eager to attempt to avenge my earlier defeat. As we were served liquid refreshment, I informed Randel of the unfortunate incident that had occurred shortly after we parted. He politely expressed his sympathies and inquired after my health. "The way they assaulted you appears to be a modus operandi likely to be repeated at the same site. Could you identify them if they were arrested?" I explained that I had not seen the faces of either of my assailants and had informed the police about the incident. "Those two felons can be apprehended. The next time the sheriff arrests me, I shall speak to him about it." Randel's impassive manner of speaking made me smile. If he was insulted by my repeated chuckling as he spoke, he showed no sign of it. Methodically placing his pieces on the chessboard, my opponent neither laughed nor smiled. He placed paper and writing implements before him to record the history of the struggle. After completing each of my moves, I discussed the Commissioners' proposed plan. He had no difficulty in plotting his moves while simultaneously conversing about the plan. He spoke highly of the competence and brilliance of both Gouverneur Morris and Simeon De Witt. The third Commissioner, John Rutherford, did not appear to be an important participant in the project. When Randel finally checkmated me, he had only a queen and a rook to my lone bishop. Instead of the two hours it required to demolish me at our last meeting, he needed over four hours on this occasion. He was amused enough by the competition to suggest that we play chess on a regular basis. We agreed to play at least once each month. As we were leaving I asked him whether he liked the proposed plan. "It is a model of reason and utility. The right angle and the straight line are usually preferable to the disorder of oblique angles and curves, particularly where matters of human convenience are involved. Beware of the baroque; it is an invitation to anarchy. Besides, the plan is my proposal." As he disappeared into the night, I warned him to be careful.

It was more than a decade later that I first heard the story, which has since become popular, of how the Commissioners arrived at their plan for the streets of Manhattan Island. According to the tale, the three Commissioners, Morris, De Witt, and Rutherford, were walking through the city one cloudy day when they stopped near a bank where some workmen had been screening gravel. With his cane, one of the Commissioners began to trace in the dirt a rough map of the island of Manhattan. At the moment when he had completed the outline, the sun shone forth from behind a passing cloud and threw across the dirt map the shadow of the gravel screen of the workmen. "That is the plan!" the Commissioners cried out in unison and adopted it forthwith. When I related the story to John Randel, he said, "Fine mythology. It always enhances a plan to have it inspired by the gods."

More than three months were to pass before I returned to Morrisania with my written critique of the Commissioners' proposed plan. During the period, many events of significance occurred. Because of John Randel's complaints, the Commissioners reported that it was not possible to complete their duties unless they and their agents were protected from lawsuits, arrests, and other vexatious interruptions. Accordingly, in the early spring of 1809 the city obtained an act of the Legislature which authorized the Commissioners and all persons under them to enter upon grounds to be surveyed, to cut down trees and do other damage, as necessary; periods of time were fixed to compensate owners for the damages. On the same date, March 24, 1809, the Legislature appointed Morris, De Witt, and Rutherford as Commissioners for dealing with the Canal Street problem. Randel informed me that the Commissioners had decided not to become entangled in the problem of the Canal Street flooding and the Collect. Morris and De Witt planned to resign together from the Canal Street Commission. Both of these events caused me to make substantial changes in my report to Morris. As the pain from the assault at the Canal Street ditch bothered me for weeks, I wondered whether the beating might have been avoided if Morris had not referred the problem for my consideration. Perhaps, on that evening, I might have taken a different route home. Perhaps not. Causation is always a difficult problem in human affairs, but one that constantly intrigues me.

With the Federalist opponents of the embargo threatening civil war if it was not repealed, in one of his last acts before leaving the presidency, Jefferson signed an act repealing it and replacing it with a limited law providing for "nonintercourse" with Great Britain and France. When British minister David Erskine announced that his country's Order in Council would be withdrawn, our new fourth President prematurely proclaimed the renewal of commerce with Great Britain. On April 24, 1809, the city celebrated the restoration of commerce with Great Britain, which was characterized by the local politicians as a triumph of Federalist policy. In the expectation that Mr. Morris would be gloating over this matter, I had resolved to restrain my own comments. My position in favor of the French, I feared, was one heresy Mr. Morris would not tolerate. If necessary, I was prepared to dissemble.

In May of that year, my mother-in-law finally succumbed to her prolonged illness. Emily was shattered by the death of her mother. During the period of mourning, our connubial combat ceased temporarily. For the first time in weeks we embraced, even though it was in a somewhat perfunctory manner. If not wholly affectionate, we were at least civil to each other. A few weeks later, the passing of Tom Paine, a man I only saw once and knew only from books, moved me more than the death of Emily's mother. I wondered if printer's ink ran in my veins instead of blood. To avoid creating similar questions in Emily's mind, I said nothing to her about Paine. He had died on June 8, 1809, in the back room of a small frame dwelling around the block from the house where Randel and I had seen him. Stories abounded of Paine's last days. It was said that Mrs. Bonneville had moved him to make him more comfortable than he was in the lodging house. He retained his wit and ideals to the end. I heard that a critic had accosted Paine and reported that he had carefully read *The Age of Reason*. "Any doubts I entertained of the truth of revelations," the person stated, "have been removed by your logic." Paine replied, "I may return to my couch tonight with the consolation that I have made at least one Christian." In his last days, two divines, a Reverend Milledollar and Reverend Cunningham, attempted to have him recognize the error of his ways. Unlike my father, Tom Paine died a philosophical death. He sent the clerics away without the satisfaction of having made a Christian of the great infidel.

It was shortly after Paine's death that I returned to Morrisania on a beautiful Sunday in the early summer. After an exchange of messages, mine sent to Morrisania with a local marketman, Morris sent his own boat to transport me. Upon my entrance to his library, he greeted me warmly, as if I were an old friend. Like a tradesman attempting to impress his wealthy patron, I placed my wares before him. I began badly with references to books and essays on philosophy and the theoretical way in which cities should grow. Morris was not impressed. "These systems inscribed in books are good only to be put in other books. The men who live in the real world are very different from those who dwell in the minds of philosophers. Observations taken from life itself are infinitely more valuable than those based on books." His critical remarks bothered me profoundly. I had always questioned my ability to write effectively about politics, war, and other aspects of history without any real experience in these matters.

Morris was excited by the collection of old city maps I had accumulated, most of them obtained from Mr. Van Zandt's extensive collection, hidden away in the cellar of The Bookworm. Among these maps were a copy of "The Duke's Plan," a draft made in 1664 to be sent to the Duke of York upon the capture of the town by the English; a detailed map from 1695 showing the subsequent development of the city under the Bolting Act; and maps drawn from surveys made in 1729 and 1755 displaying the continued growth of the city. The latter plan, Maerschalk's map, showed the beginning of a plan for the streets above the Collect and along the High Road to Boston laid out in rectangles like the proposed Commissioners' plan. Also included were later plans, including the Ratzen survey of 1766 and 1767; however, Morris informed me that the Commissioners had studied all of these more recent documents.

Because of Morris's great interest in history, he was entertained by my detailed information concerning the plan of the Piraeus by Hippodamus of Miletus in 446 B.C., which replaced old winding alleys with broad straight streets crossing at right angles in a rectangular system similar to the Commissioners' draft. That the ancient Athenians under the leadership of the immortal Pericles used such a system impressed Morris, as it had influenced me, to look at the Randel map with favor. As we both knew, the ancient Greeks have rarely been surpassed in any field of human endeavor. For purposes of presenting a modern variation on the Greek model, and as an alternative to the repetitive nature of the Commissioners' proposal, I presented detailed maps and information concerning the planning for Washington City. In 1790 Thomas Jefferson had suggested to President Washington that the streets of the new capital city be wide and at right angles, as in Philadelphia. Based on his observations in Paris, Jefferson had also favored placing a limitation on the height of buildings and a generous provision for public grounds. "It is not often that I am in agreement with Jefferson; but there are times," Morris muttered playfully. The eventual plan for Washington City was by the brilliant French engineer Pierre Charles L'Enfant. I informed Morris that L'Enfant had criticized Jefferson's proposal of houses laid out in squares with streets parallel and uniform as "tiresome and insipid" and "a mean continuance of some cool imagination wanting a sense of the real grand and truly beautiful only to be met with where nature contributes with art and diversifies the objects." Morris laughed at L'Enfant's characterization of Jefferson. "He is right about the man, but wrong about the plan." Morris noted that it was L'Enfant who had ordered the marble for Morrisania. I wondered if there was any notable person whom Morris did not know.

I placed a map in front of Morris. "L'Enfant's plan imposing radiating avenues upon a pattern of rectangular streets is one that the Commissioners might want to utilize."

Morris looked at me with disapproval in his eyes. "Please do not use that word in my presence."

"What word is that?" I asked.

"You will not find the word 'utilize' in Dr. Johnson's dictionary. The word is 'use.' "

"Oh. Then I shall no longer utilize it."

Morris roared with laughter at my rather feeble joke. Pointing to the map, I added, "Morrisania might have looked like this if Congress had adopted your brother Lewis's suggestion."

"Thank goodness it was not approved. In my dotage, instead of being awakened by the sounds of nature, it would be the cackling of quarrelsome politicians." As he laughed, Morris gestured for me to continue.

Acting as a devil's advocate, I contended that the Commissioners' proposal was not consistent with the natural terrain of the island. The hills, woods, and water courses of the island might suggest maintaining curving roads and different levels in various sections. Not only would the proposed plan eliminate variety and the natural beauty of the island, I argued halfheartedly, but also the leveling and filling necessary to reduce the island to a flat surface would cause serious problems for years to come. I concluded by reminding Morris, as his devil's advocate, that the Romans did not level the seven hills of Rome and use them to fill in the Tiber. "That is the type of criticism the Commissioners can expect," I warned.

As if in rehearsal for future defense of the plan, Morris replied that the Commissioners had discussed these matters of beauty. "Nature must always lose a portion of herself in exchange for the utility which civilization requires. A city is composed of the houses and vehicles of men. Straight streets and right-angled houses are simply the cheapest to build and the most convenient for habitation. To gain these benefits we must lose others."

We had been together for more than two hours. He enthusiastically thanked me and indicated that he would carefully study my written report. In a casual aside he asked me if I intended to write another book. It was the moment I had been patiently anticipating in all my discussions with Morris. Eagerly I told him about my new project and asked him if he could provide information about his experiences in both revolutions and at the Constitutional Convention. "If you are interested, I shall have other work for you. In due course, we will have ample time for reviewing historical matters. Now I must attend to my Sunday gathering. The guests should be arriving. I hope you can join us for a time."

After whispering instructions to his valet, Morris led me through the manor. In a great reception hall at the other side of the house, a large number of guests were already assembled. The party had commenced without us. As soon as Morris entered, people gathered about him to exchange greetings. "At last, our host has arrived," exclaimed the first man to reach Morris's side. Morris graciously introduced me to each of the persons who came over to him. Uneasy, as always, in a crowd, I forgot most of the names and their relationships to Morris almost as soon as each introduction was completed. I do recall that several of the guests were named Morris, one a Colonel Morris, all members of the great Morris clan. Most present appeared to be in their fifties and sixties, contemporaries of Morris. There were, however, a few men and women who were closer to my age. In my homespun, I felt out of place in such a richly dressed assembly. They must have wondered at the reason for my presence. Usually my insignificant appearance made me feel inconspicuous in a gathering. At Morrisania I was a dandelion in a bed of roses.

As quickly as possible, I extricated myself from the crowd to partake of the cornucopia of food and drink available to the guests. Trout, beef, turkey, sweetmeats, pies, cakes, port, sherry, claret, champagne, and numerous other delights had been placed on a long table manned by servants ready to satisfy the requests of each guest. After filling my plate, I withdrew to a quiet corner of the room and sat down. A formidable dowager sailed by, with two young women escorts. She paused in her journey and looked down at me, my mouth filled with food. "Tell us, young man, where is it you come from?" Without waiting for a reply, she continued on her way. I was uncertain whether the question was intended as an insult or was merely the superficial ballroom vapidity of the aristocracy.

"The Austrians have attacked Bonaparte in Bavaria. They are already in retreat from Abensberg. That man is invincible." A group of men stood near me discussing the latest news from Europe.

"Nobody is invincible. The man has had a splendid military career. I grant you that. But he has overextended himself. Because of the Austrians, he is unable to consolidate his victories in Spain. All of Europe will continue, like the Austrians, to rise up and fight him. As soon as he ceases to act, he ceases to reign. When he fails, and he must with so many enemies, at that moment he falls." It was clear from Morris's tone of voice that he not only expected Napoleon to fail, but hoped with all his heart for his defeat.

With my back partially turned to the speakers, I hoped not to be drawn into the conversation. In this gathering it was likely that I was the only democrat and lone supporter of the French. "What do you think, Mr. Carey?" Morris asked.

Before turning around to answer, I struggled to devise an honest response but one which would not reveal my preference for the French. "Well, the recent news from Europe is two months old. My guess is that by now Napoleon has defeated the Austrian army and taken Vienna. With the assistance of the Russians, they lost the Austerlitz campaign decisively. They simply cannot withstand the Grand Army by themselves. Remember how quickly the Prussians fell at Jena when they foolishly chose to stand alone. The Austrians should not have attacked until they had allies on land to support them."

"He is quite correct," Dr. Hoffman interjected. He was the man who thought Bonaparte to be invincible. "The Austrians have no chance without land allies. British sea power is of no use in Austria. The British and others must be more moderate in their dealings with the French. These interminable wars are fruitless."

How shocked everyone would have been to learn of the situation at that moment. As soon as I heard the news later that summer, I recalled my answer to Morris. The Austrians had indeed abandoned Vienna the month before my response; but within two weeks Napoleon had suffered his first defeat in battle at Aspern-Essling in a failed attempt to cross the Danube. Temporary as that repulse was, the news reminded me that historians, unless they wish to play the fool, should never attempt to predict the future based on the past.

"Doctor," Morris said. "Moderation in dealing with Bonaparte is a vain delusion. Until the British shackle his power, we and all freedom-loving nations will be under a constant threat of tyranny. The restoration of trade with the British is a vital step in the proper direction." Having crushed the doctor's heretical views on attempting to exist peacefully with Napoleon, Morris turned the conversation to the return of prosperity in New York expected with the end of the embargo. My honesty still intact, I slipped away.

In the course of completing my escape to the other side of the room, I stopped to listen to bits of conversation in order to determine whether the patricians were truly different from the rest of us mere mortals. Alas, all that was to be heard was the same sort of tedious small talk one hears at plebeian gatherings. The women talked about their wonderful children and grandchildren or their clothing and the finery of other guests. Most of the men discussed money. It was of no interest to me. Always an outsider on the edge waiting to withdraw, I was never a part of any group. While searching for an inconspicuous place in which to pass the time, I noticed a beautiful young woman speaking in an animated fashion to a handsome young man. She looked directly up into the eyes of the young man. Her face was radiant, smiling, eager to please and attract. It was a vivacious look I had seen many times, but never in the face of a young woman who was speaking to me. Loneliness and melancholy began to overcome me. With increased desperation I looked for a place to be alone.

After sitting on a chair in the corner for a wearisomely protracted period of some minutes, I began to feel conspicuous in my solitude. Again I arose and started to wander about the room. Inevitably I was drawn to Mr. Morris. "At least all must be equal before the law." A young man was gesticulating as if the movement of his arms might persuade Morris.

"That is not really possible," Morris replied confidently. "Where there is great inequality of fortune and society, the supposed equality of the law creates injustice. If the equal punishment for all is a fine levied by the court, it oppresses the poor who cannot afford it and does not disturb the rich. If the punishment is corporal, it degrades the aristocrat and barely bothers the beggar. After execution of the punishment, the law justly prohibits them both from sleeping in the street. Your idea of equal justice is an illusion. The poor are always with us. The wealthy are a necessity. Human progress requires men of property, detached from toil, with time to spend on intellectual pursuits. Without the leisure classes, there would be no improvements in human affairs, in art, science, and the rest. The fact is that equality is not even desirable. It is liberty which is the greatest earthly good. But you cannot have both liberty and equality together. In France—"

A young woman interrupted the conversation and began to chatter about the beauties of Morrisania. She appeared to be slightly inebriated. "How did you lose your leg?" The embarrassed listeners fell silent.

Instead of being annoyed, Morris looked amused. "Unfortunately, it was not in the military service of my country."

The young woman persisted. "Where and when did it happen?"

"Almost thirty years ago, in 1780, when I was living in Philadelphia. In the recklessness of my youth, I climbed into my phaeton with a groom while allowing the horses to stand untethered. Before I was seated, they started suddenly, throwing me to the ground. My leg caught in one of the wheels while it was turning. Badly mangled. The doctors recommended immediate amputation. I agreed, and they removed it. Damn painful. When my personal physician, Dr. Samuel Jones, returned to town, he told me that the amputation had not been necessary. Had Dr. Jones been available, I might this day stand before you as a biped."

His interrogator was unyielding. "Has the loss affected your life?"

"Yes. In at least two major ways. I was unable to accept an appointment to a post as secretary to Benjamin Franklin in Paris. Also, I have always remembered that I put on one of my stockings inside out on the day of the mishap. Each morning since that day, I have carefully surveyed the condition of my stocking before venturing out into this cruel world." Morris laughed and continued to discuss the importance of property in a civilized society. Looking rather bewildered, the young lady wandered away.

In the midst of the festivities, a trio of musicians arrived. It was not a formal concert with the seated guests playing the part of an attentive audience. Instead, the sounds of the flute, violin, and piano were simply added to the din in the room. The crowd gradually divided into two distinct groups. With a few exceptions, the older men and women gathered near the fireplace, close to the musicians. The younger persons, most of my own age, congregated at the other side of the room. Walking toward the more youthful group, I heard a loud booming voice rising above the other sounds in the room. It was disturbingly familiar to me. The speaker looked like a younger version of Gouverneur Morris. He was tall and bulky of body. Like Morris, the hair on his forehead was receding. He also possessed the same generous nose and double chin as Morris. Wearing light-colored breeches, ruffled lace about his neck enclosed in a rich dark-colored coat, he was even dressed like Morris. His dark hair was in obvious contrast to the white hair on Morris's head. In a manner completely foreign to Morris's genial nature, he spoke in a loud, vain, and boastful way about himself. In between extended moments of gorging himself with food and drink, he talked about the New-York Historical Society's celebration, planned for September, of the two hundredth anniversary of the discovery of Manhattan by Henry Hudson. It was the same celebration Dr. Hosack had mentioned to me more than a year earlier. According to the loudmouthed man, as immodestly proclaimed by him, he was to be proposed for membership in the society. He boasted about his great financial success as a lawyer and his expectations of even greater achievement. "Money has become a scarce commodity these days. Membership in the society might attract a few wealthy clients."

When he began a diatribe against Jefferson and Madison, blaming them for the scarcity of money, I remembered him. His name was David Ogden. In my youth he used to frequent a tavern where I played chess. He often gambled there. After losing, he would borrow money on the pretext of hiring a carriage to get home. It became known that he would keep the money and walk home. When one day he badgered me for money, although he hardly knew me, I timidly gave him five dollars to avoid an unseemly argument with him. He thankfully promised to reimburse me before the end of the week. After letting two weeks pass, I made the mistake of asking for the return of the money. With obvious annoyance, he dismissed me as though I were a miser beneath his contempt. Thereafter, when he saw me, he would act as if we were old friends. With a drink in his hand he would sit beside me and engage in the most trivial of conversations. In the midst of these discussions, using a most friendly tone of voice, he would give me personal advice. "Your face," he might say, "will cause you serious problems in life, but each must learn to bear his own cross." Or, he would advise, "You must learn to be less bookish and boring." To be with him became a humiliation to be avoided at any cost. Rather than risk meeting him by chance, I stopped playing chess at the tavern. Several years later I heard of a highly regarded attorney named David Ogden and wondered whether it was the same dreadful man. But we did not meet again.

It was apparent that he did not recognize me. I stood directly opposite him as he addressed four other men, sounding like an unpolished version of Gouverneur Morris. "The restoration of trade with Britain will resurrect prosperity in this city. You can be certain of that. It is only a first step. We should join with the English in strangling the menace of revolution forever. The damned Jacobins and Bonapartists are the enemy, not the British. Besides, the British navy controls the seas. They can hurt us; the French can't. It is in our financial interest to be allies of Great Britain."

My old loathing for the man tempted me to speak. But I held my tongue. It was only when Ogden began to discuss the glories of Admiral Nelson and British sea power that I made the error of opening my mouth. One of the men referred to Trafalgar and Nelson's immortal message. "What was it? England desires every man to do his duty."

Ogden corrected him. "It was 'England expects that every man will do his duty.' "

My pedagogic nature overcome my discretion. "That is correct. However, the message Nelson directed to be signaled to the fleet was 'England confides that every man will do his duty.' His subordinate suggested substituting the word 'expects' for 'confides' because 'expects' was in the vocabulary of Sir Home Popham's signal book. 'Confides' would have had to be spelled out requiring the hoisting of many more signal flags."

As I spoke, Ogden whispered to his neighbor, in a voice loud enough to be audible to all, "A pedantic boor in our midst."

Rather than admit to having heard the insult, I returned to a silent state and listened to the conversation, which continued as if my words had never been uttered. Watching the smirking faces around me, I could feel the old hostility toward Ogden rising in my heart, mixed with the humiliation of being ridiculed as if I were not present. One of the men turned the conversation to the recent death of Tom Paine. Ogden vented his hatred of Paine. "Fortunately, no Christian graveyard would accept his wretched remains. The vile atheist had to be buried on his farm in New Rochelle, in a hay field." Ogden laughed righteously at his own words.

"He was not an atheist. He wrote that he believed in one God. His book has been misrepresented by his religious enemies. No doubt, he would not have wished to be buried in a Christian cemetery." Although my tone may have been defiant, I tried to present my words as a mere statement of fact. Ogden glared directly at me.

"Sir, what is your name?" His eyes widened triumphantly at the name Carey. "Why are you of all people defending an enemy of the Catholic Church? You should be spreading popery and inquisitions in America rather than defending infidels." His loud declaration was followed by an outburst of laughter from his listeners. Too flustered to think of an appropriate reply, I slinked away like a whipped dog. "No doubt, the product of a Jesuit education," Ogden bellowed.

Feeling flushed with mortification, I rushed out of the house and walked toward the river. The sun was beginning to set. The thought of my absence from the riot at St. Peter's, with the mob chanting "papists," troubled me. I had failed to defend my own wife and mother-in-law from the bigots, and now myself. It was a bitter draught of humiliation. The sight of a boat sailing serenely back toward the city was in harmony with my wish to leave Morrisania. But the thought of returning to my unhappy home only intensified my sorrow. The sounds of flute, violin, and contented voices emanating from the distant house, illuminated by candles in the windows, evoked a woeful anguish in the depths of my soul. It was a feeling of complete separation from the joys of society, of exile from the human race. Closing my eyes, I wished, for a brief moment, to end my desolate existence. The isolation and silence of Tom Paine's hay field seemed a conclusion greatly to be desired, a fit end to long years of quiet suffering. As always, the moment of desperation passed. I knew that my miserable life must continue.

After walking slowly up the slope back to the house, I passed under the tall elm trees along the edge of the mansion. On the side facing away from the river, the house was not illuminated with candles. It was, nevertheless, light enough to see a door ajar. Without any purpose, I opened the door. In front of me was a long dark corridor with a weak source of light at the end. It was so dark inside that I used my hand on the wall to guide my footsteps. The movement was slow and uncertain. As the wall ended, my right hand hung in the air. I assumed that it was an open doorway; it was too dark to determine. Without the guidance of my hand, I continued to walk in the same direction until my fingers touched the wall again. A few more steps and the wall was gone again. A second open doorway. As my eyes grew accustomed to the darkness and drew closer to the source of the light, I began to walk at a faster pace, until I reached the door from which the light emanated. Turning to my right, I saw a single candle flickering in the corner of a room and thought I heard the sounds of muffled weeping. Enshrouded by the darkness, a human form was sitting in a chair in the corner of the room. Because of the long flowing hair, it appeared to be a woman, her left hand holding her forehead between thumb and fingers. Her face, which was covered by the hand, seemed to be looking down at the floor. As I entered the room to obtain a better view of this mournful apparition, the door creaked. She suddenly looked up at me. My heart beat wildly in a kind of childlike terror of the darkness and the unknown. It was a countenance of great beauty touched by suffering. Startled, she rose quickly to a standing position. Her shape was lovely, unmistakably female. She wore a dark dress, patched at the elbows.

"Please forgive me. I did not mean to intrude."

Before she spoke, her sorrowful smile pardoned my intrusion. "Oh, no," she replied. "I shouldn't be sitting here. You must be one of the guests." The voice was strikingly soft and gentle, truly a quality most wonderful in a woman. It was a sound that makes one interested in the possibilities of tomorrow.

"Yes. But I am the one who should not be here. I should be with the others." I was hesitant to ask her about the sounds of crying. Because of the darkness, I could not determine whether she had in fact been weeping.

"It's not my place to question the conduct of Mr. Morris's guests. I am merely a servant in this household." With her left hand she wiped something, perhaps a tear, from beneath her eye.

"Is anything wrong?" I asked.

"No, everything is fine. Truly, it is." She was dressed like a servant. Her enunciation indicated a cultivated mind. If Morris were a father, I would have guessed she was a tutor for his children.

"Do I detect a southern accent?"

"How very observant of you, sir. I was born and raised in Virginia." When I asked her why she had moved north, she hesitated uncomfortably and then replied, "For work." As she spoke briefly of her love of Virginia, I drank thirstily of that tongue's utterance. Her voice exercised a charm words cannot express. It was the call of a siren to life. There was an awkwardness and vulnerability in her voice and manner that caused me to want to embrace her and say, "You are safe, now." I resisted that unreasonable and inappropriate urge. She gazed directly into my eyes with that wondrous feminine interest I had seen so many times before directed at other men, but never at me. I expected her to look away, but her gaze remained fixed upon my face.

"My name is Daniel Carey . . . from New York City. Like you, I work for Mr. Morris."

"I'm Nancy Randolph. I've only been here a short time. Do you visit often?"

"No. This is only my second trip."

"So. You're also a newcomer. You might say we're both strangers in a strange land." There was a wonderful variety and expression in her lovely face. Many men would probably not describe her as comely. Her beauty was unique and of a higher order than mere conventional physical symmetry. She seemed to be unaware of her attractiveness. The artlessness of her beauty made her irresistible. Yet there was something disturbingly inscrutable about her. My desire to impress her caused me to stammer as I searched for the appropriate words for such a singular occasion. As we exchanged pleasantries about our work, my discomfort began to diminish.

We could not have been together more than ten minutes, when a door opened nearby and the not too distant sounds of music and voices flowed into the room. At the sound of footsteps, we both turned to the doorway. A servant holding a candelabrum entered the room. In a most respectful manner, he addressed my delightful apparition. "Miss Randolph, Mary wishes to speak to you."

"Please excuse me, Mr. Carey. I must go. It was a pleasure to make your acquaintance. Perhaps we shall meet again." She quickly vanished with the servant into the corridor. Because a door to the lighted portion of the house was left open, the corridor was no longer dark. As I reluctantly returned to the light, it seemed as if my mysterious encounter had never occurred, as though it had been the product of an overwrought imagination.

As soon as he saw me, Morris beckoned me to join him. He was speaking to the odious Mr. Ogden. "This is my nephew, David Ogden." Ogden smiled unctuously. "Meet Daniel Carey, the young man who wrote that excellent history of the city I mentioned to you. Have you met each other?"

"No. We have not had the pleasure of being introduced." In his precise lawyer's fashion, Ogden was correct. We had not been introduced at this gathering. He acted, however, as if he were meeting me for the first time. Ogden seemed to be quite at ease in his deceptive behavior, confident that I would not mention the recent unpleasantness between us. Almost all traces of my anger toward him had been removed by my meeting with Nancy Randolph. I no longer cared about him. The remainder of the soiree is a haze in my memory. My body was present, but my mind was in another part of the manor.

The boat trip back to the city was in darkness pierced by the light of the moon. The moonlight on the black water gave the voyage an atmosphere of enchantment. Thoughts about my business with Morris could not compete with the burning remembrance of Nancy Randolph. All else was forgetfulness. After so many years of wanting nothing other than to write a history, I had learned to be content without earthly delights and hope for the future. It was a state of numbness, usually without pain. Now, the youthful intoxication of passion flooded my heart. My mind told me that my longings were trivial, irrational and impossible of fulfillment. How superficial and transitory, I reminded myself, are the attractions of the physical. I knew almost nothing about her other than the wonderful look of her face and the delicate modulation of that ineffable voice. It was foolish to be controlled by such unimportant manifestations. Why should the curve of a nose or the resonance of a voice have such power over our emotions? These are external characteristics, like my pockmarked face, which should not control our destinies. Yet they do. My feelings were beyond control. I had drunk the potent elixir of love and was struggling in vain.

That night the dream disturbed my sleep for the first time. As the serpent's fangs sank into my hand, I screamed with pain and terror.

SIX

"You're having a nightmare again." The voice was harsh, without sympathy. The room was dark and cold. Although the twin wounds in my hand were not visible, the pain seemed as real as the blanket tightly clutched in my hand. In the dream, I had been standing silently as the coldness coursed through my body. Emily said I was screaming. The stoniness of the shaking administered by her made me wish to be in some other place. When we were first married, she would have gently caressed and hugged me until I regained both my consciousness and composure. After a few years of marriage that tenderness had ceased to exist. It had not vanished suddenly in a convulsive confrontation. Instead, it had eroded almost unnoticed like a rock slowly worn away by the swift waters of a stream. My mind turned away from the dreary void of my own marriage bed. I thought of Nancy Randolph and the warmth that might be found in her arms. Drifting back into dreams, I trod the long corridor to that room lit by a single candle. She was there waiting for me. Her arms outstretched, she looked up and smiled. We embraced until our mutual passion could no longer be controlled. She removed her clothing. Together we plunged into carnal oblivion. I awoke with a start. The sunlight was pouring through the window. I was alone in bed. Was it only the previous day that I had seen her? No. The intense winter cold in the room reminded me of the fact that more than six long months had passed since meeting her at Morrisania.

My only communications with Morris had been by letter. The possibility of seeing her again was contingent on the receipt of an invitation to Morrisania. It had not come. She was as inaccessible to me as if she had been in Virginia. For six months the remembrance of our meeting had filled my thoughts. In the fanciful images formed in my mind, I walked toward the flickering candlelight of that room innumerable times. She was always there waiting to speak to me and to engage in the rites of Venus. Troubling me in my waking and sleeping state, she had become a succubus. A few hundred years earlier I might have suspected her of using sorcery to bewitch me. Now we live in an age of reason. I know that I am the conjurer of the demon. For my fault, rather than being burned at the stake, I am transformed in my own eyes into a figure of pity and humor. This is not to say that I was merely overcome by lustful thoughts, although I confess to their presence. No, I had not become a mere satyr. That role was not sufficiently ridiculous. Instead my poor part was the comic one of that most pitiable of creatures, the lovesick lout lost in an idle reverie of his beloved. The infatuated peasant admiring the aristocratic lady from a discreet distance.

I had never believed in instantaneous love. Lust upon a first encounter certainly is a common phenomenon, but love requires time to develop. We had been together for probably less than ten minutes. My mind told me that love could not germinate in such a short period of time. Yet my heart, impervious to reason, was filled with an intense sympathy and longing for that beautiful creature. It was a feeling for another human being I had never before experienced. As a lover must know his beloved, I wanted to know everything about her. Constantly I wondered whether she had in fact been crying. What could have been the reason for tears? Her manner was not that of a servant. Who was she? Why had she left her beloved Virginia? Was she present at Morrisania at the time of my first visit? Was she there now? Perhaps she dreamed of me as I dreamed of her. She so filled my mind that I feared I might cease to exist without the thought of her.

The unlikely prospect that Nancy Randolph could love an unprepossessing person like me released a long buried spring of pain that had been coursing through my soul since childhood. The poisonous substance entered my mind, reopening wounds thought to have been healed long ago. My reason struggled to regain ascendancy over my heart. It whispered to me that my love was an illusion, a desire for an unattainable happiness. Even if the impossible happened and the wish became reality, it reminded me of the ephemeral nature of passion. Once attained, the goal quickly loses its value. Passion drowns in the dross of daily existence. Despite the protestations of my reason, the dreams continued to trouble me. Although I had always believed my head to be in firm control of my heart, one spasm of passion demonstrated to me the precarious hold that reason maintains over our lives. How easily reason can be overthrown by sentiment and emotion.

Not since childhood, when emotion held dominion over my being, had I been plagued by recurring dreams. Unlike Voltaire's Dr. Akakia, I did not believe dreams to be a window looking into the soul, any more than I accepted Akakia's mad expectation of men walking on the moon or the Akakian idea of raising children in silence so they will speak the original human language. Dreams, I believe, are merely nocturnal terrors and desires lurking within which are held in check by the reality of waking existence. I was determined to limit the domain of these demons to no more than those hours when I was in the arms of Morpheus. When awake, my reason would expel them from my mind. Or so I had resolved.

It is a curious fact that I was actually invigorated by my infatuation. The thought of being recalled to Morrisania gave me something to look forward to other then the endless drudgery of historical research and writing. Within days after meeting Nancy Randolph, I was totally engaged in *The Age of Revolution*. My flagging energies had mysteriously revived. Even before my visit to Morrisania I had been concerned about my ability to continue work on the book. Now, for the first time in months, I could consider with some equanimity a project which would not be completed for many years. The fact that Morris himself had agreed to provide information added an incentive to my work. As a further stimulus, Dr. Hosack had informed me of the availability of a very large cache of documents concerning the Revolutionary War. These were available as part of the collection of the New-York Historical Society. Even the political news was a tonic to my reviving interest. As I had predicted at Morrisania, Bonaparte had defeated the Austrian army in the colossal battle of Wagram. The Austrians quickly capitulated and the war had ended at Znaim in July 1809. The British attempt to invade Holland by way of the island of Walcheren failed completely. To the chagrin of the Federalists, during the summer, the British repudiated the Erskine agreement. In August, President Madison had to issue a new proclamation restoring the prohibition of trade with Great Britain as required by the Non-Intercourse Act. Although I was unhappy to see the continuation of an embargo, it was gratifying to see the Federalists swallow their pompous arguments concerning the reasonableness of the British. The great Federalist celebration in April of the restoration of trade with Great Britain had proved to be premature and foolish. Unfortunately, due to illness in September, I missed the opportunity to view the mournful countenances of the Federalists at the Historical Society's long awaited two hundredth anniversary celebration of Hudson's discovery of New York. No doubt there must have been a few democrats present to gloat over the perfidy of the British. From the account of his toast in the newspaper, I knew that Dr. Hosack had been present. There had been no mention of Morris's presence. It was some consolation that I did not have to see David Ogden honored as a new member of the New-York Historical Society. To my knowledge, he had not written any work of history. No doubt he was elevated because of his status, money, and power. It would be years before I was so honored with membership, and only because of the persistent efforts of Dr. Hosack on my behalf.

During this period, my communications with Morris were all by letter. At his request I assisted John Randel in preparing detailed accounts of the expenses of the New York Street Commissioners. As Randel had indicated during the early summer, Morris and Simeon De Witt resigned from the Canal Street Commission which was to consider the problem of the Collect. Within weeks John Rutherford also resigned. With his usual ease, Randel continued to defeat me at chess. He was, however, less successful in persuading the police to set a trap for my assailants at the Canal Street crossing. Despite his repeated requests, the sheriff refused to send a "victim" across the plank while the police waited for the thieves to act. According to Randel, the police showed no interest in capturing my attackers.

At the beginning of 1810 I was spending much of my time studying Revolutionary War documents at the Historical Society, which was then located at Government House. On the same winter's day that Emily had shaken me awake, I saw Dr. Hosack there. Although he was an active member of the society, it was the first time I had met him at that location. He was carrying the two volumes of Washington Irving's newly published *A History of New York* by Deidrich Knickerbocker. He asked me if it was worth the three-dollar purchase price.

"It is a very humorous book. I hope that the satire is sufficiently broad so as not to be confused with real history. Look for the description of Dutch Governor Wilhelmus Kieft, called 'William the Testy.' It is Thomas Jefferson in disguise." I knew that Dr. Hosack would appreciate Irving's Tory humor more than I did.

"They say the book is a parody of Dr. Mitchill's *Picture of New York*."

"That is possible. It is certainly not a satire of my *History of New York City*. You cannot satirize a book nobody has read." Although I did not intend to grope for compliments, Dr. Hosack appeared to interpret my statement in that way.

"You have nothing to worry about. Your book will survive long after Mitchill's and Irving's." Dr. Hosack was not a good prophet. Irving's book soon became immensely popular. Many readers thought it was a serious account of the history of the city under the Dutch. Its popularity assured that my book would not require a second edition. Now, almost twenty years after its publication, my history has vanished into oblivion, while Irving's burlesque is still widely read. There is, of course, always hope for the future. In 1810, the same year I first read the Knickerbocker history, Daniel Horsmanden's long-lost book of 1744 was newly published with a different title, *The New York Conspiracy or a History of the Negro Plot*. At first I hoped that my book had some effect in resurrecting interest in the terrible injustices of the New York Conspiracy. To my later disappointment, I was informed that the publisher had rediscovered the 1744 text and was unaware of my book.

"I heard that you are again going to request the Legislature to purchase the botanic garden." For the past several years Dr. Hosack had petitioned the Legislature to have New York assume the great burden of operating the Elgin Botanic Garden. Despite the support of most of the medical establishments in the city, each year the petition had failed to be enacted.

"Yes. This year I think we shall succeed. The medical schools have agreed to operate the garden under the supervision of the Regents. I simply can no longer afford the quit rent and the maintenance costs. Nor do I have the time for proper care of the place."

"Why," I asked, "are the medical schools so interested in the garden?"

"For years they have been studying the medical properties of the plants. Also, Columbia College would like to acquire part of the property for expansion." The good doctor commenced a description of the various plants grown there, the drugs that can be made from them, and the many maladies the drugs can treat. During a boring dissertation on the subject in which I feigned interest, he paused for a moment. In order to change the subject and without expecting to obtain any information, I mentioned that I had not communicated with Gouverneur Morris in almost two months.

"Is he well?"

"Haven't you heard? The old man got married." Immediately I had a premonition of the remainder of the news. "He married a woman young enough to be his daughter. Just think. Almost sixty years old and he gets married for the first time. It is quite wonderful."

While Dr. Hosack was speaking, I tried to control my increasing agitation. My voice quavered as I asked, "Who is the bride?"

"Her name is Ann Cary Randolph. She is a member of the Randolph family of Virginia. She was working as a domestic at Morrisania."

"Does she call herself 'Nancy'?" I had to be certain, even though it meant revealing my meeting with her. Dr. Hosack was surprised that I knew her. After I told him of our brief meeting at Morrisania the previous June, without revealing any details, he began to talk about her. "She is beautiful. It is easy to see why Morris finally surrendered his bachelorhood. There is something mysterious about the whole matter. Why is a member of the great Randolph family from Virginia working as a servant in New York? Morris himself has not said a word about it. I have spoken to the new Mrs. Morris twice since the wedding. She is charming and intelligent but very reserved. A little sad of heart, I suspect. When I asked her about her family, she was quite nimble in talking around the subject without revealing a blessed thing about her past. The closer you get to her, the more she draws away." His last comment puzzled me. Over the years, I have thought of it many times.

"When were they married?"

"It occurred on Christmas day. I was not present. One of the guests told me it was a complete surprise to everyone. Members of the family came to celebrate Christmas. They had no knowledge there was to be a wedding ceremony. Miss Randolph entered in the middle of the festivities wearing an old dress with patched elbows. Morris announced to the guests they were about to witness a marriage. They thought he was joking. They were flabbergasted when the wedding ceremony actually occurred before their eyes. Mr. Morris has always enjoyed surprises." In order to encourage Dr. Hosack to continue his account, I forced a weak smile. "As you can imagine, the nieces and nephews are quite upset. They were all, I imagine, looking forward to dividing a sizable inheritance. According to my informant, the Wilkins family members were visibly shaken during the wedding ceremony."

"Was David Ogden there?"

"No, I don't believe so. Many members of the family missed the dinner because of the bad weather. You can be certain that Ogden is unhappy. Everyone expected him to be the next lord of Morrisania. Perhaps he will be yet. Morris may have made special financial arrangements for his wife's needs after his death. In any case, the old man is healthy as I am. He will probably outlive us all." Saying he had to leave to deliver a botany lecture, Dr. Hosack shook my hand and departed. I was rendered almost as insensible as after the attack on Canal Street. Unable to continue working, I picked up my materials and walked home in a daze.

Sometimes I think that life is a series of long strategic retreats from dreams. We may not even be aware of the need to retreat. We wait in the hope that with the passage of time events will occur to make the dream attainable again. The goal itself may be uncertain. Groping in a new direction, it is hoped, may reveal a new path to the desired end. We blunder ahead even though defeat may be preordained. Even after recognition of the necessity of retreat, we may seek a new route back by avoiding having to pass through the painful territory we originally traversed. We may build bridges behind us to assure that a route of escape is available after the next setback. Occasionally these bridges collapse or are destroyed before we have safely completed a withdrawal. In the end, defeat is inevitable. Its open maw awaits our arrival. If we perceived that maw too clearly, we would be paralyzed into passivity. Perhaps the essential feature of the heart is to make opaque the vision of the all-seeing head. Thus we can continue the heroic but futile struggle long enough to leave another generation to try again. Perhaps the languid progress of history is the purpose of it all. Perhaps there is no purpose.

For several days after my meeting with Dr. Hosack, I was in the headlong retreat which follows a rout. So complete was my inability to work, it made me fearful that my productive life had ended in the middle of my fourth decade. The credo of my existence has been that one who never wastes a moment can accomplish great tasks over a period of years. All my life I had been slavishly dedicated to my work. With my spartan needs, I had always been able to postpone life's gratification to some distant future time. Suddenly I found myself lying in bed until the late morning, staring into empty space with no wish to begin the day. A lifetime of books, loneliness, and unrealized dreams were no longer sufficient to satisfy me. Emily's anger at my behavior was less than the contempt I felt for myself and my inability to bring myself to the writing table. Within a short time the dream of Nancy Randolph had shattered my belief that I could live without the love of another person. My solitude wearied me. My mind was empty. There appeared to be no purpose to my existence.

Unable even to read, I drifted in and out of sleep. Occasionally I would leave the bed and drown my sorrows in rum. Emily's suggestions that she ask a doctor to examine me were brusquely declined. When not in a rum-induced stupor, I often wondered about the relationship between Morris and Nancy. If I was the lovesick admirer from afar, perhaps he was playing the old fool pining for the lost pleasures of youth. At his age, I thought, they could not be passionate lovers. It must merely be a marriage of convenience to restore her to the comforts of the aristocracy. One could never know.

After two weeks, boredom and disgust at my listlessness drove me from the bed. Although work on my book was impossible, I commenced laboring at the printing press and reading newspapers and books for diversion rather than for purposes of research. One morning Emily began to chide me for my aimless demeanor. "Are you going to waste the day moping again?" The words were not spoken in a voice of encouragement. Instead, the sharpness of the tone indicated an intention to punish with multiple lashes of the tongue. Too apathetic for anger, I did not deign to respond. Emily was not turned away by my silence. She had girded her loins for a confrontation. In the absence of her mother, there was no alternative object of wrath. We were alone in the house, with no one to attack but each other.

"If you followed the religious teachings of your own family, you would not be so miserable all the time."

Unable to resist a saucy reply to a religious attack, I looked at her contemptuously. "You refuse to accept the fact that we live in a senseless universe. This entire earth is one of seven inconspicuous planets in a solar system floating in a void. So, of what importance are we? You create the illusion of hope with your ridiculous prayers, rosary beads, incense, bells, and other inane liturgical nonsense. *Hoc est corpus meum.* Hocus-pocus."

"Your universe is senseless. Not mine. I believe in God and my immortal soul. I live with hope. Not like you."

"Where is he? I see this chair, this table. But where is God? I may be condemned to the torment of living without hope, but that is better than trading my reason for fairy tales. I refuse to distrust my senses. They may sometimes lead me into error, but they are a more reliable guide to the true and the false than your mumbo-jumbo." For dramatic effect I picked up Emily's copy of the Bible, ripped out the first page, and threw it into the consuming flames of the fireplace. Due to my respect for the printed word, I was careful to select a blank page.

Emily appeared to be more shocked at seeing me tear a book than at the fact it was the Bible. "I don't know you anymore," she said, more out of sorrow than anger. She was not ready to withdraw. "You've said many times that you don't know whether or not God exists. If you would just try to believe, you may turn out to be right. You have nothing to lose." She was trying to save my soul again. I was moved to discover that she still cared, even if it was only for the residue after my death.

"Ah. Pascal's wager."

"What is that?"

"The French philosopher Blaise Pascal believed it was wiser to bet on God's existence then against it. If you bet against it and lose, you are damned to eternal hellfire."

"That is what I'm trying to tell you."

"It is a silly and childish argument, even if a famous man did make it. The Greek Gods might exist, so I will worship Zeus, Apollo, Dionysus, and the rest. Mohammed may be correct, so I will be a Muslim, also. You want me to worship your Moloch of a god who hurls those who do not grovel at his feet into an abyss of eternal suffering? Maybe if there is a God, he only punishes those who are profane enough to believe that he sentences people to endless torture merely for doubting what their poor human minds cannot comprehend. Perhaps you will go to Hell for proclaiming your nasty, vengeful, little God."

"You are so obstinate. Why do I waste my time trying to talk to you? All you do is insult me." Appearing to be at the edge of tears, she quickly withdrew from the room. At the end of every dispute she always assumed the role of the injured party. Spent were the sympathies which in the past would have caused me to console her. I did not follow her.

Within a short time thereafter I forced myself back to work on *The Age of Revolution*. For a time my thoughts about Nancy Randolph ceased. When I thought I had banished her from my mind, the long awaited invitation to Morrisania arrived. The fantasies and dreams began again. Although the excitement of visiting Morrisania might have been immeasurably greater if I had not known of the marriage, I was still intrigued and excited by the thought of seeing Nancy again. Also, it was, I had to admit, something of a blessing to be able to avoid being dumbfounded in Morris's presence by the news. Inwardly I thanked Dr. Hosack for sparing me that embarrassment.

Morris met me in his study with his usual sunny affability. He said nothing about his marriage, and I saw no sign of the presence of the new Mrs. Morris. Without wasting time on preliminary matters, he informed me of the reason for his invitation.

"Have you heard about the Canal Commission?"

"The Canal Street Commission?"

"No. The Legislature has appointed a new commission to explore the route of a proposed canal from the Hudson River to Lake Ontario and Lake Erie. The benefits to be derived from a canal were the subject of my most serious thoughts many years before I disclosed them. Even then it was treated as the vision of a schemer rather than the mature reflections of a sound mind. The simple fact is, because of the great range of mountains, we are the only state that can open up a route of navigation to the great western wilderness. A canal will make New York City the commercial capital of our nation for centuries to come. Within fifty years, it could make the shores of Hudson's river almost a continuous village. Now, we are finally to begin this great business of inland navigation." It was clear that Morris was substantially more excited about the matter than he was about the New York Street Commission. "Have you read any of the recent newspaper articles on the subject?"

Certainly I could not have answered, "For weeks I have been staring at newspapers without comprehension because of my obsession with your wife." So instead I replied, "I have been so busy writing my book, I have not been reading the news. Are you a member of the new commission?"

He picked up a copy of a joint resolution of both houses of the Legislature dated that same month, March 1810, and read me the names of the Commissioners, Gouverneur Morris, Stephen Van Rensselaer, De Witt Clinton, Simeon De Witt, William North, Thomas Eddy, and Peter B. Porter. After noting that he and Simeon De Witt would now be working together on two different commissions, I commented on the fact that the Canal Commission appeared to be carefully designed to represent both political parties. Morris agreed.

"That is evidence of just how seriously the Legislature is considering this matter. In order to avoid factional squabbling, the resolution was originally passed with the names blank." Morris pointed to a map on the table. "Last year, James Geddes completed the first surveys of some possible canal routes. My opinion is we may be able to tap Lake Erie and let the waters follow the lead of the country to the Hudson without aid from any other body of water. Of course, after studying the problem in detail, I would not be surprised to have to revise my views considerably." Although I nodded knowingly so as not to reveal my ignorance, at the time I did not fully understand Morris's statement. Only months later was I to realize that he had been referring to his infamous "inclined plane" proposal. It was my later response to the inclined plane idea, I believe, which was in part to win for me the trust of Gouverneur Morris. That trust allowed me to obtain the information contained in much of this book, or perhaps I should call it this confession.

"What caused the Legislature to become interested in the canal at this particular time?" I expected Morris to tell me about his own role in the creation of the commission. Honest and candid as always, he granted the honors to others.

"According to Simeon De Witt, who is more aware of activities in Albany than I am, the credit for the legislation belongs to Thomas Eddy and Senator Jonas Platt. Eddy, who is now a member of the commission, had the idea of appointing Commissioners to determine the practicability of extending canal navigation to the western part of the state. De Witt told me that Eddy's initial idea was the rather limited one of having the Commissioners explore a canal route from Oneida Lake to the Seneca River and then authorizing the Western Inland Lock Navigation Company to construct the canal. It was Platt who favored expanding the duties of the proposed Commissioners to explore the country as far as Lake Erie and to build a canal from there to Lake Ontario and the Hudson. Eddy feared the Legislature might reject the idea as visionary. After debating the issue all night, they drafted a resolution consistent with Platt's proposal. They took it to De Witt Clinton, who agreed to support it in the Senate. For the Assembly, they relied on Stephen Van Rensselaer. Platt introduced the resolution in the Senate and it passed unanimously. Almost immediately it was unanimously adopted in the Assembly. Two years ago I would have predicted it could not gain the support of one-third of either of those bodies. The power of an idea whose time has come is a marvelous thing to behold.

"It will be the task of the Commissioners to examine and survey the routes from the Hudson to Lake Ontario and Lake Erie. The results of the survey will determine whether the canal should be made directly from Lake Erie without descending to Lake Ontario. There has been talk by Eddy and others of relying on the services of the Western Inland Lock Navigation Company. God save us from that incompetent band of commercial cutthroats. They have exposed their charter to forfeiture by repeated neglect. They could not even clear the Mohawk River of minor obstructions. No private corporation, especially that one, should be entrusted with control of so vast and important a project. The government must do it. I intend to see that private interests are prevented from becoming a part of this project." Morris traced on a map his guess as to the most likely routes of the canal. I distinctly remember that, as one of these, he traced almost a straight line from the Niagara Falls area through Rochester to Rome to the Hudson River above Albany. Although he did also trace a route to Lake Ontario, he said it was unlikely. His straight inland route was, of course, close to the actual route of the canal completed fifteen years later in 1825. At that later time Dr. Hosack and I both became embroiled in the great controversy over who should gain history's honors as the projector of the great canal. To this day the controversy continues. Because of my later breach of faith, which I shall explain in due course, I have been unable to reveal all of my knowledge of the matter. In this narrative I shall attempt to leave a full account to posterity of my reasons for withholding certain convincing evidence in favor of Gouverneur Morris.

Having described his own views on the canal, Morris explained what he wanted me to do. "If you could gather a collection of materials on the construction of canals in this country and in other lands, it would be most useful to me. Simeon De Witt told me that several years ago a series of excellent articles on the canal proposal appeared in a Genesee newspaper. You might find those to be helpful. If you can obtain reprints of those articles, I would like to review them. Of course, anything you choose to write on the subject would be of great interest to me. During the summer, the Commissioners will be traveling into the great interior country to view possible canal routes. Receipt of your work product by no later than June would allow them to be put to the best of use."

When Morris had completed his discussion of the canal, I reminded him of his promise to provide me information for my book. "Let us begin now," he graciously replied. I asked him to commence with his recollections of his career after the New York Constitution was completed, the point where I left him in my *History of New York City*. He started a detailed discussion of the events after the state convention elected him as a delegate to the Continental Congress in 1777. He began his account with his visit to General Schuyler's headquarters at Fort Edwards after the American evacuation of Ticonderoga. He was part of a committee of general safety to report the state of the military forces in that area. Burgoyne's great army had invaded New York and was only twenty miles away at the time. With a great grasp of military strategy, Morris explained how Burgoyne had made a fatal error by not returning to Ticonderoga and sailing down Lake George to Fort George and then advancing to Albany. Instead, he plunged into the wilderness. Unable to move with any speed, he never arrived at Albany. The gathering American forces obstructed his progress through the trackless forests. Three months later his worn-out force was cut off and forced to surrender after the great battle of Bemis Heights. This battle resulted in the Convention of Saratoga, the turning point, as most historians now agree, of the Revolutionary War. "At that moment," said Morris, "with a single bold stroke, Burgoyne might have won the war. Instead, he lost it." To my surprise at the coincidence of related topics, Morris explained that it was at Fort Edwards that he first publicly announced his belief "that the waters of the great western inland seas would by construction of a canal mingle with those of the Hudson River." Many years after Morris told me of his astoundingly early suggestion as to construction of the canal, I was able to confirm his account through Morgan Lewis, who was present at the time. This evidence supports those who claim Morris as the original projector of the great canal and places him decades before other claimants. However, the question of the nature of the canal he had proposed remains in controversy.

After Fort Edwards, Morris asked to be sent to Washington's headquarters to request reinforcements for General Schuyler to use against Burgoyne. Morris and John Jay found Washington's army in Pennsylvania engaged in its futile effort to prevent Howe's army from capturing Philadelphia. Washington could spare no more than the two brigades he had already assigned to aid Schuyler. Therefore, Morris and Jay set out for Philadelphia to request the Continental Congress to send additional militia to assist Schuyler. They arrived in the city the day that Congress decided to replace Schuyler with General Gates as commander of the northern army. Morris opposed the change but admitted that Gates's appointment may have been required by the insistence of the New England delegates that their troops would not march under Schuyler's command.

Morris seemed to be transported back in time as he recounted these occurrences with a passion I did not expect for stories from three decades past. "As a close friend and ardent supporter of Schuyler, it was a bitter setback for me. We succeeded only in getting Congress to direct Washington to send Daniel Morgan's regiment to the aid of the northern army. Yet, despite the bumbling leadership of Gates, the battle was won. As a result, the French joined us. For the first time, victory seemed not only possible, but likely." I was enthralled to be discussing these great events with one of the participants. In order to increase the enjoyment of the telling, Morris skillfully interspersed his historical account with numerous amusing stories. One of those concerned a wealthy widow who attempted to appease the advancing British by serving a splendid meal to their officers upon their arrival in her town. "The British officers politely devoured the meal and then proceeded to burn her house to the ground. They were, of course, apologetic about it." He laughed as he usually did at the conclusion of an anecdote.

Upon his arrival as a member of the Continental Congress in early 1778, Morris was placed on a conference committee to reorganize the army then in misery at Valley Forge. It was there that Morris first met the Marquis de Lafayette. Their lives, I was to learn later, were to be closely intertwined at various periods over many years. "At the time, I was deeply impressed by the young man. He was only twenty years old. At a later time, my favorable opinion of him would have to be revised." After relating the cancellation of the invasion of Canada, which was to have been under the command of Lafayette, Morris described in detail his committee's work in reforming the army's system of supply and the reorganization of the army itself. At this time Morris worked closely with General Washington; it is a matter of common knowledge that he become one of Washington's closest supporters. Contrary to his usual custom in describing historical figures in critical terms, Morris spoke of Washington only in words of unreserved veneration. In fact, his worship of Washington was in such marked contrast to his cynical comments about other wartime leaders that I began to wonder if Washington's reputation as a demigod was more an historical fact than it was a legend.

While I took notes, Morris spoke for hours. Before we were interrupted, he began to describe his efforts to oppose British attempts to conclude a peace with the United States before news of the alliance with France arrived from Europe. "The British written proposals were wrapped in a packet with seals depicting a mother embracing her returning children. The British were quite shameless in their diplomacy. I suggested we refuse to read them in formal session because of several derogatory references to the King of France. If we had sent them back with a demand that the objectionable references be removed, the British could not return to negotiate without appearing to be suing for peace. In any case, the attempt to drive a wedge between the French and us failed miserably." As is well-known, Morris, as chairman of the committee to treat with Lord North's conciliation commission, performed his greatest service during the war. He presented the report that there be no peace negotiations without a prior recognition of American independence. The famous report was unanimously adopted by Congress. It was in the midst of the account of his efforts to refuse receipt of what he referred to as the "British Trojan horse" that we were interrupted by an announcement I had been anticipating with a mixture of delight and dread.

A servant entered the room and declared that Mrs. Morris had returned. I felt afflicted, as if by a sudden fever; perspiration covered my forehead. Appearing eager to great the new arrival, Morris quickly hauled his large body out of his comfortable chair with the assistance of his cane. "I have a surprise for you." He gestured for me to follow him. Before we could leave the room, Nancy entered dressed in riding clothes. She kissed her husband on the cheek. "Daniel, I would like you to meet my wife." Nervously, I bowed slightly towards her. Appearing to recognize me, she smiled as if at an old friend. In a tone of mock disappointment, Morris rebuked me for my failure to express astonishment. "Are you not surprised by this unlikely union of beauty to age?"

"I must admit, Dr. Hosack told me about your marriage several weeks ago. Please accept my congratulations."

Obviously a happy man, Morris was radiantly enthusiastic. "We do. Of course we do. Nancy, this is Daniel Carey, a brilliant young historian. He will be assisting me on the work of the Canal Commission."

For a moment Nancy remained silent. In the absence of the flickering light from a single candle, she seemed no longer to be an ethereal apparition. As a flesh and blood human being, she was as attractive as the women who invaded the citadel of my reason. Yet she was unmistakably different. The aura of great sadness had vanished; she seemed to be happy. "Mr. Carey and I met last summer during one of the Sunday gatherings." That same wonderful voice stirred up all of the emotions I had been trying to suppress since my meeting with Dr. Hosack. Morris did not seem to be surprised by the fact that we had met on a prior occasion. When Mrs. Morris invited me to join them for dinner, Mr. Morris quickly endorsed his wife's suggestion. They both insisted I stay despite my feeble protestations of not wanting to impose on their hospitality.

While we were waiting for Mrs. Morris before the meal began, I asked Morris about the tapestry in his drawing room. He described it as a picture of "Télémaque being rescued from the charms of Circe, from Fénelon." When he asked about my interest, I replied guiltily, "Mere curiosity." After Nancy had changed from her mud-spattered riding clothes into a striking white dress, we sat down to one of Morris's sumptuous meals. Instead of sitting at opposite ends of the table, Morris sat at the head of the table with Nancy close beside him at his right side. I was placed on the left side facing her. Morris spoke in praise of his cook, whom he considered to be a treasure; Morris was a man who took food very seriously. As Morris continued to talk I had to remind myself not to stare at his wife. I was afraid that my clumsy passion for her might be revealed by an idiotic expression of yearning.

He always referred to her as "Nancy," never "Ann." I wondered whether she called him "Gouverneur." I guessed it was too much of a mouthful to be used as a means of address. Nancy was very quiet during the meal, mentioning only the difficulties of riding in the early spring mud. As if in answer to my unspoken question, she did finally address her husband as "Mr. Morris." The manner in which she spoke the name was in the nature of a term of endearment rather than a mark of formality. Once, after looking for some time at Morris as he spoke to me about the progress of the New York City Street Commission, I glanced at Nancy and was surprised to find her looking directly at me. As our eyes met, she smiled at me. Instead of modestly looking in another direction, she continued to gaze directly at me. Had her husband not been present, I might have stared back at her to see whose gaze would first be averted. With Morris at my right arm, I discreetly returned my attention to him. If I had not known they were married, I probably would have assumed they were father and daughter. This conclusion would have been based not only on the obvious difference in age, but also on the restrained, respectful manner in which they addressed each other. I wondered whether in private he was more like a father-protector than a husband. They did seem to be a most unlikely pair of lovers.

During a lull in the conversation, my curiosity, and perhaps too much claret, caused my tongue to get the better of my discretion. Looking at Nancy, I asked, "How did you meet each other?" Nancy's face reddened and she seemed somewhat flustered by my inquiry.

Morris rescued her by answering my question in an unexpected manner.

Instead of talking about nineteenth century New York, he surprised me by going back to eighteenth century Virginia. "Actually, it was back in ... I would guess 1787. I was looking after Robert Morris's tobacco interests in Virginia. We had many shipments to be made to France to fulfill contracts with the farmers-general. On one of my trips, I was invited by Nancy's father to his plantation, Tuckahoe. I met Nancy's numerous siblings; but I remembered Nancy. Even as a child, she was an enchanting creature. You were ... How old were you then?

"Thirteen." From Nancy's response, I calculated that she was two years older than me.

"Do you remember meeting Mr. Morris at that time?" I was amused at my own boldness in questioning her.

"Yes, I do." She provided no additional information.

Morris chuckled. "A man with one leg is always memorable, particularly to children." As Morris began to talk about her family in Virginia, she grew noticeably uneasy. Abruptly she stood up.

"I am extremely tired from riding. Please excuse me."

For a moment, as she departed, Morris and I both sat in silence. Not appearing to be disturbed by her sudden departure, Morris continued to talk about his own past for another hour. After finishing his account of his role in the rejection of the British peace offers, he returned to the subject of his wife. "Well, you have met my wife. You must admit, I am a lucky man." Without the least hesitation, I enthusiastically agreed. "Even for a man of my advanced years, celibacy is an impious and unnatural state. A man can draw all manner of plans for happiness; but a woman is essential to execute the plan. It is women, you know, who interweave the fine threads of affection into our lives to secure all of our earthly joys. Their ambition is to inspire love, and it is in fulfilling this ambition that they make the world a tolerable place. After almost sixty years on this earth, I have never met a member of the softer sex who inspires love as Nancy does. Before you stands a contented man." He clapped me on the back as if to pass some of his happiness from himself to me. I was moved by the gesture. For one of the only times in my life, I was seized by a pang of genuine envy.

According to his customary hospitality, Morris provided his boat and servants for my journey back to the city. It would be nearly one year before I would meet Nancy again.

SEVEN

Seeing Nancy Randolph transformed into Mrs. Morris, the wife of my formidable patron, allowed me to banish her from my mind, for a time. If the banishment was not complete, at least she was no longer an obsession. The dreams stopped. Even to think of her seemed a violation of a powerful taboo. As occurred subsequent to my assignment from Morris on the New York Street Commission, I ceased work on *The Age of Revolution*. For months all of my efforts were directed at the accumulation of materials concerning the canal. After much inquiry I learned through Mr. Van Zandt at The Bookworm that the articles Morris mentioned had been written by a Mr. Jesse Hawley. Commencing in October of 1807, they had appeared as a series of essays, fourteen in number, in the *Genesee Messenger*, a newspaper printed in Canandaigua. I sent letters requesting reprints to both the newspaper and to Mr. Hawley. Then I began poring over materials about canals and assembling the pertinent information for inclusion in a report for Mr. Morris. Relying heavily on the collection in the library on Nassau Street, including the *American Encyclopedia* and the lengthy dissertation on canals in the sixth volume of *Rees' Encyclopedia*, I learned about the canal systems of China, France, Holland, Denmark, Russia, and especially the extensive system of Great Britain. From the canal of Clyde in Scotland, connecting the firths of Forth and Clyde, to the canal of Kiel in Denmark, uniting the Baltic and North seas, I discovered a vast area of human activity about which I had known nothing. Within two months I could discuss in a learned manner the 825-mile canal from Canton to Pekin, built approximately 1000 A.D., or the 180-mile canal of Languedoc, commenced and completed in the reign of Louis XIV. I could explain how Peter the Great, by construction of a small canal at Vyshny-Volochuk, linked St. Petersburg by river to the Caspian Sea, over one thousand miles away, or discourse upon the career of the Duke of Bridgewater, the founder of inland navigation in England. However, not being an engineer, I found it extremely difficult to judge the feasibility of constructing a canal connecting the Hudson and the great inland lakes. Then the bread cast upon the waters months before came back in the form of manna from heaven. Although the *Genesee Messenger* never replied to my inquiry, Mr. Jesse Hawley himself sent me copies of his fourteen essays; he even included an earlier essay printed at Pittsburgh, Pennsylvania, in a paper called *The Commonwealth*. Appearing under the name "Hercules," the essays contained a treasure trove of invaluable information. Although Hawley had not explored the ground, his calculations, based on the available information, suggested that the waters of Lake Erie and those of the Mohawk and Hudson rivers could indeed be connected by means of a canal. Estimating that a canal from the village of Buffalo, at the foot of Lake Erie, to Utica, about two hundred miles away, would average about two feet fall each mile, he recommended the construction of a canal on an inclined plane. This was the first mention of the actual term "inclined plane" I ever saw with reference to the Erie Canal.

Using rough estimates, Hawley calculated the cost of the canal at six million dollars, an amazing estimate, as future events would reveal. His projected route was also very close to the final route of the canal. In essay number six Hawley predicted that the canal would make New York City the most important port in the United States, with the possible exception of New Orleans, and that within a century the island of Manhattan would be covered with buildings and population. If correct, I thought, this prediction would make the work of the New York City Street Commissioners more useful in a shorter time than even the visionary Mr. Morris might have thought possible.

In the last seven of his essays, Hawley discussed possible sources of capital for construction of the canal and suggested various other canals that might be built in the United States in diverse areas, from Buzzards Bay in Massachusetts to the Tombigbee River in the Mississippi Territory. Morris, I knew, would be excited when he read these brilliant essays. I only regretted receiving them after completing my own written report to Morris. Perhaps, however, this saved me from merely echoing the ideas, including the "inclined plane" proposal, of a more perspicacious scholar of canals. Instead of becoming the person who proposed the pernicious idea to Morris, I could instead assume the role of one who attempted to protect him from folly. Once again, a seemingly insignificant fact, receipt of the parcel of mail from Hawley in June instead of April, may have significantly changed the nature of my later relationship to Morris and my life for the next decade and beyond. As with the purchase of the Horsmanden book, at the time I was blissfully unaware of the significance of the event.

Shortly after receiving the Hawley essays, I met with Morris at the quarters of the New-York Historical Society. Accompanied by his valet, as always, he had come to the city on personal business and to see me about the canal. As I had anticipated, he was pleased with my vast amount of information on canals, especially the Hawley essays, which we discussed in some detail. "Although I am inclined to favor the inland route as proposed by Mr. Hawley, we cannot exclude the Lake Ontario route until the Commissioners have traveled through the territory in question. Next month we shall be meeting in Albany for the commencement of our exploration of the interior country. Mr. Geddes, whose surveys favor the inland route, will accompany us." I hoped that Morris would ask me to join him on the journey. To my disappointment, he never extended an invitation.

In order to ascertain Morris's opinion on the important issue of use of Lake Ontario, I asked him a question fearing that it might appear to be naive. "Would not the Lake Ontario route save a great amount in time and cost over the direct inland route from Lake Erie? Merely construct locks in the Niagara Falls area between Lake Erie and Lake Ontario; then navigation is available on Lake Ontario between Fort Niagara and the Oswego River. Some 125 to 150 miles of canal would not have to be built abreast of the presently existing body of water."

Morris's answer revealed several factors which I had not previously considered. "Setting aside the engineering obstacles of a passage by locks between Buffalo and Lake Ontario, there are major disadvantages to the Lake Ontario route. It is a much more circuitous route. It would enrich the territory of a foreign power at the expense of the United States. Montreal, instead of New York City, could become the great conduit of commerce in this part of the world. At first glance, it might appear foolish to construct a canal abreast of 150 miles of available sloop navigation along Lake Ontario. But all of the country along both sides of an inland route will soon begin to flourish upon its completion. This prosperity will also spread to the lands along the various waterways leading to the canal. The opening of the most fertile part of the state would quickly pay for the extra cost of constructing an inland canal. Also, navigation along an inland canal would be safe from the dangers of the open sea and from enemies to the north. In time of war and with the absence of an inland route, British control of Lake Ontario would sever navigation between New York City and the western part of the state. For years I have been saying that New York is a state with a unique opportunity to use navigable canals to connect our commerce with the great western waterways. Completion of this project will assure our prosperity for generations without threat from our northern neighbors." In a characteristic way, he paused for a moment, as if to savor his next remark. "The work of the Commissioners has not yet begun, and already I sound like a politician selling his program to the great apathetic public. I will say no more. Let us first permit the Commissioners to consider the matter."

As with almost every meeting we had for the next several years, Morris spent a few hours of his time providing me with historical information for my book. It was at this particular meeting I was to learn of the origin of the great hostility between Morris and Tom Paine which lasted up to the time of Paine's death. In 1778, after the return from Europe of Silas Deane, one of the three American Commissioners who had negotiated the treaty of alliance with France, a dispute arose. It concerned charges made by another of the Commissioners, Arthur Lee of Virginia, that Deane had misappropriated public funds. Congress split into bitter pro-Deane and pro-Lee factions. Although Morris did not so characterize the affair, the fact is that the factions foreshadowed the two great political parties which were later to develop. The aristocrats, including Morris and Jay, supported Deane. The less wealthy democrats tended to favor Lee.

The particular dispute concerned the question of whether supplies furnished to the Americans by Monsieur Beaumarchais were a gift from the French government or a private debt owed to Beaumarchais. In a series of articles published in early 1779, Paine, who was then secretary to the Committee on Foreign Affairs of Congress, revealed that official papers in his possession proved that the supplies furnished by Beaumarchais were a gift of the French government and that nothing was owed by the United States to Beaumarchais as a private contributor. Because France was supposed to have been neutral at the time, the articles impugned the good faith of that nation. The French minister demanded that Congress repudiate Paine's statements. As a Deane supporter, Morris led the fight for the dismissal of Paine on the grounds that he had abused his trust by revealing confidential information insulting to our new ally. Congress adopted Morris's resolutions disavowing Paine's articles, stating that France had given no supplies to the United States before the alliance, and declaring that the United States would not conclude a treaty with Britain without the consent of France. Paine was dismissed from his office. According to Morris, Paine never forgave him. As I later learned, the paths of Paine and Morris were to cross many times over the years. Although I was surprised to find myself in agreement with Morris against Paine on this particular issue, years later, when I saw Morris's private documents about the incident, my sympathies shifted back to Paine. In his speech before Congress in 1779, Morris had referred to Paine as a "mere Adventurer from England, without Fortune, without Family or Connections, ignorant even of Grammar." For years I had constantly wondered about Morris's views about me. Upon seeing these words, I considered whether Morris had also thought of me as a member of an inferior class, without fortune or a position in society. At times, I have thought, it explained the frequent long periods during which Morris did not bother to communicate with me. I shall never know.

For the remainder of 1810 I received no word from Morris. My time was fully occupied with my book. Late in the year, I met Dr. Hosack. I congratulated him on his new position. He had recently resigned from the faculty of Columbia College to become a professor in the newly chartered College of Physicians and Surgeons. Because he saw Morris much more frequently than I did, he was able to inform me about the summer trip of the Canal Commissioners. According to Hosack, the Commissioners had all met in Albany in early July. Morris and Van Rensselaer made the trip to Lake Erie on land. The others followed the river line by boat for most of the journey. The trip lasted the entire summer. At its conclusion, Morris appeared to favor the inland route over the use of Lake Ontario. After my discussions with Morris, any other conclusion by him would have astonished me.

"I am surprised he left his wife for so long. This is their first year of marriage." Despite the belief that my obsession with Mrs. Morris had ended, at the first opportunity I found myself trying to obtain information about her.

"She accompanied Mr. Morris on the trip. They were together the whole time. Mrs. Morris told me she was exhausted by the journey."

"She is not ill, is she?"

"No. I saw her two weeks go. She is quite well. Mr. Morris is in bed with the gout. He has had recurring attacks for some time. I have tried to help him, but he has little faith in the remedies of doctors." In the hope that Hosack would provide more information about the Morrises, I continued to talk about them. Dr. Hosack changed the subject to the Elgin Botanic Garden. He had been concerned about the subject for months, especially in light of the fact that the matter had been the cause of periodic attacks on him in the newspapers. In March the Legislature had passed an act for "promoting Medical Science in the State of New York." It provided for state purchase of the botanic garden, the money to be raised by a lottery five years in the future. "Last June, the appraisers estimated the value at $103,000. Have you seen what the Republic newspapers are saying?"

"I have read some of the letters. They are vicious."

Hosack became upset as he spoke about the public attacks directed at him. "They are totally distorted. They imply that because of my influence I have been awarded a price far beyond the value of the property. One legislator, who voted for the bill, actually referred to it later as an act 'for the relief of Dr. Hosack.' Can you imagine that? What they conveniently neglected to mention is that the $103,000 was the amount to be paid in five and one-half years. That amount is the equivalent of about $75,000 paid now; so the original evaluation appears higher than it actually is. After all, I can't be expected to sell now and not receive interest for the next five years on the money to be paid then. Finally, in October I agreed to accept $74,000. The public does not seem to realize that is merely the present value of the original estimate. The lower figure seems to have ended the controversy. I have been defamed without any cause. It's an outrage."

I told the doctor I had seen nothing about the subject for months. It was a lie to spare him further embarrassment. Actually, according to the newspapers, Hosack had petitioned the Legislature to grant him various public lands entangled with the botanic garden in order to clear his title. Since the public land was about one-quarter of the almost twenty acres in the botanic garden, the argument that the amount to be paid Hosack should be reduced by one-quarter appeared to be a just one. From direct personal experience, I knew David Hosack to be a man of great generosity and concern for the public welfare; therefore, it disturbed me that malicious letters and articles in newspapers could cause me to doubt his motives, even for a moment. Perhaps it is because we cannot see into the human heart that a libel, no matter how lacking in credibility, is capable of creating doubts about our own judgments of other people. In a much more forceful way, within a few years I was to receive a lesson in the enduring power of libel. The matter troubles me to this day. Although I have a number of motives for leaving this book to posterity, it is this later defamation which has been the chief cause of the writing of this account.

Early in 1811 I received from Morris a draft of the report of the Canal Commissioners. It was in the handwriting of Mr. Morris, who, as President of the Canal Commissioners, assigned to himself the task of preparing the report. In his letter he asked me to review the report and then come to Morrisania to discuss it. The lengthy report was titled, "Report of the Commissioners Appointed by Joint Resolution of The Honorable The Senate and Assembly of the State of New York of the 13th and 15th of March 1810 to Explore the Route of Inland Navigation for Hudson's River to Lake Ontario and Lake Erie." At first glance I thought the title might indicate an acceptance of the Lake Ontario route. The reports and maps of surveyor James Geddes were appended. For one like me, who is not an engineer or surveyor, the report was very difficult reading. Opening the report in a random manner, I was confronted with abstruse technical language.

Admitting, for instance, a stream to be deep and wide in descending an inclined plane, its velocity will be accelerated. But if the inclination be not great, and the channel shoal and narrow, the friction may so counteract the descent as to retard the velocity. From these considerations, it is evident that the sum of descent must depend primarily on the quantity of water required. This in navigation ascending and descending by locks, must be greater than when carried along a plane. It must also be greater in a loose than a stiff soil.

At first I feared the entire report would be incomprehensible to me. Fighting back the fear of my own inadequacy, I carefully plodded through the report. Despite the title, it was clear that the report was a rejection of the Ontario route in favor of the overland canal. Morris argued that experience in Europe has "exploded" the idea of using beds of rivers, such as the various rivers to Lake Ontario, for internal navigation where canals are practicable. He noted that the navigation of rivers relies primarily on the labor of men, which is more dear here than in Europe, whereas canals use horses, whose subsistence is cheaper in America. After a detailed review of the topography, Morris recommended the use of an inclined plane with a uniform slope from Lake Erie to the ridge between Schenectady and Albany with some lockage from that point to the Hudson. He assumed an average descent of six inches each mile, a figure substantially different from Jesse Hawley's. The inclined plane, it was concluded, would save as much of the expense of lockage as possible. The saving would include the expense of constructing and keeping the locks in repair and the time spent and tolls paid in passing through them. It was admitted that further scientific investigation would be needed to confirm the recommendations in the report.

Morris stressed that the canal would turn the commerce of the Great Lakes to the United States, giving us a great competitive advantage over the British. The area affected, exclusive of Lake Superior, would be more than two thousand miles surrounded at a convenient distance by more than fifty million acres of land. According to the report, there was no part of the civilized world in which an object of such great magnitude could be compassed at so small an expense. Although the cost of the canal could not, it was admitted, be estimated with any precision, the report suggested a total cost of five million dollars, including the construction of locks, aqueducts, and other general expenses. This sum was characterized as small compared to the value of the commodities the canal would annually transport. The report opposed granting the project to private persons or corporations. It was contended that such a large expenditure should be made under public authority, as "too great a national interest is at stake." Not just New York, but the nation, Morris wrote, should bear the expense.

The report is another example of Morris's versatile brilliance. The man wrote as if he had spent a lifetime surveying and engineering for the purpose of canal construction. The report was so convincing that I doubted that the Lake Ontario route would ever be seriously considered again. Upon a second reading, however, I began to wonder about the feasibility of the inclined plane. If it worked, it would save the immense costs associated with locks. But to create an inclined plane canal, embankments of enormous size would be necessary to cross the valleys of the Genesee (26 feet high), Seneca (83 feet), and Cayuga (130 feet). In order to determine whether it was practicable, I discussed it with John Randel, the only man I knew with the knowledge to evaluate the idea. Randel borrowed Geddes's survey map for two days. When we met again, he declared that the inclined plane proposal would probably not work. "It is a brilliant concept. The savings on the costs of lockage would be significant. These savings may well be nullified by the need to build embankments, gigantic aqueducts, and tunnels. In my opinion, it would make more sense to build the locks rather than gamble with the other." He pointed to various locations on the Geddes maps where the inclined plane might encounter serious problems. He also pointed to places where locks would have to be placed if the inclined plane were not built. I asked Randel if Morris had requested his assistance on the canal. He replied, "Morris knows I am too busy attempting to complete the city surveys within the four-year term of the Street Commissioners. Besides, with Simeon De Witt on the Canal Commission, Morris knows he can obtain the opinion of the best surveyor in the state."

Armed with the views of Randel, I returned to Morrisania in January of 1811. A few weeks earlier many of the local bodies of water were frozen. However, in a week of thaw, my usual transportation by boat was available. Instead of a servant, Mrs. Morris herself greeted me at the door. Her head was covered by a cap, as if she were trying to hide the beauty of her dark locks. She seemed to be in a cheerful mood. Upon seeing her smile and hearing her voice, my former feelings appeared as though they had never departed. They were merely in hiding, waiting to ambush me at the first opportune moment. After one of the servants assisted me in removing my heavy winter coat and left the room, I realized that it was the first time I had been alone with Nancy since the night we met, over one and one-half years earlier. All my carefully prepared defenses crumbled. Although the fact that her husband was in the same house made my desires impossible of fulfillment, I wanted desperately to embrace her. My temples throbbed with excitement as I awkwardly attempted to engage her in conversation to prolong our brief moment together. I wondered if she was aware of my clumsy passion for her. My infatuation, I thought, must be transparent. After all, women are said to have an acute ability to perceive love in a man. If she knew, she certainly was not revealing it to me. After greeting me in her ordinary refined English, she lapsed into a self-mocking heavy southern accent. "Ah do declare. Ah don't understand how you northerners tolerate this cold." It was one of the many tricks in her bottomless bag of charms. We both smiled, and she returned to her usual mode of speech. "Mr. Morris has been expecting you. His gout is bothering him terribly. Please, try not to subject him to too much fatigue." She personally escorted me into the study. Morris's one good leg was encased in bandages and resting upon a stool.

"As you can see, I have become entirely helpless. My left leg is in better condition than my right." As he spoke, Morris tapped his wooden leg with his cane. "Nancy, would you please have something warm to drink brought in to us. Daniel must be cold. Boat trips on the East River are not very pleasant this time of year." With his cane he tapped the seat next to him several times to indicate I should sit down. Unlike his usual jovial greetings, his salutations were brusque and perfunctory. He was more interested in talking about the agonies of gout than about business. "The pain usually first seizes the great toe. Then it comes into the heel and the arch of the foot. The ankle swells last. When the attacks first began, I used to think it was an improperly fitted shoe. Now I recognize it as soon as it begins. Damned nuisance, and incurable as far as anybody knows."

"Have you tried any cures?"

"Only two. Dr. Hosack recommended a mixture of minerals and herbs combined with bathing in the ocean. Had no effect. At least it was not harmful. Dr. Hoffman gave me something called 'diaphoretic compound ipecacuanha powder.' It made me so sick, I forgot about the gout. When I recovered my senses, I realized the gout was worse than ever. Damned quackery. If one of my stallions ever goes lame, I shall give him the powder and put him out of his misery. One of my nephews recommended fright, 'the Robert Boyle cure.' Nobody has tried it on me yet. Perhaps they will surprise me some day. They could come into an early inheritance that way. Enough of my woes. Let us talk about the canal."

Nancy entered carrying hot tea, brandy, and cakes. I sprang to my feet offering assistance. She gestured for me to return to my seat. Morris chided her lovingly. "Nancy, how many times have I told you to leave these chores to the servants. You are the lady of the house."

"Once a servant, you know." Her reply could have been spoken with a sharp edge. Instead it was stated with a twinkle in the eye and in a humorously self-deprecating tone. Unlike my own household, it was clear that this husband and wife enjoyed each other's presence. It would, I thought, clearly be an evil thing to come between such spouses. Had I been dashing and handsome, a Lord Byron, I probably could not have driven a wedge between them. Daniel Carey as a rival for the lady's hand was a truly ludicrous thought. At that moment, I was resigned to my fate. Nancy could never be mine. As usual, that resignation was only temporary.

Nancy told Morris to ring the bell beside him if he wanted anything. Closing the door behind her, she unobtrusively left the room. Morris began a technical discussion of his views. It was clear from his comments on the canal that he had carefully examined all of the reports and surveys. He discussed his calculations as to pressure, absorption, and evaporation of water, the quality of the soil along the proposed route and the costs of excavations, embankments, and lockage. After his awe-inspiring display of knowledge, I was reluctant to criticize his report. In response to his questions about my views on the report, I first complimented it in every way possible. No reasonable person, I told him, could seriously consider the Lake Ontario route after reading the report. My praise for the recommendations in favor of government control of the project and the cost estimates was equally profuse. Having carefully prepared my cushion of praise, I launched my criticism of the inclined plane. "It appears to me that the construction of an inclined plane may be impracticable. The great elevation of the hills at Little Falls on the Mohawk makes it almost impossible." I identified the areas where great embankments and aqueducts would be required. Morris looked grim and unmoved.

"Without the inclined plane, too great a number of locks would be required to overcome the amount of ascent and descent. The expense of erecting the locks and the delay caused by having vessels pass through them make a substitute essential. England and France have both used inclined planes in canals. There is no reason we cannot use the same method, unless it is the load to be carried. Some experiments in this area may be necessary. But it can succeed; I am confident of it." Morris attempted to shift to another aspect of the report. I continued to be adamant in my opposition. After warning him that the inclined plane could be the Achilles Heel of the report around which the opponents of the canal would swarm, I suggested he use the idea as one of several alternatives stated in the report. He was angered at my persistence.

"I have learned from bitter experience that unusual proposals, even when bottomed on mathematical demonstrations, are treated as fanciful by those who measure the whole world with the limited standard of their own comprehension. Let the critics have their target. It may divert their attention from other aspects of the proposal." Although stung by Morris's response, I continued to suggest problems with the inclined plane. Finally, in exasperation, he raised his voice. "That is quite enough on that subject. Let us move away from it." As soon as he began reviewing another subject, he regained his composure.

Interspersed with his description of the topography in the area of the proposed canal, he gave an account of the trip to Lake Erie during the previous summer. "In early July, the Commissioners all met at the Surveyor General's office in Albany. Simeon De Witt engaged Mr. Geddes to attend us as surveyor and to show us the route he had reported favorably to the Legislature. Stephen Van Rensselaer and I made the trip by land. The other Commissioners followed the line of the rivers by boat. We were all united at Utica where we met Mr. Geddes. We met again at Rome. It was there I stated my views in favor of the inland route for the canal. The Commissioners and Geddes showed no signs of disagreement." He described the dangers of disease along the route, noting that two of their party were afflicted with the fever. At Geneva the other Commissioners sold their boats and procured carriages. He and Van Rensselaer met them at Lewiston. "We reached Buffalo in early August. The village contains approximately thirty houses and no church. When the canal is completed, it will grow swiftly as the gateway to and from the western lands. At present, it can be missed without any loss." Unlike his usual accounts, he avoided any personal anecdotes, speaking only of canal business. It was only when I asked him if Mrs. Morris had accompanied him that he mentioned her. She was so exhausted by the trip that, after returning by way of Albany, they rested at the Van Rensselaer estate for some time. Morris did lapse into one anecdote at the end of his account concerning his attendance at the religious services of the "shaking Quakers" at Lebanon Springs on the Massachusetts border. "They preach abandonment of worldly pursuits, especially conjugal pleasures. If the religion ever became universal, the human race would cease to exist. I suppose that is one way to obliterate evil in the world. But until the day of deliverance comes, we weaker mortals must continue to struggle with the problems of the world.

"The canal report should be published in March. After that, the chief thing to be done will be to acquire capital. It is the requests for funds that will bring forth the inevitable sneers of those who always condemn what they cannot understand. It will be difficult. Two years ago, Joshua Forman visited Washington to propose the canal project to President Jefferson. The President said it was a fine project for a century hence. To speak of building a canal of 250 miles, Jefferson said, was little short of madness when money was not even available to complete a small canal for Washington at a cost of $200,000. As usual, brother Jefferson is wrong. We shall raise the money." Abruptly he rang the bell and a servant answered. He was instructed to provide me a boat ride back to the city. On the way out I looked for Mrs. Morris, but she was not to be seen. My disappointment was intense.

In early March of 1811 the report of the Canal Commissioners was published, as written by the president of the commission, Gouverneur Morris. He did not send me a copy of the report or even inform me of its publication. I obtained a copy on my own. Morris had made almost no alterations in the report. It was virtually identical to the draft report I had reviewed two months earlier. The inclined plane proposal was intact. My objections had been disregarded.

Later that same month, the long-awaited final report of the "Commissioners of Streets and Roads in the City of New York" was released. John Randel permitted me to review his own report, as Mr. Morris did not condescend to provide me with a copy. This double omission on the part of Morris wounded me. To me, it was a matter of respect and courtesy to make a copy of each report available to one who had expended so much time on each project. On future occasions he would continue to neglect to inform me of matters we had toiled on together. Each time it rankled. In the back of my mind there always lurked the thought that Morris would not so neglect a gentleman of his own class. Perhaps he did view me as a social inferior, without fortune or family, not owed the courtesy due to a genuine colleague. At the time, I preferred to consider these incidents as the inadvertent omissions of a busy man.

It was of some comfort to me that the report of the Street Commissioners, unlike the canal report, did appear to reflect some changes, minor though they were, based upon my comments. The plan itself was the same with avenues numbered from one to twelve extending from north to south, and perpendicular cross streets as far north as 155th Street. Much of the report consisted of John Randel's carefully drawn maps and the results of his survey. It was in the "remarks" of the Commissioners where I perceived some response to my suggestions. For example, the report stated that "one of the first objects which claimed the attention of the Commissioners was the form and manner in which the business should be conducted; that is to say, whether they should confine themselves to rectilinear and rectangular streets, or whether they should adopt some of those supposed improvements by circles, ovals, and stars which certainly embellish a plan, whatever may be their effect as to convenience and utility. In considering that subject, they could not but bear in mind that a city is to be composed principally of the habitations of men, and that straight-sided and right-angled houses are the most cheap to build and the most convenient to live in. The effect of these plain and simple reflections was decisive. . . ." The refusal to consider circles, ovals, and stars was clearly a rejection of the ideas embodied in L'Enfant's plan for Washington City.

As to my suggestion that they leave more space in its original state, they declared, "It may be a matter of surprise that so few vacant spaces have been left, and those so small, for the benefit of fresh air and consequent preservation of health. Certainly if the City of New York was destined to stand on the side of a small stream, such as the Seine or Thames, a great number of ample places might be needful. But those large arms of the sea which embrace Manhattan Island render its situation, in regard to health and pleasure, as well as to the convenience of commerce, peculiarly felicitous." Nevertheless, they did retain the various squares Morris had shown me, along with space sufficient for a large reservoir. With some foresight, they noted that "it was felt to be indispensable that a much larger space should be set apart for military exercise, as also to assemble, in the case of need, the force destined to defend the city." Thus they proposed retaining a large open space in the midst of the city to be called "The Parade." They concluded the report by stating,

To some it may be a matter of surprise that the whole island has not been laid out as a city. To others it may be a subject of merriment that the Commissioners have provided space for a greater population than is collected at any spot on this side of China. They have in this respect been governed by the shape of the ground. It is not improbable that considerable numbers may be collected at Haerlem before the high hills to the southward of it shall be built upon as a city; and it is improbable that (for centuries to come) the grounds north of Haerlem Flat will be covered with houses. To have come short of the extend laid out might therefore have defeated just expectations; and to have gone further might have furnished materials for the pernicious spirit of speculation.

Concerning these statements, I wondered whether Morris had considered the prediction of Jesse Hawley that, as a result of the canal, the entire island of Manhattan would be covered by habitations within one century. In fact, one might consider the publication of the New York City report within weeks of the canal report as an irony of history. Work had begun on the city report three years before the canal report, so they were clearly independent of each other. Yet from the vantage point of almost twenty years after the event, it would seem that the city plan was merely a supplement to deal with the inevitable effects that construction of the canal would have on the growth of the city.

These great national works never spring up without conflict. Like all human endeavor, they are the product and the cause of constant struggle. The combat involving both plans commenced almost immediately after their publication. Those whose property was threatened by the plan of the Street Commissioners vehemently announced their opposition. Others saw the plan as an opportunity for personal profit. A few weeks after reading the city report, I met with John Randel for one of our regular chess matches. Unlike every previous time I had seen him, he showed visible signs of emotion. He was angry about the intrusion into the work of the Commissioners by a scoundrel named William Bridges. According to Randel, in December of 1810 Bridges, a city surveyor, had attempted to use his political friends to steal away from Randel the city contract for completion of the task of surveying by the placement of monuments at the intersection of each planned avenue and street. As a result of Morris's and Simeon De Witt's intervention on behalf of Randel, the city awarded the contract to him. Randel was to be engaged in this work for the next seven years. To anyone who knew Randel, it was certain that he was more concerned about the accuracy of the city street plan than about the profit to be gained. Bridges, however, was interested in money and did not cease searching for it in the various projects created in the wake of the plan. Randel was seething with outrage as he described Bridges's maneuvers. "Bridges petitioned the Common Council to give him the copyright to the maps filed by the Commissioners. My maps! Before I even knew what he was doing, he used his political cronies to obtain exclusive copies of my maps. The only condition is that he furnish sixty copies to the board at no cost and compensate me for my personal memoranda. Can you imagine? The formal request has already been made for me to furnish my memoranda to Bridges. With the support of the city authorities, he is robbing me of my own work product!" Randel had the look of an innocent who has discovered the existence of corruption for the first time.

"That is outrageous. Have you spoken to Morris or De Witt?"

"Both. They are attempting to assist me. But they say Bridges has very powerful friends on the council. Morris has suggested litigation. But that would drag on for years and cost more money than I have."

We discussed alternative methods of opposing Bridges. Finally, at Randel's suggestion, we began to play chess. Although he appeared to be concentrating on the game, he was not the formidable tactician of past contests. For the first time I managed to checkmate him. There was no glory for me in such a victory. Later that year Bridges published an engraving of Randel's map with a Bridges copyright on it. The struggle between Randel and Bridges would continue for years.

Within weeks after publication of the canal report, opponents of the canal began to condemn the report. As I had predicted, it was the inclined plane that became the chief target of critical attacks. They claimed it was fanciful and impracticable. Gouverneur Morris, as the author of the report, was ridiculed as a man under the influence of an uncontrolled imagination. Opponents rallied around the Lake Ontario route as an alternative to the proposed inland canal. On the whole, the supporters of the Lake Ontario route did not want any canal; they merely dredged up the alternative plan as a stick with which to beat the whole proposal. Nevertheless, in May of 1811, two months after publication of the report, a new law was passed adding Robert Fulton and Robert Livingston to the Canal Commission; the expanded commission was given power to make further surveys and to apply to the national and to state governments for aid in the construction of the canal.

The attacks on the canal report continued for months. I heard nothing from Morris, the continuing favorite target of the critics. It was only through David Ogden, of all people, that I learned something of the fruits of my arguments with Morris concerning the inclined plane. My meeting with Ogden was a result of the infamous "Trinity Church Riot." Because of my curiosity about the case and the opportunity to see David Ogden perform as an attorney, I attended the trial in August of 1811. The "riot" occurred at the Columbia College commencement that summer. A member of the graduating class at Columbia, J. B. Stevenson, had been appointed one of the disputants in a political debate scheduled to take place during the commencement. As was required by the rules of the college, he submitted his comments for the review of a member of the faculty, Dr. Wilson. Wilson directed him to change his statement that "Representatives ought to act according to the sentiments of their constituents." Apparently, democratic ideas were heresy at Columbia College. Stevenson objected, but Wilson required that the revision be made.

At the commencement debate the student delivered the statement as he had originally written it. When his name was later called for ceremonial delivery of his diploma, the professor interposed and the president of the college refused to confer the degree. Stevenson left the hall. A short time later he returned surrounded by supporters. He walked to the platform and demanded his diploma. It was again refused. Turning to the audience, Stevenson declared, "I am refused my degree, ladies and gentlemen, not from any literary deficiency, but because I refused to speak the sentiments of others as my own." Several student supporters, including a Mr. Verplanck, mounted the stage, condemned the faculty, and demanded the degree be conferred. The audience became excited in favor of Stevenson. They began to cheer his supporters and hiss his opponents. The provost, Dr. Mason, was hissed so loudly he was compelled to withdraw. Thereafter, the police were called to quell the wild uproar of shouting, clapping, and hissing which continued for nearly an hour. The commencement ceremony could not be completed.

The controversy continued in the newspapers, with the faculty endorsing the refusal to grant the degree while others criticized the college. Seven of the principals, including Stevenson and Verplanck, were indicted for the criminal offense of creating or assisting in a riot. The trial was held at the August term of the Court of Sessions, usually referred to as "the Mayor's Court." As Mayor of the city, De Witt Clinton presided before a jury of the defendants' peers. Three well-known attorneys, David B. Ogden, Josiah O. Hoffman, and Peter A. Jay, appeared for five of the defendants. Two defendants represented themselves. Because all of the indicted students were from leading families of the city, there was great interest in the trial.

After waiting for more than an hour, I finally gained entrance into the packed courtroom. It was the most popular entertainment in the city, bear-baiting not excluded. David Ogden eloquently argued that the students were never warned of a possible penalty for refusal to incorporate the views of a professor in a speech. Sweating profusely, Ogden declared in a booming voice that creation of a penalty after the event was in the nature of an ex post facto law. He also contended that there was no proof that a riot had occurred. "The audience merely exhibited its strong disapproval of the improper refusal to confer a degree on a deserving young man. It became disorderly only when the faculty persisted in its unjust refusal to give Stevenson his diploma. There was no violence on the part of the defendants. There was no riot. There was no crime." The spectators punctuated each of Ogden's statements with roars of increasing loudness. His impassioned plea caused such an uproar in the court that Clinton threatened to remove all of the spectators.

Mayor Clinton proceeded to undo all the effects of Ogden's speech by charging the jury that a riot had in fact occurred and that all of the defendants were involved in it. He instructed the jurors that they were bound by considerations "arising out of the public peace and the public morals, and by their regard for an institution venerable for its antiquity, to bring in all the defendants guilty." As instructed, the jury convicted all of the defendants. Clinton imposed heavy fines and even threatened imprisonment. The students were also required to procure sureties for their future good behavior. After the trial, it was said that Clinton, a past bitter enemy of the Federalists, was attempting to gain Federalist support for his presidential candidacy. I later heard that the provost, Dr. Mason, an ardent Federalist, at the time of the trial had arranged an interview between Clinton and the three Federalist leaders, John Jay, Rufus King, and Gouverneur Morris. Because of his previous denunciations of the Federalists, it was said that Clinton failed to gain their support. In the case itself, Republic sympathies were with the students, while Federalist support was solidly behind the college, a bastion of Federalism. Himself an ardent Federalist, Ogden must have extorted a heavy fee to appear in support of a democratic cause, even if the students were from wealthy Federal families. In spite of my personal enmity towards Ogden, I must admit to being impressed by his substantial skills as an advocate.

Although I never acquired any direct information on the subject, my own guess is that Clinton's meeting with Morris and the others was as much to protect the reputation of Columbia College as it was to further Clinton's political career. The year before, Dr. Hosack, who was then a member of the Columbia faculty, had told me a story about Morris that further increased my admiration for the man while establishing his continuing close ties with the college. Morris, who was a graduate of Columbia College when it was known as King's College, thought the provision of the charter of Columbia requiring the president to be an Episcopalian should be deleted. Believing that a direct attack on the provision would arouse fierce opposition, Morris and Rufus King decided to produce the desired result in a gradual manner. This would be accomplished simply by electing a vice-president of the college who was not an Episcopalian. The religious requirement for the president would soon end. Thus, as he had introduced religious tolerance into the New York Constitution, Morris shrewdly sneaked it into the charter of Columbia College.

At the conclusion of the trial, outside the courthouse, I saw David Ogden striding away from the scene of his defeat. He did not appear to be perturbed. After all, the Federalists and Columbia College had triumphed, and he had an ample fee in his pocket. I pretended not to notice him, but he walked directly up to me. To my surprise, he was amiable.

"Good to see you today, Mr. Carey. Were you amused by the proceedings?"

"Yes. It was a very interesting case. The verdict was completely unjust."

"The students can all afford the fines. What is important is that the good name of Columbia College remains untarnished."

"Then you did not believe your own argument?"

"On the contrary, as a legal matter I believe there was no riot. Nevertheless, the result does not bother me. Great institutions cannot be controlled by the rabble. The natural leadership must always govern. Otherwise, we would have anarchy."

"That is the difference between you lawyers and us historians. History

requires a greater degree of certainty than the law. You lawyers are less interested in the truth than in the results produced by the legal system."

"I would prefer to say we are looking for something more than the truth.
We protect the values of the society in which we live. The truth is only one
among many of such values."

Rather than argue with Ogden, I changed the subject. "I have not seen
your uncle, Mr. Morris, and his wife for some time. I hope they are well."
Ogden's answer pleased me.

"My uncle is quite well. These days he speaks highly of you. He told me
that if he had followed your advice, he would have avoided much of the
criticism directed at the canal report. You seem to have won his confidence.
That is not an easy task." He was interrupted by several well-wishers and bade
me good day. I was intrigued by his avoidance of recognizing the existence of
Mrs. Morris and, of course, by his comments on the canal report. Although
defeated in the battle of the inclined plane, I was apparently victorious in the
campaign. Morris, I thought, would soon communicate with me; I was certain
of it. Yet, six months would pass before I heard from him.

In the interim, I did little but work on *The Age of Revolution* and look at
the great comet that was visible in the night skies during the autumn of 1811.
There was one notable exception to my seclusion. In November of that year
a special meeting of the New York Manumission Society was called to draft
a petition for the total abolition of slavery in New York. Over the years,
most members of the society had lost their fervor for the cause. Only a small
core of members remained active. It was several of these members who remembered my appearance at the slavery debate three years earlier and asked
me to assist them in writing the petition and preparing supporting documents.
The active members had become increasingly dissatisfied with the system of
gradual manumission established by the Act of 1799. It may be remembered
that the act freed children born to slave women after July 4, 1799, with males
to become free at age twenty-eight and females at age twenty-five. As the years
passed, the problems of enforcement of the law became more difficult. Despite
the efforts of the society to halt the practice, pregnant slave women continued
to be sent out of state, where the newborn infants could be sold. Also, the
society had only limited success in preventing traders from purchasing children at low prices in New York for illegal sale beyond the state borders.
Numbers that the society had compiled indicated a decrease in the Negro
population of New York since 1799. Because it was unlikely that free or soon-
to-be free Negroes would leave the state voluntarily, the society declared that
the decline was due to kidnapping and illegal sales. The numerous acts passed
since 1800 to halt this abominable trade were ineffective. The society had
endorsed all of these acts. In 1808, for example, the penalty for kidnapping
was increased by making second offenses punishable by life imprisonment.
Since 1808 New York City had denied the use of its jails for the detention of
so-called "fugitive slaves." In 1809 the state had recognized slave marriages,
prohibited separation of husband and wife, and legitimized the children of

slaves. Despite these laws, between 1808 and 1812 the society itself had to free 165 persons unjustly held as slaves. Finally the society decided to turn away from these partial measures as insufficient; total abolition was demanded, and I became an active participant in these demands.

At first I had balked at the request to assist the society. No matter how worthy the cause, I was always hesitant to join organizations, out of both my accursed unsociability and a strong sense of the hopelessness of eliminating the injustices of this world. Yet I did finally join in the society's efforts, not with the expectation of accomplishing anything, but out of a sense of duty. If everyone refused, like me, to act on this most important of issues, the failure of reform would become a certainty. I would also yield my right to criticize others for their failure to act. I did not want the bitter taste of hypocrisy in my mouth every time I cursed injustice.

At first my worst fears about the ineffectiveness of organizations were confirmed. At one sparsely attended meeting the proponents of a proposal would carry the day. At the next meeting, with an almost entirely different group of members present, the new group would repeal the previous action. After many tedious and bitter meetings, we drafted a demand for total abolition which was adopted by the society. The effort to gain legislative enactment of the demand would continue for many years. Eventually, when I was not as unsociable a creature as I was in 1811, I would even attend the American Convention of Delegates from Abolition Societies in the role of representative of the New York Manumission Society. But that is a story for another time.

In February of 1812 Morris finally invited me back to Morrisania. He was fully ambulatory, with no sign of his earlier disabling attack of gout. He informed me that he and Nancy had just returned from a two-month trip to Washington to obtain financial support from the national government for the construction of the canal. The Canal Commissioners had entrusted this task to Morris and De Witt Clinton. Within minutes of my arrival, he showed me his draft of the Canal Commissioners' latest report, scheduled to be published in March. Although he did not mention my previous opposition to the inclined plane, the first thing he said to me about the new report was that it abandoned the proposal for an inclined plane east of the Seneca outlet. It was as if he were saying, "You were right, and I have now belatedly recognized that fact." He never made such an express apology, but I sensed that from this time he treated me with increased respect and trust. Perhaps I imagined too much, based on David Ogden's statement to me; nevertheless, my feeling has always been that my spurned advice on the inclined plane was a major cause of important future favors and confidences bestowed on me by Mr. Morris.

Morris asked me to sit at his own desk and read the report. He departed stating he would return for my opinion in a short time. Sitting alone in his study, I immediately sensed that my status at Morrisania had been enhanced. The new report indicated that the federal government had refused the offer to make construction of the canal a national project. The individual states had differing views on the New York proposal. Massachusetts, Ohio, and Tennessee had agreed to instruct their Congressmen to endorse the application of New York. Connecticut, New Jersey, and Vermont were opposed. Others favored the route by the falls of Niagara to Lake Ontario instead of the inland route. The Commissioners reported that they had again examined the advantages of the two different routes and continued to favor the inland route.

Morris used the report to strike back at his attackers.

> Things which twenty years ago a man would have been laughed at for believing, we now see. Under these circumstances there can be no doubt that those microcosmic minds which, habitually occupied in the consideration of what is little, are incapable of discussing what is great, and who already stigmatize the proposed canal as a romantic scheme, will not unsparingly distribute the epithets, absurd, ridiculous, chimerical, on the estimate of what it may produce. The Commissioners must, nevertheless, have the hardihood to brave the sneers and sarcasms of men, who, with too much pride to study, and too much wit to think, undervalue what they do not understand, and condemn what they cannot comprehend.

Morris supported his vision with calculations on the expense of conveyance by canal drawn from experience in England. Using the quantity of work that two horses and three men could do in eight hours, including wear and tear on the boats, horses, and the canal, plus interest on capital expended plus wages, which are higher in this country than in England, Morris concluded that the total expense would amount to no more than one cent per ton per mile. This conclusion meant that a ton could be moved 3200 miles by canal boat for the sum paid to transport it by wagon for only a hundred miles. It was a very powerful argument in favor of the canal, which Morris had not used before. As a result of these figures, the report estimated huge future net revenues which would repay the cost of the canal within a short time. The estimated expense of construction was raised by one million dollars, from five million in the 1811 report to six million dollars in this report. Morris concluded the report with a passage of characteristically soaring prose that could be read as a suitable epitaph for his work as President of the Canal Commission and of the New York City Street Commission:

> The life of an individual is short. The time is not distant when those who make this report will have passed away. But we can fix no term to the existence of a State; and the first wish of a patriot's heart is, that his own may be eternal. But whatever limit may have been assigned to the duration of New York, by those eternal decrees which established the heavens and the earth, it is hardly to be expected that she will be blotted from the list of political societies before the effects here predicted shall have been sensibly felt. And even when, by the

flow of that perpetual stream which bears all human institutions away, our Constitution shall be dissolved and our laws be lost, still the descendants of our children's children will remain. The same mountains will stand, the same rivers flow; new moral combinations will be formed on the old physical foundations and the extended line of remote posterity; yet, after the lapse of thousands of years, and the ravages of repeated revolutions—when the records of history shall have been obliterated, and the tongue of tradition have converted the shadowy remembrance of ancient events into childish tales of miracle—this national work shall remain. It shall bear testimony to the genius, the learning, the industry and intelligence of the present age.

It was clear from the report that Morris was sensitive about the bitter invective aimed at him as a result of the first report. When he returned to the room, therefore, I was careful to use only words of praise in order to avoid inflicting additional wounds. My reservations about partial retention of the inclined plane were kept to myself. It must be confessed that I did not want to squander the goodwill I had established in my dealings with him.

"I have no reservations about this new report. It is superb. But without financial assistance from outside the state, has the proposal any chance?"

Morris was optimistic. "The expense of this project is a mere pittance compared to the benefits. New York is now at liberty to rely on its own resources and to retain the benefit of the resulting revenues. The next step is to ask the Legislature to authorize the gathering of the necessary funds. I shall soon go to Albany for that purpose. There is now, I believe, enough support within the state. We will obtain the authorization." He discussed the report in greater detail and with more candor on his part than had been present in our earlier meetings. When he was satisfied that he had heard all my comments, he ended the discussion. "Enough of this. I have not seen you for many months. Tell me about your work."

He seemed quite interested in my report of progress on *The Age of Revolution*. Without my asking, he even renewed his offer to discuss with me his personal experiences. When I mentioned my concern about the machinations of William Bridges, he indicated his sympathy for John Randel. "I have expressed my views in Mr. Randel's favor to the Common Council. It is a political thicket in which I cannot afford to become further entangled. Bridges will lose his copyright on the maps. They are public documents. He cannot legally be given the exclusive right to them." In this opinion, Morris was to prove correct.

During our discussion, Nancy walked into the room. For an instant her surprise entrance took my breath away. She politely greeted me but was reserved and distant. Each time we met, the distance between us seemed to increase. The slight warmth that had developed as a result of our first encounter had almost entirely disappeared. I had become a stranger to her. As we had completed our business, Morris told her to join us. She sat down but seemed distracted. She spent more time looking at the flames in the fireplace than at either of us. The sorrow that was so prominent at our first meeting seemed to have returned. She complained about being fatigued from the long trip to Washington. Perhaps it was fatigue, not sorrow, I perceived. Even at that early time the thought occurred to me that the trip to Virginia might have reopened some old wounds.

Morris commented on the terrible roads and filthy inns on the route to Washington. He was, however, sanguine about future travel. "In years to come, we shall be able to complete the journey in days, instead of weeks. Just this past summer, I went to Albany by steamboat. Robert Fulton himself was aboard. I embarked at five in the afternoon and reached Albany at midnight the next night. Despite engine trouble, the return trip was almost as swift. It is truly amazing. Within five days, I dined in New York, traveled to Albany, spent two complete days there and returned. It cost only seven dollars for each passenger, with a servant at one-half the price. I calculated that by land the trip would take more than twice as long and cost three times as much. Fulton has wrought a revolution in travel. In the future, we shall be riding steamboats down the entire coast of this country."

"Did you enjoy the trip?" I turned directly to Mrs. Morris. "You must have been pleased to return to Virginia." I asked the question more out of a need to say something than out of any expectation of gaining information. She looked at me with a pained expression, as if she did not know how to respond. As he always seemed to do whenever Nancy's past was discussed, Morris bore the burden of the conversation.

"We traveled with our own carriage and baggage wagon. Went through Philadelphia and Baltimore. For this time of year, the weather was surprisingly tolerable. We were in the capital in less than two weeks. We even beat Clinton. Unfortunately, the President thought the canal bill to be unconstitutional. There are few who will challenge Mr. Madison on constitutional questions." I said nothing, but looked again at Mrs. Morris. I fancy she interpreted my look as a silent repetition of my question.

"I was delighted to see Virginia. My family and I enjoyed being united again." She blushed noticeably. With knowledge of subsequent events, I believe it is reasonable to conclude that she was lying. At least, she was being less than candid.

"Does your family live near Washington?"

"No. Closer to Richmond." As if to devise an answer, she paused. "We were actually too busy to leave Washington. But my sister's brother-in-law, John Randolph, was there. He's a Congressman. Of course, you must have heard of him." I nodded affirmatively. "He visited us. My sister Judith did also."

Morris interjected, "John Randolph made a great speech opposing Clay and Calhoun's mad attempts to drive us into a war with England. Unfortunately, we missed it. Never thought I would be in Randolph's political camp. But you know my position. War with England would be utter folly. She is all that stands between us and Bonaparte." Morris launched into a prolonged denunciation of French tyranny followed by praise of British enlightenment. I had heard it all before. Nancy said almost nothing for the remainder of the time. It was as if she were in a distant land to which our voices could not travel.

For the next several months Morris spent most of his time in Albany pressing for the enactment of legislation to provide capital for the canal. Finally his efforts were crowned with success. On the nineteenth day of June, 1812, a law was passed authorizing the Canal Commissioners to purchase the rights and interests of the Western Inland Lock Navigation Company and to borrow the sum of five million dollars for the construction of the canal. On the next day, June twentieth, the news arrived in New York City that the United States had declared war on Great Britain. These two seemingly unrelated events would bring me into contact with three persons from Morris's scandalous past in the old world where I would witness the death throes of Napoleon's vast European empire.

EIGHT

It was, I remember, a warm Saturday morning. While I was working, Emily entered the study. That, in itself, was unusual, as we generally shunned each other except at meal time and when communication could not otherwise be avoided. Looking pale and concerned, she softly declared, "We are at war with the British." The fact that the morning newspaper mentioned nothing about war with Great Britain made me skeptical about her report.

"Where did you hear that?"

"Mrs. Fitzroy told me. Everybody is talking about it."

Immediately I left the house and crossed the street to the Green Dragon Tavern. Randel and I often played chess there. In the forenoon the tavern was ordinarily almost empty. This day the usual scattered brag and whist players were not to be seen. Instead the inside of the tavern was a chaotic mob scene. The noise of the talking, shouting, and wildly gesticulating crowd was overwhelming. The proprietor, Mr. Lambert, told me the news had arrived by ship. The United States had declared war on Great Britain. "Must have to do with taking our ships and sailors," Lambert guessed. Nobody present knew why war had been declared.

From its commencement, this so-called "Second War of American Independence" was paradoxical. For years war had seemed imminent with either France or Britain; yet its actual arrival was a complete surprise. Many had expected the war to begin five years earlier when the British ship the *Leopard*, lurking, as its name would suggest, off the coast of Virginia, attacked the *Chesapeake*, killing three Americans and wounding many more. The British proceeded to remove four deserters from the American vessel, three of whom were Americans who had been impressed into the British navy. The entire country, Federalist and Republican, was outraged. Despite the provocation, Jefferson would not be dragged into war. The Embargo was the limit of his retaliation. Although the Embargo inflicted more harm on us than it did on the British, it must be admitted that the avoidance of war at all costs now appears to be a much wiser course than it did at the time. After Madison's inauguration, the new British minister, David Erskine, agreed to pay reparations for the attack on the *Chesapeake* and also announced the repeal of the Orders in Council. As mentioned earlier, Madison prematurely announced the restoration of trade with Great Britain. When the British recalled Erskine and repudiated his statements, Madison was deeply embarrassed. It has always been my suspicion that this betrayal exhausted the patience of Madison and Congress with the perfidious British. Thus, in 1812, neither was inclined to resist the demands of the War Hawks in Congress. No doubt, Madison's desire to be reelected influenced his acceptance of war. Yet at the time it was commenced, and even to this day, the war appears to be one without an immediate cause. Everyone assumed that war was declared because the British had refused to repeal their Orders in Council. Nevertheless, when the news finally arrived in America that the British had repealed the Orders in Council several days before the declaration of war by the United States, the hostilities continued. Impressment of our sailors became the stated cause of the war. But impressment had been occurring since Washington's presidency without igniting a conflict. It appeared that we had stumbled into a war not only without a cause, but also absent a purpose.

Perhaps my father was correct. He always said that men enjoyed destruction and each generation required its own bloodletting. In his twenties my grandfather had fought in the French and Indian War. At about the same age my father was a soldier in the American Revolution. Even as a child I had expected my war to appear no later than 1800. She was late, but the vicious harlot war finally invited the young men of my generation to her side as she had so many earlier generations. The majority of adults who remembered the hideous hag, hiding beneath the appearance of a beautiful beckoning harlot, had been consumed by the passage of time. The collective memory of past suffering could not be transmitted by mere words to the minds of the young. Bored by the sameness of daily peacetime existence, youths were ready once again to rush into her open arms. Even I was seduced by the siren's call to adventure and excitement never before available. She was not to disappoint me.

As Hobbes states, war may be man's natural state. It is only periodically interrupted by brief periods of peace. The annals of ancient Rome record only a few periods when the Temple of Janus was closed to signify that peace reigned supreme. According to Suetonius, it was closed only twice from the establishment of Rome to his own time. These closings appear to be in 235 B.C., several years after the First Punic War, and in 29 B.C., after the Battle of Actium. Even great Gibbon himself concludes that during the long period of peace in the age of the Antonines, the seeds were being sown for future wars as, paradoxically, the military spirit disappeared, genius was extinguished, and the process of decay began. The historian da Porto described the phenomenon: peace begets riches, riches beget pride and anger; these beget war, which creates poverty and peace; in time of peace, wealth begins to be accumulated and the cycle begins again.

This cycle is not to be found only in the ancient world. Looking back at the past two hundred years, one finds an almost endless succession of major wars beginning with the Thirty Years War of 1618 to 1648. There follow the English Civil War, the three Anglo-Dutch Wars, the continual wars of Louis XIV, including the War of the League of Augsberg and the War of the Spanish

Succession (Queen Anne's War, in America), the Great Northern War of twenty-one years' duration, the War of the Quadruple Alliance, the War of the Austrian Succession (King George's War, in America), the Jacobite Rebellion, the Seven Years War (the French and Indian War, in America), the American Revolution, and the twenty-three years of the wars of the French Revolution and Napoleon. This list does not even include the interminable wars involving the Turks, the Persians, the Indians, the Chinese, the Africans, and the South Americans, or the countless small wars which also seem to be without end. Even as I write this book, at a time considered to be an era of peace, civil war rages in Portugal, wars continue between Russia and Persia, the Greeks and the Turks, the Muslims and the Chinese, and numerous people of Africa. Is not the history of mankind the history of war?

War is the point of convergence for all of the historical forces of a period. To understand the causes and results of any war is to comprehend the political, economic, and social strands that make up the fabric of an era. In 1812 I welcomed, as a historian, the opportunity to view that part of the cycle of war which had last appeared in America when I was a child. At the time, most of the European world had been at war for the previous twenty years. By the end of 1812 it had spread into Russia, Java, Sumatra, and the Cape Colony, as Napoleon invaded the domain of Czar Alexander II and British cruisers attacked lands held by the Holland of the Bonapartes. Finally the conflagration had come to our shores. At last I would see mankind in its natural state.

To view war from the proper position, I would need the assistance of someone with influence. Accordingly, I decided to seek the aid of Gouverneur Morris at the first possible opportunity. Within a few weeks of the commencement of the conflict, the chance came in an unexpected manner. It was on a very hot July evening. In order to obtain the benefit of the cool breeze that usually wafts in from the sea, I decided to join the strollers along Battery Walk. The walk was crowded with many others who, no doubt, hoped to obtain relief from the oppressive heat. Unfortunately, there were no breezes on that humid day. As there was to be a concert that evening at six-thirty at the Battery flagstaff, many men, women, and children were slowly making their way toward the octagonal enclosure where seats, music, and refreshments could all be found. I was one of the few persons who was alone. There were families with children, ladies with arms linked to those of their gentlemen escorts, and large groups of people chatting together. For a moment I regretted not asking Emily to accompany me. But the thought of the inevitable bitter words which would have passed between us eradicated the remorse which temporarily welled up in my breast.

In the distance I saw a familiar figure pointing out to sea. The wooden leg and cane revealed it to be none other than the great man himself. Nancy was standing next to him, her arm linked to his. For a moment I hesitated to approach them. Without any expectation of such an encounter, I had gone out in old breeches and a shirt stained with printer's ink. My desire to speak to them quickly overcame reservations about my appearance. Walking toward them, I noticed the way Nancy was leaning on his arm. To my chagrin, they looked like lovers. I consoled myself with the thought that they could also be mistaken for a friendly father and daughter.

"Good evening. What brings you to the city on such a hot night?"

Morris and Nancy turned toward me. To my relief, they both seemed pleased to see me. "Daniel. How are you? Mrs. Morris wanted to get out in the boat tonight. We thought the concert would be an appropriate destination." They wished, I found myself thinking, to see what the common folk are doing.

"It's lovely here." Nancy smiled and lapsed into her comic southern accent. "With this humidity, Ah feel right at home, suh." She was radiant. Never had I seen her look so happy.

After an exchange of pleasantries, Morris began to lament the fact that funds for the canal would not be available because of the war. "You realize the canal is all but forgotten. Nothing is of interest these days but the accursed war. An important project which would create widespread prosperity is overthrown for a useless war with the wrong foe. The French have been seizing our ships for years. Is war declared against Bonaparte? Not by this government. It is utter folly. The Corsican bandit controls the continent. Britain is the only bulwark left against the great enemy of liberty, and we stab her in the back. I tell you, this war will open the gates to the torrent of Bonaparte's tyranny. It is quite mad." Morris was beginning to work himself into a rage about "Mr. Madison's War." I interrupted him.

"Did you see in the newspaper several days ago that Napoleon decreed in late April that the Berlin and Milan decrees are no longer in effect for American ships? Although we did not know it when war was declared, he had removed the last cause for conflict with France two months before the war began. Whatever you think of France, seizure of ships and sailors is now only an issue with Britain." At the time, news had not yet arrived of Britain's repeal of the Orders in Council in response to Napoleon's decree.

Morris was visibly upset by my response. "This war is not about the seizure of ships and sailors. It is about greed for more territory. They want Canada now. If Canada were still French, we would have declared war on France. Proximity is the cause of this war. Nothing else. Oh, I admit the democrats are shouting loudly about impressment. The claim is absurd. It is an argument that we are at war to protect British seamen against their own country. You look puzzled; let me explain. The figures I have seen indicate that almost all of the impressed seamen are British, not American. Since 1776 we ourselves have exercised the same right the British claim, the right to search neutral ships incident to the right of capture in war. It is unjust to make war on Great Britain for refusing to surrender a right we also claim and constantly use. It is also unwise. The most complete form of defense available to our own country is to be found in a navy. In war we must, like Britain, be able to rely on the fidelity of our own seamen. If they desert, they must not be allowed to find protection under a foreign flag. We ourselves would fight to retain the right to remove our own sailors from neutral vessels and the right to search those vessels to detect contraband of war. Yet we now wage war to destroy those very rights we value so highly. All we accomplish is to shed our own best blood to protect the worst of our enemy's subjects. On such a mad enterprise we waste our own limited treasure. It is folly. I refuse to support it in any manner." As Morris spoke, his face increasingly reddened, until he appeared to be ready for a seizure.

Nancy tried to calm him. "Please, let's not talk about the war. It's not worth your anger. You can't change what is. We are here to enjoy our personal good fortune, not to lament the woes of the world." A few words of her enchanting voice and Morris's anger subsided, like the Furies calmed by the music of Orpheus.

"Of course. Of course. I am sorry my dear. It is too wonderful an evening for that."

When his anger had abated, Nancy mischievously interjected, "Besides, I did read about Napoleon's decree from St. Cloud. Mr. Carey is quite correct."

Morris laughed as she gently tweaked his nose. "Daniel, these southern women, you know, are not like the ladies in New York. They can hold their own discussing politics. I learned that in Virginia twenty-five years ago. Still true today."

While walking in the direction of the Battery flagstaff we were halted by two acquaintances of Mr. Morris. When they began to discuss a commercial matter with him, he turned to me. "The concert will be starting soon. You and Mrs. Morris can save some seats for us. I will be with you soon." Before I could respond, Nancy placed her arm around mine and began to walk toward the portico of the flagstaff. My sleeves were rolled up, so I could feel her bare arm against my own flesh. It was the first time we had ever touched each other. My senses were ablaze; I was dazed by my good fortune. Nancy was delightfully flirtatious. As I had heard of the coquettish ways of southern women, I warned myself not to take her attentions too seriously.

"Where is your wife? Why isn't she out with you on an evening like this?"

I had never mentioned my wife to Nancy. The fact that Nancy had acquired and retained personal information about me was somewhat pleasing. "She was tired tonight. Did not want to leave the house." I felt guilty about lying.

"Well, that is her misfortune. I have you all to myself." While clasping my arm tightly, she looked into my face with great warmth. Her interest in me seemed so genuine, I wondered whether there was something more than mere coquetry in her actions.

After purchasing a pine apple ice cream for her and strawberry for me, we sat down together to listen to the music of Moffat's Military Band. Although she could easily have moved her elbow away from mine, she held it snugly against my bare arm. Closing my eyes, I wondered whether the pounding that shook my head was the beating of her heart or mine. It was that heartbeat I listened to, not the sound of fifes, drums, clarinets, and French horns. "Yankee Doodle," "Mary La Moore," "Hail Columbia," and "Rural Felicity" were mere background to the glorious music of life coursing through our bodies.

My half hour of bliss was terminated by the return of Mr. Morris. As soon as he sat down to her left, she placed her left arm around his right. When her right hand moved to touch him, our physical connection was severed. The pounding in my temples ceased. Once more I was alone.

After the concert, as we walked back to Morris's boat, I delivered my carefully prepared request. "Are you familiar with Polybius's criticism of the historian Timaeus?" Morris was taken aback by my strange, unexpected question. Before he could respond, I continued. "Polybius accused Timaeus of being a mere 'book historian,' one who had never traveled like Herodotus or seen a battle, like Thucydides. He compared that kind of historian to animal painters who draw from models and stuffed skins. You yourself have told me how much more important experience is compared to mere theory found in a book. Well, I do not wish to be a 'book historian.' I must see this war in person. Could you help me? Stephen Van Rensselaer is to be in command of the militia on the Niagara frontier. Would you write me a letter of introduction?"

Looking rather thoughtful, Morris stopped walking and turned to me. "Of course. If you wish. You realize he is as opposed to this war as I am? No matter. He is a man of honor and conscience. He will do his duty. I will send you a letter immediately. You and he can talk about the canal. On our trip to Lake Erie, I mentioned you to him."

When we arrived at the boat, Nancy took my hand and wished me good fortune. Morris promised I would hear from him soon. I watched their boat sail across the moonlight shimmering on the water until it vanished in the distance. That night I imagined myself alone with Nancy in a room with one lighted candle. As always in my musings, she did not resist my advances. My caressing hand moved slowly over her body. When I finally drifted off to sleep, I dreamed again of the long corridor and the dusty coils of the serpent.

Within little more than a month I was with a group of militia volunteers marching from Albany to the Niagara frontier over two hundred miles away. Upon receipt of Morris's letter to Major General Van Rensselaer, I gave my will and a substantial amount of money to Emily. As the only member of my family, she was named as the sole beneficiary of my estate. To my surprise, she seemed to be genuinely saddened by my departure. She did not, however, try to dissuade me from leaving. In order to find companions for my journey, I searched for information about militia units leaving for the Niagara front. On the advice of a captain in the militia, I embarked from New York City on board a Hudson River sloop bound for Albany. To assure my acceptance as a militia volunteer, I obtained, as he advised, a musket, a bayonet and belt, two spare flints, a knapsack, a pouch with a box containing twenty-four cartridges suited to the bore of my musket, and a proper quantity of powder and ball. Upon arriving in Albany, I attached myself to a militia unit of ninety-day volunteers departing for the Niagara frontier. For the long journey, I purchased an inexpensive old horse. As if to fulfill Morris's prophecies about the superiority of the inland canal route over the Lake Ontario route, especially in time of war when enemy naval units could make travel on Lake Ontario hazardous, we followed a line of march that at various places crossed the proposed canal route to Lake Erie. We even traversed some of the formidable terrain which I had used to argue against the practicability of the inclined plane.

My thirty-six traveling companions were a boisterous mob of young men, most half my own age. My first lesson in war. It is children who do the fighting. The few trained men with our tiny army placed men on the flanks of our group to warn of possible surprise attacks by Indians and Canadians. When not on roads, we passed through endless forests in stifling August heat. The odor of pine filled the primeval forests which were heavy with growth; for miles the sun was not visible in the torpid air. At times the trackless woodland was so filled with undergrowth that men a few yards away could not be seen. Fallen trees and broken ground frequently made riding on horseback impossible. We sometimes became lost in the maze of trunks and undergrowth. To pass the time, the tireless youths of our company would profane the unspoiled woods by carving fulsome insults about our British foes. To direct their energies to a more useful endeavor, the mature and knowledgeable woodsmen among us often ordered the striplings to cut spruce tops in order to make spruce beer, which, we were told, protected us from scurvy. For the purpose of producing the medicinal beverage, a generous supply of West Indian molasses was carried among our provisions in the wagons. After a week of constant marching and riding, the thrill of adventure was replaced by fatigue and discomfort relieved only by the quarts of spruce beer distributed at our infrequent stops for rest and food.

At the end of more than three weeks of marching, we finally burst out of the immense solitude of the wilderness to the glistening waters of the Niagara River, ten miles to the north of Buffalo. We marched ten more miles north along the river until we reached Niagara Falls, the most magnificent scene of nature's beauty and power that my eyes have ever beheld. The thunder of the great falls could be heard for miles before we even reached the site. For one like me, who had never before been more than fifty miles away from Manhattan Island, the sublime grandeur of that colossal cataract was enough to render the adventure worth the suffering of the journey.

Having spent the night at the falls, the next morning we continued to march northward down the river until we arrived at our destination, the village of Lewiston, headquarters of Major General Stephen Van Rensselaer. The small village is less than seven miles south of Fort Niagara, where the Niagara River flows into Lake Ontario. Van Rensselaer was in command of the entire frontier along the river, which runs for thirty-six miles through the neck of land separating Lake Erie from Lake Ontario. We arrived at Lewiston on August 23, 1812. On that day I began to keep a journal of my militia service on the Niagara. Looking at it after fifteen years, I am amazed at the legibility of my handwriting, which has degenerated into my disordered and harried scrawl of the present day. As I read the journal for the first time since it was written, it is amusing to discover my naive disappointment at the unattractiveness of the harlot war. At the time I was thirty-six years old, an age when one should know better. Except for a few facts concerning the Battle of Queenston, there is little in the journal that can be used in *The Age of Revolution*. In this personal account of my adventures, it appears to be of more relevance; so I have selected portions of the journal in the hope they will be of some interest to the reader.

AUGUST 23—*The arrival of a mere 37 militia volunteers at Lewiston creates more enthusiasm than I would have expected from the large body of troops stationed here. Like us, almost none of the men have uniforms. I am one of the best equipped men in the camp. Many are without muskets, or firelocks, belts, cartridge boxes, or even shoes.*

We are harangued by a pompous officer, Captain Hawkins, about the duties of members of the militia and the penalties for deserting before our 90 days of service are completed on November 21st. Since we joined the militia in Albany on July 30th, the members of our contingent maintain our service ends on October 27th not November 21st. Hawkins declares that the 90-day period begins upon arrival at the front and warns that penalties for premature departure include running of the gauntlet and execution by firing squad. This is not consistent with the vision of freedom of movement necessary to a historian which I held to my bosom on the long journey through the wilderness.

We are assigned to small tents, five men to a tent. There does not appear to be enough room for even three men. After placing my equipment in the tent, I inform Captain Hawkins that I am carrying a personal letter to General Van Rensselaer from Gouverneur Morris. It is clear from the sudden respect he shows me, he knows of Mr. Morris and is cautious with any person having a direct link to the General.

The General maintains his headquarters in a large tent—or "marquee," as it is called—among the tents of the soldiers, which are fixed in rows behind the village. Captain Hawkins introduces me to Major John Lovett, General Van R.'s secretary. He is a lawyer in civilian life. When Lovett hears that I am a historian sent by Morris, he is cordial and enthusiastic. He volunteers his services in assisting me to obtain necessary information. Like his fellow Federalists, he thinks the war is folly. "Unseen hands force men, who would otherwise be friends, to face each other on opposite sides of this river for purposes of cutting each other's throats." Nevertheless, he admits to enjoying his first experience in the military. There has been some fighting, he says, but since August 18th an armistice has been in effect. According to Lovett, the British repealed the Orders in Council two days before we declared war. They are holding to the armistice in the hope that the war can be terminated without an effusion of blood now that its chief cause no longer exists.

Lovett introduces me to General Van R.'s kinsman and aide-de-camp, Lieutenant

Colonel Solomon Van Rensselaer, who appears to be about my own age. The Colonel, a handsome figure of a soldier, is blatantly and disdainfully proud. When he learns that I am a historian, he makes it known that he is one of the only experienced soldiers in the camp. He was wounded in 1794 at the Battle of Fallen Timbers fought against the Maumee Indians. General Anthony Wayne, called out of retirement, was his commanding officer. It is clear that the Colonel admires himself greatly and is contemptuous of his foes. He informs me of his brilliant negotiation with British Major-General Sheaffe from Fort George. As a bluff, according to the Colonel, he threatened to end the current armistice unless all navigable waters could be used as a common highway. The British agreed to his terms. "This allows us to build up our woefully inadequate forces and supplies by using Lake Ontario," said Colonel Van R. The armistice which began on August 18th can be canceled by either side with four days' notice. "If the armistice ends," the Colonel confidently predicts, "the United States are sufficiently powerful to be victorious in this war."

Lovett introduces me to the General. The great patroon is one of the wealthiest aristocrats in this country. Yet, like Morris, he is charming and without airs. Unlike his kinsman, he dresses in civilian clothing. I would guess that he is approximately fifty years old. It is well-known that he is one of those aristocrats who considers his high rank to confer upon him the obligation of honorable, generous, and responsible behavior. He is especially generous to the poor, including the numerous tenants on his vast lands. Federalists like General Van R. and Morris make me wonder whether I belong to the wrong political party, particularly when they are compared to our own bigoted and boisterous Martling Men.

Upon reading the letter from Morris, General Van R. is very friendly. He informs me that Morris has favorably spoken about me several times. The General identifies me as "the supplier of the Hawley articles and the first opponent of the inclined plane." He thinks the Canal Commission will remain inactive until the war is over. In this regard, he informs me that his fellow Canal Commissioner, War Hawk Congressman Peter B. Porter, is also present on the Niagara frontier as Quartermaster General for the State of New York. "I will attempt to assist you in your efforts as a historian; but for purposes of equality within this camp, you must bear all the duties of other members of the militia."

After my meeting with General Van R., I explore the village of Lewiston, which is between our camp and the river. It is small, containing about 100 houses and a number of warehouses for storage of grain, salt, and flour destined for Ohio and the western territories beyond. The Canadian village of Queenston—or "Queenstown," as some call it—is less than 300 yards across the river. It appears to be even smaller than Lewiston. Our camp is at the foot of a steep precipice rising perpendicular from the ground to a height of several hundred feet. Queenston lies at the foot of similar heights across the river. The British have artillery on top of Queenston Heights opposite our own artillery at Fort Grey on top of the heights on our own side of the river.

The men appear to be mostly volunteers or substitutes for drafted men. Most are here for 90-day terms. My tent is shared with three young farmboys and one ruffian, John Fotterall, a young cutthroat from Albany. I try to avoid him. He constantly fought with the other men on our long journey to the Niagara and today continues *his endless quarreling. Fortunately, he and my other tent mates are illiterate and incapable of deciphering this journal.*

Our tent is in the rear line of tents. It is too near the necessary, which is 100 yards beyond the tents. The stench is overpowering when the wind blows in this direction. Mosquitoes are everywhere. Many of the men are ill. The soldiers have not been paid for weeks and openly grumble about it.

The men play whist in the evenings. Unfortunately, nobody in my company plays chess.

AUGUST 24—*First full day in camp. My first taste of the tedious routine of military life, which was not apparent yesterday because of the sabbath. The reveille is beat at daybreak. Every soldier must appear on parade. The companies are exercised by their commanding officers for one hour. The exercise is repeated for another hour at 4 P.M. Captain Hawkins is a petty tyrant, constantly shrieking at the men for the most trivial of offenses. Perhaps on account of my age and the letter to General Van R., he does not badger me. Because of Fotterall's threatening manner, Hawkins is also reluctant to antagonize the young bully. In the army, as in civilian life, power protects against power.*

The troop is beat at 9 A.M. and the retreat at 6 P.M. when the line is formed for roll call. The tattoo is beat at 9 P.M. At that time the men retire to their tents and the sentinels begin to challenge. Guards, two captains and two subalterns, are mounted daily. The captains' guards are in the front and rear, the subalterns on the flanks. The guards assemble on the parade ground at 9:30 A.M. and are marched off, to the accompaniment of fifes and drums, at 10 A.M. Guards are furnished with 24 rounds of cartridges. When guards are relieved, they are permitted to discharge their weapons on the parade ground. Because firing is strictly prohibited at all other times, this is the only sound of weapons heard during the day. Despite the armistice, we are warned that a musket ball fired from across the river has enough force to kill a man.

We receive food three times a day. Based on five meals, it can be stated that the food is uniformly execrable. The beef and pork are particularly bad. I may have to survive on bread and hickory nuts. Tuesdays and Fridays of each week there are to be company and battalion parades. The remainder of the time is sheer tedium and discomfort. Where is the excitement of war which lures us away from the mundane existence of peacetime?

AUGUST 25—*Catastrophe has befallen our western army. A guard of redcoats was seen moving on the opposite shore with lines of American prisoners. We have been informed that General Hull has surrendered our entire army at Detroit to British commanding General Isaac Brock. The left wing of our great invasion of Canada has disintegrated. The men are humiliated to learn that Hull surrendered without a fight.*

Lovett meets with Brock's aide-de-camp and a scarlet-coated major sent to our side of the river by the triumphant Brock, who is now in Queenston. A number of Hull's officers from Ohio are allowed, on parole, to cross to our side of the river to speak to General Van R.

True to his promise, Lovett informs me of the scope of the disaster. Hull's officers estimate the number of men surrendered at Detroit as 2200. The British officers claim 2500 to 3000. Although he had ample provisions in Fort Detroit for three weeks, Hull surrendered to a vastly inferior force of no more than 700 British soldiers accompanied by the same number of Indians led by the great Shawnee Chief Tecumseh, the brother of the Prophet. Hull surrendered without a shot being fired by him; the enemy had to fire its artillery only once. His officers hint at cowardice, or perhaps treason, on the part of Hull. Lovett says the affair casts a stain on the American character which cannot be washed away. Brock now has his entire army from the west available to attack us. Lovett says, "He can overrun the entire Niagara frontier within a few days." The great Tecumseh and his savage army are expected to be a few miles downriver, on the Canadian side, at Fort George within a few days. "By God, no matter what happens, we shall not be Hulled," Lovett declares.

Fotterall is fighting again. To avoid him, I stay away from the tent as often as possible.

AUGUST 26—American captives from Detroit continue to be paraded before us on the opposite shore. Their eyes look to the ground while their redcoated captors march at their sides with the British insolence and gleaming bayonets I remember so well from my childhood in occupied New York City. We can see the road for more than a mile filled with ragged, shoeless captives, open wagons, and guards in an unending procession of defeat. Many of our men are indignant and enraged. The loudmouths, including Fotterall, demand that we disregard the armistice and attack now. This, of course, would be madness, as the armistice is our best protection against a British attack in overwhelming numbers.

AUGUST 29—Because of the scattered firing of guns yesterday, at parade we are all reminded of General Van R.'s orders prohibiting firing in camp. Any discharge of firearms, guards excluded, is punishable by immediate confinement. Tomorrow being Sunday, even the guards are warned not to discharge their pieces until Monday. Fotterall says the next time he discharges his musket, it will be in Captain Hawkins's buttocks.

Despite the continuing fear of British attack, we have not yet heard that the enemy has given the four days' notice necessary to terminate the armistice. Because General Brock is known to be a man of honor, nobody anticipates a surprise violation of the armistice.

After seven days of military life I have doubts about my ability to withstand two more months of this agonizing tedium. My sympathy for the substantial number of deserters has increased greatly since my arrival.

SEPTEMBER 4—It is announced that, by order received from General Dearborn, the armistice will be ended at noon on September 8th. Lovett informs me that our commanding general is so far away from the front that he terminated the armistice before he knew about Hull's surrender. This lack of timely information could result in a disaster for all of us. Fortunately, because of the British concession on free use of navigable waters, we have been reinforced by several regiments of regulars and militia.

They were transported, with artillery, from Oswego by way of Lake Ontario. We have also received large amounts of pork and flour.

Now that the armistice is to end, we are allowed to fire our muskets as part of drill. After twice going through the twelve separate drill movements for loading and firing, I managed to get only a flash in the pan each time. On the third attempt, I cleaned my musket, shook the block powder from horn to pan, rammed in the cartridge, and to my surprise, the musket fired. I cannot imagine loading in the face of an attacking enemy. In any case, I hope never to have to fire at a fellow human being.

As if life is not miserable enough here, Fotterall and his friends sawed a log in the latrine, causing an officer to fall into the excrement.

SEPTEMBER 12—According to Lovett, Quartermaster General Peter Porter and other Republican officers are spreading the rumor that General Van R. is a Federalist traitor who will surrender his army like Hull. It appears that the Canal Commission will be badly split when this war is finished.

Lovett believes that General Van R. has been placed in an extremely difficult position. Governor Tompkins shrewdly appointed General Van R., his likely political opponent in the election next spring, to command in a war Van R. opposes. Van R. could not refuse the appointment without appearing to be a coward. His appointment has quelled Federalist opposition to the war. If Van R. is a successful commander, he will not be available to oppose Governor Tompkins in the spring. If he fails in war, he will be discredited as a political opponent. Either way, Tompkins and the Republicans win. Despite my democratic sympathies, I may vote for General Van R. if he runs.

Four days since the end of the armistice—no fighting.

SEPTEMBER 17—Fotterall continues complaining about bad food, no pay, and lack of action. Suggesting Gray and Fleming join him, he threatens to desert. If only he would.

Fotterall and a group of fellow dissidents, one of whom is able to write, have prepared on birch bark a notice to the officers that unless the men are paid, they will leave in eight days.

Rumor in camp is that Colonel Solomon Van R. has challenged General Peter Porter to a duel on Grand Island but Porter's seconds did not appear at a meeting to make arrangements. General Van R., I am certain, will not approve of his kinsman's conduct.

Heavy firing continues today on both sides of the river.

General Van R. has revoked the death sentence of two deserters. The prisoners, Schyler and Moore, are to be returned to duty. The General's sympathy for his men makes him popular with the troops.

SEPTEMBER 21—Terrible rainstorm continues. Many of the tents have been blown over. Continuous hail, lightning, and thunder. Our tent is filled with water; almost everything is soaked. Sleep is impossible. My boots are beginning to rot. My ankles are painfully swollen. Mud in the camp is above the wagon axles.

We have had no reinforcements in weeks. Many are sick. Even without an attack, I fear the army will disintegrate. We hear increasing numbers of stories about Indian reinforcements across the river. It is reported that the British are offering six dollars for each American scalp delivered by them. Tecumseh, they say, forbids scalping and torture, but his men, encouraged by the British, engage in these barbarous practices. One of our company from Pennsylvania describes a scalping he witnessed. The Shawnee warrior cut a circle around the scalp with his knife; then holding the knife in his teeth, the barbarian put his knee on his victim's back, tore off the entire scalp, and placed it in his belt. It is an image I find difficult to banish from my mind.

OCTOBER 7—*This is my eighth day in the hospital tent. Over my objections, the surgeon bleeds me again. He insists it is the only cure for bilious fever. Writing these few sentences exhausts me. I fear I shall never leave this accursed place. Volunteering for this agony may have been the single most foolish decision of my life.*

The rain continues to deluge the camp. It is becoming extremely cold. I seem to be one of the few who had the foresight to bring woolens.

OCTOBER 10—*My first day out of the hospital tent, and our own tent is flooded. I am too tired to do anything about it.*

Lovett visits with important information. Despite repeated requests by General Van R. for consultation with Brigadier General Alexander Smyth, the new commander of the regulars at Buffalo, Smyth refuses to meet Van R. to plan joint action. Smyth will not cooperate with the militia. According to Lovett, Smyth is a Republican appointed by Jefferson who wants nothing to do with a Federalist militia leader. Unfortunately, General Van R. has no authority over a general of the army. Because of Smyth, Van R. has had to cancel his plan for a two-prong attack against both Queenston and Fort George. An attack at both locations would prevent British reinforcements from one place being used at the other. Nevertheless, General Van R. plans to attack Queenston tomorrow beginning at 3 A.M. The men have been eager for action since receiving word of Lieutenant Elliott's brilliant exploit of capturing two British brigs (the Detroit *and the* Caledonia*) from Fort Erie. All the officers have indicated a strong disposition to act. Many of the men have threatened to leave unless there is immediate action. According to Lovett, General Van R. believes he must act now or face disgrace, or at least suspicion about his loyalty.*

Because of my weakened condition, I am not to participate in the assault. I feel both relief and disappointment at the same time. Colonel Van R. also has the fever but plans to command the attack across the river.

OCTOBER 11—*Despite the continuing deluge, the attack was scheduled to begin at 3 A.M. in bateaux from the old ferry opposite Queenston Heights. The usual landing place was not to be used. For one hour none of the boats left. Finally, the men were informed that the attack had been canceled. It seems that a Lieutenant Sims took the first boat, containing almost all of the oars for the other boats. He abandoned his boat on the Canadian side and disappeared. Many of the men think he was a spy. If so, the secrecy of the attack plan is ruined. Our wretched little war is becoming a comedy of errors, treachery, and stupidity.*

OCTOBER 12—*Lovett has informed me that the attack is scheduled again for tomorrow morning beginning at* 4 A.M. *Several detachments from above the falls are expected to reinforce us later today. General Smyth's large contingent of regulars at Black Rock will not be among them, as his mad refusal to cooperate with the militia continues. Smyth's regulars would almost double the size of the attack force.*

We have 12 boats, each of which will carry 30 men, plus 2 boats which carry 80 men in each. Colonel Solomon Van R. is to command a force of 300 selected militia, and Lieutenant Colonel Chrystie is entrusted with a force of 300 regulars. These 600 men (the first attack force) are to seize Queenston Heights and hold the area. They will all cross in two trips. It is estimated that it will take 15 minutes to cross the river and another 15 for the boats to return. The second group crossing the river is to be Lieutenant Colonel Fenwick's light artillery, supported by Major Delaney's detachment of regulars. My company and I are scheduled to cross the river with the sixth attack force. If all proceeds as planned, Lovett guesses that I will be across the river before 8 A.M. It is anticipated that 7 or 8 round trips will be necessary to move our entire force of 4000 men across the river. We have skilled civilian boatmen in charge of the bateaux. Lovett will command the artillery battery on Lewiston Heights.

In my entire life I have never been as excited or anxious. My anticipation of the adventure to come is darkened by a sense that tomorrow may be my last day on this earth. Although our chief foes are the redcoats, I am more fearful of Indian savagery, which is not constrained by the rules of war.

The storm has blown down many of the yellowing leaves. They litter the ground like so many of the corpses I expect to see on the morrow.

For the first time since leaving Manhattan, I have been visited by the dream. The attack begins in two hours.

OCTOBER 14—*Yesterday was such a day of unmitigated activity and catastrophe that I could not bring myself to write. As scheduled, the first attack force assembled at 3:30 A.M. It was raining, as usual, and extremely dark, but the rain was intermittent and not heavy. The roar of the river, which is rapid with a patchwork of treacherous eddies below the falls, drowned out the noise of embarkation. All seemed to be confusion. I counted only 12 boats.*

From a hill overlooking the old French ferry, I watched the crowded boats disappear into the night. Within 20 minutes there was firing on the other side. We later learned that a sentry almost immediately discovered the presence of the landing party. The batteries at Lewiston and Fort Grey began to fire across the river. Their fire was returned by British artillery from Queenston Heights and Vrooman's Point downriver. The darkness was broken by the flash of musket and cannon. The din, mixed with the roar of the river, was frightful.

Several of the boats, including Colonel Chrystie's, returned to our side. They had become disabled or lost in the darkness and came back to begin the crossing again. The men were becoming discouraged in the darkness and confusion. My own fear increased with each passing hour. The times for crossing fell badly behind schedule. When the third group should have been crossing, the first group was still attempting to complete its mission. By dawn only 5 boats appeared to be in operation. Several of the boats were sunk by artillery fire. Some were captured on the other side. The civilian rivermen assigned to operate the boats all disappeared. The officers replaced them with bewildered soldiers who seemed to have no knowledge of the river or the handling of bateaux. I feared for the men on the other side.

The day was gloomy with threatening storm clouds overhead. The battle was so fascinating, I did not mind standing in the mud and drizzle for hours. Shortly after dawn the American flag was run up over the British battery on Queenston Heights. My usual sense of detachment was lost in the excitement of the moment. Men cheered and hugged each other. Although alone until that moment, I joined the celebration of the men in my company. Scattered firing could be heard across the river. After 10 A.M. there were no sounds of muskets for several hours. The only sign of British opposition was the occasional firing of the battery at Vrooman's Point aimed at the few boats attempting to cross the river. At this time many of the men, including me, sat near the edge of the river and watched the spectacle while eating bread and cheese. During the lull the officers did little to fill the few available boats to ferry men across the river. Instead, most of the boat trips to the Canadian side were by a few officers and messengers who had no difficulty crossing. On the return trips the boats were filled with wounded men, many of them unconscious and begrimed with blood. Some of those who were conscious screamed in agony. Among the wounded were some soldiers who jumped into the boats to escape from the Canadian side. Nobody arrested them or forced them to return. One of the first boats to return carried Colonel Solomon Van Rensselaer, whose legs were covered with blood. Urging on his men, he was carried to the hospital tents on a litter.

Hundreds of men stood by the water's edge watching the steady flow of wounded men as if they were spectators at a bear-baiting. The returning boats were filled with bloody water. Instead of ordering units into the few available boats in the order in which they were scheduled to embark, the officers called for volunteers. Many hesitated to enter the bloody boats. Rather than returning to the far shore with boats filled with 30 men, the bateaux were leaving with no more than 10 men in each vessel. The original plan was not being followed. By noon it appeared that well over half the men scheduled to cross had not done so. As the commanding officer, General Van R. must bear the responsibility for this failure. The General himself crossed to the other side at noon.

By 2 P.M. long lines of redcoats could be seen moving up the river road on the Canadian side. These must have been reinforcements sent from Fort George five miles downriver. They were joined by Indians. Within a short time we heard the terrifying war whoops of the attacking Indians echoing across the gorge. The crashing thunder of muskets firing in unison indicated that the British regulars had joined the fray. No such sound had been heard until that moment. Our own militia and regular units could be distinguished by the scattered popping sound of individual musket fire. Shortly after the savage cries of the Indians began, accompanied by the reverberation of British volleys, men ceased volunteering to cross the river. Like the soldiers in my company,

I stood and waited for others to volunteer. My own passivity melted into the inactivity of the faceless mass of hundreds of men surrounding me like a protective shield. If an officer had directly ordered me or my company into a boat, I would have gone. Encircled, however, by a multitude of soldiers, I was not within fifty yards of an officer. Fotterall joined in the shouting by some of the men that militia could not be ordered to fight outside the borders of the United States. Some screamed it was contrary to the Constitution to send militia into Canada. Although this was nonsense, I remained silent. "If my company is ordered across, I will go," I repeated to myself. Then I waited, a silent spectator to the shame swirling around me.

General Van R. returned from the Canadian side of the river. Still in civilian clothes, he mounted his horse and rode along the edge of the river urging the men to climb into the boats. Lovett rode beside him. I was too far away from the river to hear all of the General's words. His summons was addressed to named battalions and regiments rather than to individuals. He gestured imploringly toward the heights across the river and then to the few empty boats on the shore. I heard him shout, "One-third of you can secure the victory." A few men climbed into the boats, but there were no boatmen to push them off and guide them through the treacherous eddies to the other side of the river. In a lonely position of moral superiority, they waited for others to join them in the boats. Few did. A wounded bleeding officer, who was identified to me as Lieutenant Colonel Bloom from the Niagara Falls area, mounted his horse and began to exhort and threaten the troops to cross to the other side and help their comrades. There also appeared on the scene an elderly man in a large cocked hat with a broad white belt. One of the local men from Lewiston identified him as Judge Peck. The Judge pointed frantically to Queenston. Then he fell on his knees and assumed a pose of prayer. These efforts were in vain. Although a few more men climbed into the boats, everyone else stood, with unused weapons in their hands, as if frozen to the ground. It was clear there would be no more reinforcements.

At about 4 P.M. the sounds of a furious conflict could be heard from the Canadian side. The war cries of the Indians seemed to be everywhere. For almost one-half an hour the din of cannon and the thunder of musketry continued. The cannon roared incessantly. Gradually the tumult subsided and then there was silence. A few boats with terrified men returned to our side of the river. Many soldiers could be seen throwing their arms away and attempting to swim across the swirling river to the American shore. After a few strokes they disappeared in the maelstrom. By 4:30 P.M. the firing had completely stopped. Everyone on our side knew we had been defeated. A palpable sense of shame hung in the air. If the others had moved, I have told myself, I also would have climbed into a boat; it was impossible for a few men to accomplish anything. An army must move together or not at all. In the end even those few who volunteered did not succeed in crossing to the other side. My arguments are to no avail. Shame and disgust at myself have enshrouded my soul. I fear they will never leave me.

Lovett has been rendered deaf from commanding the battery on Lewiston Heights.

OCTOBER 15—*After the battle, an armistice was entered into by both sides for the exchange of wounded and prisoners. Only militia and wounded regulars are returned on parole. Unhurt regulars will not be allowed to return.*

Many of the details of the battle are now known. Some of the first boats to attempt to land were discovered while still in the river. Many died or were wounded before reaching land. Colonel Van R. managed to land but was almost immediately wounded in five places in his leg. Although our men were trapped at the water's edge for some time, some units found a path leading to Queenston Heights. They drove off the British at the battery and raised the flag. It is said that General Brock himself was surprised at the battery. Shortly thereafter, Brock was shot in the chest and killed in an attempt to recapture the heights. Before he was wounded, Brock sent for reinforcements from Fort George. These were the redcoats who were later seen on the river road. Mohawk Indians combined with the British before the attack. Among the reinforcements from Fort George was a company of escaped slaves who volunteered to fight against the country of their former masters. Additional British reinforcements also arrived from Chippewa upriver.

General Van R. was fortifying his camp when he saw the enemy reinforcements. After their first attack was repelled by musket and bayonet, General Van R. returned to our side to bring reinforcements across the river. Our collective cowardice sealed the fate of our abandoned brethren on the Canadian side. Our men were forced off the heights. There were no boats available for a retreat, as the boatmen had all fled. Lieutenant Colonel Winfield Scott of our regulars attempted to surrender with a white flag, but the Indians paid no heed to it. He had to fight his way to the British lines in order to surrender.

Many of the militiamen who crossed did not participate in the battle; instead they hid by the banks of the river for most of the day. It is reported that our casualties number 60 killed, 170 wounded, and almost 800 men captured. Half of the prisoners are militia, half regulars. Our militiamen are to be returned to us at Fort Niagara on their parole not to serve during the war or until they are exchanged for British prisoners. Officers are to be exchanged as drawn by lot or at the direction of General Van R.

The sickly sweet odor of death still fills the camp as the wounded continue to perish.

OCTOBER 16—General Van R. has ordered a salute for the funeral of General Brock to be fired this afternoon. According to Lovett—for whom I must write my questions, as he can hear nothing—General Van R. intends to resign. The General will withdraw to Buffalo within the next few days and then return to Albany. His political career is surely ended by our debacle.

We all hope to leave this place within 11 days, when, we claim, our 90-day term ends.

OCTOBER 17—By order of our new commander, General Smyth, Lewiston will no longer be headquarters. All militia infantry are ordered to Fort Schlosser near Niagara Falls. Men are deserting in droves. Fotterall, we give thanks, is among them.

OCTOBER 27—The 21 men left from our 37-man Albany expedition prepare for departure. Captain Hawkins contends that we cannot leave until November 21st, as we arrived on August 23rd. Despite our vehement protests that our 90-day terms began *in Albany on July 30th, Hawkins cannot be moved. Williams pushes Hawkins and is arrested.*

OCTOBER 29—*Five more of our Albany contingent have deserted. Our pleas to General Smyth are denied. There seems to be no end of this misery. Most of those who have not deserted are ill.*

NOVEMBER 3—*Hallelujah! We are free to leave. Two days ago, 100 militiamen in Miller's brigade stacked their arms and departed. They were supported by others in the militia. General Miller has been dismissed. As a result of the mutiny, the men have been promised barracks for the cold weather. Because of Smyth's fear of mutinous militia, Lovett, in spite of his disability, has been able to obtain authorization for the release of those claiming their 90-day terms have ended. Sixteen of our original Albany group, joined by 12 others, depart tomorrow.*

NOVEMBER 4—*As we are preparing to leave, we are informed that word has arrived of a great victory by General Wellington over the French in Spain. The victory occurred on July 22nd at Salamanca. There is no information about Napoleon's invasion of Russia. If the French are not successful, Wellington's veterans will surely be sent here. A French defeat will assure our destruction. I seem to be the only person concerned about the news. Everyone is too eager to depart to worry about the war in Europe.*

I am fearful of the long trek back in this cold weather. Grateful to be alive, and wishing I had climbed into one of the boats for Queenston, I leave this place in sorrow and shame. War is not what I expected.

That is the last entry in my journal. On the return trip we traveled more than ten miles each day through the same endless forests we passed through in August. But this time they were filled with mud and snow. If my horse had not survived for the return trip, I never would have succeeded in completing the arduous journey. Wandering in the desolation of late autumn, we were drenched with rain and then benumbed by the cold. Except for an occasional squirrel, there was almost no game to improve our meals. Day after day we pushed through the silent wilderness until time had no meaning. My only thought was to keep up with the men for one more day, and then the next. Had many of the younger men not been sick with dysentery and other afflictions, I would not have been able to stay with them. One man died before we reached Albany on the twenty-fifth of November. Before the end of the month, I arrived back in New York City. To my surprise, Emily was pleased to see me.

I had performed a small role in the disgrace of American arms which in 1812 was complete on all fronts. In addition to Hull's cowardly surrender of the left flank of our armies and the shameful defeat at Queenston in the center, there were other humiliations. On the right flank of our "invasion" of Canada, General Dearborn led a force of six thousand men by way of the Lake

Champlain route to Canada. When the militia refused to cross the border into Canada, he retreated to his original position and went into winter quarters after a useless campaign of four days' duration.

Before the year ended there was one more act to be completed in the tragi-comic effort to invade Canada in 1812. Several months after my return to New York City, I met a militiaman who served with me on the Niagara frontier. He described how General Smyth provided the grand finale to the year of national humiliation. Within a few weeks of our departure from Fort Schlosser, Smyth issued a bombastic proclamation to the "Men of New York" which was widely printed in newspapers. "The nation has been unfortunate in the selection of some of those who directed it. One army has been disgracefully surrendered and lost; another has been sacrificed by a precipitate attempt to pass it over at the strongest point of the enemy's lines with most incompetent means. The course of the miscarriages is apparent. The commanders were popular men 'destitute alike of theory and experience' in the art of war." Unafraid of warning the enemy of his plans, Smyth continued. "In a few days, the troops under my command will plant the American standard in Canada. They are men accustomed to obedience, silence and steadiness. They will conquer or they will die." Confident in his own abilities, Smyth declared, "Shame, where is thy blush! No. Where I command, the vanquished and peaceful man, the child, the maid and the matron shall be secure from wrong. If we conquer, we will 'conquer but to save.' "

Smyth, who was known to his men as "General Van Bladder," was quickly to learn that those who live in houses of glass must take care how they throw stones. Smyth assembled his army for an attack across the Niagara River near Black Rock on the morning of November 28. The noisy preparation of his "silent" troops destroyed any hope of the attack being a surprise. Some men crossed to the British side and were taken as prisoners. Smyth was not present at the scene of the attack. He left the main body of his troops sitting in boats in cold rain and sleet from early morning until later afternoon. Finally he appeared on the scene and ordered the men to "disembark and dine." Some of the men were so enraged, they broke their muskets against trees while officers broke their swords. In disgust, General Peter Porter sent his men home. Smyth ordered another attack on November 30 against a well-prepared and alerted British position. Smyth was forced to capitulate to his officers, who ordered the troops out of the boats. They announced that regulars were to go into winter quarters and volunteers to return home. Smyth had continually to move his headquarters to be protected from his own men, who were shooting musket balls through his tent. General Porter sent a letter to the *Buffalo Gazette* accusing Smyth of being a coward and a liar. Smyth challenged Porter to a duel. With twenty men, the two generals climbed into a boat and crossed over to Grand Island in the middle of the Niagara River. One shot from Porter's pistol went over Smyth's head. This was enough to satisfy "General Van Bladder" that Porter was a man of honor. Smyth returned to his home in Virginia and the army dropped him from its rolls. It seems that I departed too early and missed the best part of the campaign.

A week after returning from the war, I read in the newspaper that Gouverneur Morris, as the First Vice-President of the New-York Historical Society, would deliver a discourse at their anniversary meeting in the Supreme Court Room in City Hall. Although not then a member of the society, I decided to attend without an invitation. The meeting was the evening of December 6, 1812. As I entered the crowded room, David Ogden was the first to recognize me. In his usual diplomatic manner, his first words to me were, "My God, you look terrible." It was true. My weight was down fifteen pounds and my skin color was pale and unhealthy looking. Even John Randel, who usually did not talk about such things, had commented on my haggard appearance three days earlier. When I mentioned my militia service for the past four months, Ogden exclaimed, "Oh, yes, I had forgotten; my uncle told me months ago." As soon as he learned of my presence at the Battle of Queenston, Ogden announced in his booming voice, "We have a veteran of Queenston here." A large group of people quickly crowded around me. It seems that I was one of the first inhabitants of New York City to return from the Niagara frontier. In fact, few of the soldiers in that sector of the war were from Manhattan. Also, General Brock's death at Queenston gave the battle a notoriety it would not otherwise have had. Since a similar scene had occurred when I visited the Green Dragon Tavern, I was not surprised by the great interest shown at my presence. Egbert Benson, the president of the society, John Pintard, and others came over and shook my hand and then stayed to listen to my account and ask questions. Dr. Hosack warmly greeted me, followed by a smiling Gouverneur Morris. They both heartily shook my hand and welcomed me back. At first so many questions bombarded me from all sides, I barely had an opportunity to speak. Ogden silenced the crowd with a stentorian command repeated several times. "Let him speak!" As this was my fourth recitation of the Battle of Queenston, I had no difficulty in recounting my experiences like a veteran storyteller. In each narration, I indicated that my prolonged illness prevented me from being among the troops assigned to cross the river. Although this was true for the abortive attempt of October 11, it was a lie as to the actual day of battle. This deception rescued me from the distasteful task of explaining my failure to climb into a boat on October 13. The crowd seemed spellbound by my account, which ended with General Van Rensselaer ordering a salute from both Lewiston and Fort Niagara in honor of his fallen foe, the victor of Detroit, General Isaac Brock, who had already become a hero even to some citizens in the United States, particularly the pro-British Federalists.

The meeting was called to order. Mr. Morris delivered a rather rambling one and one-half hour speech which I would not rank among his better efforts. He began by promising a sketch of our history from 1763 to 1783 but then spoke at length about a number of unrelated topics including the importance of law as a protector of property and liberty. His criticism of the war was veiled and surprisingly restrained. "War with the greatest naval power in the world is not a happy condition for a commercial people. Whatever may be the feelings of our sister states, our house, in all probability, will be a house of mourning." Perhaps his not being able to reveal the true extent of his opposition to the war accounted for his curiously uninspired performance. He concluded with a warning against submission to kings, stating that a republican spirit is liable to ferment and be changed to "the corroding acid of despotism." My father, who always thought of Morris as a monarchy man, might have been surprised. The speech was warmly applauded.

After the meeting adjourned and the festivities were concluded, Morris, Ogden, and Hosack came over to speak to me. "I very much enjoyed the speech, particularly the part about the way human nature remains unchanged over time. The resemblance between the nations Tacitus and Caesar have described and those who now inhabit those regions underscored the point admirably." Morris seemed pleased at my polite praise. When I asked him if Mrs. Morris was well, he shocked me by announcing that she was pregnant and that their child was expected to be born in February. Morris glowed with unconcealed joy. Although he already knew about the child, Ogden could barely disguise his distress at this new threat to his inheritance. Dr. Hosack, as the attending physician, confirmed that all was well with Mrs. Morris. Despite feeling a distinct twinge of disappointment that the object of my desire was to be a mother, I desperately tried to look delighted for Mr. Morris. Knowing the futility of my affection for Nancy, perhaps I was a bit pleased for her and her husband.

All three men asked me numerous questions about my experiences at Lewiston. Morris was particularly concerned about the role of his friend Stephen Van Rensselaer. He was gratified by my opinion that much of the blame for his friend's failure rested on the shoulders of General Smyth. "If General Smyth had sent his substantial force of regulars either to attack Fort George, as originally planned, or to participate in the attack on Queenston, General Van Rensselaer's plan would have succeeded. An attack on Fort George would have prevented the large British force there from relieving Queenston. As an alternative, the presence of Smyth's regulars at Lewiston would have assured the holding of Queenston Heights. Unlike the militia, the regulars would not have refused to cross the river. If I learned one thing from my experiences, it is that militiamen are not reliable. My idea of the military value of democratic volunteers has been shattered."

Morris nodded affirmatively. "Quite right. I am in total agreement with you. During the Revolutionary War, the militia was almost always untidy, undisciplined, and unwilling. Untrained militia cannot stand against regulars. They always flee at the sight of an unbroken line of advancing bayonets. Morgan showed they could be used at Cowpens when he allowed them to fire and then flee behind the regulars. It was merely the clever use of their natural inclination for flight. General Washington insisted that only regular troops are equal to the exigencies of modern war. Substitutes, he said, must prove illusory and ruinous. Of course, he was correct." Morris then began to denounce the war in terms much harsher than he used in his speech. "The

British repeal of the Orders in Council removed all cause for the war. Yet Madison continues the fight on the flimsy ground of impressment and manages to get himself reelected. How can democracy work with an electorate so easily duped?"

When I stated that I had not heard much about the election and De Witt Clinton's campaign against Madison, Ogden responded. "Clinton ran a two-faced campaign for the presidency. His defeat was certain well before the election. Of course, he never had the support of Tammany. The Martling Men hate him. Although he opposed the war, he has never been considered a friend of the Federalists. He sought Republican votes by favoring a more vigorous prosecution of the war. By criticizing Madison's premature declaration of war, he expected to gain Federalist votes. The fact is, he had few ardent supporters of his own and he angered the opponents of the incumbent by trying to please everyone. He represented no principle but his own election."

Morris added, "The electorate was badly divided on the issue of the war. A few more years of a war nobody strongly believes in and I fear the union may be in danger." Ogden enthusiastically agreed with his uncle, as he always did. Hosack kept his political opinions to himself. After a few more minutes of conversation, they both left.

Morris invited me to accompany him to his carriage. "I have something of importance to discuss with you." He directed the driver of his carriage to proceed to my address which, to my surprise, he knew. As the carriage moved along slowly through the dark streets, the memory of the assault at Canal Street made me grateful for the ride to my home. We sat facing each other. Morris began tapping his cane. Then he spoke. "Despite this war, which could continue for years, I have not abandoned the idea of the canal. We are still authorized to borrow up to five million dollars for the cost of construction. When the law passed last June, the expectation was that credit could be obtained in Europe. England, of course, is now beyond consideration as a source of credit. In better days, Inglis, Ellice and Company could have been very helpful. But I have reason to believe that we can borrow the money at reasonable rates from the capitalists in Amsterdam or even in Switzerland. Of course, the war on the continent will make it more costly. Nevertheless, we must proceed before interest in the canal project vanishes completely. Would you like to travel to France as my agent?" For a moment I was speechless. Morris continued. "You have told me you do not want to be a mere book historian. This is your opportunity to see the continent under the sway of the greatest conqueror since Charlemagne, or perhaps Caesar himself." Morris knew how to make his suggestion irresistible to me.

"I would be delighted to go. But I cannot possibly afford the expense of such a trip."

"That is no problem. I will pay for all of your expenses and two thousand dollars for your time."

"That is a very generous offer. Why not send somebody with experience in commercial matters?"

"You need not worry. Leray de Chaumont in Paris will provide that experience. I need a man of discretion to transport and execute my detailed instructions. The mail cannot be trusted. Bonaparte's agents open and read almost everything. When I was in Europe, I wrote in duplicate, triplicate, sometimes even in quadruplicate for an important letter in order to be certain it reached its destination. Even then the letters required months to arrive and occasionally were never received. Use of a cipher was often necessary. There is great uncertainty when letters are not entrusted to confidential persons or special messengers. I will provide you with instructions for negotiations, and you will have discretion to accept terms within certain limitations. You and Leray will have to use your best judgment. If I were younger, I might go myself. But with my gout and a newborn child in the house by spring, it is quite impossible. If all occurs as expected, I would want you to leave in the spring. You will, of course, have to run the British blockade, here and in Europe. Well, are you interested?"

"Yes. Most definitely. I will do it. And I am flattered by your trust."

The carriage halted outside my house. We talked for a few minutes more before I climbed out of the carriage. Morris indicated that the decision whether to send me would depend on information he expected within the next few months. I bade him good night and sent my best wishes to Mrs. Morris. The thought of traveling to Europe made my head spin. Before the war I had never been more than a short distance from New York City. The war was opening the world to me. On the way into the house I thought of Nancy, heavy with child. Then the idea occurred to me for the first time. She must have known she was pregnant when we were together at the concert the previous July. Her coquettish behavior toward me may have only been a manifestation of her joy. She did seem to be almost jubilant. What a fool to believe her happiness could have been related in any manner to my presence, I thought. Again I resolved to end my foolish fancies directed at one who was now about to become a mother. Also, until my departure was certain, I decided to say nothing to Emily about the trip to Europe.

It had been my intention to mention to Morris that John Randel was upset about the fact that while I was gone, in October, the Common Council had presented to the New York City Street Commissioners mounted copies of William Bridges's map of the city with a resolution thanking them for their services, which were performed gratuitously for the city. In the excitement about the proposed trip to Europe, I forgot to mention Randel. Fortunately, in January of 1813, the Common Council decided, as Morris had predicted earlier, that Randel's survey was a public record and Bridges could not be given the exclusive right to publish it. At the time, I thought the dispute between Randel and Bridges was over. It was not.

In the same month as the council's decision, news arrived of the release of some of the prisoners taken at Queenston, including the exchange of Lieutenant Colonel Winfield Scott, the gallant officer forced to surrender his command to the British. The prisoners were taken to Quebec and placed aboard a ship bound for Boston to be exchanged for British soldiers. After the exchange of prisoners, it became known for the first time that twenty-three American regulars with Irish brogues were separated from the other regulars, placed on a British frigate, and sent to England to be tried for treason. This ugly incident eventually halted the exchange of prisoners. Although I had come to expect such conduct from the British, this particular act enraged me. It was as if the Irish ancestors of my father cried out from within me in angry resentment at another outrage against them perpetrated by their historical enemies.

That spring, Stephen Van Rensselaer ran for Governor against the incumbent. Governor Tompkins easily defeated him. The Queenston fiasco was used extensively against the General. The role of General Smyth, the man most responsible for the defeat, was hardly mentioned. Smyth himself was later elected to Congress and served there almost to the present day. Now he writes religious tracts on subjects such as "An Explanation of the Apocalypse, or Revelation of St. John." In politics, virtue is frequently not triumphant. Nor is courage victorious in war. Many of the heroic men of Queenston lie shrouded in the darkness of death. The indifferent and the cowards, among whom I must number myself, have endured to witness the arrival of many another season. Sometimes I wonder which of us were the more fortunate.

NINE

In April of 1813 I was summoned to Morrisania to learn the fate of the proposed trip to Europe. Upon greeting Morris, I congratulated him on the birth of his son, an event that had occurred on February 9, 1813. Dr. Hosack had informed me of the birth of the boy, who was named Gouverneur Morris, Jr. The doctor did not indicate that Mrs. Morris had been seriously ill. Thus, I was taken aback when Morris told me that Nancy had endured a long and dangerous struggle before the child was delivered. "Mrs. Morris's condition was serious for some time. Now she has almost fully recovered her health. The boy is large and strong. It is truly a wonderful thing to be able to continue one's family line. Nothing attaches a person to life so much as the direct responsibility for a member of the next generation." As he spoke, he looked directly at the family portraits on the wall of his library. "They are both sleeping now. You will see them later."

Morris handed me a letter from Paris written in English. "The latest word from my man in Paris, Leray de Chaumont, is that we may be able to borrow the five million dollars for the canal in Holland. Switzerland is also a possible source of funds. The most likely terms are from five to seven percent for from ten to twenty years. With Bonaparte's defeat in Russia, the war in Europe should be finished by this summer. Even Napoleon cannot create a whole new army in a few months. Once the French surrender, we will be forced to make peace with the British. The restoration of peace means the canal will be built. I have written to Leray that you will be coming with explicit instructions for negotiating the loan. By the time you arrive, Bonaparte's empire may have already collapsed like a house of cards.

"The Canal Commissioners will have to pledge the public faith of the State of New York for payment of interest and final redemption of the loan. As a practical matter, you will not be able to accept more than six percent, with charges not to exceed five percent. The large size of the loan makes negotiation on economical terms a distinct possibility. I will give you all of the most recent figures on the expected costs and revenues of the canal. No doubt, the loan will be dependent on the termination of Mr. Madison's War within a reasonably short period of time. From long experience with such matters, the bankers in Europe know that a large construction project is impossible in time of war. No need to worry. This war cannot continue much longer. You should have the loan by the end of the year.

"Money will have to be spared from construction of the canal to compensate for interest from time to time. We might even be able to pay the entire interest by profits on part of the principal. They will know that a sufficient sum cannot be borrowed in this country until the payment of our war debts, which will not be for a long time. You and Leray will have to assume the position that in the absence of favorable terms from them, we are willing to delay the building of the canal until our pecuniary situation improves. If they sense impatience to begin the canal, they will demand a higher rate of interest. You must be willing to terminate negotiations and let them pursue you. There may not be any pursuit. If this war lasts much longer, we shall be unable to borrow at home or abroad. We shall have neither credit nor means.

"Last year, I proposed to borrow the money in Europe, and the Commissioners agreed. My original idea was that Leray de Chaumont would receive the money and the Commissioners draw on him for the entire amount. The Commissioners refused to allow my agent to pledge the credit of New York until the money is paid to the Commissioners here. They contended that if the agent received the money in Paris and then died, or some other unforeseen event occurred, the state might find it had lost the full amount. They would not accept my guarantee that the instrument of credit could protect the state from any such catastrophe. Therefore, it is important to remember that the credit of the state cannot be pledged until the money is actually received in this country. The documents contain that condition in them."

After completing his instructions concerning the loan, Morris handed me a large collection of documents to review and discuss with him before leaving. In order to help me with my historical research and obtain interviews with persons of authority in the French government, perhaps even with Bonaparte himself, I asked Morris if he could provide me with letters of introduction.

"Most of the persons I knew when I was there two decades ago are gone. Swept away by the Revolution or expired from old age. Leray de Chaumont can assist you." He hesitated for a moment. "There are two people. Talleyrand survives every upheaval. He is out of favor now, but he may be able to help you. Perhaps he will recollect we were once acquainted." He laughed as if to indicate that Talleyrand had good reason to remember him. "The man is a scoundrel. Although not of a criminal disposition, he is quite indifferent to the distinction between virtue and vice. You know, Mirabeau, who could have been describing himself, said of him, 'For money Talleyrand would sell you his soul, and he would be right, for he would be trading dung for gold.' "

"He sounds like a cunning rascal, a true politician. An excellent person to know."

"Oh, he is, believe me. There is also Charles de Flahaut. I knew him when he was a child. Although I have not communicated with him for many years, I think he will remember me. The last I heard, he was an aide-de-camp to Berthier, Napoleon's chief of staff. Talleyrand can help you locate him.

When we meet again, I will have the letters ready for you. By then, your passage on a privateer bound for France should be arranged." He stood up and moved to his cushioned chair. "Now we can talk about the Convention."

Because I expected to be abroad for six months to one year, I had become concerned about speaking to Morris, who was fast approaching his biblical three score and ten years, about his experiences as a delegate from Pennsylvania to the 1787 Federal Convention in Philadelphia. The proceedings of the Federal Convention were secret. Twenty-five years later, there were no published records of its deliberations. Therefore, I considered the Convention the most important of all of the historical subjects to be discussed with Morris. In spite of the fact that at the time I was still accumulating information about the American Revolution, I requested Morris to speak to me about the Convention in order to preserve my only available source on the subject. Of all my conversations with Morris, those about the Convention were of the most value. Although Morris was always a candid and reliable source of information, for purposes of corroboration, several years ago I sent my version of Morris's account of the Convention to James Madison. By letter, Madison, who was one of the most important participants at the Convention, confirmed the accuracy of Morris's account, including such details as the spreading of loose earth in front of the State House to lessen the noise of traffic in the street. He indicated that the rule of secrecy at the Convention was objected to by no delegate. Unfortunately, it seems to have remained in effect, with a few exceptions, to the present day.

Morris described the delegates and their positions on various issues. Among those he discussed in some detail were his fellow delegates from Pennsylvania, including Robert Morris, Jared Ingersoll, and Benjamin Franklin. He also talked much about luminaries like Alexander Hamilton, James Madison, George Wythe, and, of course, George Washington. As always, he spoke of Washington with a sense of awe which never failed to astonish me because it was so completely foreign to Morris's critical and often sarcastic descriptions of his fellow mortals. If Washington was a demigod, one of Morris's amusing anecdotes inadvertently presented the General as one whose pomposity may have prevented him, at least in my mind, from ascending to Mount Olympus. At the Convention, Hamilton wagered that Morris would not dare to greet the austere General with a slap on the back. The bet was for a fine meal and all the Madeira the winner could drink. Several days later, during a meal in a room crowded with delegates, Morris walked up to the seated Washington, clapped him on the back, and greeted him heartily. Washington did not acknowledge the greeting. He remained in his seat looking straight ahead without a change in the grave expression on his face. "The silence in the room was thunderous. I won the bet. But the price was so dear that an ocean of Madeira with a thousand meals could never have induced me to repeat it."

According to Morris, the year in which the Convention assembled was a propitious time. "Because the inadequacy of the government was apparent, state pride slumbered for a time and was sacrificed to a sense of right. As soon as the Constitution was promulgated, that pride reawakened, and bedevils us to this day." Morris described his various positions on the major proposals for correcting the weaknesses in the Articles of Confederation. Throughout the Convention he supported a strong and independent executive to check the excesses of the legislature. Initially, he favored the popular election of the President and opposed any prohibition of a second term on the ground that it would tend to destroy the motive to good behavior during the previous term. Later he endorsed a President elected for life subject only to a requirement of good behavior in office. He also favored a Senate for life to preserve the stability of government and to protect the rights of property against "the wayward spirit of democracy." Originally he even opposed removal of the President by impeachment, but was persuaded by Franklin to change his position. He was the author and spokesman on the floor for the final article on the presidency. He laughed as he noted that the Republicans under Jefferson and Madison had expanded the power of the presidency to limits the Federalists under Adams would have approved but would not have dared to attempt.

It surprised me to learn that as a member of the Committee of Style and Arrangement, Morris actually wrote the final version of the Constitution. He condensed the twenty-three articles of the delegates into seven and wrote the wonderful preamble. "We the People of the United States, in Order to form a more perfect Union, establish Justice, insure domestic Tranquillity, provide for the common defence, promote the general Welfare, and secure the Blessings of Liberty to ourselves and our Posterity, do ordain and establish this Constitution for the United States of America." Although admitting to disagreeing with many parts of the final document, he proudly stated that "the choice of words was mine." In his letter to me, Madison wrote, "The finish given to the style and arrangement belonged to the pen of Mr. Morris, who, like all of the other delegates, did not agree with every provision of the final document." To this day it is a fact that is not widely known. It was characteristic of Morris that he was proud of the document but did not care that his own role in its creation remained a secret. Perhaps it was the reason for his limited success as a politician; he was more interested in the result than in the praise that went with it. The applause of the mob held no attraction for him.

Concerning his preamble, he said that the "We the People" phrase really meant "We the States." Since he did not know which of the states would ratify the document, rather than enumerate the names of states, he simply wrote "We the People." He stated, "The Constitution was a compact, not between solitary individuals, but between political societies each enjoying sovereign power." Consistent with this view, he would later support the right of the northeastern states to secede from the union rather than to continue their participation in what he considered to be an unjust war.

Because of my work with the New York Manumission Society, I was especially interested in Morris's account of the manner in which the three-fifths ratio for the representation of slaves was adopted. He reminded me that the three-fifths ratio was first used in 1783 to measure the burden of taxation. Therefore, at that time, the southern states opposed counting slaves, while the New England states wanted to count them like free men. At the Federal Convention in 1787 the use of the ratio concerned the right of representation. Accordingly, the states reversed their positions. The southern states fought to count slaves as the equal of free men, and the states without slaves did not want to count them at all. "The ratio was a compromise that did not, of course, provide representation for slaves, but power for slaveowners. It was an unfair compromise. The slaveowner with five slaves would have one unit of representation for himself and three for his five slaves. The owner of five ships would have only one unit of representation for himself. If slaves were property, they should not have been treated better than ships. If they were humans, they should have been counted as humans. Instead, the Convention counted each slave as three-fifths of a human being and turned his vote over to his owner. We established our nation on this violation of the most sacred laws of humanity. In order to end the subjugation of our fellow creatures, I moved to limit representation to free inhabitants and suggested having the government purchase and emancipate all slaves. As with the New York Constitution, I failed in my attempt. Although the delegates were too ashamed to use the word 'slave' in any part of the Constitution, there was little support among them for abolition of slavery. At the end of the proceedings and for the sake of union, I even withdrew my opposition to the twenty-year delay in permitting the elimination of the importation of slaves. We simply left the problem of slavery to be resolved by future generations. I fear the sons of America will someday curse us for our failure. As with individuals, a virtuous and honorable conduct is the truest interest which a nation can pursue. When we fail to follow that interest, we later pay a heavy price for our misconduct.

"At the Convention, I also opposed the ratio because it would transfer political power away from the maritime states, whose primary interest is in commerce, to the southern states, where the chief interest is in land. I warned that those interested in land would lead us into a war for the expansion of our territory. Now, twenty-five years later, the South and West have marched us off to conquer Canada with no regard for the harm done to the commercial interests of the East."

"They are the controlling majority," I interjected.

Morris looked at me scornfully. "It is nonsense to say that the voice of the majority must be obeyed regardless of the folly and vice they preach. If we sacrifice the dictates of conscience to the caprice of the majority, we are no better than the most despicable slave subject to the whim of the sternest tyrant. That is despotism and I will not abide it. Democracy, or majority rule, is a disease from which all republics have perished except those conquered by foreign invaders. Now the natural political depravity of men, of majorities, has led us into this mad war. I fear it will blow our union flag from the masthead."

The war seemed to rob Morris of the common sense with which he was so richly endowed. When he spoke of it, he became immoderate, like the haughty aristocrat I had expected before actually meeting him. "You speak as though the war has destroyed your faith in your own Constitution."

"That was over a quarter of a century ago. In any case, it is not the war that destroyed my faith in the document. The Constitution was mortally wounded over a decade ago when Congress repealed the Judiciary Act. The judicial positions created under that act were to last during a term of good behavior. Congress had no power to suspend them except by impeachment. It was an unqualified breach of the independence of the judicial branch and an end to the rule of law. The Constitution was already violated. This unjust war now puts the union itself in peril. How long can we allow our own commercial interests to be wantonly disregarded by this political dynasty from Virginia? There is always the hope that this impious war will end their vain hope of conquest and rescue this nation from the despotism of democracy. We cannot—" As he spoke, a servant entered the room and gestured to Morris. "Ah. Nancy and the child are coming down."

"The Virginia dynasty, you mean." Morris roared appreciatively at my joke. Then he bounded out of his chair to greet his wife.

Nancy entered carrying the infant in her arms. She had gained weight since we last met at the Battery and she looked haggard. There were dark circles under her eyes. Her greeting was friendly, but subdued. She asked me about my service on the Niagara frontier. But she seemed to be only half listening. Her attention was constantly drawn away to the tiny being in her arms. When one of the servants offered to assist, she clung to the infant with a fierce maternal fervor. After ten minutes with us, during which time she barely spoke, the baby began to cry. She announced that she had to feed the child and departed. It was difficult for me to accept the fact that this maternal figure was the same ethereal being who had filled my thoughts for almost four years. Could this mother, this chameleon, I wondered, continue to trouble my sleeping and waking hours? If not, perhaps that other Nancy would vanish into a fond memory of what once was but can no longer be.

Morris smiled with paternal pride. "How she adores that child. That is what women live for. Children. We men draw our ideals from war and politics. The ideals of women come from motherhood. Is it any wonder they cherish peace and life so much more than we do?" Morris appeared ready to resume lamenting "the madness of the war." Everything seemed to remind him of it, even the sight of his wife holding his child and heir. To my relief, he did not commence another tirade concerning the struggle.

Before we parted, Morris recalled a summer day during the end of the Convention. General Washington and he left Philadelphia in Morris's phaeton to fish for trout at Valley Forge. "While I was fishing, he rode around the old camp of 1777–78 and visited the works. They were in ruins but still retained the power to recall the memories of those tumultuous years. He usually remained silent as to his thoughts about the past. But on that day, the warmth of the summer sun, our solitude, and the magic of that place to conjure memories all joined to remove his usual diffidence. He made me feel as though I were his son in whom he could confide his feelings about that troubled winter encampment. It was a day I shall cherish to the moment of my own death. Now he is only a memory. Soon I shall join him."

"Soon, we all shall."

That evening I told Emily for the first time about my plans to leave for France. Although the initial warmth of being reunited had cooled considerably, we had not argued since my return from the Niagara frontier. She was silent, but I could see the anger mounting within her. The truce was over. "How can you leave me again? You've only been back for a few months."

"I must go. It is very important both to me and to Mr. Morris. It is a wonderful opportunity to witness what I am writing about. Morris will pay all my expenses plus two thousand dollars. You will have all the money you need while I am gone. You should be glad to be rid of me. Be reasonable."

"That's all you are is reasonable. You have no emotions. You're cold as a stone."

"Emotions are unreliable. My cold reason is something you can depend on." My answer, which was meant to be humorous, enraged Emily. Perhaps it was the fact that I responded to her rising anger with a controlled, passionless monotone. The indifference within me subdued any anger that may have been lurking within.

"I cannot continue living like this." The anger in Emily's voice was barely controlled.

"Like what?"

"This! We are not a family. We lead separate lives. We may as well live in separate houses."

"It has been that way for years. So why are you angry when I propose leaving for a time? I don't understand your problem."

"I can't talk to you." She stormed out of the room. The argument, I thought, was ended. Within one minute, however, she returned and stood at the opposite end of the room as if there were an abyss between us. "It's your godlessness that makes you so—"

"What has religion got to do with this matter? You always return to the same irrelevant subject."

"It makes you heartless. You did not care when my mother died. You didn't even try to console me, you bastard."

She was beginning to shatter my indifference. I could feel the anger rising in my gorge. "How could I console you, when you refused to speak to me? Why talk about your mother? You were the one who was always fighting with her, not I."

"You have ruined our marriage. I don't love you anymore. I don't even like you."

Emily and I had many skirmishes before this one, and even a few major battles. We had always ended the hostilities with a truce or a treaty of peace. These resolutions were possible because I had never before resorted to the mayhem of the bayonet. Despite my knowledge of Emily's vulnerable points, I had always avoided inflicting wounds that could not be healed. This time I drew the bayonet and stabbed. It was not out of any pleasure in inflicting pain, but from an inability to stop.

"Oh what a splendid marriage we have. I give you the fruit of my labor and you give me the fruit of your womb. Nothing! I receive no warmth, no love, no heirs. Nothing except your constant carping." Emily winced in pain at the mention of our childlessness. It was a subject we had warily avoided discussing for years. Emily, I knew, could not bear to confront the matter. She fled the field in tears. My victory was complete; but it left a bitter taste in my mouth.

Our marriage was not a Gordian knot requiring intricate work or vigorous cutting to untie. The knot had been unraveling for many years, until a few fragile filaments remained. These had been irretrievably ripped by my single cruel statement. The power of that comment to inflict pain was greater than I had anticipated. Our childlessness, I had often thought, was the most conspicuous cause for the unhappiness of our marriage. In the years after we were first married, it had not been a matter of grave concern to either of us. With the passing of time, however, it became an obsession with Emily. She would gaze dreamily at any woman with little ones. At night she would be desirous of attempting conception. Her advances were most agreeable to me. For nature has generously matched the female's desire to procreate with the male's ardor to inseminate. When our couplings produced no issue, she lost interest in the proceedings. An unspoken indifference seeped into our household. At first Emily suggested we seek guidance from a priest. I refused to submit to any medieval church remedy for infertility, which, I suggested with hostile intent, might be to tie us naked to a post while a praying priest lashed us with miraculous rods and sprinkled holy water. Angered by my flippancy, she saw a priest without me. He said a prayer, she lit a candle, and we remained without a child. The life slowly continued to drain out of our marriage. For years we had not spoken of our failure to procreate. My breaking of the long silence was intolerable to Emily. For the three weeks preceding my departure for Europe, she uttered hardly a word in my presence. My preparations continued.

After Morris visited me in the city and provided me with additional written instructions and three letters of introduction, I made my final preparations for the long voyage. A trip to Europe was the fulfillment of a life-long yearning formed while turning the pages of hundreds of books on the history and culture of that alluring continent. At last I was to make the great pilgrimage which I had seen so many others commence from the wharves of New York. Because my crossing would be on a twenty-two gun brig, the *Rights of Man*, it would not be possible to transport the immense amount of goods others frequently carried across the Atlantic. In time of peace it was not uncommon to see passengers taking on board horses and cows, the latter to provide milk and beef, on the lengthy journey. The space available to me would be much too limited for such extravagance; nevertheless, I had to carry on board numerous items to sustain me on the six- to eight-week crossing. The supplies and food were expensive and had to be provided initially out of my own pocket. Money from Morris would only be available upon my return. Among the goods I gathered were flour, Indian meal for frying, a cask of salted beef, two hams, three chickens to provide eggs and fresh meat, several bushels of corn, a barrel of apples to prevent the scurvy, twelve bottles of wine, a keg of rum, salt provisions, two weight of tea and chocolate, several loaves of sugar, a mattress, a pillow, sheets and blankets, and an ample supply of clothing with extra gold coin and currency sewn into the lining. (Because a ship's hammock was more comfortable than the bed, I did not use the mattress and sheets.) I carried two account books, one to maintain a record of my expenditures for later reimbursement by Morris, and the second to use as a journal of my experiences abroad. To relieve the tedium of the long crossing, I included in my baggage a small library of recent histories, numerous quills for my pen, and a substantial supply of paper. Not having used French for many years, I brought several volumes in that musical tongue for the purpose of improving my fluency. Unfortunately, I possessed little experience conversing in the language of Voltaire. Rereading the adventures of Candide and Cunegonde, I feared, would not assist me in obtaining directions to Versailles or negotiating the rate to be paid for a night at a roadside inn.

Being a dutiful wife, Emily assisted me with the tedious task of packing. She spoke not one more word than was necessary to complete the work. On the day of my departure, she retreated into the bedroom without wishing me well. Not wanting to leave without bidding her farewell, I followed her to the bedroom. With neither anger nor sorrow in her eyes, she closed the door in my face. I departed without a word.

On a beautiful cloudless day in early May, I boarded the privateer, the *Rights of Man*. In order to avoid the British squadron cruising off Sandy Hook since the beginning of the war, we set forth by way of Long Island Sound, which had remained open for the first year of hostilities. At the time, the route was frequently used by ships trading with the unblockaded ports of New England. Filled with that wonderful excitement which attends an ocean voyage, I stood at the railing transfixed by the sight of the coastline of Long Island fading into the distance. To the shock of everyone, within an hour after clearing Montauk Point, a British man-of-war was sighted. Captain Tarlow, an experienced old sailor, calmly identified it as the forty-eight-gun *Acasta*, one of the vessels in the blockading squadron. Within minutes the seventy-four-gun *Ramillies*, the flagship of the British fleet, was also sighted. The captain confidently announced that we would outrun the enemy. For hours I watched apprehensively as we maintained a safe distance from the pursuers who relentlessly stalked their prey. Finally, a favorable wind drove us forward into the open sea. First the *Ramillies* disappeared on the horizon. When the *Acasta* turned about and gave up the chase, I joined the wild cheering of the crew.

The next day, in fitful winds, we sailed on more turbulent waters off the New England coast. For the first time in my life I became seasick. The pitching and rolling of the vessel combined with the putrid odor of its interior filled me with a nausea that lasted for many days. Even the sighting of porpoises could not raise my spirits. Unable to eat or drink, I sat on deck and watched the endless rising and falling horizon until my churning stomach forced me to retreat into the cramped quarters of my cabin, which was so small I had to crawl into it. Death itself seemed preferable to my perpetual misery. After two interminable weeks of rough seas, my suffering finally ended with a period of smooth waters and bright sunshine.

For the first time, I was able to dine with the captain, several of his officers, and a Frenchman named Jean Lafont, who was bound for Lyons. The table was furnished with movable cross bars to prevent dishes from rolling off the edge. Because of calm seas, I was able to disregard the cross bars and eat heartily. Captain Tarlow seemed to be delighted to have a new listener so that he could repeat the stories he had exhausted days earlier. It was clear that everyone else at the table had already been subjected to his rambling monologues. The captain proudly declared his intention of hunting British vessels in the English Channel and those attempting to supply the British army in Spain. "Maybe we'll impress a few of theirs into our service. Show 'em what it feels like." In response to my eager and welcome questions, he described the process of impressment as he had witnessed it on a number of occasions. "They like to bully our smaller ships. Show some cannon and they avoid you. They always send over a beardless lieutenant with a host of armed men. The whole crew is forced to line up on deck and pass in review by the arrogant whelp. He compares any damned seaman he wants with his protection certificate and takes the men he fancies. He piously claims the description of each seaman on the document doesn't match the lad standing before him. It's nothing but damned kidnapping. Some Brits don't even look at the papers. They drag away our boys as if they still belonged to the King. Nothing but damned British arrogance." Upon a later questioning of two ordinary seamen about the practice of impressment, I was surprised to learn that both favored the right to search and impress because they feared losing their jobs to the large number of English sailors working on American ships.

With the end of seasickness, the pain and emptiness in my heart returned. I was distressed to find myself thinking and dreaming about Nancy. Not the maternal Mrs. Morris of my last visit to Morrisania, but the mysteriously beautiful Nancy Randolph illuminated by the light of a single candle. It was this phantom, the eye-enthralling siren of my thoughts for the past four years, who filled my mind and inflamed my imagination. Whenever I thought she was gone, she returned with renewed power to disturb my tranquillity. Even the vast reaches of the Atlantic could not provide enough distance to escape her hold on my fevered dreams. With the boredom and loneliness of the long journey, I quickly surrendered to the sweetness of my musings and thought of her constantly.

Monsieur Lafont, whose English was as bad as my French, helped me to improve my ability to converse in French by providing an opportunity to practice. He also advised me on the sights of Paris, one in particular. "There is a place in Paris every visitor must see. The Palais Royal. Anything in the world a man might want is there, food, drink, singing, dancing, gambling, and women, especially women." With a lascivious grin on his face, he whispered dramatically, "The brothel at number 113, Palais Royal, will have the woman you desire. That is my guarantee to you."

"The woman I desire is back in New York."

"At 113, you will forget about her."

"I wish you were correct, but that is quite impossible."

He laughed. "You Americans are so innocent."

In the sixth week of our voyage the lookout sighted a British merchant-man headed south toward Spain. The captain gave the order to pursue. Muskets were distributed to the crew. The surgeon laid out his instruments and dressings. In case of fire, barrels were filled with water. After a chase of several hours, the *Rights of Man* pulled alongside and aimed her impressive array of cannon at the vulnerable hull of the hapless victim. The British captain immediately struck his ship's colors. Captain Tarlow ordered a prize crew to board the captured vessel and announced his intention to bring her into Rochefort. He informed me that, after the beginning of the war the previous year, as soon as American privateers began to reach the French coast, Napoleon had issued orders for the admission into any French port of all prizes captured by American ships on the same terms as if they had been seized by the French. These orders permitted Americans to avoid the risk of attempting to escort captured British ships all the way back to America. Instead the prizes could be hauled directly into French ports for immediate adjudication. As a result of the ease of seizure and reward, according to Tarlow, in the year since the beginning of the war, the English Channel and waters between Spain and England had become overrun with American privateers preying on British shipping.

There is something strangely moving about meeting the men of another ship at sea, even if it is the crew of a captured enemy vessel. After weeks of sailing on the endless desert that is the ocean, we had discovered another society of fellow human beings wandering in the same desolation. Thus, when the British seamen were brought on board, there arose an immediate spirit of good fellowship that far exceeded the relations among soldiers on land. The British captain, an amiable soul, provided us with our first news of the outside world in six weeks and the first reports of the European war more recent than February. To my surprise and relief, we were informed that not only had Napoleon's empire failed to collapse, but that within the first three months after the Russian disaster, Napoleon had assembled another grand army. In early May he had defeated the combined armies of Russia and Prussia at Lützen, the same German battlefield where the great Gustavus Adolphus had been slain almost two centuries earlier. The war continued.

Although the continuation of the war made it much less likely that a loan for the canal could be obtained, I was delighted by the news of Napoleon's continuing military success. In the preceding years of his triumphant march through history, Napoleon had captured a place in my affections far beyond any other leader of my own lifetime. To understand fully the events of the next few years, it is important to understand the extent and nature of these affections. Of course, my sympathies were naturally with Bonaparte as the representative of the ideals of the French Revolution, and I detested his enemies, the Romanovs, Hohenzollerns, Hapsburgs, Bourbons, and Hanoverians, all of whom had been struggling to retain the ancient privileges of their aristocratic families against the threat of a leader chosen by the people. But I must confess, Napoleon had become something far more important to me than a mere political leader. He was a genuine hero who transcended the issues of his era. That is not to say I approved of all of his actions; I was both fascinated and repelled by the man. Yet, my feelings for him were so great that they even overcame my detestation of the one unforgivable act he had committed. Unlike many republicans who abandoned him when he made himself Emperor with a hereditary line, my objections arose at an earlier time. During the short-lived peace of Amiens with England in 1802, which reopened the seas to French shipping, Napoleon decided to revive the French slave trade so as to provide a larger population in the Antilles and create a market for French goods. General Leclerc was sent with a large fleet to conquer Santo Domingo, which had become an independent black republic during the turmoil of the Revolution. The new republic was governed by the great black revolutionary, Toussaint L'Ouverture, who had defeated the English. Toussaint was captured by the French forces and sent to France to die in prison. I was appalled. For the first time in my life I found myself hoping for a French defeat. Fortunately, with the assistance of yellow fever, the French were beaten by the former black slaves. Their nefarious enterprise had failed.

Toussaint originally had supported the French because of the determination of the leaders of the French Revolution to abolish slavery. Bonaparte's reversal of the policy against slavery was a betrayal of the most sacred principles of the revolution. To my horror, another great republican leader, President Jefferson, supported the French plans for the subjugation of Santo Domingo because the island was becoming a base for pirates in the Caribbean, and, I fear, because Toussaint's black republic threatened the institution of slavery in the United States. During his presidency, Jefferson even signed a disgraceful statute establishing an embargo on trade with the victorious blacks of Santo Domingo. Surely it was the mad prejudice of race that caused the leaders of the two great revolutionary states, France and the United States, to refrain from supporting the refusal of Haitian Negroes to be enslaved. Nevertheless, for lack of political alternatives, I continued to support in my own mind both Jefferson and Bonaparte. Endorsement of the principles of both the American and French Revolutions would, I believed, eventually lead to the end of slavery.

My objections to Napoleon becoming an Emperor were not nearly as strong as my feelings on slavery. It was understandable that in a country like France, with a long tradition of kings, the leader selected by the popular will would choose to wrap himself in the trappings of monarchy. He was simply forced to fight an unregenerate world using the weapons of that world. Yet at the coronation itself there occurred an action so sublime as to represent the essence of my admiration for Napoleon. In the midst of the traditional pageantry of the coronation ceremony, he snatched the crown from the hands of the Pope and placed it on his own head. It was as if he were proclaiming to the world that his power did not derive from God or the established authority of religion, but instead issued from his own will. He was his own god, the leader of an aristocracy of talent. His ascendancy meant that every man would be judged by his own abilities rather than the accident of his parentage. In his life's achievements, Napoleon fulfilled the dream of every man, including me, to overcome the obstacles created by society and to perform to the limits of his own ability. As the French once said, there is a marshal's baton concealed in the knapsack of each French soldier. *Une carrière ouverte aux talents.* As long as a man who crowned himself with the approval of the people was in power, no hereditary prince could feel safe. The sovereigns of England, Russia, Prussia, and Austria fought to the death to restore the privilege of the few and eliminate the opportunity open to the many. Popular sovereignty could not be tolerated. In the years since 1815 the victors have written history to make Napoleon the aggressor. The facts are otherwise. With the exception of Spain in 1808 and Russia in 1812, it was the supporters of hereditary privilege and the wealth of the few who began each campaign against the forces of democracy—in 1792, 1800, 1803, 1805, 1806, 1809, 1813, and later, in 1815. "Liberty, equality, and fraternity" have never been principles supported by those in power. The motto of the powerful has always been "order, privilege, and exclusion." To some extent, Napoleon partook of both mottoes. Yet as long as he stood alone against the kings of Europe, who treated their subjects like personal possessions, he represented to me the immense power of the individual human being. In the perpetual war between the "haves" and the "have-nots," Napoleon represented the great masses of "have-nots." Despite the attacks on his immense achievements in the twelve years since his final defeat, many, including me, still revere his memory. Thus, it was with great excitement I arrived in the nation of the great revolutionary.

On the ides of June of 1813, after a voyage of seven weeks, we heard the long-awaited cry from aloft. "Land! Land!" In less than an hour the coastline was clearly visible from the deck. With the assistance of a pilot boat, the captain brought the *Rights of Man* with its prize into the port of Rochefort, a favorite destination of privateers preying on British ships attempting to supply Wellington's peninsular army. My joy on returning to land, in a place whose history I knew better than that of my own country, was overwhelming. The news we received upon our disembarkation added to the overflowing cup of my happiness. Less than three weeks after Lützen, Napoleon had won another great victory in Saxony, in a place called Bautzen, against the combined Russian and Prussian armies. The allied armies had retreated into Silesia and an armistice had been agreed to on June 2. Peace negotiations had begun. Not only was Napoleon again victorious, but the reestablishment of peace made it likely that a loan for the canal could be obtained.

It was a beautiful hot sunny day that made one think it was the middle of summer. Everywhere was the usual bustle of a great port. Cargo being loaded and unloaded. Wagons picking up passengers. Officials of the port transacting business with great solemnity. It could have been the port of New York, except for one disconcerting fact. Everyone was speaking a foreign language, and with a speed that made it almost incomprehensible to me. In seeking directions to a hotel, I found myself saying to each person, *"Parlez lentement, s'il vous plaît. Je ne comprends pas."* Unfortunately, instead of speaking more slowly, my listeners would talk more loudly. Inevitably, I would be forced to say not what I wanted but what would evoke a comprehensible response.

My trip to Paris was in a government coach. The coach was not at all like our uncomfortable vehicles, which are little better than wagons. It was spacious enough to accommodate more than one dozen passengers. Seven were inside; outside, three were in the front, and I sat in back with two other passengers watching the dust in the road billowing behind the coach. On the second day of travel I sat in the front and observed the postilion in action. Riding one of the four horses, with the other three harnessed in front of him, he wore enormous leather boots and an old-fashioned wig. I was pleased to see that the driver's cracking of the whip was merely to keep the horses alert while not actually hurting the poor beasts. In Rochefort I had thought myself fortunate to have acquired a book published by the government which printed the rates by the post on every stage of the journey with extra charges for the postilion. When the time came to pay, the postilion informed me that my book was out of date and that there were substantial extra charges for the drinks of the horses and the driver. There was also an extra charge for entering Paris. It must be admitted that the thrill of entering Paris was worth an additional payment. As we approached I found myself regularly stretching my neck to catch a first glimpse of that fabled city. Finally the postilion cried out, *"Là voila."* Its domes and steeples shimmered in the midday heat like a rich jewel in the midst of the surrounding countryside.

Before entering the city, the coach was stopped at the barrier by douaniers wearing dark green uniforms and immense cocked hats. For the second time since my arrival in France, I was required to show my passport before being admitted to the heart of the old world. The delay only heightened my wonder and curiosity about the city that was at the center of so much of the history I planned to write. As we drove through the city itself, I was thrilled by the beauty and magnificence of the place, the spaciousness of the boulevards, the stately buildings, the beautiful trees. Compared to such an ancient metropolis, New York City was but a backward, isolated village in the distant provinces.

Thomas Jefferson had been right to praise the limitation of the heights of the buildings and the generous amount of public grounds. A few glimpses of the wonderful variety of Paris and I was assailed by new doubts about the plan of the Street Commissioners for Manhattan—it was to be a flattened island with endless monotonous blocks. No curves, no surprises; a city, unlike Paris, of infinite predictability.

In the Latin Quarter near the Sorbonne, I rented a room at a weekly rate from an ancient crone who promised everything and, as it came to pass, delivered almost nothing. Immediately I began to explore. In the area of my hotel the streets were narrow, with gutters running down the middle of the way. In the back streets many of the inhabitants walked with nosegays held to their faces to repel the unpleasant odors all about them. Within minutes of leaving my hotel, I was almost drenched by a young woman pouring a vile liquid from the window above me. At the cry of *"Garde à l'eau"* from above, I quickly learned to jump out of the way. Many of the streets are so narrow that a person on foot barely has room to avoid being run over by the constantly passing carriages. Several times during my stay I leaped to the side of the street, only to be splashed with mud from a passing cabriolet.

On my first full day in the city, after determining that Leray de Chaumont was away for a week, I forgot all thought of business and abandoned myself to a systematic exploration of the historic places. The shadows of the dead appear everywhere in Paris. The city is filled with history. It was the history of the past half century that most interested me. The remains of the Bastille with jets d'eaux newly added to commemorate the marriage of Napoleon to Marie Louise. The Conciergerie, the prison of Marie Antoinette. The immense square, now Place Louis XV, where Louis XVI, Marie Antoinette, Princess Elizabeth, Danton, Robespierre, and many others were executed two decades earlier. The Pantheon, where one can pay homage to the remains of Voltaire and Rosseau. The colossal statue of General Desaix in the Square des Victoires. At the Luxembourg Palace, I gazed with great interest at the massive paintings of Napoleonic warfare— Marengo, Austerlitz, Jena, and Jacques Louis David's celebrated picture of Bonaparte's passage of the Alps. On another day I visited David's own painting shop in the Sorbonne and saw the huge canvas of the coronation of 1804. Unfortunately, David chose to portray Napoleon crowning Josephine instead of the placing of the crown on his own head. At a museum called the Cabinet of Comparative Anatomy, where the skeletons of most of the animals of the world are collected, I saw the grotesque display of the skeleton of the Mameluke who assassinated General Kléber in Egypt. The curator, with great relish, pointed out the burns from red hot irons visible on the bones of the right hand. He even allowed some of the visitors to shake hands with the grisly relic. The poor wretch was severely tortured but would not reveal whether others had conspired with him. All that suffering, and now no more life than a stone or block of wood. A senseless thing hanging in a museum for the entertainment of other mortals soon to follow him into oblivion.

In the Catacombs at the Barrière d'Enfer awaited an even more grisly reminder of my own mortality. Each visitor was given a candle to light his way down the narrow stairs. Fearful of being plunged into darkness, I cupped my hand around the flickering flame. At the bottom of the stairs were a number of dark passages cut out of rock. Finally our party of visitors arrived at the place where lie the mortal remains of thousands of those who trod this path before us. The bones of humans are piled into a wall of our predecessors. Layer upon layer of skulls placed in neat rows of death and decay. In the end the ugly and the beautiful, the healthy and the sick, the rich and the poor, the good and the evil, all reduced to this ultimate equality, the quintessence of dust. As I have always been quite aware of the end that awaits me and all my fellow voyagers on this planet, I was not touched by despair or even saddened by this infernal display of death's hegemony. Only upon returning to the land of the living did I feel a touch of melancholy at the sight of a wretched young boy standing alone at a corner playing a hurdy-gurdy.

My first Sunday in the city, I attended a mass at the Cathedral of Notre-Dame, that majestic edifice at the center of Paris. Although I had not been to mass for many years, since the days when my mother would drag me to church over the objections of my father, the ceremony recalled the mixed feelings of fascination and disgust I had experienced so many years earlier. Unable to tolerate the constant ringing of the small bell and incessant genuflections, I fled back into the sunlight of Paris filled with anger at those who gain power over other humans by preying on their fears of death and the unknowable. Even the Revolution had been unable to replace the god of terror with the goddess of reason. Nor had it been able to end the insatiable hunger of the god of war. At the Place du Carrousel, I watched a military parade of impressive size, the soldiers looking magnificent in their brightly colored uniforms. It was the first time I heard the military music that seemed to be omnipresent during my stay in France. The constant warfare of the previous twenty years had replaced the gentle music of peacetime with the belligerent blasts of brass and the roll of ceremonial drums. At almost every parade or concert in the city, one could close one's eyes and picture the thunderous advance of armies to the sounds of "La Marche Consulaire à Marengo," "La Grenadière," and "Le Salut des Aigles." One tune, "La Marche des Eclopés," subtitled "La Boiteuse," the lame or crippled march, was extremely popular. It was said to have been composed at Napoleon's command during the retreat from Russia the previous year. The music itself limped as if to match the stumbling steps of the survivors of the dreadful march back from Moscow. To this day I find myself humming the tune as I limp along my own private route of retreat.

Standing at the top of the unfinished Triumphant Arch in the Place du Carrousel were the great bronze horses from St. Marks's in Venice. Stolen by the Venetians when they sacked Constantinople during the Fourth Crusade, six hundred years later they had been brought to Paris by Napoleon, the conqueror of Venice. Because of the great height of the arch, I had to stand at a considerable distance from it to see the horses, so that much of their beauty was not visible. The unfinished triumphal arch itself had carved in it bas-reliefs of the capitulation of Ulm, the Battle of Austerlitz, and other great Napoleonic humiliations of Austria and her allies. In the nearby Louvre were accumulated art treasures taken from all the lands of Europe conquered by Napoleon. Many of these were soon to be taken away by the triumphant allies. Being there in 1813, I had the good fortune to see such treasures as Raphael's *Portrait of Leo X* and *Transfiguration*, which I admired but did not approve, the *Dying Gladiator*, and my favorite work of sculpture, the *Laocoön*, the destruction of an innocent old man and his two young sons in the coils of the serpent sent by a vengeful god.

After spending many hours in the Louvre, I wandered through the gardens of the Tuileries. Of particular interest to me were the numerous statues of gods and goddesses. It is said that in 1792 the sans-culottes refused to fire at two Swiss soldiers of the King who had taken refuge behind the marble statues. Rather than damage the sculpture, the leaders of the mob pricked the Swiss soldiers with their pikes until they came out to be slaughtered. The story was told to me as an example of what Europeans consider to be the triumph of civilization in the old world.

While pondering the paradox of civilized brutality, I noticed that the dirt path was beginning to be spattered by intermittent drops of rain. As the rain began to become more heavy, I ran beneath the shelter of a nearby tree. Within a few seconds a beautiful young woman with long dark tresses ran beneath the same tree and stood beside me. Her graceful movement and striking figure reminded me of Nancy. In clumsy French, I attempted to start a conversation with her. "I am sorry I do not have an umbrella to share with you." With the beginnings of a coquettish smile on her face, she turned to me. As soon as she looked into my face, she turned away and stared off into space as if I were not present. A terrible feeling of loneliness enshrouded me. I wanted desperately to seize her and have her acknowledge my presence. But the desire had no power over my paralyzed limbs; even if it did, I knew she would have fled from me in terror or disgust. Within minutes the rain turned into a light drizzle and she vanished from my side. Life in Paris, I knew, would be no different from my lonely existence in Manhattan. I carried my own solitude inside of me wherever I traveled.

Later that day I watched the rays of the setting sun striking the dome of the Invalides and fell into a deep melancholy. I spent the entire evening thinking of Nancy, both the beautiful Miss Randolph and Mrs. Morris, the mother. The different images of her filled my mind as they had ever since my departure from New York. The constant thought of her troubled me like a recurrent illness. Her face haunted my dreams at night and my days walking through the streets of Paris. Whenever I thought the fever had finally departed, it returned with a renewed fury. In the fourth year of this affliction, I began to fear that it was incurable.

To divert my mind from my feverish imaginings, I went to the theatre on two separate occasions. Once to a tragedy by Corneille, and the second time to a Molière comedy. Compared to the drama in New York, I found the French stage to be rather uninteresting. In most scenes only two persons occupied the stage, engaging in long dull speeches. There was little interest in scenery, costumes, and processions. Perhaps the French had enough pageantry outside the theatre and sought ideas within. After the failure of the plays to divert me, I decided to concentrate on my most important mission, the canal loan.

Nine days after my arrival in Paris, I was finally received by Monsieur Leray de Chaumont. It was obvious from his apartments that he was a very wealthy man. When he came out to greet me, I noticed a fleeting look of surprise and disappointment in his face at the unimpressive appearance of Mr. Morris's emissary from America. Even my newly-purchased waistcoat, knee breeches, and silk stockings could not disguise my plebeian ordinariness. Leray quickly covered over his momentary lapse with a fulsome display of charm.

"Well, you have arrived at last. Welcome to Paris, my friend." He spoke English like an American.

"You're an American?"

"Of course. Didn't Mr. Morris tell you?"

"No. He referred to you as 'my man in Paris.' I assumed anyone with a name like Leray de Chaumont must be French."

"My name is James Leray. The 'de Chaumont' comes from my estate at Chaumont. They buy our land and I buy theirs. The French, you know, have a great hunger for land in America. It has provided me with a very profitable enterprise. There is great risk, but the money is well worth it. How did you come to be involved in the canal? I would wager you own land along the planned route."

"No. I certainly do not." My indignant reply, I suspect, convinced Leray that he was dealing with a person of no consequence. After explaining my labors as a historian and employment with Morris on both the New York Street Commission and the Canal Commission, I foolishly mentioned my work as a printer. Leray had no interest in my endeavors in history, but he immediately questioned me on the size of my printing business. It was apparent that he was appalled to find himself dealing with a printer of no financial importance. Following a few perfunctory questions about my voyage, he changed the subject.

"And how is Mr. Morris? I have not received a letter from him since March. His new heir is in good health?"

"Of course, I have not seen him for two months. Everyone was well before I departed. He did give me these documents to deliver to you."

Leray quickly scanned the letter and other documents. "The latest word on the loan is not good. The bankers are now saying that a large loan to New York is impossible until peace is restored in America. They expect an American defeat. After the events of last year, it does seem likely. Based on the recent reports, Wellington's army may soon be in America. You have not heard? We just received news that Wellington has badly defeated the French at Vitoria. Southern France is now open to invasion from Spain. Austria will now probably join the coalition with Russia and Prussia. You know, I am in agreement with Mr. Morris on the only way peace can be restored. There can be no peace with Bonaparte." Leray smiled at me in the manner of a conspirator. He clearly assumed that I shared Morris's hatred of Napoleon.

He pushed a piece of paper toward me and suggested I write my address so that he could communicate with me. It was obvious that he wanted to end our brief meeting. Disappointed that he was neither discussing the loan with me as an equal nor extending any manner of hospitality, I attempted to extend the conversation. In response to my inquiries about meeting with bankers, he stated that he would inform me in the event of any such meeting. When I told him about my intention to do historical research and interviews in Paris, he suggested that I visit the archives. "I am a man of business. I can do little to assist you on matters of history. The past is of no interest to me. If I think of an appropriate person, I shall give you a letter of introduction." His tone was curt. I had intended to ask him about Talleyrand and Flahaut; but, angered by his brusque treatment, I departed. My initial wrath quickly transformed itself into dismay and profound disappointment. After traveling seven weeks on a mission of some importance, I had been treated like a boy delivering a basket of food for the evening meal.

As I was appropriately dressed, I decided to deliver my letters of introduction from Morris to Talleyrand and Flahaut. The visit to Talleyrand's house at the Rue St. Florentin was fruitless. A servant greeted me at the door and took my letter of introduction. Within several minutes he returned, asked for my address, and informed me that "the Prince of Benevento" would communicate with me at a later date. The door was closed in my face. Flahaut, I soon learned, was a brigadier general serving with the army in Saxony. My disappointment and loneliness were acute. I wished to return to New York. Entering my hotel, I was greeted by my disagreeable landlady who demanded payment of the next week's rent in advance.

In order to overcome my increasing despair, I decided to commence my research immediately. The next day was the beginning of my daily visits to the archives. Each day they would be open for six hours, from ten A.M. to four P.M. Because of the limited time there, I would eat a large breakfast every morning. For two francs my landlady served a plate of eggs, fried mackerel, coffee, cheese, wine, and bread. Fortified by this large morning meal, I would work at the archives for six uninterrupted hours and then go to a café for my evening meal. The work at the archives was tedious but rewarding. After I became a regular visitor, an elderly man, a Monsieur Monceau, who was employed there, took an interest in my work and often assisted me in finding particular materials. I began by exploring all of the documents available on the American Revolution. As the documents for some years had been carefully numbered, it quickly became obvious that many of them were out of order or missing. The documents for one year were frequently not in any comprehensible order for that year. Scattered papers were tied up in dusty cartons by months or series of months. The information was fragmentary and confusing. It was often uncertain whether crucial information was lost or had ever existed at all. Nevertheless, enough nuggets of considerable interest were to be found to encourage further research within the chaos of information. For example, there were numerous papers on the significant impression Burgoyne's defeat made on the French ministry and how the surrender at Saratoga directly caused France's decision to join the war against the British. Because all of the documents were in French, it took me a considerable amount of time to translate, abridge, and copy them. At the end of the day my eyes and head would ache. After a meal and a walk, I would usually write and then go to sleep.

Occasionally I would play twenty-one or whist with one of the residents of my hotel or watch the landlady's cabala expert play lunatic games with words, numbers, and a Ouija board. The cabalist claimed that when he wrote down his magical symbols, God became present in the letters or figures. Thus, the symbols themselves contained all knowledge, past, present, and future. Alas, if only truth were so simple to discover.

In order to lessen the tedium of perusing the documents of the American Revolution, I began to read back issues of the *Moniteur* presenting an account of daily events during the French Revolution and the period of Napoleon's rule. For 1789 to 1799 I reviewed thirty-one bound volumes of the newspaper. After 1799, when the *Moniteur* became the official journal of government, it is essential for an understanding of events. Reading the bulletins of Napoleon, I became familiar with the details of all of his military campaigns. It must be admitted that the bulletins are most useful for the official view which the government wanted the nation to accept rather than for the truth of the statements contained within them. It quickly became clear to me why the expression "to lie like a bulletin" had become proverbial under Napoleon.

Because so many of the men of France were in the army or had been killed in the wars of the previous twenty years, Paris was a city of women. They worked in the stores, cafés, markets, and even in the apothecary shops. They filled the museums and the boulevards. In one particular stall, where I frequently purchased beer, fried potatoes, sausages, and other assorted snacks, a very beautiful young woman would frequently serve me. She was always polite to me, but I do not think she recognized me from one visit to another. I was as invisible to her as to all of the other people in Paris. When she was not busy serving customers, she would sit and read. On my first visit she was reading Rousseau's *Confessions*; the next time, Voltaire's *Candide*; then Rousseau's *La Nouvelle Héloise*. On my fourth visit she was completely occupied with a copy of the poems of Ossian. In my awkward manner I attempted to begin a conversation with her. "Ossian seems to be very popular these days."

She looked up at me and smiled. "Everyone has the poems. Have you read them?"

"No. They are fraudulent, you know. Many years ago Samuel Johnson concluded they were not really a translation of Old Gaelic ballads. James Macpherson, the so-called translator, actually wrote them himself, based on original material." She was indifferent to my comments. Fearing that I was being too pedantic and possibly insulting poems which she liked, I added, "Of course, that is not to say they are bad. They may be wonderful. They are just not ancient Gaelic writings. Macpherson was . . ." She walked away, leaving me speaking to myself. For a moment I was angry at her rudeness. If I were handsome or wealthy, I thought, she would have been attentive to my words. But my anger faded into sadness. It is nature, I knew, not this young woman who is unfair. If she had been unattractive, like me, I probably would not have begun the conversation. Nature's injustice is one which even a revolution cannot overcome. It is the way of the world that lovers are to be seen everywhere while so many are languishing for want of love.

After one month in Paris, out of a frenzy of loneliness, I decided to act on Monsieur Lafont's advice and visit number 113 in the Palais Royal. With the expectation of a tryst with a prostitute, I purchased several protective sheaths in order to be able to enter the lists of Venus in full armor. As many of the best eating houses of Paris were to be found in the Palais Royal, I had been there a number of times before, but had been cautious to visit only the first floor. The Café des Aveugles, which opened in the evening after five o'clock, one hour after the archives closed, was my favorite place for dining. Despite the blockade, the café had real sugar for use in coffee instead of the dreadful beet-root sugar one had to use almost everywhere else in Paris. One could eat a splendid meal there to the music of a large orchestra of blind musicians who played until the spirits soared. After the meal I would browse through the numerous shops, on the same floor of the Palais Royal, which sold all manner of goods including expensive jewelry, books, clothes, clocks, watches, toys, and luxuries of every kind. On my first visit to the shops, I had my profile taken. Oh, how I yearned for a companion black silhouette of Nancy.

On the upper floors of the Palais Royal are innumerable rooms in which games of all kind are played. In a perfect democracy of vice, aristocrats, bourgeois, and lower classes can be found together gambling. In the outer rooms are to be found games more to my taste, billiards, chess, or backgammon. I would have liked to play chess, but the noise and tobacco fumes so filled every room that I could remain no longer than ten or twenty minutes. In the inner apartments the more serious gambling is carried on, particularly dice, cards, and "rouge et noir" tables surrounded by people playing for large sums of money at a single hazard. Persons of all ages, sexes, and classes risk their earnings every day in a frenzied search for wealth. Visitors can play or watch, as they wish. In some of the rooms where the prizes are greatest, there are tables with wines and viands, with beautiful young women encouraging visitors to purchase bottles and drink with them. In the midst of this decadence there are rooms used for scholarly pursuits. Lectures are given hourly on various topics including literature, philosophy, and science. One evening I listened to a lecture on Pierre Simon Laplace's new treatise, *"Théorie Analytique des Probabilités,"* and then considered the application of probability to the roll of the dice in a nearby room. The incongruous juxtaposition of these activities, I was told, never ceases to amaze foreigners. It seemed strange but natural to me—a collection of all of the aspects of life in Paris under one immense roof, a world in miniature.

On this night it was the subterranean apartments, the infernal regions of the Palais Royal, which I intended to visit for the first time. For the descent into depravity, I had no Virgil, or even a Monsieur Lafont, to guide me. There was no sign warning, "Abandon all hope, ye that enter here." Nevertheless, it was with great trepidation that I slowly moved into that doleful city in the bowels of Paris. With debauchery on my mind, I walked down the long, crowded arched corridor with innumerable rooms on either side stretching endlessly before me. In the first room a performer was singing bawdy songs to the delight of the tightly packed assemblage. The chamber on the opposite side of the corridor was filled with billiard players. The third room seemed to be devoted entirely to drinking. The next entrance revealed a cavernous hall containing a stage on which two naked males and two naked females were performing various sexual acts in a kind of ballet of sensuality. With open-mouthed amazement I watched the voluptuous orgy for several minutes. When two huge dogs were brought out on the stage, I quickly departed. Ahead was a gauntlet of prostitutes of all shapes and sizes waiting to negotiate with each male who passed their way. The numbers indicated I was approaching my destination, the brothel at number 113. "Want to spend the night with me, dear?" The attractive woman speaking to me was the first female in Paris who seemed to show an interest in my presence. When I hesitated, she repeated the same question to someone behind me. I was as invisible here as in any other place. "Voulez-vous coucher avec moi?" There were women and girls of all ages, each with her own relentlessly repeated question. "Like to come to my room?" A tough-looking predator placed her hand on my shoulder, looked into my face and smiled. I continued walking until an older woman with the face of Medusa stepped in front of me and thrust her hand between my legs. Several of the others laughed loudly as I jumped back away from her. Stumbling backward, I retreated toward the entrance of the long corridor. Every human being may need love, but having an ugly harlot grab my private parts in a public place was not the kind of lovemaking I desired. In a sweat of indecision and misery, I fled from the immense building and began to walk back to my hotel. I vowed never to return to the Palais Royal, at least not to the subterranean circle of those hellish regions teeming with multitudes who made one feel more alone than being in any empty room. Unable to sleep that night, I mused for hours. Nancy was in my arms, her breasts pressed against me as our tongues touched. My body melted into hers until we were no longer corporeal beings. Finally drifting off into a restless sleep, I wandered long empty corridors and awakened at the moment when the dusty coils of the serpent began to stir.

The next morning, in a state of exhaustion from lack of sleep, I returned to my tedious duties at the archives. Days flowed into weeks of dusty documents, translations, summaries, and copying. Occasionally I would break the monotonous routine with small trips to places of interest like Versailles and St. Cloud. The first significant news from the war in America arrived. During the spring an American force had embarked from Sackets Harbor and captured York, the capital of upper Canada. To my disgust, I read that our men had burned the public buildings in the city before returning to American soil. Also, Colonel Winfield Scott, who had gallantly commanded our troops on the enemy side of the Niagara River during the battle of Queenston, landed a force in boats to the rear of Fort George at the mouth of the Niagara River and captured the place by assault. The defeat of Queenston had, at last, been avenged. In contrast, the war news in Europe was very bad. Wellington was attempting to drive through the Pyrenees into southern France. Much more serious than that, during a period of very hot mid-August weather, the terrible news arrived that the Emperor of Austria, Napoleon's own father-in-law, had declared war on France. The armistice was ended. France was now at war with England, Spain, Portugal, Russia, Sweden, Prussia, and Austria. Several of these had been bribed with British gold to join the coalition against Napoleon, whose defeat appeared inevitable. In 1809, with northern Spain firmly in his control, Napoleon had a very difficult time defeating Austria alone. This time all the armies of eastern Europe were joined together against him, with the British in control of Spain and threatening Bayonne.

As one of my objectives in traveling to Europe had been to observe Napoleon's Grand Army in action, I was determined to travel toward the French army in Germany and attempt to use Morris's letter of introduction to Charles de Flahaut. After the retreat from Russia, Flahaut had become, I had learned, a brigadier general and an aide-de-camp to Napoleon. General Flahaut, I hoped, might arrange for me to meet with the Emperor himself. It was a thought which beckoned me east during my entire stay in Paris. Unfortunately, while planning my trip to Germany, I became ill with a fever very similar to the malady which had afflicted me at Lewiston the previous year. My journey was postponed for several weeks. During this time, Napoleon surprised the pessimistic Parisians and won a crushing victory against the combined Russian and Austrian armies at Dresden, the center of the French defensive position on the Elbe River. Unfortunately, during the same period, the positive effect of Napoleon's tremendous victory was wiped out as his Marshals lost four battles in Germany. Nevertheless, Dresden continued to be held by the French, and it was to that city I planned to travel as soon as my strength returned.

By the middle of September my preparations were complete. In order to be able to inform Morris that I had taken some direct action in attempting to negotiate the canal loan, I obtained the names of two bankers in Basel, Switzerland, from the reluctant Leray de Chaumont, who was so uncooperative I began to suspect that he favored delay in order to buy or sell land along the proposed canal route. On the way back from Leray's residence, I walked through the garden of the Tuileries. For the third time since my arrival in Paris, I emerged from the garden and went to the Rue St. Florentin in the hope that Talleyrand would speak to me. To my delight, the servant who had turned me away twice before announced that the Prince of Benevento would see me. He led me into an immense entryway with black and white marble floors and up a wide straight staircase to Talleyrand's apartments. With great excitement I waited in an anteroom to be received by the man Napoleon had called in public, *"un bas de soie plein de merd,"* a silk stocking full of dung. (It was probably one of the only matters on which Morris would have been in agreement with Bonaparte.) The story was that Talleyrand's only comment on the insult was, "Pity, so great a man should have such bad manners." After waiting for almost an hour, the servant at last guided me through rooms of palatial splendor into the library, where, the servant indicated, "the Prince grants private audiences." Talleyrand was standing by a bookcase. After politely but coldly greeting me, he walked, with a pronounced limp, to a chair. He used a gold-headed cane on which he leaned heavily. On one foot he wore a large rounded shoe with a metal frame extending up his leg, where it was attached to his knee with a leather strap similar to the one holding Morris's wooden leg. Like Morris, he powdered his hair in the old style. They were both of approximately the same age. "So, you are a friend of Gouverneur Morris. I knew him quite well many years ago." He spoke rapidly. Although my ability to converse in French had improved greatly after almost three months in Paris, I missed some of his words. Immediately, he noticed. "You have some difficulty in understanding the language?"

"Yes. I can both read and write in French, but it is spoken a bit too quickly for me. My mother was French but always spoke English because my father did not know the language."

"From which region of France did your mother come?"

"She was born in Canada ... Acadia. Her grandparents came from Gascony."

Talleyrand continued to speak with great speed. His half-closed eyes stared off into space. A complacently ironic smile rested upon his lips. It seemed to me that he wore a mask of indolence and indifference which disguised a penetrating intelligence. To my surprise, he knew about my mission to obtain a loan for the construction of the canal. He revealed his knowledge with some pleasure, as a subtle reminder of his own power. Leray, or his bankers, had been talking too freely. "Until there is peace, you will never obtain a loan for the canal. Unfortunately, we live in a world of kings, and a peaceable king is a contradiction in terms. The people have no respect for a monarch who does not subdue his enemies. Our sovereigns have always been aware of this unpleasant fact of life. Thus, I fear, the war will continue until one side or the other is completely defeated. No surrender, no canal."

"Surely there are reasons for this war beyond the vanity of individual leaders," I replied. "The principles of the French Revolution are in jeopardy."

"What principles are those? Nations have always gone to war. For their convenience, they manufacture religious and legal reasons to satisfy the sentimental idea that it is a matter of conscience and principle. Morality is merely the language of justification. Do not take it too seriously. Self-interest is the real mainspring of mankind." As he spoke, Talleyrand's expression was half angelic and half malicious, like a priest giving a sermon from a pulpit concealing some unspeakable act in which he is engaged. To prove his point that the war was not being fought for revolutionary principles, he cited the recent death at the Battle of Dresden of the great French republican General Moreau, who had returned from exile in America to assist the allies against Napoleon. When I mentioned the fact that I used to walk by Moreau's house on Pearl Street in New York City and that Moreau had visited Morrisania several times, Talleyrand spoke briefly of his own visit to America, which he described as "an endless forest."

After explaining my work as a historian, I grew bold. "If you could oblige me by providing letters of introduction to persons who, in your opinion, would be helpful to me, I would appreciate it. At your convenience, I would like to discuss with you your own role in government since before the Revolution."

"Perhaps at some other time. I am busy today."

"Also, I am interested in obtaining a private audience with the Emperor. I was told that General Duroc, the Grand Marshal of the Palace, is the best man to arrange a meeting with Napoleon."

"Duroc was killed by a cannonball after Bautzen. Caulaincourt, the Duke of Vicenza, is now Grand Marshal of the Palace. It may not be of any assistance to you, but I will write a letter to him in your behalf." He stood up and limped to his desk, leaning heavily on his cane and then on a chair. He quickly scribbled a letter and handed it to me. "Tell Mr. Morris I saw you on his account."

Not wanting to end my interview so quickly, I thanked him and continued to speak. "Do you think with the great victory at Dresden, the allies may agree to a negotiated peace?"

"Diplomacy is the slave of military success. It depends on force to give it weight. Unfortunately, the Emperor likes to exploit his successes beyond the weight they will bear. Suffice it to say that a negotiated settlement is most unlikely." He rang for his secretary to escort me out.

Again I thanked him for the letter to Caulaincourt. On my way out the door I turned and asked one final question. "Mr. Morris gave me a letter to General Flahaut. Do you know where he can be found?"

The mention of Flahaut's name caused Talleyrand's half-closed eyelids to open wide with surprise. "Did Mr. Morris tell you to mention General Flahaut to me?"

"He said you might know where to find him."

"Ah, of course. He is an aide-de-camp to the Emperor now. He will be with Napoleon. You should have no difficulty locating the master of Europe. He finds his pleasures by the tap of the drum. Just follow the army." He sat down at his desk and began writing. The interview had ended.

TEN

With a substantial number of Napoleons d'or, twenty-franc gold pieces, sewn into the lining of my coat, I set off for Basel by coach two days after meeting with Talleyrand. The trip was uneventful. The charge was by the distance of forty leagues, with an allowance of fourteen pounds of free baggage, a greater weight than my very light bag. At Basel, I met with the two bankers whose names had been provided by Leray. Because of my suspicions about Leray, I spoke to an additional banker. They all told me the same thing. There would be no loan of five million dollars until the wars in both Europe and America ended. Even if peace were restored, they all regarded as unacceptable the condition that the credit of New York could not be pledged until the money arrived in the United States. In spite of the fact that Leray had provided me with accurate information about the unavailability of a loan, I believed the trip to be worth the effort, if only to be able to tell Morris that I had spoken personally to a number of bankers.

From Basel, I journeyed northward along the Rhine River and then moved toward the east through Bavaria and into Saxony. The warmth of the summer was gone. The autumnal chill in the air and rainy weather made the trip uncomfortable. The horses were slow, the postilions obstinate, and the meals dreadful. Because the roads were becoming impassable to coaches due to the mud and churning of the ground by armies on the march, I purchased a horse at Chemnitz, approximately forty miles west of Dresden. As none of the inhabitants spoke French or English, it was becoming increasingly difficult for me to obtain information. I was finally able to get directions from a priest who spoke Latin. To the best of my ability to understand him, he seemed to indicate that the French army was still concentrated around Dresden. He told me to remain on the main road to Freiberg, so I continued eastward. It was early October and the leaves were beginning to change color. The fall foliage reminded me of the Niagara frontier the previous year. If one of my fellow militiamen had predicted that I would be following Napoleon's army in Germany within twelve months, I would have told him he was mad. Or, perhaps, I would not have doubted him; for, since meeting Gouverneur Morris, it seemed that anything was possible.

Many of the people in the region were very poor. There were numerous beggars on the roads. Many women worked in the fields swinging scythes in large groups. There was usually a male overseer directing them as though they were slaves on a southern plantation. After spending the night at Freiberg, the next morning I crossed the Mulde River only twenty miles away from Dresden. The highway entered a thick wood with trees on both sides as far as the eye could see. Suddenly I heard the sound of horses coming towards me. Three French cavalry vedettes stopped me and told me to turn back. Then they continued on their way toward the west. After waiting until they were out of sight, I resumed the journey to Dresden. Within fifteen minutes the thunderous sound of many horses caused me to slow my horse to a walk. At least twenty light cavalrymen closed around me. An officer shouted at me, "Where are you going? What is your business?"

"To Dresden. I have a letter for the Grand Marshal of the Palace from the Prince of Benevento." From the skeptical look on the officer's face, I could see that it was a mistake to mention the letter.

"You speak French like an Englishman," he growled. "Show me the letter!"

"I am an American," I replied while handing him the letter.

"This does not look official. You will have to come with us." He grabbed the reins of my horse and turned me around. Before it was possible to protest, I was galloping back toward Freiberg surrounded by cavalry. We rode down the main road to Chemnitz, then abruptly turned northward along a much narrower road. Within a short distance the route became blocked by a train of wagons of reserve artillery. My escort was forced to a slower speed. As I was most uncomfortable riding at the swifter pace, the crowded road was a stroke of good fortune for me. We stopped at a town called Mittweida, where rations for the men were brutally demanded from an official of the town. The cavalry officer turned me over to a captain of infantry. Standing at a distance from them, my heart sank on hearing my captor refer to me as a possible spy. As soon as the cavalry officer rode away, I informed the captain that I was an American carrying a letter to General Caulaincourt. The captain, who introduced himself as Captain Clery, was sympathetic, a good bluff soldier.

"Yes, I have the letter. You must remain with us until your innocence is proved. You'll have to march with us. We'll hold your horse."

"How am I to prove my innocence? What is the charge? Where are we going?"

"The army is concentrating at Leipsic. General Caulaincourt will be there when the Emperor arrives. We'll turn you over to the General and he can decide. Until then, please do not make any trouble and you'll be safe."

That night I was placed in a tent with three young privates, none older than eighteen. The tent was made of the same canvas linen as the one I had lived in the previous autumn. The infantry bivouac was in squares, each tent equidistant from the next, like a small city, with latrines to the rear. I closed my eyes, sniffed the air, and imagined myself at Lewiston. The meal consisted of a piece of horseflesh, cooked in the communal kettle, served with beetroot foraged from farms abandoned by the local peasants. The men ate sitting on the ground, their muskets stacked standing like the ribs of a tepee. "Even the rats starve when the Grand Army marches," one of the old veterans laughed. "Not much food here, but it's much better than Spain. You can take a piss in the fields without worrying about having your throat cut. These Saxons hate us too. But they're too fat and wealthy to fight."

My traveling companions were from a company of voltigeurs, sharpshooters attached to a regiment of the line. They had marched all the way from Spain to reinforce the army on the Elbe. Having been cantoned in Bavaria, they were attached to Marshal Augereau's corps. Because the loyalty of Napoleon's soldiers was legendary, I was shocked to hear them cursing the Emperor. "The bastard will bring us all to ruin. He doesn't know when to stop fighting." The others were agreeing when Captain Clery appeared carrying a bottle of wine. At the approach of the captain, all cursing of the Emperor ceased. He poured some wine into my cup.

"Sorry, men. Only enough for our guest. Drink up. It's good Hungarian wine." Not wanting to be treated more favorably than my companions, I took a sip and passed the cup to the man next to me. "We should be at Leipsic in three days," Clery continued. "There you can deliver your letter personally."

"Could you give it back to me?"

"Sorry. I'll have to hold it until we reach Leipsic." As soon as he left, the men continued complaining about Napoleon and his young recruits of 1813, many of whom, according to the veterans, mutilated themselves rather than face battle.

Within two days we were at the River Pleisse headed north to Leipsic. As we approached the city, the roads and fields became increasingly crowded with soldiers. In front of us were the famous mobile artillery pieces designed by Monsieur Gribeauval. Everywhere lines of infantry defiled the landscape, marching to the tap of drums and followed by long columns of supply wagons. Some of the wagons were driven by women who sold food and equipment to the men. These sutlers, who were referred to as cantinières, seemed to be accepted as part of the military. The moving horde was more than a mere army; it was a society of nomadic conquerors living in tents, whose sole purpose in life was to kill or be killed.

The roads were covered by the fresh dung of the horses of advancing cavalry. It was mixed in with the mud from periodic rain and the churning of innumerable wheels and feet. Cuirassiers in their gleaming silver breastplates and dragoons, heads protected by brass casques, galloped by, forcing the infantry to the side of the road. The uniforms of many of the conscripts were ragged from months of campaigning, their shoes torn and toes visible. After marching on foot the entire day, we arrived at a small village. Without the consent of the inhabitants, the men were billeted in houses. Five hundred rations of meat, bread, and wine were demanded and obtained. When our reluctant host, in broken French, demanded a billeting note, a fierce-looking sergeant roughly pushed him into the wall. As each house in the village was given a quota of troops to quarter, every room was jammed with six or seven men. A private sleeping next to me warmed a large stone in the hearth, wrapped it in a towel and placed it in the center of the room. Sleeping like the spokes of a wheel, the men placed their feet beside the warm stone at the hub. With the benefit of this snug comforter, and exhausted from the long day's march, I fell into a deep slumber.

At dawn I was awakened by the noise of drums and bugles. The bustle of soldiers was everywhere. Horses were fed and harnessed. Baggage was loaded on wagons. Many of the men took pots, pans, and other property from our hosts, who watched in silent resentment. Men rushed in all directions. In the distance could be heard fifes playing "Watch over the Safety of the Empire," a piece I had heard several times in Paris. The hosts of war swarmed along every road moving north. A young captain, whom I had never met before, came for me. He introduced himself as Captain Ramballe of the Young Guard. "I have orders to take you into Leipsic."

"Where is Captain Clery?"

"He left before dawn. You are now in my custody."

"Did he give you my letter?"

"Don't know nothing about a letter. You're to come with me." For the first time I became fearful for my own safety. In the general confusion I could become mixed in with prisoners rounded up by the advancing army. At any time it was possible that I could be stood against a wall and shot. In time of war, armies are notorious for their summary injustice.

Along with a large body of infantry, I marched toward the steeples of Leipsic. My horse had been lost in the confusion of the morning, but I tried not to show anxiety or anger about my treatment. We crossed a broad boulevard planted with trees and entered the city walls through a large gate. Inside the dilapidated walls there was a city of considerable size, with church steeples and towers everywhere to be seen. Within one block of the outer wall of the city, the captain led me into the cellar of a house where three disreputable-looking men were being held. The door was locked behind me with a loud, dull sound which made me wonder if it would ever again open. The room was lit by a single window higher than the head of any man. It was too small to crawl through or to admit much light. My fellow prisoners all spoke German. We were unable to communicate except by gesture. In dejection, I sat on the cold floor, my back against the moist cellar wall. It was October 13, 1813, exactly one year to the day of the battle of Queenston.

On the other side of the locked door, the guards could be heard talking. Their conversation was the only available source of information. Because the fourteenth was the anniversary of the battle of Jena, and the Emperor was one who liked to celebrate one great victory with another, they expected a battle on the morrow. After waiting for several long hours, I began to pound on the door. The guard ordered silence. I told him that I had a letter for Brigadier General Flahaut and demanded to see him. There was no response. Two hours later the guard opened the door to deliver a dismal gruel with bread and to empty the slop bucket. A second guard asked to see the letter to

General Flahaut. Fearful of losing my only other letter, I showed it to him and quickly placed it back inside my coat, explaining that it had to be delivered personally. Both guards left the room without comment.

The next day the sound of artillery could be heard in the distance. According to the conversation of the guards, Marshal Murat had engaged the advance guard of the Austrian army less than "two leagues" south of Leipsic. The Austrians had captured the nearby town of Liebertwolkwitz. My demands to see General Flahaut or General Caulaincourt were ineffectual. Two more German-speaking prisoners were added to the cell. We were fed only once during the entire day. In the evening Captain Ramballe came to speak to me. I showed him the letter to General Flahaut and told him it was from Gouverneur Morris of New York City. He asked me to repeat Morris's name but would not allow me to leave the cell.

The fifteenth was quiet. Because there was no conversation among the guards, I suspected only one was outside the door. I spent most of the day killing cockroaches. Like a vengeful god, I crushed most of them while capriciously sparing an occasional one as the spirit moved me. The sixteenth dawned gloomy, rainy, and cold. I was so miserable even the thought of Nancy failed to comfort me. Suddenly it was as if the hosts of Hell had erupted out of the earth and surrounded the city. It was nine o'clock in the morning. The immense cannonade in the distance sounded like one continuous roar. At times the building trembled with the noise. For many hours the sounds of combat could be heard from all directions. In the middle of the afternoon the bells of Leipsic began to ring. The guards outside the door spoke gleefully of a great victory for the Emperor. But the sounds of cannon continued for hours and seemed to be getting closer to the city. It was only when daylight faded from the cellar window that the sounds of battle ceased. Despair filled my heart. In the midst of a great battle and trapped in a miserable room, I was in a state of complete uncertainty as to my own fate and in total ignorance of the momentous events occurring outside.

During the night a heavy rain began to fall and continued throughout the next day, a Sunday. Only sporadic sounds of cannon could be heard from the outside. The battle appeared to have ended. The guard was silent. At nightfall Captain Ramballe opened the door and called my name. "General Flahaut says he will see you. Come with me." It was as if I had died and was brought back to life by these magic words. With a sudden burst of energy, I grabbed my coat and bag and followed Ramballe out of my prison. We walked several blocks to another house near the city wall. It was still raining. The muddy streets were filled with the shadowy figures of horses, wagons, and soldiers limping along to some unknown destination. Despite my questions, Ramballe said nothing. Silently he led me into a large house with whitewashed walls. The rooms were crowded with officers engaged in a flurry of activity. It appeared that a large number of orders were being written and sent from the room by courier. Ramballe brought me to a tall, slender young man in a gold-braided uniform. He was the very figure of a military hero. The uniform was dirty, the long legs splattered with mud, indicating the man had been doing a great deal of riding during the day. The young man dismissed Ramballe and led me into a small room containing a table and chairs.

"I have a letter from Gouverneur Morris for General Flahaut." As with Leray, I was astonished when the young man answered me in what sounded like the impeccable English of a British officer.

"I am Flahaut. May I see the letter?" As he read Morris's letter of introduction, a smile flashed across his face. "A friend of Gouverneur Morris is also my friend." He warmly clasped my hand. "Twenty-one years ago, during the massacres in Paris, he protected both my mother and me from the mob. He took us into his house and helped us escape to England. Our family is forever in his debt." His voice was hoarse but most pleasing to the ear.

"Well, you have just paid part of the debt by saving me. I've been held a prisoner for the past five days."

"Yes, I was just told today. Had I known you were here, you would have been released immediately. Battlefields are not very hospitable places. What in the name of heaven are you doing here?"

Briefly I explained my mission to France to obtain a loan, my interest in the Grand Army as a historian, my arrest and the loss of Talleyrand's letter to General Caulaincourt. He appeared almost as surprised at the utterance of Talleyrand's name as Talleyrand had been at the mention of his. I told him that Morris had suggested that Talleyrand might know where to find him. He nodded but said nothing more on the subject. In order to establish my position as a fellow soldier, I told him about my service on the Niagara frontier. Interrupting me, he said, "I am being very thoughtless. You must be famished." He opened the door and directed a soldier to have a Mrs. Rochlitz bring in some food. Within minutes a rotund, smiling old matron entered carrying a tray with bread, meat, cheese, wine, and apples. Flahaut said a few words to her in what appeared to be fluent German. Then he introduced her to me. "Mrs. Rochlitz, our gracious hostess, is the owner of this house. She is a loyal subject of the King of Saxony and, I suspect, one of the few persons in this city who still welcomes the King's French allies."

The old woman shook her head disapprovingly. In broken French with a heavy German accent, she denied that the citizens of Leipsic were disloyal to her monarch Frederick Augustus or his "beloved friend" Napoleon. "The soldiers of Napoleon are welcome in my house, always. Now, eat and be happy." As she departed, I attacked the food with the fervor of one who had survived on gruel for the past five days.

In response to my apology for bad manners, Flahaut laughed. "We are the ones who should apologize for starving an innocent man."

Between mouthfuls I attempted to converse with my benefactor. "You must be ten years younger than I am. How did one so young become a general? Have you fought in many campaigns?"

"Almost all of them, 1805, 1806 and '07, 1808 in Spain, 1809 in Austria, Russia last year and, of course, this past year. I joined the hussars in 1800 at age fifteen. At twenty, I fought at Austerlitz, my first great battle. Yesterday was the most recent of many battles; it will not be the last."

The man clearly liked to talk about himself. With my numerous questions and genuine interest in his career, I encouraged his obvious vanity. After noticing that he winced when he moved, I asked if he had been wounded. "Not since last year. The pain you see is my rheumatism. Too many nights in the cold and damp." He then enumerated his many wounds, including a near fatal one at Ems in 1809. "Last year I was almost killed at Ostrowno on the road to Vitebsk. The ball hit my aiguillette, cut my gold braid in four places and passed through my coat. Yesterday, I was in the thick of the fighting, but, as you can see, suffered not a scratch."

"Please tell me what has been happening. I have been without information for five days. I assume you have been victorious. You still occupy Leipsic and there was no fighting today."

Flahaut gave a discouraging shake of his head. "The battle will be renewed tomorrow. The fight was so fierce yesterday that both armies, I think, were too exhausted to continue today." At my repeated questions about the situation, he went into the next room and returned with a detailed map of the Leipsic area which he placed on the table in front of me. It was my first view of the geographic features of the region, which I have since studied repeatedly for the past fourteen years. Because of my presence at Leipsic, the great battles around that city have become a historical obsession of mine which has been surpassed by only one other series of events from the past. Those events I shall relate in due course. But first Leipsic and its environs must be described in order to understand the disastrous events which followed my meeting with Flahaut.

The old walled city of Leipsic is bounded on its western side by the River Pleisse and then by the Elster River. Both rivers are narrow but are so deep, and with steep muddy banks, as to be unfordable. The rivers run through a wide area of marshes and swampy meadowland which is almost impassable. Thus the only way out of the city for the French army, if it was forced to retreat back toward France, was by using a single causeway, over the two rivers and marshland extending a distance of almost two miles, before reaching the town of Lindenau and the roads to the Rhine and France. The causeway consisted of a series of bridges, including a stone bridge over the Elster River. To the north, south, and east, the old city of Leipsic is surrounded by suburbs. All around the city and suburbs on the east bank of the river are open rolling plains with occasional heights commanding the countryside. Numerous small villages are scattered across the plain. The villages can be used to anchor a line of defense protecting the city from attack.

Flahaut briefly explained what had happened during the two months from the reopening of hostilities. Much of what he related was consistent with the reports I had read in Paris before leaving. Since the end of the armistice, the French army in Germany had been fighting three separate allied armies composed of Russian, Prussian, Austrian, and Swedish units. The largest army, the Army of Bohemia, arrived with the entry of Austria into the war. This force threatened Saxony from the south. Flahaut referred to it as the "Army of the Sovereigns" because it was accompanied by the Emperor of Russia, the King of Prussia, and the Emperor of Austria. The second force, the Army of Silesia, was led by the Prussian General von Blücher, who was not then as famous as he has since become. It had been advancing steadily from the east. From the direction of Berlin the Army of the North moved forward, commanded by Crown Prince Bernadotte of Sweden. Because Bernadotte had formerly been a Marshal in the French army, Flahaut referred to him contemptuously as "the traitor." In an angry voice Flahaut declared, "He will be on this field tomorrow facing his old comrades, in exchange for British gold."

During August and September, Napoleon had successfully held back all three allied armies on the line of defense of the Elbe River. In early October, however, the armies of the North and of Silesia had crossed the Elbe while the Army of Bohemia moved northward. Napoleon was forced to withdraw from the Elbe; he concentrated his army around the area of Leipsic in an attempt to defeat the three advancing allied armies piecemeal before they could unite. In the expectation of a great victory at Leipsic, according to Flahaut, the Emperor had left large garrisons in the various cities along the Elbe, including Dresden, Torgau, Wittenberg, and Magdeburg. "Before the concentration at Leipsic," stated Flahaut, "the Emperor considered a march on Berlin; but the defection of Bavaria to our rear made that impossible." Three days earlier, on October 14, advancing allied units had been beaten back south of Leipsic. On the previous day, the sixteenth, three separate battles had been fought around the city. The battle opened on the morning of the sixteenth with the great cannonade I had heard. The Army of Bohemia attacked the approaches to Leipsic four miles southeast of the city. The advance was halted by the main French army led by Napoleon himself. "When we attacked, all of the lost ground was retaken. We broke through the allied center with General Bordesoulle's cavalry division. They almost reached the Emperor Alexander's command post, but Russian reinforcements arrived at the decisive moment and drove back our cavalry. *Le destin des états dependait d'un moment.* When word of our initial success reached the King of Saxony, he ordered the church bells rung to celebrate the victory. It was premature. On the main battleground around Wachau, neither side achieved a victory. The fighting was as terrible as any I have ever seen. Our enemies do not break as easily as they did in the past.

"North of the city, Blücher's army drove Marmont's corps back two miles. Our lines to the north are now only one-half mile outside the city between Gohlis and Eutritzsch." He pointed to the villages as he named them. "In the third battle of the day, to the west of the city, the Austrians tried to take Lindenau and cut off our lines of communication to the Rhine. Bertrand's corps has driven them back. Lindenau is safely in our hands."

"Is it certain that the battle will begin again tomorrow?"

"Yes. We fear that the Army of the North and Russian reinforcements will join the fighting tomorrow. We will be heavily outnumbered. The Emperor has ordered our lines to withdraw two miles closer to Leipsic. By tomorrow morning, the allies will discover we have formed an unbreakable semicircle around the city. Our northern and southern flanks will both rest on the river. They will have to attack us frontally. No flanking movement is possible." As he spoke, Flahaut pointed to a convex line of villages forming an arc around the city east of the river from Connewitz in the south to the suburbs of Leipsic in the north.

Flahaut seemed to me to be excessively confident. "Your situation looks dangerous to me. It is like the Russian position at Friedland with their backs to the Alle River. It is also like the position at Aspern-Essling with your own backs to the Danube. In fact, the only great battle I can think of won by an army with a river to its rear is Cannae, and that was Hannibal."

Flahaut shook his head with surprised admiration. "Well, you know a great deal more about warfare than I would have expected. You possess a discerning eye. But remember, the Emperor is our commanding officer. He has directed over fifty battles in the field and has never been defeated ... Aspern was merely a temporary setback. As always, we will be victorious. We have marched into the great capitals of the western world, Milan, Cairo, Vienna, Berlin, Madrid, and Moscow. Before this campaign is over, we shall again occupy Vienna and Berlin." He stood up and shook my hand. "I must go. I will leave you a pass to enter any of the church steeples. You will be able to view the battle from there tomorrow. You can sleep here tonight. The city is so crowded, you will not find other quarters. If you need anything, ask for Major Vernant. If God is willing, we shall meet again. Good night." He opened the door and quickly walked out of the room. I watched him as he spoke to several officers in the next room. Before he departed, he carefully straightened out his uniform and hair, intently looking at himself in the mirror. His unruffled calm in the face of death filled me with admiration for qualities which I so sadly lacked.

That night I slept fitfully on a floor covered with the bedding of sleeping officers. The next morning before dawn I was awakened by the bustle of the officers leaving for battle. After a hurried breakfast I went, pass in hand, to the nearest church with a steeple. The street outside the church, St. John's, was crammed with wounded men. A young soldier used the discarded breastplates of cuirassiers as soup kettles to make broth from the flesh of dead horses lying in the street. The inside of the church was even more crowded. There was barely enough room between wounded men for me to walk to the stairs. The sheer hopelessness of the misery about me and my desire to see the battle quickly overcame my guilt at not helping the unfortunate soldiers all about the church. It was much easier to turn away from the suffering of hundreds of men than if there had been only one miserable soldier crying for help. Perhaps I had become hardened by my experience on the Niagara frontier. In war, men become like ammunition and supplies; losses are inevitable. If a commander is sentimental about them, he becomes overly cautious and ends up losing both his men and the battle. The soldiers themselves become aware of this grim fact of life and learn to accept it, as long as they are victorious.

After climbing the stairs to the top of the steeple, I pushed my way to the front of the spectators. The clouds of the early morning had disappeared and the sun was shining brightly. As if struck by a blow, I was stunned and then dazzled by the sublime spectacle before me. It was a sight I shall never forget to my dying day. The rolling plains in front of the city were covered by vast multitudes of men and horses stretching to the horizon. To the east, the north, and the south, the entire city on the eastern side of the river was encircled by hostile forces. The allied armies, numbering in the hundreds of thousands, were drawn up in full battle array and moving forward at a stately pace. In front of them waited the dense columns of the French army, their backs to the city. In every direction lines of bayonets glittered. Banners of bright colors waved in the morning breeze. Cavalry columns in the magnificent colors of lancers and dragoons moved forward in the precise lines of a parade. Shimmering with light in the bright sunshine, the silver breastplates of cuirassiers could be seen in the distance with their plumed helmets, and spirited mounts tossing their manes as if eager to begin the fray. Hordes of infantrymen marched steadily forward in bristling formations. The sounds of drums drifted in from all directions. It seemed that the entire manhood of Europe had gathered at one place to decide for all time the future of the continent. It was an incredible, unexpected sight out of a dream. For the first time I actually understood the beauty and terror that drew men to war. Look! Look! You will never again see such a sight, I told myself. Tears rolled down my cheeks, perhaps for the thousands of men who would not live to breathe the pure air of another morning and the innumerable maimed soldiers who would later wish they had not survived the day. Or, maybe like weeping Xerxes, viewing his colossal army crossing the Hellespont, I felt pity at the thought of how brief is the whole life of man, seeing that of this multitude not one would be alive when one hundred years had passed.

Two men standing next to me watched the spectacle through a telescope they shared. Although they spoke German to each other, they understood my request in French to borrow it for a moment. Through the instrument I scanned the horizon. My eyes sought in vain for an end to the lines of advancing infantry. While looking at the massed formations spilling over the horizon and into view, I was shaken by a tremendous roar which moved the floor beneath my feet and continued for many long minutes without diminishing. Wave after wave of overpowering noise shattered the solemnity of the magnificent panorama before me. Clouds of smoke appeared in rapid succession and moved across the vast plain until many of the compact masses of soldiers disappeared behind them. Because of the proximity of the guns, the cannonade seemed worse than the one I had heard two days earlier in my prison cell. The splendid pageantry of war was swiftly replaced by its cruelty. Cavalry began to charge in a confusing variety of directions. The once orderly scene suddenly disintegrated into a chaos of men and horses in motion. The advancing lines of soldiers were enveloped by smoke through which flashes could be seen like lightning in the midst of storm clouds.

For hours I watched the battle, stupefied by its magnitude. Before long the entire countryside was dotted with burning villages. Dense columns of smoke rose to the heavens, covering over the beautiful cloudless sky. The spectators in the steeple, most speaking German, seemed to be saying, "Look here, not there." Or, "That is nothing; see what is happening to the north." Despite the fierceness of the allied attack, the French semicircle appeared to be immovable. There was no sign of yielding to retrograde movement back into the city.

To the north of the city the allies began to fire a strange weapon I had never seen before. One of the spectators identified the missiles as "rockets." They seemed to glide through the air, making a terrifying screaming sound, and within seconds a village was in flames. Long after the battle, I learned that the British had sent a special battery using Congreve rockets, which were more successful in terrifying the French troops than in inflicting real damage upon them.

When night finally arrived, the sky glowed red. Many of the Saxon villages and one of the suburbs of Leipsic was in flames. Peasants from the burning villages could be seen streaming into the city with wagons carrying all of their movable property. The battle diminished gradually after more than ten hours. The roar of the cannon ceased and the incessant rattle of musketry became the isolated sounds of single shots. The din of battle ended. A terrible silence fell across the battlefield. It was the silence of death. The cries of the wounded, men and horses, became distinctly audible, a mournful intrusion on the frightful stillness. Between the flames of the burning villages the entire plain to the horizon was speckled with the lights of countless campfires. Another day of deadly work had come to an end for the laborers of both armies.

For only the second time during the day, I descended from the steeple. The church was even more crowded with wounded. The street was filled with streams of bleeding men moving into the city. I walked back to the house of Mrs. Rochlitz in time to get a share of the officers' bread, cheese, and wine. Nobody had any information about Flahaut. The officers spoke glumly about the events of the day. A retreat would begin during the night. They blamed the defeat on the defection of a corps of Saxons in the midst of the battle. Leaving a large gap in the French lines, the Saxons had marched into the allied lines and turned their guns on their former comrades. After listening to the various accounts of the day's events, I fell into a fitful sleep.

It was still dark when Major Vernant awakened me. "The retreat has begun. We cannot hold the city for much longer. The whole army will be gone by sunset."

"Where is General Flahaut?" The news had quickly returned me to my senses.

"With the Emperor."

"Where is that?"

"The Emperor is at the Hotel de Prusse in the Rossplatz." Vernant thought that Napoleon would be leaving the city within two or three hours. He gave me directions to the Rossplatz. After hastily helping to finish the remaining bread and cheese, I took my bag and set forth to search for Flahaut and his commander. On the way out the door, Mrs. Rochlitz handed me one of her prized Borsdorf apples. She appeared to be agitated and saddened by the defeat of her monarch and his French ally. I kissed her cheek, put the apple in my bag, and said farewell.

It was another beautiful sunny autumn morning. A crowd had already gathered around the Hotel de Prusse, held back by a line of tall French grenadiers. Although the sound of battle outside the city began again and seemed much closer than the previous day, the throng waiting in front of the hotel continued to grow. After an hour a murmur of excitement rippled through the crowd. First I saw some of his officers so covered with gold lace and decorations that the color of their uniforms was barely visible. Then the soldiers cried out in unison, "Vive l'Empereur." It was the Emperor of battle himself, the famous hat, its side appearing to face front, and the gray overcoat I had seen so many times in paintings and drawings. This short, unimpressive-looking man with the massive head, standing only twenty yards away from me, had brought the armies of the entire continent to this place. Like a god of war, he seemed indifferent to the individuals stretching to gain a glimpse of him and the chaos surrounding the isolated space he occupied. His own inscrutable purposes, his will and destiny, had controlled Europe for thirteen years. But now he was only a man who had striven to achieve his goals and, like all other mortals, had finally tasted the bitterness of defeat. The colossus took a pinch of snuff and disappeared behind several giant grenadiers of the Guard. Flahaut was nowhere to be seen. The crowd quickly dispersed in an excited rush, as though in that one location the panic had been held in abeyance only long enough to obtain a glimpse of the spirit of the age.

Although it was increasingly difficult to move in the crowded streets as the retreating French army swarmed in from all sides, I made my way back to St. John's Church outside the city walls. "Friend, please kill me. Brother, please!" A young soldier, bleeding profusely from a wound to his stomach, sat with his back against the wall of a house screaming in agony. In a frenzy to get to the other side of the city and across the bridge to the west, soldiers pushed by him as if he did not exist. A grizzled old sergeant struggled out of the crowd and stopped beside the wounded soldier. Gently caressing the hair of the injured boy, he placed the muzzle of his musket an inch from the side of the boy's head. The boy gestured as if in thanks for the mercy shown to him. I averted my eyes a moment before the sound of the discharge of the musket signaled the end of another life. When I looked back, the boy was slumped over on his side and the sergeant had rejoined the swiftly-moving flow of men. The wall was stained with crimson gore.

Filled with the sounds of moaning and screaming men, the church was even more crowded than the day before. One of the wounded men lying on the floor grabbed my leg as I stepped over him. "Please, something to eat." Reaching into my bag, I placed the apple into the palm of his hand. He fervently kissed my fingers. The man resting next to him groaned some incomprehensible words. I placed my ear next to his lips. "May this day of my death bring you good fortune." He smiled at me. There were tears in his eyes.

Only a few people remained to watch the battle from the steeple. The man with the telescope was there again. The allies were near the walls of the city. To the northeast their columns stretched to the horizon. French infantry behind overturned wagons and barricades formed a line of defense near the outer Grimma Gate where I had entered the city, at what seemed to be a lifetime earlier. Units of Russian soldiers in green attacked. The opposing armies were so close to each other that lines of men could be seen stabbing at each other with bayonets and shooting their muskets at point-blank range. At some points the allies were breaking into the suburbs. Every street inside the city was jammed with a sea of soldiers all flowing in one direction, towards the causeway over the Pleisse and Elster rivers to Lindenau and the west. It appeared that the French lines would not be able to hold much longer. Immediately, I decided to join the retreat. On my way out of the church, my eyes searched in vain for the man with the apple and the one who had wished me good fortune.

The streets of the city were becoming more crowded by the moment. Buildings everywhere were loopholed to afford a cross fire against the advancing allies. The gardens around the old city were filled with dead horses, wagons, corpses, and wounded soldiers. Despite the open spaces of the gardens, it was difficult to move quickly. Inside the walls of the old city the crowds moved forward even more slowly. As the sounds of musket fire came closer, the mobs of men become more agitated. Everybody seemed to be pushing. Although the pace of the confused retreat was extremely slow, there remained no vestige of order. Herds of cattle, which the retreating soldiers were attempting to take with them, blocked the streets. Wounded men stood in dazed perplexity. Ammunition wagons, cannon, grenadiers, and cavalry all struggled forward in a tangled confusion. The men next to me pushed and cursed at those in front of them; but the mob could not move any faster. All was chaos.

The sounds of cannon thundering at the gate of the city raised the panic to a higher level. The throng was so dense, my feet were no longer touching the ground as the mob pushed forward, carrying me along in its iron grasp. Some were trampled. Terrified of falling and being crushed, I fought against the panic and nausea taking control of me. Finally, near the Marketplatz, I managed to escape into a building. On the other side I climbed out of a window into a churchyard and out of the old city through a small opening in the wall near the Barfuss Gate. Although the circular boulevard outside the old city was crowded, there was much more room to move than in the narrow streets of the old city itself. As I moved slowly toward the one avenue of escape across the rivers and marshes, the Pleisse River became visible to my left. Stray cows and horses wandered along the banks eating grass, as though all was peaceful around them. Suddenly the sound of an immense explosion dwarfed the noise of the allied guns on the eastern side of the city. In front of me to my left, about five hundred yards away, smoke and falling debris filled the air. The only bridge over the Elster River had been blown up. There were still thousands of French soldiers isolated on the east side of the rivers with the allies in pursuit on every side. Within moments a frenzy seized the remaining Frenchmen about me. "The bridge is blown!" they shouted. Without hesitation, many jumped into the river. A few men managed to fell trees from the garden and used doors as planks to cross the narrow Pleisse. I followed them across the makeshift bridge. Making my way through a large garden, I reached the steep banks of the Elster. It was obvious that the second river could not be so easily crossed as the first. A number of soldiers undressed and jumped into the muddy waters of the Elster. From windows of the houses overlooking the west side of the city, women waved handkerchiefs as if to mock the desperate men. Seeing that many of the naked men could not climb out on the other side because of the steep muddy banks, I decided not to attempt a crossing. As I turned back, a soldier fell dead at my feet. Others preparing to jump into the river were shot. Prussian sharpshooters could be seen approaching. While many more men jumped into the river to escape the enemy, I retreated among the trees in the garden. A small group of Prussian militia, the landwehr, ran up to unarmed Frenchmen standing by the riverbank with their hands up in the air and ruthlessly bayoneted them. Men swimming in the Elster were shot. One man, completely naked, managed to climb back on the eastern side. For some unknown reason, he remained unharmed. The murderous Prussians acted as if he were invisible. I comforted myself with the thought that perhaps men are trained to attack uniforms and not other men; therefore, I might be safe in my civilian clothes. Perhaps a naked man may be too vulnerable, too much like his enemies, to be treated as an object of hatred. While his comrades were slaughtered about him, the naked man stood in bewilderment. It was clear that no prisoners were being taken.

In terror I ran in the opposite direction. I tied my heavy coat into a ball and hurled it across the narrow river. With the remainder of my clothes on, I jumped into the Pleisse River and managed to struggle onto the eastern bank. I went back into the city using the same route I had used to escape it. French soldiers were firing from roofs and windows at advancing allied troops. The dreaded Prussian landwehr, wearing flat caps with crosses on the front, were everywhere. Of all of the troops I saw, these militiamen appeared to be the most brutal. Whenever they were in the vicinity, I hid. The loud cheers and beating drums of the victorious allies could be heard from every direction. The smoke of powder was so dense in the narrow streets, it was difficult to see. Attempting to get out of the path of the advancing allies, I stumbled over corpses lying in the street. After what seemed like hours of wandering and hiding, I ran into an open doorway and descended into a vaulted cellar that was crammed with men, women, and children huddled together. The day had turned very hot, and my outer clothes were partially dry. My body was drenched with perspiration from my exertions and heavy clothing. Nobody objected to my presence, so I sat in a corner by myself until the sounds of battle ceased. In the late afternoon I made my way back to the house of Mrs. Rochlitz. My fears that she would now turn on the defeated French were unjustified. She beckoned to me to enter quickly before enemy soldiers arrived. She welcomed me by giving me another ripe Borsdorf apple. It was the first food I had consumed since breakfast. Her supply of meat and bread was gone.

The main forces of the allies were marching into the city to a shower of flowers and apples from the happy residents of Leipsic. Those like Mrs. Rochlitz, who were still loyal to the King of Saxony and to Napoleon, remained out of sight. Within the hour, cossacks were pounding at the door demanding entry. Mrs. Rochlitz crossed herself while reciting in Latin a prayer she must have learned in church. *"De cossaquibus, Domine, libera nos."* To the relief of Mrs. Rochlitz and me, the cossacks were polite. They spoke only a few words of German, using hand gestures to indicate they would be billeted there. The head man had an immense curling mustache, a short whip at his wrist, and a pistol tucked in his girdle. Mrs. Rochlitz gave each of the twelve men who entered a Borsdorf apple, of which she seemed to have an endless supply. One of the men admired my coat. "Fine coat, brother." Mrs. Rochlitz translated his German into French, which she whispered into my ear. I murmured to her in French to tell him it was too small for him. The cossack shook his head in agreement. "Good, brother," he replied.

In the morning the cossacks left, taking everything in the house with them, dishes, pots, furniture, and the remaining apples. They also took my bag with my soggy journal and extra clothing. Fortunately, my money was all on my person, much of it still sewn into the lining of my coat. Even as they looted the house, the cossacks were friendly, as though their activities should be considered legal and acceptable to their hosts. Mrs. Rochlitz was content to escape with her life. To celebrate our survival, she led me into the cellar, where she cleaned off a trapdoor. We feasted from her ample emergency supplies of cheese, wine, and apples. Although she was in mourning for her beloved King of Saxony who had been taken prisoner by the allies, she ate as heartily as her guest. Lulled into a sense of security by my full stomach, I decided to risk walking about the city.

The people of Leipsic were ecstatic at their "liberation." The streets were crowded with townspeople and the allied soldiers in their uniforms of diverse colors, including Russian green, Austrian white, and Prussian gray. But it is other scenes of that day I shall never forget. A cossack dismounted his horse, made a small cut on the leg of the animal, and sucked at the wound as a means of obtaining nourishment. Other soldiers drank the blood of dead horses to quench their thirst. At St. Thomas's Church, near where I had escaped from the old city the day before, corpses were piled into neat pyramids. There were separate piles of amputated limbs. The city had become a charnel house. The stench was so overpowering, I had to cover my nose and mouth with a handkerchief. Despite the nauseating condition of the air, many wandered about searching for food. In the entire city, no food or drink could be purchased. I could find no coffee house that had beer, brandy, wine, or any other drink. With a thirst that could not be quenched, I walked to the Ranstadt Gate near the beginning of the causeway to the west, the goal of so many soldiers on the previous day. The great square, the Fleischer-platz, was strewn with discarded weapons, equipment, and the bodies of French soldiers. A severed head lay in a ditch beside the carcass of a horse. The corpses were piled high near the remains of the stone bridge over the Elster which had been blown up the day before. Bodies were scattered on both sides of the causeway in ditches. The eyes of many of the dead were still open, as if staring into the maw of death. The allies had thrown several wooden bridges over the Elster and were pouring out of the city in pursuit of the retreating French army.

In other parts of the city, wounded French soldiers sat in the street, often in puddles from the rain of the previous evening. Some ate raw horseflesh cut from the haunches of putrid carcasses. One man removed the earrings from his ears and offered them in exchange for food. Although I did not see such a sight, I heard reports of Frenchmen eating the flesh of their dead comrades. Thousands of wounded soldiers were crammed into public buildings, most still in their bloodstained uniforms. In these "hospital" areas, those who could not stand lay in the noxious effluvia from their own bodies. Open troughs were set out for the wounded who could walk. Because they were not emptied, they overflowed, covering the street with vile liquid and excrement which oozed over the cobblestones. On one street, dogs and ravens feasted on the naked bodies of the dead soldiers. At the sight, I began to retch and vomit; but I forced myself to continue the journey through these infernal regions.

Outside the city, I returned to St. John's churchyard in order to climb the steeple for one more view of the field of battle. Many of the buildings in the area had been destroyed by artillery fire. The graveyard was covered with unburied bodies resting on the graves of those who had left this earth at an earlier time. Soldiers were digging up coffins and removing the corpses. The wood from the coffins was used to provide fire for cooking. Even the realm of the dead was invaded to provide for the needs of the living.

The stench around the church was so unbearable that I decided not to climb the steeple. Instead I returned to the house of Mrs. Rochlitz. A dozen aristocratic Russian officers were now billeted there. Because Mrs. Rochlitz told them I lived there, they tolerated my presence. As they all spoke fluent French, I was able to converse freely with them. They were exuberant. According to them, the French were now totally defeated. "We will be in Paris before the end of the year" was a repeated boast of the victors. They claimed that in order to save himself, Napoleon had blown the bridge over the Elster in a cowardly sacrifice of twenty thousand or more of his own soldiers. Based on my knowledge of Napoleon's well-known personal courage and impassivity in the face of numerous battles over many years, I judged the story to be not credible. Yet, for the first time, the idea of writing the definitive account of the battle of Leipsic and the mysterious Elster Bridge catastrophe began to arouse my interest.

The next morning, after thanking Mrs. Rochlitz profusely for her hospitality and giving her ten Napoleons d'or for her great generosity, I set off on foot for Paris. In order to avoid the devastation of the advancing armies and possible arrest, I decided not to cross the bridges to Lindenau in the west. Instead, I planned to depart the way I had come, proceeding south on the eastern side of the Pleisse River to Zwickau and Hof, through Bavaria and back to the Rhine. This route out of the city, through what could have been the gate of dark Dis, took me through the battlefield of the preceding days. Even worse than inside Leipsic, the plains outside were littered with thousands of unburied corpses and bloated carcasses of horses. Crows and dogs were feeding on the offal. Boots, helmets, shakos, and weapons were everywhere. The stench was unbearable but inescapable. To this day, fourteen years later, I sometimes wake up in the middle of the night with that terrible smell in my nostrils. It shall, I fear, follow me to my death bed.

Thousands of peasants were engaged in the fields burying the bodies. Children collected discarded weapons and lead balls. Cobblers cut covers off cartridge pouches and gathered belts for use in making boots. Blacksmiths assembled piles of iron and horseshoes. Most of the bodies of the soldiers had been stripped naked, but there was still treasure to be found. I watched one group of children giggling, as if they were playing a game, while they ripped the decorations and buttons from the uniform of a dead soldier. Men are proud of war but procreate in the dark. Perhaps there is a twisted logic in the shame of bringing children into such a world.

After living from the apples in my pockets, I was finally able to purchase some food at the village of Borna. One does not realize how quickly the human body loses its strength until one survives for days with almost no food. At the village of Altenburg I managed to purchase a horse very cheaply. The angular bones jutted out of the flanks of the half-starved animal, but it was still strong enough to carry me. No doubt it was the property of a cavalryman who probably lay rotting on the plains to the north. At last I was able to flee the pestilent gorge of Avernus, without the help of Charon, the dread ferryman, and return to the land of the living.

After my return to Paris, I considered returning to New York City immediately. The charms of the old world had eroded considerably. But no one in possession of his senses crosses the Atlantic between November and March. So I decided to remain in Paris until the following spring. After a terrible retreat from Leipsic, Napoleon had arrived at St. Cloud on November 9, several days before my own return to the city. Many soldiers had died of starvation and typhus. The French army's retreat to Frankfurt had been blocked by a large army of Austrians and Napoleon's former Bavarian allies at Hanau. Despite inferior numbers and the desperate condition of the French army, Napoleon's forces crushed the enemy, another brilliant military achievement for the Emperor.

According to the *Moniteur*, Napoleon was attempting to raise an army of 300,000 more men to face the advancing allies. New taxes were imposed. The Senate had decreed conscription of those who had escaped military service in former years. It became almost impossible to purchase substitutes for service in the army. Boys of fifteen and sixteen years of age, the "Marie-Louises," were the primary recruits for the new army. The dreaded flying columns were everywhere, seizing men for the army. I myself was stopped three times and had to prove my American citizenship before being released. After the second catastrophic campaign in two years, people in the streets were openly critical of the Emperor. "He is willing to devour our children to feed his own ambitions" was a favorite complaint of the time. They referred to him as "that man" and warned, "He will destroy us all." English journals were discussed which claimed that Napoleon had blown the bridge over the Elster in an act of personal cowardice. In order to increase his popularity, Napoleon began to make surprise appearances, without a military escort, in the streets of Paris. On one of these occasions I was walking near the Tuileries when the cries of "Vive L'Empereur" drew me to a rapidly growing crowd of people in the street. Over the heads of the crowd, less than ten feet away from me, I could see and hear the great man talking to a few of the spectators. He was wearing the same costume as in Leipsic, the unmistakable hat and gray coat. It was surprising to see him spoken to as if he were an ordinary citizen. "Will the enemy invade France?" he was asked.

His voice resounded with great authority. "They may soon be here in Paris, if nobody helps me. I cannot turn them back myself. You must enlist and fight. Only then shall we maintain our glory." The huge crowd cheered enthusiastically, "Vive l'Empereur!" An aide came over with his horse and he rode away. An elderly man turned to me. "The allies will be here by year's end. He has no army left; his star has fallen." That night I returned to the Palais Royale and found number 113. After the hell of Leipsic, the Palais seemed an escape into purgatory. I succumbed with joy to the pleasures of the flesh. But Monsieur Lafont was wrong. The remembrance of Nancy burned even brighter in the dark recesses of my mind where I had attempted to exile her.

At the archives, soon after my return, I eagerly read the official accounts of the battle of Leipsic. The bulletins blamed the withdrawal to Leipsic on the defection of the Bavarians. A victory was claimed at Wachau, several miles to the south of Leipsic, on October 16. The bulletin declared French losses of 2500 men to 25,000 for the allies. Historians have since determined that the casualties were equal on that day. Another victory was claimed for October 18, the battle I had seen, despite the "treacherous" defection of the Wurtemberg cavalry and Saxon army to the enemy side. These accounts lent credence to the expression "to lie like a bulletin." It was the explanation of the blowing of the bridge on October 19 that I was most anxious to read. This was an event of historic importance which I had actually witnessed. The allies were attempting to use the event to discredit Napoleon in the eyes of his own people. There existed a historical mystery of great significance, but one of comprehensible proportions for the making of a complete investigation. A definitive account of this event by an eyewitness could be one of the most important parts of *The Age of Revolution*. What would Gibbon have done if he had been presented with such an opportunity? No doubt he would have achieved a tour de force surpassing even his account of the fall of Constantinople.

It was with great excitement that I ran my fingers across the page of the *Moniteur* containing Napoleon's bulletin of October 24, which purported to describe the catastrophe of October 19. The bulletin stated that it was a lack of ammunition that forced the French army to renounce the victories over "the armies of the whole continent" of the previous days and to retreat from Leipsic. Despite the necessity of retreat, the bulletin claimed, Napoleon refused to set fire to the suburbs of Leipsic in order to prevent allied pursuit. The Emperor could not resolve to destroy "one of the beautiful cities of Germany" and under the eyes of his loyal ally, the King of Saxony, who was so greatly disturbed by the defection of his own army. Instead, the Emperor had ordered the engineers to build mines under the big bridge over the Elster so as to blow it up when all French troops had crossed, thereby to retard the advance of the enemy. According to the bulletin, General Dulauloy had charged Colonel Montfort with this operation. Instead of remaining on the spot to direct the demolition, Montfort had ordered a corporal and four sappers to blow up the bridge "when the enemy should present himself." When the corporal, "a man without intelligence and ill understanding his mission, heard shots fired from the town ramparts, he lighted the match and blew the bridge." Although it was admitted to be difficult to gauge the losses caused by the unfortunate event, the bulletin estimated the men left on the east side of the Elster at twelve thousand. Thus the enemy, after losing the battles of the previous days, gained by the disaster of the nineteenth "courage and the ascendant of victory." I was determined to learn whether this official story was the truth or merely another bulletin of lies.

In December of 1813, after two unsuccessful visits, I was able to speak to General Flahaut at his splendid apartments on the first floor of the Rue Verte. In the short time since I had last seen him, Flahaut had been promoted to Lieutenant General and created Count of the Empire. A servant led me through a magnificent suite of rooms, befitting a count, into a large drawing room. Dressed in a splendid gold-braided uniform, Flahaut was sitting on a sofa speaking to a very beautiful woman who appeared to be at least twenty years older than himself. He seemed pleased to see me again. "So you survived Leipsic. I was unable to determine what happened to you." He introduced the woman at his side as his mother, who lived on the floor above. She smiled at me and politely withdrew. It has become a matter of great regret to me that neither the General nor I had the opportunity to mention in her presence my connection to Gouverneur Morris. If she had stayed longer, I might have even referred to my meeting with Talleyrand. I have always wondered what she might have said about them. Unfortunately, it would be more than three years before I learned the nature of the relationships among Morris, Talleyrand, and the Flahaut family.

"Madame de Flahaut is a lovely woman."

Charles corrected me in English, which he continued to use for the remainder of our conversation. "Her name is now Madame de Souza. She is remarried. You see, my father died during the Revolution. He was arrested in 1793 but managed to escape. When he heard that an innocent man was in danger of execution for aiding his escape, he surrendered himself and went to the guillotine. Another victim of the rabble." He pronounced the word "rabble" with undisguised contempt.

I marveled at the heroism of such an unselfish act. Flahaut seemed quite proud of the action of the man he referred to as his father. After I related the story of my adventures in Leipsic, he told me about the horrors of the retreat, including the spread of typhus among the soldiers. "The position we find ourselves in today is because we lost our horses in Russia."

"What do you mean?" I asked.

"So many of our horses died last year in Russia that we have suffered from a severe shortage of cavalry during this entire year. With few cavalry patrols available, the army lost its eyes and its ability to pursue after victory in the field. If we had more cavalry, the Russians and Prussians would have been routed at Lützen and Bautzen instead of being able successfully to withdraw from both fields of battle and await reinforcements. In that event, Austria would never have joined the coalition against us. Also, our infantry formations on the battlefield have had to be more dense than in the past to protect against enemy cavalry attacks. These formations have made us more vulnerable to enemy artillery. It must be admitted that this was not as great a problem at Leipsic because the Emperor ordered the infantry into formations of two ranks instead of three so the army would appear stronger by a third.

"With their advantages of superior cavalry and numbers, the allies avoided facing the Emperor on the field after the armistice ended. Instead they concentrated on beating our other armies. Within the two weeks after August twenty-third, our Marshals were defeated at Gross Beeren, the Katzbach, Kulm, and Dennewitz. The only time we won during that crucial period was at Dresden, the lone battle where the Emperor was present, and he arrived after the battle had started. I have no doubt that if the allies knew he would appear on the field, they would not have attacked Dresden. By the time of our concentration at Leipsic we were heavily outnumbered, and the allies were finally willing to confront the Emperor on the battlefield."

Using my knowledge of military history, I attempted to make a favorable impression on Flahaut. "That is the ultimate proof of the Emperor's greatness as a military leader. His enemies refused to fight any army he commanded. The only way the Romans defeated Hannibal was by avoiding combat with any army he led for many years after Cannae." Flahaut nodded in agreement.

Having established my favorable views on the Emperor, I began to question his leadership in a critical manner. "After the failure to defeat the allies at Leipsic on October sixteenth, why did you not retreat on the seventeenth before the allies received 100,000 reinforcements?"

"The Emperor thought we could win on the eighteenth and he did not want to abandon our garrisons along the Elbe, Dresden, Torgau, Wittenberg, Magdeburg, and Hamburg. We left more than 100,000 men in those garrisons when we retreated from Leipsic. That is the real disaster of the battle. Had we merely taken St. Cyr's twenty thousand men from Dresden when we withdrew to Leipsic, we would have been completely victorious on October sixteenth. That was the major error of the campaign. If we had withdrawn almost all of the soldiers in the fortresses, there is no doubt that we would have been completely victorious at Leipsic. Of course, in criticizing the decision to hold the fortresses, it must be remembered that much of our supplies and ammunition came from the fortresses to the east and not from the direction of the west. In any case, the Emperor was confident of victory and a return to the line of the Elbe. We now desperately need those troops in the fortresses; but they are lost for the defense of France." Flahaut walked about the room as he spoke. He seemed to be incapable of passing a mirror without inspecting himself.

Emboldened by the great candor with which Flahaut spoke, as if the war were already lost, I pressed him on the details of the retreat from Leipsic and the blowing of the bridge. Insofar as his response was sympathetic to Colonel Montfort, it was substantially different from the tone of his commander's bulletin. "There was a hearing at Erfurt on the affair of the bridge. General Rogniat had been ordered to throw new bridges across the River Saale to keep open our line of retreat to the Rhine. Montfort, a colonel of the engineers, succeeded him in the Leipsic area. Many of the bridges to our rear at Leipsic were blown prior to the battle to limit the threat from the allied forces west of the Elster. To his credit, Montfort wanted to build additional bridges across the Pleisse and Elster rivers for purposes of expediting a retreat, but Berthier rejected the suggestion."

"Why," I asked, "would the chief-of-staff disregard such a sensible proposal?"

Flahaut seemed reluctant to speak about Berthier's role. "I was an aide-de-camp to Marshal Berthier for many years. Let us say that he has a tendency to wait for the Emperor's orders and a reluctance to issue his own. The Emperor was too busy with the details of the battle itself to prepare for a retreat. I do not know what was in his mind on this matter. Perhaps Berthier, or the Emperor, thought that the premature building of bridges would discourage the troops. Unfortunately, the two wooden bridges that were hastily built at the time of the retreat fell apart after only a few units crossed. During the retreat, the Emperor did order the mining of the Elster Bridge with explicit instructions to Montfort that the match was not to be lit until all of our men were safely across."

"Why was Montfort not present when the bridge was blown?"

"He was unable to obtain any reliable information as to how many men were left in the city. So he decided to cross the causeway to Lindenau to receive additional information and instructions from the Emperor himself. He left a Corporal Lafontaine and four sappers with instructions to fire the mine only if the enemy was about to seize the bridge. Montfort got caught in the mob struggling across the causeway and was unable to reach Lindenau. Before he could get back to the bridge by fighting against the hordes moving in the opposite direction, small numbers of Prussian troops were seen near the bridge and some of the sappers began to yell, 'Fire the mine.' It appears that the corporal believed the appropriate moment had come and lit the fuse. Montfort, as the officer in charge of the operation, has had to bear the blame. He is a ruined man."

"Where was the Emperor at the time of the explosion?"

"He was sleeping at Lindenau and was awakened by the blast. He was enraged that the bridge had been blown so early in the day. He knew that the corps of Marmont and Poniatowski were still holding the city. Marmont escaped. Marshal Poniatowski, you know, drowned trying to swim across the Elster with a wounded arm. His body was found by fishermen several days after the battle."

"Yes. I read about it in the *Moniteur*. I saw many men die trying to swim across the Elster. A horrible sight."

"The Poles are very unhappy about the loss of Poniatowski. They are, you know, our last faithful allies, except, of course, for you Americans. Perhaps you will succeed in defeating the British for us. I fear we shall never do it." Flahaut sat down at the piano and began to play with impressive skill. The joyous tune he sang in a beautiful voice was completely inconsistent with his somber words.

Because he seemed to imply that Colonel Montfort had been made a scapegoat for the failures of Berthier, I began to question him about Napoleon's chief-of-staff. Instead of talking about Leipsic, Flahaut told me a series of humorous anecdotes about Berthier's eccentric behavior. Stories of Berthier's service as a major in the war of the American Revolution. Berthier in Egypt pining for his mistress in France, Madame de Visconti, and erecting an altar to her in his tent before which he would kneel in silent devotion. After his coronation, Napoleon chose a respectable bride for Berthier to marry. He obeyed his master but persuaded his wife to accept Madame de Visconti into his household. "The three of them live together to this day." I laughed politely and attempted to return to the bridge at Leipsic. Irresistibly cheerful, Flahaut insisted on telling one more Berthier story. "You must hear about the rabbits. Berthier was assigned to organize a rabbit shoot for the Imperial Court. With his usual efficiency, he arranged everything, food, beaters, gun bearers, and hundreds of rabbits. Unfortunately, he purchased tame rabbits instead of wild ones. When the Emperor began the hunt, the rabbits refused to run away. They must have thought the Emperor was going to feed them their daily rations of lettuce and carrots. Like an attacking cavalry corps, they charged at the Emperor in one vast horde. The beaters were unable to hold back the squadrons of advancing rabbits. The Emperor had to run to his coach to escape, rabbits falling off the top as the coach rode away. Berthier still blushes at the mention of 'those rabbits.' The Emperor will never let him forget." Flahaut laughed heartily at his own stories. It was as if he had forgotten his gloomy statements as to the future safety of the Empire. I departed with a promise from Flahaut that he would attempt to arrange an interview for me with the Emperor. According to him, Corporal Lafontaine was dead, but Flahaut promised to seek information as to the whereabouts of Colonel Montfort.

Despite Flahaut's efforts on my behalf, Montfort refused to speak to anybody unless he was ordered to do so. In January, Flahaut sent me a note that the Emperor was too busy to meet with me. However, he enclosed a letter from the Emperor himself directing persons at the archives to assist me in my work. The effect of the letter was magical. I no longer had to rely on Monsieur Monceau as the sole person who would assist me. The lackadaisical employees at the archives suddenly became my eager and respectful servants. Requests on which weeks had passed without action were approved instantly. Documents that had not formerly existed were quickly found by the staff. Assistants were even provided to me for the making of copies. Within two months I accomplished many times as much as during all the preceding months in Paris.

In late January, Napoleon left the city to confront the advancing allied armies. Flahaut departed at the same time. Paris was quickly in a state of panic at the news of the advance of the allied armies, especially the Prussians, who seemed to be the most feared by the Parisians. To the astonishment of almost everyone, news of the victories of Napoleon and his small army of raw conscripts arrived daily. Between February 10 and 14 the French won three victories in swift succession at Champaubert, Montmirail, and Vauchamps. To remove the doubts of the skeptics, 25,000 enemy prisoners were paraded through Paris. Parisians thronged the boulevards to watch the procession of disarmed prisoners, led by their generals and other officers. Napoleon was again a hero, "the savior of France."

In early March the news from the front almost ceased. For the next few weeks the *Moniteur* printed no news of the war. Panic again began to spread. The financial markets were in a state of confusion. Shares quoted at 65 one day were down to 45 on the next. One day I saw a sign on the Vendôme column beneath the statue of Napoleon: *"Passez vite, il va tomber."* Many members of the National Guard carried pikes instead of muskets. The Palais Royal was mobbed with gamblers and seekers of pleasure, including me, who behaved as though it was their last day on earth. Through the barriers of the city, crowds of peasants with their families, furniture, and livestock poured into Paris. It was obvious to everyone that defeat was imminent. It was as though I were again trapped in Leipsic waiting for the horrors of war to engulf the city.

On the morning of March 29 the Empress fled the city in a long procession of green carriages with an escort of cavalry. Standing in the rain at the Place du Carrousel, I was among the spectators watching the mournful parade. Surrounded by lancers, the Empress and her son were huddled in one of the front carriages. Inside the heavy coronation coaches, harnesses and saddles could be seen piled on the satin cushions. The crowd watched in complete silence. Early the next morning I was awakened by the roar of cannon. In order to view the events of the day, I walked toward the windmill on the heights of Montmartre. Despite the extreme cold, the faubourgs were crowded with people. It was as if the entire population was in the streets to experience the events of the day. The banks and shops all over Paris were closed. From the heights of Montmartre the sight from the steeple at Leipsic was repeated before my eyes. The same dark masses of troops filled the plains in front of the heights north of Paris. A furious battle was raging, but it was obvious that the army defending Paris was hopelessly outnumbered.

The heights, which provided a spectacular view of the battle, were filled with spectators. I stood near a church on the spire of which a telegraph was fixed. It was topped by a cross beam and two arms for signaling operated by pulleys. The station could be manned by a watcher with a telescope who could read distant messages and transmit them to the next station. It was said that in this manner news could reach Paris from as far south as Lyons within fifteen minutes. I hoped that news would suddenly arrive that Napoleon's army in the field would soon rescue Paris. No such tidings brightened that terrible day. Nobody knew where Napoleon and his army were. The vast hosts of the enemy spilled across the plains of St. Denis like the waters from an immense flood. As at Leipsic, the bayonets and standards of the armies glittered in the bright sunlight. The cheers of the allies, especially the loud Russian "hurrah," could be heard as they ascended the heights. Within fifteen minutes the Russians had taken Montmartre. By two in the afternoon the battle for Paris was over. As soon as the white flag waved from the nearby telegraph, I returned to the conquered city.

The next day I joined the crowds watching the parade of the allied armies into Paris. The French regulars had all left the city. Only the National Guard, in their blue uniforms with red epaulets, were left to make a path for the victors. The cossacks on horseback with their thick beards, long pikes, and small whips led the procession, followed by Prussian cavalry and colorful Austrian, Russian, and Prussian infantry. The crowds were amazed by the sight of Asiatic horsemen called Bashkirs who rode into view with high pointed hats, curved swords, and bows and arrows. According to the accounts of the battle of Leipsic, they had actually attacked French cavalry with their ancient weapons. As they had to shoot the arrows high into the air, instead of horizontally, in order to avoid wounding each other, the bowmen inflicted little harm on the French. Because of Benjamin Franklin's suggestion during the American Revolution that the longbow be reintroduced to modern warfare, the Bashkirs interested me. It appeared from the experience at Leipsic that Franklin's experiment would not have worked.

The allied soldiers had looped white scarves from their left shoulders. Many in the crowds interpreted this as a sign of support for the restoration of the Bourbons. I later learned that the allies wore the scarves only for purposes of recognition in battle. Nevertheless, the sign of the white scarves was taken as a signal for the royalists to bring out the white cockades and rosettes. To my horror, some Parisians began to shout, *"Vive la Roi! Vivent les Bourbons!"* Others yelled, *"À bas les droits réunis,"* as though their only interest in the midst of defeat was the repeal of Napoleon's excise taxes. The streets became so crowded that the troops had difficulty moving forward. Expensively dressed women waved white banners and bed linen from crowded windows to declare their support for the return of the ancient royal family of France. The people who had set an example for the world of liberty from Bourbon oppression were now shamelessly calling for a return to the yoke of the kings of old. A man standing next to me declared, "We marched all the way to Moscow to show the Russians the way back to Paris." When people shouted *"Vivent les Bourbons,"* the wit next to me muttered, "The Bourbons, never heard of them." I wondered how many others shared this man's views.

The crowds seemed to be impressed by the orderliness and clean uniforms of the enemy, since they had been told repeatedly that their enemies were nearly annihilated. *"Au moins, c'est un beau debris,"* was an expression repeated numerous times by cynical spectators. The splendid conditions of the uniforms of the allied troops was a surprise to me, since at Leipsic many of them had been clothed in motley uniforms stripped from the dead of both sides. From talking to French-speaking Russian officers, I later learned that many of the troops of the Czar had fought in great coats and kept clean uniforms in their knapsacks for purposes of a triumphal entry into Paris.

During the entire day I saw only one prominent display of continuing support for Napoleon. A sign on a wall declared "Long live the Emperor"; as persons walked by, they surreptitiously wrote underneath, "Approved." Hedged in by foreign bayonets, most of the Parisians visible in the streets groveled before their conquerors. At the sight of the Czar of Russia and King of Prussia, many yelled, *"Vive L'Empereur Alexandre! Vive le Roi de Prusse!"* Women crowded about the monarchs as though they were liberators. One prosperous-looking woman wearing a white Bourbon rosette knelt and kissed the foot of the Czar. Perhaps it is a virtue of Frenchmen that they submit with good grace to that which they cannot avoid. They fight desperately until valor is useless, then they surrender to their fate. Had they fought from street to street, they might have accomplished little but to destroy the magnificent city of Paris and many of its inhabitants. It is also possible that they might have held the city long enough to permit Napoleon's army to sever the allied supply lines and force an enemy retreat. To this day, I am in doubt as to which was the wiser or more honorable course of action.

After the parade, I walked through the cossack bivouacs on the Champs-Elysées. They built straw huts supported by planting their lances in the ground.

The men sat sewing their clothing and repairing their boots. They rarely moved on foot. To go from one tent to the next, they would ride on horseback rather than walk a short distance. Parisians came out with their families to stare at the strange horsemen from the east. Later, when I visited Flahaut's house, one of his servants informed me that he was with the Emperor at Fontainebleau. Flahaut had sent a message that he would never return as long as the Russians occupied the city.

The next day, April 1, the entire city was placarded with a proclamation signed by the Emperor Alexander announcing that the allied sovereigns would not treat with Napoleon or with any members of his family; however, they would uphold the constitution which the French nation chose. They invited the Senate to appoint a provisional government. Czar Alexander was staying with Talleyrand at the hotel on the Rue St. Florentin, where they both organized the new government of France. A detachment of Russian imperial guards kept people away from the house where I had met Talleyrand six months earlier and which I never succeeded in entering again. The Senate quickly established a provisional government with Talleyrand as its president. Like a cat who always lands on his feet, Talleyrand had once again flourished during a political upheaval. No matter who was ascendant, the Bourbons, the revolutionaries, the Bonapartes, the allied sovereigns, or again the Bourbons, Talleyrand always maintained his position of power. Morris despised his unprincipled nature, but Talleyrand is a prince whom Machiavelli would surely have admired.

The sovereigns Napoleon did not remove from their thrones when he controlled their capitals did not return the kindness. Under the control of its conquerors, the Senate quickly dethroned Napoleon and absolved the army and the people of the oath of allegiance to him. Shortly thereafter, Marshal Marmont, the Duke of Ragusa, surrendered his entire corps to the allies, thereby ending any chance of a French attack against the allies. Before I left, people were already using the new word *raguser* to mean "to betray." Although the news did not appear in the *Moniteur* until April 12, Napoleon abdicated the day after Marmont's betrayal. Certainly Napoleon must have wished that, of the Marshals left in Leipsic after the explosion of the bridge, it was Marmont instead of Poniatowski who had drowned in the Elster.

From a pamphlet by Chateaubriand, spread throughout Paris after its conquest, it was clear that the allies were planning to recall the Bourbons to the throne of France. "God himself," the pamphlet proclaimed, "marches openly at the head of the allied armies and sits in the Council of Kings." Napoleon was denounced as "the greatest criminal that has ever appeared on the earth," and Frenchmen were urged "to rest under the paternal authority of our legitimate sovereigns." The day I spoke to Leray de Chaumont for the last time, I showed him a copy of the pamphlet. "Of course the Bourbons are returning. Surely, you don't think the allies have been fighting all of these years to leave the Revolution triumphant." He reiterated that there could be no loan for the canal until the war between America and Britain ended. "With

Bonaparte gone, the United States can no longer obtain credit of any kind in Europe." He showed me British newspapers and journals indicating that since Leipsic, the British people and members of Parliament were expecting total victory in Europe to be followed by the defeat of the United States. British policy was the conquest of the Great Lakes and the seduction of New England into the forgiving arms of the British. "There is one benefit in that for you," Leray declared. "New England continues to refuse to support the war. To keep them friendly, the British have maintained their prohibition on extending the blockade to the New England coast. Without any great problems, you should be able to obtain a passage to a New England city from a port between Brest and Rochefort. To do so, you should leave soon, before Wellington's army takes control of the entire French coastline." He seemed eager to be rid of me.

The day after speaking to Leray, I hastened to the archives to complete my work. Monsieur Monceau, who had assisted me in the past, no longer worked there. The sullen librarian greeted me with contempt. When I referred to "the Emperor," he brusquely corrected me. "You mean your benefactor Buonaparte." Upon hearing the old Corsican pronunciation of Napoleon's name, I knew that my star had fallen with the Emperor's. My accumulated work for the previous month, which I maintained at the archives, had been seized. "You will need the authorization of the Provisional Government for its return," he said, sneering. There was little doubt that the recovery of my material could take months. Fortunately, the impounded papers concerned the period of the Directory, which was not of the greatest interest to me. Also, some of the lost material was duplicative of information from records reviewed by me during the previous August. I decided to forego any attempt to obtain its return.

On my last full day in Paris, April 10, Easter Sunday, I watched an immense religious ceremony presented by the Czar of Russia in the Place Louis XV. By coincidence, Russian Orthodox Easter, March 29 by the Russian calendar, fell on the same day as Catholic Easter in 1814. An altar had been raised at the place where Louis XVI had been beheaded twenty-one years earlier. At this symbolic site, the Emperor Alexander had an Orthodox mass celebrated. The crowd of assembled soldiers knelt on one knee with their hats off. The cavalry remained on horseback with their hatless heads respectfully bowed down. With banners, incense, and icons waving, the bearded priests chanted in Russian. To my disgust, the French Marshals and Generals, the soldiers of the Revolution, crowded in behind the allied sovereigns and Generals to genuflect and kiss the Russian cross. The huge crowd of spectators exhibited no sign of disapproval. Many of them were too young to have seen such a ceremony, with the State prostrating itself before the Church. Christianity had triumphed over its revolutionary enemy, the old Europe over the new. The ancient God of superstition and privilege had dethroned the Goddess of reason and liberty. The Age of Revolution had ended.

The next day, in profound sorrow over the events of the previous two weeks, I departed for the coast of Brittany. Following a wait of several weeks for a ship to America, and after an uneventful passage of six weeks across the Atlantic, I disembarked in Boston. Although the British had recently extended the blockade to the coast of New England, we arrived at our destination unimpeded. Since I had last trod the democratic soil of America, more than thirteen months had passed.

ELEVEN

After a year in the center of the European maelstrom, the complacency of New York City was irksome in the extreme. As always, the good burghers of the city were fully immersed in their petty concerns. Smug shopkeepers amassing money for a comfortable old age. They could not imagine the hellish domains through which I had wandered. With war all about them, they were absorbed in their insignificant provincial world. Their lack of comprehension of the abyss over which our nation now tottered enraged me within the limits of my enfeebled capacity for anger.

Because of my own carelessness, I had been ill for months. My error was, for one last time at the Palais Royal, to engage in the rites of Venus without my protective armor. The goddess of love had punished me for my negligence with a visitation from Monsieur Gonorrhea. He invaded the dominion of my body and gave no quarter. During the long Atlantic crossing, endless bleeding by the ship's doctor depleted what remained of my vitality. In spite of spending almost the entire trip resting in a hammock, I was weaker at the end of the voyage then at its beginning.

It was a warm evening in June of 1814 when the carriage left me at my doorway. I wondered whether Emily would greet me warmly, as she had upon my return from the Niagara frontier; whether time and distance had ended our private conflict. If we were to resume our conjugal relationship, it could not be until the malady had departed from my body. Her prudishness assured that I would be unable to reveal the nature of my affliction. There would, however, be no such problems arising from an end to discord and a resumption of my old mundane existence. The moment Emily opened the door, I suspected something was wrong. My arrival caught her completely by surprise; she did not appear to be pleased by my return. "You're back," was the single comment she could muster. There was only shock, with no sign of pleasure in the words. It was her dress and coiffure that made me distrustful. She had not taken such care with her appearance for many years.

"Yes. I have come home. Are you going somewhere?"

She nervously stammered as she spoke. "I was going to church ... Sit down. You must be hungry. I'll give you something to eat." Without asking a single question about my trip, she began to prepare food. There appeared to be a bit of apprehension in her indifference, which perhaps was feigned. She acted as if I had departed the day before. A cursory inspection of the house revealed that she had moved all my possessions out of the bedroom and into the guest room. No excuses for my lack of amorousness would be necessary.

Within half an hour of my arrival, there was a knock on the door. John Randel was so surprised to find me greeting him that for a moment he was speechless. Then he blurted out, "Well, you've finally returned. I have been stopping here every week since April." Cuckold's horns seemed to be sprouting from my skull. My suspicions were increased by Emily's flustered reaction to Randel's entry. It was of some comfort to me that Randel seemed genuinely pleased at my presence. Perhaps his visit was an innocent coincidence. Maybe Emily was truly going to church. Indeed, she did depart within minutes of Randel's arrival. The more I thought of Randel and Emily in ardent embrace, the more ludicrous my suspicions seemed. Emily was much too religious to engage in adultery. Randel was a doubtful candidate for the soft snares of passion. He probably would have said the same of me. Despite the improbability of an illicit relationship between two such people, the seeds of doubt had been sown in my mind.

Following a discussion of my trip to France, Randel told me of the local events of the past year. The news of Napoleon's exile to Elba had preceded my return by a week. The war in America had turned into a bloody stalemate. Perry had won a glorious naval victory on Lake Erie. But on the Niagara frontier the news was bone-chilling. At Christmastime the previous year, the British in force had crossed the Niagara River to the American side. Despite the warnings of a British attack, the front gate of Fort Niagara was left open. Before accepting a surrender, the British bayoneted sixty-seven American soldiers. They and their Indian allies then proceeded south, leaving the American side of the Niagara, from Lake Ontario to Lake Erie, a wasteland. Lewiston, Schlosser, Black Rock, and Buffalo were burned to the ground. Civilians and soldiers were massacred along the entire border. All property, public and private, was destroyed.

Although Randel was still employed in placing the monuments marking the streets according to the plan of the Street Commissioners, he was also engaged in his continuing private war with William Bridges. In competition with Bridges's 1811 map of Manhattan, Randel's map of the plan of the Street Commissioners had been displayed in April of 1814. It was to be published in the fall. In order to advertise his own map, Randel obtained a letter from Morris, as Chairman of the Board of Commissioners, praising the map as "an excellent work." Morris's letter expressly declined to enter any questions between Randel and Bridges but stated that Randel's map was more accurate than anything of the kind which had yet appeared. Bridges was incensed at the suggestion that his map was not accurate. Over a period of weeks during March and April, a vitriolic series of letters between Randel and Bridges had appeared in the New York *Evening Post*. Randel, who never revealed any emotion except in his hostilities with Bridges, later showed me the newspapers he had retained like trophies of war. Bridges contended that the Street Commissioners—Morris, De Witt, and Rutherford—had already attested to the accuracy of his map, and that Randel was not at liberty to depart from it except by special act of the Legislature. According to Bridges, Randel was a "conceited young man" arrogantly proclaiming his own infallibility. He stated that Randel had received $15,000 for his services as Secretary to the Street Commission and for placing the monuments. In contrast, Bridges lamented that he had to rely on public patronage for his map, which was made at his own expense. Bridges held out his own integrity and propriety of conduct against the "incredible astonishing accuracy to be found alone in Mr. Randel's practice." Upon reading Bridges's characterization of Randel's well-known precision, I laughed aloud. Perhaps he thought the public would sympathize with his own mediocrity rather than Randel's inhuman exactitude and proceed to purchase the less reliable map.

Randel admitted he was infuriated by Bridges's public attack on him. In retaliation, Randel sent his own response to the newspaper. The Street Commissioners, he stated, had signed his map, not Bridges's. Randel reminded the readers of Morris's letter, which praised his map as more accurate than anything that had yet appeared. Since Bridges's map had been published two years earlier, Randel concluded that his own map must be the more accurate of the two. He then accused Bridges of deceiving the city by informing the corporation that Randel voluntarily planned to furnish him with the notes and papers of the Commissioners for purposes of assisting in the publication of the Bridges map. Randel attacked as totally inaccurate Bridges's statement that he had received $15,000 for his work. With an accuracy to which I can attest, Randel reported that he was paid only $125 per month for his services; and, out of his own pocket, at a cost of more than $3500, he had special instruments made in order to increase his accuracy and save time on the project. Randel listed numerous inaccuracies in the Bridges map, which, Randel noted, had the unauthorized signatures of the Street Commissioners affixed to it. Charging Bridges with attempting to divert public attention from the errors in his map, Randel had demanded a retraction of statements injurious to him.

Randel had good cause to be seething over the whole affair. Bridges was a scoundrel who used political maneuvering in an attempt to reap the profit from years of hard labor by another man. "Anybody who knows both you and Bridges is aware of the fact that you are concerned with accuracy, not money, while Bridges is ambitious only for personal gain. Your reputation is secure."

Randel grumbled, "At least he no longer holds a copyright on the map. If he had been able to retain it, he would have won. Enough of Mr. Bridges. There is more bad news. Two months ago the Legislature reduced the size of the Parade. There was too little open space provided in the plan, and already they are nibbling at it. . . ." As Randel spoke, I tried to picture him as Emily's lover. Like most husbands, I was flattered at the idea that my wife might be desirable in the eyes of another man, as long as that man pursued her no further. It was almost inconceivable that two such people could engage in amorous mischief. He showed no signs of guilt. Yet, doubt preyed on my mind. If it was not Randel, it could be someone else. Perhaps she was with him at that very moment. The thought filled me with nausea.

After extracting a promise to resume our monthly chess games, Randel went home. Immediately I began a frenzied search of the house before Emily had an opportunity to remove any clues as to her activities during the past year. There was nothing. No incriminating letters, no suspicious clothing, no signs of the presence of another man. Even the sheets were spotless. Although greatly fatigued from my journey and the lingering effects of my illness, I remained awake until Emily came home. It was not much later than the hour she usually returned from church. I feigned sleep in our old bed. She retired to the other bedroom.

The Empress Theodora was wise to cause her husband Justinian to legislate against prostitutes. She was, it is said, concerned that as long as husbands were free to pursue their pleasures outside the home, their wives could not manage them. There was an incidental benefit for husbands, avoidance of the miseries of the clap and the suspicions about the fidelity of wives raised in the minds of philandering husbands. Better to be uxorious than to suffer such agony.

After several days of rest, I returned to Morrisania to report to my benefactor. As the boat sailed up to the familiar dock, my head throbbed with great excitement at the thought of seeing Nancy again. Nancy, Morris, and three servants were visible as I walked up the hill. The lord of the manor and his wife were sitting in large chairs, basking in the sun on the lawn in front of the great house. The baby crawled about the grass with the wild exuberance of a healthy sixteen-month-old. On seeing my approach, Nancy scooped up the infant and walked swiftly down the hill to greet me. She was even more beautiful than I had remembered. The weight of her pregnancy and the dark circles under her eyes had vanished. The enthusiastic greeting from that exquisite voice instantly made me happy to be alive, as one feels in the first warmth of the spring sunlight after a long frigid winter. She embraced me affectionately and whispered in my ear, "You must tell me about Paris." She held the child in front of me. "Isn't he beautiful?"

"That is a rhetorical question, is it not?"

Nancy laughed at my reply. There could be no doubt that the child was the object of her most profound adoration. Both she and the baby wore large bonnets for protection from the sun. As always, she seemed to be hiding her beauty. How I longed to remove that bonnet and see those long, dark, flowing locks.

Leaning on his cane, Morris stood at the top of the incline awaiting my arrival. With a firm clasp of the hand, he effusively welcomed my return. After the chilly reception in my own home, I was moved by the warmth of their greeting. We sat together in the summer heat and drank cup after cup of wine poured by a bevy of servants, all eager to please. Morris announced that as my return from France was a special occasion, we were drinking his special Tokay wine. "Notice, this bottle is sealed with the arms of Austria. It was a wedding gift from Maria Theresa to Marie Antoinette. During the Terror, I purchased cases of it from a small shop not far from the remains of the Bastille. The price was quite reasonable. Now, after all these years, the Bourbons have returned to Paris."

Nancy giggled like a young girl. "Perhaps you should return their Tokay to them."

"They may have my best wishes, but never my Tokay." Smiling broadly, Morris stood up. "A toast to the restoration of peace in Europe . . . and in America." I was relieved that he had pronounced a toast that would not cause me to choke on the wine. "A letter from Leray de Chaumont has preceded you. I know you were unable to obtain the loan. It may be of some consolation for you to learn that our government was unable to borrow a single sou in Europe to pay for the war. In any case, this past April the supporters of the Lake Ontario route were able to convince the legislature to repeal the authorization to borrow five million dollars. What would we have done if you returned with the money?"

Morris began to grumble about the war. Before he could proceed with a tirade, Nancy interrupted. "Tell us about your adventures in France."

For over an hour I luxuriated in my role as the center of attention, while relating the events of my trip. The pursuit by British ships, my explorations of Paris, the valuable materials discovered in the archives. Nancy was intrigued by my description of the Palais Royal. In the telling, my own amorous adventures there were expurgated. Morris was very attentive to the account of my meeting with Talleyrand. "I hear," Morris interjected, "he was made the Vice Grand Elector of the Empire; it was the only vice he lacked." Without telling him that I had heard it in Paris from Leray, I guffawed at Morris's joke.

Both Morris and Nancy were spellbound by my account of the battle of Leipsic. She gasped audibly at my escape from the Prussians after the Elster Bridge was blown. He agreed with my conclusion that Napoleon would not have ordered the destruction of the bridge to save himself. "The man may be a monster, but he is certainly not a coward." When I began to describe my first encounter with Napoleon, Nancy asked in an excited voice, "What does the monster look like?" Morris was interested in my meetings with Flahaut. He said nothing, however, at my mention of meeting Flahaut's mother. At the time, I paid little attention to his reaction.

Sweating in the heat of the midday sun, Morris rolled up his sleeves. He quickly noticed that I was looking at his badly scarred right arm. "This happened a long time ago, when I was fourteen years old. My old friend Morgan Lewis and I were wrestling. He overturned a kettle, spilled boiling water on my right arm and side. I was quite badly scalded and had to convalesce at home for more than a year. You can see the flesh did not grow back normally. My hand was never the same. Never could wield a musket. But I made it through this life with one arm and one leg."

"Former Governor Morgan Lewis? Isn't he now a militia commander?"

"The very same one. An old man like me, but a major general. Wonderful man."

Aware that Morris had noticed my glances at his arm, I was careful not to stare excessively at Nancy. It was most difficult for me to keep my eyes away from her exquisite face. I also had to be cautious as to my choice of words. During the course of the discussion, I covered my preference for the French with the disguise of the impartial historian. It was an arduous task for me to appear neutral while describing the fall of Paris. During my account of French women kissing the feet of the Czar of Russia and Frenchmen yelling "Vivent les Bourbons," it was most difficult not to reveal my true feelings. Morris declared he was not surprised at the fall of Bonaparte and immodestly reminded me that he had repeatedly predicted, "As soon as the Gallic Caesar fails, he falls." He thanked me for my account and indicated it would be useful to him in preparing his speech on the restoration of the Bourbons. Later he gave me a ticket to the speech which was to be made a week later.

After lunch Morris escorted me into his library, where we discussed the latest report of the Canal Commissioners. It was dated March 8, 1814. The Commissioners reported they had appointed an English engineer to ascertain the best line for the canal from Lake Erie to the Hudson. They had made further investigations of the route up to the summer of 1813, when all efforts were suspended as a result of the war. I was pleased that the report stated, "The Commissioners beg leave to remark, that they are much misunderstood, when it is supposed they recommend exclusively a canal descending according to the level of the country, like an inclined plane. On the contrary, their project embraces the system of locks as well as the other, and their opinion is that the operation must be regulated by the nature of the country, taking into view the diminution of expense and the shortening of distance." That Morris pointed out this specific passage was most gratifying to me. It was as if he were saying, "You were right and I trust your judgment."

Always uneasy about asking for money, I reluctantly presented an estimated account of the complete expenses for my trip, with apologies for loss of my account book at Leipsic. Without even looking at the amount of my estimate, Morris declared he would pay the sum immediately. Within the week, he paid the full amount with an extra $250. His note accompanying the payment characterized my estimation as "unduly low." On my way out the door, I expressed my fears about an invasion by Wellington's peninsular veterans. Morris was optimistic. "The British could take New York City if they wanted; I do not believe they will. Unless they first gain strong support for the separation of New York and New England from the rest of the country, they would gain nothing by such a major effort. Their main attack will be in the Chesapeake." He reminded me to attend his speech and I promised to be present. On my way out of the house, Nancy hugged me again. My cheek touched hers. When the stench of the battlefield at Leipsic haunts me in the middle of the night, I still try to repel it by remembering the wonderful scent of her soft skin on that faraway summer day.

The speech of Gouverneur Morris was scheduled for Wednesday, June 29, 1814, at eleven o'clock in the forenoon at the Presbyterian Church on Cedar Street. Two full days before the event I informed Emily that I would leave at ten A.M. and be gone for at least three hours. I wanted her to be confident of my absence. On the morning of the twenty-ninth I departed before ten A.M. but circled back to a hidden location for observing the entrance to my own house. For forty-five minutes I watched for a man to enter or for Emily to leave. There was no sign of activity. My behavior appeared foolish to me, but the seeds of suspicion had been planted the night of my return home. I could not be at peace until the true situation was ascertained. Although there was barely enough time to get to the church, I waited for another ten minutes, and then for an additional five. Finally, with great reluctance, I deserted my post and hurried to fulfill my promise to Morris.

There was little doubt in my mind that I would not like the event, a Federalist observance of the deliverance of Europe from "the yoke of military despotism." The *Columbian* and other Republican newspapers had been denouncing it for days as a traitorous celebration in time of war of the victory of our British enemy over America's only ally, Napoleon. Led by the Tammany Society, the Republicans were openly organizing demonstrations for that day. A few of my fellow democrats hurled epithets at me as I entered the church. My ticket was carefully examined to determine that it was not a forgery. No doubt the Federalists feared a democratic disruption of the event. The aristocratic rites had already begun. I entered and took one of the only remaining empty seats, at the rear of the church. The Reverend Dr. Mason read a portion of the Book of Isaiah.

> "And it shall come to pass in that day, that his burden shall be taken from off thy shoulder, and his yoke from off thy neck."

After a short prayer, the prosperous-looking Federalist audience enthusiastically sang a hymn of gladness. Dressed as usual for a public occasion in his unfashionable powdered wig, Gouverneur Morris hobbled up to the pulpit. He was the only man I have ever seen who could limp majestically. His deep, mellifluous voice resounded from the walls and filled the hall.

> " 'Tis done. The long agony is over. The Bourbons are restored. France reposes in the arms of her legitimate prince. We may now express our attachment to her consistently with the respect we owe to ourselves."

With great oratorical flourishes, Morris reminded the audience of the role of Louis XVI as our ally in the War of American Independence. I wanted to rise and declare that France had again been our ally against our continuing enemy and its same King, George III, in this Second War of American Independence. "How," I wanted to shout, "can we celebrate the victory of the very foe whose European armies are now massing for an invasion of our soil?" Of course, I remained mute.

"How interesting, how instructive, the history of the last five-and-twenty years. In the spring of 1789 the States General of France were convened to ward off impending bankruptcy. The derangement of their finances was occasioned by the common artifice of cheating people into a belief that debts may be safely incurred without imposing taxes."

The audience was respectfully silent as Morris reviewed the events of the French Revolution culminating in the death, before a "ferocious mob," of the virtuous monarch who had been a friend in our hour of national peril. According to Morris, the French would have to expiate their terrible crime by many years of misery. I wondered what Emily was doing. Perhaps her lover, if she had one, arrived long after the speech began. That would have been the cautious way to arrange an assignation.

"O! It was a crime against nature and against heaven. A murder most foul and cruel. A deed at which fiends might have wept. I was in Paris. I saw the gush of sorrow. I heard the general groan. Every bosom anticipated the sentence of an avenging God. It was like a second fall of man. An awful scene of affliction, guilt, and horror."

His rhetoric was overstated for my taste, but effective. I reminded myself to ask Morris about his experiences in France. It was a subject he had never discussed with me in any detail. His brief review of the struggle between the Jacobins and Girondists and the death of Danton whetted my appetite to begin discussions with him as soon as possible.

"Those who slaughtered their prince and made havoc of each other; those who endeavored to dethrone the King of Heaven and establish the worship of human reason—who placed, as representative of the Goddess of Reason, a prostitute on the altar which piety had dedicated to the holy virgin, and fell down and paid to her their adoration, were, at length, compelled to see and to feel, and, in agony, to own that there is a God. I cannot proceed. My heart sickens at the recollection of those horrors which desolated France. That charming country, on which the bounty of heaven has lavished blessings, was the prey of monsters. To tell the crimes, everywhere and every hour perpetrated, would wound the soul of humanity, and shock the ear of modesty. But where, my country! O where shall I hide the blush, that these monsters were taken to your bosom?"

My anger began to rise with this exaltation of religion over the dominion of reason. It was not like Morris to praise religion and denigrate reason. Have not those who worship God committed innumerable atrocities in his name? Do they not permit his "invisible hand" to leave generations of poor to starve in the streets while they gorge themselves on the fat of the land and pray before altars of gold, all in the name of a God who warns it is easier for a camel to pass through the eye of a needle than for a rich man to enter the Kingdom of Heaven? A chasm between Morris and me was opening beneath my feet.

As Morris reached the career of Napoleon, "the terror, the wonder, and the scourge of nations," the excitement of the crowd was palpable. Morris had the audience firmly within his grasp. Never have I been present at a more effective oration, not even his own after the death of Alexander Hamilton. It was like Antony's speech over the body of Caesar in Shakespeare's *Julius Caesar*, a great speech in an unworthy cause.

> "In the month of September, 1812, the son of an obscure family, in a small island of the Mediterranean, was at the head of a greater force than was ever yet commanded by one man, during the long period to which history extends: His brows encircled with an imperial diadem, his sword red with the blood of conquered nations, his eye glaring on the fields he had devoted to plunder, his feet trampling on the neck of kings, his mind glowing with wrath, his heart swollen with the consciousness of power unknown before, he moved, he seemed, he believed himself a god. While at one extremity of Europe his ruthless legions drenched, with loyal blood, the arid soil of Spain, he marched, with gigantic stride, at the other extremity, to round his vast dominion in the widest circle of the civilized world. Already he had pierced the Russian line of defence. Already his hungry eagles were pouncing on his prey—Pause. View steadily this statue of colossal power. The arms are of iron; the breast is of brass; but the feet are of clay. The moment of destruction impends. Hark! The blow is given. It totters. It falls. It crumbles to dust."

Now I listened with great attention. He was beginning to describe the very period I had just witnessed. Napoleon collects the renewed means of warfare and appears in force on the Elbe River to halt the victorious Russians and aroused Prussians. Again he drinks the "luscious draught of victory" and shuts his ear to the counsel of prudence. Already the history written by the victors commences its hegemony.

> "A confidence in his talents, a confidence in his fortune, have made him blind. He confides in fortune, the god of atheism, which, analyzed, is nothing more than the combination of events we cannot discover; in which, nevertheless, though unknown, there is no more of chance than there was in a comet's orbit ere Newton was born.

But the adoration of that which derives its essence from ignorance accords with their wisdom who deny the existence of that Being by whom ponderous planets, hurled through the infinite void, are compelled to move in the prescribed course, till time shall be no more. Bonaparte, elate with rash confidence eluded negotiation."

Has Morris become a Calvinist? Is everything preordained at the whim of a Divine Being? This from the same Gouverneur Morris who declared human liberty to be the supreme human value. I wondered what Nancy would say about such a speech. He did not speak in this way at Morrisania, where he always indicated a healthy skepticism of such clerical claptrap. I closed my eyes and imagined Nancy embracing me. There is a divine being in whom I can believe.

"The plains of Saxony were wasted with inexorable severity. Pestilence and famine marched, in the train of war, to thin the ranks of mankind; to extend the scene of human misery, and prepare a wide theatre for the display of British benevolence. At length, after many battles, the well-planned movements of the allies obliged Napoleon to abandon Dresden. From that moment his position on the Elbe was insecure. But pride had fixed him there; perhaps, too, the same blind confidence in fortune. His force was collected at Leipsic. Leipsic, in the war of thirty years, had seen the great Gustavus fall in the arms of victory. Leipsic again witnessed a battle, on whose issue hung the independence, not of Germany alone, but of every state on the continent of Europe. Hard, long, and obstinate, was the conflict. On both sides were displayed an union of the rarest skill, discipline, and courage. As the flood-tide waves of ocean, in approaching the shore, rush, foam, thunder, break, retire, return—so broke, retired, and returned the allied battalions, impetuously propelled by the pressure of their brethren in arms. And as the whelming flood, a passage forced through the breach, rends, tears, scatters, dissipates, and bears away its unnumbered sands, so was the tyrant's host overwhelmed, scattered, and borne away."

Angered by his reference to "British benevolence," and the applause that followed it, I almost failed to notice Morris's mistaken placement of the death of Gustavus at Leipsic, instead of Lützen. It was the only incorrect historical reference I ever heard escape from his lips. My pedantic mind seized on the error, almost as if to stifle the idea emerging in my thoughts that this celebration may indeed be traitorous. What would the members of the Tammany Society have done at the sounds of acclaim following the oxymoronic words "British benevolence."

Morris continued his account. Hard-hearted Napoleon refuses to recognize the "benevolence" of the allies and their "generous" offers of peace. He fights on.

"Again the cannon roar. The long arches of the Louvre tremble. The battle rages. The heights of Montmartre are assailed. They are carried. The allies look down, victorious, on the lofty domes and spires of Paris. Lo! the capital of that nation which dictated ignominious terms of peace in Vienna and Berlin; the capital of that nation which wrapt in flames the capital of the Czars is in the power of its foes. Their troops are in full march . . . And now see two Christian monarchs, after granting pardon and protection, descend from the heights of Montmartre and march through the streets of that great city in peaceful triumph. See, following them, half a million of men, women and children, who hail, with shouts of gratitude, Alexander the deliverer. They literally kiss his feet."

Morris was twisting my own words. I only saw two women kiss the Czar's feet. In spite of my desire to leave the church, I remained rooted to my seat to listen to Morris's concluding words of praise for those who wear "legitimate crowns" and of contempt for his own democratic form of government.

"Look there. Those kings are Christians. And thou, too, Democracy! Savage and wild. Thou who wouldst bring down the virtuous and wise to thy level of folly and guilt! Thou child of squinting envy and self-tormenting spleen! Thou persecutor of the great and good! . . . Yes, Democracy, these are the objects of thy hate. Let those who would know the idol of thy devotion seek him in the Island of Elba . . . The Bourbons are restored. Rejoice France! Spain! Portugal! You are governed by your legitimate kings. Europe rejoice! The Bourbons are restored. The family of nations is completed. Peace, the dove descending from heaven, spreads over you her downy pinions. Nations of Europe, ye are her brethren once more. Embrace. Rejoice. And thou, too, my much-wronged country! My dear, abused, self-murdered country, bleeding as thou art, rejoice. The Bourbons are restored. Thy friends now reign. The long agony is over. The Bourbons are restored."

The people sitting in front of and next to me rose in unison with thunderous applause. Despite the angry look of the man on my right, I remained in my seat, heartsick. My feelings of friendship for Morris had been irretrievably damaged. As if a member of my own family had died, my mind was filled with a profound sadness. At the sight of the smiling David Ogden, applauding as he advanced toward his triumphant uncle, I fled the church. Screaming "traitor," a group of children threw rocks at me and then ran down the street in the opposite direction. One of the rocks struck me in the back. There was no injury, except to my pride.

The speech had lasted little more than an hour. I hurried home to discover what was happening there. With the image of Emily and her lover in my mind, I burst into the room. Emily sat quietly in a chair embroidering, a half-empty glass of wine besides her. Unsmiling, she looked up at me but said nothing.

It was generally known that the men of the Tammany Society would be gathering to protest the continuation of the Federalist celebration, a public dinner scheduled for four P.M. at Washington Hall. All of the important Federalists would be there, including Rufus King, Chancellor Kent, and, of course, Gouverneur Morris. Because of poor health, John Jay could not attend. All of the foreign consuls, except the French consul, would also be present. As word of Morris's "Bourbon speech" spread in the streets, the crowd of protesters outside Washington Hall grew to enormous proportions. Although I had not received an invitation to the dinner, I walked up Broadway to Washington Hall to watch the protest. In many years, it was the first mob action by the men of Tammany with which I was in complete sympathy.

For a time the crowd, which was later estimated at two thousand persons, was boisterous but well-behaved. Then the rumor spread that inside the hall the British flag had been raised above the American. The crowd began to chant, "Traitors! Traitors! Traitors!" Having always found hostile action by groups to be repugnant to my nature, I did not join in the shouting or other activities of the crowd. Consistent with my usual behavior, I remained a passive spectator in the midst of the human activity swirling about me.

When a group of aristocratic-looking gentlemen attempted to leave Washington Hall, the throng became an ugly mob. Angry chants of "Tory! Tory!" filled the air. A hail of stones drove the Federalists back into the shelter of the building. Some of the stones were thrown through the windows of the hall. The sounds of breaking glass further inflamed the passions of the multitude. A distinguished-looking elderly man came out of the hall and attempted to address the crowd. In an entreating manner, he raised his hands to request silence. Shouts of "Tory traitor" drowned out his voice. A volley of stones forced him to retreat inside. I could picture Morris and his friends inside, complaining about the "rabble" outside, appalled by their disrespect for property. It was what Morris called "the worst of all possible dominions," the domination of a riotous mob. Although not approving of the misbehavior, I believed it had been provoked by this outrageous celebration in time of war of the victory of our own enemy.

Standing to the rear of the crowd, I noticed a solid line of constables, cudgels in hand, advancing up the street. After shouting a warning to those in front of me, I retreated to the side, away from the menacing advance of the forces of order. The constables waded into the crowd, ordering people to disperse. Those who resisted were beaten and dragged away. Suddenly, a crowd of demonstrators ran towards me pursued by flailing constables. With a speed that amazed me, I fled down the street. After running for what seemed like a mile, I stopped and, gasping for breath, looked back. There was nobody in sight.

The country was at war with itself. The next day the newspapers were filled with news of the riot. Some of the persons inside Washington Hall had been injured by stones and broken glass. Twenty rioters had been arrested. The *Columbian* accused the Federalists, particularly Morris, of inflaming a combustible atmosphere without regard to decency, duty, or honor, and with a complete absence of common prudence. The *Commercial Advertiser* accused the Republican newspapers, especially the *Columbian*, of incitement to riot. The *Columbian* was charged with being the vilest of those Jacobin newspapers mortified at the downfall of their idol, Bonaparte. No doubt Bonaparte, who detested the Jacobins, would have been amused at our provincial simplification of the complexity of European politics.

The toast of Gouverneur Morris at the dinner, printed in the newspaper, added to my anger and sorrow over the whole affair. "America—sole exception to the Christian world—may she soon be restored to the family of nations." Although he was probably oblivious to my feelings, Morris and I were separated by an immense chasm. In the heat of the moment I vowed never to work for him again. There was no more center. People were either in the aristocratic faction or the democratic faction. Thucydides had described the situation over 2200 years earlier in *The Peloponnesian War*. Society had become divided into camps in which no man trusted his fellow. "Reckless audacity came to be considered the courage of a loyal ally; prudent hesitation, specious cowardice; moderation was held to be a cloak for unmanliness; ability to see all sides of a question, inaptness to act on any." The divisions were "such as have occurred and always occur, as long as the nature of mankind remains the same; though in severer or milder form, and varying in their symptoms, according to the variety of the particular cases."

In my opinion, the day of Morris's Bourbon speech was the beginning of the end of our friendship, if it can be called that rather than the relationship between master and man. Fortunately, I did not see or speak to him for months after the event. Thus, I did not have an opportunity to reveal my outrage concerning his political views. Had we met during that intense summer of 1814, the crisis of the war, angry words may well have been exchanged and he probably would not have sought my assistance in the fall of that year on the extraordinary private matter which is the proximate cause of the writing of this book. It must, however, be admitted that my anger about the Federalist celebration subsided a bit the day after the riot, when more about the inside of Washington Hall became known. The arms and colors of the principal continental allied powers united against Napoleon—Austria, Russia, Prussia, and Sweden—were displayed in the four corners of the hall and connected to an American Eagle suspended from the center of the room. The Bourbon and American flags surrounded a picture of George Washington. The colors of the lesser allies, including Spain, Portugal, and Rome and the Ecclesiastical States, were also arrayed. But, contrary to rumor, the British flag was not displayed inside the hall. Nor were any toasts made in honor of Great Britain. Morris and the Federalists had brushed against the line of treason without crossing it.

With the completion of the annual Fourth of July ceremonies, the fever of war seized the city. On July 6 an immense British fleet appeared off Sandy Hook. The residents of the city began to fear that the tragic events of 1776 were to be repeated with another British invasion of Manhattan. The city's defenses were known to be inadequate, and many remembered the ease with which the city had been taken in the first war with George III. Canadian newspapers brought into the city reported that thousands of British veterans of the Peninsular War had boarded transports in Bordeaux and were bound for America. The British were vowing to "chastise the savages" in the United States who had stooped to become "tools of the monster Bonaparte."

Several days after the sighting of the British fleet, news arrived of a great American victory at the Battle of Chippewa on the British side of the Niagara River. A few weeks later another bloody battle, Lundy's Lane, was fought near Niagara Falls. Our troops retreated to Fort Erie, which was besieged by the British.

July brought an end to John Randel's personal war. His nemesis, William Bridges, died. When I next played chess with him, Randel expressed neither joy nor relief. As he proceeded to checkmate me with his usual expedition, his only comment on the matter was, "Bridges completed his damage to me; the reaper has come too late to assist my cause." A few months later the publication of Randel's map of New York City and the surrounding area was ordered postponed out of fear that the enemy would find its exceptional accuracy to be useful to his cause.

Emily continued to speak to me only when speech could not be avoided. After two months of observing her, I concluded that my suspicions of infidelity were probably unfounded. The return of my health failed to raise my spirits. The fall of Napoleon had removed my desire to continue *The Age of Revolution*. Instead I decided to write two less ambitious books, one on the American Revolution and a second on the fall of Napoleon, from 1812 to 1814. My writing, however, was completely disrupted by the war. In early August, Mayor De Witt Clinton appealed to the citizens of the city to volunteer their services in the construction of fortifications to prevent a British invasion. Men were asked to volunteer by craft. Without charge to the city, I turned my printing presses to the preparation of leaflets exhorting citizens to work on the fortifications. Instructions for volunteer labor were also printed. The Republicans of the Tammany and Columbia societies worked on the fortifications on Brooklyn Heights. Not to be outdone, the Federalists of the Hamilton and the Washington benevolent societies sent men to labor on the Harlem works, which were to stretch from the East River to the Hudson. Each day five hundred to a thousand men volunteered their services. So great was the fear of invasion that newspaper editors for the only time within my memory excluded all acrimonious political discussions from the pages of the daily news. For one day all newspapers even suspended publication so that their employees could work on the fortifications. Students, masons, carpenters, free colored people, and many other groups, even men from New Jersey, volunteered their services. Foolishly, I spent one full day working with my fellow democrats and seventy free Negroes from the Asbury African Church on the Brooklyn Heights fortifications. An injury to my back forced me into bed for two weeks. For each day of my convalescence, I contributed $11.25, the amount announced by the Committee of Defense as the pecuniary substitute for one day's work.

In late August the first news arrived of the British invasion of the Chesapeake and of a battle at Bladensburg, outside of Washington. On August 27 the headlines of the *Columbian* blared TO ARMS—YOUR CAPITAL IS TAKEN! It was also reported that an immense army of British veterans from Spain had moved from Montreal across the border into New York State and was advancing southward along Lake Champlain. The army was estimated to contain more than eleven thousand of Wellington's fierce warriors. They were supported by a British fleet moving down the lake beside the land forces. The city was thrown into a complete panic. I joined crowds standing in the streets waiting for news. The newspapers exhorted the citizens of New York to be prepared to defend the city to the last extremity. Panic increased with the news that the British had burned Washington to the ground and were expected to move north toward Baltimore and then on to Philadelphia. Even the British blockade of the eastern seaboard had been tightened so as to strangle commerce. Because of the starvation caused by the blockade, in August the people of Nantucket declared themselves neutral and under the protection of England. Ships were unable to enter or leave New York City. The Long Island Sound route had been closed since the beginning of the year. Governor Tompkins ordered local militia units into service. Because my official militia unit was on the Niagara frontier, I was not among those called to service. I decided to volunteer only if the British army attempted to invade New York City. For the first time in almost two years, I removed from storage my musket, bayonet, belt, cartridge box, powder and ball. If the British came, I knew that, unlike the disaster at Queenston, there could be no refusal to face them; this time they would be attacking our own homes.

The burning of Washington seemed to end all trace of political factions. At the Green Dragon Tavern, I saw a vocal Federalist strike a man who told a joke about Jemmy Madison's flight from Washington. "Our commander deserves respect," he growled to his victim. At last there were no Federalists, no Republicans, only Americans.

By mid-September the news grew even more grave. The British had landed at North Point in Chesapeake Bay and had advanced to within a few miles of Baltimore. The great British army continued its slow advance along Lake Champlain. The siege of Fort Erie continued. New York was like a city besieged. The streets were filled with infantry day and night. Cavalrymen were everywhere. Guard outposts were scattered across the city. Soldiers bivouacked in open lots. Thousands of men swarmed around the Harlem Heights fortifications which ran in a solid line across Manhattan Island. Like my father thirty-eight years earlier, I was prepared to rush to whichever sector of the city's defenses the British chose to attack. Unlike my father, I had no children to defend who might be present decades later to continue the family tradition of military service in time of peril. I felt a strange kinship to my father reaching across the mists of time. But my generation was to be the last of the Careys. I was troubled by the melancholy fact of the extinction of our line.

The invasion never came. The terrible clouds of anxiety hanging over the residents of the city were amazingly dispersed in a single day. On the morning of September 15 I was awakened by shouting in the street. "Victory!" was the cry. After dressing hurriedly, I raced out into the street and asked a young boy what he was yelling about. "We've won, everywhere!" Skeptical about this incredible report, I went off in search of a newspaper. To my delight, the boy had not exaggerated. Never was there a more joyous headline.

VICTORY! NORTH, SOUTH AND WEST! In the north the British had made a combined ground and naval assault at Plattsburg, on the western shore of Lake Champlain. The naval battle on the lake had ended with the complete defeat and surrender of the British squadron at the hands of the American flotilla under the command of Lieutenant Thomas MacDonough. The naval defeat had caused the huge British land force to give up its assault on our troops and to retire in great disorder. In the south the British attack on Baltimore had failed. The commanding officer, General Ross, the man who had burned Washington, had been slain on the outskirts of the city. The British naval attack on Fort McHenry south of Baltimore had also failed. To the west Fort Erie had been reinforced and the enemy appeared ready to withdraw from its lengthy siege. Two days later an American sortie from the fort ended the siege, and with it the last significant action of the Niagara frontier. Although we did not know it at the time, the threat to New York had been terminated.

In October the city's fortifications were completed. Manhattan remained an armed camp. The fear of future assaults continued. At the end of October the State Legislature, which had Republican majorities in both houses, finally acted in a manner which, for the first time in many years, made me proud of my own political party. A new law was enacted which authorized the enlistment of two regiments of colored soldiers for three years; with the consent of their masters, slaves were allowed to join and thereby obtain their freedom at the end of the term of service. Another small blow had been struck at the lingering traces of slavery within the State of New York.

With the canal project dead, and because of my vow not to perform any work for Gouverneur Morris, I did not anticipate making any more trips to Morrisania. The remembrance of Nancy was a continuing ache with which I had learned to live. It was with me upon awakening in the morning and accompanied me into the arms of Morpheus at night. She was an insubstantial dream, a distant, mysterious siren enticing me onto the rocks of my own hopelessness. Although for years I had seized particles of information about her like a starving man picking at crumbs, I had surrendered the expectation of learning anything about her shadowy past. Then, in the forenoon of November 2, 1814, I received the most memorable of all Morris's summonses to Morrisania. Unlike previous calls from the manor, the servant asked me to return with him immediately. It appeared to be a matter of some urgency. Without a moment of hesitation, I agreed. The vow not to work for Morris was broken in an instant.

Sitting in the boat that memorable Wednesday as it moved along the East River, I shivered in the sharp wind. Heavy clouds blocked any hope of relief to be found from the warmth of the sun. I wondered if Morris had been angry at not seeing me after his "Bourbon speech" the previous June. My guess was that he had not even noticed my absence. He could not have seen my early departure. The applauding audience was standing and I had been only a few steps from the door. Besides, in the past, months had frequently passed without any word from him.

The reason for again being enlisted into Morris's service was a complete mystery to me. While the war continued, the Erie Canal project was dead; it could not be that. My first idea was that he was calling me about former governor Morgan Lewis, his old childhood friend who had been involved in the scalding of his arm. The week before, a story about Lewis had appeared in the newspapers. As usual at that time of year, militiamen had been appealing to be allowed to go home to harvest their crops. After constant refusals, several companies of the Rockland County militia had abandoned camp. When the crops had been gathered, they returned. As punishment, they were given the extra duty of marching for hours around Harlem. Major General Morgan Lewis investigated the massive desertion. After deciding that the men had good reason for returning home, Lewis wisely granted the entire Rockland County militia a leave of absence on condition that they immediately would return to the front if called. For this compassionate act, General Lewis was removed from command of the military district. In his place Governor Tompkins, a staunch supporter of President Madison, had been appointed the new commander of the Third Military District of the United States, which included New York and a substantial part of New Jersey. My surmise was that, in order to protest the removal of Lewis, Morris wanted me to gather information on the matter, including whether the Governor of New York could be granted military jurisdiction in New Jersey. Morris, I thought, must believe time is of the essence in helping Lewis. The only other matter to occur to me was the recent call by the New England Federalists for a convention to be held in Hartford. It appeared that the opposition of the eastern states to the war was about to result in the secession of New England from the union. Morris, I hoped, surely did not expect to involve me in this sort of treason. While walking up the incline to Morrisania, I prepared my responses. Morgan Lewis was a worthy cause, but I would have nothing to do with the Hartford Convention.

Morris was sitting in his library. Unusually subdued, he did not even rise to greet me. He gestured for me to sit. "It is good to see you. I have been ill these past few weeks. My gout again, just at the time I need the vigor of youth. When a man gets to be my age, he must rely on the energy of others." He looked and sounded very tired. "I need your assistance in obtaining information about the past. That is your special skill, is it not?" I nodded affirmatively. "You have always been discreet about our work. You've never discussed it with others."

"That is true. Not even with my wife." Morris, of course, missed the irony of my response. He continued to ramble in an uncharacteristic manner. Finally, overcome with curiosity, I bluntly asked, "What is the problem?"

"Read this." He handed me a lengthy letter enclosed in a cover addressed to him. But the letter began "Madam." It was dated two days earlier. In order to see who had written it, I glanced at the end. The letter was signed, "John Randolph of Roanoke." Nancy and Morris, I recalled, had spoken to the well-known Congressman in Washington when Morris went there to attempt to obtain federal support for the canal.

"This letter is to Mrs. Morris?"

"Yes, unfortunately it is." There was a sorrow in his voice I had never heard before.

"John Randolph is her relative, isn't he? You mentioned him when you came back from Washington several years ago."

"He is the brother of Richard Randolph, the deceased husband of Mrs. Morris's sister, Judith. But read the letter. Then I will answer your questions."

Holding the pages with my hands raised to the level of my chest, I commenced reading the communication. After completing the first sentence, my hands began to tremble. Fortunately, Morris was looking away, as if he could not bear to see me read it. In order to prevent Morris from seeing the state of my inner agitation, I lowered the letter so that it rested on my lap. In all my years of examining documents, I have never read one that astonished and horrified me as this letter did.

Greenwich St., Octo. 31, 1814.

MADAM:

When, at my departure from Morrisania, in your sister's presence, I bade you remember the past, I was not apprised of the whole extent of your guilty machinations. I had nevertheless seen and heard enough in the course of my short visit to satisfy me that your own dear experience had availed nothing toward the amendment of your life. My object was to let you know that the eye of man as well as of that God, of whom you seek not, was upon you—to impress upon your mind some of your duty towards your husband, and, if possible, to rouse some dormant spark of virtue, if haply any such should slumber in your bosom. The conscience of the most hardened criminal has, by a sudden stroke, been alarmed into repentance and contrition. Yours, I perceive, is not made of penetrable stuff. Unhappy woman, why will you tempt the forbearance of that Maker who has, perhaps, permitted you to run your course of vice and sin that you might feel it to be a life of wretchedness, alarm and suspicion? You now live in the daily and nightly dread of discovery. Detection itself can hardly be worse. Some of the proofs of your guilt (you know to which of them I allude); those which in despair you sent me through Dr. Meade on your leaving Virginia; those proofs, I say, had not been produced against you had you not falsely used my name in imposing upon the generous man to whose arms you have brought pollution! to whom next to my unfortunate brother you were most indebted, and whom next to him you have most deeply injured. You told Mr. Morris that I had offered you marriage subsequent to your arraignment for the most horrible of crimes, when you were conscious that I never at any time made such proposals. You have, therefore, released me from any implied obligation (with me it would have been sacred; notwithstanding you laid no injunction of the sort upon me, provided you had respected my name and decently discharged your duties to your husband) to withhold the papers from the inspection of all except my own family.

I laid them before Tudor soon after they came into my hands with the whole story of his father's wrongs and your crime. But to return:

You represented to Mr. Morris that I had offered you marriage. Your inveterate disregard of truth has been too well known to me for many years to cause any surprise on my part at this or any other falsehood that you may coin to serve a turn. In like manner, you instigated Mr. Morris to write to the Chief Justice whom you knew to have been misled with respect to the transactions at R. Harrisons, and who knew no more of your general or subsequent life than the Archbishop of Canterbury. Cunning and guilt are no match for wisdom and truth, yet you persevere in your wicked course. Your apprehensions for the life of your child first flashed conviction on my mind that your hands had deprived of life that of which you were delivered in October, 1792, at R. Harrison's. The child, to interest his feelings in its behalf, you told my brother Richard (when you entrusted to him the secret of your pregnancy and implored him to hide your shame) was begotten by my brother, Theodorick, who died at Bizarre of a long decline the preceding February. You knew long before his death (nearly a year) he was reduced to a mere skeleton; that he was unable to walk; and that his bones had worn through his skin. Such was the inviting object whose bed (agreeably to your own account) you sought, and with whom, to use your own paraphrase, you played 'Alonzo and Cora,' and, to screen the character of such a creature, was the life and fame of this most gallant of men put in jeopardy. He passed his word, and the pledge was redeemed at the hazard of all that man can hold dear. Domestic peace, reputation and life, all suffered but the last. His hands received the burthen, bloody from the womb, and already lifeless. Who stifled its cries, God only knows, and you. His hands consigned it to an uncoffined grave. To the prudence of R. Harrison, who disqualified himself from giving testimony by refraining from a search under the pile of shingles, some of which were marked with blood—to this cautious conduct it is owing that my brother Richard did not perish on the same gibbet by your side, and that the foul stain of incest and murder is not indelibly stamped on his memory and associated with the idea of his offspring. Your alleged reason for not declaring the truth (fear of your brothers) does not hold against a disclosure to his wife, your sister, to whom he was not allowed to impart the secret.

But her own observation supplied all defect of positive information and, had you been first proceeded against at law, your sister being a competent witness, you must have been convicted, and the conviction of her husband would have followed as a necessary consequence; for who would have believed your sister to have been sincere in her declaration that she suspected no criminal intercourse between her husband and yourself?

When, some years ago, I imparted to her the facts (she had a right to know them), she expressed no surprise but only said, she was always satisfied in her own mind that it was so. My brother died suddenly in June, 1796, only three years after his trial. I was from home. Tudor, because he believes you capable of anything, imparted to me the morning I left Morrisania his misgivings that you had been the perpetrator of that act, and, when I found your mind running upon poisonings and murders, I too had my former suspicions strengthened. If I am wrong, I ask forgiveness of God and even of you. A dose of medicine was the avowed cause of his death. Mrs. Dudley, to whom my brother had offered an asylum in his house, who descended from our mother's sister, you drove away. Your quarrels with your own sister, before fierce and angry, now knew no remission. You tried to force her to turn you out of doors that you might have some plausible reason to assign for quitting Bizarre. But, after what my poor brother had been made to suffer, in mind, body and estate, after her own suffering as wife and widow from your machinations, it was not worth while to try to save anything from the wreck of her happiness, and she endured you as well as she could, and you poured on. But your intimacy with one of the slaves, your 'dear Billy Ellis,' thus you commenced your epistles to this Othello!, attracted notice. You could stay no longer at Bizarre, you abandoned it under the plea of ill usage and, after various shiftings of your quarters, you threw yourself on the humanity of Capt. and Mrs. Murray (never appealed to in vain), and here you made a bold stroke for a husband—Dr. Meade. Foiled in this game, your advances became so immodest you had to leave Grovebrook. You, afterwards, took lodgings at Prior's (a public garden), whither I sent by your sister's request, and in her name, $100. You returned them by the bearer, Tudor, then a schoolboy, because sent in her name which you covered with obloquy. But to S. G. Tucker, Esq., you represented that I had sent the money, suppressing your sister's name, and he asked if I was not going to see 'poor Nancy'? You sent this, a direct message, and I went. You were at that time fastidiously neat, and so was the apartment. I now see why the bank note was returned—but the bait did not take—I left the apartment and never beheld you more until in Washington as the wife of Mr. Morris. Your subsequent association with the players—your decline into a very drab—I was informed of by a friend in Richmond. You left Virginia—whether made a condition—or not, I know not, but the Grantor would not, as I heard, suffer you to associate with his wife. From Rhode Island, you wrote to me, begging for money. I did not answer your letter. Mr. Sturgis, of Connecticut, with whom you had formed an acquaintance, and with whom you corresponded! often brought me messages from you. He knows how coolly they were received. When Mr. Morris brought you to Washington, he knew that I held aloof from you. At his instance, who asked me if I intended to mortify his wife by not visiting her, I went. I repeated my visit to ascertain whether change of circumstances had made any change in your conduct. I was led to hope you had seen your errors and was smoothing his passage through life. A knowledge that he held the staff in his own hands, and a mistaken idea of his character (for I had not done justice to the kindness of his nature), fortified this hope. Let me say that, when I heard of your living with Mr. Morris as his housekeeper, I was glad of it as a means of keeping you from worse company and courses. Considering him as a perfect man of the world, who, in courts and cities at home and abroad, had in vain been as-sailed by female blandishments, the idea of his marrying you never entered my head. Another connection did. My first intimation of the marriage was its announcement in the newspapers. I then thought, Mr. Morris being a travelled man, might have formed his taste on a foreign model. Silence was my only course. Chance has again thrown you under my eye. What do I see? A vampire that, after sucking the best blood of my race, has flitted off to the North, and struck her harpy fangs into an infirm old man. To what condition of being have you reduced him? Have you made him a prisoner in his own house that there may be no witness of your lewd amours, or have you driven away his friends and old domestics that there may be no wit-nesses of his death? Or do you mean to force him to Europe where he will be more at your mercy, and, dropping the boy on the high-way, rid yourself of all incumbrances at once? "Uncle," said Tudor, "if ever Mr. Morris' eyes are opened, it will be through this child whom, with all her grimaces in her husband's presence, 'tis easy to see she cares nothing for except as an instrument of power. How shocking she looks! I have not met her eyes three times since I have been in the house. My first impression of her character, as far back as I can remember, is that she was an unchaste woman. My brother knew her even better than I. She could never do anything with him."

I have done. Before this reaches your eye, it will have been perused by him, to whom, next to my brother, you have most deeply wronged. If he be not both blind and deaf, he must sooner or later unmask you unless he too die of cramps in his stomach. You understand me. If I were persuaded that his life is safe in your custody, I might forbear from making this communication to him. Repent before it is too late. May I hear of that repentance and never see you more.

John Randolph of Roanoke.

My head was spinning, my tongue struck dumb. Unable to collect my thoughts or to speak, I looked to Morris to bring a merciful end to the embarrassing silence. He uttered not a word. Finally I managed to ask a question. "What does Mrs. Morris say about this?"

Morris spoke in a very subdued, almost inaudible tone of voice. "She knows nothing of the letter. I don't have the heart to show it to her. She would be mortified. She is easily upset about her past, fearful of harming me and the child. If the scoundrel publishes it, she will have to be told. We may have to prepare a response to this libel. The ravings of a madman, but I must be ready to defend against them. That is why I have called you here. As you read, the letter mentions the Chief Justice. The reference is to Chief Justice John Marshall. Twenty-one years ago, at the murder trial of both Richard Randolph and Nancy, John Marshall was one of the defense attorneys. I have known him for many years. He is a brilliant man of the law and a fine gentleman."

"Then you know for a fact there was a murder trial?"

"Oh yes. Although it occurred while I was in France, I was aware of the scandal before we were married. Before entering this household, Nancy told me all about it. Her candor blunted the arrows of later gossip. Prior to our marriage, five years ago next month, I wrote to the Chief Justice, with Nancy's encouragement. He assured me of her good character. Now, I fear, we must again ask for his assistance. I would like you to take a copy of this letter to him. With Washington burned, he must be at his home in Richmond. Speak to him as my agent. I will give you a letter of introduction. You will find him to be most agreeable. Obtain his opinions on the statements in the letter. Get as much information as you can. Use your own discretion as to what you want to ask. Tell him we may have to publish a reply. You can assure him we will not use his name. Can you do it, as soon as possible?"

"Yes," I stammered. "Of course I will do it."

"Excellent. I am deeply indebted to you. I will send a letter to the Chief

Justice warning him that you are coming. You probably will arrive before my letter."

Morris presented himself as one who had absolutely no doubts about his wife. Having recently been wracked by doubts about my wife, I was certain that Morris, with much greater provocation, must harbor the seeds of suspicion about his own spouse. I imagined Morris sitting in front of his food, wondering if it might be poisoned. The thought made me shudder. One reading of that malignant letter and the seeds of uncertainty had been implanted in my own mind. Was the angel of my dreams actually a monstrous Clytemnestra? Was she the lover of a Negro slave? The thought filled me with revulsion. As a man who had always prided himself on his freedom from bigotry and his belief in equality, I, nevertheless, trembled with loathing at the image of Nancy in the lascivious embrace of a black man. From whence, I wondered, did this disgust come? Until that moment I had not known such a pestilent pool existed within me.

Questions began to tumble into my storm-tossed brain. "The letter is from Greenwich Street. Is John Randolph in New York?" Morris nodded affirmatively. "Could I speak to him about the letter? He might provide information discrediting his own charges."

Morris thought about my request for a few moments. "Yes. Why not. He has already done his worst. He can only harm his own cause. Yes. Speak to him. See the madman for yourself." As if in disbelief at the situation, Morris shook his head, leaned back in his chair and sighed audibly.

"Why is he in New York now?" I asked. "After so many years, why does he now make such charges? It is puzzling."

"Those are excellent questions," Morris replied. "Why now? I can tell you the reason for his presence. As you may have gathered from the letter, Judith Randolph, Nancy's sister, has a son, Tudor. The father was the late Richard Randolph. The boy is a student in Massachusetts, at Harvard College. Three months ago, in early August, he and a friend, a Mr. Bruce, came to Morrisania by packet boat. Tudor was very ill. He suffers from consumption. While here, his hemorrhages became increasingly copious. We nursed the boy for months. He was too sick to leave. Dr. Hoffman and Dr. Hosack both treated him. Nancy wrote regularly to Virginia to inform her sister of Tudor's condition. Finally, Judith decided to visit her son here. She came three weeks ago. John Randolph arrived about ten days later. He had been injured in a fall and was in bad temper. He only stayed here for one day and left. His carriage overturned on Cortlandt Street and he was hurt even more severely. Two days after his departure from here, Judith and Tudor joined him in the city. We visited him in Manhattan. He was in great pain. Several days ago, he sent me a note asking that I come to town immediately, to see him. The baby and I were both sick, so he was informed that we could not leave home due to these illnesses. Yesterday I received this letter written as if to Nancy but addressed to me and clearly intended for my eyes. The man has had a long career of libeling others. Maybe he was driven mad by the pain of his injuries and whatever slights he thinks he received at Morrisania. I am not aware of any. So he attacked with this absurd epistle. It is a tale written with a madman's malevolence. Who can plumb the irrational depths of such a mind?" Morris shook his head with a dark perplexity and then was silent for a few moments. "My boy, there is nothing in this farce of life which should be permitted to put us out of humor. We must remember that both happiness and misfortune are transitory. The reverses of life merely serve to enhance our appreciation of happier moments. This too shall pass." Morris seemed to be talking more for his own benefit than for mine.

"Could I speak to the sister, Judith?"

"No. Do not discuss this with her," he replied sharply.

"Why not?"

"Just do not! Forget about her," he brusquely commanded.

I then asked Morris a series of questions about the letter itself. He seemed to be fully informed of the trial of Richard Randolph and Nancy on the charge of infanticide. In 1792 Richard, Judith, and Nancy had visited the home of a cousin, Randolph Harrison. During the night, Nancy became ill. After they left, the rumor spread that Nancy had given birth and that she and Richard had murdered the newborn child. Richard and Nancy were tried for murder. There was no evidence against either of them and they were both acquitted. But ever since, rumors had stalked Nancy, even in the North. After the trial in 1793, Nancy had continued living, as she had done before the incident, at Bizarre with Richard and Judith. Three years later Richard became sick and died. Nancy continued to live at Bizarre, for many years after Richard's death, with her sister and John Randolph, who was usually away in Washington. Finally she left Virginia and came north to seek employment. Morris knew nothing of the charges concerning Nancy and the slave, Billy Ellis, or of the alleged poisoning of Richard. In the midst of answering my innumerable questions, a servant entered and announced the arrival of David Ogden. Morris told me to make a copy of the letter, to show to Chief Justice Marshall, while he spoke to Ogden.

After a few minutes of copying the malignant message, a task most disturbing to me, I heard Ogden's familiar voice bellowing from the drawing room. As it was difficult to determine what was being said, I moved to the door and opened it wide enough to hear the conversation. Ogden sounded quite upset about his financial difficulties. He was pleading with his uncle to endorse a note for $10,000. From the conversation, it appeared that Morris had previously signed the note as an accommodation. Ogden wanted it renewed. Offering a few questions but little resistance, Morris agreed. During the two or three minutes of my eavesdropping, there was no mention of the letter. They then moved out of the drawing room. The house was silent.

By the time Morris returned, I had completed my copy of the letter. The original was returned to him. He gave me the location of John Randolph's lodging on Greenwich Street and the Chief Justice's address in Richmond. In response to my additional questions on the letter, Morris provided little more information. He carefully avoided telling me about Nancy's version of the trial, like a priest refusing to reveal the confession of a penitent. When I asked about Mrs. Morris and the child, he informed me they were out, visiting with relatives. He did not say whether the relatives were his or hers. I wished him and his family well and departed.

That night I experienced great difficulty in sleeping. My mind was filled with an endless procession of questions. After weeks of uncertainty about the activities of my wife in my own house, I worried about the impossibility of reaching any conclusions concerning events in the life of Nancy Randolph which had occurred many years earlier. How could I investigate the past of a woman with whose charms I was madly smitten? Perhaps it is the irrationality of the lovesick male, but I must confess that the charges in the letter only increased my ardor. As a fallen woman, Nancy had become even more desirable to me. There was a reality to the thought of possessing her, a possibility of fruition, which had not existed before. It was only when the light of morning pierced the darkness of the room that I finally dozed off. The dream assailed me with an intensity I had not experienced since the first night after meeting Nancy Randolph, more than five years earlier. With the pain of the serpent's fangs stabbing my hand, I awoke in terror and confusion.

TWELVE

The next morning I was exhausted. My head ached with the residue of reverberating questions from the previous day. A new thought about the letter occurred to me. Perhaps it was written for political reasons. Had there not been an attempt to smear President Jefferson by claiming that in his youth he had made improper advances to the wife of his friend John Walker? Also it was said that he had children by one of his slaves. There was the story of Alexander Hamilton's illicit affair with Mrs. Reynolds. Perhaps John Randolph was playing the role of James Callender of poison pen fame. But Morris's political career was finished; there appeared to be no reason, other than revenge for his "Bourbon speech," to attack him. It was well-known that John Randolph hated President Madison. He was in agreement with Morris on the war. Before even rising from my bed, I concluded it was not a political feud but a matter of family enmity. Did not the great Tacitus write there is no hatred so bitter as that of near relations?

After preparing a list of questions in my mind, I set forth for Greenwich Street to make a morning call on John Randolph. My knowledge of the man was limited. He had become leader of the Republicans in the House under President Jefferson. At some point he and Jefferson had become political enemies. At the time, I could not recall the reason for the split between the Virginians. Instead of joining the Federalists, he made his reputation as a political rebel hostile to both parties. He was a formidable opponent of the French, of federal construction of canals, and of any government interference with the institution of slavery. He led his own splinter faction, called the "Quids," against the war. It was almost certain I would detest him.

Turning onto Greenwich Street, I was startled to see David Ogden walking on the opposite side of the street about thirty yards ahead of me. To my astonishment, he entered the very house which was my own destination. At first I was angry that Morris had sent Ogden to see John Randolph when he had already delegated the task to me. Then it occurred to me that perhaps Morris had not sent Ogden. I waited at the corner. After less than thirty minutes Ogden emerged from the house. He did not see me as he left.

The door to the house was opened by a small, black man with a deep voice and a thick southern accent. No doubt he was one of Randolph's slaves. After announcing that Gouverneur Morris had sent me to speak to Mr. Randolph about his letter, I asked the slave if Mr. Ogden was also sent by

Mr. Morris. "He didn't say, sir" was the response. After a wait of ten minutes, I was led into a dark room. The heavy curtains, hanging to the floor, were drawn. A narrow shaft of sunlight thrust into the room through a slight opening in the curtains. A man was lying in bed, his face shrouded in darkness. The exceptionally long bony fingers of his delicate hands were visible in the sliver of light streaked across a portion of the bed like a stripe of paint. The hand gestured for me to sit down. "Gouverneur Morris sent me to speak to you about your letter of October thirty-first." There was no response. I repeated myself and was again answered with muteness. After a full minute of excruciating silence, I commented on the cold, brisk weather. There was no response.

As my eyes became accustomed to the darkness, I could see the features of the man's face. There was something grotesque about him. It was the face of a child who had been suddenly transformed into an old man. Yet he was only a few years older than I was. There were the traces of great suffering, spiritual and physical, in the childlike face. He stared at me with terrible brightness in his eyes. As if in great pain, he suddenly turned away. After another minute of silence, a disembodied voice came out of the shadows. It was high-pitched, a tenor, like the voice of a young boy or even a woman. "My head aches. I cannot tolerate the sunlight. Excuse the darkness."

The voice was so filled with pain that I felt a twinge of sympathy for the speaker. At the mention of the letter, he was again silent. I decided to talk about something else. Briefly, I spoke of working for Gouverneur Morris for the past five years on the New York Street Commission and the Canal Commission. "I have recently returned from France on a mission for Mr. Morris. I was present at the battle of Leipsic and the fall of Paris." Randolph seemed to be listening and judging me at the same time.

At last he responded. "So, you saw the end of that great scourge of mankind. A modern Tamerlane. Bonaparte is one of those malefactors of the human race who grind down men into mere material for their selfish ambition. To think we helped that monster against the British. Their navy was our only defense against him. Fools. I warned them. Give to the tiger the properties of the shark and there is no longer safety for the animals of the land or the fish in the sea ... His fall should shorten our own mad war of agrarian cupidity. You know, despite my opposition, I served in this war. During this recent business, I was a vedette." He coughed like one well on his way to the graveyard. "It is not maritime rights started this war. They wanted Canada. We need the soldiers to protect us from our own slaves. The Yankee peddlers have sown the seeds of revolt among our Negroes. They infect the slaves with the vicious doctrines of the French Revolution and Toussaint L'Ouverture. When the night bell tolls in Richmond, the frightened mother hugs her infant closely to her bosom, uncertain of what may have happened. It tolled for Gabriel and will again."

"You said that in a speech, did you not?" He disregarded my question.

"The soldiers should be protecting that mother and child from slave insurrection, not invading Canada. But Mr. Madison, our Yazoo president, has been seized by the mania of power. He wanted Canada. We must have the frozen deserts of Labrador. Washington is burned black. New England is ready to leave the union. This war may end in civil war. Canada, indeed." His high, feminine voice was filled with contempt as he inveighed endlessly about the moral corruption of our times. "The Indians were not instigated by the British. They were invaded. Tecumseh knew they must fight or die. I am part Indian myself, a descendant of Pocahontas on my father's side. You look surprised. It is quite true. Her real name was Matoaca. She married John Rolfe and left an only son, Thomas, whose only daughter married Robert Bolling of Bolling Hall. He left a son, John Bolling, one of whose daughters married Richard Randolph of Curles, whose youngest son, John Randolph, married Frances Bland. I am the only surviving issue of that marriage—sixth in descent from Pocahontas. Her proud spirit flows in my blood. It is a race, you know, that never forsakes a friend or forgives a foe. Bonaparte was our foe, not our ally. Madison turns this country into one vast prison house. He is a foe. Ross is dead. He burned our capital city but he did not incite a slave revolt. More restrained than Lord Dunmore was. I do not count Ross as an enemy. She is a foe . . . not just of me, but of your friend Mr. Morris." He paused ominously. "She destroyed both my brothers. Theodorick shriveled and died in pursuit of her. She ruined Richard's reputation, which he treasured. She stole his honor and then poisoned him. The whore must be watched. Mr. Morris has been generous to Tudor and my family. I owe him a debt of gratitude, so I have told him about his wife. He should know he is too old to sire a child. He has been warned. My conscience is clear. She is a creature one must be wary of; she creates obsessions in men." He appeared to speak more in sadness than in anger.

He might be mad, I thought, but he is perceptive. "How do you know she poisoned Richard? Your letter says you were away from home. Do you have any witnesses?" Contrary to my expectations, he answered the question.

"It is true I was not present at Bizarre at the time of Richard's death. But the facts are known to me." His face was ghostly pale. He began coughing again.

"How do you know? Who was there when Richard died?"

"Nancy, Judith, Tudor, St. George."

"Who is St. George?"

"Judith's other son. Deaf and dumb. Now we fear he is going mad." He closed his eyes, wincing as if in great pain. "Latrobe was there too."

"Who is Latrobe?"

"Benjamin Latrobe. He was Jefferson's Surveyor of Public Buildings. The position was abolished when the war started. No loss in that."

"Do you know where he can be found?"

"As far as I know, he is still in Washington, unless the British got him. He is a well-known supporter of the French party. He was there when Richard was ill. I was away . . . God must have had a purpose. I often wonder."

He groaned. "And what is the purpose of this constant agony? On my way up north, I fell down a steep, dark staircase in Port Conway. I was unconscious for some time. My shoulder, elbow, and ankle were badly injured. Those wounds are not even healed, and it happens again in New York. My idiot coachman drove over a pile of stones from an unfinished house and overturned the coach. God thinks my pain is not sufficient. He always increases it. Why? Why!? . . . But Tudor seems to be improving. I raised that boy as if he were my own. I was his tutor. Had to renew my own Latin to teach it to him. I used the plan of Horne Took. The only time I ever punished that boy was to take away his Caesar when he recited badly. I wrote a note of disapproval on the title page. When the boy read my words, he was overcome with grief. I made that boy. Took him from his mother before he could speak. I was his friend, his teacher, and his father. Then I made the mistake of sending him to Harvard. They ruined the boy in Cambridge. He was forced to live in a style of great extravagance. He had to borrow money from that woman in Morrisania. The unpardonable negligence of his teachers at Harvard shall not be forgiven by me. Never!"

Finding it least difficult to ask him questions on whatever subject he happened to be rambling, I asked about Tudor. "Did Tudor say something to cause you to write the letter?"

"Leave the boy out of it! He is a child." For the first time there was anger in Randolph's voice.

"Why did you write the letter after all these years?" He was silent. "What is the story of the slave, Billy Ellis?" No response. "What are the proofs of guilt Nancy Randolph sent you?" Silence. "Is it not cruel and unjust to write such a letter after so many years?"

Finally he spoke, but in Latin. *"Justum est bellum quibus necessarium. Inter arma silent leges."* I translated in my mind, as he spoke: "War is just, for those to whom it is necessary. In time of war, the law is silent." He gestured for me to leave. Maybe Hobbes was correct; the condition of man is one of war, of everyone against everyone. *Bellum omnium, contra omnes.* Perhaps, I thought, he considered himself to be at war with Nancy. If he were a king, his armies would have invaded Morrisania.

"As a courtesy to him, Mr. Morris asks that you not inform anyone of my visit, including his wife."

Randolph smiled grimly. "All you northern gentlemen extract the same pledge of silence."

It was fortunate I had seen David Ogden. Immediately I guessed that Randolph must be referring to him. "Did Mr. Ogden say that Mr. Morris asked you to keep silent about his meeting with you?"

"I gave Mr. Ogden the same promise I now make to you. Therefore, I am not at liberty to discuss my meeting with him. Good day, sir . . . Johnny, show this gentleman out!" He closed his eyes and returned to his own personal darkness.

Walking back to the house, I was excited about my morning's work.

Randolph had revealed nothing to strengthen his charges against Nancy. Morris was probably correct. His letter appeared to be the ravings of a madman. Moreover, I had learned two important new facts. Ogden was connected to John Randolph in some way, perhaps without the knowledge of Morris; and Benjamin Latrobe, someone outside the Randolph family, was present when Richard died. Without asking Morris's permission, I decided to attempt to see Latrobe in Washington.

The next day I began the journey south. For the third consecutive autumn since the war began, I was following another strange path through unknown forests. If it were not for the war, a steamboat could have been used for part of the trip. With the British blockade, the land route was the only one available. The trip to Philadelphia was in one of those miserable little wagons used for that route. Sitting on a bench without a back, my own backache from the summer returned to add to the general discomfort of traveling. From Philadelphia, I moved by way of Darby to Chester, on the Delaware River, to Wilmington; through Havre de Grace, which had been burned by the British; to Baltimore. The roads were muddy. The coach frequently traveled in pouring rain, the only protection from the elements being the heavy leather curtains inside. The coach was so unstable in the rutted roads that the driver constantly had to instruct the passengers to move to the left, then to the right, in order to avoid overturning the vehicle. The coach sometimes left the road to try the supplementary trails cut through the forest. It was on one of these side roads we became stuck, hub deep in the mud. Even the shoulders of four male passengers pushing the wheels could not budge the vehicle. We were forced to abandon the coach and walk in the pouring rain for over two miles to an inn.

After leaving Baltimore early on the morning of the thirteenth, I reached Bladensburg in the middle of the afternoon. It was there, more than two months earlier, our army had fled in terror before the advancing British, leaving the capital to the rewards of British benevolence. Before six P.M. I arrived in Washington after a journey of nine days. The next morning I began to explore the capital city. It was clear why Morris always referred to the city as one fit only for future residence. It was little more than a small muddy town. The streets were a morass. The main road, Pennsylvania Avenue, was a country road with rows of poplar trees planted along the sides. Like many of the other streets in the city, the avenue extended beside a long ditch filled with stagnant water. A few months earlier I would at least have been able to view the splendors of the government buildings. Whatever fascination these edifices formerly had added to this ugly city no longer existed. For, with the exception of the Patent Office, the British had burned every public building, leaving masses of blackened ruins in various desolate areas of the sparsely populated city.

The Capitol was in rubble, a solitary wreck on a desolate hill. Every window, of what must have been an impressive edifice, was charred. A resident of the city, Mr. Timothy Bailey, who was present during the British visit, told me that the enemy soldiers held a mock session in the House of Representatives. According to the story, Admiral Cockburn assumed the speaker's chair and asked, "Shall this harbor of Yankee democracy be burned?" The redcoats voted unanimously in the affirmative. Thereupon, they piled chairs, desks, and tables with books from the Library of Congress and set the chamber ablaze. The heat was so intense that, when I saw the room, the skin of the Corinthian columns had peeled and the marble was burned to lime. The Supreme Court located in the basement chamber beneath the Senate was also badly damaged; it appeared unlikely that the court would be able to use it for a very long period of time. In any case, my informant told me the court was not in session in November, and the place to seek Chief Justice Marshall was, as Morris stated, in Richmond. Although he did not know the whereabouts of Mr. Latrobe, Bailey provided me with the addresses of two people who knew him.

The British had also burned the Navy Yard, the Treasury, the War and State Department Building, and the President's House. President Madison had to abandon his residence in such haste that British soldiers ate the banquet that was to have been served to the President, members of his cabinet, and other dignitaries. When they finished their meal, the soldiers benevolently reduced the executive mansion to a scorched ruin. The British even destroyed the offices of the *National Intelligencer*, whose newspaper stories they did not approve. In an act of barbarism which could not be explained as mere revenge for our burning of the public buildings at York, they smashed the presses and threw the type out of the window. According to Bailey, Admiral Cockburn, in jest no doubt, directed his men to be certain to destroy all of the c's so the American rascals could no longer abuse his name. One could not help but compare the mildness of the cossacks in Paris with the savagery of the British in our own capital city.

To my great disappointment, I learned that Benjamin Latrobe had moved to Pittsburgh the previous year, after his position as Surveyor of Public Buildings was abolished. Thoroughly dejected at the prospect of having to travel through the wilderness to a distant place, I told myself that time did not permit such a detour. Morris had asked me only to speak to Chief Justice Marshall. Even the authorization to visit John Randolph had been granted reluctantly. My report might be useless if not timely made. Accordingly, my tentative decision was to reject the journey to the west.

Having spent the early part of another day in Washington, I could bear no more of that mournful place and set forth for Richmond. The roads in Virginia were a quagmire, even worse than those between Philadelphia and Baltimore. After a few hours in the coach, hub high in mud, one of the horses went lame. I retreated to a nearby tavern with hogs roaming about the front door. There I was treated to my first "mighty hearty Virginia welcome." It was like every other inn in Virginia I later encountered, with billiard table and bar. As soon as I entered, the landlord asked me what game I was partial to, faro, billiards, or whist. At my answer "chess," he grimaced in disgust.

The inn was crowded with boisterous fellows, drinking and gambling. As in every Virginia inn, they were almost all either "colonels" or "majors." At the bar I asked for a cider. "We don't have any damned cider here. I'll give you some decent spirits." He poured me a flagon of grog which almost burned out my throat. The food was also like the fare in every other inn, some kind of pork dish served with a disgusting pulp called "hominy," which is eaten with butter and salt. After a few meals in Virginia inns, I learned to ask for "hoecake" or "johnnycake," a delicious meal of maize kneaded into a dough and baked until brown.

When not discussing gambling, the colonels and majors talked ceaselessly about farming and horse racing. My inability to discuss these subjects, as well as my northern accent, quickly identified me as an outsider, my permanent situation no matter where I went, Paris, Richmond, or even Manhattan. After a few hours of cards and billiards, I withdrew to my sleeping quarters, a completely bare room, except for two beds and one broken bench. The bed was covered with lice. Even in the absence of these vermin, I could not possibly have slept with the constant noise from downstairs of carousing, singing, and fighting. Just as I was finally beginning to drift off, two drunken louts climbed into my bed, squeezing me to the very edge of the mattress. Three more drunks staggered into the other bed in the room. Within minutes they were all snoring, leaving me alone, exhausted and wide awake.

The next evening fortune smiled upon me. When the coach stopped at an inn for the evening, a Negro dressed in livery offered the passengers fruit and cider from a tray he was carrying. He then invited me and another gentleman to accompany him to his master's plantation, which was only a few miles from the inn. We both accepted the offer of hospitality and spent the night at the mansion of a prosperous tidewater planter. Except for the sight of a gaggle of women sitting in the middle of the drawing room working at their embroidery, the plantation was not substantially different from the inn. The master had a billiard table and insisted on playing whist, according to the rules by Hoyle. In spite of the war, the conversation was focused on dogs, horse breeding, and tobacco farming. After a peaceful night of sleep on a clean comfortable sofa, I spent the next morning, an exceedingly warm one, with the planter's family. Just before noon of that day, I witnessed a scene that was profoundly disturbing to me. Two young male slaves, about fourteen or fifteen years old, served drinks on the veranda to the gentlemen and ladies of the house. The two Negroes were completely naked. The young women of the household paid no more attention to the boys than they would to a dog walking about in its natural state. Although I have seen slaves all of my life, never has it been demonstrated to me so forcefully that they were perceived as something less than human, another species not worthy of subjection to the rules of civilized behavior.

The following day I entered Richmond, the beautiful capital city of Virginia, located by the James River. One of the first sights in the city to afflict my eyes was a procession of manacled half-naked slaves. Attached one to the other, their chains were fixed around their ankles and fastened about their waists. The lamentable sound of the clanking chains mingled with the shouts of overseers and the cracking of whips reminded me of how insular were our efforts in New York to end this monstrous institution. Upon learning that the slaves were being led to an auction, I followed them to their destination. I was determined to watch and to learn.

The auction was held inside an old warehouse in a shabby part of the city. The buyers were a prosperous-looking group of men, well-dressed, many of them smoking, drinking, and taking snuff. The sale began with the least desirable males. The first was a young man whose left foot had been cruelly mutilated for attempting to flee north. He was presented as "a good worker whose running days are past." The second male had been castrated as punishment for an attempted rape. "No longer a stud, but still a good field hand." The auctioneer made it a major point of marketability if any slave had recovered from smallpox. "This healthy young buck now has immunity from the disease; he should give you at least twenty years of faithful work."

It was clear that the real interest in the crowd was in the sale of the females, among whom were a large number of what the auctioneer referred to as "breeder wenches." Unlike New York, fecundity is a major asset in Virginia for the sale of a female slave. For as long as I can remember, it has been a liability in New York, as there are few who possess either the space or resources to be able to care for the children of slaves. In the old days in New York City, an older female slave who had never had children would always sell for more than a young breeder. In New York, I have also seen skilled slaves obstruct a sale by announcing a refusal to work for a particular bidder. In that Virginia warehouse, such conduct would have probably ended in a severe beating or worse for the rebellious black. Harsh as slavery was in the North, it was instantly observable that it could not compare with the brutality of the institution in the South.

Ten young women stood in a line, facing the audience, at the side of the platform. Several of them looked terrified. "We begin with one of our finest specimens." The auctioneer prodded one of the most attractive of the young women to the center of the platform. "Gentlemen, eighteen years old. A fine breeder wench. Look at the broad hips. Many young ones will issue from this belly." He stroked her face and arms. "The skin is tight and soft as a baby's bottom." The girl closed her eyes as if trying to remove herself from the place where she stood by escaping into the recesses of her mind. "Start the bidding at four hundred." The bids quickly increased by increments of fifty up to $550; then they ceased. The auctioneer expected more. "Look at these fine teeth, gentlemen. This is a very healthy young wench. Beautiful features for a nigger. No further bids. Well, let us see what we have here." He slowly unbuttoned the girl's dress. Then, in a sudden dramatic gesture, he violently pulled her garment from her shoulders so that she was naked down to the waist. She attempted to cover herself, but the auctioneer grasped her arms and put them by her sides. "Look at those magnificent breasts, gentlemen." He cupped one of the breasts in his hand. "You will regret your frugality later." The sound of lascivious laughter rose from the spectators. The bids commenced again with a renewed fervor. The crowd was becoming agitated. Were I born into this society with the money to purchase such a woman, would I be willing to surrender my right to engage in this activity? The twinge of envy and desire, which I momentarily experienced, answered my question for me. No surrender; only a fight to the death. While the bidding continued, I walked out of the warehouse into the bright midday sun.

There was no problem in locating the house of Chief Justice Marshall. The first person asked provided detailed directions to the "Shockoe Hill" area. The house was a simple but handsome dwelling, two and one-half stories high and built close to the street. Opening the wooden gate, I climbed several steps to the front door and rang. A boy, about fifteen years old, answered. He informed me that the Chief Justice was out doing his marketing. Following the directions of the boy, who identified himself as John Marshall's son James, I walked to the market area and asked for the Chief Justice. My eye followed a pointed finger to a tall, lanky man dressed in a slovenly manner and carrying a basket filled with bread and greens. He appeared to be about fifty-five or sixty years old. I introduced myself as an emissary from Gouverneur Morris. He had not received the letter Morris had sent him about my pending visit. "It seems you have preceded the mail from New York." He laughed warmly, in an open, friendly manner. "The postal service has been very unreliable of late. The war, no doubt."

"Mr. Morris gave me this letter of introduction in case you did not receive the other one."

Placing it in his basket, wedged between stalks of leafy greens and a loaf of bread, he suggested that I come back to his house later in the afternoon. As we spoke, numerous persons greeted him and wished him well. Some addressed him as "Judge," others as "John." It seemed that everyone in the city knew the man. Both the whites and the blacks smiled at him. As he walked away, I watched him make his way through the marketplace. He lifted his hat even to the Negroes as they walked past him. The reason for his immense popularity was plain to see. The great Federalist had the manner of a true democrat. Less than a few minutes of observing the man and I already liked him myself.

Two hours later I again rang at the door of the Marshall home. This time a Negro servant answered. He led me to the side of the house and pointed to a small brick building in the corner of the yard. "He's in his office, sir. Expecting you. You are Mr. Carey?" I walked across the spacious yard and knocked on the door.

"Come in. Come in." Marshall's friendliness immediately put me at ease. His eyes were dark and piercing, but they seemed to sparkle with good cheer and graciousness. Although I knew his politics to be much like Morris's, there was nothing aristocratic about Marshall. His simple clothes and manner were more to be expected in a frontier lawyer than the Chief Justice of the United

States Supreme Court. After joking about the untidiness of his office, he proceeded to business. "Your letter of introduction from Mr. Morris speaks of a communication from John Randolph. Do you have it?" Taking it from my hand, he told me to sit down while he read it. Within seconds of beginning to peruse the letter, he shook his head in dismay. "Dear Lord." His expressions of disbelief continued throughout his review of the letter. After finishing it, he handed it back to me as if it were something vile which he wished to discard. "I don't know what could have possessed John Randolph to write such a letter. He is, you know, a very unhappy man. He does have a facility for slander, always has. But he is more to be pitied. He is always ill, in constant pain. An irascible man. This is also a bad time for him. Last year, he lost his seat in Congress. He is upset about the Yazoo lands, flooding on his own property, the war. Tudor and St. George have both been ill . . . St. George is Tudor's brother. Since birth he has been unable to speak or hear. A great burden for the family." He paused thoughtfully. "I don't know what Mr. Morris expects me to tell you about that letter. But I would be happy to attempt to provide any information that may ease his concerns."

"You were a lawyer for the defense at the trial mentioned in the letter?"

"Yes, along with Patrick Henry and Alexander Campbell."

"*The* Patrick Henry?"

"Yes, the great man himself."

Knowing that Henry was long in his grave, I asked if Alexander Campbell was still alive.

"Campbell committed suicide many years ago. He was supposed to go to Philadelphia to argue the Fairfax Land case. That would make it . . . the summer of . . . Well, I would guess he has been gone for almost twenty years. It's hard to believe."

"Who was the prosecutor at the murder trial?" I was looking for other persons to speak to about the case."

"There was no prosecutor. In fact, there was no trial."

In utter confusion, I interrupted. "But Mr. Morris told me he knew about the murder trial. Nancy told him about it before she came to Morrisania."

"Yes. There was a legal proceeding, an examination in the nature of a preliminary hearing before Justices of the Peace to determine whether the accused were to be discharged from further prosecution or proceed to trial. A Chapter 74 proceeding, I believe it was. There was a great amount of confusion about the applicable law. It drove the lawyers to drink. You see, at the time of the hearing, many of the acts of the General Assembly were suspended while being reprinted by Augustine Davis, the distinguished, precise, but very slow printer for the Commonwealth. Nobody knew which laws to cite. I have it here somewhere. These files go back years." To my great amusement, Marshall dropped to the ground, his long legs stretched out on the floor to permit him to look through the voluminous materials on his lower shelves. Feeling somewhat uncomfortable at having the Chief Justice lying at my feet, I told him not to inconvenience himself for me.

"No problem at all." There was a long pause of several minutes while Marshall looked through his papers and books. "Amazing how memory fades," he finally muttered.

"The case was twenty-one years ago. I often forget what happened last year." Marshall was too occupied by his search to respond to my comments.

After several more minutes of silence, he rose from the floor triumphantly, in his hand a collection of the Acts of Virginia from 1736 to 1794. The volume was dated 1794. He turned to Chapter 74, with a date of November 13, 1792, and showed it to me. "Be it enacted by the General Assembly, that when any person, not being a slave, shall be charged before a Justice of the Peace with any criminal offense . . ." There followed an endless sentence which only a lawyer could understand.

"You see," Marshall interjected, "the problem was that the 1792 act was suspended at the time of the hearing in 1793. See my handwriting here. 'Chapter 67 of 1788 must apply while 1792 act suspended.' Now it comes back to me." The Chief Justice's information on the applicable law was of no interest to me; but I must admit to being charmed by his astounding willingness to accommodate my request for information, even to the point of groveling on the floor. The man was so free of affectation he could crawl on the floor and retain his dignity at the same time.

After sitting back in his chair, he proceeded to describe the case with only slightly more detail than Morris. In October of 1792 Richard Randolph, his wife Judith, Richard's brother John, and Nancy Randolph, Judith's younger sister, visited the home of a cousin, Randolph Harrison, at an estate called Glenlyvar. Nancy became sick and went to bed early. During the night, she was extremely ill. The next day bloodstains were found in her bed and on the stairs. Within a few days she recovered and the visitors left Glenlyvar. After finding a shingle with blood on it outside the house, the slaves of Glenlyvar spread the story that Nancy Randolph had given birth to a baby on the night of her arrival and that Richard Randolph had killed it. Because it concerned one of Virginia's great families, the rumor reached all the planter families of southern Virginia. Richard's stepfather, Judge St. George Tucker, advised that the only way to end the rumors was to prove them false in a court of law. Richard followed that advice. There was nobody to sue for libel, so he demanded to be tried for the crime of murder. "There was no corpse and no testimony that a baby had been born. The panel of Justices of the Peace had no choice but to discharge both Richard and Nancy. Unfortunately, the hearing itself spread the story even further. It ruined Nancy Randolph's reputation and eventually drove her from Virginia. As you can see, the scandal has pursued the poor woman to this day. At the time, I advised against a legal proceeding. Rumors tend to die out in the end. Trials become a matter of record. But Richard insisted on maintaining his own and Nancy's honor. She is still living with the consequences of that decision. . . . Who can judge? Even without a hearing, the same scandal might have pursued her."

"What did Richard and Nancy tell you happened that night?"

Marshall looked perplexed by my question. For a moment he hesitated, and then declared, "That is information I cannot divulge. A lawyer is under an ethical duty to maintain the confidence of his clients, even long after a case is concluded."

"Do you know anything of the charges concerning the slave Billy Ellis or the poisoning of Richard Randolph?"

"Of course, I knew that Richard Randolph died several years after the trial. This letter is the first I have ever heard about a poisoning. Nancy Randolph continued to live at Bizarre with her sister and John Randolph for almost ten years after the death of Richard. It does appear to be rather implausible that both the brother and wife of the deceased would tolerate the presence of his murderer in their house for so many years. The Billy Ellis story seems no more credible. The letter would seem to be the ravings of a sick man. Tell Mr. Morris that if my wife received such a letter, I would advise her to ignore it. A response will only spread the story further."

We began to discuss Gouverneur Morris. Marshall had known him for years, going back to the American Revolution. "He was in Richmond in the summer of 'eighty-eight for the ratification of the Constitution by the Virginia Convention. He wanted to be certain we did the right thing down here. He supplied me with a number of arguments in favor of ratification to use on the floor. When he was in France, I regularly received his views on the French Revolution through his friend Robert Morris, who was my client in those years. I have always admired Gouverneur Morris's ability not to mistake despotism for freedom merely because the revolutionaries called themselves 'the people' and assumed the mantle of liberty."

When he began to speak about the war, it was as if I were listening to Morris himself. Like John Randolph, he blamed it on the desire to conquer Canada and denounced it as unwise, unjust, and against the wrong enemy. Rather than listen to another Federalist tirade against Napoleon and in favor of England, I changed the subject to Marshall's great work on the life of Washington. Although I had found the biography to be filled with Federalist bias, from beginning to end, and to be somewhat dull and legalistic, there was still much to admire. "I bought each of the five volumes as it came out in boards. Despite a lack of funds, I not only paid three dollars for each volume, but had the entire set bound in leather. They are kept among my most treasured books." Marshall seemed pleased at my praise. In the course of speaking of his biography of Washington, he related his own experiences during the Revolutionary War. He had fought at Great Bridge, Iron Hill, Brandywine, Germantown, and Monmouth. He also spent that fateful winter with the troops at Valley Forge. From his book I knew him to be, like Morris, a worshiper of George Washington. Thus, when he praised Washington's great skills as a military commander, I did not dare mention the fact that Washington had repeated the same mistake at Brandywine that he had made at Long Island, allowing the British to turn his flank as a result of faulty dispositions. On Long Island it was the left flank, at Brandywine the right. Although Israel

Putnam had been the local commander, my father always blamed the disaster on Washington's "inept deployment" on Long Island. I could, however, honestly agree with the Chief Justice's praise of Washington's leadership at Monmouth, Marshall's last battle. When he talked about the unreliability of militia, I told him of my experiences at Queenston. This led to a discussion of my own work as a historian and my trip to Europe. Marshall was so interested in my account of the conflict at Leipsic, he invited me to dinner so we could continue the conversation.

When we entered the main house, Marshall cautioned that we had to minimize the noise in order not to disturb his wife Polly, who was upstairs recovering from an illness. He carefully removed his shoes and put on slippers. The meal was served by a black servant. Marshall was definitely a man who enjoyed good food and drink. Despite his consumption of enormous amounts of Madeira, he spoke almost in a whisper the entire time he was inside the house. With the expectation of having him tell me about his role in "the XYZ Affair," I described my own meeting with Talleyrand. Marshall immediately launched into a discussion of Talleyrand's unlimited corruption.

In the fall of 1797, at the time of Bonaparte's victory in Italy over the armies of Austria, Elbridge Gerry, Charles Cotesworth Pinckney, and John Marshall had arrived in Paris as American envoys. Their mission was to attempt to settle problems between France and America caused by French seizures of American ships. Talleyrand, who was then the newly-appointed Foreign Minister of the Directory, attempted to extort a bribe from the new envoys. From Marshall, I learned for the first time that Tom Paine had been indirectly involved in the affair. Not long after the arrival of the American envoys in Paris, Paine had presented them his own plan of unarmed neutrality. Despite the fact that Paine was on good terms with the Directory, Marshall had opposed his plan and nothing came of it. I mentioned Morris's account of Paine's involvement years earlier in the bribe controversy involving Silas Deane and Beaumarchais. Marshall replied, "Twenty years later and Beaumarchais was continuing the same kind of scheming. The demand for the bribe to Talleyrand came, as you know, through his agents W, X, Y, and Z. That is how they are identified in our dispatches. 'W' was that same Beaumarchais who caused trouble for Silas Deane." Marshall recalled that X was Hottinguer, Z was Hauteval, but he could not remember the name of Y.

"The names of X, Y, and Z are something I expected never to forget; yet, you see, I have forgotten. I don't know if it's old age or too much Madeira. 'Y' has simply fled my mind." According to Marshall, Talleyrand's terms were a loan of twelve million dollars for the Directory and a bribe of five thousand pounds sterling, all as a prerequisite to negotiations. Talleyrand himself never directly spoke of the bribe, or *douceur*; he only spoke about the loan. It was his agents W, X, Y, and Z who related the requirement of a *douceur*. I asked Marshall how he knew that W, X, Y, and Z were representing Talleyrand and not actually seeking the bribe for themselves.

"There was only one direct link between Talleyrand and the request for the bribe," he replied. "Although Talleyrand later denied knowledge of the bribe demands, Gerry attended a private dinner with Talleyrand, X, Y, and Z. Hottinguer again asked Gerry for the bribe, and Gerry refused. When Gerry was later criticized for his conduct in France, he claimed that the dinner was not private, but a large public event, and that only the loan was discussed at that time. The fact is that Talleyrand's well-known habit of demanding bribes together with his appearance with X, Y, and Z, at what I know to have been a private dinner, leaves no question in my mind that Talleyrand was seeking the bribe through his agents. It is beyond a reasonable doubt, a standard of proof sufficient for conviction in a court of law."

"Do you think it is also sufficient to establish the matter as historical fact?"

Marshall was puzzled by my question. "You do not mean to imply that history demands a stricter standard of proof than is required by the law? If that were the case, most famous historical works would need substitute pages in many places with blank spaces marked 'conclusions not proved.' "

"Historians deal in broader truths, not the narrow issues considered in a court of law. In the sense that much more general information is required to establish the truth of a historical occurrence, it can be stated that the proof is more rigorous and demanding than is required in a courtroom."

Marshall seemed to be amused by my argument. "Insofar as history may look at the broad question of the corruption of the Directory and its effect on American-French relations, you may have a point. Courts of law are concerned with much more narrow issues. As to Talleyrand's personal guilt, history would accept the conclusion of law." Pausing for a moment, his face suddenly brightened. "Bellamy. 'Y' was Bellamy!"

At the same time Talleyrand was betraying General Bonaparte by not fulfilling his promise to go to Constantinople to ease the way with the Sultan as Bonaparte's fleet set forth for Egypt, President Adams released the "XYZ" diplomatic documents, revealing John Marshall's and the other envoys' resistance to Talleyrand's bribery demands. Marshall returned from France a hero. I remember his triumphant return to New York City and then to Philadelphia. But I have always considered the XYZ Affair one of the great tragedies of our history. The Federalists used it to discredit those who supported the French Revolution. They maliciously spread the false idea that the French party in the United States, led by Thomas Jefferson, obeyed the commands of foreign revolutionaries and would murder their fellow Americans in their beds if the orders came from Paris. Marshall was right to refuse to accede to Talleyrand's demand for a bribe. However, he and his fellow Federalists were wrong to use the venality of Talleyrand and the Directory to discredit the democratic ideals of the French Revolution. These were the thoughts in my mind as Marshall spoke about X, Y, and Z. Because I admired and did not wish to offend my affable host, I kept my thoughts to myself.

We ended the evening by discussing the damage done to the Supreme Court chamber in Washington. The Chief Justice indicated that it might be years before the court would be able to hold sessions there. He reiterated his advice to Morris to disregard John Randolph's letter. As nothing had been said that would reveal my radical views, we parted on amicable terms. Before leaving Richmond, I learned that Marshall owned several slaves but refused, for reasons of protecting their welfare, to sell any of them. That such a brilliant, kind, and unassuming man would accept slavery was another blow to my hopes about the possibility of ever abolishing the nefarious institution.

The next day I took the stagecoach from Richmond to Fredericksburg. My plan was to remain on the stage to Georgetown and Baltimore, and then to take the mail to Philadelphia. Tired of traveling, I had decided not to seek Latrobe in Pittsburgh. It was not even certain he was still there; I did not want to risk a fruitless journey all the way to western Pennsylvania.

Delayed by muddy roads and another lame horse, the stage finally reached Fredericksburg, where we stayed for the night. Early the next morning I was awakened by the sounds of screaming and the cracking of a whip. After hurriedly getting dressed, I ran out the door of the inn toward the ghastly noise. A crowd was gathered around a Negro tied to the pillar of a house. His arms were extended and bound in front of his body so as to lay open his bare back. A bearded man, his master no doubt, was beating him mercilessly with a heavy teamster's whip. "You deserve this, don't you?" the brute yelled before striking again.

"Yes massa. I been ver' bad," the slave screamed. Drenched in blood and perspiration, he pleaded for mercy, twisting helplessly, as if his movements would help him avoid the inevitable next blow. As the whip cracked across his bleeding back, he screamed in agony. Again the master shouted the question and the slave made the same answer, which was followed by another crack of the whip.

"What did he do?" I asked the man standing next to me.

"Probably nothing," was the reply. "Rogers likes to beat his slaves."

There are few sights more horrifying than that of a human being, under the complete domination of another, treated like an expendable chattel. For a moment I wanted to intervene. After looking at the faces of the amused spectators, including several smiling young children, I thought that discretion was the better part of valor. I remembered the beating administered to me decades earlier when I attempted to halt a similar flogging on the streets of New York. No longer a foolish youth who thinks he can correct the injustices of the world, I walked away from the dreadful scene. Age had worn away the delicate feelings of my youth, which, I knew, were based on false hopes of the possibility of changing the cruel way of the world. Nevertheless, I was disgusted at my own helplessness in the face of such injustice. Despite my increase in wisdom, I had experienced a marked decrease in satisfaction with my own conduct.

It was on the Old Post Road between Baltimore and Philadelphia that I changed my mind and decided to hazard a detour to Pittsburgh. My own curiosity, combined with a suspicion that Morris was most interested in John

Randolph's charge that Nancy had poisoned her brother-in-law, compelled me to act on the piece of information that Latrobe had been at the Randolph house at the time of Richard Randolph's death. It was possible that Latrobe could transmit a vital fragment of the complete story. It was a chance I could not overlook. Thus, the day after arriving in Philadelphia, I set out for Harrisburg instead of returning to New York. The two-horse wagon crossed the Susquehanna on a flat boat poled by four men. They indicated that the crossing of the river, which was almost three-quarters of a mile wide, could only be accomplished safely in the spring and autumn, when the water is sufficiently high to cover the rocks. After Harrisburg the coach used the turnpike through Gettysburg to Chambersburg, to McConnellsburg, and through the small beautiful village of Bloody Run in the midst of the scenic rolling hills of Pennsylvania. The inns along the way were more primitive than any yet encountered. After a very cold crossing through the Allegheny Mountains, I finally arrived in Pittsburgh. The grueling trip from Philadelphia had required more than a week to complete. I wondered if the additional delay caused by this detour might be fatal to my original goal of reporting back to Morris before he was compelled to respond to John Randolph's letter.

At the time of my visit, Pittsburgh was a dreadfully ugly place. On the approach to the small, hilly city, it was difficult to see because of a pall of thick black smoke hovering about the gloomy place. Most of the streets were not paved, leaving a muddy mess like in Washington. Buildings, factories, and squalid cabins filled most city streets, with an occasional mansion incongruously appearing among the shabby structures. Only the boats on the Allegheny River presented an interesting sight. It was a place I hoped and expected never to have to visit again. Indeed, I never have returned.

Having obtained Latrobe's address in Washington, I had no problem in locating his home, a new three-story brick house on the corner of Second Street. The area was on the outskirts of town in one of the less ugly parts of the city. My greeting was not hospitable. A disheveled, small old woman with a freckled face answered the door. "Is this the home of Benjamin Latrobe?" I asked.

"It is. He doesn't want visitors!" She slammed the door in my face.

In response to my second ring, the same virago answered the door. "I've traveled all the way from New York City to see Mr. Latrobe. It is important."

Before my statement was completed, she interrupted me. "He's in no mood for visitors!" The door was closed in my face. Again I rang. This time a tall attractive woman, approximately my own age, answered the door. Standing behind her, the enraged old woman yelled, "I told him to go away."

The younger woman intervened. "Kitty, please! I will take care of this." The old woman glared at me and then disappeared from sight. "Please forgive my housekeeper. You wish to see my husband?"

"Yes. I have come from New York City to see Mr. Latrobe on a matter of some urgency." The word "urgency" was a bit extreme, but I was desperate to see Latrobe.

"Does he know you?" She was very polite.

After introducing myself, I admitted that he did not. Uncertain whose name to use, I mentioned John Randolph, as the person Latrobe would most likely know. The choice of name was a mistake. Mrs. Latrobe stated that her husband had not been well, but invited me inside while she spoke to him. Within a minute she returned to lead me into Latrobe's study. He was sitting at a desk using a strange wooden contraption holding two pens. While Latrobe wrote on one sheet of paper, the second pen appeared to duplicate his writing on a second sheet. Latrobe rose but did not offer to shake my hand. He was a tall, handsome man, well over six feet, with very dark curly hair and dark eyes peering from spectacles. His face was serious, intelligent, and worn-out with worry. He appeared to be at least ten years older than I was.

"You say you come from John Randolph." He spoke with a trace of a British accent. His hostile tone worried me that Randolph's name was not one to open doors in this household.

"Actually, I have come on behalf of Gouverneur Morris of New York concerning a letter written by John Randolph."

"Oh, Mr. Morris. Then you are welcome here." His manner changed completely. All trace of hostility disappeared.

Because he was connected to Nancy's past in Virginia, I had assumed he would not know Morris. Having been proved wrong in my expectations, I refrained from revealing that Morris had not sent me. "I did not know you were well-acquainted with Mr. Morris."

"My wife Mary and I visited Morrisania on our honeymoon, fourteen years ago. At the time, Mr. Morris and I discussed a proposed monument to George Washington. Only a few years ago, he offered me the position of engineer to the Commissioners for New York Western Navigation. Three years ago, I was expecting to visit New York to accept the job from the Commissioners. Unfortunately, the trip was canceled and I had to refuse the commission. There is nothing I have wanted to do more than work on the great canal. But, it was not to be."

Without revealing my ignorance of Latrobe's involvement with the Canal Commissioners, I told him about my role on the canal project, including the problems with the inclined plane and my trip to France to attempt to obtain a loan. Latrobe was fascinated with the canal. He was obviously a brilliant man who had extensive experience with a number of canals, including the Chelmsford Canal in England. In conjunction with Albert Gallatin's national road and canal bill, he had developed a plan for a comprehensive canal system for the eastern United States. It recommended the connection of the Great Lakes and the Hudson River, a canal from Chesapeake Bay to the Ohio River, a Cape Cod Canal, a Raritan-Delaware Canal, completion of the Chesapeake and Delaware Canal, and improvement of the Dismal Swamp Canal. He himself had been engineer of the Washington Canal and the Chesapeake and Delaware Canal. He was thoroughly familiar with the Jesse Hawley series of essays on canals in the *Genesee Messenger*. When I mentioned my work with the New York Street Commission, Latrobe surprised me again by revealing that ten years earlier he had refused the job of regulating the Collect Pond in Manhattan. He had also designed a hydraulic system for Dr. Hosack and had visited the doctor's botanic garden. It seemed to me an astounding coincidence that Latrobe was connected with two different worlds, separated by both time and location, Morris in New York City and Nancy in Virginia. Was there some connecting link, I wondered, involving Latrobe?

In response to my question about his hostile reaction to John Randolph's name, he admitted to not liking Randolph. Expecting to discover the mysterious link, I was disappointed to learn that his hostility toward Randolph had no relationship to Nancy. The enmity was the result of his architectural work on the Capitol in Washington, including the House of Representatives, John Randolph's home away from home. On the floor of the House, Randolph had accused Latrobe of extravagance and wanton waste of public money. "The man is vitriolic and malicious; he impugns the motives of anyone who disagrees with him. When I responded to his charges by revealing that the shoddy work on the north wing cost nearly $100,000 more than my work on the south wing, Randolph and my Federalist enemies were not impressed. They argued that the beauty of my south wing, its sculpture, masonry, and furniture, were proof enough of my extravagance without regard to its cost. Did you ever hear of anything so crass? The man thinks beauty itself is extravagant and wasteful." He shook his head in disbelief. "Of course, my French name did not help. From the beginning, they correctly assumed I was in sympathy with the French party in Washington. The fact that I was appointed by President Jefferson provided additional cause for the hostility from Randolph and the Federalists. I was defamed for my republican principles and French sympathies in the capital of the world's only great republic. And I am an Englishman." He laughed bitterly at the irony of his former situation.

After confessing to my own democratic principles and partiality for the ideals of the French Revolution, I sensed an intimacy with Latrobe which had not occurred with any of the other men I had met as a result of my relationship to Morris. We both suffered from a common fear of persecution for supporting the very principles on which this country had been founded—liberty, democracy, and hostility to hereditary monarchs. We were both relieved to be able to speak freely instead of in the guarded manner one becomes used to after dealing with too many wealthy Federalists. Having established a common bond with Latrobe, I told him more about John Randolph's letter to Morris than I had originally intended. He seemed completely shocked at the accusation of poisoning.

"Yes. Randolph is correct. I was present at the Randolph estate at the time of Richard Randolph's last illness. The place had a strange name . . . Don't tell me . . . 'Bizarre,' that was it."

"You had some sort of connection to the Randolph family in 1796?" His negative response to my question was both surprising and disappointing to me. It seemed that the mysterious link between Morris in New York, Nancy in Virginia at an earlier period, and Latrobe was merely a matter of Latrobe's proficiency as an engineer and architect. His presence at Bizarre was nothing more than pure coincidence.

"You see, I had emigrated to this country from England in early 1796. Within three months after my arrival in Virginia, I was hired to make a trip down the Appomattox River as an engineering consultant to the Upper Appomattox Navigation Company. In the course of my travels, I stayed at Bizarre during a very bad storm. Since my arrival in America, I have maintained a journal of my activities. There is an entry on my visit to Bizarre. I am certain of it. Should be in the early part of my journal." Pulling out a stack of papers and notebooks, he leafed through his journals. With a triumphant flourish, he placed the appropriate pages in front of me. I eagerly reviewed the passage as Latrobe read over my shoulder.

Bizarre. June 12th 1796. Another French name, but not quite applicable to Mr. Richard Randolph's house at present for there is nothing bizarre about it that I can see. My misfortunes have followed me to this house. It rained violently at Horsdumonde all the night of the 10th and yesterday morning. At eleven I mounted my horse hoping to get to Mr. Venable's last night. I rode gently through the woods following a tolerably good road, and crossing first Guinea creek and then Green creek, both of which were so swelled by the rain as to be scarcely fordable. At the distance of 10 Miles I got to Colonel Beverley Randolph's, who gave me a very distinct direction through the Woods hither. The weather was excessively sultry and a constant peal of thunder from a very black Cloud to the SW hastened my pace. About ½ past 2 o'clock I arrived at the last Gate before Mr. Randolph's house, which I found I could not shut without alighting. I then perceived that I had lost my bundle and great coat from behind my saddle containing all my drawing materials besides cloaths of some value. *Heu miserum!* My philosophy was nearly worn out before, but it quite forsook me now, and I stood at the gate absent and uncertain what to do for a quarter of an hour, to the great astonishment of those who observed me from the house, till a heavy shower reminded me of my horse and the neighbouring shelter, and I rode on to the house. I soon forgot my personal loss at finding Mr. Randolph very dangerously ill, of an inflammatory fever. He induced me however to stay and immediately sent a trusty servant to seek my bundle, who in a couple of hours returned with it safe but wet. But this was not all. The Superintendants of the river, of whom I was in quest, had passed Bizarre that very morning, and rendered all my journey fruitless. It was no comfort to me that the voyage must be equally so; for the fresh that has been for a Week in the river must have rendered an examination of it impossible. From the moment of my arrival till 8 this morning it has thundered lightened and rained incessantly. The river however remains just within its banks. Mr. Randolph is much worse. His family however have shown me every attention and kindness in their power. He died the Tuesday following.

Petersburg, June 17th 1796. Mr. Randolph was visited about noon by a medical practitioner in the neighbourhood, Dr. Smith. He appeared a man of good sense. His opinion was against the probability of Mr. Randolph's recovery, though masqued by a long string of hopes and technical phrases. The weather cleared up about noon. I dined with the melancholy family of my host and immediately after set off for Colonel Skipwiths. . . .

"The entry about the visit from Dr. Smith is from Petersburg. I assume you did not make any entries in your journal for five days." Latrobe nodded in agreement with my statement. "Then when did Dr. Smith examine Richard Randolph?"

"It was actually the day after my arrival at Bizarre, the thirteenth. I spent only one night in that mournful house."

"What did the doctor say about the cause of Richard's illness? Did you sense there might have been a crime committed, a poisoning?"

"No. Not at all. The doctor referred to the fever, I vaguely recall, as some sort of a digestive malady. My impression was that he had seen similar illnesses before and they were often fatal. That was eighteen years ago, so I do not remember it very well. He did say that Richard was very weak with a high fever and chills. His guess that the illness was fatal proved to be correct. Poisoning might have been possible, but the doctor certainly did not suspect it. There is no way to determine the matter now. Obviously, I added the last sentence to the June twelfth entry at a later date, when I first learned of Richard Randolph's death."

"The journal does not mention Judith, John, or Nancy Randolph. Do you recall anything about them?"

For a moment Latrobe stared thoughtfully at the floor as he walked about. "John Randolph was not there. Judith, the wife, seemed to be very worried. A nervous woman, not very attractive. When she spoke, it was about religion. God descending to save her Richard or some such nonsense. It never ceases to amaze me, the despotism religion exercises over the minds of men and women. She and her sister barely said a word to each other. In fact, they said little more than the usual polite phrases one uses to make a guest feel welcome."

"And Nancy Randolph?"

"A remarkable woman. There was something in her countenance that was electrical. Beautiful in an unusual sort of way, a quality the chisel of Phidias could not attain. It was the only time I ever met her. I was so enchanted by her, I drew a portrait from memory after leaving Bizarre. It should be in one of my sketchbooks." He leafed through a large pile of superb paintings and drawings of people, landscapes, buildings, insects, flora and fauna, even illustrations of the works of Ossian. In addition to his considerable skills as an architect, engineer, and scientist, the man was a very talented artist. He turned to a page with two drawings on it. "In matters of art, I prefer the beauty of nature to the activities of man; this is a beauty of nature." I immediately recognized the sketch of Nancy, by her classically sculptured nose and chin. It was a profile. Nancy was facing to the left, her eyes and forehead concealed in an intriguing manner by a large bonnet, her dark hair flowing down her back. In the upper left-hand corner were written the words, "from memory." Latrobe picked up the sketch and stared at it. "I have not looked at this for some time. Even with her face half covered, she is striking. Virginia women, you know, wear large bonnets in the summer to protect themselves from the sun. Hers certainly did create an air of mystery."

Latrobe asked me about her. Too embarrassed to speak about Nancy in any detail, I said as little as possible on the subject. Not much more than a statement that she was still remarkable after eighteen years. In response to my request to be permitted to make a copy of his journal entries concerning Bizarre, Latrobe suggested making two copies simultaneously by using his polygraph. Writing with the marvelously advanced kind of pantograph, I found the motions of the pen in my hand were duplicated by the attached pen, just as if a scribe were sitting next to me copying my work. Latrobe said he had been using it for over a decade and found it to be indispensable. According to Latrobe, it was invented by a man named Harrington, from England. It was refined by Charles Willson Peale, who sold one to him. He proudly declared he had obtained one for Thomas Jefferson. The year after my return from Pittsburgh, I purchased a polygraph for my own use; I have used it to this day, causing my home to be twice as cluttered as it would have been in the absence of the contraption.

Latrobe and I enjoyed each other's company so well that I spent the remainder of the day with him. He told me that he had not been sorry to leave Washington, "a city of malice, pettiness, slander, hypocrisy, and fraud." After Congress eliminated his position as Surveyor of Public Buildings, he moved to Pittsburgh to superintend the building of Robert Fulton's steamboats for the Ohio Steamboat Navigation Company. In this enterprise he had been the agent of Robert Fulton himself. Earlier in the year he had successfully launched a steamboat called the *Buffalo*. The estimated costs of building it had been based on an earlier steamboat, the *New Orleans*. Because costs had risen substantially since the completion of the first boat, Latrobe had to ask his partners in the east for additional money. He had bitter words for Fulton, who had refused all his requests and was attempting to terminate their relationship. "I have extended my own credit to the limit. For a mere six or seven thousand dollars, the work could be completed. Without a full statement of reasons, Fulton and the directors give me all kinds of empty excuses and then abandon me in this miserable town. They have acted contrary to all our previous agreements. Everything I have earned since coming to this country will be lost. All the work I spent years with in Washington, the Navy Yard, the President's House, the Capitol, all destroyed. They tell me the British fired rockets through the roofs of the buildings and made bonfires in rooms I spent years designing. What is the point of it all? How cheaply human life and enterprise are held by the great workings of nature—war, pestilence, and time. We like to believe we are more important in nature than other animals. But we are not. In the end, we leave nothing but a scattering of dust." For a moment Latrobe seemed to be distraught. With a look of complete despair, he sat in a chair staring silently into empty space. Abruptly he stood up and invited me to see his nearby works, where the steamboats were constructed. We walked together for a short distance through the dreary drizzling weather to a large T-shaped building containing an inactive boiler shop and foundry, a blacksmith's shop, and a central room containing a great horizontal wooden wheel. This," my host lamented, "is my ruin."

After the tour of his works, Latrobe invited me for dinner with his wife and three young children, John, Julia, and Benjamin, Jr. The fare, which was very limited, was served by the irascible Kitty, who set out my meager portions of food and drink in a manner establishing that I continued to be an unwelcome guest. It was apparent that the Latrobe family was in straitened financial circumstances. Because Robert Fulton was one of the Canal Commissioners, I was about to suggest that Latrobe might be able to obtain work on the canal, with Fulton's assistance, if the project was renewed after the war. Mrs. Latrobe's harsh words about Fulton at the mention of his name caused me to remain silent about the matter. The members of the family all complained about the dullness and gloom of Pittsburgh. When the conversation touched on Napoleon, as all talk eventually seemed to, I mentioned my presence at the battle of Leipsic. The family was enthralled by my account of the great conflict. The oldest child, John, who was eleven, seemed to have a fondness for Napoleon, which I assumed had been passed on to him by his father. Latrobe surprised me by constantly interrupting my account with very detailed questions about my movements through Leipsic. As he identified landmarks, like St. John's Church and the Marketplatz, before I named them, he would wink at his delighted children. They, in turn, would giggle at my increasing bewilderment. "How do you know so much about the streets of Leipsic?" I finally blurted out the question in a mock dumbfounded amazement. "Do you know the street plan of every city in the world?"

He paused. His wife and children smiled as though waiting for him to complete the joke. Finally, he did. "The truth is, I was a student at the University of Leipsic for three years." The members of the family roared with laughter at the revelation of the secret they all had known.

Before departing, I asked Latrobe if he could make me a copy of his sketch of Nancy Randolph. I lied and said it was to give to Gouverneur Morris. Without a moment of hesitation and with only a few minutes of effort, Latrobe made a fine copy of the drawing. To this day the sketch remains protected within one of my large volumes, a treasured memento of the great passion of my life.

THIRTEEN

Small incidents and minor personages are the individual leaves making up the foliage of history. Distanced by time from the events of the past, a historian attempts to describe the dimly perceived shape of an entire forest. Because it is an impossible task to delineate each leaf or define remote events as the sum of the individual leaves, the historian must select trees, or even clusters of trees, to recapitulate the nature of the whole woodland. Thus, in describing an epoch like the Age of Revolution, the chronicler will tend to focus his attentions on the major events and persons of the period—George Washington, Robespierre, Napoleon, the American Constitution, the Terror, the Code Napoleon, the invasion of Russia, the battle of Leipsic, and so forth. Sometimes a small portion of a major event may be of significance, like the destruction of the Elster Bridge at Leipsic. More often than not, as time passes, such smaller events are perceived as through the wrong end of a telescope.

At this time in late 1814 I seemed to have wandered from the main road and stumbled down a small path leading to a little known crossroad. There was evidence that many of the great persons of the period had walked along this path on the way to a more important part of the wood. But the path appeared to be obscure and of no significance in charting the terrain of the surrounding countryside. Certainly, no sensible mapmaker would bother to place such a tiny trail on a map of the entire area. Nevertheless, I voluntarily wandered through its interesting terrain, farther and farther away from the main road. While on this insignificant route, my eyes were drawn to a single alluring leaf. Whether this leaf ever existed or not would have no effect on the forest itself, yet I was fascinated by it. Despite the fact that it was of no importance, I could not take my eyes from it. As time passed and the leaf continued to occupy more of my attention than the wood of which it was a part, I began to think that perhaps if it were studied carefully enough, it would reveal the essence of the place and time of which it was a part. This absurd but comforting delusion, which has remained with me ever since, first passed through my mind on the long and dreary journey from Pittsburgh to New York City. When I arrived back in Manhattan in the middle of December, within six weeks of the day of my departure, it was firmly implanted in my brain.

My task was to prepare a report for Gouverneur Morris. As a historian, my custom had always been to exhaust all available documents and other evidence before reaching any conclusions. The word "history" itself comes from the original Greek term meaning inquiry and investigation. In this instance there were few documents and the available information was contradictory and inconclusive. Because of the absence of accessible witnesses, obtaining the truth required knowledge of the hidden recesses of the mind of Mrs. Gouverneur Morris. Only she, of any persons I could speak to, knew the truth of the matters in question. Perhaps only she could ever know it. Even if she proclaimed the truth, many would disbelieve her, particularly if she insisted on her innocence; none could be certain of her veracity. When a historian moves from considering outward actions to the concealed motives of individuals, he must inevitably become hesitant and uncertain. To the extent that history is biography, it is a fitful groping in the dark.

There were a number of available sources, John Randolph's letter, John Marshall's knowledge of past proceedings, Latrobe's limited observations. My own experience has been that it is better to use a single reliable source than to prepare a mosaic from many accounts. John Randolph was a source not to be trusted. Certainly a totally unreliable informant should be disregarded. But the tendency must also be avoided to becoming so repelled by an account as to assume the opposite must be true. That was a real danger in the evaluation of John Randolph's letter. In contrast, John Marshall is as reliable a source as is likely to be found. Unfortunately, even dependable witnesses frequently contradict each other. Does not Arrian warn us that the most trustworthy of writers, men like Aristobulus and Ptolemy, who were with Alexander the Great, have given conflicting accounts of important events with which they must have been familiar, such as the execution of Callisthenes? In the end I knew that conclusions deduced by surmise were the best I could produce. Perhaps Gibbon best stated my difficult situation.

> The confusion of the times, and the scarcity of authentic materials, oppose equal difficulties to the historian, who attempts to preserve a clear and unbroken thread of narration. Surrounded with imperfect fragments, always concise, often obscure, and sometimes contradictory, he is reduced to collect, to compare, and to conjecture: and though he ought never to place his conjectures in the rank of facts, yet the knowledge of human nature, and of the sure operation of its fierce and unrestrained passions, might, on some occasions, supply the want of historical materials.

By the day after my arrival in New York City, I had completed a written report for Morris. In response to my note, delivered by a marketman, informing him of my return, Morris requested my presence the next day at the Tontine Coffee House. I arrived punctually and found Morris, in the midst of a group of his Federalist friends, engaged in an animated discussion about the Hartford Convention which had recently convened. Without interrupting the conversation, he greeted me warmly with a handshake and a smile. One of the group did not look favorably on the proceedings at Hartford. "For the New England states to be considering secession in the midst of a war with a foreign power is unacceptable. And you all know how opposed to this war I am."

Morris interrupted. "It would not bother me if the convention voted for secession. The union should be prized, but only so long as it stands for freedom. When we are forced to prostrate the credit of this nation for an unjust war, that freedom is destroyed. The debt for this monstrous conflict should be repudiated. Massachusetts, Connecticut, Rhode Island, and Vermont were right to refuse to turn their militias over to federal command. They should continue to refuse. The simple fact is that the people of the East can no longer reconcile their interests with the inhabitants of the South and West. . . . No need to look so worried. I have been in communication with Harrison Grey Otis. Secession is not a probable outcome. Too many moderates. Much will depend on a change in the three-fifths ratio. We all know that Massachusetts has many more freemen than Virginia but has fewer votes for the election of the President. Is it any wonder that three out of four Presidents have come from Virginia? They have now controlled the office for twenty-two of twenty-six years, and Madison has two years left to serve. When I was in Congress, the slave states got from three-fifths of their slaves a bonus of fifteen representatives in the House, more than the combined delegations of Connecticut, New Hampshire, and Rhode Island. The East can no longer tolerate it."

Morris's more moderate listeners, followers of Rufus King, no doubt, agreed with Morris on the need to change the three-fifths provision of the Constitution. But they were adamantly opposed to secession and charged the New England states with hypocrisy for refusing to turn their militias over to the federal government while demanding that President Madison use federal units to recapture the occupied portions of Maine.

Morris was not flustered by their arguments. "Gentlemen, those hypocrites now assembled at Hartford will, if they are not too timid, be hailed as the patriots of their generation. The Hartford Convention is a star in the east, to be observed with a renewed hope for the future."

Speaking not a word, I was content not to be asked to comment on the disgraceful proceedings at Hartford. When the discussion was finally concluded, Morris and I adjourned to a private room. Although he was interested in receiving my report, he did not appear to be a man greatly concerned about the matter.

Eagerly, I asked, "Have you told Mrs. Morris about the letter?"

"Mrs. Morris knows that Jack Randolph has attacked her character. She says he is a malicious liar. Of course, that was well-known before he sent his malignant epistle. . . . So, what did Chief Justice Marshall tell you?"

After delivering my written report, I summarized the most important points. Morris was surprised at Marshall's statement that there was no trial, only a preliminary hearing. As to the Chief Justice's assertion that there was no evidence of a baby having been born, Morris remained completely unmoved. He did, however, seem to be pleased by Marshall's conclusion that it was unlikely that John Randolph and Nancy's sister Judith would have permitted her to remain at Bizarre if they suspected her of poisoning Richard. Marshall's recommendation that no reply be made to John Randolph's letter evoked the first emphatic comment from my audience of one. "He is probably correct. Responses to slander generally serve no useful purpose other than to give wider circulation to the original lies."

Briefly I described my meeting with John Randolph. Morris was interested in the revelation that Benjamin Latrobe was present at the time of the alleged murder of Richard Randolph. Uncertain as to whether he would be angry about my unauthorized visit to Latrobe, I hesitantly told him about my journey to Pittsburgh. Morris showed no signs of annoyance, nor of gratitude, for my extra effort. He merely noted that he had wondered what took me so long. With great interest he read my copy of Latrobe's journal entry. He seemed pleased that Latrobe had told me that neither he nor the doctor had harbored any suspicions of poison. It must be confessed that I presented all of the information in a light most favorable to Nancy. Accordingly, I emphasized such points as Latrobe's statement that Dr. Smith had seen others with a similar fever. Beyond what he had already said, Morris revealed no sign of his own thoughts as to my conclusion that John Randolph's letter contained the totally unreliable accusations of a malicious, sick man, one who could be insane. "There is one more thing I must tell you, although it is with some hesitation."

Morris's interest seemed to be aroused. "Proceed," he murmured impatiently.

"Is there any connection between John Randolph and your nephew, David Ogden?"

Morris's eyes widened noticeably at the question. "None of which I am aware."

After describing how I saw Ogden enter Randolph's lodging in New York and Randolph's statement to me that Ogden had extracted a promise to remain silent about his meeting, I paused before proceeding with such a sensitive subject. Morris urged me to continue.

"I hope you will not think I am overstepping my bounds. The fact is . . . I knew David Ogden years before meeting you. My judgment of his character has been that he cares only about money and has no scruples about harming other people to obtain it." Morris did not show any signs of anger. I said nothing about overhearing their discussion at Morrisania on the day Morris showed me the letter. "It is mere conjecture on my part, but I suspect that Ogden's fear of being disinherited by your marriage and the birth of your child may have caused him to act in a wrongful manner. This is difficult for me to tell you . . . I think he must have known something about Mrs. Morris's past. Tudor's presence in your house may have given him the opportunity to dredge up the past in an attempt to discredit your wife and even to cast doubt on the paternity of your son." I had expected Morris to become angry and interrupt me. He remained silent and completely calm.

"Thank you for your candor. Your efforts on my behalf will be fully compensated. I shall read your report with great interest." There was a lack of warmth in his manner which immediately troubled me. I feared having done something Morris would not tolerate. He coolly shook my hand and hobbled out of the room leaning heavily on his cane. The sound of his wooden leg on the floor gradually faded out. For a considerable period of time I sat alone in that silent room thinking I might never again visit Morrisania.

Morris proved to be correct about the moderation of the Hartford Convention. Shortly after the adjournment of the convention, which sat from December 14, 1814, until January 5, 1815, its report was published. After referring to the dissolution of the union as a subject not to be considered in time of war, except as a matter of absolute necessity, the report suggested it might later be considered in time of peace, and then abandoned the subject of secession. The states were advised to devise measures to protect their citizens from the proposed conscription law in order to nullify the exercise of federal power in the northeast. It was suggested that the states be permitted by Congress to withhold from national taxes money for their own militias. Seven amendments to the Constitution were also proposed. These included the abolition of the representation of slaves (the three-fifths ratio), a limitation of embargoes to sixty days, a requirement of a two-thirds vote by both houses of Congress for a declaration of war, and a provision prohibiting the same state from providing a President twice in succession. Morris's hopes for more drastic measures were dashed. In an open letter he ridiculed the timidity of the convention. Unfortunately, I never had an opportunity to discuss the Hartford Convention with the great man. As I feared, a long period of silence between us had begun.

One month after the end of the Hartford Convention, in the forenoon of February 6, 1815, news of the battle of New Orleans arrived in New York. The previous December, a British force of 7500 Peninsular War veterans, under the command of Sir Edward Pakenham, brother-in-law of the Duke of Wellington, had landed near New Orleans with the intention of seizing that city and control of the Mississippi River valley. After two weeks of skirmishing, on January 8, the British twice attacked the American forces behind their entrenchments. The casualty figures were so astonishing, I did not believe them at first. The British lost over 2000 killed or wounded with an additional 500 captured; Pakenham and his two senior officers were slain in the attack. The Americans lost only 7 killed and 6 wounded. The British, contemptuous of the American defenders, had, as I assumed, made a futile frontal assault against fortified positions, the same arrogant error they had made at Bunker Hill four decades earlier. The repulsed British forces withdrew. The fact that our soldiers had so completely routed the conquerors of Napoleon's armies in Spain thrilled the nation. The city celebrated with an eighteen-gun salute from the forts. Tammany Hall and several other buildings were illuminated for the occasion. Despite the exceptionally cold winter weather, I was so elated by the news that I walked across the frozen Hudson River all the way to the New Jersey shore. It was a rite of celebration I had not performed since the vanished days of my youth.

Five days later the war ended for me in much the same way it had begun. Late in the evening of Saturday, February 11, I was working in my study. Shortly after the sounds of a commotion in the street reached my ears, Emily entered the room.

"People are shouting, 'Peace.' Can you hear them? I think the war has finally ended." The fact of Emily's entry into the room to speak to me was more startling than the news she announced. Since the beginning of the war almost three years earlier, she had not crossed the threshold of that room in my presence. There was a softness in her voice, an absence of hostility, which astonished me, as if a ghost had returned from the distant past.

"Let's join the celebration," I meekly suggested. Instead of refusing in her usual brusque manner, Emily surprised me by bringing our heavy winter coats and hats into the room. Together we walked into the cold night air. A light snow was gently falling on the streets, which were covered with the rain-soaked remains of an earlier snowstorm. Two young men were standing by a snowbank outside our home yelling, "Peace!" They informed us that the news had arrived with a British sloop. A treaty had been signed in Europe; the war had been terminated.

Emily and I walked up Broadway. She remained a discreet distance away from me. Within a few blocks the street was filled with a sea of rejoicing men and women. Many were shouting, "Peace! Peace! Peace!" Some carried torches which illuminated the wild scene. In some houses candles were lit in the windows. In others, windows were flung open, from which people waved handkerchiefs and joined in the exuberant chant of "Peace!" As we mingled with the throng of singing, shouting celebrants, Emily and I were pushed together. For the first time in years she grabbed my arm and clung to it. Church bells pealed throughout the city. Cannons firing salutes in the distance were audible over the noise of the wildly boisterous crowd. Emily looked up at me and smiled. She spoke but I could not hear her voice. My gestures indicated she could not be heard. "It's difficult to believe," she yelled. "It's finally over."

After two hours in the snow it became too cold to remain outside. We deserted the crowds and walked back down Broadway. Although we were no longer thrown together by the encircling mob, Emily continued to cling to my arm. At a street corner several blocks from our home, we halted to warm ourselves beside a huge bonfire surrounded by shivering revelers. It seemed most strange to have Emily holding me as though we had never quarreled. Without a word about the bitterness of the past, by a few simple gestures and actions, intimacy had been mysteriously restored. That night Emily and I slept together in our old bedroom. The war had indeed ended.

With the conclusion of the war the newfound unity of the political factions disintegrated. The Common Council selected an official day of celebration. When it was discovered it was the same day as the one previously chosen by the Washington Benevolent Society for its annual dinner, the Republicans moved the day back so that the celebration would be free of any taint of Federalism. One week after the news of the end of the war arrived, the terms of the treaty and the fact of its ratification reached the city. The treaty exacerbated hostilities between the political parties. The Federalists loudly proclaimed that the terms of the treaty proved the war had been useless. To my chagrin, I found it difficult to disagree with the Federalist position. That is not to say that the American negotiators at Ghent were unsuccessful. The British wanted the peace to be on the basis of *uti possidetis*, permitting them to retain what they had conquered, including a considerable part of Maine. The American negotiators demanded a return to the *status quo ante bellum* and obtained what they were seeking. With some minor exceptions, the British accepted a complete return to the conditions existing prior to the war. But the treaty did not address the stated causes of the war. There was no mention of impressment or blockade, no guarantees of free trade or sailors' rights. The treaty was silent about boundaries, commercial rights, or control of the Great Lakes. Although slavery was not an issue dividing the warring countries, the United States and Great Britain did pledge to secure the abolition of the slave trade; since both countries had already prohibited the importation of slaves, they could comply with the treaty by doing nothing. For this, Washington, York, and numerous other cities and towns were in ruins. Years before their time, thousands lay buried in the earth. Countless others were maimed in body and spirit, their lives shattered by the conflict. Like most other wars, it was a bloody, senseless struggle. As Morris and the Federalists claimed at the time, when a nation identifies a specific claim as the cause of a declaration of war and then concludes a treaty of peace which contains neither a grant of the matter claimed nor a reservation of the question for future adjustment, that nation has abandoned its claim.

Most Americans, however, agreed with the Republican declarations that the war was a glorious success. With some merit to their position, my preferred party contended that there was no need to mention free trade or impressment in the treaty because these matters ceased to be issues when Britain's war with France ended. America, it was argued, had resisted by arms what she asserted to be wrong until that wrong ceased. Also, a republic of free men proved itself able to withstand the onslaught, on land and sea, of the most powerful nation in Europe. America, they proclaimed, had earned the respect and admiration of the entire world. In a second war against George III, our nation had preserved the freedom she had won in the first war for American independence.

Few could disagree that there were elements of madness in the war. America had declared war chiefly because of the damage inflicted on her shipping by the British Orders in Council. At the time of Madison's war message to Congress in 1811, impressment had become a dead issue. But in the middle of 1812, several days before the United States actually declared war, the British withdrew the Orders in Council. Thus, the chief cause of the war ceased to exist before war was declared. With the Orders in Council gone, impressment had to be resurrected as the primary reason for continuing the struggle. The war became a conflict insisted on by the South and West in defense of the maritime rights of the North; but the North opposed the war. In such a mad struggle, it was most appropriate that the final great American victory at New Orleans occurred a fortnight after the signing of the treaty of peace.

It must be noted that I am not in agreement with Federalist claims that the battle was utterly useless because it was fought at a time when the war had already ended. For, the Federalists forgot that the peace treaty did not become effective until both parties ratified it. When the battle occurred, the treaty had not yet been ratified by King or Parliament, nor by the President and the Senate. In fact, the great battle was fought over five weeks before Senate ratification. Clearly, it is incorrect to assert that the Battle of New Orleans occurred in time of peace. Nor was the battle entirely useless. Had the perfidious British won it, they might have found a pretext for retaining the lower Mississippi. Did not the British in 1802 sign the peace of Amiens with Bonaparte in which they expressly agreed to return Malta to France? Although France did not violate the treaty—and it must be stated that Sebastiani's report on the reconquest of Egypt, the First Consul's yelling at Lord Whitworth, and French actions in Switzerland and Piedmont, were not violations of the treaty—the British refused to restore Malta. The simple fact is that the British never let treaties or the plans of others interfere with their own insatiable ambition for empire.

What a memorable year 1815 was. Before the British had even received word of the American ratification of the Treaty of Ghent, news of the escape of Napoleon from Elba arrived in London. When the news reached New York in the early spring of that momentous time, I could barely contain my glee. Emily criticized me for being more concerned about events which did not concern me than about my own daily existence. Her remark, I thought, exhibited a complete lack of understanding of my life and work.

Nothing like Napoleon's return had ever occurred in the history of the world. With eleven hundred men and four cannon, he landed in France. As he marched northward, all the soldiers sent by the King joined him. Just as there were constant placards on the Vendôme column when I was in Paris, new placards appeared which did much to explain events. One of these placards, later described to me by a witness to the events in Paris, stated, "Napoleon to Louis XVIII: My good brother, it is useless to send me any more troops; I have enough." With barely a single shot being fired or bridge being damaged, Napoleon marched across France all the way to Paris. With little more than a wave of his hat, he reconquered France.

The people of Paris welcomed the return of the Emperor with great rejoicing in the streets. Less than a year before his return, I had witnessed a celebration at his downfall. How does a historian explain such a phenomenon? Certainly the perfidy of the allies had much to do with it. During 1813 and

1814, while I was in Europe, they had proclaimed they were waging war against Napoleon, not the French people. However, when the allies emerged victorious, they stripped France of her natural frontiers and brought them back to the line of January 1, 1792. Along with humiliating terms of peace, the Bourbons, who truly learn nothing and forget nothing, attempted to restore the privileges of the old regime. The people would not permit the loss of rights gained over the period of a quarter of a century of revolutionary struggle.

The victors, who have written the histories since 1815, present Bonaparte as an international outlaw escaped from his cage. They fail to mention the utter bad faith of the allies and the Bourbons. Napoleon's wife, Marie-Louise, was prevented from returning to him. Her own father, the Emperor of Austria, arranged her seduction by the handsome Count von Neipperg. Her child, the son of Napoleon, was held in Austria as little more than a hostage. The Vatican even ruled that Napoleon's marriage to Marie-Louise may have been invalid, bringing into question the legitimacy of Napoleon's heir. The Bourbons failed to pay a single franc of the pensions which had been promised to the Bonaparte family in return for Napoleon's abdication and retirement to Elba. Less than four months before the escape from Elba, Louis XVIII approved a decree confiscating all the houses and other possessions of the Bonaparte family. Even Czar Alexander admitted that such acts were in violation of the terms of the Treaty of Fontainebleau. Little wonder that Napoleon did not remain on Elba, entrusting himself to the mercies of the monarchs of Europe. Yet as soon as he fled the island, those same monarchs, citing the very treaty they had disregarded, declared him to be an international outlaw.

My own excitement at the return of Napoleon intensified with the news that, after his arrival in Paris, he had issued a decree abolishing the French slave trade. This, after Talleyrand at the Congress of Vienna had succeeded in blocking efforts to secure general acceptance of an article abolishing that trade. What the Bourbons had refused to do upon their restoration, Napoleon accomplished with the stroke of a pen. In addition, a new liberal constitution was written by Benjamin Constant and censorship of the press was abolished. In April "L'acte additionel" was promulgated, whereby the franchise was extended, liberty of worship guaranteed, the state church abolished, and remnants of privilege eliminated. At last Napoleon had returned to his original role as the embodiment of the principles of the French Revolution. Finally, my support for the demigod could be without reservation. So great was my excitement at this miraculous resurrection, I resumed work on *The Age of Revolution*. For the first time in many years I became indiscreet about my personal views and openly espoused the cause of the French. Had I still been working with Morris, we might have engaged in some interesting and heated arguments. But during the entire period, I heard and saw nothing of the great man.

The news from Europe seemed to be the reverse of the events I had witnessed while there. The Paris crowds cheering the allies in 1814 were supporting Napoleon in 1815. Even the Saxon regiments, under the command of Wellington, those soldiers who had changed sides and fired on their French ally during the battle of Leipsic, mutinied. They ran through the streets of Liège, shouting, "Long live the King of Saxony! Long live Napoleon!" After attacking the Prussians, the Saxons were disarmed and sent back to Germany. Such startling events convinced me that the forces unleashed by the Revolution could no longer be suppressed. Alas, my hopes were quickly dashed. The euphoria of April, May, June, and July was obliterated by the news of Waterloo which reached New York in early August, six weeks after the battle had occurred. Eighteen-fourteen had indeed been the end of the Revolution; 1815 was a mere epilogue. So thrilling was that epilogue, however, that I resolved to continue to work on *The Age of Revolution* in the original ambitious version conceived years earlier. To this very day I have labored on that vast project. Napoleon's return sentenced me to a life of incessant drudgery. His Waterloo has become my Calvary.

Waterloo was a disastrous but thrilling climax to the career of one of the greatest military commanders in the history of the world. None can deny Napoleon a place in that pantheon, in which I would include Alexander the Great, Napoleon, Genghis Khan, Hannibal, Scipio Africanus, Julius Caesar, Wellington, and Frederick the Great. (Had Napoleon died between 1808 and 1812, his name would surely have to lead the rest.) Waterloo was only the second time in history when two of the most illustrious commanders had faced each other on a field of battle. The first, of course, was Zama, where Hannibal succumbed to the genius and good fortune of Scipio. Some might contend that Pharsalus or Lützen were such battles; but I would not include Pompey, Gustavus Adolphus, or Wallenstein in my pantheon of incomparable military leaders.

This unusual matching of immortal masters of war together with the decisive nature of the great battle have caused Waterloo to eclipse the fame of all previous Napoleonic battles. No doubt, the British genius for promotion of their own has added to the renown of the engagement. In fact, the battle was not a decisive event in the history of the world. Even if Napoleon had routed the British and Prussians, the remainder of his armies would have been hopelessly outnumbered by the hordes of Russians and Austrians advancing from the east toward the borders of France. The implacable hatred of Czar Alexander and the Emperor Francis for Napoleon and his revolutionary army would have made a peace settlement most unlikely. Although many have already forgotten, Leipsic was actually a more significant battle than Waterloo. Perhaps the fact of my presence at Leipsic may have swayed my judgment, but I doubt it.

During my brief period of euphoria, prior to receiving the news of Waterloo, I wrote to General Charles de Flahaut at the Rue Verte in Paris. My letter enthusiastically congratulated Flahaut on the return of Bonaparte. In order to support my praise for the return to republican principles, I enclosed a preliminary version of a section of my book, copied with my newly purchased polygraph, in which I compared Napoleon and Frederick the Great both as military commanders and as leaders of their nations. As it had become the fashion to compare the enlightened rule of Frederick to the tyranny of Bonaparte, I attempted to prove the superiority of Napoleon's broad-minded leadership. One of the best means of comparing the humaneness of governments, I believe, is to examine the manner in which they treat the most despised members of society. In this regard, the treatment by the two leaders of the Jews was particularly instructive for purposes of my argument. Under Frederick's laws, Jews were not allowed to live outside the large cities in Silesia and West Prussia. Jewish servants were not allowed to marry. In order to promote the sale of porcelain, Frederick, by decree, required that any Jew who wished to marry must first purchase a complete service of the best porcelain; the huge expense prevented matrimony among poor Jews, unless they could obtain assistance from their communities. On certain solemn occasions, Frederick, the great "philosopher-king," even required by decree that Jews sit on coffins, dress in funeral clothes, and hold slaughterer's knives in their hands. In contrast to such medieval barbarity, Napoleon's treatment of the Hebrews was perhaps the most enlightened in the history of Europe. Wherever his victorious armies passed, the walls of the medieval ghetto fell. He called forth an assembly of the Jews based on the Great Sanhedrin of ancient times in order to cause Jews to become assimilated citizens of France. Thereafter, Jews were granted religious freedom and political rights in all of France, except Alsace and Lorraine. In most of the communities of Germany and the remains of the Holy Roman Empire under French control, edicts of equality for the Jews were placed into effect. The Inquisition was ended. For the first time in European history Jews were permitted to become free citizens of the states of Europe. After the first defeat of Napoleon in 1814, the old Jewish restrictions and persecutions were restored all over Europe, and continue to this day under the laws of the "enlightened and merciful" monarchs Mr. Morris so admired. The pendulum of history had swung once again. Europe has returned to the religious monarchical tyranny which existed prior to 1789. After the thirteen long years since 1814, I fear that this new age of darkness will not end in my lifetime.

Three years after mailing my letter with the material on Frederick and Napoleon, long after I had forgotten it, I received a response. Flahaut explained the reason for the long delay. Some months after Waterloo, General de Flahaut had fled to England in order to avoid the wrath of the restored Bourbons. When my letter arrived in Paris in 1815, it was hidden by a servant. It lay forgotten, but unlike Marshall Ney, General de la Bedoyère, and so many others loyal to the Emperor, it managed to survive the White Terror of the aristocrats. Thirty-three months after it was sent, the letter was finally received by General de Flahaut in London. Thus began our correspondence, which has lasted for almost a decade. In that memorable first letter, written in impeccable English, Flahaut enthusiastically approved of my comparison between Frederick and the Emperor; he encouraged me to include it in my book. He also told me about his life since my departure from Paris. After Napoleon's first abdication, he had reluctantly joined most of the other officers of the army in signing an adhesion to the King's government. He described his swift repentance, like that of many others, of accepting the return of the monarchy. To my amusement, he recounted the horror of Parisians at the news of the burning of Washington, causing Englishmen all over the city to be pelted with garbage. As soon as the news of Napoleon's escape from Elba arrived in Paris, Flahaut went into hiding to avoid arrest by the King until he was able to join the wild celebration which swept the country upon the Emperor's return to power. With great sorrow he noted that his beloved Marshal Berthier had refused to rejoin the army. Berthier's name was struck from the register of the Marshalate. Overcome by remorse, Flahaut thought, Berthier jumped from a window in Bamberg after watching an allied army march by on the way to reconquer France.

In the new government Flahaut was given the assignment of reorganizing the army. He was present with Ney all day at the battle of Quatre Bras. Although he said he was reluctant to speak badly of the dead, he was quite critical of Ney's lack of planning during the campaign. After Quatre Bras and Ligny, he was actually present when Napoleon directed Marshal Grouchy to pursue the Prussians "with your sword in their backs" and "to remain in communication with your left wing." Grouchy's failure to execute these orders has already achieved the status of legend. After Waterloo, Flahaut was with the Emperor in the square of the Imperial Guard. He rode away with Napoleon, who was so fatigued he could not prevent himself from falling asleep. Flahaut proudly described how he prevented the unconscious Emperor from falling from his horse. "All night," he wrote, "I rode knee to knee with the Emperor." Following Napoleon's departure for Rochefort, Flahaut participated in the action of Rocquencourt at which the advancing Prussians were repulsed. After Paris was handed over to the Prussians, it was Talleyrand who prevented his name from being placed on the King's list of persons to be banished or executed. He referred to Talleyrand as his "guardian angel." It is probably the only time that man has ever been placed among the seraphim.

Talleyrand's assistance gave him the time to arrange his escape to England. Two years later he married Margaret Mercer Elphinstone in Edinburgh; ironically, his bride is the daughter of Admiral Lord Keith, the very man who had charge of Napoleon after Waterloo on the British ship the *Bellerophon*. Flahaut admitted that this father-in-law was horrified at the marriage of his daughter to a man loyal to Bonaparte. "Love conquers all," he wrote, "even the opposition of the British navy." By the time Flahaut's letter was received, in 1818, I had learned of how interested Morris might have been in the contents of the correspondence. Unfortunately, by that time, all hope had long since passed of ever restoring my communications with Gouverneur Morris.

During that distant and eventful year of 1815, I yearned to renew my relationship with Morris. For months I had hoped to learn of the events which followed the receipt of John Randolph's letter. I had expected to discover if

Nancy had been shown the letter and, if so, her response to it, including the effect of my report on that response. But for months there was not a word from Morris. In a futile effort to speak to him, I wandered about the fringes of Robert Fulton's funeral in late February, thinking that Morris, as President of the Canal Commissioners, would attend the rites for his fellow Commissioner. I did not see him. John Randel's contacts with Morris also seemed to have ended. The Legislature's reduction of Union and Market Place, in April of 1815, aroused Randel's opposition, but he heard not a word on the matter from the former President of the Street Commissioners. Out of desperation, I wrote a letter to Morris requesting the opportunity to discuss his years in Paris at the beginning of the French Revolution. When no response was received, I became convinced that my comments on David Ogden, his beloved nephew, had irretrievably offended him.

During the summer, Dr. Hosack informed me that Mr. and Mrs. Morris and their son had been away for months, visiting Morris's estates in the northern part of New York. When I wondered aloud about not having heard a word from Morris in nine months, Hosack stated that many of Morris's old friends had not seen him for a considerable period of time. "He seems to have withdrawn from society," Hosack declared. "It often happens to people who become old and infirm." Although I did not reply, my thoughts were that John Randolph's libel and not old age had driven the Morrises into seclusion.

For months I buried myself in the problems of history and the great period of revolution, recently concluded. With such a broad subject, I could not concentrate on a single leaf or tree of the forest in order to gain an understanding of the period. For, in this instance, there was a force at work greater than the forest itself—war. From belligerent colonists throwing tea into Boston Harbor, through the American Revolution, to the storming of the Bastille, from the conquests of Napoleon to his defeat, it was clear that *The Age of Revolution* was a story of conflict. After three years of direct experience with the catastrophes of warfare, I found myself contemplating more than ever before the relationship between war and history. It appeared to me that war was not, as Gibbon called it, the disgrace of human nature; it was human nature itself. It pervaded every historical period and affected every human institution. I even began to agree with Locke's characterization of slavery as a state of war continued between a lawful conqueror and a captive. Hobbes was correct. Life is a state of perpetual war. There are those who object to histories which describe a thousand battles which settled nothing, in a compilation of disconnected facts overwhelming the mind without explaining anything. To the extent these criticisms are aimed at the emphasis on political and military history to the exclusion of the history of art, commerce, and the human mind, they are justified. Certainly the construction of an important canal or the writing of a great book is a part of history as much as is the slaughter of thousands in the snow at Eylau. However, those who object to history as a description of endless butchery, who would avoid the subject of war, are averting their eyes from an essential part of history in order to transform it into something palatable. The inescapable fact is that war is a persistent and major strand in the complex fabric of the story of humanity. It usually reveals the primary historical forces at work in a particular period. Before a war, much of the activity of men and governments consists of preparation for the next war. Thus, a number of events prior to the Thirty Years War become incomprehensible unless it is understood that the Hapsburgs insisted on control of the Val Telline, the key pass between Italy and Austria; given British and Dutch control of the seas, the pass provided the essential route of land communication for the entire Hapsburg Empire. During a conflict, armies grow to enormous proportions and, along with huge groups of camp followers, form a class which lives on the rotting carcass of war. During the Thirty Years War the generals themselves were terrified their troops would mutiny if they learned of the existence of peace negotiations. After a state of belligerency ends, the boundaries are usually drawn in such a manner as to create the causes of the next war. The Peace of Westphalia, ending the Thirty Years War, was, like most such treaties, a mere rearrangement of the map of Europe in preparation for the next struggle, the victors having chosen the best lines for defending what was gained by the previous effusion of blood. In the brief periods of peace scattered throughout history, there usually exist large armies eager to engage in warfare and not inclined toward peaceful activities. When the Roman Emperor Probus attempted to have his fierce legionaries engage in the peaceful work of draining swamps while he foolishly announced his hope of establishing universal peace and eliminating the need for a standing army, his troops mutinied and butchered him. That is not to say that armies can never be used for peaceful purposes. Louis XIV used his soldiers to build an aqueduct to bring water to Versailles. Frederick the Great was able to have his army drain swamps and build dams. But Louis and Frederick also kept their men entertained with a steady diet of slaughter.

Weapons themselves have major consequences in the shape of events. Gunpowder, which spread much faster than did knowledge, caused the concentration of power in the hands of the monarchy as the only authority able to raise the money necessary for modern firearms and cannon. As a direct result, the power of both the Church and the City-State rapidly deteriorated. The distinctions between peasants and knights began to vanish when a base-born baker or shoemaker became capable in battle, by use of firearms, of taking the life of a wealthy gentleman clad in armor and mounted on horseback. The spread of equality into armies can be seen in our own day in the light infantry tactics of the soldiers of the French Revolution. Instead of being under the direct supervision of officers, light infantrymen in Napoleon's army were allowed to fight alone or in small units. Wherever these unique soldiers have moved, they have left a fervor for the ideas of liberty and equality in their wake.

War is omnipresent. For Machiavelli, it was the only branch of knowledge necessary for him who governs. And what of those who are governed? One need only regard the daily violence in the streets of the city to conclude that conflict is all about us, even in peacetime. Men use force against each other in the streets for trifles, or out of vanity, or for pure love of destruction. The conflict in the bosom of the family manifests itself in the relations among families and beyond. The war of individuals and families merely repeats itself in the sphere of international politics. The incoherent mass of overlapping conflicts spreads out in concentric circles, as is seen when many rocks are simultaneously thrown into a pond, until the complexity of the struggles increases beyond the comprehension of an individual person. *Bellum omnium pater.* War is the begetter of all things. Unfortunately, that which is begotten appears to be without purpose or meaning. The battles and people of history are all ephemeral. It is only war which survives to repeat itself in endless cycles of misery.

My study of history has always been accompanied by the hope it would help to illuminate the future. Perhaps by understanding war, I thought, one could discover how to eliminate it; maybe progress is an inevitable part of the process of history. But the collapse of revolutionary ideals has ended my ideas of progress being linked to history, which now appears to me to be a series of disconnected events rather than a logical process. The more I examine the past, the more grim appears to be the future. Men do not seem to learn from the errors of others. Each generation refuses to heed the mistakes of its parents. The children are compelled to repeat them, to have to learn the bitter lesson again and again.

By the autumn of 1815 my own future was beginning to trouble me more than the future of mankind. Within months I would attain the age of forty. My own mortality was becoming a palpable reality. Conscious of the great speed with which more than one-half of my allotted biblical three score and ten years had passed, I was painfully aware of the shortness of the remainder of my life's journey. With increasing frequency I found myself staring at funerals and cemeteries, contemplating the inevitability of the grave. After the severance of my relationship with Mr. Morris and the end of the war, my life had again become stale and flat. It was as though the six wonderful years with Gouverneur Morris, the most memorable of my life, had never occurred. Emily and I had also returned to our former mode of living. Although there was an absence of conflict between us, our life together was also without passion. My days of forced celibacy were over, but I was as lonely as at any time in the past. Even in the midst of an attempted plunge into carnal oblivion, Emily would introduce the petty concerns of the day. There was no escape from my mundane existence.

It has been said that a woman is a young man's mistress, a companion for middle age, and the nurse of an old man. Emily was little more than a companion while my yearnings were those of a young man. How I longed to see Nancy again. She alone, I knew, could restore me to life.

When my hopes were at a low ebb late in 1815, a series of events began which renewed my expectation of reestablishing a working relationship with Gouverneur Morris. Two of the Canal Commissioners, De Witt Clinton and

Thomas Eddy, with the assistance of Judge Platt, started a movement in New York City to revive the canal. Cards of invitation were sent to one hundred men to meet at City Hall. Although not invited, I followed the proceedings with great interest. Judge Platt openly urged the formal abandonment of any consideration, even in part, of the inclined plane. Clinton was appointed to head a committee to persuade the Legislature to continue the work which had halted with the declaration of war. Meetings were held in support of the canal at Albany, Buffalo, Canandaigua, Geneva, Onondaga, and Utica. As a result, more than 100,000 citizens petitioned the Legislature to build the canal. Even the Common Council of New York City addressed a memorial to the Legislature in favor of the project.

In March of 1816 the Canal Commissioners made their first report in two years. John Randel, who continued to be friendly with Commissioner Simeon De Witt, obtained a copy and showed it to me. The report urged the Legislature to furnish funds to hire a professional engineer. Stating there were few competent persons available in Europe, it was suggested that an American be hired for the job. There was not a word in favor of inclined planes, even for portions of the canal. To my great shock and surprise, the last page of the report did not contain the signature of the President of the Canal Commissioners. Immediately, I asked Randel why Morris had not signed.

"Simeon De Witt told me that Morris was adamant on the subject of using the inclined plane at certain points along the canal route. He also wanted to hire a European engineer, even though Mr. Weston, the Englishman, refused the job. Simeon supported Morris's draft report. All of the other Commissioners voted against him and prepared their own report. Morris was deeply offended by his loss of influence. He refused to sign the report and has withdrawn from active participation. The other Commissioners have been proceeding without him." Unfortunately, Randel knew nothing about Morris's personal life.

The news of the search for an engineer did cause me to write to Benjamin Latrobe in Pittsburgh with the expectation that he might be interested in the position. To my great disappointment, I received no reply. It was some time later that I learned the Latrobe family had returned to Washington the previous year. Latrobe was engaged in the restoration of the Capitol. He had never received my letter.

One month after the publication of the report of the Canal Commissioners, my hopes of working again with Morris on the canal were completely obliterated. On April 17, 1816, the Legislature enacted a law providing $20,000 for making additional surveys and plans. Part of the statute altered the composition of the Canal Commission. Gouverneur Morris, and his ally Simeon De Witt, were no longer Commissioners. General Peter Porter, who was then busy determining the boundary line between the United States and Canada, was also not reappointed. The new Canal Commission consisted of Stephen Van Rensselaer, De Witt Clinton, Samuel Young, Joseph Ellicott, and Myron Holley. I was acquainted only slightly with Clinton, and did not look forward to discussing my heroic activities at Queenston with my former commanding officer, Stephen Van Rensselaer. My association with the Canal Commissioners, I knew, was at an end.

That summer the chill in my soul was not to be thawed by the warm sun of the season. For reasons nobody has been able to explain, there was no heat of summer in 1816. Several times it actually snowed. It was so cold the snow stayed on the ground for days when people ordinarily would be swimming. The harvest was disasterously bad. Some proclaimed it was a sign of God's wrath; the Day of Judgment, it was prophesied, was near. My mind was too engaged with the loss of the glories of Morrisania to be concerned with the termination of God's grace. The hopelessness of ever seeing Nancy again was painfully apparent to me. Once again, by an act of the will, I attempted to smother the flame burning in my heart for her; as always, it could not be extinguished. While endeavoring to write the history of the period from 1775 to 1815, for now there was a definite ending to my chronicle, I found myself wondering constantly about the personal history of Nancy Randolph, which coincided almost perfectly with the years of *The Age of Revolution* and of my own life. It must be admitted, I would have preferred to write the story of her life rather than the history of the age. Is not love the desire to know another in every way? It was inevitable that numerous historians would write about the great period recently concluded. Except for me, who would ever be interested in preserving the story of that one historically insignificant life?

Twenty long months had passed since I had last spoken to Gouverneur Morris. Suddenly the opportunity arose to see him in the flesh. In August of that miserable summer of 1816, Dr. Hosack informed me that Morris, as the new President of the New-York Historical Society, would be delivering the principal address on the occasion of the 207th anniversary of the discovery of New York. The meeting of the society was to be held at City Hall on September 4, 1816. At the time, no doubt because many of the members considered me to be a papist, I had not yet been invited to join the society. Knowing of my eagerness to speak to Morris, Dr. Hosack encouraged me to attend the meeting.

The day of the speech was a cold, rainy Wednesday. Summer had run its course without the intercession of warm weather. Just before the beginning of the speech, the great man entered the room with Dr. Hosack by his side. There was no doubt that he had visibly aged since I last set eyes on him. His walk was slower and more laborious than his previous energetic gait. His skin color was a sickly white. Cane in hand, he limped to the podium. In a voice as impressive as it had always been, he delivered a speech on the nature of history. As the new President of the Historical Society, he questioned history itself, the so-called "science of human nature." Facts, he declared, as well as motives, are frequently misrepresented in history. Events are attributed to causes which never existed, while the real causes remain concealed. Perhaps, he stated, more useful knowledge of the nature of man may be derived from the perceptions of Shakespeare than from the writing of Hume. Insofar as the Bible revealed human nature, he found it most instructive as a clue to all other history. A profound knowledge of human nature, he stated, was a necessary attribute of a good historian.

Morris declared that history and law are sister sciences which support and enlighten each other. His comments on war were of particular interest to me. War, he stated, "fruitful as it is with misery and woe," is nevertheless "medicinal to a nation" infected with foreign pollution and other ills such as the excess of selfish enjoyment. It was only when Morris began to speak about religion as essential to society that I began to find myself in disagreement with his words. Desiring to be in as friendly a mood as possible, I labored to stifle unpleasant memories of his odious Bourbon speech.

At the conclusion of his presentation, he was surrounded by well-wishers. Like a teacher encircled by eager students, he answered questions about the themes of his discourse. One perceptive questioner asked him if his praise of Shakespeare and the Bible, as useful for understanding human nature, implied that it is individuals who control history. Morris shook his head in disagreement. "No. Certainly not. In the study of historical facts, we too often ascribe to individuals the events which are produced by general causes."

As this was a subject dear to my heart, I entered the fray with my own question. "Surely you do not mean to say that a great leader, like Napoleon, does not control events by the strength of his individual will. For example, if Napoleon had died in Moscow in 1812, the war in Europe would not have continued for an additional three years."

Morris smiled at my question and acknowledged my presence with a slight nod of greeting. "Bonaparte is an extreme example of the power of an individual to affect history. Of course, he had the assistance of his patron saint, Beelzebub." For a few moments loud laughter interrupted his reply. "The tendency with strong leaders is to conclude that they occasion everything. My own experience indicates that it is the great mass of the people who control events, including the actions of those leaders. History can aid us to foresee what will be the conduct of a mass of men in given circumstances, just as it is possible to predict what an individual will do by means of a knowledge of his ruling passions and weaknesses. Otherwise, Providence has reserved to itself the knowledge of future events." Before he could continue with his answer, he was asked about the Treaty of Ghent ending our war with the British. "Treaties are very frail things," he replied. "It is good fleets and armies directed by prudent leaders which are to be relied on. With the need for wise leaders in mind, I hope that Rufus King will soon be President of this great country." The group surrounding him loudly applauded his sentiments, in anticipation of a return to federal leadership with the November elections. Morris bid farewell to the crowd and then gestured for me to remain with him.

"It has been a long time, Daniel. I hope all is well with you." His manner was friendly.

"Yes, all is well," I replied. "And how goes it with you, your wife and son?"

"They are both in excellent health, despite this wretched weather. I have been ill quite frequently. The sicknesses depart but, as you can see, leave traces of their passage. Old age is a trial, believe me. By depriving us of our health and friends, God gradually severs us from this world we must at last leave." He sighed audibly. The exertion of delivering his speech appeared to have tired him. I wondered if his statements about his poor health were meant as an apology for not speaking to me for so long a period of time.

"Did you receive the note I sent you last year?"

"You sent a note? I have no recollection of seeing it. What was the subject?"

"I wanted to speak to you about your experience in France during the Revolution . . . for my book."

Morris appeared to be confused. "No. I never received it. We were away for a considerable period of time. You, of course, are welcome to visit Morrisania. We can have a long discussion on the subject, like old times. It has . . ." He looked up at the approach of David Ogden from across the room. To my surprise, Morris whispered to me, "My nephew intends to give us the pleasure of his company so we may not have the pleasure of his absence." I wondered if this was Morris's way of informing me he was not angry about my statements against Ogden.

"Very fine speech, Uncle. But you look tired. You should be leaving." Ogden said nothing to me. He did not even acknowledge my presence.

"I shall be spending the remainder of the day with Dr. Hosack. You need not trouble yourself about me." There was a trace of annoyance in Morris's voice. Ogden grasped him by the arm and began to walk away. Morris turned to me. "When the time is right for a visit, I will send you a note." He and Ogden disappeared in a cluster of people on the other side of the room. It was the last time I ever saw Gouverneur Morris.

Two months passed. No invitation was received from Morrisania. November fifth was election day. James Monroe was running against Rufus King for the presidency. Daniel D. Tompkins, Governor of New York for almost a decade, was seeking election as Vice-President. With New Yorkers on the ballot on both the Republican and Federalist sides, the newspapers were filled with stories about the election. Two days later I was reading one of these accounts in the newspaper when I was jolted by a brief notice. My limbs grew weak. A shudder coursed through my body. It was an obituary for Gouverneur Morris.

At 5 o'clock yesterday morning at his seat at Morrisania, the Honorable Gouverneur Morris, after a short but distressing illness, in the 65th year of his age.

The funeral had already taken place at Morrisania that same morning.

FOURTEEN

The man who had dominated my life for the past eight years was no more. He had departed this world forever at the very time I was expecting to re-establish my relationship with him. Although still stunned by the initial shock of his death, I began to think about Nancy. What would her future be now? The doubts about her which had been planted by John Randolph's letter assailed my mind. Could there have been a fever like the one which carried away Richard Randolph? I had to learn the nature of the "short but distressing illness" which caused the death of the great man.

It had been years since I had been to Dr. Hosack's house. Nevertheless, within days of the death I arranged to use Hosack's library as a pretext for speaking to him. Meg, one of the family servants, answered the door. She introduced me to a young man who was new to the house. According to Meg, during a snowstorm the previous year, he had appeared at the door dressed in tattered clothes and asking alms. Dr. Hosack took him into the household and he had been living there ever since. It was another example of Dr. Hosack's extraordinary generosity which to this day has never ceased to astonish me.

After I had been working in the library for several hours, Dr. Hosack came home. He greeted me in his usual genial manner and questioned me on *The Age of Revolution.* Hosack was interested to learn that, like David Hume's authorship of the *History of England,* I was writing my work beginning with the most recent period, 1812–15, and working back to the time preceding the American Revolution. After a short discussion of my limited progress, I mentioned my surprise at the death of Mr. Morris.

"It was not a surprise," Hosack interjected. "He was not feeling well after his speech at the society. You saw how he looked. He spent the night here. Two days later he became ill and was indisposed for some time."

"What was the nature of his illness?" I attempted to appear as disinterested as possible.

"He suffered from chills and fatigue. Complained of a pain on the right side of his head and face. Other aches and pains. The illness of an old man."

"Did he have a fever?"

"There were some days when he suffered from a slight fever, according to his account. Nothing serious. Why are you so interested in his symptoms?" Hosack seemed to be amused. "You sound like one of my colleagues."

"I hope you do not mind my questions. But I am curious. Is there . . . Is it possible that poison could have been involved in his death?" I was embarrassed by the strangeness of my own question and the revealing quaver in my voice.

Dr. Hosack's reply startled me. "So, you know about John Randolph's letter."

"Yes. But how . . ."

"How do I know about it?" To indicate that was my question, I nodded. "I never actually saw the letter. But John Randolph showed it to several persons. It was common gossip for a time. I was told he accused Mrs. Morris of a number of atrocious deeds, including the poisoning of his brother many years ago. What do you know of the matter?"

After noting that Morris had sworn me to secrecy, I briefly explained, in as cryptic a fashion as possible, I had gathered some information to use for a possible response. Hosack was amazed when I revealed my ignorance as to whether there had ever been a response.

"Mrs. Morris herself wrote the response. I never saw it, but there was more talk about it than the original letter. Caused a sensation among Morris's relatives and friends. It was very lengthy, I know. She accused Randolph of being a malicious slanderer. I am told she did an excellent job of characterizing him as a dishonorable liar. She conceded to having been betrothed to another brother, Theodorick Randolph. She said she considered him her husband in the eyes of God. Although I understand the letter was ambiguous on the point, she seems to have admitted being delivered of a child back in Virginia."

"Did she say who the father was?" By this time my curiosity was undisguised and ravenous.

"As I said, I did not read the letter. The implication was, I believe, that the father was her betrothed, Theodorick, the one who died before the child was supposedly born."

Overcome with a passionate desire to see Nancy's response, I asked who might have a copy, other than Mrs. Morris herself. Dr. Hosack's answer was not encouraging. "I learned about the letter and the response from Harmanus Bleecker. He had not seen them either. Bleecker heard about them from David Ogden. Morris must have shown them to Ogden. They were quite close, you know." The thought of seeking the document from Ogden filled me with a sense of utter defeat. If I could examine any document known to be in existence, Nancy's response would be my first choice. But the last person I would ever ask for such a favor was David Ogden. Based on Ogden's deliberate refusal to acknowledge my presence at the Historical Society, I was convinced that Morris had revealed my accusations to him. That blackguard would perform no service for me.

Dr. Hosack explained that Nancy had been very upset about the whole affair. It may have been, he guessed, the primary reason for the withdrawal of the Morris family from their customary sociability. The cause of Morris's death, he also indicated, had nothing to do with poison. "He died from a stricture in the urinary passage. He never had great faith in doctors. One probably amputated his leg without sufficient cause. So on his own, he attempted to force a whalebone through the obstructed passage and only succeeded in greatly increasing his final agony. A terrible way to die."

After my meeting with Dr. Hosack, I resolved not to dwell in the past. My only salvation was in my work. But even while writing my history, I was haunted by Hosack's revelation about Nancy's response. It confirmed my anxieties about the fact that the exploration of the past is a never-ending task. After years of arduous work, a historian achieves a partial approximation of the truth. At some later date his conclusions are discredited by the discovery of a new document, one such as Nancy's response to John Randolph. I was beset by a sense of futility. Worse than the uncertainty as to ever being able to reconstruct the truth was a gnawing feeling of having been used and then abandoned by Morris. After all of my efforts on his behalf to provide information about Randolph's letter, he owed me the courtesy of informing me about Nancy's reply. Would he have treated one of his aristocratic friends in such a disdainful manner? I was also haunted by regrets for speaking to Morris about David Ogden. Perhaps, if I had said nothing, Morris would have informed me of Nancy's rejoinder. Now I would never know; my doubts would never be resolved.

In order to escape my private torment and the monotony of endless historical research and writing, I became increasingly active with the New York Manumission Society. Within two months after Morris's death I was assigned to a ten-man delegation sent to Albany to plead with Governor Tompkins, then Vice-President elect, who himself had long been a member of the society, to support legislation to end all slavery in New York. Without any hesitation, Tompkins agreed to submit a special message to the Legislature for total abolition of slavery in New York within one decade. True to his words, shortly before he departed for Washington, Tompkins sent the special message on January 29, 1817. At the end of March the Legislature enacted a law, effective on July 4, 1827, freeing all Negroes who were not then liberated before that date by the gradual emancipation act of 1799. Unfortunately, before the act was passed, the Senate added an amendment relieving masters of the obligation to support aged slaves freed by the legislation.

The society's efforts over a period of many years to achieve total abolition had at last been realized. The law was retroactive and was estimated to provide for the uncompensated emancipation of approximately ten thousand Negroes. No doubt, had I not been included in the delegation, the law still would have been enacted. In fact, Tompkins was so predisposed to emancipation, I suspect he would have filed similar legislation if there had been no delegation. Nevertheless, my trip was most gratifying. It reawakened within me a belief in the possibility of human progress.

The year 1817 was also a momentous one for the Erie Canal. Although my role in the canal project was at an end, I continued to follow its development with great interest. The new Commissioners, with De Witt Clinton as their president, issued an elaborate report in March of 1817 containing the recommendations of various engineers. Shortly thereafter, despite the almost unanimous opposition of members from New York City, the Assembly passed legislation which for the first time would authorize the actual building of the canal. One member had to explain the obvious to the representatives from New York City. "If the canal is to be a shower of gold, it will fall upon New York; if a river of gold, it will flow into her lap." Under the leadership of Martin Van Buren, the authorization bill also was enacted in the Senate. In both houses the legislation passed by narrow margins. But in the five-man Council of Revisions, the last barrier to approval of the canal, there were serious problems. Judge Platt and Judge Yates were strong supporters of the canal. Chief Justice Thompson and Acting Governor Tayler were opposed. The fifth and decisive vote belonged to Chancellor Kent. In the course of discussions, the Chancellor revealed that he was not inclined to commit the state to such an enormous project until public opinion was united in its favor. The close votes in the Assembly and Senate demonstrated that opinion was divided. The vote appeared to be three to two against the canal.

As the judge who had six years earlier upheld the conviction for blasphemy of a poor drunk named Ruggles, for the offense of standing before a tavern door and misusing the names of God and the Holy Spirit, Chancellor Kent was not a man greatly admired by me. However, on this occasion he would redeem himself in my eyes while another man who I had respected for many years made a fool of himself. Unexpectedly, the longtime object of my admiration, the same man who, a few months earlier, led the fight to abolish slavery in New York State as its Governor, appeared on the scene as Vice-President Daniel D. Tompkins. Again his action was decisive, but in an unanticipated way. At the moment of decision, Tompkins entered the council chamber to speak against the canal bill. He declared that the peace with Great Britain was only a temporary truce; therefore, instead of wasting limited resources on a canal, New York State should employ its credit and revenues for the eventual renewal of the war with the British. This Republican speech was too much for that ardent Federalist Chancellor Kent. Rising from his seat, he loudly announced, "If we are to have war, or to have a canal, I am in favor of the canal, and I vote for the bill." Thus, by a three to two vote, the Council of Revisions endorsed the Erie Canal. The law was passed on April 15, 1817. With great ceremony, ground was broken on the fourth of July of that same year near Rome, New York, on the summit dividing the waters flowing to the Hudson from those flowing to the St. Lawrence.

With credit still difficult to obtain in Europe, and President Monroe's new administration having no more interest in the canal than had its predecessors in Washington, I expected that the canal project would wither for lack of funds. In fact, as one of his last official acts in office, President Madison had vetoed legislation to apportion among the states the dividends on stock owned by the federal government in the United States Bank, a loss of $90,000 each year for the State of New York. But the canal legislation of 1817 created a board, known as the "Commissioners of the Canal Fund," which produced an ingenious financial solution. The canal fund was created by using a number of different methods—a tax on every passenger making a steamboat trip of over thirty miles on the Hudson River, imposing a duty on salt manufactured in New York, using the proceeds of lotteries, duties on sales at auctions, and a tax on all lands lying along the route of the canal within twenty-five miles on each side. Although the tax on steamboat passengers was suspended and no money was raised from lotteries or the tax on land along the canal route, the financial plan was successful primarily because of the salt and auction duties. Accordingly, the great canal was paid for by New York State herself, without the assistance of any other state, Washington, Europe, or even Leray de Chaumont. Mr. Morris would have been pleased with such a shrewd answer to the difficult financial problem.

Shortly after the death of Gouverneur Morris, I sent a note of condolence to Mrs. Morris. There was no reply. During the next six months I worked increasingly and with a renewed fervor on *The Age of Revolution*. In my absorption, I succeeded in driving Nancy Randolph-Morris from my mind. She became a distant memory, like my childhood, something lost forever in the mists of the past. But even time could not obliterate the remembrance of Nancy Randolph, nor could death still the vital spirit of Gouverneur Morris. Again the summons came, and again I answered the siren's call.

Not long after the enactment of the canal legislation, on one of those spring days on which the earth seems to be renewing itself, Mr. Morris's man appeared at my door, like a shadow from the past. With his customary flourish, he handed me a note and announced he would wait for my reply.

My dear friend:
As one of his last requests, my husband asked me to provide information which might be useful to you. I would very much appreciate it if you would come to Morrisania. Select the day and I will be there.
Most respectfully, I am your humble servant.
Ann C. Morris

As in days past, I accepted the invitation without hesitation, choosing the next day for my visit. A wait of two days would have been unendurable. Then I sat down in a futile attempt to control with reason the irresistible emotions invading my breast. For the remainder of the day I was not fit for anything else.

The next morning, a beautiful spring day, I set forth as if for a day of research in the library. I said nothing to Emily about Morrisania. She would have asked what business I could have in that place now that Mr. Morris was deceased. She knew me too well. Any discussion of Mrs. Morris would have revealed my inner agitation. In the presence of Emily, the name of Mrs. Morris was a dangerous one which could injure us both. For that reason, in all preceding years, I had mentioned it to Emily only once or twice; I resolved to continue my silence.

It had been two and one-half years since my last visit to Morrisania—that unforgettable day Morris showed me John Randolph's letter. The boat glided up to the familiar dock. It did not seem possible that the house was no longer occupied by the great man. As in days past, a servant solemnly led me into the library. In place of Mr. Morris, Nancy was sitting at the desk writing. Almost three full years had passed since I had last seen her, shortly after my return from Europe. She had aged. Yet, dressed in white, she was still the vision incarnate of my dreams. She arose from her chair and gracefully walked toward me, her hand extended in greeting. There was a distinct gravity in her manner, without the hint of a smile. Was she truly the bereaved widow or merely playing the part convincingly? As soon as she began to speak in that wondrous voice, the essence of femininity, all doubts were resolved in her favor. The tilt of her head, her flowing black locks, the movement of her hips, all created an impression of beauty which quite overwhelmed my defenses. Within a few moments I was firmly within the grasp of those marvelous powers which had held sway over me for so many years.

The conversation quickly turned to Gouverneur Morris, whose spirit still seemed to dominate the house. She thanked me for my note of condolence. Surprised that she remembered it, I apologized for missing the funeral, explaining that the news reached me too late. She described the course of his final illness which had lasted for almost three weeks. He knew he was dying. "That last day, he looked up at me and smiled. As he held my hand, he said, 'Sixty-four years ago, it pleased the Almighty to call me into existence, here, on this spot, in this very room; and now shall I complain that He is pleased to call me hence?' " She recited the words easily, as though she had told the story many times. "He asked me about the weather. I told him it was a fine day. He turned to me. 'A beautiful day, yes, but . . .' He mumbled some words and his eyes closed as the breath left his body. He was gone." A tear ran down her cheek. "He was a wonderful man, goodness itself. I miss him deeply."

In the midst of my clumsy attempts to console her, I wondered whether she knew about my role in the matter of John Randolph's letter. Revealing to her that Morris had asked me to investigate might lead her to the conclusion that he had retained doubts about her. Anxious not to inflict further pain, I resolved to say nothing unless she mentioned the letter first. She said not a word about it. Instead she turned her attention to the reason for her summons. "My husband regretted he could not help you more with the preparation of your book. When he knew he would be unable to speak to you, he told me to permit you to examine his letter books and diary up to the time of his return from Europe. He said they contain much interesting information about both our own revolution and the French Revolution. He expressed full confidence in your discretion to choose what you wish to use in your history." She led me to a table piled high with books of various sizes and colors. "Of course, I cannot let this material leave Morrisania. But you are welcome to come here during the week to examine the documents. Let us say any time from Monday to Thursday each week."

"Wonderful! I will be here on those days, whenever the weather permits.

Very generous of you." Although excited by the prospect of reading the voluminous materials spread like a treasure before my eager eyes, I was utterly thrilled at the idea of visiting Nancy several days each week. The well-known reluctance of widows to part with large collections of family archives, even for short periods of time, is a common hazard for historians. In my situation it was, I thought, a gift from the gods. But one must beware of such gifts. The road of wishes fulfilled is fraught with peril.

My expressions of gratitude were, no doubt, breathless and overwrought. In my lovesick state I was quite unable to contain my exuberance. Nancy invited me to begin work immediately. She stated she was going riding and would visit me later in the day. In my presence she informed the servants that I would be working with the documents during the week "for the next few months." They were instructed to assist me with my requests and to provide a boat back to the city each day when I was ready to leave. Then she left me alone with the precious papers. At once I began to survey the extent of the magnificent trove. It was immense, a historian's delight. There were eight volumes of diaries bound in vellum. Double clasps locked each book. Unlike the others, which were brown, the first volume was green. It began on March 1, 1789; the eighth volume concluded on January 5, 1800. They contained Morris's daily accounts of his life in Europe during the French Revolution, a subject we had never discussed in any detail. The writing was not easy to read. The books contained a substantial amount of ink-stained corrections and deletions. At random I selected the third volume. It covered a period extending from April 1790 through April 1791. After beginning to count the pages, I noticed they were numbered in the corners. The volume contained 372 pages. It would require many weeks, I estimated, just to review the diaries, and there were numerous other books. In addition to the diaries, there were many books containing official, consular, commercial, and private letters in separate volumes. These extended over the same period as the diaries. Rubbing my hands over the vellum covers, I considered with delight the prospect of seeing Nancy every week for months.

On the other side of the table were additional books, containing information going back to the period prior to the First War of American Independence. A book of "law entries" dated 1771 to 1772 contained notations as early as 1752, the year of Morris's birth. At random, I opened the book to an early page. An entry dated 1762 stated, "Present, Hon. Daniel Horsmanden, Esq., C.J." The name shocked me. It was the man who wrote the book on the New York Conspiracy, the very work whose fortuitous purchase had started me down the path to Morrisania and these private writings of Gouverneur Morris. While gazing at the name Horsmanden, written in a strange hand, not that of Mr. Morris, I felt for a moment as if I had stumbled upon my destiny. The notation had been made fourteen years before my birth and had awaited my arrival for fifty-five years. At that instant I believed my life was within the firm grasp of a power beyond my control. My fate was staring me full in the face.

The sensation quickly passed and I commenced my exploration of the papers. There were a number of interesting documents prior to 1789, many of these from the period of the American Revolution. Among these was a fragment of an old speech in 1779 containing Morris's denunciation before Congress of Tom Paine, during the Silas Deane affair. On the back of the paper were written the words "taken down from memory to obviate misrepresentation." The previously mentioned reference to Paine, as a "mere Adventurer from England, without Fortune, without Family or Connexions, ignorant even of Grammar," leaped off the page at me. The harsh words about one of my boyhood heroes pained me deeply. I wondered whether Morris had secretly held the same disdain for me, a person without money or a place of importance in society. The old wounds began to bleed.

The reference to Paine was one of many scattered through the papers. Another name appearing constantly in the documents was that of Lafayette, also one of my youthful heroes. In a series of letters between General Washington and Morris, then a member of the Continental Congress, I found the first of these references. General Washington wrote, "In a word, although I think the Baron (von Steuben) an excellent officer, I do most devoutly wish, that we had not a single foreigner among us, except the Marquis de Lafayette, who acts upon very different principles from these which govern the rest." Morris would meet the young Lafayette at Valley Forge and be impressed by his mature judgment. The documents for the next twenty years, however, would reveal that Morris did not hold Lafayette in much more esteem than Paine. Ironically, Morris would personally be confronted with the same problem as to both men—their imprisonment in foreign lands.

In 1781 Morris became the assistant to Robert Morris, who was in charge of superintending the finances of the United States. During this time he did not carefully retain copies of letters and documents, as he did at other periods of his life. However, I did discover a report in which he originated a new plan for American coinage. In 1782 he proposed a national decimal system exchangeable for the currency of the states with fractional units. The system contained a minimum unit for small purchases which was called the "quarter." He then developed a decimal hierarchy of coins based on fractions of the Spanish silver dollar. Under Gouverneur Morris's proposed system, one hundred "pennies" would equal one dollar. Two years later, in 1784, a new committee under the leadership of Thomas Jefferson adopted a revised version of the Morris decimal system. They rejected his minimum unit as too small and used the dollar as the basic unit, which, as Morris recommended, could be subdivided into one hundred pennies. This revised plan was adopted by Congress in 1786 and has, of course, remained the basis of our coinage ever since. It was another part of Morris's remarkable career with which I had not then been familiar.

After he finished working as Assistant Financier, he continued to work for Robert Morris on matters of private business. In this regard, he spent months in Virginia in 1785 working on tobacco and land speculation. I searched in vain for a reference to Nancy Randolph. As she would have been only ten or eleven years old at the time, I did not expect to find anything; nevertheless, I looked for the name with great eagerness, as though its discovery would explain a part of her mysterious past. For the remainder of the 1780s until his departure for Europe, he lived and worked in Philadelphia. To my great disappointment, there were no documents concerning the Constitutional Convention. The Convention's famous rule of secrecy seemed to have extended even into the private papers of one of its most prominent delegates. In one of his letters he did state that Alexander Hamilton had requested that he join in writing the "Federalist" essays in support of the ratification of the Constitution. Morris did not mention the reason for declining the request. At the time he was probably too busy; for, in 1788, he spent additional months in Virginia engaged in the vast mercantile affairs of Robert Morris, who had entered contracts for supplying tobacco to France. Although there were many references to various members of the Randolph clan, again I could find nothing about Nancy.

On that first day, in the midst of my initial cursory review of the documents, Nancy entered the room with her four-year-old son. Robust and rather large for a four-year-old, the boy boldly approached me and began to prattle about his friend, who was named Michael. Although awkward in talking to children, I knew that a simple way to ingratiate one's self with a mother is to treat her beloved child with utmost respect and delicacy. Clumsily, I engaged young Gouverneur in conversation. "You like Michael, don't you?"

"Oh, yes." The boy's smile and high-pitched voice were, it must be admitted, endearing.

"Why do you like him?"

"He's my best friend."

"Why is he your best friend?"

" 'Cause, I like him."

Nancy and I both laughed simultaneously at the child's response. Her irresistible smile convinced me of the efficacy of engaging her affections by doting on the boy. I resolved to do so whenever the opportunity arose.

That afternoon the three of us dined together. The servants were to provide lunch for me on all of my future visits; Nancy and the child were not usually present for the meal. The servants rarely knew, or would reveal, where they had gone. The customary response to my inquiries was, "They are away for the afternoon." That first day was an exception; I was the honored guest. Despite the melancholy air about her, Nancy played the role of gracious hostess. She wore the mask of a contented and untroubled existence which we all affect for those who are not our intimates. How I longed for her to remove the mask and to tell me about her past, about her suffering. But she smiled and spoke about the child, the food, the weather, and most frequently of her departed husband. How he loved to quote Shakespeare and Swift. His hatred of gambling and snuff.

"He always said that persons around a card table are the dullest of company. 'They are mute and deaf,' he would say. 'They neither talk nor listen while they engage in the dull drudgery of cards.' " She lowered her voice as though she could imitate the great man's booming voice. It was comical, and done with great affection. "When he occasionally agreed to play for small stakes, to be sociable, he would always give his winnings to the servants. To make me happy, he would also consent to be my partner in a game of whist. Always, he wanted me to be happy." As she spoke she played with the child, who she often called "pumpkin." Constantly I had to compete with the boy for her attention. Whenever the little imp interrupted me in mid-sentence, it became clear she was listening to him and not to me. Before I had a chance to communicate with her in any meaningful way, she was gone. I was discouraged. She remained a stranger.

That evening I told Emily about the wonderful documents that had become available to me. As expected, she displayed no interest in my historical research. "That's good," she said, and continued with her baking. The news that I would be spending several days each week at Morrisania evoked no greater interest. "Just tell me which days you won't be home for lunch." She asked no questions about Mrs. Morris, and I said not a word on the subject.

Within a few days of my first visit I was deeply immersed in the diary from the period of the French Revolution. Morris arrives in France early in 1789 and begins his diary on March first of that momentous year. How characteristic of the man; it is as if the major events of history follow him wherever he goes. Although the purpose of his trip to Europe is private business, he had obtained letters of introduction from George Washington to important public persons, including Rochambeau, Lafayette, and Thomas Jefferson, the American minister to the French court. Morris is not one to separate himself from the great public matters of the day. His primary business appears to be to settle a claim of Robert Morris against the Farmers General for tobacco shipped to France by contract. Another important part of his mission is to find purchasers, with the assistance of Leray de Chaumont, for large tracts of uninhabited lands in New York, Pennsylvania, and the Fairfax estate in Virginia.

I quickly discovered that this information is not clear from reading the diary alone. Morris's activities in Paris could only be understood by reading the diary together with contemporaneous letters contained in the various letter books. It appeared that Morris had copied every important letter he wrote into the volumes of personal or commercial correspondence. These letters appear in his books without his signature, frequently two letters on a single page. Many of the letters sent to him in Europe were without signature, probably as a caution in case they were read by others. Morris himself wrote the dates and names on the envelope of each letter. He must have spent hours each day in composing and copying. Latrobe's polygraph could have considerably extended the hours available to him, although it is difficult to imagine him increasing his massive production of work.

The diary itself seemed to be intended for his private use, perhaps as an aid to his memory, and not for the amusement of others. He usually recorded only the external events of the day—who he met, where he went, what was discussed, and almost always the state of the weather. Although the diary and letters are not introspective, they revealed more of the inner man to me than did eight years of personal contact. As one who always learned more about life from books than from my association with people, I was fully content to be communing with a dead man through his words written on paper. It is the only way I have ever succeeded in entering the secret places of other lives and comparing those hidden experiences with my own. And what experiences Morris enjoyed. I was fascinated, titillated, and even shocked by those wonderful books.

Having arrived in Paris early in that historic year, 1789, Morris begins meeting with various aristocrats, most of whom are unfamiliar to me. However, many of the names in the diary, like the Marquis de Lafayette and Thomas Jefferson, would be recognized by any reader. Morris seems not to like nor respect either of these two ardent supporters of democracy. When he spends an hour with Jefferson, he writes that it is at least fifty minutes too long. Lafayette, who, he says, is hated by both the King and Queen, has principles in accord with a republic. In contrast, he writes, his own principles are drawn only from human nature and ought not therefore to have much respect in this "Age of Refinement." On the third week after the diary begins, there enters one of the principal characters, Madame Adèle de Flahaut. It is none other than the striking woman introduced to me by Charles de Flahaut as his mother upon my return from Leipsic. My memory of her was vivid, and I attempted to imagine how she looked when she was twenty-five years younger. She speaks English and is "pleasing" to Morris. "If I might judge from appearances," he writes, "not a sworn Enemy to Intrigue." Although he does not mention it for some time, she is a writer of novels. Adèle is twenty-eight years old and married for ten years to sixty-three-year-old Comte de Flahaut, who lives in apartments beneath her own in the Louvre. The Count and Countess de Flahaut are among the lesser members of the nobility who cannot afford to be part of the court at Versailles. Morris is then thirty-seven years old. In 1789 he was four years younger than the humble historian who was reading his diary in 1817. I recalled the beautiful face, figure, and curling chestnut hair of General de Flahaut's mother, and anticipated what the diary would reveal.

At first Adèle is merely one of many attractive women who Morris encounters and views with the eye of the hunter. He is introduced to Madame Rully and writes that her fine eyes seem to say she had not antipathy for the gentle passion. "Nous verrons," he notes. Always ready for further exploration of the possibilities, he comments, "We shall see" after each encounter with another beauty. He writes like a veteran of the wars of the Paphian Queen, Aphrodite. Since he lives at the Hôtel du Roi and she at the Louvre, it is natural that he meets Adèle by accident while walking at the Tuileries. By the last day in March he commences his regular visits to the Louvre. Adèle, he states, is an elegant woman, by no means deficient in understanding, and with a good disposition. *Nous verrons.* On one of his initial visits he has an engagement to view the paintings and statues with Adèle. When he arrives at the Louvre, she is in bed and says she had forgotten their plans. A member of her family is present. Her husband enters. What may have been intended by Adèle as, what the French call, a *rendez-vous mal compris*, has miscarried. Morris laments that a scene his imagination has painted very well turns out good for nothing. The idea occurred to me that perhaps Charles is the son of Mr. Morris and Madame de Flahaut. But Charles told me he joined the army in 1800. Thus, I thought, he must have been born several years prior to 1789. Yet there was no mention of his existence.

On another visit to Adèle's apartment, Morris meets the Bishop d'Autun. At first I did not realize the identity of the clergyman who had married Adèle to the Comte de Flahaut. Then, after numerous meetings between Morris and the Bishop, it became clear that this political man of the Church was Talleyrand himself. The clergyman, who had become a bishop only two weeks after Morris began his diary, is involved in the political turmoil seething throughout the city. Ten thousand soldiers have been ordered into Paris to deal with a possible insurrection. In order to save the state from bankruptcy, due to an immense national debt, the King has convened the Estates General for the first time since 1614. On May 4 Morris goes to Versailles to witness the procession the day before the opening of the Estates General, the event which many, including me, would mark as the opening act of the stirring drama of the French Revolution. At Versailles, Morris shares a window with Adèle. In his diary and in letters, Morris describes the scene. The King is saluted enthusiastically with "Vive le Roi"; but Marie Antoinette receives not a single acclamation. The magnificent procession includes the Swiss and French Guards. To maintain the traditional distinctions among the orders, the royal court requires that the ancient costumes from the previous meeting of the Estates General, 175 years earlier, be worn. The clerics appear in the brilliant violet cassocks and scarlet capes of their order. The nobles dress with their customary magnificence, in gold-trimmed mantles and white plumed hats. The common people of the Third Estate are compelled to wear plain black mantles in order to emphasize their subordination in the hierarchy of society.

On May 5, 1789, the Estates General open, and again Morris attends. The King sits on a raised throne, the Queen slightly below him. They are surrounded by the princes, princesses, ladies and gentlemen of the court. The representatives of the clergy, three hundred priests of all colors—scarlet, crimson, black, white, and gray—sit in front of the ministers. In front of the Marshals of France, facing the clergy and equal in number, sit the representatives of the nobility. On benches reaching across the hall facing the stage are the delegates of the common people. An old man who has refused to dress in the drab costume prescribed for the Third Estate receives long and loud cheers. Mirabeau is hissed. The King speaks and receives such acclamation that the tears flow from his eyes. The Queen is greeted with silence. Because he is not a Frenchman, Morris believes he has no right to express his sentiments.

In vain he encourages those who are near him to acclaim the Queen. Finally, after the long, boring speech of Necker, the popular Director General of Finances, for the first time in months Marie Antoinette hears the shout of "Vive la Reine." Morris is pleased. At dinner that day he discusses the great issues of the day with members of the Third Estate. Morris favors voting individually, *par tête*, in forming the constitution, but once it is formed, voting by order. Under such a constitution the clergy and nobility would always outnumber the commons, two to one. Voting individually, the Third Estate, with the assistance of sympathetic clergymen, would outnumber the other two orders, thereby possessing a controlling majority of the government. The stage is set for the next act of the great drama. Morris writes in his diary, "Gods! What a Theatre is this for a first Rate Character." At this point even he cannot forsee just how stupendous is the nature of the drama about to unfold before him. Many of the greatest characters, Brissot, Marat, Danton, Robespierre, Saint Just, Desmoulins, Hébert, and the despot, who Morris will later predict must emerge from the turmoil, are as yet unseen. They wait to make their entrances and exits on the great stage of history.

The three estates, as required, meet as separate bodies. Within the next two months the Third Estate will demand that the clergy and nobility join them or else the representatives of the common people will organize themselves into a National Assembly. The Bishop d'Autun is among those opposed to merging the clergy with the Third Estate. His views will later change. Lafayette is part of the nobility but he is in sympathy with the Third Estate. He will remain a man of the people. After a period of mounting tension, the Third Estate finally declares itself the National Assembly on June 17. The declaration denies a separate existence to the other two estates, which are legally equal. In moving without the sanction of the King, the common people have denied his divine right to be the sole source of all authority. By acting on the opposing theory of the sovereignty of the people, as proclaimed by Rousseau and the American Declaration of Independence, the representatives of the French people are formally in revolution against the established order. The deputies of the Assembly are locked out of their hall. As in 1614, it appears that the Estates General is to be unceremoniously terminated by the crown. Dr. Guillotin, a deputy from Paris whose invention for humane execution will soon evoke widespread terror, suggests that the Assembly take possession of the old tennis court building at Versailles. There the deputies bind themselves by the famous Oath of the Tennis Court not to separate until the constitution of the kingdom has been established and placed upon a sound basis. At the news, Paris is aflame with revolutionary excitement. Three days later the King commands the deputies of the Assembly to disperse and resume their sessions as separate estates. Mirabeau tells the King's messengers, "Go and tell those who sent you that we are here by the will of the people and nothing but the power of the bayonet shall drive us forth." On the next day the majority of the clerical deputies join the National Assembly, followed one day later by forty-seven deputies of the nobility. The French Guards mutiny and refuse to act against the people. Lafayette submits a proposal for the Declaration of the Rights of Man, written with the assistance of Thomas Jefferson. At the behest of the nobility, the King orders the popular Necker to leave the country. Paris is alarmed at the dismissal. Camille Desmoulins calls the populace of Paris to arms. With considerable bloodshed, the people of Paris storm the Bastille. The people have joined the Revolution commenced by the politicians.

During the turbulent first half of 1789 Morris is a distant witness busily engaged in his own private business, financial and amorous. He receives an anonymous billet from a lady containing a declaration of love. After writing an ambiguous answer to his unknown admirer, he directs his servant to follow the messenger. Adèle de Flahaut and a Madame Roselle are among the suspects. Morris continues to visit Adèle at the Louvre on a regular basis. Usually company is present, including the Bishop d'Autun. Two different women inform Morris that their nuptial bands do not constrain their conduct; he is indifferent to their suggestions to begin intrigues. Although he exchanges "looks of reconnaissance" with numerous women, his eyes remain firmly on Adèle. In the French manner, many women entertain Morris as they make "la toilette." He describes them dressing and undressing, except for the shifts, and washing their armpits with water from Hungary. At one point Adèle, when he is more familiar with her charms, entertains him while she is taking a bath. Milk is poured into the water so that it is opaque, concealing from view her nude body. Would that I had been so received during my brief residence in Paris.

One day in June, Morris strolls through the Palais Royal. From her window a young lady invites him to pay a visit. He accepts and goes upstairs. A closer look at the woman convinces him that her health has been impaired by her attentions to the "physical necessities" of her fellow creatures. Morris laments her illness, which she denies. To render him more sensible of her charms, she locks the door and puts the key in her pocket. Morris asks her if she is acquainted with the police. Her knowledge, he discovers, is equal to her elocution. She is registered in their archives, as is the means by which she earns her daily bread. She demands payment for her time. Morris looks at his watch and decides to wait. Finally she surrenders and opens the door. Because he refuses to pay for her time, she shouts at him, "with a Profusion of Expressions whose Excellence consists more in Energy than in Elegance." Contrary to his own amorous inclinations, Morris manages to maintain his chastity throughout his early adventures in Paris. He waits for Adèle. Finally, on June 21, she begins to show signs of wanting a more intimate friendship. Appearing to be inclined to make him her confidant, she speaks to him of certain affairs of gallantry in which she has been told he was once engaged. He assures her that these are idle tales and that he respects the lady in question. Nevertheless, Adèle persists in her belief. She asks what he means by "respect." He replies that he has never lost his respect "for those who consented to make me happy on the Principles of Affection." He knows this idea will dwell in her mind, "because the Combination of Tenderness and Respect with Ardency and Vigor go far towards the female Idea of Perfection in a Lover."

During these months prior to the fall of the Bastille, Morris is in frequent communication with Thomas Jefferson, who in 1785 had succeeded Benjamin Franklin as the American minister to France. Morris himself will later succeed Jefferson in this position, to be followed in turn by James Monroe. Not since Socrates taught Plato who instructed Aristotle who in turn was teacher to Alexander the Great, the pupil who spread their lessons to the world, have such extraordinary men succeeded each other in an unbroken series. But unlike these heroic teachers of ancient times, Morris has no interest in receiving instruction from Jefferson. In May, after a long conversation with the American minister, Morris confides to his diary, "I think he does not form very just Estimates of Character but rather assigns too many to the humble Rank of Fools, whereas in Life the Gradations are infinite and each Individual has his peculiarities of Fort and Feeble." In June, Jefferson requests that Morris stand for Houdon's statue of Washington, a work commissioned by the Virginia State Legislature. Morris, I suspect, must have been flattered to provide the torso supporting the head of the only living man he viewed as a true unblemished hero. Morris reserved no such admiration for Jefferson. In their political discussions, Morris favors use of royal authority to prevent destruction of the privileged orders. Noting that he and Jefferson disagree in their system of policy, he states that Jefferson, with all the leaders of liberty in Paris, desires annihilating distinctions of order. "How far such Views may be right respecting Mankind in general is I think extremely problematical, but with Respect to this Nation I am sure it is wrong and cannot eventuate well." This is not to say that at this early stage Morris was opposed to reform in France. In a letter to George Washington he declares that he has every reason to wish the patriots may be successful. He later writes in his diary, "Oh! My Country, how infinitely preferable that equal Partition of Fortune's Gifts which you enjoy! Where none are Vassals, none are Lords, but all are Men." In short, he supports a republican government in America but does not believe it transferable to the inhospitable soil and the royalist institutions of France.

Although Lafayette, like Morris, supports a constitutional monarchy in France, his views are closer to Jefferson's. At a dinner late in June, Morris sits next to Lafayette, who informs him that he injures the cause because his royalist sentiments are continually quoted against the "good" party. Morris replies that he is opposed to democracy from regard to liberty. The democrats, he says, hold views which are totally inconsistent with the materials of which the French nation is composed. They are going headlong to destruction; the worst thing which could happen would be to grant their wishes. Lafayette responds that he is sensible his party is mad, and he tells them so, but he is determined to die with them. Morris declares it would be better to bring them to their senses and live with them. Lafayette is determined to resign his seat and is encouraged by Morris to do so. Morris warns that if the Third Estate becomes violent it will fail. That very day, Mirabeau and the Third Estate defy the King's messenger and refuse to disperse.

On the day the Bastille falls, Morris, who is sick with a fever, is visiting a Monsieur Le Couteulx. A person enters and announces that the Bastille is taken; the Governor of the Bastille and the Prevost des Marchands have been beheaded. The mob is carrying the heads in triumph through the city. The fall of this citadel, Morris writes on July 14, is among the most extraordinary things he has ever met with. That same day he visits Adèle. She is anxious about the safety of her foolhardy husband, who joins them in a discussion of whether he should flee the city. For Morris this would be a consummation devoutly to be wished, but he tries not to interfere. He scribbles a few lines of verse in English for Adèle about his fever, which conclude:

No Lover I. Alas! too old
To raise in you a mutual Flame.
Then take a Passion rather cold
And call it by fair Friendship's Name.

Her husband asks for a translation and looks foolish at the words about being too old to excite passion.

After the fall of the Bastille, the events in the diary quicken, as if to synchronize with the pace of activities in the streets of Paris. Lafayette, who was elected vice-president of the Assembly on July 13, is chosen commander of the new militia of Paris two days later. He organizes the militia as the Paris National Guard, giving it the blue, white, and red cockade which is to become the French tricolor. On July 20 Morris advises him on a complete plan for the militia. Lafayette tells Morris he is tired of his own power. He has commanded 100,000 men, has marched his sovereign about the streets as he pleased, and even prescribed the degree of applause the King should receive. Although Lafayette says he wishes to return to private life, Morris believes he either deceives himself "or wishes to deceive me; a little of both perhaps." Morris then writes, "But in Fact he is the Lover of Freedom from Ambition, of which there are two Kinds, the one born of Pride, the other of Vanity, and his partakes most of the latter." As I read these comments, I wondered whether it was Morris, not Jefferson, who did not form very just estimates of character.

That same day, Morris has a long visit with Adèle. He tells her he cannot consent to be only a friend. At present, he declares to her, he is his own master with respect to her, but it would not long be the case. Having no idea of inspiring her with a passion, he has none of subjecting himself to one. Besides, he is timid to a fault. I laughed aloud at Morris calling himself timid. He knows it to be wrong but he cannot help it. Adèle thinks it is a strange conversation, and "indeed so it is, but I am much mistaken if it does not make an Impression much greater on Reflection than at the first Moment. *Nous verrons.*" Although Morris's assault on Adèle's defenses is of no historical interest, I found myself taking more detailed notes on his private affairs than on events pertaining to the French Revolution. The idea of writing a book about Gouverneur Morris had begun to creep into my mind. I even imagined using his masterful amorous tactics on his widow. "Nancy, I can no longer consent to be nothing more than a friend." The idea was ludicrous but tempting.

Shortly after July 14 Morris accompanies Adèle on a visit to the Bastille. They view the inside of the fortress, which "stinks horribly." The storming of the castle, Morris writes, was a bold enterprise. He is interested in storming another fortress. The day after the visit, Morris describes an infamous atrocity. Joseph François Foulon, who had been charged with provisioning the army before Paris, is discovered in hiding. The populace demands his death for having monopolized the grain supply and having suggested that in time of famine they eat hay. Lafayette attempts to restrain the mob with words but fails. The crowd drags Foulon from the Hôtel de Ville and hangs him from a lamppost. Morris writes,

> After Dinner walk a little under the Arcade of the Palais Royal waiting for my Carriage. In this Period the Head and Body of Mr. de Foulon are introduced in Triumph. The Head on a Pike, the Body dragged naked on the Earth. Afterwards this horrible Exhibition is carried thro the different Streets. His Crime is to have accepted a Place in the Ministry. This mutilated Form of an Old Man of seventy five is shewn to Bertier, his Son in Law, the Intendt. of Paris, and afterwards he also is put to Death and cut to Pieces, the Populace carrying about the mangled Fragments with a Savage Joy. Gracious God what a People!

The next day Morris receives a note from Adèle asking to see him. They dine together and continue the conversation about his need to be more than her friend. His words have made the impression he expected. To cure him of his passion, she avows a "marriage of the heart" with another. He writes, "I guess the Person. She acknowledges it and assures me that she cannot commit an Infidelity to him. By Degrees however we come near to it." He leaves to take tea with Jefferson. Morris does not yet reveal in his diary who Adèle's lover is.

When the time came for me to return to the city by boat, I found it difficult to cease reading. It was Thursday, and I could not return for four days. Never in my life had I been so involved in the private life of a fellow human being. Thinking about Morris's courtship of Adèle de Flahaut, I attempted to imagine his conquest of Nancy Randolph. Was he, I wondered, the same kind of man, as in 1789, when he pursued Nancy twenty years later? Or did he choose to play the paternal role of protective benefactor? That day Nancy saw me off at the dock. She continued to be friendly but distant. I longed to break through her indifference.

Upon my return to the diary on the following Monday, it did not take long to learn the results of Morris's strategem. He believes Adèle has accepted the fact that she must be his. If she does not feel love, he writes, she imitates it admirably. He notes that people deceive themselves more in believing the duration of love than in its existence. Its existence is frequent, its duration rare and depending upon an uncommon union of physical and moral energies in one lover which may not be fully excited by corresponding qualities in the other. He visits Adèle again and they have "a little wild Chit Chat." She takes precautions against a scene of passion. "But we convince each other of our very warm Esteem and that Opportunity might perhaps ripen this Esteem into active affection. *Nous verrons.*" Finally, on the next day, July 27, four months after his walk with her at the Tuileries, he wins the object of his desire. After dinner with the Jefferson family, he goes by appointment at five to visit Adèle at the Louvre. She is at her toilette. Her husband enters. "She dresses before us with perfect Decency even to the Shift. Monsieur leaves us to make a long Visit, and we are to occupy ourselves with making a Translation. We sit down with the best Disposition imaginable, but instead of a Translation . . . The misfortune is that I am obliged to undertake the Translation." The next day he visits Adèle again. Her husband is there but his business elsewhere. *"Madame est difficile. Mais enfin _____ ."*

On the next day, July 29, Morris leaves for London on business. Unlike their meetings the previous two days, his leave taking of Adèle is "Perfectly platonic." He will not return to Paris until the middle of September. Many of the nobles fleeing from Paris at the same time will not return for many years, some not for a quarter of a century, in the wake of the victorious allies entering Paris after the defeat of Napoleon. As Morris saw many of them leaving Paris a generation earlier, I saw them returning to the city before my own hasty departure in 1814.

By the time of Morris's return to Paris, the new constitution has been adopted. After learning that the National Assembly has agreed to a single legislative chamber and a suspensive veto of the King, he writes, "This is travelling in the high Road to Anarchy and that worst of all Tyrannies, the Despotism of Faction in a popular Assembly." As always, I was astonished at his eerie ability to foresee future events. Adèle is out of the city, but the following week she sends him a note. Upon receipt of a letter from him announcing his return, she has traveled 180 miles to see him. He takes this as proof of her sincerity. "A feeble Health, a wretched Carriage, a bad Road, and worse weather: charming Sex, you are capable of every Thing!" Although she is tired, they resume "performing the rites" they had begun before his departure for London. After their passionate reunion, they visit a convent to see an old English nun who had educated Adèle years earlier. According to Morris, the old woman has an air of Tartuffe about her. After the visit, Adèle does not permit him to leave the carriage until the rites are performed once more. Her visits to the convent appear to stimulate the suppressed passions of her youth. The next day when he calls on Adèle, she is out, but her servant encourages him to await her return. While he does so, he writes a poem of love.

Whilst I wait the Approach of the Nymph I adore,
To hasten the Moments along
Thine Aid, charming Cupid, I fondly implore
And pour thus my amorous Song:
Come lovely Woman, why so long delay?
Oh! come and take me from myself away.

When blest by her Presence I gaze on those Charms
Which the Bosom of Age might inspire
How I pant to encircle the Nymph in my Arms,
How glow with incessant Desire!
Come lovely Woman, why so long delay?
Oh! come and take me from myself away.

When she listens at last to my amorous Zeal
And kindly consents by a Kiss,
No Words can the genial Transport reveal
No Sound but the Murmur of Bliss.
Come lovely Woman, why so long delay?
Oh! come and take me from myself away.

During this period the famous daughter of Necker, Germaine de Staël, attempts to attract Morris with her leer of invitation. Like Adèle, she is married and has a lover. Morris suspects that a few interviews would stimulate her curiosity to the experiment of what can be effected by a native of the new world who has left one of his legs behind him; but he is interested only in Madame de Flahaut. At his next meeting with Adèle, she tells him he never would have succeeded in possessing her if he had not declared he would abandon her society if he could not be her lover. As Morris had anticipated, his bold stratagem was a perfect success.

Although not given to prudishness, I confess to being shocked by the diary entry of October 1. Adèle, who is apprehensive about her activities, and Morris decide to take care for the future until her husband returns. Then they plan to exert themselves "to add one to the number of human Existences. This is a happy Mode of conciliating *Prudence* and Duty." It is not only the fact that Morris plans to deceive the husband as to the paternity of a child to be conceived, but also Morris's delight in the act of deluding the old man which amazes me. Several days later, on the historic day of October 5, Morris dines at the Louvre with Adèle and the Bishop d'Autun. The diary entry the next day again startles and amuses me. Four days after agreeing to have a child with Morris, Adèle tells him of the "importunities" of the Bishop. She says that if the Bishop abandons her, she is lost. The mysterious lover is at last revealed to be none other than Talleyrand. It appears that she has a weakness for men with only one good leg.

Aware of the fact that his lady is a coquette, Morris tells her to follow her own inclinations. She tells him she is hurt by his reasonableness and insists she will be only his lover. That same day, Morris writes in his diary, "A Host of Women are gone towards Versailles with some Cannon. A strange Manoevre."

The early days of October 1789 are momentous days for the Revolution. On October 1, the royal court at Versailles sponsors a banquet to secure the attachment of the army. Stories reach Paris that after the King and Queen entered the banquet hall, the nation was omitted from the toasts, white cockades were distributed, and the tricolor—emblem of the new order—was trampled under foot. News of the banquet creates a tempest in Paris similar to Necker's dismissal prior to the storming of the Bastille. The crowds are told the court feasts and mocks the Revolution while the people of Paris starve. By October 5, Paris is close to insurrection. A crowd led by six thousand women, including that fiery daughter of a peasant Theroigne de Mericourt, who is mounted on horseback and dressed in a costume of war with sword and pistols, marches on the palace at Versailles. The King receives a deputation of women who demand bread for the people. He accedes, but the wild crowd outside the palace is not so easily appeased. Lafayette arrives on the scene with a large force of the National Guard. Morris writes that Lafayette was forced to march to Versailles guarded by his own troops, who suspect and threaten him.

The next day, October 6, Versailles is invaded by the populace. A sea of pikes and muskets flood the palace. The crowd forces its way into the bedchamber of the Queen, who flees to the King's apartments. Breaking down doors and killing guards, the angry mob pursues. Lafayette and the National Guard intervene barely in time to save the King's bodyguards and to prevent the invasion of the King's apartments. To calm the crowd, Lafayette appears with King, Queen, and Dauphin on the balcony and addresses the crowd. Wishing to reconcile Marie Antoinette with the multitudes, Lafayette respectfully kisses the hand of the woman who detests him. After this drama, the crowd escorts the royal family to Paris. The long period of royal residence at Versailles is at an end. One hundred and seven years after Louis XIV abandoned Paris for Versailles, the people force the return of the King and Queen to the Palace of the Tuileries. The great events of the Revolution will now be near the windows of Morris at the Hôtel du Roi and Adèle de Flahaut at the Louvre.

On October 6, Paris is all in tumult. The royal family is expected to arrive later in the day. Morris dines with Adèle in the afternoon. She is hurt that he will not promise to marry her. She says she appears despicable in his eyes from having had a lover. He assures her that this is not the reason for his refusal. When she demands his reasons, "with all the Arts of wily Woman working to her Purpose," he replies it is foolish to make engagements depending on so many contingencies. They can discuss it when they both are free. She is not satisfied and begins to cry. Morris then pleads a prior promise on his part and also refuses to violate her prior engagement to Talleyrand. He writes, "Strange Sex! which insists thus on being deceived." Adèle hits upon an expedient. She wants Morris to ask release from his promise in case they are free to marry. She asks for a plain gold ring, and he promises it. She tells him that he must wear the ring. He replies that she must get the Bishop to do that. They quarrel. Finally she swears eternal fidelity to him. "So I find I have a Wife upon my Hands indeed . . . I submit." Soon they learn of the events at Versailles—that the Queen was forced to flee from her bed in her shift and petticoat and with her stockings in hand to the King's chamber for protection. Morris's love and the Revolution have reached a crisis on the same day.

The tempestuous love affair continues. On the eighth, "a vile rainy day," with sweet discourses and kisses Morris teaches his lovely scholar all he knows, but finds that she has very little to learn on any subject. He then purchases her ring. That same day Morris and Lafayette discuss the dangerous political situation. Morris has little respect for Lafayette's abilities as a leader. He writes that Lafayette is unaware that he lacks both talent and information; he means ill to no one but has the need to shine—*"Besoin de Briller."* After seeing Lafayette, Morris dines with Adèle and the Bishop. Talleyrand wants to get rid of Necker and take his place as minister of finance. Morris supports this suggestion. He later notes that Talleyrand is engaged in an affair with none other than Necker's daughter, Madame de Staël. After the Bishop leaves, Morris and Adèle close as lovers what they had commenced as politicians.

The next day Morris suggests to Lafayette that Talleyrand be appointed minister of finance. Lafayette refuses, stating that the Bishop is a bad man—false. Morris defends Talleyrand and tells Lafayette that with the Bishop he gets Mirabeau. Lafayette is surprised because the two men are enemies. The Duke de La Rochefoucault enters and joins the discussion. Morris finishes the day in the embraces of Adèle.

In the course of reading Morris's paper, I could not help comparing my own visit to France with his adventures in the same country. He arrives on private business and within months, in the midst of a historic crisis, is personally advising the leaders of the nation in matters of governance while engaging in a wild love affair with a beautiful married woman. Other ardent females pursue him. On my visit to Paris, I lived almost in complete solitude. The only persons of importance I encountered were as a result of the influence of Gouverneur Morris. Other than the whores at the Palais Royal and my landlady, there was barely a woman in Paris who would look at me. Is it appearance, wealth, birth, connections? Perhaps it is a mixture of all of these. For a select few, life is predestined to be a banquet; for most others, there is only starvation. In the end, it is a matter of the run of the celestial dice.

On October 10 Morris returns a cold answer to a note from Adèle. She begs to see him. He goes to the Louvre and speaks candidly of his feelings. She is surprised and hurt to hear him tell her he does not love her. At length, he consents to bury his dissatisfaction. Although the diary does not explain the reason for this sudden frost, it appears to involve Adèle's continuing relationship with the Bishop. Despite their constant clash of wills, the next day

Morris and Adèle join in "fervent Adoration to the Cyprian Queen, which with Energy repeated conveys to my kind Votary all of mortal Bliss which can be enjoyed." He leaves her "reclined in the sweet Tranquillity of Nature well satisfied." Later that same day Morris leaves the Bishop with Adèle. Although she has every opportunity to betray him, Morris writes that he has every confidence in his mistress. Three days later Morris is with his lover when she receives a note from the Bishop. When she insists he depart before the Bishop arrives, he acts coldly and refuses her embraces. This disconcerts her very much until he "confers the Joy repeatedly." The next day Adèle glows with satisfaction as Morris and the Bishop sit together agreeing with each other's opinions. "What a triumph for a Woman!" he writes. Morris again leaves them together, risking heroically the chance of having an unfaithful mistress. He writes, "What Self Denial for a Lover."

Two days later Morris visits Adèle, who is suffering from pains she has had for years as a result of a wound suffered in the delivery of her child. Morris's other prescriptions have not worked. This time he exhibits "another Medicine which works Wonders," causing the roses to blush on her cheeks and her eyes to sparkle. After a visit to Adèle's old nun at the convent, which as usual excites her desires, they return to the Louvre and again celebrate the Cyprian Mystery, the rite of Aphrodite. As Morris is departing to permit Adèle to receive the Bishop, she uses an expression of contempt for Talleyrand. Morris realizes he can wean her from all regard for the Bishop; but, Morris notes, he is the father of her child.

What I had begun to suspect while reading the diary was true. Charles de Flahaut is the son of Talleyrand. For the first time I understood the surprised expressions of Talleyrand and later Charles when I mentioned one to the other. In 1818, when Charles's reply to my lost letter to him was received by me, I read with great interest the passage about Talleyrand's having kept Charles's names off the list of Napoleon's officers who were to be punished for abandoning the King before Waterloo. Without the knowledge gained from reading Morris's diary, I would never have understood the real cause of this act of mercy. How little our eyes impart to us about the reality lurking beneath the mirrored surface of existence.

On October 28 Morris visits the Louvre and finds the Bishop, Adèle, and their son having dinner. The diary merely states that the son arrived on that day. It appears that the four-year-old Auguste-Charles-Joseph de Flahaut de la Billerarderie has been staying in the country. When the Bishop leaves, Adèle dwells upon her child and weeps. Morris wipes away her tears, mingling, he says, the sexual with maternal affection. This bliss opens the female heart to lavish profession of endless love. Morris coolly writes, "She means every Word of it now, but nothing here below can last forever." As usual, there appears to be much calculation and sangfroid as to Morris's dealings with his friend. On the last day of 1789 Adèle barely avoids having real cause to weep for her son. Outside the convent, Charles is attacked by a large dog. Adèle is badly frightened, but Charles is saved for the future service of his Emperor.

The rectangular relationship among the lovers begins to turn into a comedy. The Bishop and Morris frequently arrive at the Louvre together to find the old husband in the way of both suitors. On one occasion Morris begins to make love to Adèle. Before they can complete the rites of passion, the Bishop enters. After some discussion, Morris leaves his friend and the Bishop together. Considering the state of expectation to which Adèle was raised, Morris thinks the chances are greatly in the Bishop's favor. He later writes that a commerce which is smooth and uninterrupted palls. If difficulties do not arise, they must be created. Although a woman would not thank a lover who purposely gives pain, it is nevertheless true that she derives her great pleasure from that pain. In this regard, he declares at a social gathering that a woman of sense and learning is more easily seduced than another. Having perhaps a higher sense of duty, she feels pleasure proportionately greater in the breach. The mingled emotions of delight and regret lead her on further and faster than another would go. After listening to his remarks, an old woman declares his opinion to be abominable but just.

During this period the new constitutional monarchy achieves stability. Late 1789 to the middle of 1791 is to be one of the less turbulent periods of the revolutionary years. Next to the King, Lafayette becomes the most powerful man in France. The King gives him command of the regular army in the area of Paris as well as of the Paris National Guard. Devoted to popular sovereignty, Lafayette advises the King to cooperate with the National Assembly. In spite of Lafayette's exalted status, Morris continues to have contempt for his talents. He predicts that Lafayette will be used by others because he lacks talent to use them. He speaks to Lafayette and finds only vaulting ambition which overleaps itself. "This Man's Mind is so elated by Power, already too great for the Measure of his Abilities, that he looks into the Clouds and grasps at the Supreme. From this Moment every Step in his Ascent will I think accelerate his Fall." Morris's powers of prediction are not to be disregarded. One morning before the commencement of winter, he enters the salon and predicts snow. The company thinks him wild and rash; that evening it snows heavily. His predictions about Lafayette are to prove as accurate as his weather forecast.

At this time Tom Paine, who is living in London, appears in Paris. Paine has designed a model of an iron bridge in London and wants Morris to see it. Despite their past enmity, the two men, to my surprise, see each other regularly as if they are old friends. Morris has not the harsh words for Paine which he uses for that other republican, Lafayette. He praises the "half way arguments" which form the "excellence" of Paine's writings. He even admits that Paine's conceptions and expressions are splendid and novel, if not always clear and just. Morris also meets Cardinal de Rohan of the infamous Diamond Necklace Affair which unjustly discredited Marie Antoinette. The Cardinal was once the lover of Adèle's beautiful sister Julie, who used to drive about with the Cardinal disguised as a young cleric. It seems that the rule of celibacy among the French clergy is in grave danger whenever Adèle or her sister are about.

In February of 1790 Morris plans to travel to London on an informal mission for President Washington. Up to the time of his departure, Adèle and Morris continue to perform the lovers' part together. He writes in his diary that they make use of every means in their power to perpetuate the noble family of Adèle's husband. "It is a great Pity," he states, "that our Efforts have hitherto proved unsuccessful." On the day before his departure, the lovers engage in their last embrace for many months. The Bishop arrives and leaves angrily. Adèle follows him out. When she returns, she is upset. In response to Morris's inquiry, she informs him that the Bishop has reproached her with infidelity in the most injudicious terms. Morris bids adieu to his tearful lover, who declares her intention to write a letter to the Bishop.

During the first few weeks of my visits to Morrisania, Nancy and the child were frequently not in view. When present, Nancy was often moody and unpredictable. On the bad days, her greetings were perfunctory and brief. At other times she seemed to be happy and would spend some time chatting with me. On those more amicable days, she would usually enter the library to provide me with extra paper, ink, or quills, with a knife to sharpen the quills to my liking. Flattered by her attentions, I luxuriated in them like a cat resting in the sunlight. We would talk about trifling matters. Often the conversation concerned her child—his problems as an infant when teething, his fear of dogs, or his delightful prattling. When the child was present, I unfailingly attempted to curry favor with his mother by talking and playing with him.

"How did you get to be four so fast?"

"I growed," the boy shyly replied as he fervently embraced his mother's leg. How I envied those little arms.

Nancy would invariably smile or chuckle at the boy's answer as I gained her attention by continuing to amuse him. I would have preferred to use one of Morris's amorous strategies, but one can be cool to attract another only when that other has previously shown some interest. Nancy was far too distant for my use of such maneuvers. When I asked if she had read the diary, she answered, "I only glanced at them briefly; some day I will read them." My occasional references to events in the diary indicated that Nancy knew little about the contents including her late husband's liaison with Adèle de Flahaut.

When Nancy approached the library, I could always recognize the familiar sound of her footsteps. My heart would pound with excitement as she came near. But the disappointment caused by her brief, infrequent visits was acute. She shared none of her innermost thoughts with me. No more than a superficial conversation could be expected. I began to feel like Tantalus, confronted with the thing he most desired always slightly beyond the reach of his outstretched arms. Better, I thought, if she did not visit me at all. Reading about Morris's amorous adventures merely inflamed my imagination. My mind would wander as I attempted to guess the nature of his courtship of Nancy. Did he approach her in the same cold, scheming manner which he used with Adèle? Had Nancy been merely a young woman seeking shelter from the storm of life in the protective arms of an older man, or was she a tempestuous lover like Adèle? Perhaps, I thought, if Morris maintained a diary at the time he began to court Nancy, the truth, or at least part of it, could be revealed. Surely he must have retained his correspondence from the period after his return from France. Maybe Nancy's response to John Randolph's letter was among these later documents. Because Nancy was living with him, it did seem unlikely that he would keep a diary as honest about Nancy as it was concerning Adèle. Nevertheless, I became so obsessed with the idea of reading the later documents that I fell into rash imprudence.

One day when we were speaking about the diary and the events of the French Revolution, I casually asked Nancy if Morris's diary and letters continued beyond the volumes in my possession. "Oh yes!" she answered. "He kept his diary and correspondence to the time of his last illness. When he instructed me to let you see the materials up to 1800, I asked him if there was anything in the later volumes which might be of interest to you. He said they were of little historical value and should remain confidential. Otherwise, I would have given you all of the books."

"Of course. His last request should be followed precisely." My heart sank with disappointment. My direct question had been a major blunder. There was no longer a proper way to request the later volumes. If only I had held my tongue until a pretext for seeking them could have been devised. If only . . .

On February 17, 1790, Morris leaves on his mission to England. Traveling through Antwerp and Amsterdam on private business, he meets a Madame Caton who favorably receives his advances. Unfaithful to Adèle, at least in his heart, he laments the fact that time and opportunity are wanting for that consummation which is devoutly to be wished. He arrives in London on March 27. In order to determine the purpose of his mission, a careful review of the letter books for the period was necessary. There, I found excellent material for my history, including a brilliant letter from Morris to President Washington describing the course of the French Revolution. A letter from Washington to Morris, from New York, dated October 13, 1789, sets forth the instructions for Morris's official but informal mission. Morris is to press for speedy performance of the peace treaty between the United States and Britain, including provisions for putting the United States in possession of frontier posts, and payment of compensation for Negro slaves who were carried away during the war. It is ironic, but one of the frontier posts the British refused to evacuate was Fort Oswego, which controlled the future route of the Erie Canal. As to compensation for slaves, the southern states had been opposing the payment of debts contracted with British merchants before and after the War for American Independence until the British paid for the Negroes removed from the United States. This matter would eventually be addressed in the famous "British debt" litigation. Morris is also directed to inquire whether the British contemplate a treaty of commerce with the United States and the nature of the proposed terms. In his negotiations with the Duke of Leeds, the British Foreign Secretary, Morris gradually discovers that the British intend to breach their treaty with the United States by keeping the frontier posts and withholding payment for the slaves. They also are not interested in a treaty of commerce. He informs President Washington that Britain feels so confident in her greatness, that it is an unfavorable moment to obtain advantageous terms on any bargain. At the suggestion of Tom Paine, who has returned to London, he also speaks to the Duke of Leeds on the impressment of American sailors. Morris tells Leeds, "I believe, my Lord, this is the only instance in which we are not treated as aliens." He later meets with Mr. Pitt himself, who approves of the idea of certificates from the Admiralty of America for the purpose of proving the nationality of American seamen. Twenty-two years later many men, including me, would take up arms in a war based in large part on the failure to settle this issue. Before I knew him, Morris was engaged in weaving the fabric of my destiny. But even he is helpless in the face of British arrogance. Morris's diary indicates that at this time there is much conversation about a man who roams the streets of London cutting and wounding women with his knife. It appears from the negotiations that Morris would have made as much progress in bargaining with the madman as he does in speaking to the representatives of the British government.

In the course of his residence in London, Morris frequently sees his Tory brother, General Staats Long Morris, Captain John Paul Jones, and Tom Paine. For the first time in the diary, Morris shows displeasure toward Paine, who constantly borrows money from him. Expecting the loans will not be speedily repaid, Morris tells Paine he is a "troublesome fellow." Nevertheless, he does visit Paine's model of an iron bridge. As to female companionship, he remains solitary and writes he will continue so unless he joins one of the "Cyprian Nymphs"; but these connections are not consistent with his ideas. He remains faithful to Adèle.

After a long trip through Flanders and the Rhineland, during which he is unsuccessful in selling wilderness lands in New York, Morris returns to Paris on November 6, 1790. He has been away for almost nine months. He meets with Leray de Chaumont and they lay their plans for the sale of lands in America. Although Adèle claims to be happy to see him, they do not immediately resume their passionate encounters. Instead they begin to quarrel. Adèle continues to receive Talleyrand, and also has acquired a new admirer, Lord Wycombe, a young Englishman. She informs Morris that he must permit her to receive the Bishop and to deny herself to him. In Morris's absence, Talleyrand has regained Adèle's affections. However, she does agree to return Morris's ring if she is unfaithful to him. In visiting her, Morris now assumes the modest timidity of a young lover "who feels for the first Time." Within a week after his return to Paris, Morris is able to engage Adèle in sentimental caresses, after which "we proceed with Energy to the last Act, which is forcibly impressed and as a natural Consquence her Heart is opened." She declares the Bishop shall not have her. Four days later, during a ride in Morris's carriage, she says she wishes she had not received his caresses so she can meet the

Bishop with a heart more at ease. Morris coolly proposes they break off all further connection. Adèle is not agreeable to this suggestion. So instead of ending their relationship, they visit the convent once again and "sacrifice to the Cyprian Queen in the Retreat consecrated to Chastity," the apartment of the abbess herself.

Believing Adèle to be an unfaithful coquette, Morris plans to recover his dominion over her by feigning indifference in order to stimulate the desire to retain his love. His stratagem appears to be successful. She informs him that she has quarreled with the Bishop, who is jealous of Morris. Yet two days later the whole mad business begins again, with Adèle wanting to meet the Bishop without having any reason to reproach herself. Morris threatens anew to end their connection. Talleyrand, Wycombe, and Morris all continue to stumble over each other at the Louvre, each man jealous of the others. Adèle accuses Morris of having a regular plan of inflicting pain upon her. Stating his wish is to give her pleasure, he denies her accusation. Yet he again confides to his diary that it is strange but true that the pain arising from the apprehension of losing a lover is essential to the pleasure a woman finds in possessing him.

The battle of lovers continues until the delicate equilibrium is upset by the political turmoil swirling about them. On February 24, 1791, Adèle finds in a blank envelope a will written by the Bishop making her his heir. Because of the Civil Constitution of the Clergy by which the State has begun to assume control of the Church, most clergyman, who had previously favored reform, have become open enemies of the Revolution. On the day his will is found, Talleyrand has consecrated the first two elected Bishops and fears assassination at the hands of the defenders of the Catholic Church. Paris is in turmoil. Talleyrand has resigned as Bishop to become a civil administrator. Adèle is in great agitation, as she fears the former Bishop of Autun will be killed by the clergy. The crisis passes and Talleyrand remains unharmed. Like a cat, he always touches ground on his feet. Within a week Morris and Adèle are again performing the nuptial act and quarreling frequently. Morris becomes suspicious and jealous when he sees a screen in front of Adele's bed to prevent a sudden view by anyone entering her apartment. In order to gain ascendancy over Adèle, he regularly resorts to his tactic of bringing her to a state of uncertainty about him. It never fails to excite strong emotions on her part. She asks him if he would marry her if she became a widow. At first he declines to answer. When pressed, however, he asks how she can ask such a question after what she has revealed of Talleyrand's influence over her. She later tells him he must have wonderful power over his own mind to love only to a certain point and no more. She informs him she will never marry Talleyrand because she cannot go with him to the altar without first confessing to her connection with Morris. Repeatedly she touches on Morris's refusal to say he will marry her. The quarreling becomes so persistent, he proposes a final separation, as she cannot love him without hope of a future union. She is terribly upset. For many weeks they are cool to each other. Morris begins to look at other possible lovers. He flirts with a Madame de Nadaillac. He comes near to consummation with his new "friend," but she is refractory, talking much of religion and morality at the crucial moments. By late May of 1791, just before he departs for England again, Morris renews his relationship with Adèle and they recommence engaging regularly in the "pleasing act."

During the period of his quarrels with Adèle, Morris witnesses the great spectacle of the funeral of Mirabeau. He meets the great scientist Lavoisier, who will later fall victim to the guillotine. Tom Paine arrives in Paris and visits Morris regularly. A perfect example of Morris's ability to see both sides of a philosophical argument is his comment that there are good things in both Burke's *Reflections on the French Revolution* and Paine's rejoinder attacking Burke, the splendid *The Rights of Man*. Paine openly speaks to Morris of the fact that Morris was among his enemies in times past. Morris frankly acknowledges that he had urged Paine's dismissal as Secretary of the Committee of Foreign Affairs during the War of American Independence. They remain friendly enemies.

While Morris is in London working with Benjamin Franklin's Tory son Temple on the sale of Robert Morris's Genesee tract, he learns of the attempt by the King and Queen to flee from France. He correctly predicts that if they are retaken, it will suspend for some time all monarchical government in France. The royal family is captured on June 21, 1791, at Varennes. They are brought back to Paris as captives, the Queen's hair having turned gray during the two-day flight. By the time of Morris's return to Paris on July 2, the King has been suspended from office. For the first time the press begins openly to call for the establishment of a republic. Paine drafts a manifesto demanding, in the name of the American republic, the establishment of a French republic. Even the moderates begin to turn against the monarchy. The attacks on aristocrats recommence. As in the summer of 1789, châteaux are burned. Morris writes that, because he lodges near the Tuileries, it is likely he will see a battle beneath his windows. He also notes that Lafayette was near to being hanged for his failure to prevent the escape of the royal family. The Marquis is beginning to suffer the consequences of attaining too great an elevation.

Four days after the great July 17 riot in the Champs de Mars, during which Lafayette is almost killed while trying to control the mob, Morris and Adèle quarrel. He tells her their connection will soon terminate, later giving as a reason the fact that her friends dislike him. Once again Morris's stratagem succeeds. Attentive to removing his displeasure, she complains of the continuing cold cruelty of Talleyrand and engages in a series of dangerous, passionate meetings with Morris. Prior to a gathering at the Louvre, with the doors all open, visitors expected, and Adèle's husband present in the apartment below, they risk discovery and celebrate the nuptial rites in the passage while Adèle's friend is engaged in playing the harpsichord in the drawing room. A few days later they indulge their passions in the afternoon and then dine together. That same evening, at eight-thirty, they again engage in lovemaking outside on the quai between the Louvre and the Tuileries. Morris writes, "Had the Coachman turned his Head he must have viewed this edifying Scene." Several days thereafter, Morris, Adèle, and her friend Mademoiselle Duplessis dine at the Louvre. Because Duplessis does not understand English, they are able to engage freely in the conversation of lovers. Talleyrand visits. After he leaves, Duplessis retires to a window with a book. Because she is nearsighted, Morris and Adèle are able to caress each other without fear of being seen. Adèle becomes so animated, they proceed to perform their usual ceremonies, "which are fully accomplished in the Presence of Mademoiselle." For weeks they engage in such lustful scenes. Then one day Adèle informs Morris that her husband has written her a letter insisting on his rights. She has refused and expects an altercation. Two days later, as anticipated, Adèle quarrels with her husband upon her refusal to admit his embraces. She does, however, accept those of Morris in their private hours of joy. Yet, once again, Adèle begins to hint that they must begin to confine themselves in future to a pure friendship. Morris reflects and tells his friend she is perfectly right. He declares he will absent himself until he has formed another relationship. It is a stroke she does not expect. Their strange minuet of passion and restraint begins anew. As usual, he plays the cool lover and rejects her advances until she begs him to renew their love. He later writes, "Everyone is taken at the Price he puts on himself, if taken at all, and the great Art consists in placing the Merchandize at as high a Value as it will bear." The problem for me, I thought, while reading these words, is to be taken at all. Nancy must want me before I can increase her desire for acquisition by placing a high price on myself. It is an opportunity, I feared, never to be won.

During this period, the King accepts the new constitution of 1791. As a consequence he is liberated from his arrest. Among Morris's papers, I discovered a copy of a letter in French to His Majesty, Louis XVI. Morris recommends that the King attempt to win the support of the people by providing them with bread. As a man of business, Morris himself has plans to become personally involved in supplying grain to the French government. Perhaps he also has unselfish motives, as his diary indicates he is strongly committed to the constitutional monarchy. He weeps at news of the King's despair and is gladdened by the monarch's restoration to limited power. He regularly consults with the King's ministers on matters of governance. But the real power resides in the new Legislative Assembly. That Assembly contains the seeds of its own destruction. Its predecessor, the Constituent Assembly, had adopted a proposal of Robespierre to the effect that none of its members could be eligible for the next Assembly, thereby excluding many of the moderate leaders of the Revolution.

Like Morris, Lafayette supports the constitutional monarchy. However, because the King and Queen despise him, he resigns his command of the Paris National Guard and retires to Auvergne in the belief that the Revolution has ended. In a letter to Robert Morris, his agent, Gouverneur states that Lafayette's sun seems to have set unless he puts himself at the head of the republican party, which, like the nobles, is opposed to him. Morris writes, "All this results from Feebleness of Character and the Spirit of Intrigue which bring forward the Courtier but ruin the Statesman. I am very sorry for him because I believe he meant well."

Early in 1792 Morris departs for England again. I wasted days reading his bulky correspondence on the sale of land. Morris's business in Europe appears to have been a great success. Leray de Chaumont informs him that all of the lands in the State of New York are sold. In London, Morris is able to concentrate on other business. He does not even have to worry about his rivals. Lord Wycombe is in America, and Talleyrand is in London for some time, attempting to negotiate with the British. Morris later writes President Washington that Talleyrand's mission was a failure because the British ministers consider him a prime mover in the Revolution, which they view with horror. Also, Talleyrand's personal reputation for corruption is offensive to persons who pride themselves on decency of manners. In another letter to President Washington, Morris writes that the former Bishop d'Autun is not exemplary in the matter of morals. "Not so much for Adultery, because that was common enough among the Clergy of high Rank, but for the Variety and Publicity of his Amours; for Gambling, and above all for Stock Jobbing. . . ."

Tom Paine is also back in London. Morris reads the second part of *The Rights of Man* and tells Paine he is fearful it will get Paine punished. He notes that Paine himself is drunk with self-conceit while his book causes great indignation. Paine thinks he can bring about a revolution in Great Britain. Morris thinks he is more likely to bring himself to the pillory. Morris's fears for Paine's safety are well-justified. Paine will be indicted for treason, escape to France before the trial, manage to be elected to the French National Assembly, and be thrown in jail as a sympathizer with the moderate revolutionaries, the Girondins.

While he is in England, Morris receives the news that the United States Senate has confirmed his appointment as Minister Plenipotentiary for the United States at the Court of France. The controversial appointment by President Washington takes eighteen days and splits the Senate 16 to 11. The confirmation occurs on January 12, 1792. Morris receives formal notification on April 6. As the new minister, Morris's letters begin to provide much more interesting information for inclusion in my history. His friend Alexander Hamilton, then Secretary of the Treasury, sends him a letter which provides a cipher for their future correspondence. President Washington is to be Scoevola; Vice-President Adams, Brutus; Secretary of State Jefferson, Scipio; Senator Robert Morris, Cato; Senator Aaron Burr, Soevius; Representative James Madison, Tarquin, etcetera. A letter from Secretary of State Thomas Jefferson informs Morris of his appointment; he is instructed to send secret communications through a M. de la Motte at Havre and is provided a cipher for his use as minister. In a series of letters, Jefferson states his amicable policy toward revolutionary France. A most interesting private letter from President Washington accompanies Jefferson's letter of notification. In it the President explains the reasons for the Senate's opposition to his appointment of Morris.

Philadelphia Jan 28th 1792

My dear Sir,

PRIVATE

Your favor of the 30th of September came duly to hand, and I thank you for the important information contained in it.

The official communications from the Secretary of State, accompanying this letter, will convey to you the evidence of my *nomination*, and *appointment* of you to be Minister Plenipotentiary for the United States at the Court of France; and my assurances that both were made with *all my heart*, will, I am persuaded, satisfy you as to that fact. I wish I could add that the *advice & consent* flowed from a similar source. Candour forbids it—and friendship requires that I should assign the causes, as far as they have come to my knowledge.—

Whilst your abilities, knowledge in the affairs of this Country, & disposition to serve it were adduced, and asserted on one hand, you were charged on the other hand, with levity, and imprudence of conversation and conduct.—It was urged, that your habit of expression, indicated a hauteaur disgusting to those who happen to differ from you in sentiment; and among a people who study civility and politeness more than any other nation, it must be displeasing.—That in France you were considered as a favourer of Aristocracy, & unfriendly to its Revolution (I suppose they meant Constitution).—That under this impression you could not be an acceptable public character—of consequence, would not be able, however willing, to promote the interests of this Country in an essential degree.

—That in England you indiscreetly communicated the purport of your Mission, in the first instance to the Minister of France, at that Court; who, availing himself in the same moment of the occasion, gave it the appearance of a Movement through his Court.—This, and other circumstances of a similar Nature, joined to a closer intercourse with the opposition Members, occasioned distrust, & gave displeasure to the Ministry; which was the cause, it is said, of that reserve which you experienced in negotiating the business which had been entrusted to you.—

But not to go further into detail—I will place the ideas of your political adversaries in the light which their arguments have presented them to my view—viz.—That the promptitude with wch your brilliant, & lively imagination is displayed, allow too little time for deliberation and correction; and is the primary cause of those sallies which too often offend, and of that ridicule of characters which begets enmity not easy to be forgotten, but which might easily be avoided if it was under the control of more caution and prudence.—In a word, that it is indispensably necessary that more circumspection should be observed by our Representatives abroad than they conceive you are disposed to adopt.—

In this statement you have the pros & the cons; by reciting them, I give you a proof of my friendship, if I give none of my policy or judgment.—I do it on the presumption that a mind conscious of its own rectitude, fears not what is said of it; but will bid defiance to and despise shafts that are not barbed with accusations against honor or integrity;—and because I have the fullest confidence (supposing the allegations to be founded in whole or part) that you would find no difficulty, being apprised of the exceptionable light in which they are received, and considering yourself as the representative of this Country, to effect a change; and thereby silence, in the most unequivocal and satisfactory manner, your political opponents.—Of my good opinion, & of my friendship & regard, you may be asured—and that

I am always—Y^r. affect^e.

Go. Washington

In his response to Washington's letter, Morris answers like a repentant son to his displeased father.

London 6 April 1792

George Washington Esq!

Philadelphia

My dear Sir

I receive this Instant your Favor of the twenty-eighth of January, and I do most sincerely thank you for the Information which you have been so kind as to communicate. I know how to value the Friendship by which they were dictated. I have always thought that the Counsel of our Enemies is wholesome, tho bitter, if we can but turn it to good Account & in Order that I may not fail to do so on the present Occasion *I now promise you* that Circumspection of Conduct which has hitherto I acknowledge form'd no Part of my Character. And I make the *Promise* that my Sense of Integrity may enforce what my Sense of Propriety dictates. . . .

Morris returns to Paris on May 6, 1792, to assume his position as the Minister of the United States at the very moment when the Revolution is about to enter its most violent period. For a new element has been added to the turbulence within France. On April 20, 1792, France declared war on Austria, which is actively opposed to the Revolution. It is not yet known that Louis XVI and Marie Antoinette are engaged in treason, secretly revealing the military plans of the French government and inviting European monarchs to send their armies to overthrow the Revolution. The declaration will begin a period of twenty-three years of hostilities during which the Bourbon monarchy will cease to rule in France. Morris is aware that it is a fateful moment for both himself and the Revolution. He correctly predicts a period of anarchy to be followed by the reestablishment of despotism. He writes to Jefferson, "On the whole, Sir, we stand on a vast Volcano, we feel it tremble and we hear it roar, but how and when and where it will burst and who may be destroy'd by its Eruptions it is beyond the Ken of mortal Foresight to discover."

Unlike his previous arrival from London, Morris returns to a friendly Adèle de Flahaut. Together they look for a new residence for the American minister. Morris hires a large house with a stable of horses in the Rue de la Planche, across the river from the Louvre. Although Adèle and Morris resume their squabbling, they will continue to sacrifice on the Cyprian altar until the events of the Revolution prevent their adulterous coupling. On June 3 the new American minister meets the King and Queen for the first time. Morris notes the feebleness of the King's disposition. The monarchy has only two months to live. Morris writes to Jefferson that the best picture he can give of the French nation is that of cattle in a thunderstorm. In a later letter to the Secretary of State, he states that the moderate men are attacked on all sides by those who want to eliminate the effects of the Revolution and those who want to go further and introduce a republic. "I cannot go on with the Picture for my Heart bleeds when I reflect that the finest Opportunity which ever presented itself for establishing the Rights of Mankind throughout the civilized World is perhaps lost and forever."

Seventeen days after Morris meets the King, the cattle panic. On June 20 an armed multitude invades the Tuileries. For several hours the King and his sister are held by a mob in a crowded room. They are subjected to threats and insults. Many moderates are angered at the treatment of the royal family; they rally to the throne. Lafayette, who has become a general of the army fighting on the frontiers, hastens to Paris to denounce those who attack the constitution from within while the army bleeds to defend it from enemies outside the state. Morris meets with Lafayette and tells him that a popular government is good for nothing in France; an aristocratic constitution is needed. Lafayette states a preference for the American Constitution but with a hereditary executive. Morris replies that in such case the monarch would be too strong and would have to be checked by a hereditary senate. Lafayette attempts to arrange to address the National Guard for the purpose of restoring its loyalty to the crown. Marie Antoinette ruins the plan, stating that any fate would be better than being saved by Lafayette. He returns to his frontier command.

The volcano is about to erupt. For the first time in his diary Morris complains of being sleepless for nights at a time. On many mornings of that long passed summer of 1792, he is tormented by a "nervous heaviness." Anxiously I read on, knowing the precise number of days before the cataclysm. In the diary Morris cryptically refers to receiving money from the King. It is only much later, when I arrived at the papers of 1796, that I discovered an undated document in French written in Vienna and addressed "Son Altesse Royale." In the document, Morris speaks of himself in the third person. It makes clear that he had good reason for being nervous during the summer of 1792. At that time, it appears he was engaged in a plot to get the royal family out of Paris. In the document of 1796 he explains to the King's daughter that the King had asked Morris to supervise what was being done in his service and to become guardian of his papers and money. On July 22, 1792, the King sent Morris 547,000 livres of the royal funds. In the letter to the King's daughter, Morris accounts for the use of the money and returns the remainder. There is no mention of these royalist activities in Morris's reports to President Washington or Secretary of State Jefferson. Contrary to his promise to the President, he has not acted with circumspection.

During that same month of July 1792, Morris receives a message from John Paul Jones that he is dying. Morris goes to his bedside and writes the sick man's will. Morris leaves and later returns with Adèle and the Queen's first physician; but Paul Jones is dead. Morris will later be criticized for not arranging a large funeral for the American hero. Morris defends himself by stating he had no right to spend the money of the heirs of the United States on "such follies" as a "pompous funeral."

On July 25 the Duke of Brunswick, commander of the allied army, issues his infamous manifesto to the people of France announcing his intention to sweep away the Revolution and threatening Paris with a never-to-be-forgotten vengeance if the royal family is again mistreated. The defenders of the Revolution are left with no alternative but resistance to the death. On the day of the issuance of the manifesto, Morris encounters Talleyrand on the stairs at the Louvre. Talleyrand politely expresses his misfortune to come always as Morris is leaving. Morris writes that he will have that misfortune frequently. Despite mounting tumult in the city and his own personal danger, Morris continues his amorous encounters with Adèle. They again perform the nuptial rites in the convent while awaiting the arrival of the abbess. On August 2 it is extremely hot as they embrace with difficulty in his carriage. The August heat continues for days. Morris visits the court and learns that the royal family and retinue were awake all night expecting to be murdered. Adèle informs Morris that her husband has behaved brutally and threatened separation. The cuckold too has finally rebelled. The heat does not end; Paris is in great agitation. At last the volcano erupts. Morris's entry for the historic day is simple and concise:

> Friday 10 August.—This Morning M.ʳ de Monciel calls and his report is tranquilizing but shortly after he leaves me the Cannon begin, and Musquetry mingled with them announce a warm Day. The Château, undefended but by the Swiss, is carried and the Swiss wherever found are murder'd. The King & Queen are in the National Assembly who have decreed the Suspension of his Authority. Madame de Flahaut sends her Son and comes afterwards to take Refuge. I have Company to dine but many of those which were invited do not come. Mʳ. Huskisson, the Secretary to the british Embassador, comes in the Evening. He gives a sad Account of Things. The Weather continues very warm or rather, extremely hot.

Approximately eight hundred of the King's defender's fall in battle or are slaughtered while retreating. Almost four hundred of the attackers are reported as casualties. The infant constitutional monarchy is overthrown. The second revolution has established a republic in France. The middle is gone. The struggle is now between monarchists and radical republicans. Lafayette, more afraid of the Jacobins than the Austrians and Prussians, flees the army with a number of his officers and takes refuge with the enemy. He is thrown into prison by the Austrians, where he will languish for five long years. Morris writes, "Thus his circle is compleated. He has spent his fortune on a Revolution and is now crush'd by the wheel which he put in motion. He lasted longer than I expected."

The day after the upheaval, Morris is again sleepless. The weather remains hot as the new order takes hold. The house of the American minister is filled with those seeking refuge. Many request passports from Morris. He appears to turn none of the uninvited guests from his door. A number of armed men enter his residence and demand to search it for hidden weapons. Morris refuses and files a formal protest. He obtains an apology from the new government. The diplomats join the flight from Paris. Morris writes to the Secretary of State on August 22, 1792.

The different Embassadors and Ministers are all taking their Flight and if I stay I shall be alone. I mean however to stay unless circumstances should command me away because in the admitted Case that my letters of Credence are to the Monarchy and not to the Republic of France it becomes a Matter of indifference whether I remain in this Country or go to England during the Time which may be needful to obtain your Orders or to produce a Settlement of Affairs here. Going hence, however, would look like taking part against the late Revolution, and I am not only unauthoriz'd in this respect, but I am bound to suppose that if the great Majority of the Nation adhere to the new form the United States will approve thereof; because in the first place we have no right to prescribe to this Country the Government they shall adopt, and next because the Basis of our own Constitution is the indefeasible Right of the People to establish it.

Among those who are leaving Paris is the Venetian Embassador. He was furnish'd with Passports from the Office of Foreign Affairs, but he was nevertheless stopp'd at the Barrier, was conducted to the Hôtel de Ville, was there question'd for Hours and his Carriages examin'd and search'd. This Violation of the Rights of Embassadors could not fail (as you may suppose) to make Impression. It has been broadly hinted to me that the Honor of my Country and my own require that I should go away. But I am of a different Opinion, and rather think that those who give such Hints are somewhat Influenc'd by Fear. It is true that the Position is not without Danger, but I presume that when the President did me the honor of naming me to this Embassy it was not for my personal Pleasure or Safety, but to promote the Interests of my Country. These therefore I shall continue to pursue to the best of my Judgment, and as to Consequences they are in the Hand of God.

Gouverneur Morris will be the only foreign ambassador in Paris during the Terror.

The September massacres begin. The panic commences on September 2. Morris and Adèle see a proclamation that the enemy are at the gates of Paris. They know this report must be false and expect the worst. She is taken ill with concern about the fate of her friends. The populace are told they cannot march to the frontiers and leave their families at the mercy of the aristocrats and priests who have been arrested since August 10. That afternoon many of the refractory priests are slain. Mobs attack prisoners throughout the city. For days, thereafter, the entries in the diary are dreadfully repetitive:—"Monday 3d.—The murdering continues all Day. I am told there are about eight hundred men concerned in it . . . Tuesday 4.—The Murders continue . . . Thursday 6.— There is nothing new this Day. The Murders continue and the Magistrates swear to protect Persons and Property." Still in the house of the American minister, Adèle sends for a Monsieur Bertrand of the cavalry and pays him for saving the life of her husband. Talleyrand hopes to obtain his passport; he urges Morris to procure one and quit Paris. Leray de Chaumont takes his leave. Morris remains. In a letter to Jefferson, he describes the massacres.

> . . . We have had one Week of uncheck'd Murders in which some thousands have perish'd in this City. It began with between two and three hundred of the Clergy who had been shut up because they would not take the Oath prescrib'd by Law and which they said was contrary to their Conscience. Thence *these Executors of speedy Justice* went to the Abbaye where the persons were confin'd who were at Court on the Tenth. These were dispatch'd also, and afterwards they visited the other prisons. All those who were confine'd, either on the accusation or Suspicion of Crimes, were destroy'd. Madame de Lamballe was I believe the only woman kill'd, and she was beheaded and emboweled, the Head and entrails paraded on Pikes thro' the Street, and the body dragg'd after them. They continu'd I am told in the Neighbourhood of the Temple until the Queen look'd out at this horrid Spectacle. Yesterday the Prisoners from Orleans were put to death at Versailles. The destruction began here about five in the afternoon on Sunday the second Instant. A Guard had been sent a few days since to make the Duke de La Rochefoucault prisoner. He was on his way to Paris under their Escort with his wife and Mother when he was taken out of his Carriage and killed. The Ladies were taken back to La Roche Guyonne where they are now in a State of Arrestation. . . .

The Vigilance Committee later reports 1079 have been slain out of 2639 confined in prisons. Danton urges overcoming the royalists by terror. In his famous "Toujours de l'audace" speech before the Assembly, he declares that in order to overcome the enemies of France "we need audacity, more audacity, and France is saved." Marat relentlessly demands that the enemies of France must be slaughtered. Once the dogs of war are unleashed there is no turning back. Leaders and followers must support the Revolution or perish in the rivers of blood swirling about them.

On September 20, the day of the Battle of Valmy and the repulse of the invaders of France, Tom Paine, a member of the National Convention, calls on Morris, who learns that the moderate Brissotine faction is desirous of doing mischief to the American minister. The next day the entry in his diary is sardonically brief. "Nothing new this Day except that the Convention has met and declar'd they will have no King in France. The Weather is foul."

Morris's correspondence is filled with letters concerning the plight of Lafayette. Morris is cool toward helping him. Unable to see how the United States can claim him from a foreign power at war with France, Morris writes, "My opinion is that the less we meddle in the great Quarrel which agitates Europe the better will it be for us, and altho the private feelings of friendship or Humanity might properly sway us as private Men we have in our public Character higher Duties to fulfil than those which may be dictated by Sentiments of Affection towards an Individual." This from the same public man who secretly handles the funds of Louis XVI and plots the King's escape from Paris. The same feeling of disgust rises in my gorge as afflicted me during Morris's Bourbon speech. The dead man has the same power over my emotions as he possessed when he was alive. It must be reported, Morris would later redeem himself in my eyes by taking steps to assist Lafayette upon the request of the imprisoned man's family.

The date of September 30, 1792, in the diary caused me to pause. At first I could not identify the reason for my hesitation; then it occurred to me. In distant Virginia events are occurring on this night and the next morning which will profoundly affect Morris's future. Nancy Randolph has perhaps given birth to a child, or perhaps not. Because of the events of this day, she will be charged with murder. Eventually she will have to flee to New York. There she will marry Gouverneur Morris and bear his only son and heir. If it were not for the events of that day, I would probably never have seen Morris's letters and diary, or even Nancy herself. Unsuccessfully, I attempted to recall what my sixteen-year-old self might have been doing at the time. It is strange that a person living in an entirely separate world may set off a chain of events affecting the lives of others at some distant time and place. There can be no doubt that remote events concerning individuals affect our personal destinies and even the lives of those yet unborn. Do individuals affect the great events of history in a similar way? Morris would deny it, but I suspect it is so. The entry in the diary of September 30, 1792, reads, "Nothing extraordinary this Day. . . ."

Despite the bloody events of the Revolution, Morris's sympathy for the French people, expressed in his letters of the period, surprised me. In one letter he writes that he is not offended at what is done by the people because they cannot be supposed to understand the law of nations and they are in a state of fury that renders them capable of all excesses. "It is not possible to say either to the people or to the Sea, so far shalt thou go and no farther, and we shall have I think some sharp struggles which will make many men repent of what they have done when they find with Macbeth that they have but taught bloody Instructions which return to plague the Inventor." In another letter, he declares:

> I wish much, very much, the Happiness of this inconstant People. I love them. I feel grateful for their Efforts in our Cause and I consider the Establishment of a good Constitution here as the principal Means, under divine Providence, of extending the Blessings of Freedom to the many millions of my fellow Men who groan in Bondage on the Continent of Europe. But I do not greatly indulge the flattering Illusions of Hope, because I do not yet perceive that Reformation of Morals without which Liberty is but an empty Sound.

By October, out of concern for the safety of himself and of others, Morris begins to confide little more to his diary than the weather and the state of his health. Finally, on January 5, 1793, he writes,

> The Situation of Things is such that to continue this Journal would compromise many People, unless I go in the Way I have done since the End of August, in which Case it must be insipid and useless. I prefer therefore the more simple Measure of putting an End to it.

The remainder of that volume of the diary contains nothing but empty pages. For the next twenty-one months his letters are the only available source of information.

By the time Morris ceases making entries in his diary, Adèle, Talleyrand, and their son Charles have all fled to England. Adèle's letters to Morris in 1793 indicate that she wants to divorce her husband and return to her lover in Paris. For her own safety, however, she decides to await the verdict in the trial of the King. The guillotine will decide her future. As Charles himself told me years later, his "father," Monsieur de Flahaut, who was in hiding, gallantly surrendered himself to save the life of a man who had helped him. The execution of Adèle's husband will make a divorce unnecessary. But before she even knows of her husband's arrest, the death of the King persuades her that a return to Paris would not be safe. She remains in England and writes novels. She is unable to return to Paris while Morris is there.

In a letter to Jefferson dated January 25, 1793, Morris describes the end of life's journey for Louis XVI.

The late King of this Country has been publicly executed. He died in a manner becoming his Dignity. Mounting the Scaffold he express'd anew his Forgiveness of those who persecuted him and a Prayer that his deluded people might be benefited by his Death. On the Scaffold he attempted to speak but the commanding Officer, Santerre, ordered the Drums to be beat. The King made two unavailing Efforts but with the same bad Success. The Executioners threw him down and were in such haste as to let fall the Axe before his Neck was properly plac'd so that he was mangled. It would be needless to give you an affecting narrative of Particulars.

As Morris predicted, the bloody instructions given to the people return to afflict the teachers. In June of 1793 the Jacobin leaders overthrow the Girondins and usurp the authority of the Convention. Power in France is in the hands of the Jacobin Club ruling through the Committee of Public Safety. The Reign of Terror begins. Marat is assassinated. On October 15, 1793, Marie Antoinette is executed. By the end of the same month, the leaders of the Girondins are brought to the guillotine. The tumbrels roll continuously as the factions exterminate each other. The Hébertists are condemned. Danton, Desmoulins, and their followers fall to the guillotine. Finally, on July 28, 1794, Robespierre and his followers are executed. The factions pass like flickering shadows in a magic lantern.

These momentous events will be reviewed by historians for generations. No doubt they will consider causes, effects, motives, and men. They will argue, revise, and reinterpret. Yet, in the face of these great occurrences, I found myself thinking about contemporaneous events in distant Virginia. What happened there to the Randolph family? Where could I discover those motives, those causes, those effects? The fitful shadows of the past fluttering by on the pages of Morris's papers were no longer the images I wished to see. I sought an entirely different magic lantern show.

It was at the time I was examining Morris's rather guarded correspondence during the Terror. One morning I arrived at Morrisania earlier than usual. Nancy was sitting in my customary place, busily writing. At my entrance she looked up with surprise. "You're early today." There was neither pleasure nor displeasure in her voice. She seemed to be distracted. Gathering her papers, she promised to be out of my way in a moment. I told her there was no need to hurry on my account. Without replying, she stood up, apologized for being in my way, and left the room carrying her materials.

Displeased with the coolness of her greeting, I sat down at the desk and began to brood about her instead of concentrating on my work. After a few minutes I noticed that the receptacle for wastepaper on the floor contained a substantial amount of paper torn into tiny shreds. With the reverence due to possible sacred objects, I removed a handful of the scraps. To make so many small pieces, the paper would have to have been folded and ripped many times, as if the person shredding the paper did not wish to leave a trace of what had been written. I placed some of the fragments on the desk in front of me and tried to decipher them. The numerous bits and pieces made no sense in their fragmentary state. It was apparent they could not be converted into an intelligible form within a short time. Carefully using the side of my hand as a broom, I removed all of the pieces and placed them in my pocket. As a replacement for the purloined fragments, I shredded five or six sheets of paper and placed the scraps in the receptacle.

That night, after Emily had gone to bed, I spent hours trying to restore the documents to their original state. The fact that there were numerous sheets of paper, all with writing on both sides, rendered my task almost impossible. Only the jagged edges of a few tantalizing fragments could be made to fit together. These included some aimless scribbling, the names of several foods, and a few enigmatic, incomplete words. One of these appeared to be "revenge" with the *r* missing. Finally I surrendered all hope of solving the perplexing puzzle. In a state of utter frustration and fatigue, I threw the offending scraps into the fireplace and watched them shrivel into blackness as they were quickly consumed by the flames.

FIFTEEN

What Nancy meant to me has been stated; but there was something more. Beyond my desire for her, or love, if that is what it was, she inspired in me a kind of nameless dread accompanied by a hopelessness as to my ability to decipher the truth about her or any other matter. Love is more than carnal longing. It is also the need to obtain knowledge about another person. To know that other in more than the biblical sense. When one has achieved a certain age beyond the ripeness of youth, when the grave becomes a palpable reality, there can arise a will to throw off the mask of polite society in order to communicate directly and honestly with those one loves. Perhaps it is society's manners, or its morals, but it leaves us groping blindly as we blunder down life's path in a haze of idle chatter. Voltaire once said that words were invented to hide feelings. Unfortunately, Nancy and I remained enshrouded in a fog of words. As often as it was attempted, I could neither throw off my mask nor cause Nancy to remove hers. To me, she remained as opaque as the milky water in Adèle de Flahaut's bath.

In the end we are each alone. By concealing its innermost self, each soul remains solitary, wrapped in gloom, entrapped in its own deceptions and unable to gain entrance to the soul of another. Perhaps the heart and mind of each person must remain unread by his fellow travelers in this life. As Morris wrote in a letter in 1792, one can only guess at the mind of another:

> Things of a public Nature are very public. As to such as are kept or attempted to be kept secret, every different Person has a different Tale and a different Opinion, which last depends more on the observer than on the Thing itself. In a misty Morning Objects appear not in their true Shape, and every Eye beholds the Thing it pleases, because Imagination comes in to supply The Defect of Vision.

My limited knowledge of Nancy's past combined with my imagination could provide an idea of the truth about Nancy Randolph Morris. But that idea remained utterly vague and elusive. The fact is that after so many years, Nancy had become to me an object of awe-inspiring reverence. Though commanding respect, she also filled me with despair at the incoherence of my vision. Her presence evoked memories of my initial youthful encounter with the finite nature of my own existence. She inspired in me that same feeling of dread, veneration, and wonder when I first contemplated the immense void that is the universe and realized that one lifetime is not time enough to penetrate its mystery.

One day not long after the fourth of July of 1817, Nancy entered the library with quills and extra paper for me. Following the exchange of our usual greetings, I mentioned that in ten years from the past July fourth slavery would be completely abolished in New York as a result of the law passed the previous March. After referring to her late husband's valiant endeavors to eliminate slavery in the state many years earlier, I said, "Mr. Morris would have been gratified to witness the final eradication of the institution he detested."

With that condescending look southerners always have when a northerner raises the issue of slavery, she forced a smile. "No doubt, he would have been pleased. But I wonder if a mere change in the law is sufficient to resolve the problem. I grew up in a society of slaves. In childhood, they were my protectors and playmates. Later, my friends and servants. I know all about slavery. In his will, my brother-in-law emancipated his slaves. Many of the poor creatures ended their days in misery and crime. Don't misunderstand me. I favor freeing slaves. But there must be preparation. A slave needs to be educated, to be provided a means to earn a living, maybe even a plot of land. Each master has to take care of his own. You can't cure the world of its ills without tending to your own garden first." As if hurling an accusation, she looked directly at me and asked, "Are you close to any Negroes?"

"No, none." I wanted to say that I was not close to any whites either but, out of embarrassment, did not. "One can conclude slavery is evil without ever meeting a slave. It's a matter of principle."

"You men are always talking about principles. Half the human race is enslaved. Nothing is said about justice for them."

If her words had not been spoken in such apparent earnest, I might have thought she was joking. "What do you mean?" I had no notion to what she was referring.

"Women. You are, I believe, acquainted with some of them. For the pleasure of men, they are rendered weak and vain by indolence and frivolous pursuits. They are generally in an appalling state of ignorance and dependence. They are trained to let men take responsibility for them. Like slaves, they too need education to enable them to earn their own subsistence. From my own experience, I know that without education there can be no real freedom from dependence on others. How many young girls become the dupes of lovers and are ruined at an early age? How many fallen women do you see wandering about the streets of Manhattan? Once a woman's reputation is stained, she cannot maintain her station in life. She has lost all value to her male benefactors and her family. Unless she is very fortunate, she has no means of support other than prostitution." She hesitated; her voice trembled. "I myself was thrown friendless into the world. Because of the kindness of others, I was one of the fortunate few who escaped such a fate. You cannot imagine—" Beginning to lose control of her emotions, she stopped speaking, took a deep breath, and quickly regained her composure. She never completed her statement. Instead she straightened out the books on my desk and left the room, telling me to call her if I needed anything.

For the next few weeks after Nancy's startling outburst, I saw little of her. On the few occasions when we met, she was always in the presence of the servants. We exchanged a few brief pleasantries. She said nothing more about our previous extraordinary conversation. Although eager to continue to discuss the subject, I was not granted an opportunity. Each day, I hoped for another chance to peek behind her mask. Each night, there was only disappointment. It must be told that I did observe small things about her which pleased me. She was unfailingly courteous and helpful to the servants. A stranger observing her behavior might have thought she was one of them, instead of mistress of the house. She also possessed an unusually gentle manner with animals, especially horses and dogs, which she seemed to cherish with a fervor surpassed only by her adoration of little Gouverneur. There was not a trace of the malevolent creature described in John Randolph's letter.

In lieu of conversation with Nancy, I communicated with her late husband by continuing to explore his private chronicles. From January 5, 1793, until October 12, 1794, he discontinued his diary. After an unbroken river of words for four years, there was nothing but a profound silence as to his daily life. Only his letter books remain to provide information about his activities during the Terror.

It is often forgotten that it was at this time that the Convention outlawed slavery in all of the French colonies and extended the rights of citizenship to all men without regard to color. The decree of universal liberty freeing the slaves was celebrated in Notre Dame, which had been renamed the "Temple of Reason." In a letter to Jefferson, Morris described the celebration of the Feast of Reason in the newly-named cathedral. He relates how the opera girl Saunier, who is very beautiful but "next door to an idiot," asked the painter David to invent for her a dress which should be more indecent than nakedness. According to Morris, the painter had genius enough to comply with her request. In a kind of opera performed at Notre Dame, she represented "Reason" and was adored on bended knees by the President of the Convention and other principal characters. Religious relics were burned. "At this spectacle," Morris concludes, "the devout will unquestionably be scandalized" by this "strong experiment on the national feelings."

During this period, Morris purchased a country house with about twenty acres of land at Sainport, almost thirty miles away from Paris. In a June 1793 letter from Sainport, Morris reveals that he suspects Tom Paine is intriguing against him, "although he puts on a face of attachment." He explains that Paine visited his house even more drunk than usual and through his insolence revealed his "vain ambition." When Paine was expelled from the Convention on a motion excluding foreigners and was thrown into the prison of the Luxembourg, the American minister was asked to help his old acquaintance. At first Morris does almost nothing to assist Paine. Scornfully, he informs Jefferson that Paine is in prison where he amuses himself by publishing a pamphlet against Jesus Christ. According to Morris, Paine would have been executed with the rest of the Brissotines if the Jacobins had not viewed him with contempt. He informs Jefferson that he cannot claim Paine as an American citizen because of his foreign birth and his naturalization in France. In any case, he asserts, such a claim would be inexpedient, ineffectual, and perhaps fatal to Paine. Nevertheless, at the request of the prisoner, he later reluctantly claims him as an American citizen, to no effect. Of Paine he writes, "in the best of times, he had a larger share of every other sense than of common sense, and lately the intemperate use of ardent spirits has, I am told, considerably impaired the small stock which he originally possessed."

After spending the first ten months of 1794 in prison, Paine would gain his release through the politically more sympathetic James Monroe, Morris's successor as American minister to France. In an angry letter to President Washington, later withdrawn by Paine, the author of *Common Sense* accused the President of treachery in doing little to save him from prison. He also angrily attacked Gouverneur Morris, whom he considered to be a most unfortunate choice for American minister.

> His prating, insignificant pomposity rendered him at once offensive, suspected, and ridiculous; and his total neglect of all business, had so disgusted the Americans, that they proposed drawing up a protest against him. He carried this neglect to such an extreme, that it was necessary to inform him of it; and I asked him one day, if he did not feel himself ashamed to take the money of the country and do nothing for it? But Morris is so fond of profit and voluptuousness, that he cares nothing about character. Had he not been removed at the time he was, I think his conduct would have precipitated the two countries into a rupture. . . .

It was one of Paine's hostile letters to Washington, printed in the anti-Federalist *Aurora* in Philadelphia, and the false accusation that Paine was an atheist, which made him an outcast upon his return to America. At the time of his death in 1809, Paine was a hero to me; and Morris was, in my eyes, a member of the villainous aristocracy which had unjustly vilified him. My strong feelings of outrage at the mistreatment of Paine, just before I was assaulted on my way home after seeing him sitting alone in his room, are still vivid in my memory. It must be admitted, however, that seven years of acquaintance with Morris and later access to his private papers have tempered my original harsh judgments. To this day Paine remains in my pantheon of republican heroes. But now I am able to understand and even to sympathize with Morris's hostility to the man. The vivid blacks and whites of the days of my youth have faded into the blurred gray vision of a traveler who has wandered for one-half a century through this woeful world.

It was the wildly indiscreet activities of Citizen Genêt, the French chargé d'affaires in America, which caused the removal of Morris from the position of American minister to France. Genêt attempted to force the United States into war on the side of France by arming privateers in American ports to attack British shipping. These actions had the opposite effect and brought the United States close to war with France, not England. When the United States demanded Genêt's recall, it was Morris who delivered the message to the Jacobin government. In retaliation for the action against Genêt, and because of Morris's open hostility to the Revolution, the French government demanded Morris's recall during the bloody summer of 1794. After his successor, James Monroe, arrived, he left Paris for the last time on October 12 of that year. As he prepared to leave France, he began his diary again. He had originally planned an immediate return to America. Then he changed his mind. Perhaps desirous of witnessing the great events unfolding in Europe, he decided to stay for one more year. Four years would pass before he finally departed. It is not clear from the letters or diary why he chose to remain in Europe for so long. Perhaps the lure of Adèle de Flahaut, even more than personal business or interest in events, was the decisive reason.

Just before he leaves France, a Madame Simon arrives to wish him farewell. It appears that during the months he did not maintain his diary, she had been his mistress. She spends the night with him and they part in the morning with "strong emotion." He leaves Sainport on October 14, 1794.

Shortly after commencing his travels outside France, he is cheated at various inns. He pays with good humor and writes, "The art of living consists, I think, in some considerable degree in knowing how to be cheated." It is a remark that will be applicable to events later in his life.

After traveling through Switzerland, Morris reaches his destination at Hamburg in early December. He takes up lodgings in nearby Altona, chief city of the Duchy of Holstein, which adjoins Hamburg. Although there is no indication of his having obtained any news about Adèle de Flahaut for a long period of time, he receives a letter from her. Writing from Switzerland, she asks Morris to aid her in helping the twenty-two-year-old Duke of Orleans. On April 1, 1795, Adèle arrives with a "Mr. Muller," apparently the young Duke, who, as a possible heir to the throne of France, is traveling incognito. Morris obtains a house for Adèle in Altona. It appears from the diary that Morris and Adèle did not resume their lovemaking. What happened to the passions of past days is not stated. After two months of this chaste arrangement, Morris leaves suddenly for London. His first guest there is the ten-year-old Charles de Flahaut, accompanied by a Mr. Smith, who is taking care of the child in the absence of his mother and father. At this time Talleyrand is in America, unable to return to France because his name is on a list of proscribed exiles. From London, Morris travels through England and Scotland. On October 14, 1795, en route to Glasgow, he admires the local canal and its succession of locks. "When I see this, my mind opens to a view of wealth for the interior of America which hitherto I had rather conjectured than seen."

As he had told me many years later, he was contemplating the use of canals many years before the proposal for the Erie Canal had been conceived. Back in London, Morris meets John Quincy Adams and is introduced to George III. The King is surprised to learn that his American visitor is the brother of his own general, Staats Long Morris.

For almost a year Morris does not mention Adèle, until in May of 1796 he learns of the intended marriage between Adèle and M. de Souza, a Portuguese minister to Denmark. Upon reading this, I immediately recalled that in Paris, Charles had introduced his mother to me as Madame de Souza. The month following receipt of the news, Morris returns to Altona. He takes Adèle for a coach ride and she tells him about "her Portuguese lover." His love affair with Adèle is finished. He quickly leaves Altona. Two months later Talleyrand returns from America. According to Talleyrand's *Memoirs*, which Morris disliked intensely, perhaps because they mention Adèle only once and him not at all, Adèle asked him not to land at Hamburg because she feared his presence would be an obstacle to her marriage to de Souza. Morris and Talleyrand appear to have been undone in the same manner and at the same time.

Morris journeys to Berlin, Dresden, and Vienna. After his lack of success with Adèle, he is again prowling about in search of women. He is unsuccessful with both Madame de Nadaillac, a previous acquaintance from Paris, and Madame de Fontana, who in the midst of lusty embraces is overtaken by a "whim of virtue." In spite of the presence of a troublesome husband, Morris has a passionate affair with a Madame de Lita in Vienna. Thereafter, he travels through Dresden to Leipsic, where in his carriage he worships on the Cyprian altar with Madame Crayen, who is the pursuer rather than the pursued. Their encounter is so ecstatic, she informs Morris that she thinks she has conceived; she follows him to Berlin, where they engage in the nuptial rites daily. On March 31, 1797, he returns to Hamburg, visits with Adèle, and receives the news that his longtime employer and friend Robert Morris is financially ruined. That signer of the Declaration of Independence, financier of the American Revolution, and fabulously wealthy merchant and banker will spend the next three years in debtors' prison. When Robert Morris finally gets out of prison, Gouverneur takes him to Morrisania. By providing him with a substantial annuity, Morris leaves his old friend with the means to live comfortably for the rest of his life, which in fact lasts for only a few more years.

By 1797 Lafayette had been imprisoned for more than four years. As American minister to France, Morris had written numerous letters concerning the plight of the unfortunate prisoner. At first he feared that claiming Lafayette as an American citizen would draw the United States into a war if a request for his release was refused by the allies. However, when he learned that Lafayette needed money, he directed the banker of the United States at Amsterdam to provide ten thousand florins; Morris held himself individually responsible for the amount. Later, he loaned Lafayette's wife, Adrienne, 100,000 livres from his private funds to enable her to discharge her husband's debts and to meet her daily expenses. In late 1793 Madame de Lafayette herself and many of her relatives were arrested by the Jacobin government. Letters to Morris from various persons, including Madame de Staël, Madame de Lafayette and her sister, acknowledge the fact that he saved Adrienne from execution by writing letters warning the French government that the execution of Lafayette's wife would lessen the attachment of many Americans to the French republic. Morris's efforts failed to save other relatives of Lafayette. Five days before the end of the Reign of Terror, Adrienne's grandmother, mother, and one of her sisters were executed.

After her release from prison in Paris, Madame de Lafayette and her two daughters voluntarily joined Lafayette in his prison at Olmütz. Thanking him for his previous efforts, Adrienne's sister again asked Morris for his assistance. In Vienna he sought their release by speaking to Baron de Thugut, the Austrian Chancellor. His efforts were not successful. It appears to have been Bonaparte's victory over Austria in the First Italian Campaign that forced the release of Lafayette after five years of harsh imprisonment. On the eve of the Peace of Campo Formio in October of 1797, Morris is present when Lafayette is brought to Hamburg for formal release, as an American citizen, to John Parish, the United States consul in that city. In his diary Morris writes, "He professes much gratitude for my services, but this I do not expect, and shall indeed be disappointed if it ever goes beyond profession." But Morris was disappointed. In a letter written to Chief Justice Marshall a decade later, Morris states, "it appeared to me that M. de Lafayette chose to consider himself as freed by the influence of General Bonaparte, and I did not choose to contest the matter, because, believing my application had procured his liberty, it would have looked like claiming acknowledgements." By the time of the letter to Marshall, Morris's relationship with the Lafayette family had ended unpleasantly. Morris had become displeased with Madame de Lafayette's attempts to avoid repaying his loan of 100,000 livres. She claimed that the value of the livre had greatly increased in value since the time of the loan. The matter was not finally concluded until 1804, when Morris agreed to settle for 53,500 in new currency instead of 100,000 in old livres plus interest. Relying on his knowledge of the "art of knowing how to be cheated," he drops his claim for additional payment while indignantly complaining of his debtor, "There is no drawing the sound of a trumpet from a whistle."

In 1798, after another year of wandering about the continent, Morris decides to leave Europe. Before departing, he learns of Cornwallis's defeat of the French army in Ireland and Nelson's destruction of the French fleet at the Battle of the Nile. Bonaparte's army is stranded in Egypt. Turkey has declared war on France. The defeat of revolutionary France appears to be imminent. It will not happen for another sixteen years, during which time Bonaparte will bestride the entire continent.

Morris unwisely begins his Atlantic crossing at the late-in-the-season date of October 4, 1798. The horses he attempted to bring back from Europe do not survive the arduous journey. His ship does not arrive in New York City until December 23. Morris is greeted by many of his old friends and by his devoted nephew, David Ogden. On January 5, 1799, he returns to Morrisania, where he arrives at dusk after an absence of more than ten years.

During the period of reviewing the diary and letters for Morris's final year in Europe, I was afflicted by a strange illness, a high fever without any of the other symptoms which for me usually accompanied a fever. For days I was too weak to leave my bed. By means of a marketman, I sent a note to Nancy explaining that I would be absent from Morrisania until the illness ran its course. To my surprise, Emily was unusually solicitous of my health and spared no effort to assure my comfort. After a week, when the fever showed no signs of abating, she sent for Dr. Hosack. Although he was much too exalted and expensive to be our family physician, Emily insisted on requesting his services because of his well-known skill in treating fevers. Within hours of receiving Emily's note, he appeared at our home. I apologized for bothering him, but he would not hear of it. Cordial, as always, he protested that he was flattered to be called to my home. He seemed to be sincere; I found it difficult to believe that with his busy schedule he would welcome a new patient, and a poor one at that. Unlike any other doctor who had ever examined me, he admitted to not knowing the cause or cure of the illness. To the astonishment of both Emily and me, he refused to bleed me. "My colleagues are too quick to resort to the lancet. *Primum non nocere* was Hippocrates' rule. 'First do no harm.' My experience has been that rest is the best cure for a fever like yours. Drink fluids and remain in bed. The fever will probably pass without any other treatment."

Emily was impressed when the good doctor began to discuss my book with me. His interest in it, no doubt, meant more to her than all my statements over the years as to its importance. After she left the room, Hosack asked about my progress on Morris's papers. Having described the richness of the historical information to be found therein, I expressed disappointment at finding no reference to the only story I had once heard about Morris during the French Revolution. According to the tale, Morris's luxurious carriage was surrounded by an angry mob shouting "aristocrat." He opened the door and thrust out his wooden leg. "An aristocrat. Yes! One who lost his leg in the cause of American liberty." The crowd applauded and permitted Morris to proceed on his way.

"It is amusing," I said. "With all of the wonderful stories in his diaries and letters, the one best known to everyone is probably apocryphal." I then proceeded to relate some of Morris's adventures in Paris, including reference to his many amorous encounters. "I never realized the old man was such a rake in his younger days."

Hosack laughed. "That was no secret. For years he had a reputation as a man with a weakness for the ladies. John Jay always used to say that Gouverneur is daily employed in making oblations to Venus. Some people claimed he lost his leg trying to escape from a jealous husband. Jay once told me he was deeply grieved when Gouverneur lost his leg. At the time, he said, he almost wished he had lost a different part of his anatomy."

David Hosack is as near to being a man without blemish as any person I have ever met. Fortunately, he has one weakness, which has made it most stimulating to share his conversation. At least with me, he has always been a most informative gossip. Unable to let our conversation about Morris's amorous inclinations pass without further comment, he surprised me with his next comment. "Knowing what you do about our late friend's love of the fair sex, you will, I presume, be less likely than many others to believe the stories questioning the paternity of young Gouverneur." It was obvious that Hosack was interested in observing my reaction to his provocative question.

"Who would say such a thing? I've heard no such stories." My heart was pained at the thought of poor Nancy again being slandered. There seemed to be no end to the attacks concerning her virtue.

"The unhappy former heirs to the Morris fortune would like to remove young Gouverneur so they can restore their claims to the estate. The birth of the child, you know, was a dreadful blow to the hopes of the nephews and nieces. For some time, David Ogden and Martin Wilkins openly referred to the boy as 'General Cutusoff.' " Hosack laughed and shook his head with disapproval at the same time.

It took me a moment to realize that Morris's nephews had been punning with the name of the victor of the Russian campaign of 1812, General Kutusov. "They can joke about the boy. But have they actually claimed Morris was not his father?" It had long been my assumption that Ogden had given up the battle when John Randolph's letter failed to have the desired effect on his uncle. In fact, the war was continuing.

"Some members of the family have told me that David Ogden has been claiming that the father of the boy was a servant at Morrisania. From what Morris told me before he died, I would not doubt the stories."

"That he was not the father?"

"Oh, no, no, no! That David Ogden was spreading rumors. Morris suspected that Ogden had encouraged John Randolph to write the letter accusing his wife of all those terrible crimes. If Ogden could do that, he is capable of anything." Hosack again shook his head, as if to indicate amazement at the extent of human greed. "The family, you know, never accepted his wife. Shortly after Morris died, the Historical Society resolved that a portrait of its late president be purchased. As one of the officers, I was directed to ask Mrs. Morris for her assistance. She was pleased by the request and wrote the artist, Thomas Sully, in Philadelphia. She asked him to make a copy of a portrait of Morris owned by Morris's niece. Gertrude Meredith was the name. Sully wrote back that he was willing to make the copy but Mrs. Meredith refused to lend it. She brazenly announced she did not want Mrs. Morris to have a copy of her uncle's portrait. I was amazed at the refusal, and wrote to Mr. Meredith on behalf of the society. The request was again refused. Mr. Meredith replied he could not state the reasons in the letter. We finally had to obtain a portrait through other means."

"Does Nan . . . Mrs. Morris know about the rumors of her son's parentage?"

"She most certainly does. As you can imagine, she is very upset about the whole matter. A few weeks ago, she told me she would no longer passively endure the family's abuse. I believe she meant it. A very spirited woman, that one. At the time, she made a curious remark. 'For too long I have bowed down before false gods.' I don't know what she meant. I should have asked."

Although Dr. Hosack's unusual method of treating my illness eventually proved to be successful, the information he imparted to me must have aggravated my malady. Shortly after he left, my body felt as though it would be consumed by its own heat. Emily bathed me in cold water and spirits to ameliorate my condition. Within a few days the fever did finally abate. Too weak for several days more to travel to Morrisania, I could muster only enough strength to escape my boredom by wandering across the street to play chess with John Randel. It was our first meeting in several months. He was in good spirits. After seven years of difficult work he had finally completed placing the monuments, or iron bolts in rocks where monuments were impracticable, marking the precise intersections of each street and avenue on the plan of the Street Commissioners. The monuments went as far north as the planned 155th Street. His final report was in the hands of the Common Council. At the time, his interest was turning away from the streets of Manhattan to the work recently begun on the Erie Canal. He hoped to take some part in that great project and was already critical of a portion of the planned route from Schenectady to Albany. As a former acquaintance of Gouverneur Morris, he might, I thought, be able to provide some additional news concerning Nancy. After a few hints about Hosack's information, it became clear that he knew nothing about the tribulations of Mr. Morris's widow. That evening he routed me twice. The first game was completed so quickly, we proceeded to a second one. My mind was not on pawns and knights. My only thoughts were for the queen of Morrisania.

Finally, after an absence of two weeks, I planned to return to Morrisania on a Monday. But for three long days a pelting rain, combined with concern about the frailty of my condition, kept me at home. By Thursday the sky was still cloudy but the deluge had finally ceased. Because the decision to return was made on the morning of my departure, there was no opportunity to inform Nancy I would be resuming my work. With the hope that my unexpected presence would be warmly received, I arrived at Morrisania in a marketman's boat. There were no other boats at the dock. Simon, the old servant who answered the door, was surprised at my arrival. He informed me that Mrs. Morris and her son had departed for the city only one-half an hour earlier. Escorting me to the library, he left me at the door. Although it was still summer, the room was exceedingly cold. There was no sign of the diary and letter books. Except for two unfamiliar volumes, the desktop was empty. The first book was a novel by Frances Burney. The second was *Vindication of the Rights of Woman* by Mary Wollstonecraft. I was familiar with the second book. After its publication in 1792, the *Vindication* had been very widely discussed. But interest in the rights of women seemed to vanish at the same time as did sympathy for Citizen Genêt and the French Revolution. It had been many years since I had seen the book. Opening to the first page, I glanced at a marked passage in the author's introduction:

> The conduct and manners of women, in fact, evidently prove that their minds are not in a healthy state; for, like the flowers which are planted in too rich a soil, strength and usefulness are sacrificed to beauty; and the flaunting leaves, after having pleased a fastidious eye, fade, disregarded on the stalk, long before the season when they ought to have arrived at maturity. One cause of this barren blooming I attribute to a false system of education, gathered from the books written on this subject by men who, considering females rather as women than human creatures, have been more anxious to make them alluring mistresses than affectionate wives and rational mothers; and the understanding of the sex has been so bubbled by this specious homage, that the civilized women of the present century, with a few exceptions, are only anxious to inspire love, when they ought to cherish a nobler ambition, and by their abilities and virtues exact respect.

I had forgotten how well Wollstonecraft wrote. To my amusement, I had also failed to remember that the dedication of the book was to Talleyrand, "late Bishop of Autun," who had attempted to justify the exclusion of one-half the human race from participation in government under the new French constitution of 1791. The author warned Talleyrand that women may be convenient slaves, but such slavery will degrade both master and servant. One part of my mind had always retained a certain sympathy for Wollstonecraft and the cause of equal rights for women. On the other hand, I must confess, there is a great deal of wisdom in Samuel Johnson's observation that nature has given woman so much power that the law cannot afford to give her more. Turning the pages of the book, I wondered whether it was Wollstonecraft or Nancy who had been speaking to me when we last talked about slavery. In the hope that Nancy had left some residue of her thoughts on paper, I searched for some scraps of her writing. There were none.

Eager to resume work on the Morris papers, I went through the empty house in search of someone to give me the books. Simon, the old servant who had greeted me, was the only person near the house. He was sitting in a chair outside, gazing at the spectacular view. When I informed him that the books were not in the library, he seemed slightly befuddled. "Oh yes. We put 'em away, didn't we." With painful slowness he walked back into the library and began opening and closing draws to the desk until he found a key. Then he ambled over to a closet on the other side of the room. His hands shook so much, it was only with great difficulty he managed to place the key in the lock. The door opened, revealing three shelves filled with the familiar books. It was the bottom of the closet, however, that immediately caught my eye. There were additional books I had not seen before. After we removed the top three shelves of books and carried them to the desk, the old man locked the closet and returned the key to its place in the desk. Trembling with anticipation, I waited until Simon was gone. After assuring myself that nobody was near the library, I unlocked the closet. There were five more volumes of the diary, from January 6, 1800, to October 19, 1816. In addition, there were numerous letter books, private and commercial, covering approximately the same period. Knowing from previous experience that the books could not be reviewed with great speed, I immediately devised my plan of action. I removed the ninth volume of the diary and one letter book of the same time period. After locking the closet, I placed the new books on the desk, among the other volumes. With the revelation of the closet and key, it was my expectation that I could peruse the later books at leisure without being discovered. Like Adèle de Flahaut, Nancy Randolph, I knew, would eventually make her appearance on the stage of Morris's past. As that drama unfolded, I intended to be an involved spectator.

Since Nancy's strange outburst hinting at her troubled past, we had exchanged only a few words. She seemed to be avoiding me. On account of my illness, for more than two weeks I had not seen her at all. On the day of my return to Morrisania, she did not return before my departure. But the following Monday she greeted me upon my arrival at Morrisania and a wondrous thing happened. As she welcomed me, I looked directly into her eyes and told her that I had missed her. Appearing to be embarrassed, she blushed and averted her eyes. There was a slight smile on her lips. As soon as the words escaped my mouth, I knew they had made a favorable impression. The success of my greeting, however, was beyond my wildest expectations. It was as though I had spoken some magic words that shattered the long-standing barrier between us. That very day, she twice visited the library to chat with me. For the first time I sensed she was not merely being polite. She actually seemed to enjoy my companionship. It is true she revealed little about her past, but we discussed all manner of topics. The progress of my book, Morris's experiences in Europe (Adèle excluded), her joy in being a mother, and her love of novels were all subjects of our discourse over the next few weeks.

One beautiful day she invited me to ride with her about the vast estate. She was a wonderfully skilled rider, and it was only with great difficulty I was able to follow her. After the excursion, we shared lunch together in the warm sunlight in front of the house. Little Gouverneur was busy playing with one of the servant's children, so our conversation was blissfully without interruption. We talked a great deal about my early life in New York City. She seemed fascinated by the poverty of my childhood and my early exploits in the British-occupied city. About her own youth in Virginia, she spoke not a word. When she did talk, the conversation was about her interest in novels and drama. From her numerous references to various books, it was clear that she was a voracious reader. Two of her favorites were Richardson's *Pamela* and *Clarissa*, neither of which I had read. She was greatly moved by Clarissa's death. She said it "released the heroine from a pitiless world in which human beings torment each other and themselves." When she discussed these books, I noticed she mispronounced several words that are rarely used in conversation. It left me with the distinct impression that at one time she had escaped into a private world of books which she rarely had discussed with others.

She defended fiction as not just mere entertainment, but as serving a profound moral purpose. "*King Lear* impresses upon the reader the importance of respecting one's parents more than even the biblical command to 'honor thy father and mother.' And what of *Tom Jones*? Has there ever been a more vivid picture of English country life?"

At last she had named two works of literature familiar to me. After agreeing with her evaluation of the Shakespeare masterpiece, I declared my reservations about Fielding. "Although I have not read many novels, I did seek out *Tom Jones* after learning that Gibbon thought it an exquisite picture of human manners. He said it would outlive the Hapsburgs and the Palace of the Escurial. You know of my unbounded admiration for Gibbon. But I disagreed with his assessment of the book. The author tells the reader what is in every character's mind. Who possesses such omniscience other than God himself, if there is a God?" She seemed undisturbed by this indication of my religious skepticism. "Such absolute knowledge does not coincide with any reality existing in this world. We are all forced to view life through our own eyes; we can never enter the minds of others."

Nancy was amused by my criticism. "I never considered that to be a problem with any novel. In a book like *Tom Jones*, the author creates all of the characters and tells us about each one of them, including their thoughts. It is true, this permits a perspective on the world we can never have. That is one of the very elements that make novels so uniquely entertaining and revealing. They present a richer, more profound view of life than is possible through one person's eyes." We argued and laughed at each other's comments. There was an intimacy between us which had never existed before. My own long-suppressed words of love were so close to the surface, I feared that I might blurt them out at the wrong time and pop the expanding bubble of our new friendship. In expectation of a proper moment, I cautiously bided my time. Nancy saw only my public facade; there was a private Daniel Carey in the room with us who spoke only to me. No doubt it was the same for her. My hope was that one day the two hidden phantoms who hovered about us would also begin to converse with each other. Then the last obstruction between us would truly be eliminated.

During these wonderful weeks, while our friendship bloomed, I hoped to discover something in the letters and diary that would reveal a passageway to the hidden Nancy Randolph Morris. For many years after 1799, however, there was not a word about her.

After his return from Europe, Morris settles into his life as a resident of New York. He commences expensive renovations, he says fifty or sixty thousand dollars, at Morrisania. He purchases a Negro slave and, to my relief, immediately emancipates him. He visits Robert Morris in debtors' prison. His nieces and nephews, especially David Ogden, Martin Wilkins, and Gertrude Meredith, press their wealthy uncle for financial assistance. He writes a letter to retired President Washington urging him to return to the presidency. Instead of being able to welcome his idol back to politics, he speaks his funeral oration in New York City. For Washington expires only a few days after Morris's letter is sent. The following year he returns to public life. He is appointed United States Senator from New York and travels to the capital in Philadelphia, which within the year is moved to Washington. To my surprise, Morris openly disapproves of Federalist attempts to elect vice-presidential candidate Aaron Burr as President instead of presidential candidate Thomas Jefferson when the two Republicans receive the same number of electoral votes without indication of who should be President and who Vice-President. In a letter to Alexander Hamilton, Morris writes, "Not meaning to enter into intrigues, I have merely expressed the opinion that since it was evidently the intention of our fellow citizens to make Mr. Jefferson the President, it seems proper to fulfill that intention." After witnessing the excesses of the French Revolution, Morris did not perceive Jefferson as the devil incarnate seen by his Federalist friends.

Much of the material concerning his senatorial term, including his unsuccessful leadership against repeal of the Judiciary Act which caused him to lose faith in the Constitution, need not concern us here. His term as Senator expired in March of 1803 and he returned to private life. Most of the time he remained at Morrisania caring for his farm, receiving visitors, and engaging in extensive correspondence on business and politics. Several months each year he spent traveling, often to his new lands in the wilderness of New York State. It is clear from his financial records that the basis of his fortune rested on his successful speculations in such land.

Except for a brief affair with another married woman, in Philadelphia, there appear to have been no lovers in Morris's life, at least none mentioned in his diary. Impatiently I awaited the entrance of Nancy Randolph. There was not a word about her. I began to think she would not appear until 1808 or 1809, the year I met her and she married him. My thoughts on this matter would prove to be correct.

July 11, 1804, was the day of the infamous duel between Alexander Hamilton and Aaron Burr, the Vice-President of the United States. For my book on the history of New York City, Dr. Hosack had given me his account of the famous confrontation. The two antagonists met early in the morning on the part of the Jersey shore called the Weehawk, the same place where Hamilton's own son Philip had been mortally wounded in a duel three years earlier. Dr. Hosack, the surgeon mutually agreed on by Burr and Hamilton, came in a boat with General Hamilton and his second, Mr. Pendleton. So as not to be a witness, Hosack waited in the boat until the sound of the shot. In running to the fallen Hamilton, he had to pass Burr and his second, Mr. Van Ness. As Hosack went by, Van Ness coolly covered Burr with his umbrella so that the doctor would not be able to swear that he saw the Vice-President on the field.

Dr. Hosack found Hamilton half sitting on the ground in the arms of Pendleton. He barely had enough strength to say, "This is a mortal wound, Doctor." The bargeman helped carry the unconscious man to the boat where Hamilton regained consciousness. Despite his fatal wound, he had the presence of mind to be careful of his undischarged pistol. "Pendleton knows I did not intend to fire at him," Hamilton moaned. Although he suffered terribly for the remainder of the day, Hamilton showed great concern for his wife and children, who were at his bedside while Hosack tried to ease his pain.

Morris's diary entry of July 11 states that his nephew Martin Wilkins told him that General Hamilton was killed in a duel with Colonel Burr. On the twelfth Morris goes to town, where Wilkins informs him that Hamilton is still alive at Greenwich. Morris visits his wounded friend and is overcome with grief. After regaining his composure with a tearful walk in the garden, Morris sits by Hamilton's side until he expires. He remains to watch Dr. Hosack open the body. The ball had broken one of the ribs, passed through the liver, and lodged in the vertebrae, which had been shattered. Morris wrote, "A most melancholy scene—his wife almost frantic with grief, his children in tears, every person present deeply afflicted, the whole city agitated, every countenance dejected."

One of my first vivid memories of Gouverneur Morris is his delivery of the oration at Hamilton's funeral. At the time, he was so moved he could not continue the speech. Aware of the anger of the great crowd he addressed, Morris was careful to warn the people not to let indignation lead to any act in violation of the law. With great emotion he reviewed Hamilton's virtues, his great talent, integrity, and patriotism. Even I, who was not then personally acquainted with Morris and was not an admirer of Hamilton, was deeply moved. It was curious to read years after the event that Morris did not think his speech was a success. He wrote:

> I speak for the first Time in the open Air, and find that my Voice is lost before it reaches one-tenth of the Audience. Get through the Difficulties tolerably well: Am of Necessity short, especially as I feel the Impropriety of acting a dumb Show, Which is the Case as to all those who see but cannot hear me. I find that what I have said does not answer the general Expectation. This I knew would be the Case— It must ever happen to him whose Duty it is to allay the sentiment which he is expected to arouse.—How easy would it have been to make them, for a Moment, absolutely mad!

How utterly amazed I would have been at the time, if someone had told me that the impressive one-legged speaker would become one of the most important persons in my life.

In reviewing the diary and letters after 1800, I discovered numerous references to Morris's early ideas on the canal. From 1800 to his death, the subject was frequently on his mind. While reviewing this material, I did not know it would be useful, but copied much of it in any case. It would create problems for me at a later date. The diary and letters contain substantially less information about Morris's work as chairman of the Street Commissioners of New York City. He appears to have delegated much of this work to Simeon De Witt and John Randel. Reading Morris's papers indicated to me how minor a part I played in the great man's life. My assistance in the matter of the street plan for Manhattan is not even mentioned, and he barely alludes to my assistance on the canal. That there was hardly a recognition of my existence was not unexpected. But it was a surprise for me to read the diary for more than three months into 1809 without a single reference to Nancy. Then, on April 23, she is finally mentioned. The notation is that Morris drove to a tavern and "after breakfast brought home Miss Randolph of Virginia, who had arrived from Connecticut." Not a word about how Morris and Nancy were brought together. It was two months after Morris brought Nancy home that I met her for the first time. At that encounter, she had told me she had only been at Morrisania for a few weeks. While reading the entry for April 23, I experienced a sense of relief to have something Nancy had stated to me corroborated by an independent source. It was an insignificant piece of a very large puzzle but it had been confirmed as the truth. If I could not know Nancy in the biblical sense, I intended to know her at least in the historical sense.

The diary contains no other significant reference to Nancy until Christmas day 1809, when Morris wrote, "I marry this day Anne Cary Randolph. No small surprise to my guests." Unlike his relationship with Adèle, Morris does not record the intimate details of his private life with Nancy. My expectations frustrated, I turned to the letter books in the hope of discovering additional information. Fortunately, there was indeed more to be found.

Shortly after his return from Europe, in a letter to his friend John Parish, the American consul at Hamburg at the time of Lafayette's release from prison, Morris stated his thoughts on marriage.

> I don't know but you are right in the Idea, that I should provide to myself a Help Mate—the rather as I believe there is but little Help to be found in the Circle of one's Acquaintance. In sober Seriousness, I should not hesitate, if I could light upon such a Person as Mrs. —— and light up in her Bosom such a Flame, as would on such an occasion warm my own. It is not good say the Scriptures for man to be alone, and When the Winter of the year adds its Frosts to the Winter of Life, I suspect that the long Evenings may grow somewhat dull—and force me to town. But sufficient unto the Day is the Evil thereof. I trust myself to the Stream of Time, and float as Fate may order, fully convinced that the best Pilots know very little of the matter.

Three years later, he continues to surrender himself to fate, but in a less optimistic manner.

My friend, I fear it is my Fate to work as long as I live. I had rather not, but we are not Masters of our Road in travelling toward the grave.

I have built no castle, but a pretty good House at Morrisania, on the foundation of that in which I was born and in which my parents died. There I believe my Wanderings must end.

In a letter to Robert Morris in 1803, he continues to speak of marriage. He writes that if he meets the enchanting Yankee he was told about, he will endeavor to oppose the power of reason to the fascination of the enchantress.

I have, you know, in my drawing-room the picture in tapestry of Telemachus rescued from the charms of Circe by the friendly aid of old Mentor. In truth, my friend, marriage, especially at my time of life, should be more a matter of prudence than of passion. Good sense and good nature are of more importance than wit and beauty and accomplishments.

When he finally does decide to marry, his choice, an accused murderess, could certainly not be characterized as an act of prudence.

Perhaps, for some years after that letter, Morris thought his adventures with the ladies had come to an end. The first sign of Nancy does not appear in the letter books until six years later, when they exchange a series of epistles. On March 3, 1809, he writes a letter addressed to her at Stratford, Connecticut. It appears to be a response to a communication from her which is not included in the letter book.

Talk not of Gratitude my dear but communicate so much of your Situation as may enable me to be useful. I once heard but have no distinct recollection of events which brought distress into your family. Dwell not on them now. If we happen to be alone you shall tell your Tale of Sorrow when the Tears from your Cheek may fall in my Bosom.

He reminds her, as I once heard him say on another occasion, that in brooding over her misfortune, she should not forget that the sufferings of life are essential to its enjoyment.

The Incidents of Pleasure and Pain are scattered more equally than is generally imagined. The Cards are dealt with fairness. What remains is patiently to play the Game; and then to sleep.

Six days later he writes another letter to her, stating that their last letters have crossed in the mail. "You ask for my sentiments on a Subject about which I am not sufficiently disinterested . . . I can only answer that I will love you as little as I can." Although not entirely clear, this response implies that he will attempt to restrain his strong feelings for her.

His next letter appears to respond to her questions concerning an offer to assume a position as housekeeper at Morrisania. He writes that the numerous ladies who visit his house have never harbored an idea injurious to the virtue of his housekeepers, and they are correct, for he has never approached her predecessors "with anything like desire." He informs her that none but a "reduced gentlewoman" can command the respect of his servants, but she herself will not be a mere servant. "I can only say that our real relation shall be that of friends." He notes that her salary will be the same as he now pays "because appearances are best supported by realities." He concludes by assuring her that his esteem and affection are undiminished and perhaps are increased. This statement seems to refer to her revelations about the past. The following month, his diary indicates, she arrived at Morrisania.

Following the passage of seven months' experience with his new housekeeper, he contemplates marriage for the first time in his life. Before committing himself to such a bond, on December 2, 1809, he writes a letter to Chief Justice Marshall.

> You have perhaps heard that Miss Randolph, the daughter of our old friend of Tuckahoe, is in my house and has the care of my family ... I hear that the World, that is to say the Gossips, male and female of New York, circulate Sundry Reports respecting this unfortunate young Lady, founded on Events which happened while I was in Europe. I presume that no particular malevolence is directed at her, but if she can be depicted in black colors, it may serve as a foundation for calumny against me. It will be argued that I would not treat with Respect a Person so undeserving unless there existed between us an illicit connection ... I am not so vain as to believe that the World would give itself so much trouble about me if I stood alone, but connected with so many worthy Men as fill the federal Ranks, it may serve a valuable Party Purpose to affirm a Stigma on any one of us, however inconsiderable he may be personally considered. Now it is from Consideration for friends I esteem and by no means from Solicitude about the idle Gulping of those who take a little Scandal as a Relish to their Dinner or their tea that I lay a small tax on your Goodness. The Object of this letter is to ask you frankly the Reputation Miss Randolph left in Virginia, and the Standing she held in Society, for my Government.

Marshall's response, dated December 12, was separate from the other letters in the book. He wrote that he was pleased that Morris was extending his protection "to that unfortunate young lady." The infanticide charge, he informed Morris, "was very public and excited much attention." He stated, however, "Some circumstances adduced in support of it were ambiguous, and

rumor, with her usual industry, spread a thousand others which were probably invented by the malignant, or magnified by those who love to supply any
defects in the story they relate." The letter continued by informing Morris
that Judith, Richard Randolph's wife and Nancy's sister, the person "who had
the fairest means of judging of the transaction and who was most injured by
the fact if true," permitted Nancy to live in her home while Richard lived
and for many years after his death. As to the general opinion of society,
Marshall reported, "Many believed the accusations brought against Miss
Randolph to be true, while others attached no criminality to her conduct and
believed her to be the victim of a concurrence of unfortunate circumstances."
He added that "those ladies with whom I am connected" were among those
who did not consider her to be a criminal. He concluded by informing
Morris that Nancy ceased appearing in public but continued to be received in
the homes of many who "were not disposed to condemn because the world
had pronounced an unfavorable sentence."

On the same page of the letter book containing Morris's inquiry to
Marshall of December 2 appears Morris's response, dated December 28, 1809,
to Marshall's letter. He thanks the Chief Justice for his reply of the twelfth,
which had reached him a day or two before the wedding. As a result of
Marshall's letter, for which he is "very much obliged," Morris wrote that he
had prepared a short contract containing a release of dower and offered it to
Miss Randolph. In other words, according to a lawyer I consulted, he appears
to have given Nancy an antenuptial contract in which, in exchange for proper
consideration, she released the interest in his real estate given by law to a
widow during her lifetime. Certainly not the act of a passionate lover without
reservations about his bride. Morris's letter continues:

> This was the first Declaration made of my wish, tho' I had per-
> ceived in her Manner that Good Will and amusing Conversation had
> produced that Effect on her Mind which ought not to be expected by
> People of my age. On the twenty-fifth, we were married. Your candor
> makes it my Duty to explain more than I shall to others my conduct.

He informs Marshall that he already knew the facts in Miss Randolph's
case and "was satisfied." She had most of the qualities he wished in a wife,
good sense, good temper, cleanliness, and a developing knowledge of house-
keeping. "On Beauty, I lay no Stress, but if I did, she has her Share." Fortune
never entered his calculation; he has enough to be content. The only important point was her reputation. As to that, he set down all her relations had
said as nothing. Persons capable of persecuting a relative so young are unworthy of credit. So grievous a charge, he writes, "must inflict a Wound which,
heal it as you may, must leave a scar." The malevolent will condemn and the
charitable will acquit. But among the honest and well-meaning there must be
a difference of opinion, and against this opinion he considers Nancy's "fifteen
years of irreproachable Conduct, under Circumstances where the common

fortitude is sufficient to support Virtue." Of course, at the time Morris wrote of the years of good conduct, he was unaware of the charges that Nancy later poisoned Richard and consorted with a black slave. To this day I wonder if he would have gone ahead with the marriage if he knew of these other allegations.

Morris's expectant heirs, David Ogden, Martin Wilkins, and his other nieces and nephews, were, no doubt, appalled by the marriage. Nevertheless, after the event, the diary indicates, Ogden continued to visit Morrisania. His personal views are not mentioned. However, shortly after the marriage, Morris responded to a letter, not among the papers, from his niece Gertrude Meredith.

> My dear Child
> I received your letter of the 3rd Last Evening and perceive in it two Charges; viz., that I have committed a folly in marrying, and have acted undutifully in not consulting you. I can only say, to the first, that I have not yet found Cause to repent, and, to the second, that I hope you will pardon me for violating an Obligation of Which I was not apprized . . . If I had married a rich Woman of seventy the World might think it wiser than to take one of half that age without a farthing, and, if the World were to live with my Wife, I should certainly have consulted its Taste; but as that happens not to be the Case, I thought I might, without offending others, endeavor to suit myself, and look rather into the Head and Heart than into the Pocket.

He concluded by hoping that his niece would approve of his choice when he and his new wife have the pleasure of receiving her at Morrisania. In response to Morris's letter, Mr. Meredith immediately sent a conciliatory reply wishing Morris happiness in his marriage and inviting Mr. and Mrs. Morris to visit them in Philadelphia. From what Dr. Hosack told me, it is clear that the Merediths in the end did not approve of Morris's wife. Even after Morris's death seven years later, they refused her request to use his portrait.

In 1810 Morris was appointed President of the Canal Commission. Among the voluminous papers from his incessant work on the project, I did find correspondence between Morris and Benjamin Latrobe. Morris had invited Latrobe to join the Canal Commission as an engineer. Latrobe refused the offer unless he was granted a position with life tenure. At the end of his letter Latrobe wrote, "Should I come to New York, few circumstances will give me more pleasure than to see at the head of this family a lady whom I had known in Virginia, who may recall my visit to Bazaar in 1797." If Latrobe had consulted his own notebook, he would have recalled the place was "Bizarre" and the year 1796.

The lady from Virginia continued to visit me regularly. It was with a mixture of joy and anxiety that I received her visits. Nothing pleased me more than to speak to the temptress of my dreams. With every visit there always existed the delightful, but unlikely, possibility she would act in the same wanton way she did in my overheated imagination. But I was constantly fearful that one day she would notice my reading included books which were not supposed to be in my possession. It was fortunate for the continuance of my work, though not for the fulfillment of my desires, that she almost never approached close enough to the desk to see what I was perusing. One day, however, she asked me if I had experienced any difficulty in comprehending her husband's handwriting. Without anticipating the results of my response, I told her that there often were words or phrases which were undecipherable. Immediately, she arose from her chair, walked over to the desk, and offered to assist me in the interpretation of Morris's writing. Fortunately, I reacted quickly to the danger of discovery. As she approached, I placed my hand over the book in front of me, hoping the gesture would not be suspicious. I told her that one of the earlier books had given me great difficulty. Not wanting her to think I was near the end of the books given to me, I selected the sixth volume of the diary, which began in late 1795. Together we reviewed some of the difficult entries. She was quite skillful in deciphering her husband's writing. It was a matter of some regret that I could not request her assistance on the more interesting letters of 1809 concerning her early meetings with her future husband.

As she had done many years earlier at the Battery concert just after war had been declared, she sat close beside me. In that distant summer of 1812 I thought she was flirting with me in a most serious manner. When I later learned she was pregnant at the time, I realized words of love from me would have been disastrously improper at the time. It was essential, I reminded myself, not to misconstrue her motives. What seemed a flirtation to me might well be an innocent passing of time for her. Stifling my intense desire to touch her, I coolly discussed the relationship between Morris and Lafayette mentioned in the diary before us. As the dispute over Lafayette's debt to Morris had ended the connection between the two men in 1804, Nancy knew little. She was fascinated to learn the details of her husband's role in the release of the Lafayette family from the infamous prison at Olmütz. At her urging, I related all I knew about the connection from Valley Forge to the joyful reunion with Lafayette at Hamburg. Of the later dispute over money, I said not a word.

The following week I read Morris's diary entry on his return from supporting the canal legislation in Albany, on June 23, 1812. "Dear, quiet happy home." Nancy must have told him she was pregnant. It was only a few days later at the Battery that I had sat next to Nancy, our arms touching. The entry in the diary strengthened my resolve to do nothing unseemly, unless I was certain Nancy would welcome my advances. That certainty, I feared, would never exist.

In advancing through the diary and letters, I finally approached the period of most interest to me, the events leading up to John Randolph's letter and the aftermath. There were no signs of any unhappiness between Morris and Nancy in the period after the birth of the child. In October of 1813, when I was at Leipsic, Morris, traveling in the wilderness lands of New York, wrote a letter in verse to his wife.

> Kiss for me, my love, our charming boy
> I long to taste again the joy
> Of pressing to his father's breast
> The son and mother. Be they blest
> With all which bounteous Heaven can grant
> And if among us one must want
> Of bliss, be mine the scanty lot.
> Your happiness, may no dark spot
> Of gloomy woe or piercing pain
> Or melancholy ever stain.

But pain and woe were soon to darken Nancy's happiness.

In the summer of 1814 Morris recorded in his diary his pleasure with his royalist Bourbon speech. "I pronounce an oration of Triumph to celebrate the Downfall of Bonaparte and the Restoration of the Bourbons with the consequent peace to Europe. This oration tolerably well written and in part well delivered." He notes that the audience were satisfied but says nothing of the riot outside Washington Hall that evening. Shortly after the Bourbon speech, on July 29, 1814, he wrote a letter to John Randolph thanking him for his remarks of approbation concerning the speech. He hopes that the nation will be rescued from "the Despotism of Democracy" embodied in the war. He then notes his deepest sympathy for Judith Randolph in her "domestic calamities." This seems to concern some unhappy event concerning her son, the deaf mute St. George Randolph. Morris writes that St. George's "malady" might have been prevented by permitting St. George to indulge in "amorous dalliance" to ease the pain consequent to his attainment of young manhood and the realization of the desperate loneliness attached to his condition. Morris mentions Tudor's illness and invites both Judith and John Randolph to come to New York where Judith will find "a comfortable house, an affectionate sister and a good friend."

On August 4 Tudor had arrived at Morrisania from Harvard. On August 13 John Randolph thanks Morris for his invitation. "The cause to which you direct my attention as the immediate excitement of St. George's malady has not escaped our attention. It occurred to me on the very first view of his situation, poor fellow." Randolph states his expectation of visiting Morrisania within the next month and sends his "best wishes to Mrs. Morris." On August 22 Morris writes a letter to John Randolph stating that he himself is prescribing for Tudor but feels himself in an awkward situation. As always, he has little faith in doctors.

> If anything sinister should happen much will be laid, and perhaps justly, to the Charge of my Presumption. On the other hand, I am

persuaded that a Phisician would probably direct a Treatment injurious perhaps fatal. Allow me my dear Sir to urge on you this as an additional Reason for coming on and for bringing Mrs. Randolph with you.

He concludes by stating he has "not a Shadow of a Doubt that to hear you and his Mother are on the Road would do him more good than any Medicine."

In the diary there follow numerous references to the course of Tudor's illness, his continuous hemorrhages and visits, upon the request of Mrs. Morris, from Doctors Hosack and Hoffman. In October, Judith arrives at Morrisania, followed shortly thereafter by John Randolph. Because Morris himself had been indisposed for some time, the entries in his diary at this critical time are maddeningly brief. At Morrisania something must have occurred to anger John Randolph; after staying only one night, he leaves for New York City. Perhaps Nancy or Tudor said something to him. Or maybe he left to seek medical assistance for the injury he had suffered prior to his arrival. In his malicious letter, sent several days later, he wrote that he had seen and heard enough in the course of his short visit to satisfy himself that Nancy had not amended her life. To my profound disappointment, I could find nothing about the receipt of the malevolent Randolph letter, not even a copy of the letter itself. Worse than that, there was no sign of Nancy's response. Morris notes the visit of David Ogden to renew his note for $10,000, but writes not a word about the letter which was then troubling him. On reading his diary, one would not even know it existed.

It is only in the letter books that there is an indication that something is amiss. During the period following the receipt of the vicious attack on his wife, Morris corresponded with various persons in defense of his wife's reputation. On December 26, 1814, he wrote to John Randolph's stepfather, Judge St. George Tucker, in Williamsburg, Virginia.

> Your goodness cannot persuade itself that Mr. Randolph originated the Calumnies of the anonymous letter you have returned. It is nevertheless a fact. At no distant Day, shall be transmitted to Virginia the copy of his Letter to her sent open to me, after having been exhibited to, at least, four Persons in New York. In this Letter he more than insinuates those malignant absurdities, with the avowed Objects of tearing us asunder. The Root of his Torturing Engine to rend my heart strings was the fact which she confided to him and to you. But her Candor had secured her against the Assault. She would not, tho perishing from want in Connecticut, enter my house even as my Servant without telling me all her story.

Morris adds that he took Nancy to his bosom from the knowledge of her virtues. The only effect of Randolph's letter was "disgust" at the breach of a trust so sacred. According to Morris, Randolph was more successful with others. None but the male members of his family shared dinner at his house the previous day. He concludes, "Thank God, we find in our selves and our Child a Compensation for the Society which has been driven away. Time will, I trust, bring back as much of it as is worth having."

On December 31 Morris wrote his friend David Ford in New Jersey. He hopes that Ford and his wife will not be deterred from visiting by the "absurd tales" of John Randolph. "What may have prompted that Madman's Malevolence, it is hardly possible to conjecture. When Mrs. Morris communicated an Idea of his Slanders to her friends in Virginia, they were so far from believing him to be the Author of them that they all entreated her not to believe it but to attribute the Invention to the Malice of their Common Enemies." Morris predicts that Randolph will meet a flood of indignation for his "unprovok'd Malice and most improbable falsehood." He continues, "In the meantime, his foul Slanders have been believed by those who, hating her, desire to believe whatever may destroy her Peace." Those who give their reason fair play will revolt at "such a Tissue of contradictory words." He ends the letter by stating he will say no more on the subject, "of which I have not written so much to any one else.

On January 22, 1815, Morris writes about the war to a Mr. Randolph Harrison at Clifton, in Virginia. He ends the letter with a reference to his personal troubles.

> Our Boy is well and exceeds the Promise of his earlier Day. He begins to prattle. His Blandishments and my tenderest attentions are required to soothe his Mother's Anguish. *She never deceived me.* Her health is sinking under Wounds inflicted by Relations, whom she believed to be friends. I trust that she will not perish. The Hand of a just Judge will press heavily on them and restore her to the Happiness of which you were a Witness.

What of David Ogden during this period? On December 20, 1814, Morris wrote Ogden referring to John Randolph's letter.

> When you were here last and mentioned to me having received many letters from Mrs. Morris attributing to you unworthy Motives, I assured you that I knew nothing of them. On reflection, I am apprehensive that you may extend the meaning of this assurance to a long letter part of which she read to me written immediately after the receipt of an anonymous Epistle which contained almost all the aspersions cast on her character by Mr. Randolph with the addition of some new matter. . . .

Morris assures his nephew that the part communicated conveyed nothing improper and was written to Ogden as one disposed to defend the reputation of Mrs. Morris as far as it can be defended on grounds of reason and truth. "God forbid that on any occasion you should go farther." (It is not clear that sarcasm was intended here.) Thus, even before my report was made to Morris, it appears that Nancy was at war with Ogden, and Morris was perhaps trying to restore the peace between them.

During the following year, 1815, Ogden dined many times at Morrisania. It must have been most difficult for Morris to entertain his nephew and maintain peaceful relations with Nancy. In February of 1815 he writes Ogden congratulating him on the return of peace to the nation, which, Morris hopes, will prevent a separation of the states. In March, Morris writes Judith Randolph that Tudor was "a principal agent" in the transactions which excited Judith's "indignation and abhorrence." Morris writes that Judith's solemn assurances convince him that she did not participate in the slanders. That same day, he sends Judith's letter of assurances to Ogden and suggests he show it to his acquaintances who may have wrongly supposed Judith was involved in the plot to destroy her sister's name. He directs Ogden not to show Judith's letter to the ladies "who greedily swallowed and zealously propagated the Slanders against my wife." It would be idle to correct, he declares, where there is no hope to amend.

It was a shock for me to learn how widely known, at least among Morris's circle of acquaintances, were the contents of John Randolph's letter. In my accursed seclusion from society, I had heard nothing about the matter beyond what Morris, and later Dr. Hosack, had told me. Numerous others knew about the scandal which I had assumed Morris had shared only with me. My perceived role as confidant to Gouverneur Morris dwindled in my mind to the insignificant thing it truly was.

One day late in the summer, while I was in the midst of reading Morris's correspondence from the latter part of 1815, Nancy entered the library and sat in a chair near the desk. It quickly became clear that the mood was upon her to converse with me. At first she spoke only of trivial matters. Apprehensively concealing the letter book in front of me, I said nothing. Suddenly she was silent. We looked at each other and she smiled. "You northerners are so very reserved. You never ask about anyone's personal life. Are you not curious about me, even a tiny bit?"

Taken aback by an invitation which seemed to be a gift from the gods, I could only muster a feeble response. "We are fearful of offending by treading on forbidden ground . . . Of course I am curious. Tell me all about yourself." She smiled enigmatically and remained silent. I could not ask about John Randolph's letter or many other matters which were not supposed to be known to me. My dissembling had gone on too long. It was too late to admit my knowledge. If only I had known earlier of how many shared that information. Careful not to reveal the extent of my knowledge, I asked her how she came to Morrisania. Her response was extremely guarded. She related how after her mother's death, her father, Thomas Mann Randolph of Tuckahoe, had married a young woman not much older than his own daughters. Because of Nancy's unsatisfactory relationship with her stepmother, and her refusal to marry a husband selected by her father, she left home. When I asked her about her problems with her stepmother, her response was, "We just did not like each other." She stayed for a time at Monticello with her brother, who had married Thomas Jefferson's daughter, Martha, who Nancy called "Patsy." Then she lived at Bizarre with her sister Judith and Judith's husband, Richard Randolph. "I was betrothed to Theoderick, Richard's younger brother, but he became deathly ill and wasted away before our eyes. His death was the beginning of my sorrows. You men don't understand how difficult it is for a woman alone to survive in this world. We are kept hopelessly sheltered from life, without means to earn our own subsistence. Our sole purpose is to provide entertainment for men. When the bloom of youth begins to fade, we become useless. Our own beauty becomes a curse."

The influence of Wollstonecraft was evident in her words. But I said nothing about seeing the book on her desk. Instead, I asked her if she loved Theoderick. She replied, "Although we were not married, I considered him my husband before God. When Theo died, I was on my own. For a time, I continued to stay with Judith and Richard. But when Richard died, his property was inherited by his brother John. You've read of his political career. You know what a spiteful and malicious man he is." Her characterization of John Randolph, I acknowledged, was generally accepted by the world.

"It was impossible for me to stay entombed in that loveless house with Jack Randolph and my sister. When he accused me of taking as many liberties in his house as if it were a tavern, I left. I was poor and dependent on others, living by my skill with the needle and other housework. By bestowing my hand, I could have avoided destitution. There were opportunities, you know. But my heart revolted at marrying without love. So I continued to struggle. Finally, at the invitation of my cousin, I moved to her house in Newport, Rhode Island. Then I became a teacher at a school in Stratford, Connecticut. When Mr. Morris, an old friend of my father, learned I was teaching there, he invited me to come to Morrisania as his housekeeper. His previous employee had provoked his servants to riot, so he said he was looking for a gentlewoman, who could command respect, to take charge of his household. As always, he was most generous in his offer. I accepted."

"That first night I saw you at Morrisania, were you crying, alone in that room? You do recall our first meeting?" I asked plaintively.

"Oh yes. I remember it well. I cried often in those days. I had been ill and destitute for so long. I thought Morrisania might provide only another temporary refuge. But fate was kind to me. We were married. You know the rest."

Nancy's brief account perplexed me. After voluntarily offering to tell me about herself, she gave an incomplete account of her past which deleted the most important events. Her reticence about the past, for the most part, continued to be unyielding. As she continued to talk, I realized it was not about her past problems she wanted to speak. Her mind was on her present woes. At first she described her financial problems. Years before, when David Ogden had purchased vast amounts of northern lands, Morris had given his nephew a substantial mortgage loan and had also become his surety. According to Nancy, Morris did not even bother to record the mortgage until it was discovered that Ogden's assurances—that he was satisfying his numerous creditors—were false. Ogden had expected to be named executor of Morris's estate, a position which would have permitted him to conceal his devious financial schemes. "That scoundrel," Nancy said, uttering the words with venomous contempt, "stole more than $100,000 from the estate. Just to pay our employees, the final medical bills, and the funeral expenses, I had to sell sheep, cows, horses, hogs, furniture, plate, and even the contents of the cellars."

In response to my expressions of amazement about her financial problems, Nancy shook her head and hands as if to indicate those matters were trivial. "But it's the lawyers' bills that are ruining me. You see, I have begun a lawsuit against David Ogden. It's not just for the money he owes. He still thinks he, instead of my son, can inherit Morrisania. The villain has attacked both my child and my honor by claiming that my husband was not the boy's father." Her voice quavered as she spoke these words. Otherwise, she revealed not a trace of emotion. The face she presented was one of outrage accompanied by a resolve of iron.

Before I could ask how Ogden could possibly claim Morris was not the father, Nancy broached the subject of her own accord. "After the baby was born, Ogden began telling people that the father was one of our former servants, David Dunn. Anyone who knew poor David would laugh at the charge. He was just a poor, honest, Irish waiter, a totally harmless man. Shortly after he left our employ, I foolishly wished, in front of some guests, he would come back to Morrisania. That was all the opening David Ogden needed. The man is a monster of greed and treachery!"

"If Ogden had no basis for his stories about David Dunn, you should be able to prove he slandered you."

"That's what I thought. My lawyers have already begun to speak to witnesses. They tell me Ogden only expressed a belief that my own son was not Gouverneur's child. But he never made what they call 'a positive statement of the fact.' Whatever that may mean. Ogden, you know, is a lawyer. It seems he told some relatives that little Gouverneur looked like David Dunn, but he never said David Dunn was the father. Oh, he's a clever liar."

"You don't have to convince me of David Ogden's vicious nature. I knew him twenty years ago. He was the same villain then as he is now."

Nancy listened with great interest to my stories about the young David Ogden. Our shared hatred of the man, I believe, brought us closer together. In response to my question as to why Morris tolerated such a villain for so long, Nancy told me that Ogden was the child of Morris's favorite sister, Euphemia. "Even if his nephew was a scoundrel, my husband believed it was his duty to take care of Euphemia's son."

I asked when Nancy had become aware of Ogden's plots. Without hesitation, she responded. "Immediately after our marriage, it was obvious to me that he and his cousin Martin Wilkins were my enemies. They saw me as a threat to their inheritance, but they bided their time. Except for an occasional comment about their dislike for me, I said little to my husband. I did not want to be the one to break his bonds with his family. Shortly after our son was born, Morris learned of their open hostility from family members and others. They were not discreet in their enmity. 'No need to get mad,' he would say. 'They shall reap the fruits of their efforts in due course.' "

My report to Morris about Ogden's intrigues with John Randolph was clearly no blinding revelation to him. It only corroborated a long-standing hostility with which he was fully familiar. My modest efforts on Morris's behalf had been of little consequence. The die had been cast before I was recruited to visit Richmond. The results, I believe, were ineluctable, and certainly not to be changed by the exercise of my poor powers.

After Nancy left the library, I spent the remainder of the day glancing through the diary for 1816, searching for hints of Morris's attitude toward Ogden. There was no sign of a breach in the short entries for that final year. The nephews, Martin Wilkins and David Ogden, continued to dine at Morrisania frequently. After his inaugural discourse as President of the Historical Society, Morris became indisposed. On October 19, 1816, more than two weeks before his death, the final entry appears in the diary. "A little frost last night." Beneath that final statement, in a large scrawl, were the words of another.

Oh my adored, my best of Husbands, Had I been told this was to be the last morning we should leave our chamber together—the last night we should reenter it together—I should have thought my Heart would Burst. I had traced the suffering of your mind from the first Detection of David Ogden's villainy. I had participated in all those sufferings. The helpless age of our Infant prevented my sinking—by claiming double care.

On the top of the right-hand page, the scrawl continued.

The gracious remains of this wise and Virtuous Man are preserved in three Coffins. The First having been made without a Leaden lining, I trust in God I shall be laid down by this kindest of Friends, this tenderly beloved Husband.

After speaking to Nancy, my desire for information became insatiable. I was no longer content to wait for my gradual review of the papers to be completed. Having made certain that nobody was present outside the library, I removed the key from the desk, opened the closet, and removed the last letter books. In a matter of minutes I discovered Morris's final letter, dated

July 16, 1816, to his old friend John Parish. It was convincing evidence that John Randolph's letter and David Ogden's plotting never succeeded in shaking Morris's love for his wife.

> I will, then, assure you that I indulge the same friendly Senti-
> ments which we felt at parting on the banks of the Elbe nearly sev-
> enteen years ago. How large a Portion of human Life! How eventful
> a Period in the History of Mankind!
> I lead a quiet and, more than most of my fellow Mortals, a happy
> life. The woman to whom I am married has much genius, has been
> well educated, and possesses, with an affectionate Temper, Industry
> and a Love of Order. Our little boy is generally admired. The senti-
> ments of a father respecting an only Child render his Opinions so
> liable to Suspicion that Prudence should withhold them even from a
> friend. I will only say, therefore, that some who would have been
> more content had he never seen the Light acknowledge him to be
> beautiful and promising. His parents, who see him almost every Min-
> ute of every Day, are chiefly delighted with the Benevolence that
> warms his little heart.
> You may, then, opening your Mind's Eye, behold your friend as
> he descends, with tottering Step, the Bottom of Life's Hill, supported
> by a kind Companion, a tender female friend, and cheered by a little
> Prattler who bids fair, if God shall spare his Life, to fill, in due time,
> the Space his father leaves. He will, I trust, bequeath a Portion larger
> than his Heritage of Wealth and Fame. Nevertheless, looking back, I
> can, with some little Self-Complacency, reflect that I have not lived
> in vain; and at the same Time look forward with Composure at the
> probable Course of future events. At sixty-four there is little to desire
> and less to apprehend.

Within an hour a cursory review of the letter book and other papers uncovered what I had hoped to discover—the will of Gouverneur Morris. In fact, there were two of them. The first, made in 1809, was highly favorable to David Ogden, Martin Wilkins, and the other nieces and nephews. It was superseded by a later will executed less than two weeks before his death. It provided the final convincing proof of the strength of the testator's attachment to his wife.

> I, Gouverneur Morris, declare this to be my last Will and Testa-
> ment, of which I name my friend, Moss Kent, and my wife, Ann
> Cary Morris, Executor and Executrix, hereby giving my said Execu-
> tor ten thousand dollars for his care and trouble in executing that
> office.
> Item, I confirm the ante-nuptial contract, by which I settled on
> my wife twenty-six hundred dollars a year; moreover, I give to her,

during her life, my estate of Morrisania, with all the stock thereon, and also all my plate, furniture, and carriages; and it is further my will, that the improvement, which may become necessary, shall be made at the expense of my estate; and, in case my wife should marry, I give her six hundred dollars more per annum, to defray the increased expenditure, which may attend that connexion.

Item, I give to my son, Gouverneur Morris, the whole of my estate, saving and excepting such bequests, as may be in this my will, and such as I may hereafter think proper to make. If it should please God to take him away, before he arrives at full age, or afterwards, not having made a will, I then give my estate to such one or more of the male descendants of my brothers and sisters, and in such proportions, as my wife shall designate; but in case she shall have made no such designation, I then give my estate to Lewis Morris Wilkins, son of my sister Isabella, on condition, that he drop the name of Wilkins, and bear the name and arms of Morris.

Item, I give to my nephew, Gouverneur Wilkins, twenty-five thousand dollars, to be paid to him when he shall have arrived to the age of thirty, provided his conduct shall be, in the opinion of my Executor and Executrix, such as becomes a good citizen.

In witness whereof, I have hereunto set my hand and seal, this twenty-sixth day of October, one thousand eight hundred and sixteen.

David Ogden and Martin Wilkins had indeed lost the struggle for the fortune of Gouverneur Morris. How I would have enjoyed seeing Ogden's face at the reading of the will, at the moment of learning of the total triumph of his enemy. A lawyer acquaintance of mine has informed me that in all his years of practice he had never seen a will which increased the bequest to a wife who remarried after the testator husband's death. Morris had written years earlier that the art of living consists in great degree in knowing how to be cheated. Perhaps he considered his last will and testament to be the final and best means for demonstrating how well he had mastered that art.

The next day, a Wednesday, I set forth for Morrisania with great anticipation. After so many years, the barriers between Nancy and me were collapsing. At last, she was beginning to confide in me as a friend. Because as a lover she had visited me in my dreams the previous night, I warned myself against ridiculous hopes and incorrect perceptions of my true status in her life. "Do not make a fool of yourself" was my precept for the day.

The boat ride to Morrisania that morning was exceptionally difficult. Treacherous winds almost capsized the marketman's small boat. The winds howled in an unusually ominous way. "Nature's way of telling us to beware," commented the boatman. By the time of my arrival, dark storm clouds were visible in the distance. Nancy was not at the door to greet me. Simon, the ancient servant, led me into the library. It was quickly apparent that I had forgotten to return to the closet two of the volumes which were not supposed to be available to me. They were under three other books. Nobody had seemed to notice them. But a vague sense of anxiety troubled me. I turned back to the beginning of 1816 for a careful perusal of the diary for the last years of Morris's life. The entry for January 1 was striking.

> Another year is buried in the abyss of a past eternity. What the coming, or, rather, the arrived year may bring is known only to the Omniscient. But we know that, whatever may be its course and incidents, they will be what they ought to be.

No doubt Morris would have written those words even if he knew that death was waiting for him on the road to 1817.

Within the hour, heavy winds began to batter the house. It became dark as night. The windowpanes rattled. The sounds of a heavy rain augmented the atmosphere of solitude which dominated the room and permeated my thoughts. It was too dark to read. My mind wandered. With my eyes closed, I watched the succubus Nancy Randolph, dressed all in white, enter the room. Without a word she walked up to the desk and began undoing my clothes. She ran her hands gently over my body. The experience was so intense as to attain the palpable reality of the most vivid of dreams. As the spirit and I consummated our union, we were interrupted by the prattling of a young child. The flesh and blood Nancy entered the room holding the hand of her son. She was wearing the same white dress as the apparition who had preceded her entrance into the room. To my recollection, I had never before seen the dress. The coincidence between the vision and the reality shocked me into a state of stunned speechlessness. After greeting me, Nancy lit several candles. The dark spell of the room was broken. She fixed a piercing eye upon me, so that I was unsettled by the intensity of her stare. Perhaps realizing she had crossed society's vague line of what is permissible, she averted her eyes. Smiling coquettishly, she declared she would leave me to my business and play with little Gouverneur.

Looking forward to my next encounter with Nancy, I was able to accomplish very little that morning. In the afternoon we dined together. Because the constant demands of the child required most of Nancy's attention, there was a scarcity of significant conversation. However, as the storm had grown more severe, Nancy did say that it appeared the weather would keep me a "prisoner of Morrisania," at least until the next morning. Agreeing with her assessment of the storm, I apologized for any inconvenience. She replied that there was no problem; I could use an empty bedroom on the second floor. She smiled and lowered her eyes, leaving me in a state of lovesick confusion. It was the opportunity of which I had dreamed for many years. A night, I feared, which would overwhelm my carefully prepared defenses and cause me to play the fool by testing the reality of my own imaginings.

Sixteen

The crowds of unfamiliar faces pass me on the street. Once again the old man whose skull has penetrated his visage. The closet laced with cobwebs. The small casket falls to the cold marble floor. The dust-covered coils begin to move. I know it is a dream, but it troubles me. Waking with a start, I think for a moment it is that night at Morrisania. The clock will soon strike. It is time to act. The pain in my rotting teeth informs me of my misconception. My breast fills with a dull ache of disappointment. There will be no second opportunity. The road has no more turns. My bedroom is filled with piles of unread books. Notes clutter the floor up to the very side of my bed. *The Age of Revolution* still summons me to greatness. It is all vanity.

As I conclude this book, this diversion from my major work, it is ten years since my night at Morrisania. Twenty years since I purchased the book on the New York Conspiracy which set me on my path. Two decades ago, 1827 seemed a lifetime away. Now, those thousands of days appear to have passed in an instant, like a fleeting dream. This book will be finished in my fifty-first year; I am almost as old as Morris was when I first met him. So much time has passed. Yet, in the moment of waking, the fever of full desire burns anew. What was first felt for Nancy Randolph so long ago has not been buried under a decade of silence.

Work on *The Age of Revolution* will continue. It is true, as my father once told me, the quest for knowledge never palls; it is the only thing to last for a lifetime without growing stale. The other side of the coin, however, is that the quest suffers from the distinct disadvantage of being incapable of completion. The newly published biography of Napoleon by Walter Scott, on the table beside my bed, reminds me of the reason for my discomfort. Working backward from 1815, I thought the period from 1805 to 1815 was at last finished. Certainly my lengthy account of the Battle of Leipsic had long ago been completed to my satisfaction. After extensive research and thought, I had concluded that Colonel Montfort was responsible for the premature destruction of the Elster Bridge. He should have remained at his post, as ordered, to be available to make the judgment on lighting the fuse. But Napoleon and Berthier were much more culpable for not having the foresight to build several additional strong bridges the day before the final retreat. Withdrawal across the one overcrowded bridge was so slow that another hour or two for the retreating soldiers would not have saved many lives. It was the lack of additional bridges, rather than the premature destruction of the single remaining span, which caused the loss of the rearguard. Although my conclusion appeared to be correct, my entire account of the Elster Bridge incident was thrown into doubt by Scott's new book. He correctly reports that Colonel Montfort was publicly denounced as the person who out of negligence or treachery left his post in the care of a subordinate. But Scott further claims that the only officer by the name of Montfort in the engineer service of the French army was at Mentz when the battle occurred. He quotes Marshal Grouchy, who wrote, "One would wish to forget the bulletin, which, after the battle of Leipsic, delivered to the bar of public opinion, as preliminary to bringing him before a military commission, Colonel Montfort of the engineer service, gratuitously accused of breaking down the bridge at Leipsic." Of course, as the one blamed for the defeat at Waterloo, Grouchy may have wanted to imply that he, like Montfort, was being made the scapegoat for the failures of others.

Also contrary to my account, which has Montfort charged at Erfurt, Scott writes that neither the Colonel nor the noncommissioned officer were ever brought to a court-martial. To the extent that Scott questions the official accounts of the incident, he implicitly resurrects the claims that Napoleon destroyed the bridge to protect himself. Even Morris refused to believe such nonsense. Nevertheless, another portion of my book is thrown into doubt. It is like fighting the Hydra. One head is cut off and two more grow in its place. The writing of history, it seems, can never be perfected. Once again I must write to Charles de Flahaut for a clarification of the Elster Bridge incident.

Time has laid down in the dust so many of the great men of the Age of Revolution. Franklin, Washington, Hamilton, Paine, Morris, Adams, Jefferson, and many others are gone. Napoleon himself, a man of my own generation, died six years ago. Prometheus chained to the rock of St. Helena. Even the colossus of his age has been swept away by the deluge of time. The ordinary folk I have known since youth have begun to vanish, one after another, from the stage of life, insubstantial mortal shadows. A number of them were snatched away in the nightmare summer of 1822.

For the past five years I have lived alone in the empty silence of my house. Emily was among those to meet the ferryman in that mournful summer of yellow fever. Without leaving the city, both before and after our marriage, we had both survived many previous summers of fever—1795 through 1799, 1803 and 1805, when there were over two hundred deaths in the city. Even in 1819, when the fever broke out in the vicinity of the Old Slip, we did not leave our home, although we did consider it when the stock exchange moved away from Wall Street. During different earlier outbreaks, we had each contracted a slight fever, and we believed ourselves to be immune. In June of 1822, when the fever appeared in Rector Street, a part of the city previously free from the ravages of the dreaded illness, there was universal alarm. By late July the fever was spreading fearfully. The rumors of pestilence were everywhere in the city; they traveled faster than the epidemic itself. On every street people began to leave their homes. Carts and wagons were laden with furniture, clothing, and cooking utensils for the trek to Greenwich and the country beyond. They were inevitably accompanied by lines of sullen adults, grim parents, and weeping children. Stores and houses were boarded up. For days the streets were filled with long lines of frightened humanity in flight to the north. For those of us who stayed in the city, all manner of protection was tried. Handshakes were discontinued. People walked in the middle of the street so as to avoid contamination from they knew not what. Bonfires were lit in the street to ward off the pestilential air. Many believed that smoking tobacco could provide protection. It was not uncommon to see women and children smoking cigars. The most popular method of protection was vinegar. It was sprinkled generously on clothes and soaked into kerchiefs which were wrapped about the face. In those days of horror, spectral figures muffled in vinegar-soaked rags regularly haunted the streets in all parts of the city.

Within a short time the lower portion of the city became completely desolate. Fearful of the unseen death hovering everywhere, and the lack of supplies in the city, Emily and I decided to leave for the country the next morning. We spent the afternoon and early evening selecting the limited number of items we would be able to carry with us. Among these would have to be numerous valuables which could not be left behind, as they would be stolen by the inevitable plunderers who descended on the abandoned areas. At supper Emily complained of exhaustion and went to bed early. Within the hour she began to shiver with chills. She had become feverish. I knew it must be the plague. By morning there was no longer any doubt. Her limbs were too weak to support her. Burning with fever, she lay almost lifeless in bed until forced back to consciousness by paroxysms of vomiting. After helping her to drink water, which she desperately craved, I waited until she dozed off and ran into the street to find our regular physician, Dr. Shaw. I was astonished at my good fortune in meeting him as he left his house. Although he complained about the many patients he had to visit, he promised to come before two P.M. He did not appear. By six P.M. Emily was worse. The vomit was bilious with black blood of a malignant appearance and odor. She drank water from the pitcher with the eagerness of one dying of thirst. When she fell asleep, I set forth for Dr. Hosack's house. It was getting dark. Except for a few ghostly figures wrapped in vinegar-soaked cloaks, the streets were almost deserted. In spite of the summer heat, I was the only person without a cloak. The silence was broken only by the occasional shrieks and lamentations of the survivors. The terrible unseen foe had brought life in the city to a halt.

The door at Dr. Hosack's house was answered by the young man he had taken into his home some years earlier. He informed me that the doctor had been visiting houses all day, and suggested leaving a message. After scribbling a note, I hastened back to Emily. Despite the substantial distance back to my house, the only sign of life in the street during the return journey was a hearse, driven by two Negroes, moving slowly along the street. It was the night, I knew, which was reserved for the removal of the dead.

Upon my return, Emily was sleeping. The floor was covered by the bilious effusion from her diseased stomach. The skin on her forehead was burning; her face was swollen and jaundiced. I hastily filled the pitcher at the well and tried to force as much of the fluid into her as she could swallow. After changing the sheets and cleaning the floor, I sat in a chair and stared out the window into the blackness of the night. The terrible silence and desolation of the city was creeping into my spirit. A kind of panic began to envelop my mind. It was the moment of utmost terror for me. I thought of a childhood friend who had died of the fever in the summer of 1819. Also of Benjamin Latrobe, who was carried away by yellow fever in 1820 in New Orleans, according to the news accounts, on the third anniversary of his son's death from the same cause in the same city. Almost all of the neighbors had fled from the presence of the invisible scourge. Uncertainty as to the manner of avoiding it filled me with a sense of complete helplessness. The blow could fall at any moment, and I was unable to protect myself. For one dark moment I even considered abandoning Emily and fleeing to Greenwich. Instead I arose, soaked a cloth in vinegar and held it to my face. I imagined Nancy Randolph, distant and unattainable. What is life to me, I thought, that I should be so afraid of losing it? The moment of panic passed.

Early the next morning the sound of Dr. Hosack's carriage stopping in front of my building awakened me from a fitful sleep. I welcomed him with profuse and sincere expressions of gratitude. Because of his copious writings on yellow fever, I hoped he might actually be able to save Emily from the maw of death. Following a brief examination of the patient, he confirmed the obvious. It was yellow fever. "Your wife is in very serious condition. There is little we can do with the epidemic form of fever. Bleeding and use of mercury do not seem to help. My own experience has been that the mild sudorific treatment of the disease provides the best chance of saving the patient. There is little you can do but force fluids into her. Every few hours put her in a cold bath to control the fever. That, and hope for the best. A few do recover. Only a few when it's this far along." Noticing my vinegar-soaked cloth, he indicated there was no proof that vinegar was of any use whatsoever. Suddenly he collapsed into a chair. Looking tired and discouraged, he admitted he had been working with only a few hours' rest each night for weeks. "We simply cannot control it," he said.

In response to my question about the cause of the epidemic, he stated it was unknown. "It is thought to be related to the black plague. Has many of the same symptoms. Dr. Benjamin Rush of Philadelphia believed it was caused by the miasma from decaying vegetable matter in wet and marshy places. Some say it is stagnant air in our narrow, filthy alleys. Others claim it is imported by persons carrying the disease from abroad. The foreigners, they say, transmit it by bodily contact. All of these theories may hold some part of the truth. I tend to support the view the contagion is a combination of mephitic air and filth seeping into the drinking water. You know, for many years I fought to clean up the Collect for those very reasons. But the fact is

we have not yet established the cause with any kind of certainty. Some day
... perhaps." He did not have the look of a hopeful man. "Rush recommended copious bloodletting as the only method of treatment. That I have
never supported. Those with the fever are too weak to survive such treatment.
I refuse to use it." After informing me of the incorrectness of the belief that
blacks are immune to the disease, he told me he had many other patients to
see. As if rested, he arose from the chair with renewed vigor. While opening
the door to leave, he urged me to bathe Emily in cold water within the hour.

"Can she recover?" I asked.

"God only knows." He rushed to his carriage, which I watched disappear
around the corner. I was filled with admiration for a truly extraordinary man.

For the next few days I followed Dr. Hosack's instructions. Emily showed
no signs of improvement. On the fifth day after the onset of the fever, Emily
lapsed into a coma. The following day Dr. Hosack visited again. Gently, he
informed me that she would die within the next several days. Two nights later
she was gone. I removed the sheets, which were tinged with a frightful yellow
and gangrenous black substance. For some time I stared at my wife's lifeless,
naked body. Her yellow face was haggard and contorted with a look of solitary agony. Her eyes were partially open, her mouth grotesquely twisted, her
hair in disarray. There never had been anything mysterious about Emily in
life; but now she had become so by crossing into the land from which no
traveler returns. Nothing was left of the woman I had known for so many
years but this hideous shell of a human being.

Having wrapped the corpse in a clean sheet, that same evening I engaged
the attendance of a hearse. Two burly black men came and carried the remains
to a wagon containing two other bodies. In mournful silence we rode together
to a freshly dug hole in the ground. The three bodies were hastily thrown
into the pit and covered over with lime. Wearing the white mourning scarf
which had accompanied me to the funerals of my parents and sister, I neither
cursed nor prayed to God. What can one say when observing the fragility of
human life in the face of nature's brutality? Through the abandoned, dark
streets, I returned to an empty home.

Emily was one of the early victims of the pestilence. In August the epidemic became worse. The Board of Health directed that high board fences be
erected to close off infected districts. The interment of bodies in various cemeteries was forbidden because of overcrowding. Some churchyards were so full
that they were raised several feet above the level of the adjacent streets. The
Custom house, post office, banks, and other businesses, including printing
establishments, were moved to upper Broadway, Greenwich, and other areas
outside the city. Courts were closed. The wharfs were entirely bare of ships.
In order to disinfect the atmosphere in the lower part of the city, lime, char-
coal, and ashes were spread on the ground. The streets near the Battery were
barricaded at the upper ends. Everywhere, houses were boarded up and deserted. Country people ceased bringing their produce to market. The usual
sources of subsistence were eliminated. Many relied on the Relief Committee

for their meager supplies of food. As there existed no more stores in the lower part of the city, I had to walk miles to the least affected areas to purchase food. In these areas carts were regularly employed to remove furniture and goods into the country north of the city. The streets in parts of the city were strewn with debris and filled with hogs, dogs, and cats devouring the offal in the gutters. An occasional corpse was left to decay in the streets. It was never as ghastly as Leipsic at the time of the battle, but it was somehow more shocking to see such desolation enveloping my own city.

A whole new city arose several miles north of the Battery. The formerly empty fields were filled with temporary wooden buildings out of which business was conducted. This makeshift city included coffee houses, grocery stores, barber shops, banks, insurance offices, and even auctioneers' sales rooms. After the death of Emily, I remained in my neighborhood only long enough to care for an old man, on the floor below, who had been abandoned by his family. When he died of the fever, I moved to a shack in the fields north of Greenwich for the months of September and October. It was only after a slight frost occurred at the end of October that the fear of the plague began to dissipate. Except for certain dangerously infected areas, the Board of Health announced it was safe to return to the city. Before resuming the occupation of houses, we were instructed to ventilate, cleanse, and purify them. According to the newspapers, it was estimated that of 120,000 inhabitants of the city, less than 10,000 had remained within the city limits during the epidemic. To the surprise of many, there had been only slightly more than 400 cases of the fever, of which 230 were fatal.

Had there been no other deaths, the pestilence would have been disastrous to me. For in spite of our bickering over the years, the loss of Emily affected me severely. During the months after her death, I was unexpectedly plunged into a deep melancholy. I became almost insensible to the concerns of daily life. The reasons for this profound grief were not entirely clear to me; but the sorrow existed and had to be borne. The only person with whom I had a continuing relationship was gone forever. The bond had not been a satisfactory one, yet it was my only daily link with the living. With the end of my hopes concerning Nancy, there had been a partial, if not entirely satisfactory, reconciliation between us. Life became predictably monotonous, but at least tolerable. Emily accommodated me. Though I hated being accommodated, it was better than sleeping alone. Once she was gone, I knew that the remainder of the time allotted to me in this vale of tears would be spent in almost complete solitude. Henceforth, I would wake alone, eat alone, and sleep alone. My prolonged mourning was for myself, I suppose, as much as it was for Emily.

During the epidemic I had thought of Nancy. I knew she was safe at Morrisania. Long ago, Morris had told me one of the reasons Lewis Morris had used to argue for Morrisania as the capital of the United States—the fever had never touched there during the many times it raged within the city. In November my assumptions about Nancy's safety were confirmed. To my great astonishment, I received a brief note of condolence from her. She wrote that Dr. Hosack had informed her of my "recent bereavement" and she wished to send me "an expression of sympathy." Although I had not heard from her for five years, my former hopes were instantly revived. There existed a reason, illusory as it was, to return to the land of the living. Perhaps, I thought, Nancy had avoided me only because I was a married man. Now that we were both without spouses . . . Immediately, I wrote a note thanking her for her statement of sympathy and expressed the wish that we could resume our former connection. As always with Nancy, I was affected with voluntary blindness. There was no response. Yet the hope her note kindled in my bosom was sufficient to return me to life and my labors on *The Age of Revolution*.

In 1824 there began a series of great public events, one each year for the next four years, which recalled the past for the public and evoked in me the memory of Gouverneur Morris. The first of these occasions was the one which most enthralled the entire populace of New York City. In fact, the whole country was held spellbound for many months. In that year, Congress adopted a resolution inviting Lafayette to visit America as the guest of the nation. When the hero who had been in Europe for over forty years accepted, the excitement in this country was stupendous. It was as if George Washington himself were returning from the grave to bless the fruits of American independence. The exact date of arrival of Lafayette's ship in New York City, his first stop, was unknown. Thus when the *Cadmus*, an American merchantman, arrived on a beautiful Sunday morning, the city was not fully prepared to receive the only surviving major general of the American Revolution. That he had arrived on the sabbath forced the delay of his triumphal entry into the city. All were supposed to be busy communicating with God; they could not desecrate the sabbath by greeting the legendary hero from the past. The delay did, however, grant city officials an additional day to plan the festivities while Lafayette stayed with Vice-President David Tompkins at his home on Staten Island.

The following afternoon I joined the throngs of spectators who jammed the Battery to witness the arrival of the beloved Frenchman, who was frequently referred to as the "Prisoner of Olmütz" and "Guest of the Nation." The great man was venerated in the new world as George Washington's young general and as the symbol of the struggle for constitutional government and equal rights in the old world. To me, he was that and much more—almost a personal acquaintance from the pages of Morris's diary and letters. The general excitement grew as a huge fleet was sighted accompanying Lafayette from Staten Island to the Battery. The cannons roared and church bells rang. Tens of thousands of people surged forward to greet the hero. The bands played "Hail Columbia," "See the Conquering Hero Comes," "Où peut-on être mieux qu'au sein de sa famille?" and "La Marseillaise." No doubt Lafayette had not heard the last melody for many years. The roofs of houses, every window facing the sea and every foot of ground, were crowded with wildly enthusiastic spectators. Women waved white handkerchiefs. Old soldiers wept.

Fathers held their sons high to glimpse the revered ghost from the past. Before he disappeared into the multitudes at Castle Garden, I was only able to catch a fleeting view of the distant figure.

The opportunity to see the hero at close range would occur two days later. He had accepted an invitation to visit the New-York Historical Society with his son, George Washington Lafayette, in order to receive their honorary memberships. Fortunately, by the time of the visit, I had become a member of the society. When De Witt Clinton succeeded Gouverneur Morris as president of the society, Dr. Hosack had become corresponding secretary and later vice-president. In 1820 Hosack succeeded Clinton; not long after that, the new president gained my admission as a member despite the opposition of David Ogden. Thus, on that memorable day, I was assigned a prominent place among the crowd packed into the New York Institution in City Hall Park. In order to accommodate the huge throng, the society's rooms and the apartments of the Literary and Philosophical Society were thrown open.

Dr. Hosack waited in his carriage outside City Hall until General Lafayette left at two P.M. So many thousands of people crowded in front of the building that the carriage could barely move. Accordingly, the president and his guests arrived at the society much later than had been anticipated. The increasingly loud roars of the crowd informed everyone inside of the progress of the triumphal procession. Finally the great man appeared at the side of Dr. Hosack. Like the Red Sea before the upraised staff of Moses, the men and women quickly parted to make a path for the guests. Lafayette was a tall, impressive-looking man, then sixty-seven years old, dressed in the plain clothing of a citizen. He wore no medals. His copious head of reddish-brown hair appeared to be a wig. Walking with a cane, he limped noticeably from what many assumed to be the wound he received at Brandywine, where my father was also wounded. I later learned from Hosack that the limp was the result of a fall on the ice in Paris many years earlier. The few people to whom I later mentioned that fact responded, "Let it be a wound from Brandywine." All preferred the myth to the fact. The General's son was about forty years old and much shorter than his impressive father. I wondered how he felt, constantly standing in the colossal shadow of his father.

Dr. Hosack and General Philip Van Courtland conducted Lafayette to the chair of honor, which had once belonged to Lafayette's late monarch, Louis XVI. It had been presented to the society by Gouverneur Morris, who had brought it back from Europe along with the royal Tokay wine. Above the chair, in a space decorated with revolutionary emblems, hung a portrait of the twenty-seven-year-old General Lafayette. Thus there stood before us the young, slender warrior, the memory of every mind's eye, and the old, somewhat rotund statesman whose return had resurrected that splendid image from the past. The minutes of the special meeting held the previous day were read aloud with the resolution electing Lafayette and his son honorary members. Then Dr. Hosack arose and addressed "General Lafayette." I was pleased not to hear the doctor making the error of addressing him as "Marquis." From the time of his arrival in New York, Lafayette had openly disavowed the title numerous times with the simple comment, printed in the newspapers, "Since the Constituent Assembly of 1790, I have ceased to bear the title 'Marquis.' "

The president of the society presented the General with a copy of his honorary membership in the Historical Society:

> "In the name of this institution, I also tender to you their congratulations upon your safe arrival, which affords you the opportunity to witness the happy condition of that country in whose behalf the sword of your youth was drawn, and personally to bear your testimony to the blessings which have followed the achievements that have been accomplished by the united efforts of a Washington, and his illustrious companions in arms. General, my bosom glows at the associations which these events bring to our recollection, and every heart in this assembly throbs with inexpressible emotions at the sight of the hero who this day enters their hall, and confers a lasting honor upon the sittings of this Society.
>
> "Long, long, Sir, may you live to enjoy the homage so justly due, and spontaneously offered from the hearts of a free and grateful people, for the services you have rendered to this nation, to the world, to liberty, and to the ever memorable establishment of the only example on earth—a pure unmixed republican form of government."

Lafayette rose from Morris's chair and accepted in English spoken with a charming French accent. Briefly, he expressed his gratitude for the honor bestowed on him, and concluded by declaring his hopes for the spread of the republican form of government to other parts of the world:

> "The United States, Sir, are the first nation, on the records of history, who have founded their constitutions upon an honest investigation, and clear definition of their natural and social rights. Nor can we doubt, but that, notwithstanding the combinations made elsewhere by despotism and aristocracy against those sacred rights of mankind, immense majorities in other countries shall not in vain observe the happiness and prosperity of a free, virtuous, and enlightened people."

After the ceremony was repeated for Lafayette's son, the honored guests were introduced to the members of the society. Standing within a few feet of Dr. Hosack and Lafayette, I was able to observe the manner in which the great man conducted himself. Consistent with Morris's description of the man, he seemed to thrive on the adulation of the multitudes. His behavior was a striking mixture of ease and charm. When complimented on his English, he responded, "And why should I not speak English, being an American just returned from a long visit to Europe?" Asked how long he would be staying in New York, he stated he would be leaving in two days to arrive in Boston, as promised, for the Harvard commencement. Every awestruck person who approached him, he greeted with undiminished politeness and affability. Each tearful old veteran of the Revolutionary War was embraced as though he were a personal friend. Many of the veterans greeted the General with a question about the past. "Do you remember who began the attack at Brandywine?"

With only a moment of hesitation, Lafayette would answer the question in one way or another. "Let us see. It was the Jersey troops."

Inevitably the old soldier's face would light up at the response. "Yes! So it was; and I was with the Jersey brigade!"

When those who greeted him had nothing to say, he would ask, "Are you married?" To an affirmative response, Lafayette would reply, "Ah, lucky man." When the next man answered in the negative, the General smiled and whispered, "Ah, lucky man." With the ladies, he gallantly avoided such jokes.

At an opportune moment I slipped in near the end of the line. My planned greeting was calculated to capture his attention. It was widely known that Lafayette was an ardent opponent of slavery. Several years after the end of the American Revolution, he obtained General Washington's approval to undertake a scheme to promote the gradual emancipation of slaves in America. As an experiment to prove that it could be done, in 1786, before he lost his great fortune during the French Revolution, he purchased the plantation of "La Belle Gabrielle" at Cayenne, in Guiana. All of the slaves on the plantation became tenants. The plan was to educate and otherwise prepare all of them for their eventual emancipation. Lafayette became so busy elsewhere, he turned the project over to his wife. The outbreak of the French Revolution brought the experiment to a premature termination. All of the slaves on the Cayenne plantation were liberated by Lafayette and his wife. For his efforts, in 1788 Lafayette had been made an honorary member of the New York Manumission Society.

At the moment of shaking Lafayette's hand, before he could ask if I was married, I declared, "As a fellow member of the New York Manumission Society and of the Historical Society, it is an honor to meet you." Then, speaking in French, I stated my admiration for his efforts against slavery, including the experiment at Cayenne. His face lit up; he seemed to be both surprised and moved by my comments.

"There is nothing I consider to be of greater importance than the restoration of our Negro brethren to the rights of man." He spoke in English, as though he wanted those around him to hear his response.

Because he seemed not to be eager to end our brief conversation and move on to the next person in line, I continued to speak. "I am an acquaintance of General Charles de Flahaut. You knew his mother, I believe, Adèle de Flahaut."

"Ah. Madame de Souza. And how do you know that?"

"Gouverneur Morris sent me to Paris on business. It was through him that I met General de Flahaut. Also, I have had the honor of reviewing Mr.

Morris's private papers for use in a history. There were many references to you in the documents."

Lafayette responded in French, spoken with great speed. "I hope these references were not all unflattering." He laughed. "You should know, I hold great affection in my heart for Mr. Morris, for the great services he rendered my wife and children when I was in prison. He was a distinguished statesman. But in his communications with the royal family, he presented me as an extreme republican. This encouraged the King and Queen to disregard both my advice and the opinions of the French people . . . We had our differences, but let us not speak ill of the dead. I thank you for your kind words." As I turned to leave, he began to speak again. "General de Flahaut and his mother have been in England for many years. I have not seen them for some time. If I meet them again, I will relate our conversation." In response to his request, I told him my name. Then I informed him that I too was a veteran of the American Revolution. "As a child, I used to throw rocks at the redcoats occupying New York City." He smiled broadly and returned to receiving those in line. Dr. Hosack looked at me and raised his eyebrows in mock amazement, as if to ask, "How is it you have so much to say to a man you never met?"

Following his trip to Boston, Lafayette was back in New York City less than three weeks after his departure. During this second visit, when Lafayette was informed of plans to view the city schools, he insisted that the plans include a stop at the African Free School operated by the New York Manumission Society. Unfortunately, I was not told of this arrangement or I would have attempted, as a member of the society, to see the conquering hero again.

Much of the remainder of Lafayette's return trip to New York was linked to the mounting excitement about the soon to be completed Erie Canal. The French citizens of the city held a great banquet for the guest of the nation in Washington Hall. According to accounts of the event, the banquet table was eighty feet long and sixty feet wide. The centerpiece, which extended the full length of the table, was a miniature representation of the canal—a tube filled with water on which tiny canal boats floated through a landscape of grass and tiny trees. When Lafayette left the city for the second time, he traveled by steamboat, appropriately named the *James Kent*, up the Hudson to Albany. From there the party went with five canal boats to the point where the great canal runs into the Hudson River. Thereafter, Lafayette spent almost a year traveling through the great country he had helped to establish. To Philadelphia, Baltimore, Washington, and Richmond, where he was welcomed by an address from Chief Justice Marshall. At Monticello he was the guest of Thomas Jefferson. Congress voted him $200,000 and a complete township, from land to be selected by President Monroe, for his services to the country. After traveling through the South, he came up the Mississippi to St. Louis. Everywhere he received a tumultuous welcome. By June he was back in New York State, where he traveled on sections of the Erie Canal and participated in a ceremony conducted by Stephen Van Rensselaer, President of the Board of Canal Commissioners. Again he traveled to Boston to officiate at the laying of the cornerstone of the Bunker Hill Monument on June 17, 1825, the fiftieth anniversary of the great battle. For one last time he returned to New York City to participate in the Fourth of July celebration. Finally in September, after another visit to Washington, he departed for France.

Lafayette was a prophet without honor in his own land. At his departure from France, police had brutally broken up demonstrations in his honor. While he was in America, news of this incident, and of the prohibition of any stories in the French press about his triumphal visit here, caused a wave of outrage against the Bourbon monarchy. Upon his return to France, crowds of admirers who gathered to greet him were attacked by detachments of Royal Guards with sabers drawn. Many were wounded or arrested. Numerous women and children were trampled. For the first time since the early years of the French Revolution, excluding the brief furor concerning the Peterloo massacre, I was pleased to find my fellow citizens aroused en masse against royalist tyranny in Europe. Once again I began to hope that the Age of Revolution had not ended in 1815.

The month after Lafayette left the United States was the occasion for another major festival in New York. On October 26, 1825, after eight years and four months of continuous labor, the Erie Canal was completed. At the decisive moment, the message was dispatched by artillery telegraph which proclaimed the great news from Lake Erie to the Atlantic Ocean. The salute of artillery was formed by a battery five hundred miles long in celebration of the glory to come of the State of New York. The canal boat *Seneca Chief* began its voyage over the completed canal from Buffalo, starting a vast celebration which would last for more than a week. It was not until November 4 that the great fleet of canal boats and steamboats, which had joined the *Seneca Chief*, arrived in New York City. Once again there was another mammoth celebration to rival the pageantry of a triumphal procession in ancient Rome. All over the city the bells rang. The air was filled with martial music. Thousands filled the streets. New York City's position as the metropolis of the new world was secure.

The early opponents of the project had called it a big ditch in which were to be buried the treasures of New York, watered with the tears of posterity. Once it was completed, however, the canal had only supporters. Governor De Witt Clinton, considered by many to be the "father of the canal"—it was often called "Clinton's ditch"—addressed the crowd.

"Standing near the confines of the ocean, and now connected by navigable communications with the Great Lakes of the North and the West, there will be no limit to your lucrative extensions of trade and commerce. The valley of the Mississippi will soon pour its treasures into this great emporium through the channels now formed and forming, and wherever wealth is to be acquired or enterprise can be attempted the power and capacity of your city will be felt, and its propitious influence on human happiness will be acknowledged."

The endless speeches about money were followed by numerous ceremonies throughout the city. The great fleet moved up the East River to the salute of cannon. Finally, a tremendous armada gathered into a crescent shape stretching for miles in the water in front of the city. The ceremony of uniting the waters of Lake Erie with the Atlantic was performed by Governor Clinton. After more speeches, Dr. Mitchill, whose dreadful book on New York helped send my history of New York City into oblivion, poured out the contents of several vials containing the waters of the Elbe and many other famous rivers. Mitchill then delivered an interminable address. This was followed by salutes, civic processions, illuminations, fireworks, and balls in an orgy of celebration. It was all quite entertaining, but completely lacked the profound emotion accompanying the return of Lafayette. There is always something more moving about the remembrance of the past, tragic or triumphant, as compared to the empty rejoicing over an uncertain future.

During one of the gatherings at the Battery, I glimpsed a woman who looked like Nancy Morris. Plunging into a sea of unfamiliar faces, I frantically attempted to reach her. It was like trying to rediscover a single pebble on an immense beach. If present, she was swallowed up by the crowd and vanished without a trace. I spent the remainder of the day unsuccessfully searching for what was probably a momentary illusion. If Nancy did visit the city, she must have been disappointed. There was virtually no recognition of the major role her husband had performed in the creation of the canal. In fact, during the entire celebration, the only reference to Gouverneur Morris which I saw or heard was at the Lafayette Ampitheatre. Above the proscenium were inscribed the names of all the Canal Commissioners since the project began. Except for this inconspicuous recognition of his role, Morris was a forgotten man. As so often happens in public life, the credit for a great project is taken by those in a politically advantageous position from which they can sound their own trumpets. I was upset by this unjust omission of the true father of the canal, the man who had been reviled as a wild visionary for proposing the idea. It was to correct this injustice that I became involved in the scholarly debate, which had been proceeding for some time, as to the origin of the Erie Canal.

As President of the Historical Society, Dr. Hosack had become enmeshed in the debate to the point of stating his own opinions concerning the creation of the Erie Canal. He concluded that there were four classes of persons responsible for the canal. In the first class he included those who predicted the union of lakes and rivers of the west with the ocean without reference to the specific plan. Among these persons he placed Cadwallader Colden, Surveyor General of the Province of New York early in the last century, Sir Henry Moore, Governor of the province in the latter half of the past century, and even George Washington. Hosack included the name of Gouverneur Morris in this class of early promoters of the general idea of inland navigation. But he omitted Morris's name from any of the other three classes: those who conceived the practicability of connecting the Hudson River with Lake Erie or Lake Ontario; those who planned the method of the direct internal communication to the Atlantic; and those who caused it to be accepted as public policy and to be constructed. It was clear to me that Morris was the only person who belonged in the first three categories and possibly in the fourth. Instead, Hosack awarded much of the credit to lesser men like Elkanah Watson, Thomas Eddy, and Jonas Platt. De Witt Clinton clearly played the most prominent role in actually completing the canal. Because Morris had died the year before construction had begun, he was ineligible to be included in any competition for those honors.

In order to persuade Dr. Hosack of the correctness of the claim that Morris was the originator of the idea for an Erie Canal, I obtained a statement from former Governor Morgan Lewis, Morris's boyhood friend who had accidentally scalded Morris's arm in the course of a youthful frolic. As Morris himself had once told me, Lewis recalled that in 1777 at Ford Edwards, after the evacuation of Ticonderoga, Morris had stated that some day "the waters of the great western island sea would, by the aid of man, break through their barrier and mingle with those of the Hudson." Hosack concluded that the statement demonstrated the general concept but was not specific enough to admit Morris to his second class of those responsible for the canal. As a result of having read Morris's letters and diary, I knew that he had written general descriptions of the canal on numerous occasions, long before any of the other claimants to the idea. Yet, because my access to these documents dated after 1799 was unauthorized and illicit, I could not use them. Accordingly, I urged Dr. Hosack to ask Mrs. Morris for a release of Morris's documents on the canal for a review by the Historical Society. In this regard, I volunteered my services in speaking to Mrs. Morris and in selecting the relevant documents. Unfortunately, Hosack decided that such a proposal would be more appropriate from him as both president of the society and a personal friend. During one of his visits to Morrisania, he made the request in person; but Nancy refused. She declared that at a later date she herself intended to publish many of her husband's papers. Hosack informed me that her intention to publish was due to the fact she was still searching for ways to pay the debt on Morris's estate, which was large despite the successful settlement of her legal claim against David Ogden. It was at this time that I conceived the idea of writing a full account of the origin of the canal using the unauthorized documents. My plan was to delay publication for many years so as to establish Morris's proper historical role in the development of the plan without revealing my breach of trust to either Nancy Morris or Dr. Hosack, the only two people whose goodwill I valued and who also knew about my restricted access to Morris's papers.

In my opinion, the only two contenders to the title of originator of the idea for the Erie Canal were Gouverneur Morris and Jesse Hawley, whose series of detailed essays on a canal from Lake Erie to the Hudson had appeared under the name "Hercules." Because Hawley's articles were published in 1807 and 1808, the claim that Morris was the "originator" could be established by proving he had proposed the idea at an earlier time.

A number of documents from among Morris's papers proved he was the first to conceive of the idea. Among these were two particularly striking statements. In 1800 Morris visited Lake Erie and wrote a letter about his journey to his friend John Parish. He described traveling along the Niagara River, above the falls, to Fort Erie near Buffalo.

> Along the Banks of this Stream, which, by Reason of Islands in it, appears to be of moderate Size, we proceed to Fort Erie. Here again the boundless Waste of Waters fills the Mind with renewed Astonishment. And here, as in turning a Point of Wood the Lake broke on my View, I saw, riding at Anchor, nine Vessels, the least of them above a hundred Tons. Can you bring your Imagination to realize this Scene? Does it seem like Magic? Yet this Magic is but the Early Effort of victorious Industry. Hundreds of large Ships will in no distant Period bound on the Billows of those inland Seas. At this Point commences a Navigation of more than a thousand miles. Shall I lead your Astonishment to the Verge of Incredulity? I will. Know then that one tenth of the Expense borne by Britain in the last Campaign would enable Ships to sail from London through Hudson's River into Lake Erie. As yet, my friend, we only crawl along the outer Shell of our Country. The interior excels the Part we inhabit in Soil, in Climate, in everything. The proudest Empire in Europe is but a Bauble compared to what America *will* be, *must* be, in the Course of two Centuries, perhaps of one!

The second notable statement appears in Morris's diary for September 12, 1803, when he was on a journey to his lands in St. Lawrence County. At the confluence of the Onondaga, Oneida, and Seneca rivers, he noted that the canal must follow along these rivers and Oneida Lake.

> It seems to me that a Canal should be taken from the Head of the Onondaga River, and carried on the Level as far East as it will go, and, if practicable, unto the Mohawk River; then, in as direct a Course as Circumstances will permit, to Hudson's River, making Locks as the Descent may require. This Canal should, I think, be five feet deep, and five and forty feet wide. A Branch might easily be carried to Lake Ontario; the fittest harbor would be I believe at Oswego.

He would later turn away from the use of locks to an inclined plane. But the idea of an overland canal connecting Lake Erie with a branch to Lake

Ontario and the Hudson River appears in Morris's writing years before Hawley's articles of 1807–1808.

Not content with only the various entries in the Morris papers, and in the hope of gathering additional corroborating information, I arranged a game of chess with John Randel, who had become obsessed and then indirectly ruined by the canal. At the time of my meeting with him, Randel was trapped in a slough of despond caused by a dispute much more harmful to him than his earlier battles with William Bridges. An imperfect world had not been kind to one with Randel's need for precision and perfection. The Canal Commissioners, after Morris, had almost hired him as the engineer for the Erie Canal. For reasons which he refused to discuss, he never acquired the position. Instead he was employed in the examination of a difficult portion of the canal. In 1822 he published a pamphlet in which he proved that Judge Wright, the principal engineer on the canal, had unnecessarily extended the canal nineteen and one-half miles and wasted $630,000 by choosing the circuitous route around the Mohawk River from Schenectady to Albany instead of the direct route. A few years later Wright gained his revenge. In 1824 Randel became the contractor for the eastern section of the Chesapeake and Delaware Canal. It was his great misfortune that Judge Wright was chief engineer on the project. According to Randel, Wright informed several members of the Board of Directors that he would not deal with Randel. After quietly obtaining the support of the majority of the board, Wright had them falsely declare, without stating any specific reasons, that Randel had abandoned his contract. As a result, Randel received no remuneration for nine months of work, and he eventually lost over $15,000, a loss he could not afford to suffer. His reputation was severely harmed to the point of endangering his future prospects.

Randel was not interested in playing chess. In his continuing bitterness over his personal misfortune, he could only lament the unfairness of this world. "I see nothing but hypocrisy, selfishness, malice, and injustice. It is intolerable. Mankind is despicable. Where is the interest in truth for its own sake? I am declared a villain for proving that over $600,000 in public funds has been wasted either by stupidity or willful miscalculation. What is wrong with speaking the simple truth, especially when it can be established by mathematical calculation? Why do so-called men of honor take the side of a scoundrel like Wright? Justice was on my side, but I lost. Wright is a base deceiver and he won. Where is justice?" Randel's face was red with anger. Life had finally pierced the armor of his scientific detachment.

"Perhaps we must learn to live with the fact that the world is not fair. It is the nature of mankind—"

Randel interrupted. "I can never accept such a world. It would be preferable not to be a part of it."

After inveighing against the hatefulness of the human race for well over an hour, Randel fell silent. Taking advantage of his desire for the triumph of truth, I mentioned how history was already being rewritten by the living to eradicate the fact that Morris was the original proponent of the Erie Canal. It was my intention, I declared, to correct the record for posterity. Randel was enthusiastic about the idea. "Oh yes. Let the deserving dead triumph over those thieves of honor." He informed me that his mentor, Simeon De Witt, had always maintained that Morris originally conceived of the idea. We both agreed that a statement to that effect from the man who had been the Surveyor General of New York for one-half century would be persuasive. Thus, Randel consented to arrange a meeting for me with his old friend.

De Witt, an amiable old gentleman, who was formerly one of the New York Street Commissioners and a Canal Commissioner, provided me with a decisive piece of proof. "There is no doubt," he said, "that the idea of a direct communication by canal between Lake Erie and the Hudson originated with Gouverneur Morris. He was the first man I ever heard mention it. In 1803, by sheer good fortune, we both put up for the night at the same inn in Schenectady. It was at that time he first mentioned to me the project of 'tapping Lake Erie,' those were his own words, and leading its waters in an artificial river across New York to the Hudson. I objected to the idea as unrealistic. The intermediate hills and valleys, I argued, presented insuperable obstacles. His response was *'Labor improbus omnia vincet.'* The result, he said, would justify any labor and expense. I mentioned the idea to Mr. Geddes in 1804 when he was a member of the Legislature. Geddes related it to Jesse Hawley. That information, no doubt, inspired Hawley to write his essays on the subject." Immediately, I noticed that De Witt's chance meeting with Morris occurred on the same trip that inspired Morris to describe, in his diary entry of September, 1803, a canal using locks as the descent required. For my future use, De Witt gave me a written account of his meeting with Morris.

To confirm De Witt's account, I wrote to James Geddes, the well-known surveyor. Geddes agreed in writing with De Witt's story and added to it. "The idea of saving so much lockage by not descending to Lake Ontario made such a lively impression on my mind that I frequently inquired into the practicability of the project. When Mr. Morris's notion of constructing a canal across country from Lake Erie to the Hudson River was made known in the interior of the state, the scheme was met with approval and spread with incredible rapidity."

The last person of some renown to discuss Morris's role with me was General Peter Porter, one of the men displaced as a Canal Commissioner at the same time as Morris. Porter contended that had Morris remained as President of the Board of Canal Commissioners, the canal would have been completed in larger dimensions. "Morris," he wrote, "not only originated the idea, but would have made it a much greater project than the one actually built." Morris's posthumous claim to be the originator of the idea of the Erie Canal had been proven to my satisfaction.

Morris had once predicted that the effect of the proposed canal would be to make the shore of the Hudson River, in fifty years, almost a continuous village. According to my expectations as to the possible longevity of Mrs.

Morris and Dr. Hosack, my account of the origin of the canal probably could not be published for almost fifty years. It occurred to me that at such a distant time the question of who conceived of the idea for the canal would be of little interest to the residents of that "continued village." What might engage the attention of posterity, I thought, would be a more personal account of Gouverneur Morris, not only as the originator of the canal, but also as major actor in the American Revolution, ardent opponent of slavery, draftsman of the United States Constitution, father of the American system of coinage, minister to France, chairman of the Board of New York Street Commissioners, President of the Board of Canal Commissioners, amorous adventurer, and husband to Ann Cary Randolph. To make the story credible, I would have to explain how this information, much of it confidential, became known to me. Thus, I decided to cease writing *The Age of Revolution* for a time in order to concentrate on my own personal perspective of that age, to explore the interstices of great events. If *The Age of Revolution* were never completed because its author was drowning in a sea of partial, conflicting accounts of innumerable events, this less ambitious book would save a small portion of my life and labors from the onslaught of time. As Gibbon conceived the idea of his great work in "the ruins of the Capitol," so I imagined this book in the rubble of my own incomplete history. Gibbon's work filled nearly twenty years of his life; my book would recapitulate twenty years of mine. My title came from a footnote in the last chapter of Gibbon's great work, wherein the speech of Glaucus in Book VI of *The Iliad* is mentioned. Seeking out the reference in Homer, I found a melancholy speech befitting my own mournful state of mind:

"As is a generation of leaves, so is that of humanity. The wind scatters the leaves upon the ground, but the live forest burgeons with leaves again in the season of spring returning. So of men one generation grows while another dies."

It was on the ninth anniversary of the breaking of the ground for the canal that a coincidence occurred which seemed almost miraculously to mark the passing of the generation of the American Revolution. On July 4, 1826, the fiftieth anniversary of the Declaration of Independence, there was another great celebration in New York City. The bread and circus for this event included a massive parade and a public feast for ten thousand people. Robert Fulton's son was presented with a gold medal commemorating the completion of the canal. Three similar medals were sent to the three surviving signers of the Declaration of Independence, John Adams, Thomas Jefferson, and Charles Carroll. The transitory public festivities were quickly overshadowed by events in New England and Virginia. On July 6 the news reached the city of the death of John Adams at the age of ninety-two. Two days later the newspapers reported the death of Thomas Jefferson at the age of eighty-three. What startled, amazed, and awed everybody, including confirmed skeptics like me, was the fact that both signers, and former Presidents of the United States, had died on the same day, July 4, 1826, the fiftieth anniversary of the very document they had both labored to produce. Orators and persons in conversation everywhere spoke of "the finger of Providence." Many claimed that the circumstances of the passing of Adams and Jefferson proved the Declaration of Independence to be the eternal word of God. Emily would surely have chided me for my skepticism in the face of such "obvious" proof of the existence of a Divine Being. For the fiftieth anniversary, Thomas Jefferson himself had written the New York Committee on Arrangements that he thanked Providence for the preservation of the lives of the three surviving signers. It has enabled them, he wrote, "to witness the wisdom of the choices then made between submission and resistance." After Jefferson's death, his son-in-law, Thomas Mann Randolph, who was both the former Governor of Virginia and the brother of Nancy Randolph, wrote the Common Council of New York City. "I cannot refrain from congratulating the Common Council on their being the first to call the attention of the instructors of the people in religion to the miraculous Euthanasia of those two venerable Patriots— Few of the miracles recorded in the sacred writings are more conspicuous."

Everybody saw the hand of God in this event. Even I found it difficult to devise a natural explanation. Yet, are not we human beings prone to search for meanings in coincidence while we disregard the thousands of other times when no such coincidence occurs? Is not the odd event simply a manifestation of the rules of probability described by Monsieur Laplace? Occasionally the roll of the dice will produce a very unusual outcome which is fondly remembered long after the ordinary results are forgotten. Famous men are born and die each year; the dates are quickly disregarded. But when Galileo and Shakespeare are born in the year of Michelangelo's death and Newton is born in the year of Galileo's death, the clerics claim it is proof of the divine intent to replenish the world with genius. Perhaps there is in fact a natural explanation for the conjoined deaths of two national demigods on the half-century anniversary day. Thomas Mann Randolph's letter to the Common Council reported that an eminent doctor had predicted at eight P.M. on July 3 that Jefferson would die within the hour. But the old man wanted to live to see the day of celebration. Maybe each human being possesses an inner strength which permits him to fight off death for a short time in order to arrive at a time or event of some importance to that person. Do not we all know of instances when dying persons delayed their departures from this life until they were able to converse with friends or relatives? No, I see no proof of the existence of God in the events of July 4, 1826. The life of man is of no more importance than the life of a mosquito. If there is a God, he shows equal indifference for both creatures. These unusual occurrences are to me no more than another manifestation of random events connected by the unintelligible rules of mysterious fortune.

The truly extraordinary occasions are when men themselves achieve human progress toward the creation of a world governed by the golden rule. Such a rare event occurred exactly one year after the improbable joint departure of Adams and Jefferson. On July 4, 1827, the year in which I am now concluding this book, the 1817 legislation abolishing slavery in the State of New York finally went into effect. Unlike Lafayette's visit, the opening of the canal, or the fiftieth anniversary of the Declaration, there was no great public celebration, at least among white people. Many had declared it could not be done. Human bondage, they argued, is as old as war, and war as ancient as human nature; neither one could be eradicated. Yet in the State of New York, it had been accomplished. It must be admitted that total emancipation had been a closely fought battle. James Tallmadge, whose antislavery resolution opened the Missouri Compromise debate, had proposed in 1821, during the New York Constitutional Convention, that slavery be abolished immediately in our state. The proposal was rejected along with a suggestion that the 1827 termination of slavery be guaranteed by the state constitution. Fortunately, threats to repeal the 1817 legislation also were not acted upon. Unfortunately, my former political party, to its eternal disgrace, did successfully sponsor amendments to the state constitution to increase the property qualification for Negroes to vote, from $100 to $250, while abolishing it for whites. In New York blacks are now free, but their rights as freemen have already been substantially and unjustly impaired. Yet there is reason for optimism. Twelve of the twenty-four states have now abolished slavery. Furthermore, the Missouri Compromise excludes slavery from all parts of the Louisiana Purchase north of the southern boundary of Missouri. This progress is more than Morris would have expected when he fought slavery in the constitutional conventions of both his state and his nation. Were he alive today, he might reject his former pessimism about slavery eventually leading us into a national cataclysm. Having finally reached the long-anticipated date of July 4, 1827, the end of slavery in New York, without bloodshed, I am hopeful about the eventual extinction of the nefarious institution throughout the rest of the country. It can no longer spread north; it cannot survive in an isolated South.

There are now eight surviving members of the original ten-man delegation from the New York Manumission Society which traveled to Albany in 1817. We had successfully pleaded with Governor Tompkins to submit a special message for the total abolition of slavery in New York. As a former member of that delegation, I was invited to Albany for the small Emancipation Day celebration. The most memorable part of that commemoration was a moving speech delivered by Nathaniel Paul, the impressive pastor of the African Baptist Society in Albany. As many of us "are passing down the declivity of life and fast hastening to the grave," he intoned, "how animating the thought that the rising generation is advancing under more favorable auspices than we were permitted to enjoy, soon to fill the places we now occupy." The minister's speech was punctuated by the joyful cries of his congregation. "Amen! Hallelujah!" The minister's black brethren sang, and they wept for joy. During the speech, I actually believed that optimism and happiness might bloom in my breast. By the next day gloom had regained its customary position of primacy in my bosom.

Shortly after my return from Albany, the old dream again began to invade my sleep. Almost ten years to the day of my last visit to Morrisania, the dream descended upon me with an astonishing intensity. That very morning, I decided to do no writing for the entire day. Instead, as in the days of my youth, I would follow my irresistible impulse and wander through Manhattan Island all the way to where Morrisania shimmers in the distance across the Harlem River. After looking at Latrobe's sketch of young Nancy Randolph, I set forth on my long day's journey. It was a disquieting trip which filled me with a strange sense of foreboding. The city is so different from the way it was in the days of my youth. I felt like Irving's Rip Van Winkle or one of the seven sleepers from the ancient fable. Many of the places of my childhood have ceased to exist. The empty fields are filled with buildings. The old houses have been replaced. The Collect where we used to fish in summer and skate in winter has been covered over. What was once a marsh is concealed by an overlay of streets of expensive brick edifices. Canal Street is now majestic in appearance; the ugly system of Dutch architecture has vanished. Many of the new houses are of white marble. Oil lamps are being replaced by gas lights throughout the city. The familiar street names are being changed. Garden Street, between Williams and Broad, where I once lived, is to be called "Exchange Place." The houses will be numbered. Even the old Boston Post Road is to be abandoned by the city as a public highway. Since Dr. Hosack sold it, the Elgin Botanic Garden has been almost entirely neglected. Its former beauty lies in ruins.

The growth of the city is almost beyond belief. It has spread so fast that Greenwich is no longer a separate village. Instead it is a mere extension of the city. Churches are everywhere. There is scarcely a large street without one. Many more are in the process of construction. Despite the intervening years of revolution here and in France, the tyranny of superstition continues to be triumphant over the minds of men. Looking at these monuments to clerical control, I sense futility and hollowness lurking beneath the glittering surface of this new city. Mankind does not profit from the experience of its predecessors. Each new generation is endlessly condemned to repeat the old errors. Poverty, misery, and crime thrive in the new city. The rich continue to prefer throwing away their wealth to sharing it with the poor. War will, no doubt, come again and continue until exhaustion restores the peace. Then, after a time of tranquility, it will return once more. History seems but a circular repetition of growth and decay, peace and war. At least, it is my wish that the next generation will be more fortunate in its war than was my own. Morris, Jay, King, and Hamilton had the glorious war for freedom from British tyranny. My generation drifted into an inglorious struggle without any discoverable purpose.

Even in time of peace this interminable discord of human nature continues. One hears little of John Randolph until news of one of his duels appears in the press. Last year he fought Henry Clay with pistols on the banks of the Potomac. Neither was wounded. The most recent news indicates an associate editor of the *New York Courier & Enquirer* has been shot and killed in another duel at Weehawk. Even Dr. Hosack recently sent Cadwallader Colden with a challenge to Dr. Watts. Fortunately, the only result was an apology. If a man like Dr. Hosack cannot peacefully live with his medical colleagues, there can be little hope for the rest of us.

Walking northward through the city, I periodically encounter John Randel's stone monuments, or iron bolts, marking the intersection of every street and avenue on the plan of the Street Commissioners. The streets are marked out to a distance of seven miles. The relentless flat squares which are to be the future of the city no longer please me. The harsh parallel and perpendicular lines are disturbing in some strange, inexplicable way. It is all too straight, too rational. The natural beauty of Manhattan is beginning to be destroyed. In the area of Corlears Hook, hills of great magnitude have been leveled. This flatness will one day extend across the whole island. The beautiful hills and valleys will be gone forever. Trying to imagine the endless flat avenues which will one day thrust straight to the north, I walk toward Morrisania. Like my life, the rigid squares stretch out before me with no variation, leading to an unseen but inevitable end. We have made the future and it is wanting.

At last I enter the open country north of the city. Farms, swamps, and thickets continue to exist. The autumn leaves are beginning to fall, reminding me of Octobers long since past. While walking, I find myself humming "La Marche des Eclopés" for the first time in many years. From the top of a hill the Harlem River is visible. Across the water is Morrisania. The house is sheltered from my eyes by the huge elm trees in front. My mind is filled with images of Nancy. Even after ten years, she leads me from dream to dream. In a joyless, corrupt, meaningless world, she still shines for me in the darkness. The difficulty of our parting continues to be a painful memory. Even after all these years, cupid's arrow is deep embedded in my heart and the wound has not completely healed. I sit by the river and watch the flowing water. Like the dark stream of time sweeping all before it into the void, the unfordable river separates me from my own past. But memory effortlessly carries me across the broad channel to that night ten years earlier, the only one I ever spent at Morrisania.

The terrible storm was still raging. When the usual time for my departure arrived, there was no doubt that Nancy had been correct earlier in the day when she announced the weather would make me a "prisoner of Morrisania." After dinner, when the child had at last gone to bed, she continued the conversation about her lawsuit. She required no prodding on my part, nor did she feel compelled to make any kind of an introductory statement. In the abrupt way she took up the sensitive subject, there was an intimacy which surprised and pleased me. "My lawyers have told me that the members of my husband's family will be of no assistance in my case. The prevailing opinion of the relatives is that my child is not my husband's. The worst part of it is they say their opinions are not based on any statements by David Ogden."

"That is to be expected," I responded. "They simply will not help the person who destroyed their hopes of future wealth. By protecting David Ogden, they serve their own selfish interests. If he wins, they win. But they have nothing to support their opinions other than worthless gossip. They have no evidence, do they?" I watched carefully for her reaction to my question.

Nancy blanched. She did not reply. Her silence affected me almost as much as the sound of her voice. Her eyes shadowed over in rage and then grief. Regaining her composure, she told me about her nephew Tudor's illness, how she cared for him at Morrisania, and the visit of his mother and John Randolph. "After my health had sunk under the burden of twelve weeks of caring for him, he uttered the most dreadful, unfounded calumnies about my conduct as a wife and mother. He spoke them to his dear uncle, Jack Randolph." She then related that John Randolph, while still in New York, had written a letter addressed to her but intended for Morris's eyes. She referred to the charges about driving away her husband's friends, and "lewd amours" with servants. But she said nothing about earlier events in Virginia. "My husband read it. He didn't believe a word of it. He knew they were nothing but malicious lies."

"What I cannot understand is why two of your own relatives from Virginia would make such statements. Unlike David Ogden and the others, they had nothing to gain from your husband's estate. Why would they do such a thing?" Like an acrobat on a tightrope, I had to proceed carefully so as not to state more than Nancy thought I knew. Only when she revealed the whole story of her past would I be able to ask all of the questions which troubled my mind.

"David Ogden played a part in it. Of that, I am certain. He had numerous opportunities to speak to Tudor when he was here. He filled the boy's head with falsehoods about me."

"But why would Tudor believe such calumnies coming from a stranger?"

She bit her lips and nervously ran her fingers across her face. Her facade of calm began to crumble. "I may as well tell you." Her voice quavered with emotion. Her breath consisted of irregular gasps. "At the age of eighteen, I was charged with murdering my own newborn infant." Tears ran down her cheeks. "The charges were false. What never happened could never be proved. The court found me to be innocent. But my reputation was ruined. That is why, in the end, I had to leave Virginia. I was nearly driven to despair by my accumulated woes." Her voice was hoarse. She struggled to prevent grief from overwhelming her power of speech. "The slanderous lies followed me north. They caused me to lose my teaching job at Stratford. Morris heard of my plight from an old friend of his. He offered me the position here. By the time Tudor and his uncle revived the tales, my husband knew about them and was not impressed. He trusted me completely. I would truly have to be a monster to betray such a wonderful man."

"What of your sister Judith? Did she support her son in his lies?"

"No. She wrote us that she took no part in the slander and disassociated herself from Jack's charges. Now she's gone. She died last year. I'm all alone, except for the baby." She could barely finish speaking. "The attacks on me I can bear. I'm accustomed to them. But to slander an innocent child . . ." She began to weep openly. As if to leave the room, she arose from her chair. Quickly getting out of my own chair, I walked to her side and feebly placed my left hand on her shoulder. She buried her face in my bosom. I put my arms about her. It was the timid comfort of a priest for his parishioner rather than the ardent embrace of a lover. After a few moments she regained control and disengaged herself from my cautious embrace. "You must be wondering about me. So many charges from so many people." She began to weep again. "Why haven't I told you this before? I suppose it's because . . ." She never completed the sentence. Instead, she ran from the room.

Nancy did not appear downstairs for the remainder of the evening. It was the servants who showed me to my room. That night I lay in bed thinking only of her. At last she had revealed to me a part of her dreadful past. The wall between us had almost completely collapsed. In my entire life I had never felt closer to another human being. My own emotions were elevated to heights never before experienced by me. I wanted to reveal my own feelings to her. But my reason and natural caution continued to warn against precipitate action which might be unwelcome.

The rain continued to pound on the windows and roof. The wind howled outside. Upon hearing sounds of human activity in the long corridor, I opened my door a crack and peered out. Dressed in her nightclothes, Nancy held the hand of her child, who was staggering as though half asleep. She led the boy into the room across the one from which she had come. Within a minute she returned alone to that room and closed the door. For a long time I watched until the candles in the corridor flickered out. She had not left the room. The house was completely silent. It was after midnight.

My head throbbed with the knowledge she was sleeping at the other end of the corridor. I wanted desperately to speak to her. To hold her in my arms again, but this time to have the full pleasure of her person. What words could be spoken? What if she protested my intrusion into her bedroom? My only purpose, I could say, was to tell her how moved I was at her confiding in me. How nothing she had revealed lowered in the least my high estimation of her character. If she withdrew with distate from my touch, I was prepared. "Please do not confuse an act of spontaneous affection for an attempted seduction." A ridiculous statement for an uninvited guest to make in a woman's bedroom in the middle of the night. Perhaps Morris's approach to Adèle could be used. "Nancy, I can no longer bear to be no more to you than a mere friend." I decided to forget the prepared speech. Resting in the bed in a cold sweat, I attempted to convince myself to abandon the whole absurd venture. Nancy would think me ridiculous, or even worse, a scheming seducer. The visits to Morrisania would be at an end.

My decision would be made when the clock struck one. Time seemed to stop as I listened to the endless ticking of the clock. Finally, it rang once. As if frozen to the spot, my legs remained on the bed. A mysterious force held me back. Honor, fear, and numerous other elements in an unknown mixture of parts. My endeavor had miscarried. My head had triumphed over my heart. With a mixed feeling of relief and disappointment, I remained in bed listening to the sound of the rain. My limbs were weak. Gradually my mind drifted off into the arms of Morpheus. Blessed oblivion.

With a sudden start, I awoke. My candle still burned. It was fifty minutes after one A.M. Shall I go when the clock strikes two? With detachment which had not existed an hour earlier, I considered my situation. A nocturnal mood had taken hold of me. The darkness and silence of the middle of the night seemed to have stifled my earlier doubts. I wanted to throw off my own mask and reveal my deepest feelings to Nancy. The clock struck two. Without hesitation I picked up the remnant of the candle flickering in the room. Driven by an uncontrollable urge, my feet carried me to the door without consulting my mind. My hand lifted the latch. The long corridor was dark and silent as a tomb. Out of fear of being hurled into darkness, I cupped my hand around the flickering flame of the candle and walked slowly toward my destination. Although able to see, I ran my hand along the wall as if blinded by the dark. In spite of my nocturnal fortitude, fear began to creep back into my heart. As if a fever had suddenly seized me, my face was soaked with perspiration. My hand began to tremble. The door to Nancy's bedroom was in front of me. I paused and tried to calm myself. If there was happiness in this life, this was my one chance to seize it. If there is a God, I told myself, as though God could care about such insignificant matters, fortune would this night smile upon my efforts. Her beauty, the irresistible strength of my own feelings, could not be wrong. They must be a manifestation of God's existence. I entrusted myself to the benevolence of fate, to the chain of circumstances which had brought me to this place. The door opened before me. The room was dark. The rain beat steadily on the windowpane. I walked toward the large bed on the other side of the room. My heart was pounding wildly. The light moved across the darkened bed. It was empty. The covers were neatly folded beneath the pillows. Nobody had slept in it. Something was in the corner to my left. As I turned, the candlelight revealed a rocking chair with Nancy's white dress folded over it. In a kind of terror at the unexpected, I quickly retreated back into the corridor and shut the door.

Where could she have gone? The boy might have been frightened by the storm. In order to comfort him, she must, I thought, be sleeping in his room. Without hesitation, I opened the door opposite her room and walked quietly to the bed. The little boy was sleeping soundly. He was alone. Closing the door behind me, I hastened back to the safety of my own bed.

My head ached with fatigue and excitement. My nocturnal feeling of invincibility had vanished utterly. Perhaps Nancy was downstairs sitting in a chair or writing in the library. Or maybe she was sleeping with some lusty young stable boy. I no longer possessed the will for further exploration. My mind was too exhausted to consider the possibilities. Sometime after the clock struck three, sleep rescued me from my bewilderment.

The next morning the sun was shining. After almost twenty-four hours, the storm had passed. When I awoke, it was after eleven A.M. Had the whole thing been a dream? The door to Nancy's bedroom was ajar. The bed was neatly made. The rocking chair stood in the corner but the white dress was gone. I had indeed been there. Expecting to continue my conversation with Nancy, perhaps even to discover where she had gone that night, I proceeded downstairs. The servants provided me with breakfast. They informed me that Mrs. Morris and the boy had gone out early that morning. Hoping Nancy would visit me during the day, I resumed my work in the library. She never came.

When I arrived home that evening, Emily was extraordinarily pleased to see me. She had been concerned about my safety and afraid I would be foolish enough to attempt to return home in that fearful storm. That night she granted me the full enjoyment of the nuptial bed. My body was present; my mind was with Nancy.

During the next two weeks, I completed my work on Morris's papers. There was not a trace of Nancy's response to John Randolph's letter. Each day, I waited for Nancy to visit me in the library. She did not appear. I saw her only once. In the middle of the day I left the library to take a breath of air outside. In the sunlight with her child in her arms, she was speaking to Simon, the old valet. On hearing my greeting, she turned toward me. "Oh, hello," she said. "I hope your work is going well." She listened quietly to my affirmative response and a few inane comments. In a polite but perfunctory manner, she replied, "That's good. I'm glad to hear it. Will you be finished soon?" She avoided looking into my eyes.

"Within one or two weeks." Before I could continue speaking, she had acknowledged my response, turned to speak to Simon, and then walked away. It was as if we had not been friendly during the preceding weeks, as if our intimate conversations had never occurred. The barriers had been reconstructed. We were strangers again. After completing my work, I continued going to Morrisania for another two weeks in the hope of speaking to her. She avoided me. How I staggered beneath the weight of that silence. My pain transcended the limits of my own loneliness. It created an immense sympathy which extended to that great community of those living without hope in silent desperation. In my situation, I recalled Herodotus, the saying of Solon to Croesus, that no one of the living might be called happy.

Bored with the empty hours of awaiting a visit that never came, one day I announced to the servants my work had been completed. I left a note of gratitude for Nancy, expressing the hope that we might see each other again. Then, for the last time, I departed from Morrisania. She never responded to my note. Within a week I wrote a letter. "My love for you is hopeless, but boundless and indestructible." It was never sent. I fed it to the flames. Except for her note of condolence upon the death of Emily, for ten years I have not heard a word from her. She has vanished into my past.

I continued my writing. My days were filled with an acute awareness of the tedium of the passing of time. The repeated rituals, from rising in the morning to falling back into unconsciousness at night, were connected by unbroken hours of sorrow, by the melancholy memory of what might have been. I ceased my writing. Whatever vitality had been present in earlier days dried up, crumbled into dust, and blew away. Only an inner void survived. Any remainder of my youthful hopes had finally expired. The winter of my life had begun. My desire to rival Gibbon vanished. The unproductive months passed into years. The unread books and half-written pages filled my room. I persevered and survived my own inactivity. Finally I returned to *The Age of Revolution*. Yet the sorrow remains to this day. Unlike pleasure, it never quite exhausts itself.

The unanswered questions fill my mind. If I had not purchased the Horsmanden book of the New York Conspiracy, would my life have changed completely? The fate of each person seems to be woven of gossamer threads. If one seemingly insignificant portion is removed, perhaps the entire fabric unravels. Why had Nancy withdrawn her friendship? She may have been ashamed of what she had revealed to me. Or I might have failed to do or say something she had expected of me. Perhaps the irretrievable moment of opportunity, when she cried in my embrace, had passed without my realizing it. Instead of acting spontaneously, I had relied on my reason and permitted the precious moment to slip away forever. Whether my own failure to act was virtue, cowardice, or something else, I did not even know. It is possible that her coldness had a cause of which I was unaware. Did I inadvertently reveal that I knew too much? Or had she discovered that I was reading diaries and letters in violation of her trust? Perhaps she was not a martyr but, in truth, the monster described by John Randolph. Had she borne a baby many years before? Had she committed numerous crimes, or was she the innocent victim of malicious gossip? I possessed no answers. It may be that nothing human is calculable except life ends in death.

Often I have recalled the words of Dr. Hosack about Nancy shortly after I met her for the first time. "The closer one gets to her, the more she draws away." For a moment our two solitudes had come together; then they separated forever. Since then my own solitude has wearied me sorely. Yet sometimes I think she might dream of me as I dream of her. For a brief moment I had actually learned that love is not a fairy tale. It does exist, at least for a few brief, fleeting moments. If there be any mortal who derides the unseen world, let him consider the power of love and ponder the invisible forces which govern mankind.

It is my hope that the writing of this book will help to exorcise my unseen demons. Some contend that a book is not a success unless it survives for at least a century. According to the standard, no author ever has the satisfaction in life of knowing his book has succeeded. Since this book will not see the light of day while its author and principals still live, I will not even experience the satisfaction of having it published. By the time it is read, my characters will be as distant to its readers as Pericles or Ben Franklin are to me. As they fade into the past, the events will, no doubt, lose some of the enchantment and importance they once possessed. Yet they may continue to live for some as those vanished beings live within me. Because human nature changes so little, I am confident readers yet unborn will understand and sympathize with my account. A piece of the past may yet continue to live in my words, and posterity may forgive me my breach of faith in relating this story. If not, forgiveness be damned. That the story survives is all that matters.

As I sat by the river looking toward Morrisania, it began to drizzle. The land across the river faded from view. Millions of drops spattered on the flowing river. It is true. One cannot step in the same river twice. All is flux; nothing endures. This world is like a vast body of water flowing into eternity. As everything is annihilated, in some mysterious way everything continues to exist. Arising from the moist bank of the river, I turned my back on Morrisania and the dreams of my youthful self. I shall not gaze again on that which is not to be granted in this life.

The countryside rushes by my eyes. After what seems like a short journey, it becomes the city. The gas lights are already illuminated. The color of the light is whiter and more brilliant than the old lamps, without the former smoke and smell of oil. In the light of a new age the crowds look the same as in days long past. In search of some evanescent satisfaction, they rush about where so many other men and women trod before them. Soon, like me, they will all be gone, spirits vanishing at the rising of the sun. But, like me, for the moment, they hurry home, before the darkness falls.

PART II

THE PAST

Bliss was it in that dawn to be alive,

But to be young was very heaven!

WILLIAM WORDSWORTH

THE PRELUDE

(THE FRENCH REVOLUTION

AS IT APPEARS TO ENTHUSIASTS)

Mary Harrison stared into the darkness. She was exhausted but could not fall asleep. Her head ached. The unseasonable chill in the air caused her to pull the blanket over her eyes. Only the first day of October and it seemed like the middle of winter. In order to warm herself, she moved closer to her husband, who was snoring noisily beside her. Little Carter Henry, thirty-four days old, was finally asleep. His cradle, only a few feet away, was barely visible in the blackness. One month old and the child already had a fever. Thomas, born the year before at Clifton, had never been as much trouble. Mary had just looked in on him. The angelic little boy was sleeping soundly in the next room, faithful old Mammy Dilsey on the trundle bed beside him.

It was a mixed feeling of satisfaction and discontent, Mary thought, that was keeping her awake. Not just that alone. There was more. A vague but profound dread. It was not only the baby's illness or the feeling that she herself might be falling ill. Her visitors, she was certain, were partially responsible. No doubt it had been a mistake to invite them to Glenlyvar so soon after her delivery. If all had been well with them, the visit would have been tolerable. But the guests had been troublesome from the moment of their arrival. As soon as Nancy stepped out of the carriage, it was apparent that she was ill. Then Judy announced she did not feel well. Dinner was a shambles.

Perhaps it was so many hours in the carriage over those dreadful roads. Jack, of course, did not mind the ride. Thirty miles on horseback would bother him not at all. The man was foaled, not born. His first visit to Glenlyvar, and within an hour after dinner he was off riding to visit someone else. Although he looked a bit more worried than usual, Dick did not seem fatigued by the long ride. Yet he was rather irritable with Judy. And poor Archie. Mary heard herself whispering her brother's name aloud. Still lovesick over Nancy. For over a year she has not shown the slightest interest in him; yet he persists. But then, all the men play the fool in her presence. She enchants them without even trying, the little bitch. Thank the Lord I didn't have a sister like that. Poor Judy once told me the first word she learned to spell was D-R-A-B. 'Too bad Judith is so D-R-A-B,' her aunt used to say when she walked into the room. Even a gentleman like Dick pays more attention to Nancy than to his own wife. Mary thought of how close the two couples had always been. She and Judy were almost the same age as each other, and so were their husbands. Her marriage had been less than five months after that of Judith and Richard. All four of them cousins to each other. Judy's first child born only five months earlier, John St. George. Something about that child was not right. Perhaps that was one reason for Judy's lack of concern about leaving him at Bizarre. She spoke as though she were relieved to be away from him. Mary knew she could never leave her infant for so many days. That difference between them troubled Mary.

She thought of the day of her own marriage to her cousin Randolph Harrison. Dick, Judy, and all their other friends carrying gifts from Clifton to Glenlyvar. Dick walking with a chair, Judy with a looking glass. Everything so lovely in the brilliant sunlight of early spring . . .

The massive, shadowy figure moved slowly out of the darkness. Who could be here at this time of night? Mary wondered. White eyes glared at her from the other side of the room. Gradually they moved closer. It was an enormous, muscular black man, naked from the waist up. His head was shaved. A cruel, savage expression flickered across his barbaric face. Her eyes moved down his massive upper arm, along his sinewy forearm webbed with veins, to the powerful hand grasping a terrifyingly long knife. He ran the point of the deadly blade along the side of the cradle. The infant began to cry. Mary sat up with a start. Her body was covered with perspiration. Instantly she knew it was only a dream.

She wished she had never heard those dreadful stories about the slave insurrection in St. Domingo. White children slaughtered in their beds. Women raped and murdered. Plantation owners disemboweled. Mr. Armistead's words about the inexorable and bloodthirsty Negroes in the West Indies still reverberated in her head. Daughters torn from the arms of their fathers. Wives dragged away from husbands. "Their naked bosoms inflaming the brutal passions of the ruthless blacks who satisfied their lust and then cruelly butchered their victims." These St. Domingo stories of the past year were indelibly printed on her mind. The fact that the patrols, with dogs, had been out every night for months failed to overcome her fears. She knew that her family was surrounded by potential enemies.

The baby's cries were turning into screams. Gently removing little Carter Henry from the cradle, she climbed back into bed. Randolph Harrison continued to sleep soundly beside her. The soft sucking of the infant at her breast calmed her somewhat. The child continued to feel feverish. Judy had given St. George to a black mammy, she thought. "Like being an animal, suckling a child," she had told Mary. Fool, Mary thought, she is missing one of the most wonderful experiences in this life.

Having returned the satisfied infant to his cradle, Mary again started to drift into sleep. Suddenly, a loud scream shattered the silence of the house. "Now what?" Mary asked herself as she shook her husband awake. After a second scream, Randolph Harrison opened his eyes. "What is it?" he muttered in a state of total confusion.

"It's from upstairs," she answered. As if another scream were required to get them out of bed, they both waited for a few moments. There was a quiet knock at the door. Mr. Harrison opened it. It was Nancy's maid, holding a lighted candle. He could not remember her name.

"Massa say get de laudnum for Miss Nancy." The fifteen-year-old Negro girl looked frightened.

"You tell them I'll be up with the medicine in a minute." As Mary answered she was already rising out of the bed. Relieved at his wife's response, Harrison jumped back under the warm covers. The room was extremely cold. Only a few sparks flickered in the fireplace.

Candle in hand, Mary unlocked the medicine chest. Instead of returning upstairs as directed, Nancy's servant had followed her to the chest. "Stupid girl," Mary muttered to herself as she handed the bottle to her. The servant quickly disappeared up the stairs. After a brief stop at the necessary, Mary, with candle in hand, anxiously mounted the stairs to the unfinished room above. At the top of the staircase she looked to her right at the bed in the outer room. Judith reclined on the mattress looking intently back at her. Richard was not with her.

"What is wrong with Nancy?"

"I don't know." Judith seemed strangely calm. It was as if she were trying to disguise her emotion. "She may be having one of her hysterical fits. Colic wouldn't make her scream that way." Wordlessly indicating she wanted to engage in no further conversation, Judith looked away.

It did not surprise Mary that Judy was not caring for her sister. She never could tolerate being near sick people. Mary turned to her left and reached for the door of the inner room. It was bolted from the inside. She was surprised. Then she remembered the spring catch on the door was broken. The bolt was the only way to keep the door shut. She knocked. Immediately, the bolt was unlatched. With a sound of urgency in his voice, Richard Randolph asked her not to bring the candle into the room. "Nancy's in great pain. She cannot bear the light in her eyes."

The choked voice of Nancy Randolph confirmed her brother-in-law's statement. "Yes. Please don't bring the candle in here."

Placing the candle on the floor outside the door, Mary entered the room. There was a pungent smell in the air; a candle had recently been extinguished. Enough light was emitted to make it possible to see Nancy in bed. Eyes avid with curiosity, Mary scanned the dark, cold room. Richard stood on one side of the bed. On the other side Mary recognized Nancy's maid, Polly, who had fetched the laudanum. Behind Polly the bewildered child Virginia sat on a pallet next to her sister Nancy's bed. Poor little girl, she should not be here, Mary thought. "Virginia, go back to sleep." In response to the command, the seven-year-old girl quickly scampered out of the room.

"The laudanum seems to have had an immediate effect. Nancy's already improved." Richard's apprehensive voice contradicted his optimistic words.

Nancy held the covers tightly around her body. She whispered weakly, "I do feel better."

After her various offers of assistance had been declined, Mary had the distinct impression that her presence in the room was neither welcome nor necessary. "I have to get back to the baby; he's still feverish," she announced apologetically as she moved out of the room.

"Please don't stay if the baby needs you," Nancy urged.

While picking up the candle, she noticed that Judith had turned away from the door of the inner room. Uncertain whether Judith was sleeping, Mary said nothing more. She returned down the narrow stairs to the bedroom and climbed back into bed. Mr. Harrison was again snoring peacefully. I was told marriage was the merging of two souls, Mary thought. Why do I feel so alone?

As it always did, the first light of day awakened Randolph Harrison. So that he could rise with the sun, he insisted that the curtains never be drawn. Through the window the autumn leaves could be seen blowing across the circular drive at the front of the house and swirling around the planks and shingles stacked in piles in the front yard. He could stare for long periods of time at his estate, Glenlyvar. The name had been taken from his wife's favorite poet, the sublime Ossian. "Shady glen" it meant. It was a lovely place, and when the house was completed it would, he knew, be splendid.

Before the rising bell in the kitchen was rung, Harrison was already dressed. From the frost on the windows he knew that damage had been done by the premature cold. "More work and less money," he said to one of the house servants. "It's always the same. We haven't even finished cutting the tobacco, or planting the barley and rye." Harrison was a frugal man and proud of the fact. He intended to remain one of the few plantation owners not drowning in debt. He did not even have an overseer. "They steal more than they save," was his usual comment. Instead he worked side by side with his slaves. They respected him for it. At least, he believed they did. To the constant irritation of his wife, he repeatedly expressed his aversion to any kind of luxury. When he had denounced wasteful expenditures the evening before, young John Randolph had retorted in his usual manner with an appropriate contradictory quotation.

> "O reason not the need; our basest beggars
> Are in the poorest things superfluous.
> Allow not nature more than nature needs,
> Man's life's as cheap as beast's."

"King Lear," Jack announced. Mary laughed and applauded. Harrison forced a smile. He had never read the play. Looking at Richard, he declared, "Your brother certainly knows his Shakespeare." Everyone expected Dick to attempt to surpass Jack with a witty rejoinder. But Richard, appearing to be lost in thought, said nothing. Both he and Judy, Harrison noticed, had been uncharacteristically quiet. Nancy had been sick before; Harrison had never seen them so concerned. Richard and Judith were not yet married three years, yet Mary and he had sensed there was trouble between them. He never understood what Richard had seen in Judith. A handsome, wealthy man like Richard Randolph could have had any lady in Virginia. Why, Harrison wondered, did he settle for a commonplace woman like Judith? Over the years the thought had occurred to him many times.

Harrison ran his finger along the frosted windowpane. What a night! A sick baby, screaming, servants at the door, then those footsteps up and down the stairs in the middle of the night. This visit by the Randolphs had certainly commenced very badly.

After breakfast Harrison went upstairs to help Richard provide Nancy with a fire in the hearth. Richard had little to say. Half hidden under the covers, Nancy remained silent. From what Harrison could observe, she looked terrible, white as a sheet. There was also an unpleasant sickly sweet odor in the room. Female problems, he thought to himself.

Mary chided him when he came back down. "Don't you notice anything? There's blood on the stairs. There was blood on the pillowcase. The sheets and quilt on the bed yesterday are gone."

"Must be having her monthly," he replied.

As if to heighten the dramatic effect of her announcement, Mary paused for a moment. "Oh, it's much worse than that. Dilsey tells me Nancy miscarried last night."

Harrison was shocked. "How would she know that?"

"She spoke to Nancy's maid. The one who asked for the laudanum. When I went upstairs last night, she was in the room with Nancy and Dick."

"Dilsey was in the room?"

"No, the maid . . . Polly. She was reluctant to speak. But Dilsey says she said enough. It was a miscarriage."

"My God! She didn't look pregnant. Who was the father?" Harrison's voice betrayed the horror of the thoughts beginning to invade his mind. Mary's challenging silence drew the thought from his lips. "Oh, not Richard, I hope . . . She attracts men like ants at a picnic, and he always had a weakness for a pretty face. But it could have been anybody, even your brother Archie."

"Archie?" The incredulous expression on his wife's face quickly revealed her rejection of the suggestion. "That is most unlikely. Theo's a better guess, and he's been dead for over half a year."

"Well, don't ask any questions. Be discreet for once in your life. The less we know about it, the better."

Polly stepped out on the veranda. It was another cold morning. Because she had not brought clothes with her for such weather, she held a blanket tightly around her shoulders. It was only the second full day at Glenlyvar, and she was eager to return to Bizarre. She was not comfortable in a strange house. With her mistress sick, there was nobody to protect her from the sharp tongue of Judith Randolph, who had been in an exceptionally foul mood since their arrival late on Monday afternoon. Polly surmised the reason for the bad temper, but that did not make it any easier to tolerate. Then there were the slaves of Glenlyvar, especially fat old Mammy Dilsey. They were almost strangers to Polly. Yet just because she was a slave like them, they expected to be treated as though they were family. Asking her questions about Nancy's screaming and the bloody sheets. But they were not her people. Polly's family was at Tuckahoe. Even the slaves at Bizarre were not yet close to her; she had known most of them only since Nancy had moved to Bizarre to live with her sister Judith. Although Nancy was white, Polly trusted her far more than fat old Dilsey. They had grown up together at Tuckahoe. Nancy was almost like an older sister. Polly had been hurt by the way Nancy abandoned her when gentlemen came courting; but in her heart, Polly had remained a faithful friend. When Nancy left Tuckahoe after her father's new wife arrived, old Colonel Thomas Randolph had given Polly to Nancy. He presented her the deed and said he didn't want his daughter to lose her "pet."

Two male slaves walked into the front yard carrying axes on their shoulders. As they walked, their footsteps crunched on the leaves. Chopping wood for the fireplace, they began to sing together:

"A col' frosty mo' nin'
De niggers feelin' good.
Take yo' ax upon yo' shoulder
Nigger, talk to de wood."

They marked the blows by the lines of the song. First one chopped, then the other. On the last line they both moved together shouting the word "talk." Intently, Polly watched them work until there was nothing in her mind except the sound of the song and the thud of the axes. Even the cold had ceased to bother her. She savored the moment of tranquility.

"It be cold again." The old man had walked up to her without being noticed. "Got my winter clothes on. Dat old nigger cloth jus' like needles." Scratching his arm to indicate his discomfort, he continued to chatter about matters of no interest to Polly. Old Esau, she recalled, was his name. Dilsey had introduced the old man to her. Polly knew he wanted to gossip about her mistress. Impatiently, she waited for him to speak up on the subject.

"How's Miss Nancy today?" He had finally arrived where he wanted to be.

"She's feelin' po'ly again." Polly barely concealed her annoyance at his prying.

Old Esau could see there was no point dancing around the matter. "What happened, night fo' last? Tell me, chile."

"Dat's de white folks' secret. Ask dem."

"White folks ain't got no secrets. Dey's wrapped deyselves wid niggers. Ain't nothin' dey do, we ain't list'nin' an watchin'. Dey hurt you if dey can. Don't protect 'em, gal. Dey don't deserve it. I seen blood under dat pile o' shingles. Told Massa Harrison. He don't even look. Know what he say? 'I don't see nothin' dere.' "

At that moment Mr. Harrison came out of the house. "Esau, tell Jim I want to speak to him."

The old man looked down at the ground and shook his head submissively. "Yassuh, massa."

Harrison stepped off the veranda and walked toward the slaves with the axes. "You don't need two of you to chop wood, damn it." For a moment Polly looked directly into Old Esau's eyes. Without speaking another word, she adjusted the blanket around her shoulders and went back inside the house.

The tall, flaxen-haired youth stood outside the entrance to Nancy's room, trying to calm himself before entering. The features of his face were delicate, almost feminine in appearance. Those features had been a distinct advantage for most of his nineteen years. The women had all petted and spoiled him, telling him what a beautiful child he was. Suddenly, in the past few years, his body had shot up over six feet. He had expected to enter manhood looking like his brother Richard, who, many said, was the most handsome man in Cumberland County. At a minimum he had assumed he would be no less attractive than his brother Theodorick. During adolescence, however, something had gone terribly wrong. His shoulders were narrow, his chest unimpressive, and his small upper torso was connected to immensely long, skinny legs ending in large, awkward feet. He detested his long arms and fingers almost as much as his legs. He felt like a clumsy ibis whenever he entered a room filled with the staring eyes of strangers. The world, he knew, relied heavily on appearances, and his was not a prepossessing one. Worse yet, his voice had remained high and squeaking, like that of a boy who has not yet blossomed into manhood. People had commented to his face on his "rich soprano" or "falsetto." Those even more cruel had told him he sounded like a woman or a castrato. The sound of his own voice had become unbearable to him. At times, during his extended prostration from scarlet fever that summer, he had wished not to survive. After his recovery only weeks earlier, the doctor told him he had been to the edge of his grave. At the time, he had wondered if it would not have been preferable to have joined his father, mother, and brother Theo on the far side of the River Styx. With increasing anxiety he found that prospect more attractive than the possibility of living the remainder of his life as a "castrato."

Although the matter of his appearance and masculinity had been a concern for several years, it became a torment whenever he was in her presence. The thought of that painful scene over a year before at her eldest sister Molly's home at Presque Isle filled him with uneasiness whenever he was with her. Before speaking to her, he attempted to erase it from his mind. Taking a deep breath, John Randolph entered the room with a sudden surge of determination.

Her back against two pillows, Nancy was sitting up in bed. She looked at him with an utter lack of interest. He wished that his hideous birdlike body would melt and resolve itself into a dew. In desperation he thought that perhaps the apathy in her face was due to her illness and not to his presence.

"Hello, Jack. How long have you been back?"

"Just this past hour. Dick tells me you've been ill all week."

She confirmed Richard's account. To fill in the awkward silences, John spoke about the unusually cold weather. He was delighted, he reported, that the frost had killed off all the flies he so detested. Like the old days, he tried to interest her with talk about horses, dogs, racing and hunting. It was of no use. She was not interested in how he spent the week on his horse "Star." Whatever slight spark had once existed between them was gone. The conversation was disturbingly perfunctory.

Abruptly Nancy asked, "When did you leave Glenlyvar?"

John was wounded by the fact she seemed to know so little about his presence or absence. "Monday, after dinner. Not long after you went upstairs ill. The house seemed a bit crowded. You know I can't stay in the same place very long. I was surprised when Dick told me you were sick all week."

"What else did Dick tell you?"

"Not very much. He said you had a touch of the colic."

Nancy looked away from him. "Yes," she replied weakly, "a touch of the colic." She gradually slid down in the bed. When she was no longer sitting up, she turned away from him. As if going to sleep, Nancy Randolph pulled the blanket over her face. The interview had been abruptly terminated.

Sorrowfully, John Randolph walked out of the room. Perhaps it's only her illness, he thought. She was not hostile. Or am I deceiving myself again?

1793

Two of the most notorious cases heard in many years were tried within one month of each other in the spring of '93. The Randolphs of Bizarre and Judge St. George Tucker, a member of the clan by marriage, were directly interested in both of them. The first case was a matter that some said should never have been brought to court. But the Randolphs insisted, and they were a family accustomed to controlling events.

It has long been stated that nothing is good enough for a Randolph except another Randolph. Certainly many have held that against the family. The heights from which a Randolph could fall were lofty indeed; and fall several did that winter and spring, into the dung heap with an indecorous crash. The less fortunate snickered at the rumors that swept out of the Piedmont, into the new year, through the Tidewater, and across the state. Although at the time there was nothing more than gossip, Judge Tucker was shocked at the magnitude of the scandal involving his own stepson. With the assistance of Judge Tucker, however, the Randolphs transformed the rumors into something far more entertaining.

The triumphs and tribulations of the Randolph family had amused Virginia society for as long as anybody could remember. During the 120 years since the advent of the patriarch, William Randolph, they had intermarried and multiplied until they controlled a substantial portion of the Old Dominion itself. William was not much older than twenty when he arrived in Jamestown in the early 1670s. The progenitor of the race of Randolphs, a man who believed in connections, William quickly ingratiated himself with Henry Isham, who was well-established on the south side of the James on his plantation, Bermuda Hundred. Before he had been in the new world for a decade, William had courted and married Henry's daughter, Mary Isham. Using his many connections to aggrandize himself further, William benefited greatly from the failure of Bacon's Rebellion in 1676. Within eight years he had acquired, from the confiscated estate of Bacon's partner, Colonel Crews, property on Turkey Island, which became his family seat. From the estate of Nathaniel Bacon himself, which had escheated to the King, William came into possession of several large plantations, including Curles. From this base of landed power, William Randolph of Turkey Island and his wife, Mary Isham of Bermuda Hundred, became the Adam and Eve of Virginia. Nine children sprang forth from their loins. Six of these founded great family lines—William

II of Chatsworth, Isham of Dungeness, Sir John of Tazewell Hall, Edward of Bremo, Thomas of Tuckahoe, and Richard of Curles. Elizabeth, daughter of William and Mary Isham Randolph, married Richard Bland, thereby establishing another great dynastic line, but one without the name of Randolph. It was Frances Bland, the widow of a Randolph and the great-granddaughter of Elizabeth and Richard Bland, whom Judge Tucker had married, connecting himself to the great Randolph dynasty.

Generation after generation the Randolph cousins married each other, until relationships became a tangled web of genealogy. In one way or another, each of the great family lines descending from William and Mary Isham Randolph was involved in the scandal that shook the aristocracy of Virginia early in 1793. Isham of Dungeness was the grandfather of Thomas Jefferson, Secretary of State. Jefferson's daughter Martha, by her marriage to Thomas Mann Randolph, Jr., the brother of Judith and Nancy Randolph, was to become an innocent participant situated near the core of the scandal itself. The great-grandson of Thomas Randolph of Tuckahoe, John Marshall, would defend the honor of the Randolph family. Thomas of Tuckahoe was also the grandfather of Thomas Mann Randolph, Sr., the father of two children who required their honor to be defended.

Thomas Mann Randolph, Sr., married Ann Cary of Ampthill. They had thirteen children, three of whom died in infancy. The other children in order of birth were Mary ("Molly"), who married her cousin David Meade Randolph of Presque Isle; Elizabeth; Thomas Mann Randolph, Jr., who married his cousin Martha Jefferson; William, who married his cousin Lucy Bolling Randolph; Judith, who married her cousin Richard Randolph; Ann Cary ("Nancy"); Jane Cary; John; Harriet; and Virginia ("Jenny"), the youngest, who became seven years old on January 31, 1793. Their mother, Ann Cary Randolph, died in 1789 at the age of forty-four. It was said that her widower could not live without his horses or society. Thus, it was no surprise when he married the year after his wife's untimely death. What was unexpected was the age of his new bride, Gabriella Harvie, who had not yet attained the age of twenty. Thomas Mann Randolph's children, especially those daughters who were older than their new stepmother, objected strenuously to his swift betrothal. The beautiful but unpleasant Gabriella was deemed unsuitable. Their protests fell on deaf ears. The marriage took place at the bride's home in Goochland County. Only the bride's parents were invited to the ceremony.

It was Richard of Curles who married Jane Bolling and thereby brought the blood of Pocahontas into the Randolph family. The late Ann Cary of Ampthill was the granddaughter of Richard of Curles. Her daughters, including Judith and Nancy Randolph, were, therefore, descended in the fifth generation from the daughter of Powhatan. The blood of Pocahontas also ran in the veins of the sons of Richard of Curles, one of whom, John Randolph of Matoax, married his cousin Frances Bland. They had three sons, Richard Randolph of Bizarre, Theodorick Randolph, and John Randolph. Frances Bland Randolph became a widow in 1775; three years later she married St.

George Tucker, who thus became the stepfather of Richard Randolph and a principal participant in the great scandal of 1793.

St. George Tucker, Judge of the General Court at Richmond, was fully informed about the genealogical intricacies of the Randolph family. In fact, there appeared to be little knowledge that Judge Tucker did not possess. A man of immense learning, he aspired to attain the kind of versatility achieved by his wife's relative, Thomas Jefferson, Tucker's lifelong friend and the man he admired above all others. Poet, playwright, essayist, musician, inventor, soldier, lawyer, professor of law, judge, and ardent anti-Federalist, St. George Tucker shared many of the characteristics of his friend Jefferson. Yet there were important differences between the two men. One of the most significant of these was the fact that Tucker was not a native of Virginia. Nine years after the birth of Jefferson, Tucker was born at Port Royal, Bermuda, on June 29, 1752. The sandy white beaches, salty breezes, and tall palmetto trees, which made the island seem like paradise to visitors, were not enough to compensate for the lack of opportunity for an ambitious young man. Before he was twenty years old, Tucker emigrated to Virginia. After a year at the College of William and Mary, he began his legal training with George Wythe, Clerk for the Virginia colonial legislature in Williamsburg. Shortly thereafter, he was admitted to the bar and began his practice in Williamsburg. Greatly influenced by his teacher, he decided to join the colonials in the war against England. He quickly became an enthusiastic and active supporter of the revolutionary cause. At the commencement of the conflict, he conducted a successful expedition to Bermuda, capturing large amounts of military supplies which were used to assist General Washington's siege of Boston. Later in the war he outfitted ships at Charleston with indigo to be used in the trade for salt, arms, and ammunition. Although Tucker did not speak openly about his business, it was widely believed that he accumulated a considerable amount of money in this wartime trade. As a colonel of the Chesterfield County militia, he served with distinction at the Battle of Guilford Court House, where he suffered a minor bayonet wound. He later took part in the siege of Yorktown and he witnessed the surrender of Cornwallis in October of 1781. At that time he became acquainted with General Washington and the Marquis de Lafayette, a man he was later to revere as the embodiment of the republican spirit of France.

Although Tucker despised religion as the imposture of priestcraft, it was during one of his rare appearances at a church service that he met Frances Bland Randolph, the strikingly beautiful widow of John Randolph of Matoax. The following year, 1778, he married Frances, who had inherited several large estates upon the death of her husband in 1775. One of these estates, the family plantation Matoax in Chesterfield County, was where Tucker and his wife chose to live with her three sons. At the time of the marriage, Richard Randolph was eight years old, Theodorick was seven, and John five.

By all appearances, St. George Tucker's marriage had made him a very wealthy man. But to those familiar with the financial condition and curious will of the late husband of Frances Bland, these appearances were deceptive.

John Randolph of Matoax left to his wife the plantation at Matoax, consisting of 1305 acres and numerous slaves. To his eldest son Richard he devised his Bizarre plantation in Cumberland and Prince Edward counties on the Appomattox River. To his second son Theodorick he left his land on the Staunton River below the mouth of the little Roanoke in Charlotte County, forty miles from Bizarre. The youngest son, John, inherited the remainder of the land on the Staunton River. The executor was directed to divide the Negroes equally among the three boys, who were to be educated in the best manner possible "without regard to expense."

The provisions of the will conveying the Roanoke lands to Theodorick and John contained a curious condition. Each son was required to promise he "don't sell, swap or part with" any of the land to one Paul Carrington, or any of his children, living on or near little Roanoke. According to the will, Carrington cheated the testator's brother Ryland out of £570 in a bargain for 310 acres on the opposite side of the little Roanoke. The will stated that the purpose of the provision was so that his three sons would feel to the present day "the villainy of Paul Carrington." These unusual sections of the will were to create the belief that a feud existed between the sons of John Randolph of Matoax and the powerful Carringtons, whose family seat was located in Cumberland County.

Ryland, the brother of the late John Randolph, was not only responsible for the feud with the Carringtons, but he was also the primary cause of the shadow of debt that darkened the family's future for many years. In order to save Ryland after he squandered his fortune, his loyal brother John had given a mortgage on his entire property, except for his favorite body-servant Syphax, to the firm of Capel and Osgood Hanbury of London. Then the revolution had intervened and thrown into doubt the status of all such debts owed to British creditors. St. George Tucker, like almost every other man of property in Virginia, feared that the peaceful settlement of outstanding issues with Great Britain, especially the all-important issue of British debt, would mean the legal seizure of all the Randolph property to satisfy the debt to the Hanburys of London.

One year after Tucker's marriage, Frances began to bear him children of his own flesh. Anna Frances Bland Tucker, called "Fanny," was born in 1779, Henry St. George Tucker in 1780, Theodore Thomas Tudor Tucker in 1782, and Nathaniel Beverley Tucker in 1784. To all of her children, Frances Bland Tucker was a beloved mother who gently attended to all of their needs. In spite of her husband's open hostility to religion, she insisted that the children be given religious instruction in the Church of England. It was said she could charm a bird out of a tree by the music of her tongue. She used that remarkable gift to encourage her sons to read aloud and practice oratory, a skill she considered to be of great importance in achieving worldly success. In contrast to his wife, St. George Tucker was an austere and rigid parent. Although not a harsh disciplinarian, he did go so far as to designate his household "Fort St. George," posting "garrison articles" for the conduct of his children. Nevertheless, the Randolph boys loved and respected Tucker as though he were their real father; and Tucker treated them as if they were his own sons.

In late 1787 Tucker became engaged in the struggle to prevent Virginia's ratification of the proposed federal constitution. As an ardent believer in the sovereignty of the states, he found himself in the camp of Patrick Henry, a man toward whom he bore some hostility, and opposed to James Madison, John Marshall, and other men he deeply respected. Although fear of federal power and the consequent threat to the authority of the Commonwealth of Virginia provided sincere motives for his opposition, he also believed that a strong central government would resolve the impasse over payment of the prerevolutionary claims of British creditors, thereby plunging himself and his family into financial ruin.

During this period of intensive law practice combined with active opposition to the federal constitution, Tucker was too busy for many weeks to return from Richmond to Matoax to care for his wife, who had fallen ill. Her condition rapidly deteriorated; by the time Tucker returned to Matoax, she was at death's door. Frances Bland Tucker died in January of 1788. Tucker buried her at Matoax next to her first husband. In death she returned to the Randolphs.

In the summer of that same year, the Virginia Convention met in Richmond to consider the ratification of the federal constitution. The convention became the occasion for one of the greatest social gatherings in years. While the politicians debated, the city entertained a tremendous influx of visitors. During a trip to the races at Richmond, Richard Randolph introduced his stepfather to his future wife, Judith Randolph, daughter of the well-known breeder of horses Colonel Thomas Mann Randolph. They were later to be married on the last day of 1789. On that hot day at the races, Colonel Tom introduced Tucker to his guests, the immensely wealthy Robert Morris of Philadelphia, the financier of the revolution, and his handsome one-legged assistant, Gouverneur Morris. The Morrises, who were not related to each other, were visiting Virginia on business related to Robert Morris's monopoly of the tobacco trade with France. A delegate to the Constitutional Convention in Philadelphia the previous year, Gouverneur Morris was quietly assisting the federal side in the ratification debate in Virginia. When the one-legged man quoted the preamble to the proposed constitution, Tucker chided him. "It should not say 'We the people' but rather 'We the states.' The ultimate watchmen over the central government should be the states which ratify the document."

Mr. Morris had smiled at him. "I do believe Mr. Henry has made that point several times in debate. I myself have no objection whatsoever to 'We the states.'" The man appeared to be so well-informed concerning the details of the various articles of the federal constitution, Tucker asked him about the effect ratification would have on payment of British debts. Gouverneur Morris's response had not been encouraging. "The Treaty of Paris provides that the debts can be collected. Under the new constitution, that treaty would become the supreme law of the land. Debtors would be wise to obtain the best conditions for payment while there still exists some doubt on the matter."

With Mr. Morris's learned opinion in mind, Tucker soon after ratification wrote to his stepsons.

> You will have heard that the Constitution has been adopted by this state. That event, my dear children, affects your interest more nearly than that of many others. The recovery of the British debts can no longer be postponed and there seems now to be moral certainty that your patrimony will all go to satisfy the unjust debts from your papa to the Hanburys. The consequence, my dear boys, must be obvious to you. Your sole dependence must be on your personal abilities and exertions.

Contrary to Tucker's beliefs, recovery of the debts would continue to be delayed.

Not long after the conclusion of the convention in Richmond, Tucker reestablished himself at Williamsburg. He became a judge of the General Court in the newly reorganized state judiciary and was afterward appointed professor of law at William and Mary College, succeeding his old mentor, George Wythe. In 1791 he married for the second time. His new wife was Lelia Skipwith Carter, widow of George Carter and daughter of Peyton Skipwith. Lelia's young children, Charles and Polly, joined his growing family. In 1792 a son was born to the Tuckers; named after his father, the boy was called "Tutee." That same year, his stepson Theodorick died at Bizarre. Toward the end of the year rumors of a profoundly disturbing nature reached the ears of St. George Tucker. Richard Randolph, his favorite among his stepsons, was accused of having committed incest and infanticide. The mother of the child was rumored to be Nancy, the sister of Richard's wife.

Disgusted with himself, St. George Tucker pushed away the page of verse in front of him. Since the rumors had begun, Tucker found himself unable to concentrate on "The Probationary Odes of Jonathan Pindar, Esq." or anything else. Despite the fact that these pages were already late for publication, he could not complete them. They were to have been sent to Freneau's *National Gazette* in Philadelphia the previous week. But his satire of Hamilton, Jay, Adams, and wealthy Federalists, speculating with their purchased paper, had come to seem frivolous in the face of the problems faced by his stepson. The honor of the family was in jeopardy. Action was necessary.

Tucker turned from his poetry to his astronomical observations and then to his plans for extending the first floor of his house. The two-story structure in the northwest corner of Courthouse Square in the heart of Williamsburg was too small for his expanding family. Within minutes he vigorously pushed his plans to the side of the desk. Again he picked up his volume of Virginia statutes. After glancing at the applicable provisions for the third time in the past hour, he closed the book and walked to the window. The streets were quiet. Tucker could see Richard outside in the garden, talking to his nine-year-old half brother, Beverley Tucker. Yelling wildly with youthful exuberance, the smiling little boy ran behind the hedges. Richard turned to the doorway of the house. His face was as sorrowful as Tucker had ever seen it. Judge Tucker was not a man of dark moods, but he was suddenly filled with grief for the past and an overpowering dread of the future. Perhaps it is fortunate, he thought, Frances did not live to see this day. Her first son facing a fiery ordeal of public humiliation. Her second son dead little more than a year. The youngest boy banished by his own choice from William and Mary as a result of a meaningless duel with a classmate. Looking out across the street, Tucker noticed the grazing goats eating the overgrown grass. Not only his own family, but the city itself was beginning to degenerate. It was as if an illness in the body politic had infected the individual citizens. Since the end of the revolution and the moving of the capital to Richmond, Williamsburg had been in serious decline. The politicians, lawyers, and tradesmen who had created the vibrant spirit of the city had gradually disappeared. The Palace had been destroyed by fire. The trees and shrubbery were badly neglected. The buildings had deteriorated so much, there was talk of tearing many of them down in order to provide materials to rebuild the remaining structures.

When a glorious city like Williamsburg can decay and die, Tucker thought, what hope is there for short-lived man? The glory days of the past would never return to this city. As he had many times in the past few months, Tucker recalled the wonderful scene when the Continental Army confidently marched into Williamsburg just before the siege at Yorktown. Accompanied only by Rochambeau and a few officers, General Washington himself rode into town. It was while leaving to organize a parade of his brigade, Colonel St. George Tucker rode by the General. "Colonel Tucker, if I am not mistaken." So surprised had Tucker been by this recognition, he was rendered speechless. Within moments after the encounter the Marquis de Lafayette swiftly rode up to Washington. Overwhelming joy was on their faces. Lafayette embraced the General as though he had found his long-lost father. The ecstasy of being recognized by Washington quickly faded in the light of the ardor shown by the great man toward his spiritual son. Those brilliant days would never return. Beverley came running around the corner screaming as loudly as he could. Richard seemed to break free of his reverie. He returned to the porticoed doorway and entered the house.

Within a few minutes Richard would be returning to the library to discuss the subject again. Tucker hoped that they could at last agree on a plan of action. Of Frances's three sons by John Randolph, Richard had always been his favorite. John, the youngest, was too thin-skinned, too emotional, and too irrational to satisfy Tucker's strict standards. He had never expected anything of Theodorick. It had not been a surprise when the boy died young, no doubt the victim of his own dissipation. Richard, however, had been almost the perfect stepson, respectful, obedient, and considerate. It was Richard who, he believed, had caused the other boys to treat him as if he were their real father. Tucker was also pleased by the ease with which Richard had accepted his new family. He treated Lelia with great respect. Charles and Polly seemed to like him as much as Fanny, his half sister, and Henry, Tom, and Beverley, his half brothers. Now twenty-three, Richard seemed to Tucker a young man who could achieve almost anything he wanted. He had been a brilliant student. Even his teacher, George Wythe, a man not easily impressed, had admired him. His sturdy, handsome features, together with manners like old polished silver, assured his success in society. Yet, Tucker had been perplexed by Richard's open dislike of the legal profession and his willingness to withdraw from society to the comforts of his plantation. Tucker wondered whether his lack of self-discipline, that touch of indolence, had been an unfortunate inheritance from his father. After all, Frances had often complained about her first husband's lack of ambition.

When the rumors about Glenlyvar had first reached them, Tucker and his wife had dismissed them as absurd gossip that would soon vanish. The stories, however, persisted; they became so widespread in Cumberland County that Richard, Judith, and Nancy had fled. For eight weeks, from January to March, they visited Tucker's home in Williamsburg. The Judge observed their behavior very closely. Richard had been gloomy most of the time. Under the circumstances, watching a treasured reputation for good character destroyed by idle gossip, what man would not be weighed down by sorrow? And Richard, more than many others, had always been thin-skinned about his reputation. Judith had seemed more disturbed by the deafness of one-year-old St. George than by the stories concerning her husband and sister. She constantly lamented the injustice of her only child's affliction. On occasion she even exhibited a marked aversion for the poor little boy. It was clear that the cross of St. George was a burden she would not bear easily through the years. Judith and Nancy had spoken little to each other. But Tucker had never observed a genuine closeness between the two sisters. Both sisters had refused to discuss the matter of the rumors with Judge Tucker. Whenever possible, they avoided the unpleasant subject; when discussion was unavoidable, they denied the event had any significance. In private, Richard had conferred with his stepfather concerning the events at Glenlyvar. Based on these conversations, Judge Tucker had concluded that the scandal concerned Nancy and Theodorick; poor Richard, he thought, was merely the innocent victim of the dissipated life of his late brother.

During the extended visit, on numerous occasions, Judge Tucker and Richard had talked about what could be done to discredit the ugly rumors. Richard wanted to confront his accusers but could not determine the appropriate manner of doing so. Without any conclusions being reached, the Randolphs had departed from Williamsburg. In less than two weeks Richard had returned. Picking up the letter that had preceded Richard's visit, Tucker read it again. It had been sent from Tuckahoe a few days earlier, on March 14, 1793.

> You will no doubt, my ever dear Father, be much astonished when I tell you that, by the time you receive this, I shall be far on my return to Williamsburg; and you will be yet more surprised at hearing that I mean to spend the summer in one of the Northern States. Since I saw you, I have been informed that the late horrid and malicious lie, which has been for some time too freely circulated, has been, by the diligent exertion of those timid enemies (whom I have not been able by any insult to force to an interview) so impressed, during my absence, on the minds of every one, that a public enquiry into it is now more than ever necessary. Having endeavored, by every method I could devise, to bring William Randolph to a personal explanation of his conduct, and to give me personal satisfaction for his aspersions of my character, and finding that no insult is sufficient to rouse his feelings (if he has any), I have at last urged Col. Tom to bring an action of slander against him. This will bring the whole affair once more before the eyes of every one, the circumstances, from beginning to end, of the persons accusing and accused will be seen at once, and the villainy of my traducers fully exposed. When this is done, I shall once more know the blessing of a tranquil mind!

Before leaving Williamsburg, Richard had tentatively decided on a public inquiry in the nature of an action of slander. But the idea of having Colonel Thomas Mann Randolph sue his own son William for slandering William's own sister and brother-in-law was, Tucker thought, absurd.

> The reasons for my determining to spend the summer to the north are as follows. In the first place, my feelings would be continually wounded, during the time taken up in such an enquiry, by seeing no one whose mind was not impressed unfavorably towards me that I would not support it silently. Again, Nancy's situation would be yet worse than mine from the same causes, on account of the delicacy of her sex and sentiments. For this reason, she will go with us, and, while the most important enquiry that could take place is going on, we shall be out of the way of that observation, which could do nothing but wound our feelings! But what weighs with me more than all is the situation of my beloved wife! When she left Williamsburg, she had extracted from me a promise not to say anything more, or make any further enquiry into the abominable story. To satisfy her mind, I made the promise, hoping that, when I arrived here, I should find that the force of truth and a conduct on our part, dictated by conscious innocence, had prevailed over the dark and little calumnies of cowardly enemies. The reverse being the case, I am

obliged to go on with the enquiry, and that in the most public manner. It would be impossible for me to avoid innumerable broils, were I to stay in Virginia. My mind has been so exasperated by the villainous conduct I have met with that I know not what I might do in a moment of passion; perhaps what might embitter every moment of my future life; probably what would be fatal to my beloved wife in her present situation! I cannot answer for myself, if I remain in this scene of villainy and base atrocious calumny. I therefore avoid it. When I see you, my beloved Father, I will speak more fully and unburden a heart loaded with the basest injuries! The share of the crop of the lower plantation now due to me will enable me to effect my purpose, and I will thank you either to sell so much of it, or, if you prefer keeping it together, to raise the probable amount of it on the credit of the tobacco.

You will see us in a short time; at farthest the day after your rect. of this. Our joint loves to all the family. Assure my dear Mrs. Tucker how more than ever we feel ourselves bound to her. Adieu my most tenderly beloved father, and do not give yourself uneasiness on my account, as I hope soon to be redressed and at peace! Yours most filially affect.

RD. RANDOLPH.

At their last meeting, Richard had mentioned the possibility of dueling with those who had impugned his honor. Fearful that Richard would return to this desperate idea, Tucker had now devised a new approach to the problem, which he hoped would resolve the matter and end all talk of combat.

With an unpleasant scowl marring his handsome countenance, Richard entered the library. Lack of sleep was beginning to affect his usual sweet nature. He denounced those family members who had been spreading the rumors, with harsh words for each of the miscreants—William Randolph, Judith and Nancy's brother; Mary, their eldest sister; Gabriella Harvie Randolph, who Nancy referred to as "my spiteful, malicious stepmother"; and Mrs. Carter Page, Judith and Nancy's meddlesome "Aunt Polly." There was a fury in Richard's voice as he spoke. "Even Peyton Harrison, I hear, has joined in the gossip. I would expect it from strangers and servants; they owe us nothing. But our own friends and relatives! It is intolerable! My only satisfaction may be on the field of honor. There are times when bloodshed cannot be avoided."

Judge Tucker was alarmed by his anger. "A passionate man is a scourge to both his family and himself. Your brother has had to leave William and Mary. He cannot even show his face in Williamsburg. A fine young man like Robert Barraud Taylor almost killed. What satisfaction is there in that?" Before a word could escape Richard's mouth, Tucker continued his protestations. "You know what I think about dueling. Are you going to challenge every gossip in the county? That would be more appropriate for John. He could have killed that Taylor boy. For what? The correct pronunciation of a word?"

"Charging me with murder is a bit more serious isn't it? Besides, it was Taylor who challenged Jack." Richard's voice continued to be filled with rage.

Tucker was not accustomed to such a disrespectful tone of voice from his stepson. In an attempt to be conciliatory, he disregarded the outburst. His new proposal, he hoped, would terminate all discussion of violence. "There is a peaceful way to defend your honor. Use the law. You can challenge the world to prove the charges against you. Like a duel, you place your own life at risk. But you threaten nobody else's. That is true honor and courage." Seeing Richard's interest piqued by his words, Tucker handed him the open book and pointed to the applicable statute, Chapter 67 of the Acts of 1788. As Richard read, Tucker explained. "It's a special examining court, a 'called court' to consider evidence. Any person charged before a Justice of the Peace with any criminal offense can receive a preliminary examination in the County Court. All you have to do is convince one justice that the case should be examined. The justice then summons all material witnesses to appear before the justices of the County Court within ten days. The assembled justices consider whether the charges should be dismissed or tried before a jury in the District Court."

"Who would make the charges to the court?"

"That is the beauty of this procedure. Although it is somewhat unorthodox, you could ask that the charges be brought against yourself. You confront the slanderers directly by challenging them to prove their calumnies in court."

"What would the charge be?" As he realized the seriousness of Tucker's proposal, Richard began to look concerned.

"The same one as in the rumors, murder."

"Wouldn't an action for slander be a bit safer? If I lose, they don't hang me." Richard's tone was sarcastic, but Tucker was undaunted.

"It would be difficult to prove slander. The burden of proof would be on your shoulders. You know little of the tales people have repeated. Nobody has put the charges in writing. The case would degenerate into an argument about who spoke what words. At best, you might strike one or two heads from the hydra. That is the nature of a personal action for slander. You can challenge only one person at a time. A criminal case places you against the entire people of Virginia and the burden of proof is on the state. You strike at the heart of the hydra, not at one of its many heads. By placing your own life at risk, you establish your credibility and preserve your honor at the same time. Actually, the risk is quite minimal. There is no prosecutor before a called court. There would be very little evidence. Usually, the complainant supplies the witnesses against the defendant. In this case, you would initially be both the complainant and the defendant. Without a reasonable prospect for conviction in the District Court, the case would have to be dismissed."

Richard continued to look worried. "But there would be evidence. Under oath, I would have to admit the miscarriage. The truth of part of the rumors would be proved. Poor Nancy would be publicly humiliated. The family honor would be lost. It's quite impossible."

Tucker's denial was confident and forceful. "No, that would not happen. You would be the defendant. A defendant cannot provide evidence in his own behalf or against himself even if he wants to. Because of the irresistible temptation to perjury, a defendant's testimony is considered untrustworthy. In other words, you are not competent to be a witness for yourself. The slaves, of course, Negro or mulatto, cannot testify in any proceeding against a white person; that is statutory. Judith cannot testify either for or against you because she's your wife. That is a matter of common law."

Richard waited expectantly. Tucker said nothing more. "I knew about the husband-wife rule. But what of Nancy? There is no prohibition on sisters-in-law. Or have the pettifoggers created a rule for that?"

As always, Judge Tucker was irritated by Richard's scornful words about lawyers. Richard had often indicated that he would rather work his plantation than sink to the chicanery and low cunning required of a lawyer. Not wanting to be provoked into an argument on an irrelevant subject, Tucker disregarded the biting remark. "It has long been a maxim of the common law that no person can be compelled to give evidence against himself. The privilege against self-incrimination, at least at common law if not in our Constitution, extends to women. Nancy can simply refuse to testify. What other evidence is there except for the gossip of those who have no firsthand knowledge of the matter? The justice of the peace might well dismiss the case without referring it to the County Court. Certainly the called court, if it gets that far, would dismiss. In all my years of experience I have never seen a called court send a case to the District Court for trial where two circumstances are present—lack of strong evidence, and the defendant is a respected citizen of the county. If you were a stranger to Cumberland County, there could be problems. But you come from a respected family; you are a freeholder. There will never be a jury trial in this case!" With a triumphant flourish, Tucker concluded his presentation.

Richard was not convinced. "The Carringtons are on that court. We have no open feud. But the tobacco inspectors often give me trouble. Two years ago they wanted to burn a good part of my crop. They are, you know, appointed by the court. I've always suspected it's the Carringtons who instruct them to create difficulties for me."

"You have no proof of that, I am certain. Even if it were true, they would not dare to trifle with a murder case. I admit the possibility of unforeseen circumstances. That always exists. You need a reliable lawyer. I suggest Alexander Campbell. He is experienced in criminal cases and nobody knows the law better than that man."

Richard agreed. "You know I like Campbell. If we can get him, he would be splendid."

"To be certain, I would also suggest John Marshall. In the past few years he has surpassed even Campbell. Few lawyers can present a more carefully reasoned argument. He is your cousin; he might take the case without a fee."

Shaking his head in disagreement, Richard indicated his displeasure. "The man looks shabby, he speaks like an uncouth backwoodsman, and I don't know him very well."

"Let me tell you a story about Marshall. Every lawyer in Richmond has heard it. Some years ago, an elderly gentleman from the country arrived in Richmond to present his case to the Appeals Court. He asked the owner of his hotel for the best advocate in the city. 'John Marshall' was the immediate response. But when he was introduced to Marshall he was not impressed. Marshall looked too young, he was dressed in his usual careless manner, and he was eating cherries from the hat he was carrying. So the old gentleman spoke to the clerk of the court. 'Can you recommend a lawyer for me, not too expensive?' The answer was swift. 'John Marshall's the best in the city and not costly either.' The old man had already dismissed that suggestion. Marshall was not his idea of an attorney. He wanted one of the wealthy-looking city lawyers. At that moment, in walked a dignified lawyer in a black coat and powdered wig. 'That's the man for me,' says the old gent, and gives him ninety-five guineas out of the one hundred he brought to Richmond for the case. That was a very large fee at the time. Then he went to the courtroom to watch the argument. As fate would have it, the lawyer in the powdered wig was opposed by John Marshall in a different case. As soon as the argument was over, the old gent realized he had made a terrible mistake. The powdered wig was a pompous ass and no match for the brilliant man with the hat full of cherries. So the old man told Marshall what happened. After apologizing, he asked if Marshall would take the case for the remaining five guineas. Marshall laughed about the power of a black coat and wig. He accepted the case for five guineas. Of course, he was victorious." At the conclusion of the story, Tucker was pleased to see that Richard was amused. It had been weeks since he had seen Richard's gentle smile.

"You have made your point. If Campbell agrees to Marshall, I'll hire him. That would be two of the British debt lawyers. Why not engage Patrick Henry and make it three?"

Tucker thought Richard was joking. Nevertheless, he was displeased at the suggestion. His dislike for Henry went back to the early years of the revolution. Patrick Henry, who was then Governor, had summoned Tucker and requested him to undertake an expedition to the West Indies. According to his custom, Tucker was to depart with a cargo of indigo and return with arms and ammunition for the soldiers of Virginia. The Governor provided part of the funds for the expedition. After successfully completing the dangerous voyage, Tucker reported to Governor Henry's office in Williamsburg. To his chagrin, he had to appear twice before he could gain entrance. The Governor did not even ask him to take a seat. While standing like a person of the lowest rank, Tucker delivered his lengthy report. Governor Henry uttered not a word of commendation. His only comment was, "I think you paid too much for the indigo." Tucker had departed in a state of indignant fury. He did not forget nor forgive.

Judge Tucker had never told the story to his stepson. He knew that this was not the time to do so. As a man of reason, he had to explain why Henry was not the proper lawyer for the case without reference to an ancient grudge. "Everyone knows Patrick Henry is a great orator. I've told you many times of my admiration for his ability as a speaker. I heard the great speech at St. John's Church. At the 1788 Convention, his speeches were unsurpassed. But he appeals to emotion, not reason. He persuades by arousing anger and prejudice against his opponents. He is a good lawyer to engage if you're guilty, not if you're innocent. The people know that. When he wins an acquittal, it is generally considered to be a reward for his great performance, not a vindication of the defendant. In your case, you will be fighting for more than a dismissal of the charges. After the case is finished, you want people to believe in your innocence. Believe me, Patrick Henry is not your man." Richard did not appear to be convinced. In desperation, Tucker clumsily attempted to appeal to his stepson's emotions. "At the Convention of 'eighty-eight, Henry, you recall, argued against excessive power in the hands of the federal government. I remember when he said, 'They'll free your niggers.' The Convention laughed, but his low argument turned some votes against ratification. I agreed with his ends but not his means. I would not want that kind of argument made in your behalf."

Richard blanched. Tucker thought that his stepson, who was vehemently opposed to slavery, would be offended by Henry's statement. He was not. "When it comes to slavery, Patrick Henry is one of the most honest men in Virginia. He says it's morally wrong but admits he's too lazy to surrender his slaves. I can't claim to be any better." As if in self-disgust, Richard's voice faded into inaudibility. "As to his representing me, you may be right. But with Henry, I'm convinced we could not lose the case. Let me think about it."

"You do agree with my proposal to submit to a preliminary examination ... don't you? Remember, a dismissal of charges by a called court is final. It has the same effect as an acquittal. You can never be charged again with the same crime."

Anxiously moving the leg resting on his left knee back and forth, Richard sat silently for a few moments. "I will do it upon one condition. You must leave the conduct of the case to me. I will decide what the lawyers must know. It is for me, not you, to protect our family's honor in the way I see fit. Agreed?"

"Agreed!" Tucker enthusiastically shook his stepson's hand. "I am proud of you, Richard. I feel like old King Henry the Fourth. There is a story about William Gascoigne, Chief Justice of the King's Bench. Prince Hal, the King's son, demanded the release of one of his servants on trial before the Chief Justice. When Gascoigne rebuked him for his interference, the Prince drew his sword. The Chief Justice reminded him that his conduct was an affront to the law and the King, as represented by his judges. The Prince submitted to the court and was taken into custody. When the incident was reported to the King, he rejoiced, saying, 'How much am I bound to your infinite goodness,

O merciful God, for having given me a judge who feareth not to administer justice, and a son who can thus nobly submit to it.' "

Although they often disagreed with each other on matters of politics, Alexander Campbell and John Marshall were amicable associates. They were, after all, fellow Masons, Marshall being Grand Master of the Masons. Over the years, they had worked together on a number of cases, including the most closely followed litigation in the Commonwealth, the British Debts case. Despite Marshall's increasing opposition to the French Revolution and his support of Hamilton and the Federalists, Campbell, an ardent Republican, admired and respected him, as did virtually every member of the Richmond bar.

While Richard Randolph spoke, the two lawyers sat quietly. Alexander Campbell, dressed impeccably in a black coat, ruffled shirt, silk stockings, and the other habiliments of the successful lawyer, listened to the story with a gloomy expression on his face. If it were not for his expensive clothes, he would have been physically unimpressive. His clothes, he knew, saved him from dullness, an affliction fatal to lawyers seeking clients. In contrast, John Marshall was in his usual state of disarray. His hair tied sloppily in a queue at the back of his head, his plain linen shirt hanging over his breeches, which were unbuckled at the knees, he looked as though he had just arisen from bed after spending the night in those same clothes. Unlike Campbell, however, he was physically striking—tall and slender, ruddy complexion, black hair and piercing dark eyes. Because his practice was almost exclusively civil, Marshall was uneasy about handling a criminal case where a client's life might be at stake.

There was nothing extraordinary in the tale Randolph related. The family had been visiting their cousins. His sister-in-law Nancy became ill. His wife Judith asked him to administer laudanum. Nancy, who was frequently ill, had suffered colic, hysterical fits, and some menstrual bleeding. Except for Richard himself, the only others who had entered Nancy's room that night were her maid, her seven-year-old sister, and Mary Harrison, the mistress of the house. "If these rumors, all based on unfounded gossip, had not begun, I would have forgotten the entire incident," Richard declared. Marshall carefully wrote the names of the potential witnesses, even those he knew were not competent to testify. After explaining St. George Tucker's arguments for using a called court, Richard waited expectantly for the reaction of the lawyers.

Campbell spoke first. "If it is feasible to obtain a preliminary examination, and if the evidence is as you say it is, Judge Tucker is probably correct. There would be nothing to prove any criminal activity had occurred that night. The case would have to be dismissed. The problem, as I see it, is there exists no basis for getting a justice of the peace to hear the case. Perhaps after we obtain the depositions of those hostile to you, some semblance of a prosecution case will appear. Our job as defense lawyers will be to uncover evidence against our own client—in small amounts, of course. Damned unusual."

Marshall was not so confident. "With all due respect to Judge Tucker, I am not in agreement with his proposal. Before charging yourself with murder, you should weigh the advantages against the disadvantages. Judge Tucker has given you the most favorable picture of a called court. Consider the problems. First, all you have now are rumors. Gossip and rumor are like snow. For a short time, they are present everywhere; but they soon melt away and are forgotten. A court proceeding will produce written documents. They will become part of the legal history of the community and remain in existence permanently. Second, any lawyer will tell you that the results of litigation are never certain. Surprises are to be expected. Persons commit perjury, judges fail to follow the law, and juries are completely unpredictable. Because most of our justices of the peace are not members of the bar, their rulings are exceptionally difficult to foresee, particularly on issues of the common law. Third, in your case, you have a special problem. Four of the justices of the peace in Cumberland County are Carringtons. That means one-quarter of the justices may be hostile to you at the commencement of the case. Those are men who will be holding your life and reputation in their hands. Fourth, these days the causes in our courts are more numerous than they can decide. Anyone familiar with the dockets will tell you they are crowded with lawsuits which will not be determined during the lives of some of the litigants. In good conscience, I cannot recommend that a person who claims to be innocent demand that the courts charge him with a crime. It is a very questionable use of our court system. If you insist on going to court, Mr. Campbell has suggested to me the use of a statute against divulgers of false rumors as an alternative method."

"It's an old procedure, goes back about one hundred and thirty years," Campbell interjected. "It was reenacted as Chapter 112 last year. You can bring a person spreading false news into the County Court. He can be fined and bound to good behavior in the future."

Richard interrupted. "That's no better than suing for slander. I would have to bring suit against half the people of Virginia. No. Judge Tucker and I agree. That type of case provides no relief for me."

"Well then, my advice to you is to disregard the rumors. They will eventually disappear." As if he were advising a close friend, Marshall spoke softly and with great sincerity. "Passion can sometimes make its victim act against his own interests. Please, be cautious about this no matter how unbearable the gossip is at the present time. This too shall pass."

Richard was not persuaded. "It is because those tales are intolerable to me that I've come here. If you don't want to take the case, I will engage another lawyer."

Marshall replied in a reassuring tone of voice, without any trace of anger. "I did not say I would not take the case. I merely want you to be fully aware of the possible disadvantages of the course you are proposing."

"Yes, I understand. But will you take the case?"

Marshall and Campbell looked at each other. Campbell spoke first. "Let us take the depositions of some of the potential witnesses. Then we will speak to Joseph Carrington. Next month, he is the presiding justice in Cumberland. If the prospects appear to be favorable, we will proceed."

"We will have to speak to your wife and her sister," Marshall added. He was curious to see the response his statement would evoke.

Richard Randolph did not appear to welcome the suggestion. "But my wife can't testify in the case. Nancy would be too embarrassed. She refuses to discuss it with anyone. Judge Tucker says she can claim the right against self-incrimination and refuse to testify. Why speak to them?"

"Even if they don't testify, either one or both may reveal some helpful or crucial information." Marshall was unequivocal. "We must speak to them."

Campbell interjected, "They won't even have to leave Bizarre. We will visit." After a short conference with Marshall, he stated, "Sometime next week. We will inform you."

"One other thing," Marshall added. "Try your hand at a letter to be published in the newspaper. State your grievance as to the rumors; then declare your intention of presenting yourself before the court to answer the charges any person wants to make."

"Leave yourself an alternative," Campbell advised. "Say that if they refuse to come to court, they can publish the charges in the newspaper. You will refute the charges by your own detailed response. You may smoke out a few scandalmongers who are too cowardly to confront you directly. At your next meeting, we will review the letter with you. By then, we may be able to advise you on the appropriate time for publication. In the interim, avoid all confrontations. If you succumb to a duel, you defeat the whole purpose of going to court."

Alexander Campbell carefully arranged his business in Cumberland County so that during his days away from Richmond he would make the best possible use of his time. An admirer of *Poor Richard's Almanac*, Campbell firmly believed that time was a commodity not to be squandered. On a beautiful morning in early spring, he and his amanuensis, Mr. Isaac Lanier, set out in Campbell's new carriage for the countryside of Southside, Virginia. After the miserable cold of winter, Campbell always enjoyed escaping from the city into the rolling hills and endless green forests. It usually helped to dispel the gloom he wrestled with during most of the year. His unsuccessful marriage to his cousin Lucy Fitzhugh was a major cause of his continuing unhappiness. Never a happy person, at the time of his marriage five years earlier he had been surprised to find himself enjoying life for the first time. Within a year, when he gradually came to realize his wife did not share his affection, he lost all hope of achieving true happiness in this life. He resigned himself to the grim fact that he would live out the remainder of his days without joy and without hope. It was an onerous burden, but he kept it to himself. In the face of increasing physical discomfort from aches and pains of an undetermined origin, he also played the stoic. The mysterious illness caused a disturbing diminution in his powers. He had begun to notice a marked amount of loss in the daily work he could accomplish. His father, the Reverend Archibald Campbell of Westmoreland County, had raised his sons to endure bravely the hardships of life. Faithful to his father's teachings, Campbell suffered in silence.

The dense fragrant woods, the gentle sounds of running streams, and the endless blue sky had gradually created within Campbell a mood of tranquility. This blissful state was regularly interrupted by large bands of armed men on horseback kicking up clouds of dust along the road. Ever since the news of the insurrection in St. Domingo, the patrols had been visible in every area. The minor abortive slave revolt in Norfolk the previous year also caused increased patrol activity. Campbell noticed there were far fewer Negroes walking along the roads than in past years. Lack of a proper pass could be fatal. At a minimum, infliction of the biblical thirty-nine lashes could be expected, even by those who had proper passes. Most of the patrollers were poor whites who did not own slaves. For many of them, the opportunity to beat slaves, as though they were masters, was irresistible; there was great pleasure to be found in bleeding black flesh and screams of pain.

All of this activity to control slaves, Campbell knew, was making his own work more difficult. Inspired in part by the news from St. Domingo, the General Assembly in 1792 had undertaken a thorough revision of the many laws concerning slaves. While these new laws were being reprinted, a substantial number of the Acts of the General Assembly were suspended during the period from December 28, 1792, until October 1, 1793. In the interim there existed great confusion among the members of the bar as to which laws were in effect. Campbell thoroughly disapproved of such disorder in the very principles that governed an ordered society. If the lawyers did not know which laws were in effect, he asked repeatedly, how could the common people be expected to obey them? In order to prevent unpleasant surprises in the course of a trial or of other legal business, Campbell took precautions to assure that he had available copies of the new statutes with a complete list of those that had been suspended. He had even prepared a table containing both the new and old chapter numbers. On several occasions during his trip through Southside, Virginia, his careful preparation had already served to enhance his status among his fellow lawyers. Information, he believed, was power.

Having completed their business in the countryside within three days, Campbell and Lanier arrived at Bizarre a day earlier than expected. The plantation consisted of almost two thousand acres along both sides of the Appomattox River. One part of the estate was in Cumberland County, the other in Prince Edward County. The area was sparsely settled; not a house or person was to be seen for miles. As the carriage approached the plantation house, it passed hundreds of slaves working in the fields. "Not a white face to be seen," Lanier commented sardonically. "Maybe the insurrection has already succeeded out here."

At that moment a man on horseback darted out from a cluster of trees and rode alongside the carriage. Speaking with a noticeable British accent, he introduced himself as Richard Knowles, the overseer. From his slurred speech and the glazed look in his eyes, Campbell concluded that he had been drinking under the shade of the trees while his charges sweltered in the hot sun. "Mr. Randolph's away on business today. Wasn't expecting you chaps until tomorrow. Mrs. Randolph is here, though." Campbell was not contented. John Marshall had suggested that Campbell take the depositions at Bizarre because Richard trusted him and would urge full cooperation. The master's absence could, Campbell feared, be a strong hindrance to the successful completion of the interviews.

The overseer led them to the stable, where two slaves took charge of the horses. After clumsily dismounting from his horse, Knowles guided them past a large enclosed area containing a number of separate buildings. The overseer explained that the high fence surrounded the kitchen, smokehouse, woodhouse, spinning and weaving house, and various other structures. The enclosure was locked at night; only the mistress, Judith Randolph, had the keys. "After we heard about St. Domingo, Mrs. Randolph had the fence built. She does not trust the niggers the way she once did."

Mrs. Randolph did not appear to be pleased to see her visitors. After the slaves were directed to provide food and drink for the guests, she strongly suggested that no questioning take place until the return of her husband later in the day. Campbell insisted that he had to be on his way back to Richmond that same day. "Your husband's presence is not necessary for the taking of depositions. We require only a few hours. We can begin with you."

"Richard told me I would not be able to testify because we are husband and wife. Of course, I would like to speak in his behalf. If my testimony is not allowed, there is no reason to take a statement from me, is there?"

Campbell realized immediately that he was dealing with a formidable woman; Judith Randolph could not be intimidated into doing anything she did not want to do. "It is true, your testimony cannot be used in court either for or against your husband. Nevertheless, it can assist us in preparing for the examination of other witnesses. Please." In response to Campbell's gesture in the direction of the closest chair, Judith sat down on the edge of the sofa as if she were prepared to bolt at the least provocation. In an attempt to relieve her obvious sense of anxiety, Campbell began with a series of simple questions. Without any opposition she revealed that her husband had been born on March 9, 1770. Her own date of birth was November 24, 1772. They were married at the end of 1789 and had one son, John St. George, who was one year old. The Harrisons of Glenlyvar had informed Campbell that the child was deaf. The lawyer was tempted to ask Judith if the child's condition had caused problems between her and her husband. Fearful of the skittishness of his witness, he avoided the subject. When she described her relationship with her sister Nancy as being very close, Campbell asked his first difficult question. "Was your sister Nancy pregnant last September, as the stories have indicated?"

The muscles around Judith's mouth tightened noticeably. Campbell wondered if her anger was directed at him, the gossips, or somebody else. After hesitating for a moment, she spat out one word, "No!"

"Nancy was engaged to Richard's brother, Theodorick, early last year. Could he have impregnated her before he died?"

A ferocious expression of hostility flashed across Judith's face. "I just told you she was not pregnant. Don't you think I would know if my sister was expecting?"

"Tell me what happened on the day of your arrival at the Harrisons' house last October." Campbell glanced at Lanier to make certain he was recording Judith's words.

"Nancy was ill that night. I was not feeling well either. I asked my husband to go into her room and drop her some laudanum. After he did it, he returned to bed. If it were not for these malicious rumors, I would have forgotten the whole thing. That is all there is to tell." She rose from her chair.

"Please, just a few more questions." Judith did not resume her seat. "Could a stillborn child have been carried out of the room without your knowledge?"

She responded in a harsh, grating voice. "I have told you my sister was not with child. Whose child could it have been? This is quite pointless. Talk to Nancy. I'll send her in. I have nothing more to say."

As she departed, Campbell shouted, "Would you answer my questions if your husband told you to?"

In an indignant voice she yelled back, "No."

Campbell could not help but compare Judith to his own virago. From his bitter personal experience, he knew that a belligerent, sharp-tongued woman dams the current of her husband's affections. Once this occurs, it is very difficult for her to remove the obstruction. An attractive sister living in the same house could present an appealing alternative. With great interest he awaited her arrival.

Within minutes after Judith stormed out of the room, Nancy Randolph entered. Before the incident at Glenlyvar, Campbell had been briefly introduced to the wife of St. George Tucker's stepson. The sister was a complete stranger to him. At first sight she was clearly not a promising witness for the defense. Her combination of cool beauty and warm allure lent credibility to the stories about her, particularly when she was compared to her ill-favored older sister. Because she seemed reluctant to speak, Campbell carried the conversation for the first few minutes. After explaining her right not to incriminate herself, he asked her if she wished to testify in court.

"This is all very embarrassing to me. I would rather not speak in public about the details of my illness, if that is possible."

The seductive voice was an immediate warning to Campbell of the dangers of using her as a witness. The plain wife with the harsh voice, Campbell thought, compared to this lovely creature, was in itself enough to convince any man of the plausibility of the gossip. "No need for you to worry. If you do not wish to be a witness, your testimony cannot be compelled. But to assist us in Mr. Randolph's defense, it would be helpful for you to answer a few questions. Your statement will be for our use only, not the court's." Nancy nodded her assent.

Once again, to put the deponent at ease as was his custom, Campbell began with routine questions. Her actual name was Ann Cary Randolph, after her mother, Ann Cary of Ampthill. Her birth date was September 16, 1774. Campbell thought to himself that if the proceeding were an inquest, her testimony would be barred because she was a minor. "Why are you living here with your sister instead of with your father at Tuckahoe?" As with most of his questions, Campbell knew the answer but wanted to hear what Miss Randolph had to say.

"Not long after mother died—it has been over three years now—my father married again. His wife, Gabriella Harvie, is not much older than I am. My father is old enough to be her grandfather. My sisters, Molly and Elizabeth, and my brothers Tom and William, are all older than she is. Like me, they didn't approve of the marriage. Judy was opposed also."

"You all thought your father an old fool?"

"We thought he was being unwise. She wants my father's property, not my father. There was constant bickering. Tom became very angry when my father told him he would not be receiving all the land he had been promised. My father said he was saving it for his new children by Gabriella. I was the oldest daughter living at Tuckahoe. Life there became intolerable. To get away from my stepmother, I visited my father's sister. After that, my youngest sister Jenny and I stayed for a time with my sister-in-law, Patsey, at Monticello."

"Your youngest sister is 'Virginia,' your sister-in-law, 'Martha Jefferson Randolph'?"

"Yes. Those are their real names. I also visited with my oldest sister Molly—'Mary,' if you prefer—at Presque Isle."

"That is Mrs. David Meade Randolph?"

"Yes. Two years ago, I accepted an invitation to live here at Bizarre with Judy."

"Your father told me you refused to marry the man he chose to be your husband."

"Oh yes. I left home for the last time to avoid a marriage hateful to me. He was much too old. When I marry, it will be an affair of the heart, not a property transaction." Nancy produced one of her most dazzling smiles. "Later my father would not approve the man of my choice."

"That would be Theodorick Randolph?"

At the mention of the name, Nancy's smile quickly vanished. "My father told me he would not permit me to marry a man whose property was threatened by British debt. He insisted I marry a man of clear and substantial estate."

"He permitted your sister to marry Richard, whose property is encumbered by the same creditors?"

"True. But he liked Richard, and he was the first, not the second."

"You were engaged to Theodorick?"

Eyes to the ground, Nancy nodded affirmatively.

"Do you recall the date of his death?"

"The middle of February, last year."

"At the time he died, were you pregnant with his child?"

"No." Her eyes remained fixed upon the floor.

"Were you ever pregnant by any other man?"

"No! Those stories are false." There was a hint of petulance in her voice. Campbell was skeptical. He sensed insincerity.

"Several of the persons I have interviewed told me you have shown an undue fondness for your sister Judith's husband, and he for you. Do you deny this?" Nancy murmured inaudibly. "I cannot hear you," Campbell bellowed.

"We are like brother and sister. Nothing more. Dick has been kind to me since Theo's death, that's all."

"One of our witnesses describes your affectionate scenes with Richard as beginning months before Theodorick's death?" Campbell watched closely for the reaction to his question. Nancy's face turned red. She began to sob.

"It's not true. Who would say such a thing?" she cried. "Judy would not tolerate such behavior." She wept openly.

After she had regained her composure, Campbell reviewed the testimony of other deponents. There were no surprises. She denied all accounts implying guilt on her part and confirmed statements tending to prove her innocence. Her answers were swift, confident, and effective. She characterized her condition at Glenlyvar as "a simple illness," the blood as menstrual blood. The stain on the shingles was "malicious gossip," she proclaimed. "If the rumors had not begun, I would have forgotten the entire incident."

Campbell looked at his amanuensis to make certain he had written down that response. "You all seem to agree very closely on that point."

"I have no fear of a trial," she responded haughtily. "What never happened can never be proved."

After Nancy read and signed the document, Campbell told her that he wanted to speak to the female servant who had accompanied her to Glenlyvar. "If you wish" was the calm response. He could detect no trace of anxiety in her voice. Nevertheless, he concluded that she was not as convincing a liar as her sister.

Warned by both Mrs. Randolph and Miss Nancy that she might be questioned, Polly had been anxious for days about the visit of the lawyers. Their arrival had brought an unexpected benefit. Mrs. Randolph was too preoccupied to fuss about Polly's chores. This was one day she was not going to exhaust herself with Judith's endless orders to clean—the chamber pots, the floors, the stairs, the furniture, the windows. The woman was never satisfied. She could not bear to see a slave sitting down, not even her sister's own maid. For once, Polly knew, she would be left alone, at least until the lawyers were finished.

Polly loved to look at the pictures in the many books stored in various locations in the big house. The master did not mind, nor did Miss Nancy. But whenever she caught Polly looking at books instead of finishing her chores, Mrs. Randolph was furious. The arrival of the lawyers had filled Polly with cold fear. Yet she could not miss an opportunity to look at the books while the mistress of the house was occupied with her company. Stealthily, she pulled out her favorite volume, a Bible filled with pictures. The opportunity was present, but the enjoyment was not. Even the cherished image of Moses leading the children of Israel across the Red Sea could not calm her mounting terror. Barely paying attention, she turned the pages without enthusiasm. Those she usually studied intensely were passed over without pause. Her stomach began to ache. It turned into a cramp, low in her pelvis. "Not now; not so early," she said to herself. Just a few years earlier she thought she could refuse to participate in the disgusting activity described by the older women. Now she knew better. The moisture was there; it was the curse. Quickly, she ran up to Nancy's room to take one of her mistress's washable cloths.

With the low, heavy cramp crushing her innards, Polly wandered past the high fence enclosure outside the big house and down toward the narrow muddy river coursing through the plantation grounds. She walked to her favorite place, where an old gnarled beech tree stood beside the river. Leaning her back against the old tree, she rested her feet on one of the large twisted roots. With her eyes closed, she listened to the sound of the birds and the humming of the insects. Hopefully, she waited for the cramp to drift silently away like the muddy water of the Appomattox.

Having rested for what seemed like hours, Polly returned slowly to the big house. Passing the household servants' quarter, she noticed Daddy Syphax sitting in front of his cabin, smoking his pipe. Polly enjoyed talking to the old man. Having been with the Randolph family for sixty years, he possessed an endless collection of stories about the slaves, the family, and their numerous plantations—Cawsons, Matoax, Roanoke, Bizarre. Syphax was proud of the fact that he was the only piece of property considered too valuable by old Master Randolph to be included as part of the mortgage to the British. The self-proclaimed favorite body servant of old John Randolph, then of Richard and young John, he loved to tell tales of the revolution. One of his favorites was about the family flight from Matoax when the traitor Benedict Arnold invaded Virginia. Syphax had been assigned the job of driving the carriage containing Mrs. Frances Tucker, her two-year-old daughter Fanny, and little Henry St. George Tucker, born only five days earlier. Colonel St. George Tucker rode along beside the wagon. Essex was in charge of Richard, Theo, and seven-year-old John, who rode a horse by himself for the first time in his life. "Ain't never got him untached from dat horse since" was the one line of the story that never changed. Otherwise, the details of the story varied with each telling, until over the years it had grown into an epic tale of the revolution.

As Polly walked by, Syphax gestured to her to stop and talk to him. He was puffing on his corn cob pipe in his customary way. "You sho loves dat pipe," Polly commented as she walked toward his rocking chair.

" 'Tain't a matter of love, chile. But it's a pow'ful lot o' easement. Blow dat trouble 'way in de smoke." He smiled benevolently. "Where you goin' in such a hurry, gal?"

"Lawyers here to ask de questions. I'se goin' to be a witness."

"Chile, you never be a witness in de white man's court. Thousan' niggers see a white man kill someone; dere ain't no witnesses. White folks does as dey please; darkies do as dey can. De law is made for de white man, not fo' us. You be careful what you tell. Can't help you, but it can bring you a pow'ful lot o' trouble."

It was Nancy who brought Polly to the door of the study where Alexander Campbell was waiting. Looking into Polly's eyes, she forced a smile. Polly knew what she had to do.

Campbell began with questions about Tuckahoe. Lanier sharpened his quills with his pocket knife. As soon as Lanier began to write, Polly would hesitate and stumble over her words. "You can leave the room," he told Lanier. "This is not a deposition." After Lanier's departure, he explained that Polly would protect her mistress by telling the truth.

Having overcome her initial fears, Polly described how Nancy suddenly decided to leave Tuckahoe after constant fights with her father and his new wife. As a gift, Colonel Thomas Mann Randolph gave Polly to his daughter. She then accompanied her mistress to the homes of various relatives, including Nancy's brother Tom at Monticello and sister Molly at Presque Isle. Then they came to Bizarre.

"How does Miss Nancy get on with her sister Judith?"

On the way back from church that day long ago, Polly walked in back of the two sisters. Nancy made jokes about the preacher. "You don't talk that way about a man of God." As usual, Judith was irritated by Nancy's misbehavior. Nancy wandered over to the greenery at the side of the road. "Get away from that, it's poison ivy!" With mischief in her eyes, Nancy looked back at her sister. "What is?" she asked. "That," replied Judith, pointing to it. "How can you tell?" Judith became angry. "Those white berries and the three glossy leaves." Without hesitating, Nancy pulled up her skirts and placed her bare leg into it. Standing with one foot next to the ivy, she looked defiantly at her older sister and laughed.... As soon as they arrived back at Tuckahoe, an outraged Judith related the incident to her father and mother. Colonel Tom laughed. "If she has sinned, she has decreed her own punishment." Her mother said nothing. Judith glared at her parents. "She's never wrong, is she?" The next day Nancy had the rash on her leg. Polly assisted with the lotion. While Nancy stoically held the compress on her leg, Judith chided her for gross stupidity. "Now I know what it's like," Nancy calmly stated. Judith flew out of the room in a rage.

"Dey loves each t'other, like sisters." Polly smiled meekly.

"Tell me about Miss Nancy and Theodorick."

Polly thought of the story Essex had once told her about a giant plantation where some of the field slaves had never seen the master. One day a white man rode by a slave named Isaac and asked about his master. "We never seen him," says Isaac. "I hears he whups his house slaves even when dey's good." Isaac didn't know he was speaking to the master himself. Next day, he was sold south to Georgia, the worst punishment of all. "Never talk bad 'bout one white man to 'nother," advised Essex.

"Dey was friends," replied Polly.

"Was Theodorick the father of Miss Nancy's child?"

Polly could almost feel the coarse blanket she held to her face that night when she heard them. It was so cold, Miss Nancy let her sleep near the fireplace. It was a man's footsteps she heard walking softly to Nancy's bed. Polly thought her mistress was sleeping. From the sound, she could tell he kissed her. "Who is it?" Nancy asked, all startled. "It's me," he said. "Let me fuck you." She pushed him away. "No!" she whispered in an excited voice. "I need to fuck you," he commanded. "No," she said, but not loud. "Please, no." In a swift motion he pulled down her blanket and got on top of her. She made no sound. Her nightgown was pulled up. After a short time their breaths fetched short and quick. Their bodies moved together, up and down, up and down. The breaths got louder and heavier. Then there was no sound until he left the room. When the night began to break into dawn, she could see her mistress was still awake, her eyes wide open. Miss Nancy never said a word about it.

"She never had no chile," responded Polly.

"Other folks tell me she had a baby at Glenlyvar and you were in the room. Virginia was in the room with you."

"She's jus' a chile. Jenny didn't see nuthin'."

Campbell had spoken to the seven-year-old girl at Tuckahoe. She said Nancy was sick; she was in the room for only a few minutes. Campbell was desperate to learn the truth, if only for his own peace of mind. The need to know seized him with a brutal force which shaped his lips. "The master, Richard Randolph, was in the room with you. He told me you were there when the child was born. Now tell me the truth! Don't think you can fool with me." Even if it was a slave, Campbell felt himself soiled by the filth of his own lie. Polly began to whimper, then to sob. He grabbed her brutally by the arm. "Tell me!"

"De baby was dead borned."

"How old did it look?"

"Don't know." She was weeping with a look of terror on her face. "It was small, real small."

"Was Richard Randolph the father?"

"Don't know."

"Did he act like the father? Was he kind to Nancy in that room?" Campbell's voice was ferocious. He continued to squeeze Polly's arm tightly and shake her as if she were a disobedient child.

"Massa Randolph, he good to everyone, even de slaves."

"Did you ever see them together when they acted like lovers?"

Polly grasped the pitcher of water in her hands. She knocked on the door softly. There was no answer. She opened it. Richard and Nancy were startled. She had tears running down her cheeks. He had tears in his eyes. They were both standing; all their clothes were on. "Put the water down and please leave, Polly," he said. It wasn't long after that Nancy told her they were going back to Tuckahoe. Then her stepmother wrote the horses were lame and couldn't fetch her. "My father has so many horses, I lost count; and she says there are none to get me." While tearing up the letter, she laughed bitterly.

"I never see dem like dat. Dey rode off on de horses all o' de time. But I never seen dem dat way. I don't know nothin' 'bout dat." She was weeping hysterically. Campbell released her arm from his iron grip. His fingers hurt from the sustained effort. He was pleased with the results.

"What you are proposing would be a waste of the court's time. There is no complainant, no corpus delicti, no evidence. The correct procedure, gentlemen, is the Commonwealth declares the defendant has committed a crime and then has to prove it. You have it backwards. Your client says nothing happened and wants to force his way into court to prove it. Tell him to disregard the gossip and go about his business." Joseph Carrington sat back in his chair. Mayo Carrington was silent.

John Marshall and Alexander Campbell knew they would have to persuade these two men before the courts could be used as a forum for proving Richard Randolph's innocence. Joseph was presently the presiding justice of the peace for the Cumberland County Court. The more formidable of the two, although he was twelve years younger, Mayo was Joseph's chief advisor, as well as his kinsman and fellow gentleman justice. Because of the system continued by the constitution of 1776, Campbell and Marshall were dealing not with two mere members of the local judiciary, but with the leaders of the most important political organization in the county. The justices of the peace of the county courts were selected by virtue of their positions as the most prominent freeholders in the county. They were appointed by the Governor for life. In practice, vacancies were filled upon the nomination of the remaining members of the county court. The Governor was chosen by the legislature. Because few men were elected to the Senate or House of Delegates without the approval of the county courts, the justices of the peace of the various counties formed an aristocracy that effectively controlled the executive, legislative, and judicial branches of state government. They also selected the members of the Court of Appeals as well as the candidates for the federal Congress. Various county officers, including the sheriff and county clerk, were appointed by the Governor only with the endorsement of the justices of the peace. The justices also exercised county legislative, executive, and judicial powers, including the fixing of local rates of taxation. Within the confines of Cumberland County, their family seat, the Carringtons were indeed formidable foes.

"All our client asks," Marshall stated, "is that he be given an opportunity to answer in court any charges made against him. If you approve, he will publish this announcement and then present himself before you for a decision as to whether the case is to be heard before a called court." Marshall handed the draft letter to Justice Joseph Carrington. Exhibiting a keen interest in the matter, Mayo Carrington arose from his chair and read the letter over Joseph's shoulder.

To The Public

My character has lately been the subject of much conversation, blackened with the imputation of crimes at which humanity revolts, and which the laws of society, have pronounced worthy of condign punishment. The charge against me was spread far and wide before I received the smallest notice of it—and whilst I have been endeavouring to trace it to its origin, has daily acquired strength in the minds of my fellow-citizens.

To refute the calumnies which have been circulated, by a legal prosecution of the authors of them, must require a length of time, during which the weight of public odium would rest on the party accused, however innocent—I have, therefore, resolved on this method of presenting myself before the bar of the public.

Calumny to be obviated must be confronted—If the crimes imputed to me are true, my life is the just forfeit to the laws of my country— To meet and not to shrink from such an enquiry as would put that life in hazard (were the charges against me supportable), is the object of which I am now in pursuit.

I do therefore give notice, that I will on the first day of the next April Cumberland Court appear there and render myself a prisoner before that court, or any magistrate of the county there present, to answer in the due course of law, any charge or crime which any person or persons whatsoever shall then and there think proper to alledge against me.—Let not my accusers pretend an unwillingness to appear as prosecutors against me in a criminal court. The only favor I can ever receive at their hands is for them to stand forth and exert themselves in order to obtain my conviction.

Let not a pretended tenderness towards the supposed accomplice in the imputed guilt, shelter me. That person will meet the accusation with a fortitude of which innocence alone is capable.

If my accusers decline this invitation, there yet remains another mode of procedure which I am equally ready to meet. Let them state with precision and clearness the facts which they lay to my charge and the evidence whether direct or circumstantial by which I am to be proved guilty in any of the public papers.—Let no circumstance of time or place nor the names of any witnesses against me, be omitted. The public shall then judge between me and them, according to other rules than the strict rules of legal evidence.

If neither of these methods be adopted in order to fix the stigma which has been imposed upon me, let candor and impartiality acquit me of crimes which my soul abhors, or suspend their opinions of my guilt until a decision thereon can be obtained in some other satisfactory mode.

Richard Randolph, Jun.

March 29, 1793

Mayo finished reading the letter before Joseph. "I have read the depositions you have taken up to this time. Together with the witnesses produced by this letter, there may be enough evidence for a preliminary examination. In fact, you may be sorry you requested one." Mayo Carrington's chilling tone caused Campbell to wonder whether the whole idea might be a serious mistake. For Richard to place himself at the mercy of the Carringtons, who may still hold some unstated enmity toward him, was dangerous, perhaps even foolhardy. That his associate was harboring similar fears was clear from the expression on Marshall's face. Carrington is suggesting the possibility of a guilty verdict, Campbell thought, and he is unaware of the content of the statements by the slaves.

"Let us assume we go forward with this case," Joseph declared. "Some of the depositions indicate that slaves reported incriminating evidence. None of them can testify. The defendant cannot testify. There was no deposition from the alleged mother. Will she testify?"

Campbell answered. "I spoke to Nancy Randolph. She assured me of her innocence. The poor girl is distraught. Her reputation is irretrievably ruined. What man would have her now? She is terribly embarrassed about discussing the intimate details of her illness. We would request that she be excused from testifying. As gentlemen, you could not wish to inflict further suffering on a young girl. Besides, the same reasons preventing the defendant from testifying essentially apply to her. Her testimony should be considered as incompetent as the defendant's. Please, leave her out of the case."

"Would you attempt to invoke the privilege against self-incrimination for her?" Mayo asked.

"We really did not think it would be necessary. But, if the occasion arose, we would consider it, to protect Miss Randolph." Although he had expected a threat to call Nancy, Campbell was careful to leave the answer in doubt.

Opening a book on the desk in front of him, Mayo began to read aloud from the Virginia constitution. "I quote from Section 8 of the Declaration of Rights. 'That in all capital or criminal prosecutions, *a man* hath a right to demand the cause and nature of his accusation, to be confronted with the accusers and witnesses,' etcetera, 'nor can *he* be compelled to give evidence against *himself.*' As you can see, the language of Section 8 does not extend to women any more than it does to slaves; it only applies to white men who have entered a state of society."

Campbell immediately contested the point. "It is certainly arguable that the constitution of the Commonwealth gives women the privilege against self-incrimination. In any case it need not be argued. The maxim of the common law is '*nemo tenetur prodere seipso,* no person shall be compelled to give evidence against himself.' Historically, it has applied to women as well as men, and to witnesses as well as to defendants, in both England and Virginia. There are many cases ruling that neither parties nor witnesses are required to answer if it would expose them to public disgrace or infamy."

Marshall added, "In this we merely follow the Law of Nature which commands every person to try to preserve himself. Blackstone is clear on—"

Mayo Carrington interrupted. "Please, do not quote Blackstone and the common law of England to us. I've read Blackstone. The man tells us that to deny witchcraft is to contradict the revealed word of God. He worships British tradition. He would stifle all legal innovation by reference to the general custom of the law. Did we rise in revolution to be governed by the dead hand of monarchy? The common law of England is an engine of oppression which must be rooted out of this Commonwealth. Instead of these endless codes of British law, we should adopt principles agreeable to our republican form of government. These old English authorities answer no other purpose than to increase the influence of lawyers. We will not be bound by the quirks of Coke and Blackstone. It is common sense, not common law, which governs this court."

Campbell was prepared for this line of argument. Since the revolution, it had become very popular. "I must call attention to our own Virginia statute of 1776 which states that the common law of England, all statutes or acts of Parliament made in aid of the common law prior to the fourth year of the reign of King James the First, and which are of a general nature, shall be considered in full force. The common law privilege against self-incrimination has roots that extend back to Magna Carta. As judges, you are bound to follow the legislative law of this Commonwealth." Campbell had some doubts about the strength of his own argument. The right against compulsory self-incrimination had not become firmly embedded in English common law until the struggles of Lilburne and the Levellers succeeded in the time of the Long Parliament and Cromwell. He was also aware that the Acts of 1792 had declared that statutes or acts of Parliament had no authority in Virginia; because his arguments related only to the common law, he decided the 1792 act was irrelevant to the discussion. Nevertheless, he was becoming increasingly apprehensive of the dangers of submitting to the notoriously arbitrary and capricious justices of the county courts. In the end, he knew the justices of the peace would follow their own private whims, without reference to the requirements of law. Thus, the moderation of Mayo's response surprised him.

"You may be correct on this point," Mayo declared. "Let us assume Nancy Randolph will not be a witness. After all, if Richard Randolph is convicted, she becomes a potential defendant. Of course, if the charges are dismissed against him, there could be no case against her. What of the wife, Judith Randolph?"

Both Campbell and Marshall were amazed at the suggestion that a wife could testify in a case concerning her husband. Even Joseph appeared to be shocked by Mayo's question. Fearful of belaboring the obvious, Marshall replied, "It is the general rule that a husband and wife are regarded as one person in law. Being the same person in affection and interest, Judith Randolph can no more give evidence for her husband than he can for himself. As a general principle, to allow such testimony would create domestic dissension and invite perjury. It is unheard of to take the oath of a person under so great a bias. Is this truly a point to be argued?"

Mayo Carrington was better prepared than Marshall or Campbell had expected. "Yes, we know all about these principles. The wife's legal existence is suspended. Husband and wife are one flesh but the husband owns that flesh." To demonstrate his familiarity with the law, Mayo recited with impressive speed, as if by rote. "Mr. Marshall, you have quoted Blackstone to us. Permit me to cite him back to you. Concerning cases of *feme covert*, he reminds us there are exceptions to the rule. For example, if the husband assists another to rape his own wife, she can testify against him. Lord Audley's Case, I believe. On an indictment for bigamy, the first wife cannot be a witness but the second can."

Marshall did not hesitate in his answer. "In the bigamy case, the marriage to the second woman is void. Thus, when she testifies, it is not as a wife. In the rape case, the husband is a principal in a crime with another directed against his wife. The allegation in our case is murder. The victim would be the child, if it existed, and not the wife. The exceptions in Blackstone are not applicable to Mr. Randolph's situation."

Mayo Carrington persisted. "If your client engaged in intercourse with his wife's sister, he is guilty of incest and adultery. Is his wife not one of the principal victims of those crimes?"

Concluding that Carrington would not concede this point, Marshall abruptly decided to alter his course. "I believe it is well-established in this Commonwealth that a wife cannot testify either for or against her husband in a case like this one. However, Colonel Carrington, if you believe the law is to the contrary, we would be delighted to have Mrs. Randolph testify for her husband."

With an alarmed expression on his face, Joseph interrupted. "This argument is quite interesting, but I believe that Mrs. Randolph cannot be allowed to testify in behalf of her husband." Although silent, Mayo appeared relieved to be extricated from the coils of his own argument. For a few moments the two justices conferred with each other in whispers. "We agree," Joseph announced. "You may publish the letter. The case will be brought before me as a single justice on April twenty-second. That gives you more than three weeks to prepare your case. Based on the depositions submitted to me, I will then decide whether to refer the case for a preliminary examination. We strongly recommend you take the depositions of Mrs. Martha Jefferson Randolph, Peyton Harrison, and any who come forward as a result of the publication of your client's letter." Joseph stood up to indicate the meeting was concluded. "I shall see you on the twenty-second. Good day to you both."

As Polly folded the clothes, she watched her mistress for signs of distress. Richard was soon to depart for the Cumberland County Court House. Perhaps, by the end of the day, they would know whether there would be a trial. Sitting on the edge of her bed, Nancy Randolph languidly brushed her hair. Usually she sang quietly to herself while she performed this ritual. On this day she stared silently out of the window.

There was a knock on the door. "Come in," Nancy answered in her soft voice. When there was no movement at the door, she repeated herself. Richard Randolph entered the room. Nancy looked surprised. Since before the visit to Glenlyvar, seven months earlier, Polly had not seen him in the room.

"I cannot use this." He held what appeared to be a letter in his hand. "It is very generous of you but—"

Nancy interrupted. "Polly, would you please leave the room." Polly observed that Richard had been unaware of her presence. Hurriedly, she folded the petticoat in her hand and placed it in the closet. Without a word she left the room. Richard closed the door behind her.

Polly walked down the corridor to determine whether anyone else was upstairs. There was not a sound. Stealthily, she returned and placed her ear on the closed door. The voices from inside the room were audible; she could not comprehend the words. A burning smell came from behind the door. After looking down the corridor again to be certain she would not be seen, Polly dropped to her knees and placed her eye at a small crack in the door. Richard was holding a burning document in his hand. When the flame got too close to his fingers, he threw the paper into the hearth. He began to walk toward the door. Polly scurried around the corner and listened to his footsteps on the stairs receding into silence. She returned to the room. The sparks were still flickering in the hearth. Feigning ignorance, Polly declared, "I smell smoke in here."

"It's nothing, Polly." Standing beside the window, Nancy looked outside. Polly suspected she was waiting for the master to ride away to the court.

"What did he want?" she asked boldly.

"Nothing, Polly. Forget you saw him in here."

Polly looked into the fireplace. Except for a small pile of blackened ash, it was empty.

The jailer opened the cell for Brett Randolph. Although Richard Randolph had been a prisoner for only three days, he looked utterly disconsolate. His letter to the public had appeared in several newspapers early in April. Since he had publicly announced his intention to appear before the County Court in April and render himself a prisoner, he could not have been surprised to find himself in jail. Depositions had been presented to Justice of the Peace Joseph Carrington, who ordered Richard Randolph arrested on a magistrate's warrant dated April 22, 1793. He was to be held in jail by the sheriff for the seven days prior to a preliminary examination by the sixteen justices of the Cumberland County Court.

There is nothing like the slamming and locking of a jail door to awaken feelings of the most profound distress in a prisoner. Many is the man who has hanged himself in a cell after the meaning of that dismal sound penetrated into the depths of his soul. After only one day as a prisoner, Richard in desperation had summoned his cousin, Brett Randolph. Ten years older than Richard, Brett was as close to him as a brother. Brett was astonished by Richard's request. Although the prisoner had already engaged two of the most distinguished members of the Richmond bar to defend him for a considerable sum of money, he had instructed Brett to ride out to Long Island in Campbell County and offer Patrick Henry up to seventy pounds to represent him at the hearing scheduled for April twenty-ninth. "I cannot risk failure," he had told his cousin. "Campbell is competent. Marshall does not inspire me with confidence. I don't think he believes in taking this case to court. It is Henry who will assure victory."

Sitting in a dark corner of his cell, his back resting against the wall, Richard did not look up when Brett Randolph entered. "Bad news," Brett reported. "Mr. Henry refused your offer."

As if waking from a nightmare, Richard stared blankly at him. Suddenly, the significance of the message was comprehended. He groaned, then stood up. "Why? Did he give a reason?"

"After he read your letter, he told me he was just recovering from an illness and is too unwell to make the long trip. Also, he claimed to be busy preparing for the British Debts case next month. He said he thought his fellow counsel in the debts case were already representing you. When I confirmed his statement, he said he had the greatest respect for both Campbell and Marshall. 'If you have them,' he said, 'you don't need an old man like me.' "

"He is probably right. But I feel so uneasy. For the first time in my life, I find myself actually wishing for my death. . . . Oh, don't look so alarmed. I am not a man for self-destruction."

For a long period of time Brett attempted to encourage Richard. His assurances were to no avail. "My own brother-in-law writes me, 'I defy you to transfer the stigma to your deceased brother.' What hope is there for me if Tom Randolph feels that way? Until now, I never thought of the gallows as a possible end to this business. Now it seems quite real." With a look of complete despair, Richard threw himself down on his filthy bed and stared at the ceiling.

"Let me speak to Campbell and Marshall to get them to approve the hiring of Henry. If I tell Henry they have no objections, maybe he'll agree. These lawyers, you know, are very fearful of insulting each other."

Richard's response was immediate. "Try it. If they agree, go back to Henry and offer him double the original amount."

Two days after his first visit, Brett Randolph again rode through the Piedmont countryside, mile after mile of forest interspersed with tobacco and cornfields. Less than five months earlier, Patrick Henry had sold his farm in nearby Prince Edward County and moved to distant Campbell County. Brett cursed the bad timing of the move. His body still ached from the first bone-jarring ride to Henry's home. Finally, after many hours of riding with only a brief stop for lunch by a muddy creek, he arrived at Patrick Henry's estate, known as "Long Island," on the Staunton River. A mulatto servant led him to a clump of trees in the back of the house where Mr. Henry was sitting on a chair in the shade. A tin can of water and a pile of books were on the table beside him. Next to Washington, he was the most famous man in Virginia; since Washington had become President, Henry was perhaps now the best loved. He looked older than his fifty-seven years. Stooped over his book, he wore spectacles, hanging loosely on his nose. Except for straight, long hair on the back and sides of his head, he was bald. Even sitting, it was clear he was a tall, thin man. Squinting, he looked up at Brett Randolph. "Won't take no for an answer, sir?"

"I would, but Richard Randolph won't. He is still in jail, you know. He has authorized me to offer you double the amount we discussed."

Henry's face was extremely wrinkled. His bright blue eyes, small and deeply set, twinkled at the prospect of increasing his considerable fortune. It was well-known that in his old age Mr. Henry was eager to improve his financial situation by accumulating as much property as possible to leave to his immense brood of children and grandchildren. "How much is that?"

"Seventy pounds . . . originally. Now he is offering one hundred and forty pounds. Also, Mr. Marshall and Mr. Campbell have informed me they have no objection to your joining the defense."

"Well, I am feeling much better today. It will give me a chance to discuss the debts case with them. I reserve the highest veneration for those honorable gentlemen." He spoke as if he expected his words to be repeated to Mr. Marshall and Mr. Campbell. For a few moments Henry meditated. Then he shouted in a loud, booming voice, "Dolly!" On hearing his master's call, one of the slaves ran to the house. Within a minute Mr. Henry's wife, a woman considerably younger than her husband, came out.

"Is something wrong?" Undisturbed at being interrupted, she appeared to be concerned about her husband.

"This gentleman informs me that Richard Randolph is very anxious that I should appear for him. He is now offering double the previous amount. One hundred and forty pounds is a very large sum. Don't you think I could make the trip in the carriage?" The question appeared to be rhetorical. It was clear to Brett that Henry had decided to accept the offer.

"If you think so, dear. You are the best judge of your own health."

"The preliminary examination is in three days, on the twenty-ninth," Brett reminded him. As it was customary to pay the lawyer before his appearance in court, Brett handed Richard's note for £140 to Patrick Henry.

After checking the note, Henry scribbled a brief letter to his new client. "Give this to Mr. Randolph. Also, please inform Campbell and Marshall I would like to discuss the case with them on the twenty-eighth. The time and location are in my letter. Dolly, please provide the young man with some refreshment before he leaves . . . and get me my Blackstone."

Alexander Campbell angrily drummed his fingers on the table. Even if it was Patrick Henry, it was humiliating to bring a new lawyer into the case the day before the crucial preliminary examination. Then to be kept waiting almost an hour for his arrival. It was intolerable. In addition, Alexander Campbell did not like Patrick Henry. The great revolutionary, the man who only five years earlier had fought against the ratification of the federal constitution, had become conservative in his old age. Henry now opposed the revolution in France and supported the Federalist government in Philadelphia. No doubt, he endorsed President Washington's Neutrality Proclamation, announced the day Richard Randolph was arrested. France, the only other republic in the world, was now at war with Britain, the greatest enemy of the United States, and the Federalists in Washington declare neutrality. Of course, Jefferson himself had agreed to the issuance of the Neutrality Proclamation. That being the case, Campbell thought he might be able to support it. Regardless of Henry's position on neutrality, his politics had become anathema to Campbell. Marshall, of course, shared Henry's political views. But it was impossible to dislike the younger man. After all, Marshall was Marshall. If his politics were Federalist, no man was more democratic in his dealings with his fellow mortals. His humility and unfailing good nature disarmed all his political adversaries. Campbell envied the man's calm acceptance of the travails of life.

For his part, Marshall was not the least disturbed by the intrusion of Henry into the case they had so painstakingly prepared for the past month. "If our client wishes to retain Patrick Henry, that is his prerogative." So Marshall had calmly stated when they were first informed of the offer to Henry. There had been not a trace of sarcasm or rancor in his voice. No doubt Marshall was genuinely honored to work beside Patrick Henry. As a young member of the Culpepper Minutemen during the revolution, Marshall and his fellow soldiers had the words "Liberty or Death" sewn in large white letters on the breasts of their brown linen hunting shirts. In Marshall's heart, Henry was second only to Washington among his political heroes.

The two attorneys sat together in a private room in the Cumberland Court House Tavern. Marshall calmly drank Madeira and joked about ribald country matters. Campbell was not amused. Without much success, he attempted to steer Marshall away from his amusing anecdotes. Just as he succeeded in engaging Marshall's interests in the complexities of the laws concerning infanticide, Patrick Henry and his servant drove by the window in a dust-covered carriage. Campbell watched through the window as the young black man jumped out of the carriage with a leather bag in hand. He turned to assist his master, who laboriously climbed down from his seat.

"Please, sit down. You make me feel old with these displays of respect." Stooped over, Henry slowly walked to the table and sat down next to Marshall. He refused an offer of Madeira. "Only water for me," he declared. "I've studied Grotius and Vattel. I'm ready for British debts but not for to-morrow. Permit me to hear the sordid details."

"Have you read the letter to the public?" Marshall placed a copy of the *Virginia Gazette and General Advertiser* in front of Henry.

The great man lowered the spectacles that were on his wig instead of his nose. "Execution of Louis the Sixteenth . . . This is old news."

"No, just below that."

"Oh yes, I have seen it. Randolph's challenge to the public. This is an old newspaper . . . April third." He pushed the paper away from him. "Situation in Europe is becoming quite bad. England, Holland, and Spain have joined the war against France. The proclamation of neutrality is very wise. We must not become entangled in these endless European wars."

Campbell pompously and loudly cleared his throat to indicate his dis-agreement. "The proclamation may be wise at the present time. But France will perceive it as an attempt by Hamilton and his friends to undermine her republican form of government. Britain is our real enemy. At this moment, she is attacking our ships and impressing our seamen into the royal service. Perhaps we should quietly be supporting France to the limits of British tol-eration of our assistance."

"France is not a republic. It is a country led by a small group of blood-thirsty atheists." Using his right hand as the blade of a guillotine cutting off the fingers on his left, Henry gestured to show his contempt for the govern-ment of France. "These revolutionaries have formed the mad idea of spreading their doctrines of equality to people not ready for such ideas. In St. Domingo, we see the horrible results. Our own young people walk about calling each other 'citizen,' as though these godless madmen were to be emulated. Heaven forbid it! I am deeply disturbed by the growing hatred of religion among our own children."

"Do you object to deism?" Campbell asked.

Henry answered forcefully. "With me, deism is but another name for vice and depravity. From its first appearance, the religion of Christ has been at-tacked by the philosophers and wise ones. The puny efforts of men like Paine have been helpless to halt the complete triumph of Christianity. No matter how bloody, political movements are powerless to interfere with God's will."

Without endorsing Henry's religious remarks, Marshall agreed with the criticism of the French Revolution. "It is true. These Jacobins are pursuing an abstract system for the attainment of questionable goals through an ocean of blood. They disregard law. The execution of the King was illegal under French law. The general amnesty of the Constituent Assembly two years ago cleared him of any prior misconduct. After 1791, the new constitution protected him because the ministers bore the exclusive responsibility for the acts of the government. Also, no positive law existed for the prosecution of the King at the time his crimes were allegedly committed."

Campbell was going to interrupt. Marshall did not give him the opportunity. "The violence is so widespread, all the ambassadors have fled from Paris except our own minister; and armed men have broken into his house in Paris. Thousands of prisoners have been massacred. The less we meddle in this business, the better. Except, I would want our government to attempt to free Lafayette. I served under him at Brandywine and Monmouth, you know. He is a great man and a true republican, unlike the present French leaders."

Henry was astonished by Marshall's outburst. "You seem to know a great deal about this. I had not heard our minister's house was attacked."

"My client, Robert Morris, is in direct communication with the minister. They are close associates, you know. He passes the news on to me. The situation in France is worse than what you read in the newspapers."

Unwilling to argue with both Henry and Marshall, Campbell changed the subject. "Gentlemen, we have more pressing matters. You seem to forget, the hearing is tomorrow."

After explaining the problems to Henry, the two younger men reviewed each deposition and the statements of those who would not be testifying. Even Campbell thought that Henry's comments were perceptive. "If slaves could testify," Henry stated, "we would be in serious trouble, as would, I suppose, every slaveowner in Virginia."

Campbell interrupted with one of his frequent scholarly comments on the law. His tone was sarcastic. "In ancient times slaves could testify, but the evidence was given under torture. We have made great progress in this Commonwealth. Rather than use torture, we simply exclude their testimony. In the end, it is a matter of power, is it not?"

"Yes, it is a matter of power," Marshall replied. "And that power resides in the legislature. It is a statute that forbids the use of slave testimony. In a court of law, we are bound to obey the legislature."

"Yes, fortunately for us, there will be no slave testimony," Henry stated. "As the case stands, the most dangerous witnesses are Jefferson's daughter, Martha, and Mrs. Carter Page. Martha cannot be attacked directly. She is not hostile to our client. The best approach is to place an innocent interpretation on her story. On the other hand, Mrs. Page is the enemy. She will have to be destroyed by a frontal assault. We could also use a denial. Why not let Nancy Randolph testify?"

Campbell was vigorously opposed to the suggestion. "She does not want to testify, and Richard Randolph supports her in this. The Carringtons have agreed she is in a position similar to the defendant. It's just as well. On the stand, she could break down and seriously harm our case. She is quite distraught over the whole affair. Her beauty will not support our position either. If it were my decision, I would admit the birth of a stillborn baby and explain that Theodorick, the dead brother, was the father. Our client, however, wants to prove he and his family are without sin. Otherwise, he would never have taken the case to court."

For a different reason, Marshall was opposed to using Nancy Randolph's testimony. "We cannot bring forward any witness we think would commit perjury. The facts in the deposition can be interpreted in a light favorable to our client. An honorable defense requires that we go no further. As members of the bar, we cannot present untruthful testimony."

Henry laughed. "What do lawyers have to do with truth? Only God knows the truth. Our job is to protect our client. A Christian lawyer who defends a client he suspects is guilty is merely obeying the commandment to 'love they neighbor.' The truth will take care of itself." There was no trace of hostility toward Marshall in his remarks. It was clear that Henry liked Marshall, as did everyone else. For his own unstated reasons, Henry agreed that Nancy Randolph would not be called as a witness.

Alexander Campbell did not criticize Marshall's statements; but he did think them to be hopelessly naive. It was to be expected from a man who handled almost no criminal cases. Campbell warned Henry about the feud with the Carringtons. The feud, combined with the fact that most of the justices of the peace were not members of the bar, made the results of the case dangerously unpredictable.

"If only our system could be changed to have the lawyers select the judges," Henry noted. "The eagerness of our brethren to be rid of their ablest competitors would assure the choice of judges of the most outstanding ability."

Late into the evening the three lawyers discussed the case. Candles had to be brought into the room so that the meeting could continue. While Marshall and Campbell consumed immense amounts of Madeira and claret, Henry would drink only water. After many hours of conversation, they parted. Henry's final suggestion was to have the two sisters sit together. "Appearances," he advised, "are often determinative."

Consistent with the wishes of Richard Randolph, it was agreed that Henry would cross-examine the witnesses and make the concluding argument. Campbell and Marshall were to act as Henry's assistants, speaking as they thought appropriate. Deeply insulted by his diminished role in the case, Campbell departed in a huff. Marshall was pleased that his client's life was in the capable hands of the man he considered to be the greatest orator and criminal lawyer in Virginia.

It was a warm windless spring morning in Southside, Virginia. Although it was too late for the lilacs, numerous other fragrant flowers were everywhere in bloom. The birds warbled in the resplendent green trees. The roads were dry and easy to traverse. As his old-fashioned topless stick gig passed through the pastoral scene, Alexander Campbell was barely aware of the surroundings. It was court day in Cumberland County.

For the roads to be crowded was not unusual on court day. The country fair aspect of the event in each region always attracted farmers, merchants, clients, and lawyers, as well as the idle and curious. The higher courts, including the District and Superior Court sessions, sat only in the spring and fall in locations central to five adjacent counties. It was the monthly sitting of the County Court that was the great local attraction. At these sessions, there was always much in the way of diversion for itinerant lawyers. Campbell did not approve.

Campbell's vehicle passed over a rude stone bridge. The gurgling sound of the brook below could be heard. Ahead, large clouds of dust from the road were swirling about in the air. Within a few minutes the road was filled with carriages, riders on horseback, and pedestrians. Because of the notoriety of the case, Campbell had expected a larger crowd than usual, but not such an immense throng. He wondered whether word of Henry's presence had become widely know. For when Patrick Henry appeared at any court, the crowds were always enormous.

It was almost a mile to the courthouse, and scores of horses were tied along the sides of the road. People could be seen sleeping under wagons. Some had even raised tents. No doubt, the ordinaries in the area had been filled the night before. Customers must have been sleeping three to a bed. With the chaos in the road, Campbell decided to walk his horse the remainder of the way to avoid frightening the creature. It was clearly an exceptional day for business and pleasure. Stalls selling food were everywhere besieged. On the opposite side of the road an auction and a cockfight were simultaneously in progress. Black and white faces surrounded the site of the combat, so that only the sounds of the fighting birds revealed the nature of the exciting event. On both sides of the road horses were being bought and sold. One enterprising young man was showing off his prize stallion with a view to having the animal cover the mares of those willing to pay the fee. An old man loudly invited spectators to visit the raree-show "over yonder." The Cumberland County Court House Tavern was thronged. The rowdiness outside indicated that the drinking had begun early. Those with a taste for violence could choose between the brawl outside the tavern or the flogging of a Negro to the rear. Some official was administering the biblical thirty-nine strokes of the whip.

At last Campbell noticed Marshall on the courthouse green, engaged in a game of quoits. From a considerable distance the sound of the heavy iron quoit ringing the meg could be heard. Few men could hurl quoits with more accuracy than John Marshall. In his usual manner, Marshall was negligently clad in loose-fitting old clothes which appeared to have been worn for weeks. His hair was uncombed and his boots dirty. His long legs were in knee breeches and stockings, with the knee buckles carelessly unfastened. In his characteristically unhurried way, he joked as he moved into position for his toss. Watching Marshall at play made Campbell even more anxious than he had been. "Oh, like brother Marshall, to be blissfully undisturbed by today's solemn events," Campbell mumbled to an old lawyer acquaintance.

A quoit in each hand, Marshall stood, tall and ungainly, with his long arms hanging loosely by his sides. Using the full force of his body, he hurled the first quoit and overshot the meg. Without changing his position, he moved the second quoit into his right hand and gently threw it. Ringing the meg, it appeared to have fallen closer than the quoits of any of his opponents. Marshall shouted exuberantly. His opponent, a fellow attorney, stepped up to make his throws. The first struck the meg and bounced away from it. The second landed directly on top of Marshall's closest quoit. "By rule of law, I am the victor," Marshall yelled. "The right of the first occupant extends to the heavens. *Cuius est solum, eius est usque ad coelum.*" The other lawyers joined in Marshall's laughter at his own mock pomposity.

As soon as Marshall saw Campbell, he left the game and retrieved his books. Without a word they walked together toward the courthouse. A long line of people had already formed. An officious court officer blocked them at the door. The opportunity to exercise his suddenly important authority could not be wasted. "Have to go to the end of the line," he snarled.

His hair powdered and tied with a silk ribbon, wearing an expensive dark coat, ruffled shirt, and silver buckles on his shoes, Campbell stared contemptuously at the meddlesome intruder. "Sir, you are speaking to Mr. Randolph's counsel." Looking crestfallen, the court officer gestured for Campbell to pass. Then he blocked Marshall's entry. Campbell put his arm on Marshall's shoulder. "This is Mr. Marshall, also counsel for the defense." A look of disbelief crossed the man's face as he stepped aside.

Patting the man on the back good-naturedly, Marshall smiled. "It happens all the time, my good man." After spitting into a box of sand placed outside the courtroom for that purpose, Marshall followed Campbell into the courtroom.

Within a few minutes the two lawyers looked out the window to determine the cause of the commotion outside. As was to be expected at the presence of the man for whom two separate counties had been named, an honor given to no other Virginian, pandemonium reigned when Patrick Henry arrived. Crowds swarmed about him. As was his custom, he handed out copies of Soames Jenyns's *View of the Internal Evidence of the Christian Religion,* which were carried by his servant. "Read it and give it to your neighbor. Stop the spread of atheism." As though in the presence of a saint, those close by touched him reverently. He handed the last copy to one of the lawyers who had been playing quoits. "Sir, I hope you will not take me for a traveling monk," he declared. The lawyer laughed politely. With the last book gone, he walked into the courtroom carrying his leather bag stuffed with legal papers. The court officer nodded respectfully as he passed.

The hour for the commencement of court approached. The principals arrived. Appearing to pay as little attention as possible to the gawking spectators, Judith and Nancy Randolph climbed down from Mrs. Shore's carriage and entered the courthouse. They were accompanied by John Randolph and his friend Robert Banister. Although John had been at Glenlyvar during part of the crucial week the previous October, he had heard nothing about the rumors of infanticide until Banister had revealed them to him. Martha Jefferson Randolph, several months pregnant, arrived with her husband, Thomas Mann Randolph, Jr. Some of the other witnesses were forced to explain their way around the court officer barring entry to all except those he chose to favor. Being among the most distinguished citizens of the county, the sixteen Gentlemen Justices had no problem gaining entry. The life of Richard Randolph rested in the hands of his fellow Cumberland County aristocrats. The last of the sixteen to arrive was Henry Skipwith of Horsdumonde, who was serving a dual role as one of the justices and also the county sheriff in charge of the safe delivery of the prisoner. If St. George Tucker was correct, in the absence of overwhelming evidence of guilt, these men would protect one of their own. That was the sustaining hope of the defendant's friends and counsel.

In the custody of two burly guards, Richard Randolph was led to the place reserved in the courtroom for the defendant. After seven days in jail he looked bedraggled, worried, and somewhat unmanned by his ordeal. Within a few minutes of the entrance of the prisoner, the sixteen Gentlemen Justices, in a stately procession, filed to their seats on the raised bench in front of the courtroom. "All rise!" the court officer cried out as the justices of the peace marched into the courtroom. "Be seated!" he commanded. The distinctive sound of bodies moving in unison at the cry of the officer filled the courtroom with anticipation of the drama about to unfold.

At the prompting of Joseph Carrington, the presiding justice, the clerk stood and rapidly read aloud from a document in his hand. "At the court held for the County of Cumberland on this twenty-ninth day of April in the year of our Lord one thousand seven hundred and ninety-three for the examination of Richard Randolph who stands committed and charged with feloniously murdering a child said to be born of Ann Cary Randolph, known as Nancy Randolph, present: Joseph Carrington, Mayo Carrington, Thomas Nash, William Macon, Nelson Pattison, John Holman, Ben Allen, Henry Skipwith, Joseph Michaux, Anderson Cock, Cary Harrison, Walter Warfield, Benjamin Wilson, Codrington Carrington, Archer Allen, and Nathaniel Carrington."

Joseph Carrington began to speak. The noise from outside the courtroom drowned out his words. The court officers had left the double doors open so that those standing near the door could hear the proceedings inside. The long line of those waiting to get into the full courtroom stretched out across the courthouse green. The events occurring inside were passed along the line to those waiting outside.

"Close the doors!" As the court officers attempted to push the doors closed, the crowd outside shoved back. An uproar commenced outside the court. The magnitude of the commotion halted the proceedings. Finally, in desperation, Joseph Carrington countermanded his order. The tumult gradually ceased. "We will leave the doors open so those outside can hear. Should there be any more disturbances, those outside this courtroom will be forcibly removed from the premises!"

After waiting until silence was restored, Carrington continued. "This is a preliminary examination held pursuant to Chapter 74 of the Acts of 1792 within the required period of not less than five nor more than ten days after the issuance of a warrant to the sheriff by a single justice of this court. This court is to examine whether the prisoner may be discharged from further prosecution or shall be tried for murder in the District Court."

Campbell stood up. "May it please the court. This hearing is held under Chapter 67 of the Acts of 1788 because Chapter 74 of the Acts of 1792 has been suspended until the first of October of this year." Joseph Carrington frowned at the interruption. Campbell noticed Henry rolling his eyes at what he considered, no doubt, to be a pedantic intrusion serving no purpose except to antagonize the justices. Nevertheless, Campbell sat down pleased with himself. He had served notice that the justices would be held to the strict letter of the law and not the rough country justice usually dispensed in these backwater courts.

With a note of irritation in his voice, Carrington picked up the thread of his introduction. "The charge is murder. That is when a man of sound memory, and of the age of discretion, unlawfully kills any person under the Commonwealth's peace, with malice aforethought, either expressed by the party or implied by law, so that the party wounded or hurt dies within a year and a day. When the law makes use of the term 'malice aforethought' as descriptive of the crime of murder, it is not to be understood in the narrow restrained sense to which the modern sense of the word 'malice' is apt to lead one, a principle of malevolence to particulars; for the law by the term 'malice' in this instance means that the fact has been attended with such circumstances as are the ordinary symptoms of a wicked heart, regardless of social duty, and fatally bent upon mischief. And whenever it appears that a man kills another, it shall be intended prima facie that he did it maliciously, unless he can make out the contrary by showing that he did it on a sudden provocation or the like.

"The particulars of this case involve a charge of infanticide. I call the attention of my fellow justices to the law on this subject. If a woman be quick with child and by a potion or otherwise kills it in her womb, this is a great misprision but not a felony. However, when a man counsels a woman to kill her child when it is born and she afterwards does kill it in pursuance of such advice, it is murder and the man is an accessory to the murder. Or, if he himself kills it, he is guilty of murder. . . . How does the defendant plead to the charge of murder, guilty or not guilty?"

Richard Randolph stood up. "Not guilty!" The voice was not as forceful as his counsel would have wished.

"We shall hear the various witnesses in the order agreed upon by counsel so as to provide a roughly chronological description of the events in question. Call the first witness."

Carter Page entered the witness box. Joseph Carrington directed that the oath be administered unless religious scruples would not permit it. With a nod of his head the distinguished-looking witness indicated his willingness to take the oath. The clerk addressed him. "You are brought hither as a witness and by the direction of the law I am to tell you, before you give your evidence, that you must tell the truth, the whole truth, and nothing but the truth."

As the oath was administered, John Marshall placed his summaries of the deposition evidence on the table before him. Inconsistencies between the testimony in court and the previous statements in the depositions would be most useful to Patrick Henry on cross-examination. Justice Carrington informed the witness that the court desired him to state what he knew of events pertinent to the charge of murder. Page softened the statements in his deposition. Because he is Richard Randolph's uncle, he explained, he often visited Bizarre. "I have frequently seen Mr. Randolph and Miss Nancy together. She is, of course, his sister-in-law and they live in the same house. I am aware of no criminal conversation between them."

Mayo Carrington interrupted. "Sir, you have deposed that you saw them kissing and appearing to be fond of each other."

"Yes, I did."

"And did you not notice an apparent alteration in her size in the spring of last year?"

Campbell whispered to Marshall, "It appears the Carringtons are going to play the part of prosecutor today." With a look of dismay on his face, Marshall nodded his agreement.

"She did seem to put on some weight. But I had no other reason to suppose her to be pregnant."

Carrington continued to question the witness. He could evoke no other incriminating statements.

At the close of Page's statement, Patrick Henry slowly arose from his chair. Despite the fact that his shoulders were stooped like those of a feeble old man, he was still impressively tall. Although not as careless of his appearance as Marshall, he took no great care in his dress. The plain brown cloak, which had been thrown over his shoulders when he arrived, was draped across the table. His brown wig was haphazardly placed on his head, revealing a high intelligent-looking forehead. He wore spectacles. No doubt, many in the audience were disappointed to discover a common old gentleman in front of them instead of the fiery orator of legend. His voice was clear but disappointingly soft. His questions were routine. Page agreed he had seen many relatives, mother and son, uncle and niece, brother-in-law and sister-in-law, kiss each other and indicate a familial fondness. He also admitted that the fondness shown between Nancy and the defendant was not clandestine. "And this alteration in size, you noticed it in May, more than four full months before the events at Glenlyvar. Is that not correct?" At Page's affirmative answer, Henry sat down in a nonchalant manner, as if to say that there is nothing of importance here. "No more questions, your honors."

The next witness was Martha Jefferson Randolph, daughter of the Secretary of State of the United States, Thomas Jefferson. Because of his duties in Philadelphia, her distinguished father was unable to be present. His reputation for honesty and integrity, however, had attached itself to his daughter. It was a force to be reckoned with. Martha was tall and lanky; some said she was a delicate feminine likeness of her famous father. Her blue eyes and reddish hair were striking. Her rather ordinary face was animated by an acute intelligence. All three lawyers for the defense knew that her sweet voice and gracious manner exuded a natural goodwill which made a poor target for hostile cross-examination. She would have to be handled gently and with great deference.

After explaining that for the past three years she had been the wife of Thomas Mann Randolph, Jr., the brother of Judith and Nancy Randolph, she told of a visit to Bizarre in September of 1792. As had been expected, her testimony was troublesome. On or about September 12, 1792, in the presence of Nancy, she had a conversation with Judith Randolph. "We were talking about treatments for the colic. Among other medicines, I mentioned gum guaiacum as an excellent medicine for colic; but I observed that it was dangerous in some instances because it could produce an abortion. At the time of the conversation, Miss Nancy was silent. A few days later, on the following Friday, I received a request to send some gum guaiacum to Bizarre for the use of Miss Nancy. Soon after the application was made to me, I sent it to her, but not in considerable quantity."

Justices Macon and Holman asked the witness several questions which elicited no damaging responses. Then Mayo Carrington joined the interrogators. "Did you suspect Miss Nancy was pregnant?"

Martha was silent for a moment. "She did seem to be unhappy. The request for the gum guaiacum made me think of my warning about its power to produce an abortion. At the time, it occurred to me that her illnesses might have been caused by pregnancy. The amount I sent was only a small quantity. My book of medicines indicated that more could be given to a pregnant woman without producing any mischief."

Although her testimony was damaging, Martha Randolph's manner was that of one attempting to tell the truth without harming anyone. The three lawyers for the defendant conferred briefly. Henry then proceeded to ask a series of innocuous and boring questions. Gradually he worked his way to the sensitive subject of the medicine. "Like calomel, is not gum guaiacum a medicine that is used to treat many kinds of illnesses such as colic, gout, and skin disorders?" Martha agreed with the suggestions contained in his question. He continued with a long list of other maladies and quietly concluded his examination. "So, Miss Nancy's use of gum guaiacum could have been entirely innocent and unrelated to a pregnancy."

"Yes, that is entirely correct."

As Martha Randolph returned to her seat in the audience, Campbell was struck by the expression on her husband's face. With a look of extreme hatred, Thomas Mann Randolph, Jr., glared at the defendant. That is not going to help us, thought Campbell. Most of the justices, he was relieved to see, were looking in the other direction at the next witness, Mrs. Carter Page.

Mary Cary Page was the sister of Judith's and Nancy's deceased mother. Although she was their "Aunt Polly," she was only eight years older than Nancy. The defense lawyers had identified her as the most hostile and dangerous of all of the witnesses. According to Richard, she had been one of the chief purveyors of the damaging rumors. When he had been asked why she would spread stories harmful to her own family, Richard Randolph could only respond, "I wish I knew."

Campbell, who had not been the one to take her deposition, was relieved to hear her speak. The voice was sharp and grating. Unlike Martha Randolph, she was not a person who naturally evoked the sympathy of her listeners. If Henry continued his listless cross-examination, Campbell was prepared with a few questions of his own. However, he did expect some fire from Henry on this particular witness. After all, Mrs. Page was the daughter of Henry's old political enemy, Archibald Cary, who had once threatened to plant a dagger in Henry's heart if he attempted to become a dictator.

"For many years, I have been a frequent visitor at Bizarre. Before March of last year, I did not suspect a criminal correspondence between Mr. Richard Randolph and my niece, Nancy. Even after the death of Theodorick, there appeared to be harmony in the family. One day last spring, I did overhear Mrs. Randolph say that Mr. Randolph and Nancy were only company for themselves. That statement certainly set me to thinking. But my actual suspicion of a criminal intercourse between them was founded on their obvious fondness for each other. I began to notice that affection about the end of March or early April of last year. In May, I noticed Nancy's shape begin to alter. She was melancholy and ill most of the time. She avoided undressing and going to bed in my presence. My suspicions were aroused."

Mrs. Page needed no questions from the Carringtons to provide damaging evidence. She poured forth her story with great eagerness and more than a hint of malice. "One day, I overheard a conversation between Nancy and her maid. Because I was suspicious of her situation and desirous of learning the truth, I approached the door to her room. It was locked, but I could see through a crack. Nancy was undressed. She appeared to be pregnant. She asked the maid whether she looked smaller. The maid said she seemed to be larger. Then she complained of her ill health. That was all I observed. Another time, I saw her look down at her waist and cast her eyes up to Heaven in silent melancholy. Her pregnancy, I thought, was plunging her into despair." Mrs. Page tried to appear sympathetic to the plight of her niece. She did not succeed.

"It was not long after, I heard she had been delivered of a child at the Harrisons' home. I informed her of the stories that were being circulated about her and suggested that she put it in my power to contradict them. My niece's reply was impudent and uncooperative. 'If my denial will not satisfy you,' she said, 'I can give no further satisfaction.' It was not the response of an innocent person."

In the same manner as he had handled the previous witnesses, Patrick Henry commenced his cross-examination peacefully. However, as he continued to ask questions, a strange transformation occurred. Adding to his apparent stature, his stooped frame straightened. His voice became penetrating, his movements animated. Spectators leaned forward in rapt attention, their emotions rising with Henry's. This was the Patrick Henry they had been waiting to see. The powerful intonation, dramatic pauses, and the gestures of an actor, all created an intensity of feeling that had not previously been present in the courtroom. "You quote Mrs. Randolph as stating that her husband and Miss Nancy were only company for themselves. Did she not also say to you that Mr. Randolph was generally out tending to the plantation and Miss Nancy upstairs in her room?"

"Yes but—"

"Just answer the question, Mrs. Page. You conveniently omitted the other statement, did you not?" Henry circled about the witness, addressing his words both to her and to the judges.

"I did not omit it. I—"

"You testified that when her shape began to change, Miss Nancy was unwilling to go to bed in your presence?"

"Yes, that is correct."

"Is it not a fact that for many years before these events you often visited Bizarre?"

"Yes."

"Yet you cannot recall Miss Nancy undressing and going to bed in your presence on these other occasions. Can you?" Henry waved her deposition in his hand. Mrs. Page was silent. *"Can you!?"* The loudness of Henry's voice seemed to intimidate the witness.

Her reply was an abjectly meek "no." When Henry announced he could not hear her, she was forced to repeat her negative answer. In a gesture of scorn and preparation for the next question, he turned his back on her. There followed a series of rapid questions concerning the conversation between Nancy and her maid. At the defiant tone of Mrs. Page's responses, Henry moved his spectacles from his nose to the top of his wig. Those who had seen him before knew that this gesture meant he was about to declare war on the witness.

"You say she asked her maid whether she was getting smaller. Have you ever heard of a pregnant woman decreasing in size rather than increasing?" While asking the question, he pulled in his stomach and slumped his shoulders forward. At the orotund pronunciation of the word "increasing," he pulled his arms back, spread his feet apart, placed his hands on his waist and thrust out his belly. A wave of laughter swept across the courtroom. "Are you unaware of the facts of human reproduction?" The laughter increased. Mrs.

Page's face grew red with anger. Unable to make herself heard, she spluttered with frustration. Henry paused until the laughter subsided. "Was it your custom to sneak about your niece's room?"

"I am not accustomed to pry," the witness answered haughtily.

"Then it was duty compelled you to pry."

"Yes, that is correct," Mrs. Page agreed reluctantly.

"You have told us you were looking through a crack in the door." As if lowering his body to peek into a keyhole, Henry clumsily spread his legs. His knees pointed in opposite directions. He gestured in a ridiculous fashion. The laughter commenced again. In his most ludicrous manner he asked, "Did you peep with your left eye or your right?" As Henry avidly looked first with one eye and then the other, gales of laughter swept across the courtroom. Mrs. Page turned crimson with embarrassment. Other than the witness, it was difficult to find a face not convulsed with laughter. Tragedy had quickly been converted to low comedy. Many of the judges covered their mouths in order to hide their broad smiles. Henry knew that laughing judges are not likely to be in a mood to convict.

For a full minute, until the laughter completely subsided, Henry remained silent. Then, in a sudden dramatic gesture, he turned to the court, threw up his hands, and shouted to the heavens, "Great God deliver us from eavesdroppers."

Marshall had been thrown into a paroxysm of laughter which continued as Henry concluded his cross-examination. Campbell had finished smiling before most others in the courtroom. He knew that Mrs. Page's testimony had effectively been destroyed. Yet it had nothing to do with the truth of the matter. The demolition of the witness had been accomplished by emotion, not reason. In the eyes of Campbell, Henry was a great actor but not a good lawyer.

With a description of the arrival of the Randolphs at Glenlyvar on Monday the first of October, Randolph Harrison began his testimony. "It was immediately before dinner. I assisted the ladies out of the carriage. Miss Nancy had a close greatcoat buttoned 'round her. I observed no sign of pregnancy." John Marshall placed a large mark beside the same testimony appearing in the summary of the deposition before him. "As soon as she entered the house, Miss Nancy complained of being unwell and laid down on the bed. Almost immediately after the meal—she did not eat—she went upstairs to her room. Later, my wife and Mrs. Randolph went to her bed. She was very ill. My wife told me she took essence of peppermint, which she was accustomed to use for the colic." Harrison continued at some length describing the unfinished rooms upstairs, the loud screams during the night, and his wife's handing the laudanum to Nancy's maid. "After Mrs. Harrison returned, she told me Miss Nancy was improved. We went to sleep again. During the night—I was not completely awake—I heard a person come down the stairs, and, a short time later, return upstairs. From the weight of the step on the stairs, I assumed it was Mr. Randolph coming down to send for a physician.

"The next day, I entered Miss Nancy's room to lay the hearth so she could

have a fire. There was nothing unusual, except she was very pale and ..."
As if uncertain of the appropriate words, he hesitated. "There was a disagreeable flavor. At the time, I had no suspicions of childbirth. It never entered
my mind until information was given by a Negro woman that Miss Nancy
had miscarried."

Campbell jumped out of his chair. "I must remind the court that, under
the provisions of Chapter 77 of the Acts of 1785, or temporarily suspended
Chapter 103 of the Acts of 1792, the testimony of a Negro or mulatto is not
admissible except against Negroes or mulattoes. What Mr. Harrison was told
by a servant cannot be considered by the court."

With a look of irritation on his face, Joseph Carrington replied, "We are
quite aware of the law on this subject and will apply it in a proper manner.
Please continue with your statement, Mr. Harrison."

"On Wednesday, Mrs. Harrison, with Mrs. Randolph and her husband,
rode to a store. Miss Nancy kept to her room but she did get out of bed. That
day I heard a report among the Negroes that the birth had been deposited on
a pile of shingles between two logs." Immediately, Campbell was on his feet.

Joseph Carrington gestured for him to return to his seat. "We are aware
of your objection on this point. Any statements by Negro servants will not
be used against your client. Mr. Harrison, you did observe some physical
evidence concerning the rumor, did you not?"

"Yes. About six or seven weeks afterwards, I saw a pile of shingles between some logs. They appeared to be stained." He awaited the next question.
When it did not come, he continued. "On Thursday, I observed the disagreeable flavor again in Miss Nancy's room. On Friday, or Saturday, our guests
returned to Bizarre."

Campbell again objected "This story about the shingles is meaningless
without the testimony of the servants. It should not be considered." The
presiding judge indicated that the court would discuss his objection when the
justices deliberated.

Before commencing his cross-examination, Henry spoke briefly with his
colleagues. With his spectacles firmly on his nose, Henry turned to the witness. "When your guests arrived at your home, you have stated, Miss Nancy
had a coat buttoned tightly around her. You saw no sign she was with child,
did you?"

"None at all." To each of Henry's questions, Harrison made a similar
negative response. Henry was very gentle with the witness, a man who was
clearly disposed to interpret events in a light most favorable to the defendant.

"The footsteps in the night you thought were Mr. Randolph's, they could
have been someone else's, could they not?"

"Oh yes. Servants frequently passed up and down the stairs during the
night. It could have been one of them."

"You have also told us that originally you had no suspicions of a child
having been born. These came later, not from your own observations, but
from statements by Negroes. Correct?"

"Yes. I thought Miss Nancy had a hysteric fit. She was subject to them.

I was told she had a fit two or three days before. The disagreeable odor, I thought, was caused by something totally different from childbearing."

"You testified that you saw a stained shingle six or seven weeks after these events. The shingle could have been placed there long after the first week of October, could it not?"

"Yes, certainly. Also, I could not determine the cause of the stain. It could have been any number of things."

"There has been testimony about friendly relations between Mr. Randolph and Miss Nancy. Did you observe anything which disturbed your sense of decency?"

"No. There were some familiarities between them—hugging, kissing on the cheek, and the like. Some might have considered it imprudent. I have too high an opinion of the both to entertain any suspicion of a criminal correspondence. Other than illness, I noticed nothing unusual in the behavior of Mr. and Mrs. Randolph and Miss Nancy while they were our guests. About three weeks later, our family visited Bizarre. Mr. and Mrs. Randolph behaved to each other in the usual way, except that Mr. Randolph was somewhat crusty. Miss Nancy was fully restored to health. She spent much of the time riding her horse."

"So, if it were not for the malicious rumors, the visit to your home would have been an ordinary occasion not worth remembering."

"Yes. That there would be a trial for murder for the events of that night was beyond my wildest imaginings."

Mary Harrison testified immediately after her husband. She repeated her husband's description of the arrival of the guests almost exactly. Without being asked, she stressed the fact that Miss Nancy did not appear to be pregnant. "After supper, Mrs. Randolph and I went upstairs to inquire about Miss Nancy's condition. She looked very sick. She said, I believe, she had taken her gum guaiacum."

Mrs. Harrison then related a full account of her visit to Nancy's room later that night. The screams, the request for laudanum, the door fastened by a bolt, and her brief discussion with Nancy and Richard Randolph were described in minute detail. Thereafter she had returned to bed and had only a vague remembrance of footsteps coming down the stairs. She did not know who it was. "The next morning, I saw some blood on the pillowcase and some on the stairs. There were no sheets and no quilt on Miss Nancy's bed. I entertained no suspicion unfavorable to her until one of our Negro women told me she had miscarried." To remind the court of his objection, Campbell stood by his chair. Before he could speak, Joseph Carrington declared that his objection was noted.

"Later, I had an opportunity to examine the bed more closely. It appeared as if an attempt had been made to wash it, but the stain was not removed. To wash it properly, I had to take all the feathers out. Guests do become ill, you know. Everything I saw could have an entirely innocent explanation. That is my belief—nothing extraordinary happened that night."

With a benevolent expression on his face, Henry approached the witness. "In your deposition, you stated, did you not, that after supper it may have been Mrs. Randolph who suggested Miss Nancy take her gum guaiacum as usual?"

"Yes. I forget whether it was Judy—I mean, Mrs. Randolph—or Miss Nancy who mentioned the guaiacum. In either case, it seemed quite proper to me."

"Did Mrs. Randolph appear to be alarmed at the time, as one would expect if she thought her sister was about to be delivered of a child?"

"No, not at all."

"Did Mrs. Randolph show the signs of resentment one would expect if she suspected her husband of being the father of her own sister's child?"

"There was no sign of that whatsoever. I have seen her upset by family illness. That night she demonstrated nothing more than ordinary concern for a sick person. There were no hints of improper behavior. In fact, as my husband has mentioned, we visited Bizarre a few weeks later. There appeared to be complete harmony between Mr. Randolph and his lady."

As Mary Harrison left the witness stand, Henry bowed his head respectfully. "Thank you, Mrs. Harrison, for your candid testimony."

Mary Harrison was followed at the witness stand by her mother-in-law, Susanna Randolph Harrison. The lawyers for the defense were certain she would be a helpful witness. They were not disappointed. As soon as she heard Nancy was unwell, the old woman explained, she came from Clifton to visit her. "That was Tuesday. Miss Nancy was not well enough to see me. Her sister, Judith, told me she had been very ill and was resting easier. I was informed that Miss Nancy had been kept awake most of the night and had been calmed by laudanum. The day before the Randolphs left Glenlyvar, I sat in the room with Miss Nancy for a considerable time. There was no mark of her having been delivered of a child. No milk, no fever, or any other sign. Mrs. Randolph was as cheerful as I have ever seen her. There was no reason to suspect a child had been born. Utter nonsense, if you ask me!"

Mrs. Wood, a midwife and neighbor of the Harrisons who examined Nancy's bed at Glenlyvar, testified that there were appearances that would justify the suspicion of a birth or abortion, but that another cause might have produced the same effect. Justice Nash inquired as to that other cause. "Why, plain old monthly woman troubles. Don't you have a woman, judge?" The crowd roared with laughter.

Mrs. Brett Randolph, six years older than her cousin Richard, was not as fond of him as was her husband. Based on her hostility at the time of taking her deposition, Campbell was apprehensive about her testimony. He was relieved to hear her friendly tone. The influence of her husband had, no doubt, lessened the severity of her testimony. During her frequent visits to Bizarre, she stated, she never saw any signs of ill will between Mr. Randolph and his lady or between the sisters. Mayo Carrington interrupted. "Did you not depose that Mr. Randolph was more attentive to Miss Nancy than to his wife?"

"Yes. But I assumed he was attentive because Miss Nancy was so saddened at the death of Theodorick, Mr. Randolph's brother. Miss Nancy was, you know, betrothed to Theo."

Carrington continued. "And did you not depose that Miss Nancy's size had increased in a manner consistent with pregnancy?"

"Her size did increase so as to admit of a possibility of her being pregnant. It could also have been caused by illness. I was told that at the time of the visit to the Harrisons, Miss Nancy wore a close gown without any loose covering to conceal her shape. I saw her shortly after her return. Her size was diminished, but her obvious improvement in health may have been the cause."

Archibald Randolph, Mary Harrison's brother and unsuccessful suitor for Nancy's hand, took the stand. John Marshall leaned over and whispered to his colleagues, "Beware of unrequited lovers."

Dressed like a dandy, Archibald made an impressive appearance until he opened his mouth. The splendor of his clothes merely served to draw attention to the dullness of his voice and manner of speaking. After describing how he "waited on the ladies" on the trip to Glenlyvar, Archibald stated that he had observed no change in Nancy's size. He was not involved directly in any of the events after supper that night. However, three days later Nancy passed through the room in which he was sitting. She complained of being extremely weak. After beginning to ascend the stairs, she called to him for assistance and rested for some time on his arm. He noticed a disagreeable smell but had no unfavorable suspicions until Randolph Harrison's brother, Peyton, informed him that she had miscarried.

Mayo Carrington halted his testimony. "Did you not state in your deposition that as early as 1791 you had entertained suspicions that Mr. Randolph and Miss Nancy were too fond of each other?"

"Yes, but long before the visit to Glenlyvar, I had entirely relinquished those suspicions. Miss Nancy became attached to Theodorick Randolph. He was the one she was with most of the time."

The justices and the lawyers for the defense spared Archibald the agony of recounting his lack of success in courting Nancy Randolph. When his testimony ended without his being interrogated on the subject, he bounded from the witness stand with the eagerness of a schoolboy whose failure to do his lessons remains undiscovered by the teacher.

Peyton Harrison, Randolph Harrison's brother, confirmed Archibald Randolph's testimony. Upon being told by a servant that Miss Nancy had miscarried, he thought himself bound by his friendship for Archibald to inform him.

Henry approached the witness. "The information you passed on to your friend was based on the rumors of servants, was it not?"

"There was more—"

"Just answer the question, yes or no," Henry thundered.

"Yes, but—"

"No more questions," Henry announced disdainfully as he returned to his seat.

"But what?" interjected Mayo Carrington.

"The rumors seemed credible to me because I had perceived a fondness between Miss Nancy and Mr. Randolph last spring."

After Peyton Harrison returned to his seat beside his brother, Justice Joseph Carrington addressed the court. "It is my understanding that the remainder of the deponents will not be called today because they have all stated they knew nothing of the matter."

"That is correct, Your Honor," Henry responded. "But we request leave of the court to call two additional witnesses on the part of Mr. Randolph."

Joseph Carrington glanced at Mayo, who made no sign of disapproval. "Proceed, Mr. Henry."

"We call to the stand John Randolph, the brother of the defendant."

Because no formal deposition had been taken from the witness, for the first time during the proceedings John Marshall began to write at a rapid pace in order to summarize the testimony. As an addition to his previously prepared deposition summaries, he scribbled "On the Part of Mr. Randolph" at the top of a new page. In spite of the unusual falsetto voice of the witness, there was something compelling about his testimony. It was clear, concise, and artfully stated. Marshall had no problem committing it to paper in a shortened form.

"While we were both in Philadelphia, my brother Theodorick told me that he was engaged to Miss Nancy. Not long after that, he died of consumption. That was on February fourteenth of last year. Some months before the events at Glenlyvar, I returned to Bizarre. In consequence of Theo's death, Miss Nancy was in very low spirits. My brother Richard and his wife both warned me not to mention Theo to her. On one occasion, I forgot the admonition and spoke about him. When Miss Nancy heard the name, she burst into tears." John looked at the front row of spectators. Judith was looking directly at him. Sitting next to Brett Randolph, Nancy's eyes were fixed on the floor. It was as if she were ashamed to look into the face of another human being. John was fearful that the steadfast aversion of her eyes would make an unfavorable impression on the judges. He reminded himself that his brother's life was in jeopardy.

"The most perfect harmony subsisted in my brother's household. I had often observed how much fonder Mrs. Randolph was of Miss Nancy than of any of her other relations. In like manner, my brother was protective of Miss Nancy in her profound sadness over the loss of Theo. His wife supported him in this protection of her own dear sister's feelings.

"Although I spent much time with Miss Nancy, I saw no signs of pregnancy. She continued to dress in her usual manner. She never wore stays. From her pallid and emaciated appearance—there was a greenish-blue color under her eyes—I thought she labored under an obstruction. This condition became worse during the ride to the Harrisons. After we arrived at Glenlyvar, I saw nothing extraordinary, other than the worsening of her health. At the Harrisons', I did sit in the room with her several days after October first. The disagreeable smell mentioned by the other witnesses lingered in the room. On the return from Glenlyvar the next day, I sat with Miss Nancy in the carriage and did not detect the odor. Other than an improvement in her complexion, I noticed no change in her after we returned to Bizarre. Her size remained the same. Shortly after our homecoming, Miss Nancy was regularly riding on horseback according to her usual custom."

After further questions extracted no significant additional information from John Randolph, Brett Randolph, Richard's cousin, was called by the defense. Henry knew exactly what he was going to say. Brett was the only witness Henry had the opportunity to examine prior to the hearing. As the bearer of Richard Randolph's offer of a large fee, Brett would be, Henry knew, a most sympathetic witness. And so he was. His statement precisely corroborated the testimony of John Randolph. Brett testified he had often visited the family without ceremony. He had observed the most perfect harmony among the members of the family and had no cause whatsoever to suspect a pregnancy or criminal conversation. Neither the judges nor the attorneys for the defense asked any questions. As soon as Henry solemnly announced there were no more witnesses, the courtroom buzzed with excitement at the anticipated denouement of the proceedings.

Patrick Henry commenced his closing statement. The most profound silence enveloped the courtroom. Even the persistent noise ceased from those seeking a more favorable location at the open doors to the courtroom. No sounds were to be heard except from the lips of Patrick Henry. Using long pauses that riveted the attention of his listeners, he spoke with great earnestness and emotion. "May it please Your Honors. I speak in support, according to my powers, of the honor of an innocent man. For this is not truly a case of murder. There is no proof of a crime. It is a case of a man who chose to submit himself to the majesty of the law rather than to spill the blood of some scandalmonger in a pointless duel to the death." Pausing for dramatic effect, Henry gestured to the heavens. " 'Thou shalt not kill' is the commandment of God. Richard Randolph is here today because he chose to obey the law of God by submitting himself to the law of man.

"To force this honorable man to suffer the harsh ordeal of a trial is to reward those who spread malicious gossip in this land. It is to encourage every slave in this Commonwealth to tell tales about his master. It is to permit subversion of the sacred rights to life, liberty, and happiness by the mere whisper of words. Take these rights from us, these precious jewels, these greatest of all blessings, and you take everything." As if to represent the despair which would follow the loss of these treasures, his voice faded into a prolonged, melancholy silence. Suddenly the voice reappeared in a booming explosion of words. "If you find against Richard Randolph, the slaves of Virginia will be empowered to destroy their lawful masters and our way of life, without resort to weapons. Tongues will become their cutting blades. St. Domingo will be their model."

Alexander Campbell was appalled at Henry's words. They were a blatant appeal to fear. It had never occurred to him that St. Domingo had anything to do with the proceedings. Yet here was his colleague transfixing the audience by an emotional appeal to irrelevant subjects. The man should have been an actor, he thought. The people are always swayed by this dishonest kind of rhetoric; but I shall never stoop to it, even if it is effective.

With almost no reference to the facts of the case, other than the statement that Miss Nancy's physical condition was consistent with dropsy and a number of other maladies, Henry's summation continued for almost an hour. Pushing his old brown wig to the side of his head, he attacked eavesdroppers and gossips. He drew a heartrending portrait of Judith Randolph and her one-year-old son deprived of husband and father. He appealed to patriotism. Finally, he turned to the Bible. "In concluding, Your Honors, I find it necessary to trespass one more time on your patience. I shall take the liberty of reading from Matthew. A lawyer asked Jesus a question to test him:

" 'Teacher, which is the great commandment in the law?'

"And he said to him, 'You shall love the Lord your God with all your heart, and with all your soul, and with all your mind. This is the great and first commandment. And a second is like it, you shall love your neighbor as yourself. On these two commandments depend all the law and the prophets.'

"In this case both of these sacred commandments have been violated, not by the defendant, but by his accusers. To bear false witness against one's neighbor by way of spreading malicious lies is to dishonor both God and the Golden Rule. To free Richard Randolph from the stigma of these false accusations is to love thy neighbor and to protect thyself. To find against Richard Randolph is to give the victory to slander itself—

"Whose edge is sharper than the sword,
    whose tongue
Outvenoms all the worms of Nile, whose breath
Rides on the posting winds and doth belie
All corners of the world.

"I implore you, restore to this man his honor, his good name, his family, and his liberty. Justice demands nothing less."

At the end of the oration, many of the spectators burst into applause. Justice Joseph Carrington called for silence. In a state of exhaustion, Patrick Henry slumped into his seat. The old man had expended his remaining strength. His face was pale, his breathing irregular. He whispered to Marshall, "I think my malaria is upon me; it's that time of year."

Alexander Campbell had to interrupt Justice Carrington's remarks to inform the court that both he and John Marshall would also be making concluding statements. The Gentlemen Justices did not looked pleased. Campbell did not care. He intended to instruct these country bumpkins as to the correct rules of law to be applied, whether they wanted the instruction or not. In excruciating detail he reviewed the history of the British and colonial law of murder, the cases concerning the absence of corpus delicti, and the rules that prevented the testimony of the defendant and his wife. In his concluding remarks, he delved even further into the past. "The Roman Emperor Antoninus decreed that cases of doubt must be resolved in favor of the accused and that a man is innocent until proven guilty. The *Digest* of Justinian ascribes to the Emperor Trajan the principle, it is better that the guilty should remain unpunished than that the innocent should be condemned. These are fundamental principles of civilized law which have been established over time to prevent injustice. They must be followed here. It is a common error to suppose that men in the present generation are endowed with greater moral insight than those in the past. Do not make that error by disregarding the rules which have protected Virginians and their forefathers for centuries. Under the common law as it has been transmitted to us, this case must be dismissed for lack of credible evidence." There was no applause for Campbell. Many spectators, and a few justices, had ceased listening to him. Not wanting to lose their seats to those outside, many of the spectators tolerated what they perceived as a boring lesson in legal jargon.

It was clear to John Marshall that the justices did not want to listen to another speech. "Everyone in this courtroom is fatigued with this lengthy hearing." Marshall was interrupted by scattered expressions of approval. "The Commonwealth would never have prosecuted this case without the insistence of the defendant, who seeks to restore his reputation in this community as a man of honor. There is insufficient evidence to proceed to a trial. Restore Richard Randolph's honor to him. Justice requires it." There was silence until Marshall sat down. Then the brevity of his remarks earned him loud applause.

In order to confer in private, the Gentlemen Justices departed from the courtroom. The defendant was removed by the agents of the sheriff. Those wishing to leave the courtroom while reserving their seats were given passes by the court officers. Within less than an hour the defendant returned, followed by the justices. When the courtroom was restored to silence, Justice Joseph Carrington announced the decision of the court. "The charges against Richard Randolph are dismissed on grounds of insufficient evidence. The defendant is free to . . ." Carrington's statement was drowned out by the loud roar of approval that filled the courtroom and extended to those outside. No doubt many cheered for the victory of Patrick Henry rather than the freeing of Richard Randolph. Spectators ran up to shake Henry's hand. Campbell and Marshall were slighted by the crowd. Although pleased by the result, Campbell was upset by the lack of recognition of his efforts. Delighted by the verdict, Marshall heartily shook the hand of Richard Randolph, who was surrounded by friends and relatives.

In the mist of the tumult, Justice Carrington called for order. It was several minutes before quiet was restored. As Carrington made his statement, the silence became a murmur of excitement. "This court has also decided that justice requires a determination be made as to whether a magistrate's warrant shall be issued for the arrest of Miss Nancy Randolph. If the warrant is issued, a preliminary examination shall be held within five to ten days from this date." Nancy Randolph cringed in disbelief. She covered her face with her hands. An expression of unmitigated horror passed across Richard Randolph's countenance. Judith remained stone-faced. Campbell and Marshall were instantly on their feet objecting. Henry, ashen-faced, remained seated.

"Your Honors," Marshall protested, "the evidence is the same as that just heard in the case of Richard Randolph. We request dismissal at this time of the charges against Nancy Randolph."

With a sneer on his lips, Mayo Carrington answered. "The evidence is not identical. The court refers you to 21 James the First, Chapter 27. The statute provides that if any woman is delivered of a child, which if born alive by law is a bastard, and she endeavors privately to conceal its death by burying the child or the like, the mother shall suffer death as in the case of murder unless she can prove by one witness, at least, that the child was actually born dead— Allow me to finish, Mr. Campbell. The statute was introduced into our code in 1710 and is still in force."

Campbell was enraged. "That act was reported to the General Assembly as still in force last year. It was then repealed." He shuffled through his papers. "I refer you to the Report of the Committee of Revisions to the Governor of June 23, 1792. The committee reported a bill to prevent the destroying and murdering of bastard children with sections taken from the Act of 1710. That bill was not among the acts passed in 1792. Clearly, the Assembly intended to repeal the Act of 1710."

"This court disagrees with you, sir. The 1792 acts have not yet been printed. Even if they were, you yourself have reminded us repeatedly that the revisions of 1792 have been suspended until October of this year. Furthermore, if they were not suspended, you have not mentioned any direct repeal of the 1710 act, only a legislative failure to act on a revised version of the statute." Mayo Carrington smiled, a country boy triumphant over the lawyer from Richmond.

Campbell was not ready to surrender. "If we could delay this proceeding until the journals of last year's legislative session are available, it would—"

Joseph Carrington interrupted. "The problem in this case is the difficulty of proving whether a child was born alive. The 1710 act resolves the problem by shifting the burden of proof to the mother to establish the child was not born alive. This court rules that the statute is in effect. We will now proceed with the hearing on the issuance of the warrant."

John Marshall responded. "That old law is an unjust legacy from the harsh laws of England whose ties with us are now severed. It makes the concealment of death presumptive evidence of the child's having been murdered by the mother. Even if it is now in force, a point we do not concede, it has no applicability to this case. The statute presupposes the birth of a living infant or a stillborn. In this case, there is insufficient proof of an infant *en ventre sa mère*, no evidence of the birth of a child and, other than a stained shingle found six or seven weeks after the event, no evidence of any kind of concealment. In short, the statute is not relevant to the facts of this case. We ask for dismissal of the case on the same evidence you have just heard as to Richard Randolph."

Justice Joseph Carrington conferred briefly with his brethren on the bench. "We rule that the statute is applicable to Nancy Randolph."

"Then we request," Marshall declared, "a postponement to prepare for this unexpected hearing. Until this moment, we have been given no notice of it."

Patrick Henry slowly rose from his chair. "Your honors, my heart is oppressed with the weight of responsibility for the life of a young woman depending on the exertions I may be able to make on her behalf. I do not feel well enough to proceed today. I hope the court will indulge me and postpone this hearing."

"The court is only proposing to hold a brief hearing on the issuance of a magistrate's warrant. If the warrant is issued, we will grant the full ten days to prepare for the preliminary examination. You may now have one hour."

"Two hours," Campbell urged. "We have not had food or drink since this morning."

"No evidence heard today need be repeated. It shall remain in effect as to Nancy Randolph. Court is in recess for two hours."

Henry stood by shakily. With the grace of an enfeebled old courtier, he announced, "We submit to the superior wisdom of the court."

The three lawyers for the defense adjourned to a private room in the Cumberland Court House Tavern. While liquid refreshment was served, they discussed the unanticipated situation. Campbell and Marshall shared a bottle of claret. Looking utterly exhausted, Henry drank only water. "Gentlemen, I am afraid my condition will require you to bear the burden of the defense for the remainder of the day. I can be little more than an observer. Every year around this time, I become susceptible to malaria. It's either that or old age."

"It is clear," Campbell declared, "the justices want us to call Mrs. Randolph as a witness. No doubt, she will commit perjury; but they have given us no alternative. The Carringtons are more spiteful than we expected."

Marshall objected. "One of the first things George Wythe taught his students was that if a lawyer thinks a witness is going to commit perjury, he cannot use the witness. With some misgivings, I agreed to the theory that no child was born because the admissible evidence is all circumstantial. But we cannot now affirmatively place a direct participant on the stand who will lie about what she saw and knows. Besides, regardless of what the court said, on this evidence they cannot possibly release Richard and then arrest Nancy. They would look like fools."

"I've seen these country courts do much more stupid things," Campbell answered. "I fail to see why we cannot call Mrs. Randolph as a witness."

"As lawyers, we have a duty never to engage actively in conduct which lends itself in any way to perjury. We cannot present evidence we think is untrue." Marshall's tone of voice was adamant. "Our system of justice forbids it."

"It is a fool's delusion to think there is justice in this world. There is neither justice nor injustice. Only the caprice of fortune. The law is devoid of moral content. It is merely the exercise of power. The strong do as they wish. The weak bear it as they can. If we wanted the truth, we would let the slaves testify. Don't tell me we exclude their testimony to protect the truth. It's ourselves we are protecting."

Marshall was not offended by Campbell's harsh, sarcastic response. "We went down this path last night. You can play the part of Thrasymachus if you wish; but the point is not slave testimony. The General Assembly has removed any discretion in that area. The issue is whether we choose to use perjured testimony."

Campbell was becoming annoyed. "The point is protecting our clients. The truth, if there is such a thing, is always framed in ambiguity. It is never absolute. My opinion is that Judith Randolph will perjure herself. I may be wrong. Perhaps she has told the truth. I have had clients who admitted their guilt to me; but I was uncertain about the truth of their confessions. The ancient Hebrews, you know, did not permit confessions to be used as evidence. They thought a statement incriminating oneself was inherently unreliable. They may have been correct. If a client tells me he committed a crime and I refuse to represent him or let him testify, what do you think the effect would be? It would not be to promote truth. The client would hire a new attorney and not be so candid with him. He will have learned it is necessary to deceive his own lawyer. The legal system will be even further away from the truth, whatever that may be. Spare me sermons about truth and justice. Let us defend our clients."

Henry spoke for the first time. "This type of situation always presents a difficult problem. I have confronted it many times before. My own conclusion, developed over many years of difficult experience, is that a lawyer's task is not to determine guilt or innocence. Our duty is simply to present evidence so that others can make that determination." He turned directly to Marshall. "We are in the middle of a hearing. If you attempt to withdraw or indicate to the court, in some manner, that you do not approve of the testimony of Mrs. Randolph, you may fatally compromise the chances of Nancy Randolph."

Henry could see that Marshall did not agree. Pausing to catch his breath, he wiped away the perspiration pouring from his brow. "On the other hand, a lawyer does have a responsibility to the court to preserve the integrity of the process of determining the facts. There is no satisfactory solution to this conundrum. In matters of competing principles, we often must choose among several, all equally attractive . . . or unattractive. So, John, let me propose a compromise. Brother Campbell can take a proper deposition from Mrs. Randolph which he can introduce to the court. You need not participate. You can present the closing statement you were just prevented from using in Mr.

Randolph's case. If you prefer, you can refrain from referring to any of Mrs. Randolph's testimony in your statement. Agreed?"

For what seemed like an eternity to Campbell, Marshall was silent. Finally, he spoke. "I accept. I'll send Mrs. Randolph in to you. While you engage in your foul lawyer's tricks, I'll return to the courtroom and revise my virtuous statement to the court." In his endearingly self-mocking manner, Marshall laughed as he left the room.

The courtroom was lit with candles bathing everything in a quivering light. As Marshall wrote, it seemed to him that the earlier hearing had occurred on a day long ago in a different place. In this proceeding, he knew, he would be the principal attorney. He had little more than an hour to prepare. Taking a new sheet of paper, he wrote at the top, "Upon the trial of Miss Nancy before the Magistrates." Anticipating the content of the deposition being written at that very moment, he summarized the incomplete and unsigned statement Campbell had extracted weeks earlier from Judith Randolph. The problem of disassociating himself from the expected perjurious statement perplexed him. Hesitantly, he held his pen above the paper. The idea abruptly set his pen in furious motion. "I did not myself hear the testimony of Mrs. Randolph; it was delivered to me by Mr. Henry & Mr. Campbell." He was satisfied. It did not refer to Judith's testimony and did not indicate to the court any disbelief in it. With his original notes for a closing argument before him, he quickly wrote a new statement applicable to the changed legal circumstances of this most peculiar case. As was his custom, he did not refer to a single legal authority when he could dispense with such citations. He planned to let the facts speak for themselves.

The courtroom was filled. In a frenzy of activity, Marshall continued to write. Alexander Campbell placed the new deposition in front of Marshall, who was relieved. There were no surprises.

Justice Joseph Carrington addressed the assemblage. "This hearing is for the purpose of determining whether a magistrate's warrant shall issue for the arrest of Ann Cary Randolph, known as Nancy Randolph, for the reason that on the first day of October in the year of our Lord one thousand seven hundred and ninety-two said Ann Cary Randolph, not having the fear of God before her eye, did feloniously, willfully, and with malice aforethought kill the bastard child delivered of her and did conceal the death of said child. All evidence taken in the preliminary examination of Richard Randolph this day before this court of the County of Cumberland shall be applicable to the present proceeding. Do the attorneys for the defendant have additional evidence to place before this court?"

Declaring that he offered in evidence the deposition of Mrs. Richard Randolph, Alexander Campbell walked toward the bench. "Sir," Joseph Carrington replied, "it is not customary to receive depositions when the witness is available in the courtroom."

Campbell was visibly annoyed. "Your Honors, it is not customary in a magistrate's hearing to present anything other than depositions."

Mayo Carrington responded for the court. "Sir, the reason for the custom is so as not to require the repeated presence of witnesses at multiple hearings. It is for the convenience of witnesses and lawyers. Since Mrs. Randolph is present, we will hear her testimony. The deposition is not acceptable."

Campbell nodded at Judith Randolph, who was pale with fright. With the passive eyes of one beyond help, Richard Randolph looked away from his wife. Her head down, arms tightly embracing her body, Nancy Randolph continued to observe the floor; her face was not visible to the many curious eyes staring in her direction.

With a forced vigor, Judith Randolph moved to the witness box. Her voice was strong and confident as she swore to God to tell the truth, the whole truth, and nothing but the truth. At the direction of the court, she addressed her remarks to the events of early October 1792. "The visit to Mrs. Harrison last October," she began, "made no impression on me at the time. If it had not been for the later infamous reports, the incident would have entirely escaped my memory." After a detailed description of the occurrences immediately following the arrival of the Randolphs at Glenlyvar, she recounted the events of that night. "When Nancy began to scream, my husband was already asleep. Although exhausted and sick myself, I did not sleep for a moment. Nancy's complaints kept me awake the entire night. A very sudden change in the weather prevented my getting out of bed during the night, as I was fearful of taking cold. I remember it was very difficult to awaken my husband. When he was finally awake, I asked him to go into my sister's room and drop her some laudanum. At first, he was reluctant to go. He said Nancy had the hysterics and would soon be easy. After I asked him again, he got up and went into her room. It was extremely cold. I remember he did not put on his coat. He sent Polly, Nancy's maid, to fetch some laudanum. Shortly after she returned, Mrs. Harrison came up the stairs. I told her about Nancy's hysterics. Then she went into the room and stayed only a short time. I saw everyone who went into and came out of Nancy's room. There was no way of going out of Nancy's room without passing immediately by my bed. The two rooms were so close together that the slightest noise in one could be distinctly heard in the other. A candle burned all night in the room where I slept. I did not doze. A child could not have been born or carried out of the room without my knowledge. The suggestion that such an event occurred is absurd. I would have known if my sister was pregnant. She was not. After Richard came out of the room, he returned to bed. He did not go down the stairs until the next morning. Of that, I am certain."

The Carringtons closely cross-examined the witness. Despite repeated attempts to establish inconsistencies in her story, she steadfastly refused to change any part of her testimony. "There was nothing improper in the relationship between Nancy and my husband," she asserted. "Foolish gossip" was the way she characterized such stories. "Anyone who knows my husband is aware of the fact he is a perfect gentleman. His extra attention to Nancy was to soothe her hurt over the death of Theodorick. Nothing more. I encouraged it."

Judith admitted discussing the use of gum guaiacum with Martha Jefferson Randolph in the presence of Nancy. "Patsey spoke of it so highly as a medicine for the colic that we obtained some from her and gave it to Nancy when she was ill. It worked very well. I never considered its power to produce abortions because Nancy was not pregnant." She denied ever having told Mrs. Page that Nancy and Richard were company only for each other. "I know I never said it because there was no basis for ever making such a statement." She concluded strongly. "The truth is simple. No improper conduct occurred on that night or any other night. Our family is God-fearing and honorable. Nothing ever passed between my sister and my husband that could have created suspicion in even the most jealous mind. This hearing, we trust, will vindicate the honor of our family."

Alexander Campbell was pleased. Judith's testimony had improved the case for the defendant; and she had served as the one witness required by the statute. If the ancient act created a presumption of wrongdoing, Judith had provided the necessary rebuttal. Campbell was confident. The case was won. With a tone of great assurance, he announced that John Marshall would make the closing statement for the defense.

Marshall looked down at his notes. Having heard the testimony of Judith Randolph, he could no longer pretend to be unacquainted with it. Nevertheless, he thought he could proceed with a clear conscience. His argument had been prepared without it. "Your honors, for this entire day, you have heard the evidence relevant to this case. There appear to be five circumstances which would excite suspicion against Miss Nancy Randolph. Let us examine each one of them without favor or prejudice.

"First. That Mr. Randolph and Miss Nancy were imprudently fond of each other. I believe there is no man in whose house a young lady lives who does not occasionally pay her attentions and use fondnesses, which a person prone to suspicion may consider as denoting guilt. The sister of his wife is, perhaps, of all others, the person for whom he would show the most fondness. But there was something peculiar to herself in the situation of Miss Randolph, which might well mingle with a fondness for her an unusual degree of tenderness. She had been nursed in the lap of ease and indulgence; she had been accustomed only to wish and to find her wishes complied with. Suddenly, her father's house was no longer a home for her; she experienced a reduction in her condition of life and something of asperity among her relations. She was turned out into the world on her own, dependent on the hospitality of her older sisters and brothers, until at last she came to reside at Bizarre, the home of her sister Judith and her sister's husband, Richard Randolph. What is most important, she had loved the brother of Richard Randolph. When that brother was no more, she felt his loss deeply. In these circumstances, is it surprising that the attention of Richard Randolph should be somewhat particular? No, it is not. But had they been conscious of guilt, they would have suppressed any public fondness and would have avoided all public intercourse. This they did not do. Richard Randolph did not hide his affection for his sister-in-law, because it was entirely innocent. There was no consciousness of guilt. Furthermore, this conduct towards each other was under the very eyes of Mrs. Randolph and the various relatives and friends who visited the house. If they were guilty lovers, would they have so conducted themselves? Certainly not! Richard Randolph did not hide his affection for his sister-in-law because his intentions were honorable. Nancy Randolph did not object to such public displays of fondness because she knew they were entirely innocent. Any other conclusion would be contrary to human nature."

Campbell was amused at the differences between John Marshall's and Patrick Henry's arguments. As orators, one was the complete antithesis of the other. Unlike Henry, Marshall did not use his voice or gestures for dramatic effect. There were no adornments, no great energy of expression, no appeals to emotion or prejudice. Marshall's appeal was to the luminous purity of reason and common sense. Campbell approved. Although he doubted it, he hoped the judges, even if not moved, would find the conclusions reached to be inescapable. To John Marshall's questions, there was only one kind of answer—not guilty.

"Second. The appearance that Nancy Randolph was pregnant. That there was small increase in Miss Randolph's size is not denied. But an increase in size could be produced by a cause other than pregnancy. Let us then look into the testimony for the truth. In May, Mr. and Mrs. Page observed a change in shape which they thought indicated a pregnancy. If they were correct, Miss Nancy must then have been advanced three or four months; for every person knows that a fact of this sort is not discernable in a young woman, not seeking to conceal it, until about that stage. By the first of October, then, she must have been eight or nine months gone, and of the size of a woman about to be delivered. Was this so? Mrs. Martha Randolph saw her in September. Although suspicious of her situation, she did not speak of any increase in size. Mrs. Page herself saw her at the same time, so did Mr. Page, yet neither of them spoke of an increased alteration of shape. Mr. and Mrs. Brett Randolph visited familiarly in the family. They saw her without ceremony. They had heard the suspicions and saw nothing to warrant them. Mrs. Brett Randolph observed such an increase of shape, as Mr. and Mrs. Page observed in May; but she says another cause was adequate to the effect. Mr. John Randolph, who was continually in the house, saw no cause for suspicion. Mr. Archibald Randolph, who was a suitor, and one who had suspected an improper familiarity, did not suspect a pregnancy. Had she been near a delivery, he could not but have observed it. Mr. Randolph Harrison, who took her out of the carriage, declared that she had her close greatcoat buttoned 'round her and that he had no suspicion of pregnancy. This increase in size, then, observed by Mr. and Mrs. Page in May, must be ascribed to a cause which would leave the person stationary and not produce a continual growth. Those of us familiar with the ways of nature know that a woman who is visibly pregnant at four months does not become less so after eight. The laws of nature, as observed by us all, inform us that Miss Nancy Randolph's condition must have been due to something other than incipient motherhood."

Marshall paused to glance at his notes on the table. Approaching the bench without his notes, he continued to address the justices, who listened intently. "Third. The application of gum guaiacum knowing it to be a medicine to produce abortion. This medicine was calculated, it has been said, to produce abortion and also to remove obstructions. It might then be designed for the one purpose as well as the other. If Miss Nancy was near a delivery, it would have been unnecessary to take this medicine to procure an untimely one; had she sought to procure an abortion, it would have been in the early state of her pregnancy. Yet the evidence clearly indicates the medicine was sent for in September, not in May. An application could have been made by means of an accomplice, without being known for whom, and medicine might have been procured which would have been infallible; yet the medicine was openly requested without any attempt at concealment. In fact, she would have taken it at home, where the whole matter would have been concealed, and not abroad where discovery was inevitable. But the evidence is that she took the gum guaiacum at the Harrisons'. This is not the conduct of one trying to be aborted. Again, all of the evidence viewed together indicates innocence."

Marshall timed his perambulations about the courtroom so as to be back at his notes upon the conclusion of his third argument. Before launching into his next point, he quickly reviewed his notes. Then he confidently strode back toward the justices. "Fourth. The appearances at Mr. Harrison's house. The illness at Glenlyvar might have been produced by pregnancy or another cause. The screams were proof of pain, but not of pain sought to be concealed. Mr. Randolph was sent into the room to help his sister-in-law. His own wife was ill. The request that the candle should not be brought into Miss Nancy's dark room was natural from a person in pain, who had been taking laudanum. The person who came downstairs appears from the evidence not to have been Mr. Randolph. The blood and all the appearances upon the bed could have been produced by birth or illness, as those declare who saw it. The sight of it produced no suspicion until a servant said there had been a miscarriage. Let it be remembered that suspicions had been propagated and had probably reached the servants. In this situation, any suspicious appearance would be considered by them as full proof. Had there been any appearance of a child, we would expect some evidence of its existence would have been shown. The story of the shingles has no weight. Had the fact been as supposed, no person on earth would have deposited the birth on a pile of shingles. All we really know is that a stained shingle was found six or seven weeks after the event. It is not even known that the stain was caused by blood. And, remember, Mrs. Randolph showed to those who saw her none of that apprehension and extreme misery which would have been the certain consequence of her knowing the situation of her sister."

Marshall again glanced at his notes. As they indicated, this was the appropriate place to refer to Judith Randolph's testimony. He had circled the sentence "Her situation gave her the best opportunity of knowing the fact, and she contradicts it." For a moment he hesitated. The sentence remained unspoken. He continued his presentation.

"Old Mrs. Harrison saw Miss Nancy soon after the events in question, and she testified the defendant had none of those marks which are the consequence of childbirth. The smell mentioned by several witnesses is consistent with either a stillborn or an ordinary female illness. At Glenlyvar, Miss Nancy did not remain in her room, as would be expected if she had given birth; and, immediately on her return to Bizarre, she resumed her usual exercise of riding on horseback. The most perfect family harmony still subsisted. Thus, it is clear that the events at the Harrisons' home are not only consistent with the complete innocence of Miss Nancy Randolph, but also tend strongly to prove that innocence.

"Fifth and last. Miss Nancy's refusal to comply with the request of Mrs. Page for an examination. No person will deny the imprudence of this; and, if that unfortunate young lady be innocent, she has abundant cause to regret her refusal. But the most innocent person on earth might have acted in the same manner. We all know that the heart conscious of its own purity resents suspicion. The resentment is still stronger when we are suspected by a friend or relative. It must be remembered that at the time of the refusal, the subsequent extent of the rumors was not known. At that moment, the pride of conscious innocence was sufficient to produce the refusal.

"The friends of Miss Randolph cannot deny that there is some foundation on which suspicion may build; nor can it be denied by her enemies that every circumstance may be accounted for without imputing guilt to her. In this situation candor will not condemn or exclude from society a person who may be only unfortunate. In this proceeding at law, justice cannot find against such a person in the absence of the requisite proof. The case should be dismissed. There exists no cause for the issuance of a warrant."

As Marshall resumed his seat, there was a polite smattering of applause. Campbell enthusiastically shook his colleague's hand. Appearing more ill by the moment, Henry could only produce a sickly smile.

The sixteen Gentlemen Justices required less than fifteen minutes to confer. Campbell's confidence was justified. The case against Nancy Randolph was dismissed. Weeping openly at her vindication, Nancy remained seated. Her sister gave her a polite but unenthusiastic hug. Richard and John Randolph escorted the sisters to the carriage through a sea of staring faces. As Alexander Campbell and John Marshall stood by the carriage congratulating Richard Randolph and his brother, the tall quick-tempered older brother of Nancy and Judith, Thomas Mann Randolph, pushed into the space beside Richard and glared into his face. "Remember my letter."

John Randolph jumped between the two men. "I hope you mean nothing personal by this."

Thomas Mann Randolph did not deign to look at the younger brother.

His answer was directed to Richard. "I meant what I said, sir." Without another word he plunged back into the crowd to make his way back to his wife Martha.

The legal proceedings were finished. The long wait for the verdict of society was just beginning.

Mary and Randolph Harrison were greatly distressed by the aftermath of the hearing. As a result of the great interest in the affair produced by the legal proceedings, the rumors about the events at Glenlyvar continued to spread. The stories were on everyone's lips. The decision of the court seemed to have convinced few of the innocence of the accused. Even St. George Tucker decided it was again necessary to place the dispute before the public.

Judith later told Mary Harrison that before the hearing, St. George Tucker had asked her to write a letter containing her version of the events at Glenlyvar. At the time, he had thought she would not be able to testify because Richard was the only defendant. Without telling Richard, she had written the letter at Matoax and had given it to John Randolph to carry to Judge Tucker in Williamsburg. Only six days after the hearing, Tucker himself wrote a letter to the public. He declared that the eight weeks Judith, Richard, and Nancy had spent together in his house earlier in the year convinced him of the truth of Judith's statement. Tucker's own letter and Judith's, with a brief letter from John Randolph, appeared in the May 15 issue of the *Virginia Gazette and General Advertiser*. Judith's letter stated that the visit to Glenlyvar had made no impression on her mind at the time, as Nancy's illness appeared to be only a minor complaint of the stomach. The letter was consistent with her testimony in court. What was said to have happened could not have taken place because of the proximity of the two rooms; and perfect cordiality and harmony had always existed between Nancy and herself.

Judge Tucker had written in his letter to the *Gazette*:

> The acquittal is sufficient for every legal purpose; but the public mind is not always convinced by the decisions of a court of law. In cases where the characters of individuals are drawn in question, there lies an appeal to a higher tribunal; A COURT OF HONOR!

When he read Tucker's statement in the newspaper, Randolph Harrison was astonished. "Is he threatening a duel if the slander continues? I thought he wanted Richard to go to court to avoid the very thing. Doesn't he realize that continuing to discuss this in the newspapers perpetuates the sordid business?"

Before she answered her husband, Mary Harrison read the entire statement. Shaking her head in dismay, she agreed. "There can be no doubt about it. It will only prolong the agony. Is there no end to it?"

Shortly after the appearance of the Tucker letter to the public in the

Gazette, Mary Harrison became more upset on receiving a distraught letter from Judith. She informed Mary that she had been in a state of complete misery even before they had met each other at the Cumberland Court House. "I scarce know whether I should have suffered so much had I doubted my husband's innocence, for then I confess my esteem for him would have been so diminished that I should not have felt what I did on his account, but perfectly conscious of that, as I have ever been, & still dreading the diabolical machinations of his & Nancy's unprovoked (but not less rancorous) enemies, words are inadequate to express what my weak mind endured." Judith's letter continued. "My health is very bad, indeed so much have I suffered lately, both in body and mind, that I much fear that a few months will put an end to my troubles in this world; neglected & thrown off by all whom I once fondly relied on."

Horrified, Mary showed the letter to her husband. "It's difficult to believe this is Judy writing. She actually says if she is unfortunate enough to have another child, I alone, except for Dick, would be the only person she could call upon to befriend her children. Has her own family so completely abandoned her?"

Thus, it came to pass that, shortly after the hearing, the Harrisons visited Bizarre. Their worst fears were realized. Judith had lost a substantial amount of weight. Dark circles around her eyes disfigured her face, which had the appearance of one who had not slept for days, She barely spoke. It was as if her spirit had died, leaving behind the empty shell of a body which continued the motions of daily living. Poor little St. George, who received no attention from his mother, was entirely abandoned to the care of servants. Even Judith's house, which had always been spotlessly clean, had an untidy, neglected look about it.

Mary tried desperately to rouse her cousin's spirits. With little St. George in her arms, she attempted to engage Judith in conversation. She was able to evoke only apathetic one-word responses. Occasionally, Judith would mumble a few complete sentences of a surpassingly mournful meaning. "My mother always said life was a disaster waiting to reveal itself; now I understand what she meant." It was only when a dish fell on the floor with a loud crash that Judith responded to the world about her. The failure of poor, deaf St. George to react to the noise caused Judith to stare at her child with a look of complete despair. Within moments she withdrew to her apathetic state and vacant look.

Nancy spent most of the time in her room. Her maid, Polly, said she was reading. But when Mary entered her room, there was no book in sight. Nancy sat in her chair looking out the window. She appeared to be restored to her former condition of good health. Her youthful exuberance, however, had vanished. "The best part of my life is over," she lamented. "Who will have me now?" She spoke about her father's illness, bemoaning the fact that her own family did not want her to visit him, although he could be dying. Showing a spark of her old spirit, she proudly declared she could not bear to see her stepmother, Gabriella, in any case. Then she returned to self-pity. "Sometimes I fear I'll have to spend the rest of my life in this wretched house. An old spinster, imprisoned in her sister's home." She began to sob, then the tears poured out of her uncontrollably. Mary feared she was going to have another hysteric fit. Only Polly was able to calm her. "Hush," she said quietly while stroking her mistress's hair. The maid coaxed Nancy to take a nap before the afternoon meal. As soon as Nancy was safely in bed, Mary returned to the calm of her own bedroom. "That girl only thinks of herself. She is the cause of this catastrophe, and she only talks about her problems. What about her sister?" Her husband indicated his agreement to mollify Mary. To his male friends, however, he stated that the women were all too harsh with Nancy. "If she were homely," he said, "she'd receive a lot more sympathy from the ladies."

Richard was away from the house most of the day. Everyone assumed he was overseeing the field hands. Nobody knew where he actually could be found. At mealtime he finally appeared. The host gallantly attempted to converse as if life had been restored to its former felicity. The false cheer only increased his guests' uneasiness at the pall of melancholy enshrouding the house. With Nancy and Judith each acting as if the other were not present, the mealtime conversation languished and died.

After spending only one night at Bizarre, the Harrisons fled from that scene of overwhelming domestic misery. With great relief they retreated to the sweet tranquility of Glenlyvar. For a substantial period of time neither Randolph nor Mary Harrison suggested another visit with the Randolphs of Bizarre.

There was only one person in the world before whom John Randolph would remove all of his clothes and display the body he considered to be so hideous. They plunged into the water together and swam out to the rock. The relief from the sweltering heat caused a smile to flash momentarily across Richard's face. "My God, you're actually smiling," John chided his brother.

"What do you mean by that?" Richard muttered as he pulled himself onto the slippery rock.

"It's you. You're melancholy as a Baptist." Richard did not respond.

John Randolph adored his older brother. Nobody was more dear to him. When they swam together, John would always recall Richard's rescuing him from a watery grave so many years earlier. He could still close his eyes and feel Richard grabbing his arm just as he was giving himself up for the last time. The recollection never failed to fill him with an intense desire to live. But now John was hurt by Richard's continuing silence, his failure to confide in his own brother. Although John had been present at Glenlyvar for part of that fateful week in October, Richard had told him little of the disturbing events that had occurred in his absence. It was from a person who was not a member of the family, Robert Banister, that he had first heard the scandalous rumors. Richard claimed he had not mentioned it to John because nothing significant had happened. Despite John's questions, Richard would never explain the blood on the stairs, the gum guaiacum, and the stories of the slaves. Before the hearing he was silent. After it he would only say, "You heard the evidence; there is nothing more." John was pained by his brother's continuing refusal to speak to him or ask his assistance. It was Brett Randolph, not John Randolph, Richard had sent to obtain the services of Patrick Henry. It was St. George Tucker he asked for advice. John could think of only one instance in which Richard had entrusted him with secret information about the scandal. Not long before the trial, he had shown John the letter from Thomas Mann Randolph, Jr. "I defy you to transfer the stigma to your deceased brother," Richard's brother-in-law had written. "I will wash out with blood the stain on my family," the letter had threatened. As they departed the courthouse, the threat had been renewed.

"Tom still has not sent a challenge, has he?"

"No, and I don't expect he will." Richard was perfectly calm about the threats from his brother-in-law. "Tom is hotheaded. He barks but doesn't bite. Besides, he knows I'll never engage in a duel with him."

For some time they both sat on the rock, quietly baking in the noonday sun. John broke the silence. He announced that he had finally written the letter to St. George Tucker pleading with his stepfather and guardian to permit him to go to Europe to fight for the French republic.

"You're wasting your time, Jack. I've told you that. He will never give you permission."

"I'll be twenty-one next year. Then I won't need it."

"You'll still need money. Only a fool would go. Despite what Citizen Genêt is saying, they don't trust foreigners. Be assured, your reward would be either prison or the guillotine. Just because I oppose neutrality does not mean I would take up arms for a foreign power. I'll fight the British on our own soil but not in Europe. The revolution will survive or die according to the will of the French people. Save your blood for your own country."

If any other person had made such a statement to John, he would have vehemently attacked him as a royalist. His great respect for his brother silenced him. Although he loved the French Revolution with the passion of youth, he adored Richard even more. And, in his heart, he knew Richard was right. Rather than argue with his brother, he changed the subject. "Come to Richmond with me. The Debts case will be splendid. Henry, Campbell, Marshall, and Innes will all be there. If they lose, we could both be paupers. You wouldn't even be a freeholder. You could actually lose your right to vote. Just think of the excitement. It will be like having your entire fortune bet on one horse race. In fact, the bet is already made. How can you possibly miss it?"

After years of living in debt, that attached to his patrimony and his own gambling debts from his profligate days as a student, John despised being a debtor. As a religious zealot yearns for redemption, he longed for the independence of solvency. For him, the relationship of debtor to creditor was akin to that of a slave to his master. To be a debtor was a lowly state indeed. The British Debts case, John hoped, would finally remove the sword of penury that had been hanging by a thread over his family for as long as he could remember. The tongue of Patrick Henry would finally save him; he intended to witness the golden moment.

Richard was of an entirely different mind. "I've told you I won't go. What happens in the case doesn't matter to me. I intend to pay back every debt contracted by father. Mother always recognized it as a true debt. It has to be honestly discharged. If that means losing everything, so be it ... I've seen more than enough of Henry, Campbell, and Marshall. You go and tell me about it."

"Don't withdraw from the world. You can't be a hermit for the rest of your life. Please, come to Richmond!"

Richard did not say another word. Without a look back at his brother, he dived into the water and swam to shore by himself.

Thus, the month after Richard's trial, John Randolph attended the British Debts case unaccompanied by his brother. His stepfather's warning reverberated in his mind. If the British creditors won the case, the patrimony of both Richard and John would all go to satisfy the "unjust debt" owed by their father to the Hanburys of London. If Richard could not bear the idea of his father's debt left unsatisfied, John welcomed freedom from debt in any form. If the Virginia debtors won the case, he would at least have a choice as to whether to make payments to the Hanburys. Richard's life had been in jeopardy the previous month. His own, John believed, was the prize one month later. Unlike the hearing at Cumberland Court House, however, the fortunes of most of John Randolph's friends and relatives were at stake in the litigation in Richmond. For years St. George Tucker had been trying to resolve the debt problems left by John Randolph, Sr. Tucker's own inheritance, through his first wife, as well as the fortunes of his stepsons, were inextricably linked to success in the case. Thomas Mann Randolph, Sr., and all of his children, including Thomas, Jr., Judith, and Nancy, were all affected. As a result of the momentous litigation, the financial condition of almost every important plantation owner in Virginia was at risk. In short, it was the kind of confrontation John Randolph relished.

The problem was an ancient one in the former colonies. Because of the unavailability of manufactured goods in Virginia, the custom had developed of ordering from England. Toys, saddlery, furniture, clothes, or elegantly bound books, the goods of the mother country poured in an unending stream into Virginia in exchange for hogsheads of tobacco and shipments of corn and wheat. Upon their arrival in England, there were charges on the colonial crops—duties, freight, import and cocket, primage, cooperage, porterage, and others. The profit margin was extremely small. Distant British factors sold the crops for the plantation owners and then spent the money as their purchasing agents. Few Virginians were present to impose the rules of commercial fairness on either transaction, the selling or the buying. The prices of colonial goods were kept low, the prices of British manufactures high. The factors made double and triple profits on the transactions. The planters fell deeper into debt. When debt payments could not be met, heavy interest was charged. When the obligations might have been paid, the British currency laws were revised to make payment of debts almost impossible. With the revolution had come salvation for the colonists. Many of the colonies repudiated debts owed to British creditors. Virginia passed laws tantamount to confiscation. In 1777 the Virginia Assembly enacted legislation permitting citizens to rid themselves of debts owed to British subjects by paying the money owed into the state treasury. Under the so-called sequestration acts, the debts were to be paid in Virginia currency. In expectation of the eventual complete repudiation of British debts, many did not pay the state. But as Virginia currency depreciated in wartime, it became advantageous to pay. The great families of Virginia, including many branches of the Randolphs, paid the required amounts into the Loan Office. Another confiscatory act was enacted in 1779. In 1782, Virginia, which was responsible for nearly one-half of the British debt, passed a law, like those in many other states, barring any legal actions to recover British debts. The great burden appeared to have been removed. With the end of the War of American Independence, however, the treaty of peace between America and Great Britain provided, "It is agreed that creditors on either side shall meet with no legal impediment to the recovery of the full value in sterling money of all bona fide debts heretofore contracted." When ratified several years later, the United States Constitution provided that the federal judicial power extended to cases involving citizens of the United States and those of another country. As soon as the federal court opened in Richmond, pursuant to the enactment of the Judiciary Act of 1789, hundreds of lawsuits were filed by British creditors. The first of these cases to be tried was *Jones v. Walker*. The case was first heard in 1791. Dr. Thomas Walker was sued for a pre-revolutionary debt of £2151 by the surviving partner of the British mercantile house of Farrel and Jones. The outstanding members of the Virginia bar participated on both sides of the case. John Wickham, John Starke, William Ronald, and John Baker represented the plaintiff-creditors. The defendant-debtors joined together to procure the assistance of the most able lawyers available to them—Patrick Henry, Alexander Campbell, John Marshall, and the colossally tall James Innes. When one of the original jurists, Justice Blair, became ill after the 1791 hearing, no decision was rendered. In the interim, the plaintiff William Jones died. To prevent delay, the companion case, *Ware, Administrator of Jones v. Hylton*, was scheduled to be heard in Richmond for the May term of 1793. On the bench for the Circuit Court of the United States at Richmond were Judge Griffin, the District Court judge on the original case, and two new justices of the United States Supreme Court, Chief Justice John Jay of New York and Justice James Iredell from North Carolina.

John Randolph had carefully studied the case. For one of the few times in his life, he regretted not having completed his legal education. To be part of this great event, the fortunes of so many of his neighbors dependent upon the eloquence of the speakers, was one of the few things in his life he fondly desired. As a participant in his brother's trial, he had experienced, in a direct way, the ability of men to exercise power over the lives of others by little more than oratory. It had been a revelation to him. Now the stakes had been extended from one family to the solvency of the people of the Commonwealth of Virginia. It was, he told his friends, more exciting than a match race. This game was of historical significance.

In anticipation of the presentation of Patrick Henry that day, the crowds packed the courtroom at an earlier hour than usual. Even the windows behind the bench were filled with spectators. John Randolph pushed his way through the crowd until he was close to the bench. He knew that Henry's argument had lasted for three days in the fall of 1791. No matter how long it continued this time, he intended not to miss a word.

As soon as the judges entered the courtroom, John realized he was close enough to hear them speaking to each other. Early in the day's proceedings Justice Iredell expressed some doubt about the stories he had heard about Patrick Henry's abilities as a speaker. Certainly the appearance of the man belied his reputation. During the discussion of several abstruse legal points, Henry rested his head on the bar, like one too old and enfeebled to speak. When he was finally called to address the court, he rose slowly to his feet. The courtroom became as completely silent as at Cumberland Court House the month before. "I beg Your Honors' forbearance. It is a great hardship to put the laboring oar in the hands of a decrepit old man trembling with one foot in the grave. Pray, do not charge my infirmities to the great cause of my client."

John Randolph chuckled to himself. He had seen Henry play the part of the feeble old man. The diminished expectations of his audience would soon accrue to enhance the perception of his performance.

The great orator began slowly. He read extensive extracts from Grotius and Vattel on the effect of the law of war with regard to debts. According to these learned sources, he contended, when two nations are at war, either one possesses a right, pursuant to the laws of nature and of nations, to remit to its own citizens debts that they may owe to the enemy. As of the fourth of July, 1776, the government of the British monarch in this country, he stated, was dissolved and the Commonwealth of Virginia became sovereign as to the debts of its citizens. The laws of Virginia, concerning debts, passed during the late war, he argued, were properly enacted out of the exigencies of war. He compared, at length, the critical situation of America to that of Rome threatened by the army of Hannibal, after the terrible defeat at Cannae. As he spoke, Henry looked around the room at the judges and spectators, many of whom were participants in the late War of Independence.

"I need only refer to your recollection for our pressing situation during the late contest; and happy am I that this all-important question comes on, before the heads of those who were actors in the great scene are laid in the dust. An uninformed posterity would be unacquainted with the awful necessity which impelled us on. If the means were within reach, we were warranted by the laws of nature and nations to use them. The fact was, that we were attacked by one of the most formidable nations under Heaven, a nation that carried terror and dread with its thunder to both hemispheres."

His voice rising and falling dramatically in a sermonic chant, he recalled, for an audience that needed little reminding, the horrors of the execution of the war by Great Britain—the nation, he reminded everyone, of the creditor-plaintiffs.

"Our inhabitants were mercilessly and brutally plundered, and our enemies professed to maintain their army by those means only. Our slaves carried away, our crops burnt, a cruel war carried on against our agriculture—disability to pay debts produced by pillage and devastation, contrary to every principle of national law. From that series of plenty in which we had been accustomed to live and revel, we were plunged into every species of human calamity. Our lives attacked—charge of rebels fixed upon us—confiscation and attainder denounced against the whole continent; and he that was called the King of England sat judge upon our case—he pronounced his judgment. . . ."

He continued by referring to the plaintiff's contention that at the conclusion of the war the Treaty of Peace of 1783 revived the confiscated debts owed to British creditors. Denying that the treaty revived the debts, Henry argued that the treaty was not even in effect, as a state of war continued to exist between the United States and Great Britain. Ten years after the signing of the agreement, he stated, Great Britain continues to violate the specific provision by refusing to return Negroes, the property of American citizens carried off during the war; by the forcible holding of Forts Niagara and Detroit; and by supplying Indians, who are at war with the United States, with arms and ammunition.

As he spoke, the weight of his years seemed to fall from his shoulders until he was fully erect, speaking energetically in a loud booming voice. His gestures were powerful, his pauses highly dramatic, as at the Cumberland Court House. To John Randolph he seemed like a first-rate four-mile racehorse, sometimes displaying his full power and then slowing down before the next burst of speed. He was a demigod, a great fleet-footed stallion transfigured into the shape of a man. When Henry had reached his full powers, Justice Iredell sat with his mouth open in wonder. John Randolph laughed to himself at the disbelief in the eyes of this unbeliever, listening to Henry ridicule the "sacred rights" of creditors.

"Though every other thing dear to humanity is forfeitable, yet debts, it seems, must be spared! Debts are too sacred to be touched! It is a mercantile idea, that worships Mammon instead of God. . . . What authority can they adduce in support of such conclusive preeminence for debts? No political or human institution has placed them above other things. If debt be the most sacred of all earthly obligations, I am uninformed from whence it has derived that eminence. The principle is to be found in the day-books, journals, and ledgers of merchants; not in the writings or reasonings of the wise and well-informed—the enlightened instructors of mankind."

Henry raised his hands solemnly so as to contrast the grandeur of the instructors of humanity with the petty principles of the moth-eaten merchants. His solemn pause called for a response from his audience which he duly received. As if by unspoken command, the audience burst forth with loud applause and shouts. Justice Iredell turned to Chief Justice Jay. "Gracious God! He is an orator indeed." A large contingent of ladies in the rear of the courtroom applauded passionately. A fire was kindled in the breast of John Randolph. The dream was firmly implanted—to be an orator who could move the hearts of men in the settlement of the great issues that determined the fate of nations. Like a great cloud passing the sun, for a moment it blotted out the light of his earlier dreams of love and domestic bliss. These were, he thought, the trivial hopes of personal contentment. The hopelessness of ever fulfilling them had created a void in his spirit waiting to be filled. For a time on this day the need for a new dream was satiated. John Randolph wanted to move the world with words.

1796

With a piercing sympathy, Isaac Lanier watched his employer glumly peruse the recently delivered opinion of the United States Supreme Court. It was not a surprise. Word of the judgment in *Ware, Administrator of Jones v. Hylton* had preceded the delivery of the March 7 opinion by several days. Nevertheless, it was apparent that Alexander Campbell was distraught. The opinion confirmed the end of the litigation concerning the great matter of the British debt cases in the manner in which a funeral removes all doubt of the indisputable fact of death. Momentarily, Campbell turned away from the pages in front of him. Unable to bear the expression of utter misery on the advocate's face, Lanier pretended to be busily engaged in copying a document. Campbell returned to his reading. Within moments he was shaking his head in dismay. "There is no escape from this ruling, Isaac. All our debt clients are now in the shadow of debtors' prison."

Less than three years earlier it had been this same case, *Ware v. Hylton*, that had been the cause of uncharacteristic exultation on the part of Campbell. Little more than one month after the victory in the notorious Randolph murder case, the federal circuit court had ruled for the defendant debtor on one of the defensive pleas. Payment to the state loan office under the Virginia sequestration law of 1777 had been held to be a valid defense to the claims of creditors. Campbell, John Marshall, James Innes, and especially Patrick Henry were widely declared heroes of the Commonwealth of Virginia in the continuing struggle against British tyranny. Justice Iredell's opinion for the majority—Jay had dissented—had been most gratifying to the attorneys for the debtors. "However painfully I may at any time reflect on the inadequacy of my own talents," Iredell had written, "I shall as long as I live remember with pleasure and respect the arguments which I have heard on this case: they have discovered an ingenuity, a depth of investigation, and a power of reasoning fully equal to anything I have ever witnessed, and some of them have been adorned with a splendor of eloquence surpassing what I have ever felt before."

Campbell had been pleased, Lanier knew, by the fact that Iredell's opinion had rejected Henry's lengthy argument based on Britain's alleged continuing breach of the peace treaty of 1783. The Circuit Court had ruled that the treaty could not be held to be void by a court of law until Congress first declared it had been breached. Iredell had also expressly rejected Chancellor George Wythe's 1793 opinion in the case of *Page v. Pendleton*, announced only days before the appearance of Iredell's opinion. Wythe, the great scholar of Virginia law, had asserted that the right of a foreign creditor—though a former enemy in war—to recover a debt could not be confiscated. Instead of the positions of Henry and Wythe, it had been the arguments of Marshall and Campbell that were triumphant. In short, Justice Iredell had concluded that under the 1777 act of sequestration, which was adopted by the sovereign state of Virginia at a time when even the Articles of Confederation were not in force, the payment of the debtor to the Commonwealth's loan office had discharged the debt; and the treaty of peace with Great Britain did not retroactively revive the right of creditor against debtor. To Lanier and others, Campbell had proudly pointed out the fact that Justice Iredell had repeated the very words of his argument, "I cannot therefore bring myself to say that the present defendant, having once lawfully paid the money, shall pay it over again."

As a result of the victories in the Randolph murder case and the British debt cases, Campbell had become a celebrity in Richmond. Finally able to place the bitter memory of his unsuccessful first marriage behind him, in September of 1793 he married Miss Hetty Hylton, the oldest daughter of William Hylton, originally of Jamaica. In less than three years the taste of triumph had turned to ashes in his mouth.

Campbell's hatred of Patrick Henry, Lanier knew, made the Supreme Court ruling more difficult to bear. Because Henry had retired, he was not available to argue the British Debts case before the Supreme Court in Philadelphia. Only Marshall and Campbell had appeared for the debtors at the February sitting of the Court. Not only would people blame them for the defeat, but undoubtedly many were already saying that the judgment of 1793 would have been affirmed if only Patrick Henry had been present. It was a bitter blow to Campbell's pride.

Campbell pushed the opinion away and turned to Lanier. "In my entire career at the bar, this is the single most important case. To end like this. Thousands of our citizens in ruin." He shook his head with self-pity. "How could Washington appoint a man like Samuel Chase to the Supreme Court? Chase's opinion is our worst fears brought to life. That man has no respect whatsoever for state sovereignty. To him, the federal government is all powerful. He leaves the states with nothing." Campbell swiftly turned the pages of the opinion. "Listen to this drivel," he said.

> "I wished to decline sitting in the cause, as I had been counsel, some years ago, in a suit in Maryland, in favor of American debtors; and I consulted with my brethren, who unanimously advised me not to withdraw from the bench. I have endeavored to divest myself of all former prejudices, and to form an opinion with impartiality."

Campbell pounded his fist on the table. "Impartiality! That man is the most fervent Federalist partisan I've ever met. It was our grave misfortune he joined the court only five days before we argued the case. Five days!"

Lanier meekly interrupted Campbell's tirade. "The court was unanimously against us. Chase was only one of four."

"The other opinions are short and of no account. Paterson, Wilson, and Cushing add little. It is Chase's opinion which is ruinous to republican principles. He giveth with one hand and taketh away with the other. First he says that the Virginia sequestration act was a valid exercise of state power to confiscate debts owed to the British. But then he writes that Congress possessed the power of conducting the war against Great Britain. Listen to this.

> "The authority to make war, of necessity implies the power to make peace; or the war must be perpetual. I entertain this general idea, that the several States retained all internal sovereignty; and that Congress properly possessed the great rights of external sovereignty."

Campbell furiously turned the pages of the case. "It gets worse.

> "There can be no limitation on the power of the people of the United States. By their authority the State Constitutions were made, and by their authority the Constitution of the United States was established; and they had the power to change or abolish the State Constitutions, or to make them yield to the general government, and to treaties made by their authority. A treaty cannot be the supreme law of the land, that is of all the United States, if any act of a State Legislature can stand in its way."

Once again Campbell cursed the name of Samuel Chase. "He says the fourth article of the treaty of peace intended to destroy all lawful impediments to the recovery of debts, past and future, and the law of Virginia is destroyed because it is an impediment. The game is over. Daniel Hylton is ruined. Our planters are now a form of property owned by the great mercantile houses of London. Henry was right eight years ago when he warned us this federal constitution would devour state sovereignty. I thought he was exaggerating. But, for once, the bag of wind correctly predicted the future. With this opinion, they can now destroy our most sacred institutions."

Lanier had never seen Campbell so upset by a case. "You shouldn't blame yourself, sir. Both you and Mr. Marshall were superb. All of us who heard your presentation were proud to be Virginians. Any Virginia court would have accepted your arguments. I'm certain of it."

"Marshall's argument was too clever. He believes in federal supremacy, you know. Once he even told me we did not fight the revolution to avoid our just debts. It was the Randolph trial all over again. He tailored his argument to suit the needs of his conscience and placed himself before his clients. His approach was to try to reconcile the sequestration law and the treaty of peace by rational interpretation. Inconsistent laws cannot be made consistent by mere sophistry. It was an ineffective tactic."

"That did not appear to me to be the situation," Lanier replied.

"Of course it was, " Campbell snapped. "Instead of arguing the federal government could not nullify a state act, he simply claimed that the language of the treaty—that creditors must meet with no lawful impediment to the recovery of all bona fide debts—did not apply. No need to look so bewildered. It's a simple matter. It was conceded by the creditors that Virginia at the time of passing the sequestration act was an independent nation. War being a state of force, Virginia acted lawfully to terminate the debts owed by her citizens to British creditors. Since the debts had lawfully ceased to exist, Marshall argued that the words of the treaty referring to creditors and bona fide debts did not apply to the case at hand. There were no debts owed, he claimed, by those who paid into the state loan office. He simply construed the treaty without discussing the power of Congress to take away a vested right by treaty. He left it to me to contend that Congress lacked the power to repeal the laws of the several states or to sacrifice the rights of individuals. It was I who argued the rights of Virginia as a sovereign state. But the crowds followed Marshall about as their hero. You were there. Barely a single person congratulated me." As he spoke, Campbell's voice cracked with bitter emotions.

Lanier attempted to calm his boss. "The Commonwealth will surely compensate those who paid debts into the loan office; and the Jay Treaty provides for the arbitration of the debt question. All is not yet lost."

"The Jay Treaty is a disgrace," Campbell angrily replied. "It usurps the power of our own judiciary. It doesn't even address the question of payment for our stolen slaves or the impressment of our seamen. It is simply another surrender to the British and a betrayal of our allies in France." Suddenly his voice softened. "Whatever happens under the treaty is not the point. I have failed personally. Nothing can redeem this defeat. Nothing."

"Sir, there is blood flowing from your mouth."

Campbell did not seem to be disturbed. Calmly, he wiped his handkerchief across his lips. "So there is. So there is." He sat back down at his desk. "You know, Isaac, my personal life has not been a happy one. If I could begin again as a child and live it a second time, I would not want to. I thought Hetty had restored me to joy. But it was only an illusion. My youthful hopes were resurrected and then cruelly destroyed. She was worse than Lucy . . . I saw Lucy recently. She was with that minister from up north." Campbell turned his face away from his amanuensis. "In the end, the practice of law has always been the final citadel of my life's satisfaction. Now even that has been breached." Again Campbell's voice cracked with emotion. "They say, you know, when troubles come they come not as single spies, but in battalions. Shakespeare, I believe." He wiped the moisture from his cheeks. "Please forgive this display of weakness."

Lanier was astonished. In all his years in the service of Alexander Campbell, he had never seen the man reveal his emotions about personal matters. "It is God's will. We must accept it."

Campbell was instantly enraged. "What has God to do with it? Do you really believe a great father in the sky watches over us? If it is so, he must delight in cruelty. All this obsequious thanking of God for his bounties when things go well and attributing mysteriously benevolent motives to him when disaster strikes. It is all utter nonsense. There is chance and there is this." Holding up his hand in front of Lanier's face, he pinched his own flesh. "This is the only will there is. When it is gone, there is nothing!"

"I am in great dis-tris."

"That's 'distress.' "

"Dis-tress. Let us fall into de hand of de Lord, for his mercy is great; but let me not fall into de hand of man."

"That is excellent, Polly. Your reading has improved immensely." Nancy closed the large Bible.

Polly smiled broadly. "I like dem stories 'bout David. Dey's very interestin'." Nancy had originally chosen a novel for the reading lesson. It had been Polly who insisted on the Bible.

As she always did after they read together, Nancy began to get into her riding clothes. Polly assisted her. The two had grown closer than at any time in the previous ten years. It was when Nancy began to extend her dominion over men that she had begun to neglect Polly. Although only a child of nine at the time, Polly had resented it. Since the trial, however, Nancy had become isolated. For her to be invited to visit another household was an unusual event. There were no more beaux. Judith treated her more like an unpaid servant than a sister. They rarely spoke to each other except about domestic chores and little St. George Randolph, who was left for the most part in the care of Nancy and the servants. Judith seemed to have an aversion to her deaf four-year-old boy. With the birth of Tudor, only seven months earlier, she devoted even less time to her elder son. Although she did not nurse the infant, she spent much more time with the new child than with the old. Nancy was alone. But as Syphax said, "Bad weather is always good for somebody." Polly's mistress had returned to her.

In the past two years Nancy had begun to teach Polly to read. It was their shared secret. Polly knew that Judith would not approve. No doubt she would say servants should be working, not reading. Furthermore, a slave who could read and write might cause serious trouble, by writing conspiratorial messages and forging passes. Since the news of St. Domingo and all the stories about slave plots, especially the one in Norfolk in the summer of '93, Judith had begun to act more distrustfully than ever toward her servants. On a large ring at her waist, she carried all the keys for the household, including the one for the enclosure surrounding the work cabins adjacent to the main house. Even the old trusted household servants were not allowed to use the keys; and all slaves were watched closely by the mistress of the house.

Richard Randolph continued to treat all of the slaves with great trust; but he would not interfere with any of the rules established by his wife for the domestic servants. The master and mistress of the house remained apart from each other on all matters, including the location of their bedrooms. As to the slaves, she left the field workers to him. The household servants were her domain. There was only one general rule in effect for all servants. The master would not permit the whipping of any slave without his signed authorization. Nobody, not even the overseer, requested it. From past experience everybody knew Richard Randolph would refuse to sign.

Polly adored the master. Since the trial, she had heard stories about his consorting with some of the pretty "high yaller" slave girls. Sally, Judith's maid, had even bragged that the master had begun to give her the eye. Once, she claimed, he even placed his hand on her shoulder. She said no. According to Sally, she was surprised when he turned and walked away. "I shoulda shut my mouth," she had said. Polly found the story difficult to believe. Sally was, she knew, given to the telling of tales. Yet secretly Polly wished Richard Randolph had come to her. She would not have refused him. But she would never have the opportunity. She was not "fetchin' " like Sally. The mirror told her that.

As she assisted Nancy in putting on her riding boots, Polly asked the question that had been on her mind. "Are dey goin' to sell some of de slaves?"

"Why do you ask?"

"Marster Richard and Judy is always talkin' 'bout debts. She say de court require he gotta pay dem now. If marster ain't got de money, he goin' to sell slaves. We know dat. Everybody is scared."

"You can tell everyone there is no cause for worry. I've heard of no plans to sell anyone. Dick has never sold a slave and he never will. People have been talking because the Supreme Court ruled that some old debts to the British have to be paid. Dick always planned to pay them in any event. Believe me, there's no reason for concern." Nancy picked up her leather gloves and walked down the stairs.

Polly listened to the rhythmic thud of the boots on the stairs. She was not worried about herself. She belonged to Nancy; and Nancy had no debts. As Polly knew, her mistress also had no money. Colonel Thomas Mann Randolph, her father, had died in November of 1793. His wife Gabriella made it clear that Nancy would not be welcome at the funeral. The Colonel had always lived in a style of elegant hospitality well beyond his means. He died mired in debt. Just before his death he had distributed most of his property to favored members of his family and to two creditors who held the mortgage on his property. Nancy was not among the recipients of his generosity.

The Colonel's many other creditors were unable to collect from his estate. His executors, Nancy's brothers William and Thomas Mann Randolph, Jr., claimed the estate did not possess the assets to pay them. Nancy had mentioned it to Polly. "I'll never have money," she said, "but at least I'm not drowning in debt like my brothers."

As soon as Nancy rode off, Sally came running to Polly's side. Sally was a beautiful quadroon who could almost pass for white. She was, Polly thought, dreadfully stupid. It amused Polly when white visitors to the house would speak to Sally as though she were not a servant. Sally would stare at the speaker with a blank expression, say "yassuh" or "yas ma'am" and disappear. In contrast, Polly was always treated as if she were invisible. The white folks would speak about highly personal matters in front of her, as if she were not there. "You visible, all right," Daddy Syphax had told her. "Darker skin worth mo' on de slave market. Some o' dem mulattoes can pass fo' white and 'scape to de north. Ain't nobody goin' to mistake you fo' a white gal."

"Nobody's here. I show you de paper now," Sally whispered excitedly.

In her mind Polly quickly accounted for everybody. The master was away in Richmond. Always traveling from stable to race course, John Randolph was almost never home. Most recently off to visit friends in South Carolina and Georgia, he had been gone for months. Mrs. Dudley was visiting relatives. Nancy would not be back from her ride for hours. Little St. George was taking a nap. "Where's Missus?"

"She still workin' in de spinnin' house. De baby's sleepin' dere."

The upstairs was empty. There appeared to be no servants downstairs. Polly thought for a few seconds. "You sure you know where t'is?"

"I seen him put it in de trunk in his room."

"Can you find de key?" Polly was extremely cautious. They would be in serious trouble if they were caught. She knew the paper had to be important. Mr. And Mrs. Randolph had been quarreling about it for some time. Sally had been the first to mention it. "Soon's I come in dey done shift off sudden to talkin' about dinner," she said. Polly herself had once brought drinks into them while they were talking about it. The master had it in his hand. Immediately they had begun to use strange foreign kinds of words. Then they told her to leave. She had listened at the closed door. Mrs. Randolph said, "We can use that money to pay the debts." He told her to lower her voice. "I will not lower my voice!" she had yelled. "Only weaklings have such morbid sensibilities. Do you want to disinherit your own children?" She stormed out of the door so fast that Polly had almost been caught in the act of eavesdropping.

Stealthily the two young women entered the master's room. "Is it right to do dis?" Sally asked apprehensively.

"Dat's a question you shoulda settled before you brung me here," Polly angrily whispered. "We's here. Let's do it."

Sally fumbled with the drawer and pulled out a key. Polly opened the closet. The trunk was on the floor, with records piled on top of it. Polly placed the key in the lock. It opened without any difficulty. Quickly she removed the papers on top of the trunk, carefully keeping them in the original order. Together they pulled the heavy trunk into the light. The top made a squeaking sound as it opened.

"Dat's de paper, on top. De lines is de same. What do it say?" Sally asked impatiently.

"Go outside and watch de stairs. Tell me if anyone is comin'."

Sally obediently left the room. Polly began to read. It was frighteningly long, perhaps as many as five pages of the Bible; and it was in handwriting that was much more difficult than printed letters. "Too All whom it may concern, I, RICHARD RANDOLPH . . ." Polly skimmed the writing until she saw the words "my last will." She knew that was something people write for after they die. Panic began to grip her. She could not understand most of the words—"retribution, usurped, iniquitous." Finally, in the fourth paragraph, she saw the words she understood. "I do hereby declare that it is my will and desire, nay most anxious wish, that my negroes—all of them—be liberated, and I do declare them by this writing free and emancipated. . . ." Tears ran down her cheeks. For a moment she saw herself as a free person. Her vision became blurred. But she knew she was not Richard Randolph's slave. This paper would not free a slave belonging to Nancy. The voice of Sally at the door startled her. "You scared me."

"Someone's walkin' downstairs."

In a state of terror, Polly hurriedly returned the document to the trunk and locked it. "Help me put it back in!"

Within seconds the job was done. The locked trunk was returned to the closet, the papers placed back on the top. They both ran out of the room. Polly hastened to the stairs. On the lower floor Essex could be seen. He was unaware of her presence. The key was still tightly grasped in her hand. She ran back into the room and placed it in the drawer. After walking briskly to Nancy's room, she crumpled into the trundle bed and closed her eyes. She was nauseated with fear.

"What it say?" Sally asked.

Polly knew that anything she told Sally would immediately be all over the plantation. "Nothin'. It's marster's will. It tells who gets de land after he's dead."

The unexpected deaths had taken a heavy toll on Judge St. George Tucker. Two children had passed away in the previous year. Richard's half brother, Theodore Thomas Tudor Tucker, had died in April of 1795 at the age of thirteen. The following September "Tutee," Judge Tucker's beloved three-year-old son by his second wife, Lelia, had slipped away. Theodorick, his stepson, was only four years in the grave. Tucker looked haggard; yet his spirits were high. His constant activity seemed to insulate him from the vicissitudes of daily life.

Judge Tucker and Lelia agreed that Richard was showing the first signs of breaking out of the web of misery that had entrapped him since the commencement of the rumors about Glenlyvar. Richard's old charm had returned. His anger at the world appeared to have dissipated. As in the past, Richard flirted with his seventeen-year-old half sister, Fanny, a sickly faded flower who desperately wanted a beau. She was delighted. Richard's sixteen-year-old scholarly half brother, Henry St. George Tucker, worshiped him as the brilliant older brother Henry hoped to resemble someday. Only Richard's morose twelve-year-old half brother, Nathaniel Beverley Tucker, was unhappy in spite of Richard's visit. Beverley had always shown a marked preference for John. Because John had not accompanied Richard to Williamsburg, Beverley was pouting.

With a strong note of irritation in his voice, St. George Tucker chided his son. "Bev, I told you Jack will not be back from Savannah for some time. You don't listen to me."

"You never said that," Beverley snarled defiantly. Before dinner was over, the temperamental twelve-year-old son ran out of the room in a rage, slamming the door behind him.

"Let him sulk. He'll be back." Although she was still mourning the death of her beloved "Tutee," Lelia gallantly attempted to be cheerful. With everyone else, she laughed at the discussion of John's letters from South Carolina and Georgia. In his continuing love affair with the French Revolution, John Randolph had taken to addressing people as "citizen" and "citess." His letters were dated according to the revolutionary calendar. Thus, as soon as Judge Tucker began reading one, the recitation of the date, "Five Germinal, fourth year of French Republic, twentieth of Independence," produced loud affectionate laughter from the group.

After dinner Richard and his stepfather retired to discuss the primary reason for the visit—Richard's will. By letter, Judith had pleaded with the judge to persuade his stepson of the folly of emancipating all of his slaves, either in his last will and testament or at an earlier time. Tucker was fully prepared to reason with Richard. His intention was to persuade his stepson to look to his head and not to his heart.

"You know, son, I have always abhorred the institution of slavery. It is irreconcilable to the principles of democracy. It is inconsistent with the moral beliefs which are the basis of our form of government. If we truly believe in our republic, we must learn to regard Negroes as our fellow men and as equals under the law, except, of course, in those particulars where nature may have given us some advantage. When an effective remedy for slavery is found, I believe that at that moment the golden age of our country will begin. George Wythe and I have been teaching that lesson to our students for years. The question is how to accomplish the end of slavery. You know as well as I do, it is not a simple problem. You've heard that old saying—'Slavery is like a wolf; it's dangerous to hold by the ears but even more dangerous to release.' "

Richard grinned. "I've never agreed with that. A wolf held by the ears is much more dangerous than one running free in the woods."

"That may be so. But we now have it by the ears. The question is how to release the beast without being devoured. The fact is, it is not practical to liberate the slave population immediately. It would produce the most dreadful consequences. The calamity in the West Indies provides a solemn warning to us all. In the North, immediate emancipation is possible only because they have very few slaves. In Massachusetts it was done by a single stroke, a clause in their state constitution, as interpreted by their Supreme Judicial Court. I have corresponded with several members of the Massachusetts bar concerning the case. They agree the situation in Virginia is entirely different. If it were accomplished here in a single stroke, there would be no means of subsistence for the many who are freed. These people are accustomed to be ruled with a rod of iron. They are not ready for freedom. They would soon become idle, miserable, and a serious danger to the rest of us. More than mild restraint would be necessary."

Richard appeared to be unperturbed by Tucker's discourse. With a gleam of mischief in his eye, he said, "O ye of little faith."

Judge Tucker was not amused. "This is a serious matter, and I want you to consider the consequences in a serious manner." When Richard removed the smile from his face, Tucker continued. "Unlike states in the North, we have a religious establishment which is not in favor of ending slavery. I have always told you that it is a fundamental tendency of religion to impede improvements in society. Religion is a boundary prescribed by human folly; it obstructs the application of reason to the solution of human problems. That is a fact of life in Virginia, and we must learn to live with it. We also live in a society where, over the years, we have learned to justify the subservience of the black race by inculcating our fellow whites with a belief in their own superiority. These widespread prejudices make the inhabitants of this commonwealth an inappropriate group for accepting the idea of immediate emancipation. Most important of all, to all of our neighbors, the Negro is nothing more than a type of property which legally cannot be taken away without providing just compensation. The simple fact is, we must find a middle course between the continuation of slavery and the possible release of hordes of starving marauders who would like nothing better than to avenge themselves on their former oppressors."

As if to demonstrate that he would not be intimidated, Richard stared directly into his stepfather's eyes. "The very conditions you've described eliminate the chance of finding any middle course. It must be done as an act of revolution against an unjust order, the way the French accomplished it two years ago."

"Remember it was Virginia, almost twenty years ago, which was the first community in the civilized world to prohibit the traffic in slaves," Tucker interjected.

"Yes, and it is to encourage such revolutionary acts that men of goodwill, who are able to do so, must now set an example by manumitting their slaves." Richard spoke with great passion. It was that very emotion which Tucker knew he must overcome by the light of reason.

"You, my dear boy, are not one who is in a position to do it. I dare say, *Ware versus Hylton* will cost you one-half of your property. You cannot afford to free two hundred slaves in addition to paying your father's debts. That would be pure folly. Even Jefferson himself is planning to sell at least twelve of his slaves this year to satisfy his creditors. You know how hostile he is to buying and selling human beings."

"I will not sell my slaves. That is not an option for me. The British Debts case changes little. I wrote the will before the decision was published, with the knowledge the court might uphold the rights of creditors. You know I've always intended to pay the debts. At worst, I will now have to postpone the day of emancipation, possibly until after my death. If that is the situation, my will is truly the last opportunity for action. Of course, I cannot do it immediately. For a few years, I'll need the profits from my crops to pay the debts. But at the first moment I am financially able, I will free every one of them, so help me God!"

Tucker looked skeptical. "That moment may never come. Many others—"

Richard was adamant. "It will come sooner than you think. I'd do it now if I could. For me and my children, slavery is an inherited curse. It makes masters indolent and weak. It corrupts our children. They quickly learn to imitate the idleness and despotism of their fathers. You know, as well as I do, the horrible abuses around us. I shudder to think of the creatures who now possess such monstrous power over their fellow beings. Only a few weeks ago, I read about a monster who whipped a fourteen-year-old boy to death."

Tucker shook his head in agreement. "Such black-hearted scoundrels should not be allowed to own Negroes. But they are only a small number of criminals. The courts can take care of them. A man like you should not make personal decisions based on aberrations like that."

"Is it an aberration? That kind of cruelty is an inherent part of the system. Many of those who are given absolute control over the lives of men, women, and children become brutal despots. I've seen it too many times—young children brutalizing their Negro playmates or—"

Tucker was growing impatient. "We are arguing in circles. I'll concede everything you say. The system is unjust and must be eliminated. We are in agreement. In the same manner we now curse past generations, posterity will, no doubt, curse us if we fail to resolve the problem. The question is, how to do it? You can't free slaves without preparation. It would be like abandoning your children. In a short time they would be lower than the most miserable peasants of Europe or the poor in northern cities. Even Montesquieu warns against large-scale emancipations. You probably remember the passage where he recalls that when the Volsinien slaves won liberty, they voted themselves the right to sleep with the brides of freeborn men."

"No, I don't recall that. And my people will not be lower than European peasants. I intend to give each family a few acres to work."

"Yes, Judith mentioned that. It is all very admirable. But it will not solve the problem. There are few men as generous as you are."

"That is not—"

Like all judges, Tucker was not accustomed to being interrupted. He was becoming visibly irritated by his stepson's stiff-necked opposition. "Richard, just listen for a moment." In a gesture of surrender to his stepfather's wishes, Richard sat back and folded his arms. "For some months, I have been working on a general plan of emancipation. When it is completed, I intend to submit it to the General Assembly. The plan, I believe, is liable to the minimum number of possible objections. It is so gradual, it will barely affect the interests of slaveowners and creditors of the present generation. But it will achieve its end soon enough to save posterity from the catastrophe which is inevitable if nothing is done. It is my solemn hope that we, unlike our forefathers, will not be accused of permitting the disease to fester and spread until it over-whelms our civilization."

Tucker opened a book of his notes. "The 1791 census shows that the present number of slaves in Virginia is immense—no less than 292,427. That is nearly two-fifths of the entire population of the Commonwealth. Think of the disaster if some day they revolted against their oppressors. But prudence forbids precipitate action. As I have said, the slaves' habits of obedience and submission, together with the assumption of superiority by whites, makes the slaves unfit for freedom and the masters unready for equality, at this time. Immediate emancipation is financially impossible. We cannot afford to com-pensate so many owners for a government taking of so much property. Nor could we deal with the general famine which would undoubtedly ensue. Also it is not now practical to incorporate so many blacks into the state. The opposition to any such measures would be overwhelming. In contrast, my proposed system will be acceptable, I hope, because it will not be completed for more than one hundred years. In summary form, here is how it would work: First, females born after the adoption of the plan would be free and transmit freedom to all of their descendants."

Richard quickly interrupted. "Present owners would object to the loss of those females. And who would support them when they are children?"

"Please, be patient. Listen to the whole program before you criticize it . . . Second, to compensate those owners for maintenance of the freed slaves dur-ing infancy, these slaves would have to serve the persons who would have been master until the age of twenty-eight years. At age twenty-eight, the freed slave would receive twenty dollars and necessary clothing. If these things are not voluntarily done, the courts would enforce performance upon complaint.

"Third, all Negro and mulatto children would be registered with the clerk of the County Court for purposes of record-keeping. Questions of doubt due to failure to register would be decided in favor of the slave's being considered twenty-eight, unless otherwise proved.

"Fourth, the children of Negroes and mulattoes not otherwise provided for would be bound to service by overseers of the poor until age twenty-one. As compensation for their trouble, the overseers would receive fifteen percent of their wages from the persons hiring them.

"Fifth, no Negro or mulatto would be capable of taking, holding, or exercising any public office. They would have no voting or property rights, other than an ability to enter a lease for not more than twenty-one years. They could not bear arms. Nor would they be able to contract matrimony with a white, be an attorney, juror, or witness in any court. Of course, they could testify against one of their own race."

Richard looked surprised. "Where is the justice in such a system? It is a violation of the democratic principles you claim to support." Richard's comments were subdued in tone. From long experience, he knew his stepfather would provide a reasonable response.

"I admit these restrictions favor prejudice. Who of us is free of it? Anyone proposing a plan for the abolition of slavery must accommodate himself to the prevailing feelings against blacks. Otherwise, the plan will never be accepted. We must compromise with prejudice in order to overcome it as an obstacle to the progressive development of mankind. Besides, these restrictions of rights would serve a valuable purpose. Disarming Negroes would calm the general apprehension of violent attacks arising from past injustices. Although I am opposed to the banishment of Negroes, I wish not to encourage their future residence among us. I fear the races cannot live together except by the entire subordination of one to the other. Denial of their most fundamental privileges would incline them towards seeking their rights in some other place. The immense unsettled territory on this continent provides many possible locations for establishing new settlements in climates more congenial to their natural constitutions. The territory of Louisiana and the two Floridas would afford a possible asylum for those who choose to become Spanish subjects. It is not unreasonable to hope that time would eventually remove from us a race of men we wish not to incorporate with us; or, it would obliterate those prejudices which now prevent incorporation.

"Some slaveholders will, no doubt, claim they possess a property right in unborn children. But, I believe, even the most stubborn slaveowners could be convinced that, for reasons of sound policy, their rights over other men cannot extend to lives not in being. In reality, no man can be deprived of what he does not possess.

"Dr. Franklin has estimated that the people of America, including Negroes, double their numbers in about twenty-eight to thirty years. Thus, the present 300,000 slaves will be nearly 600,000 by 1830. In sixty years, there will be 1,200,000 in Virginia. If we do not begin now, what will be the size of the problem then?"

"On that point, I am in total agreement with you," Richard interjected. "That is why I am beginning now."

"The difference between us is that the effects of my plan will not be experienced immediately; they will—"

Richard interrupted again. "Do not compare dogs and mules. I have no plan for saving society. I am merely acting to correct injustices within my own grasp."

Judge Tucker disregarded his stepson's remarks. "They will be very gradual. By my calculations, the total number of slaves will not be diminished for forty years after the plan is adopted. For thirty years, the number will actually increase. After sixty years, the number of slaves will be approximately one-third of the number at the commencement of the plan. The number of blacks under twenty-eight and bound to service will be as great as the present number for most of the period. It will require above a century for no more slaves to exist in Virginia. My detailed calculations are in this draft. Read it and we can discuss it tomorrow.

"The magnitude of the present problem is obvious to any thinking man. It stupefies the mind to attempt to imagine the type of bloodstained code required to hold two and one-half million Negroes in bondage ninety years from now. If we do not begin to resolve the problem now, I have no doubt that future generations will be amazed at our stupidity and shortsightedness.

"My proposal attempts to address the whole problem. Your action does not. I always taught you and your brothers to judge the moral nature of an act by asking whether the world would be a better place if each person imitated your action. Think of your will in that way. The result of each slaveholder following your example would lead to famine, civil insurrection, and eventually to utter chaos. Use your mind and not your heart."

Richard took St. George Tucker's draft in his hand and started for the door. "I'll read this tonight, father. We can discuss it again tomorrow. But I can tell you now it will not change my mind. It is my mind I have been using. You know what it told me? Follow your heart and you will do the right thing. Disregard it at your own and your children's peril. Slavery is a gangrenous limb that must be removed now or it will be fatal to the entire body politic. It can't wait one hundred years. Am I some kind of Cassandra? Can't you see it too?"

"It's your decision, Richard. Judy is quite unhappy with it. You are the one who will have to live with her. If you decide to emancipate, by will or by any other means, please remember one thing. Do not, under any circumstances, allow your slaves to learn of your intention until the time of its execution. Since the adoption of the manumission law fourteen years ago, I've seen too many cases of slaves murdering masters to advance the day of freedom. Your safety depends on complete secrecy. Remember, do not let your servants know they are the beneficiaries of your death. Generosity can be fatal in this world."

The servants in the big house did not approve of Polly's habitual visits with the field slaves. "I has no 'quaintance wid dat class," Mulatto Nan would often say in a contemptuous voice as Polly set out for the quarters. Saturday evening or Sunday afternoon was the usual time for these visits. That is when the field slaves celebrated with a brief festival of eating, drinking, singing, and dancing after five and one-half days of drudgery. The end-of-the-week merriment in the quarters provided Polly a relief from the sober atmosphere of the house, where the servants were constantly under the eyes of their demanding mistress. "Always have to look busy even when dere ain't no work to do," Polly would complain. After a full week of back-breaking labor, the field slaves were usually amused by the complaints of one of the privileged house servants. But they did agree it would be a terrible thing to be under the eyes of the whites from early morning until late at night.

"Can't never sit when Missus Randolph 'round. She say colored not to sit in de presence of whites. If she got nothin' fo' you to do, you stands until she talks." To the delight of her listeners, Polly imitated the terrible glance of Judith Randolph. "The marster, he don't care. If you tired and wanna sit down, he tell you to do it."

In the old days before the trial, it was difficult for house servants to get away from the big house. When the conch shell was blown at noon on Saturday, work was finished for the field slaves until the next Monday morning. But in the plantation house it was the time when visitors usually came. That meant extra work for the domestic servants on Saturday and Sunday until the guests left. By that time, the field slaves were back at work and too tired to receive company in the evenings. Since the trial, however, all that had changed. There were very few visitors at the big house. For the first time, it had become possible for Polly to join the field slaves' festivities at the end of the week. She would simply ask Nancy for permission. It was almost always granted. If Judith saw her leaving, she would usually complain; but in the absence of guests, she would not interfere with her sister's servant on the days that the servants had come to regard as their own.

Since she had surreptitiously read Richard Randolph's will, Polly had been deeply troubled. While talking to others, she found it difficult not to blurt out information of such staggering importance to her fellow slaves. How could she not mention the possibility of freedom for most of the slaves of Bizarre? Yet she knew if she told anyone, the information would travel like wildfire through the slave quarters. It would only be a matter of time before the master and mistress of the house heard about it. They would soon learn it was Polly who had opened the master's trunk. Sally would talk. Although she had never heard of a slave from Bizarre being sold or whipped, Polly realized her offense was serious. Something dreadful could happen. Nancy might be forced out of Bizarre. The two of them would have no place to live. To avoid being sent away, Nancy might agree to sell her. The thought of being sold south to a cotton or sugar plantation filled Polly with horror. She could conceive of no more terrible fate.

The glow of sunset had faded before Polly visited the slave quarters. She was too worried to join the celebration swirling about her. She watched the dance but did not participate. The music of the fiddler was loud and joyful. To her, it seemed to be miles away. Cuffee, the only man who ever had her, was there. Since he had struck her and called her a "black bitch," she would have nothing to do with him. He did not seem to care. Except for Polly, he danced with almost every woman present. She was glad he avoided her. His brute presence filled her with disgust. Dancing with a big smile on his face, shaking every part of his body, he looked harmless. Polly knew better. Beating out the rhythm of the music, the others clapped juba to the dance.

"Old black bull come down de hollow
He shake hi' tail, you hear him bellow;

When he bellow he jar de river,
He paw de earth, he make it quiver.
Who-zen-John, who-za."

Before the song was finished, Polly was on her way to the cabin of Jinna, the old conjure woman. Finally she had built up enough courage to accomplish what she had set out to do. The field slaves talked about Jinna all the time. She could do almost anything, including cure the sick, interpret dreams, and foretell the future. Polly had concluded that she was the one to solve her problem.

Smoking a corncob pipe, the old leather-skinned woman sat on the dirt floor of her cabin. Polly entered. A single candle illuminated the small room. The conjure woman stared at her as if she could see clear through her. "I work up at de house—"

"I know who you is, chile. What's troublin' yo' mind?" The old woman's voice was gentle.

In an instant Polly felt she had come to the right person. Her words had been carefully prepared. "I have a friend at 'nother plantation. She kin read. Last week, she seen a paper. De marster done writ out a will. Dat's a paper dat tells—"

"I know what a will is, gal."

"De will free all his slaves when he die."

"And she want to be free?" the old woman asked.

"No. Dat aint' it. She de slave o' de marster's brother. She afraid to tell 'bout it. She be sold south if dey learn she read dat paper."

"How old de massa?"

" 'Bout same age as Marster Randolph." Polly was becoming uneasy. She feared the old conjure woman would understand whose will she was really talking about.

"De massa could live till he be old man. Dere be many slaves waitin' fo' him to die."

Polly shuddered with fear at the way she spoke. "But he been a good marster," she responded.

"Ain't none of 'em no good. Dey lives off de sweat o' blacks." Her voice was filled with anger. Polly shook her head in disagreement. The old woman's voice was softened. "If he be a good one, it ain't de same as bein' free." The old woman closed her eyes and blew puffs of smoke through her rounded lips. Abruptly, she looked into Polly's face. "Dem slaves got to poison de massa. Got to be done right. If de white folks suspects a killin', ain't no slave gonna be freed. You understand?"

Polly was afraid it would come to something terrible like this. "Good never come from doin' bad," she protested in a quivering voice.

"To hurt de buckra ain't bad, 'specially when de dyin' o' one give freedom to so many. Is de life o' one white mo' important den freein' so many blacks? De colored man is a one-armed man; can't do what a two-armed man do till he be free."

Polly continued to disagree. "It just ain't right. Can't aks a person to do dat."

"Yo' friend kin decide dat. I kin make a pow'ful poison—chopped horse's tail, grave dirt, whiskey an' arsenic. Put it in de massa's medicine when he sick, ain't nobody gonna suspect a killin'."

Polly backed out of the cabin. "I talk to my friend 'bout it." As fast as her legs would carry her, she ran back to the house. Her worst fears had been realized. In her mind, she cursed Sally for telling her about the paper. She cursed herself for discussing it with anyone.

In the late spring, Citizen John Randolph returned to Bizarre. The previous year, Henry Rutledge, John's old friend from his college days in New York, had called at Bizarre. As usual, John was away, riding from one racing field to another. Missing the visit of Rutledge had filled John with a burning desire to see his old companion. After placing himself deeper in debt by borrowing money to defray the expenses of the trip, he had set out for Rutledge's home in Charleston. Following his stay in South Carolina, he continued south to visit his friend Joseph Bryan in Georgia. The entire arduous journey of over fifteen hundred miles had taken five months. Upon his return, Richard announced that his brother had finally coalesced into his horse; he formally dubbed him "the centaur."

John was pleased by the affectionate greeting he received from both Richard and Judith upon his return. It did not take much time, however, to recall the mournful state of the household he had departed. Judith and Richard eagerly spoke to him, rarely to each other. He was their only real company, except for Mrs. Dudley, who was of little interest to anyone. It was apparent that John provided a cushion between his brother and sister-in-law. They were not happy with each other.

To John's chagrin, Nancy continued to be cool. Although he was brimming over with interesting stories about his trip, she remained indifferent to him. At meals, she listened quietly to his stories, but she added little to the conversation. At other times, she avoided him completely. Although he continued to hope she would be friendly, as in years past, his pride would no longer permit him to take the first step. Too many times, he had been rebuffed by her. The last time was two long years earlier, not long after her father's death, when his offer of assistance had been coldly rejected. She had indicated her unhappiness at having to continue living at Bizarre. Impetuously, John had replied, "Come live with me at Roanoke." Her infuriating answer made him wish he had not opened his mouth. "Roanoke?" she had said, with a cruel smile. "I'd rather live here."

Most of John's stories concerned horse racing. He related tales of countless visits to paddocks and race courses, of magnificent horses with remarkable hind quarters and marvelous speed, and of low gamblers who assumed the airs of gentlemen while they plundered with unblushing audacity. He especially delighted in describing his own victory in a race with the handsome Sir John

Nesbit, a visiting English aristocrat who was the darling of the ladies of Charleston. From the narrative, it was difficult to determine which he enjoyed more—defeating the Englishmen or the lothario. On one occasion he told how General Washington's horse, Shark, won the Jockey Club Purse of four hundred guineas. He ended the story with a toast to the General's horse, concluding with the words, "and to President Washington, may he retire or be damned." When Judith expressed shock and dismay at such a toast, John defended himself by denouncing Washington's surrender to the British with his acceptance of the Jay Treaty. "His horse ran with great credit; the President has not. He has made himself an enemy of the French Revolution and our republic. Pray this is his last year in office. Another term and we shall have a monarchy."

John spoke constantly of the hardships of riding day after day over muddy roads and through dense forests. Often, in the middle of winter, he had to sleep on the cold ground wrapped in his bearskin. Even for a centaur like Randolph, the trip had been exhausting. Shortly after his return home, his favorite horse, "Jacobin," died. He attributed the death to "Carolina distemper"; his servant said it was the hardship of the journey. But more than the countless horse races he witnessed and the difficulties of the trail, one peculiar event appeared to have captured his imagination. He had arrived in Georgia in the midst of an enormous, violent uproar over a political scandal which the local people called the "Yazoo Frauds."

In 1795 the Georgia legislature had passed a law that conveyed to four land companies more than thirty-five million acres of fertile lands extending from Georgia all the way to the Mississippi River. The price had been $500,000, less than one and one-half cents per acre. Many of the new owners were prominent northerners, including Justice James Wilson of the United States Supreme Court and Robert Morris, the great land speculator and financier. Shortly after the sale it had become known that most of the legislators who had voted in favor of the transaction were bribed or intimidated into supporting it. Only the intervention of members of the legislature who had opposed the sale prevented many of their colleagues from being hanged by enraged mobs. Angry meetings were held in every hamlet of the state. Finally a new legislature was elected. Three months after the enactment of the original legislation authorizing the sale, the new legislature declared it to be null and void. As part of the new law, all documents relating to the sale, including the original law, were to be publicly burned. John personally witnessed a ceremonial public incineration of the original legislation, as well as the burning in effigy of several of the perpetrators, including General James Gunn, United States Senator from Georgia. "While all this was going on," John related, "the fraudulent buyers had the audacity to begin selling the Yazoo lands to speculators from all over the country. Never in my life have I seen so vile a flaunting of the law by the buyers and sellers of corruption." Although he spoke of the Yazoo frauds with the fervor of a Baptist preacher denouncing sin, even John Randolph expected that this distant event would soon fade into nothing more than a memory. He could not have imagined that time would eventually weave it into the fabric of his own life.

In spite of the lengthy journey he had just completed, John became restless almost as soon as he came back. Never as easy as when he was in the saddle, he could not wait to escape the stifling atmosphere of Bizarre. Within days of his return, he persuaded Richard to accompany him on a ninety-mile trip to Petersburg and their old family home at Matoax, only three miles from that city. Two years earlier, at the entreaty of Richard, John had sold Matoax for £3000 in order to pay a portion of his substantial debts. At the time, with the encouragement of his brother, he had taken up permanent residence at Bizarre.

It was a sentimental visit to Matoax for the two brothers. Sitting on horseback overlooking the old estate, they exchanged childhood memories. John talked fondly of their beloved mother. To John's surprise, Richard, for one of the only times John could recall, spoke of his personal life. He lamented the fact that a wife's love, unlike a mother's, is not unconditional. "Remember one thing, Jack," he said, "married women make poor wives."

John laughed. "I've heard it said marriage is the grave of love."

Richard gave no sign that he was jesting. As he spoke, he looked sorrowful. "You have children, and you're at the mercy of chance. Your own happiness is hostage to theirs. Great enterprises are no longer feasible." He spoke wistfully, almost as if he were alone. "Had I remained a bachelor, you know, I would not have lost my good name. I'm no longer certain it matters—the respect of strangers. In the end, it's all vanity."

At that moment John wanted to ask him about the scandal. Because he knew of Richard's reluctance to discuss it, he remained silent. Richard looked him in the eye. "Remain a bachelor, if you can."

"I must," John replied. Richard did no ask what he meant. John was not even certain he had heard.

After the visit to Matoax, the brothers rode directly to Petersburg. While visiting his old friend John Thompson, John fell ill. When Richard rejoined him at Thompson's house, he found his brother in bed with a serious fever. They had seen each other only days earlier; but Richard greeted his brother with a whispered question, their traditional salutation. "What have you read?" John smiled weakly at this reminder of their common bond of affection as "blood-related bookworms." According to John, he was suffering from bilious fever. Richard contended it was exhaustion. The doctor agreed with John and bled him.

For the first time, Richard told his brother about the will he had written while John was away. Initially, John was displeased. He objected to the emancipation of any slaves until their creditors were satisfied. "I wish by a word I could make them all white," he protested, "but it is not as simple as that." After Richard explained his views and described his meeting with Judge Tucker, John reluctantly acquiesced. "If father disagrees, then I support you." They embraced each other.

Richard remained in Petersburg until John appeared to be recovering. Then he left for home by way of Richmond, where he had legal business to transact. It was the last time the two brothers ever saw each other.

John St. George Randolph stared at the rain beating on the window. The four-year-old was barely tall enough to look through the pane. As if trying to touch the drops on the windows, he poked at the glass with his finger. A sudden crash of thunder exploded through the house. The little boy did not react. Nancy Randolph placed her sewing on the sofa. She walked over to the child and kneeled beside him. Gently, she rubbed his back. He smiled mischievously. Lifting him off his feet, she gave him a great hug. He giggled with delight. Nancy pointed at the toy animal at his feet and then hugged herself. Little St. George understood. Imitating his aunt, he picked up the toy and hugged it. Nancy kissed his tiny, soft cheek. Then she returned to her sewing. With his toy in one arm, St. George continued to trace his finger over the dripping pane of glass. Suddenly he began to point at the window while emitting the strange guttural sounds he made whenever he was excited. Once again Nancy put down her sewing. Quickly she walked to the window. "Polly," she exclaimed, "there's a man out by the gate." Polly joined her mistress at the window. A stranger was standing in the rain, holding his horse's reins in one hand.

Upon entering the room, Judith joined the group staring out the window. "Well, just don't stand there gaping," she said contemptuously. "Tell him to come into the house." Without a moment's hesitation, Polly opened the front door and beckoned the stranger to enter. The rain began to come down in torrents. After hesitating for some time, the stranger finally climbed slowly back on his horse and rode toward the house.

The man was drenched. Having relieved him of his horse, the servants assisted him in removing his outer garments. Judith placed her sewing out of sight. As mistress of the plantation, she was obliged to maintain an appearance of leisure. She greeted him with the hospitality customary to the countryside. Speaking with a distinct British accent, he introduced himself as Benjamin Latrobe. The tall, dark-haired visitor thanked Mrs. Randolph profusely as he quaffed the hot rum thrust into his hand by one of the servants.

"What brings you to Bizarre on such a dreadful day?" the mistress of the house inquired.

"I am an engineering consultant of the Upper Appomattox Navigation Company. We are completing preliminary surveys of the river. We hope to make it more navigable by flatboat and barge. I was to have met the two directors of the company at Horsdumonde. I stayed there last night. Mr. and Mrs. Skipwith were most hospitable. When my associates did not arrive this morning, I set off in search of them. Their names are Venable and Epperson. Have you by any chance seen the gentlemen?"

"No. I regret to say we have not. There have not been any visitors here for some time. We are always pleased to receive guests. You are most welcome to stay for as long as you wish."

"Thank you. Most generous of you. But I need only trouble you until the weather clears." As he spoke, Latrobe could not prevent himself from gazing at the beautiful young woman who had been introduced as the sister of the mistress of the house.

Responding to his glances, the young woman spoke. "You have a very distinct British accent, Mr. Latrobe. Have you been in Virginia long?"

"No, not long at all. I arrived in Norfolk only three months ago." After describing the hardships of his fifteen-week voyage to Virginia by way of the Azores, he declared his admiration for the beauties of the new world. Nancy interrupted the small talk by asking him if he had brought his family to Virginia. Shaking his head to indicate a negative response, Latrobe stated, without emotion, that his wife had died in England three years earlier. When he noticed the mistress of the house glaring at her younger sister, he quickly changed the subject. "Is the master of the house present?"

Judith answered in a hushed, solemn voice. "He's asleep upstairs. For the past few days, he's been very ill with a high fever." Latrobe apologized for arriving at an inopportune time. Both women assured him that if Mr. Randolph knew of his presence, he would insist that the visitor remain. As she spoke, Judith rang a small bell on the table in front of her. Immediately Polly and Sally entered the room. Judith turned to the servants. "Would one of you look in on Mr. Randolph?" Turning back to her guest, she continued the conversation.

"Is fever common in this region?" Latrobe inquired. "It seems to be prevalent in the area. Yesterday, Mrs. Skipwith informed me that she has labored under a fever and ague for the past five years. All of her family has a similar problem."

"We have fevers occasionally," Judith replied, "but certainly not like that."

"In riding about this area, I noticed that many of the trees have been cut down to the water's edge. That can admit fog to creep up the valley, bringing fever with it."

"I never heard of that, Mr. Latrobe," Judith answered. "We are most grateful for your scientific advice."

While the guests were engaged downstairs, Polly entered Richard's room. His face covered with perspiration, he lay unconscious on the bed. His breathing was uneasy. Polly stared at the pitcher of water beside the bed. Almost detached from the harsh reality of her own thoughts, she realized the old conjure woman would advise that this was the moment to give him the poison. Everyone in the household was occupied downstairs. The master was so ill that the effects of the poison would surely be blamed on his illness. The poison itself was hidden only a short distance away. Within one minute she could have it in her hand.

It was only the previous Sunday that the vial had been given to her. As soon as Polly had arrived among the field slaves, she was told that Jinna, the conjure woman, was seeking her. The old woman had handed her the vessel with the deadly liquid in it. She said it was the "medicine" she had recommended to free her friend's master of his misery. Although she did not want to take it, Polly did, out of fear of being the object of the old woman's wrath. She was certain that Jinna knew that her friend was merely a story. The commanding look on the conjure woman's face meant only one thing to Polly—poison Richard Randolph and free the slaves of Bizarre. She was terrified. Now they would expect her to do it, to commit murder. If she did not, she was a traitor to her fellow slaves. If she failed, someone else would do it. As she fled back to the plantation house, she wished she had never spoken to the old woman. In her entire life, she knew, it was one of the most foolish acts she had ever performed.

Polly wiped the perspiration from the face of the master. Then, without hesitation, she closed the door to the room behind her and returned downstairs. Within the hour Sally informed Judith that the master was awake and eager to greet their guest.

It was Judith who brought Latrobe into Richard's room. She stayed for only a moment, leaving the two men alone with each other. The sick man attempted to sit up in bed; he was too weak to do it alone. Latrobe assisted him. In spite of his illness, Richard appeared to be alert enough to understand Latrobe's description of his business. "Stay with us tonight," he suggested. "You can continue searching for your two friends when the weather clears." Richard spoke in such a hoarse, weak whisper that Latrobe had to bend forward to comprehend his words.

"I have to go out again before it gets dark. I lost a bundle from behind my saddle. It contained all my drawing materials and some clothes. Also my greatcoat . . ."

"No need to worry. I'll send one of the servants out to look for it." Richard summoned a young slave. In the boy's presence he told Latrobe to describe the route he took to Bizarre. As soon as Latrobe had recited his approach to the house, the young black declared confidently he would find what had been lost. "Now you can remain without any worry. We cannot have it said a visitor was turned away from our house in a deluge like this one." Latrobe accepted his defeat and agreed to stay until morning.

That evening Latrobe dined with the family. The sorrowful atmosphere he attributed to the illness of his host. Mrs. Randolph and Nancy were joined by a Mrs. Dudley, who was introduced as Mr. Randolph's cousin from North Carolina. She did most of the talking. After describing herself as "the daughter of the sister of Richard Randolph's mother," she prattled about various recipes for fevers. Her favorite was calomel, sassafras tea, and ten drops of laudanum, three times daily, with bleeding as necessary. "Richard is quite ill, you know. He could expire. I've seen it happen before in such cases."

Speaking without any visible sign of emotion, Judith's response appalled Latrobe. "If it please God to call him from this vale of tears, we must accept

His will." The abrupt sound of a chair sliding along the floor accompanied by the clatter of silverware on a plate followed immediately. Without a word Nancy Randolph departed the room.

Latrobe attempted to change the subject. "Why is this house named 'Bizarre'? I see nothing at all bizarre about it."

"That was the name of the house which formerly stood on this spot," Judith explained. She appeared to be undisturbed by her sister's sudden exit.

During the course of the meal, a servant girl brought in Mrs. Randolph's infant. She introduced him to the guest as her son, Tudor. She said not a word about any other children.

Before supper was completed, the slave who had been sent out in search of Latrobe's lost bundle returned in triumph. "Found 'em dis side o' Green Creek," he announced proudly. With great relief, Latrobe searched through his bag. Everything was slightly damp, but it was there. He profusely thanked the slave and Mrs. Randolph. She smiled demurely and declined his offer to reward the slave.

Although exhausted, Latrobe did not sleep well that night. When it was not thunder and lightning disturbing his sleep, it was the sound of people running up and down the stairs. He assumed the activity was due to servants and members of the family ministering to the sick man.

Early in the morning, Latrobe dressed and left his bedroom. The rain continued to fall in torrents. He walked into the parlor. Mrs. Randolph was in dirty clothes, her hair in disarray, scrubbing the carpet on her hands and knees. Startled, Latrobe pretended he did not see her. Intuitively he knew it was as improper to see the mistress of the house engaging in such menial tasks as it was to see her nude. He hurried on to another part of the house.

Nancy Randolph sat on the floor playing with the deaf child. As soon as Latrobe entered the room, the young woman turned around to greet him, an inviting smile on her face. The child was oblivious to their conversation. "How is Mr. Randolph this morning?" the guest inquired.

"He had a very bad night. His fever is worse. We've sent for the doctor."

Intrigued by the young woman, Latrobe attempted to learn more about her. She was evasive. He could determine little except that she was unmarried and had lived at Bizarre with her sister for five years. "Don't you feel isolated out here in the country? There are so few houses."

"I never knew the day could be so long. I fear I shall die of monotony." Coming from another, the response might have seemed petulant. In Nancy Randolph's seductive tones, it was redolent of opportunity.

Latrobe could not understand how a woman of such obvious charms tolerated so lonely an existence. "I hate work but always stay busy because I detest being bored even more." Aware that she was listening intently to his words, perhaps even displaying a hint of interest in him as a man, he was emboldened. "A young woman with your beauty must have a beau." She did not speak. "No doubt, your young man will rescue you from this life of tedium." Before she could respond, Mrs. Dudley sauntered into the room and usurped the conversation. The mood of growing intimacy was instantly shattered. Present only in body, Nancy withdrew completely from the discussion.

To his regret, Latrobe did not have another opportunity to speak to Nancy Randolph alone. The house bustled with servants, children, and Mrs. Dudley's incessant chatter. Shortly after Latrobe finished tuning the harpsichord—done at his own suggestion—the rain stopped. The family doctor arrived to examine Richard Randolph. In private, following his examination, he informed Latrobe that the prognosis was not good. The doctor had seen many similar cases of what he called "an inflammatory fever." Few, he whispered to Latrobe, survived. "Do not say anything to the family. One never knows. It could be something quite different from what I suspect."

After dining with the melancholy family once again, Latrobe thanked them for their hospitality under such difficult circumstances. Mrs. Randolph graciously thanked him for his company and assistance. Her sister remained quietly in the background. Early that afternoon, Latrobe set off along the muddy road back to Horsdumonde, where he hoped to find his elusive associates.

From an upstairs window Polly watched the lone horseman disappear behind a small hill. She was relieved. For her, the departure of the guest meant the passing of temptation. She had made up her mind. At the first opportunity, she intended to dispose of the vial.

"Give me the bedpan," Dr. Smith gruffly bellowed at Polly. Pulling it out from beneath the bed, she handed it to him. Like a priest studying the entrails of a sacrificial animal, he looked at it. Appearing to know what must be done, he handed it back to her.

The patient breathed with difficulty. The doctor held the arm hanging over the side of the bed and cut with his lancet. The blood ran freely into the bowl in his hand. Richard watched the red pool with interest. "You didn't cut deeply enough," he advised in a whisper.

"It is enough," the doctor replied gravely. "If I take more, it will diminish your strength too severely."

When he had completed the bleeding, the doctor held out his hand. Polly gave him a bowl with water. Wetting a cloth, he wiped perspiration from the patient's face and neck. Without looking at Polly, the doctor spoke to her. "Your mistress should be here doing this as often as possible."

"Missus Randolph don't like to be 'round sick people. But Miss Nancy and de servants are takin' care of it."

Dr. Smith placed his medicine and instruments back in his bag. "Ask your mistress to come here," he ordered. For a moment Polly was tempted to summon Nancy. Knowing it was no time to be literal, she sent Sally downstairs to fetch Judith.

The wife of the sick man stopped short of entering the room. The doctor handed her a note he had written. Polly overheard part of his directions. "Give your husband calomel and other purges. An emetic would be helpful.

Do you have tartar?" Upon receiving her affirmative response, he indicated that a half grain mixed with calomel would be sufficient. Together they walked down the stairs.

Within minutes after the doctor departed, Judith returned. She ordered Polly to call Miss Nancy from her room. Standing behind her mistress, Polly watched the face of Judith Randolph while she brusquely issued directions to her sister as if she were speaking to a servant. "I'm exhausted. I haven't slept for two days. Watch Dick tonight. Wake me only if you need me. Here are Dr. Smith's directions and a recipe for tartar emetic. The ingredients are on the table downstairs. Give him one dose tonight." Without another word she turned away, walked to her bedroom, and closed the door.

Polly followed her mistress down the stairs. For a few minutes she watched her struggling to mix the emetic. Nancy read the recipe carefully and studied the labels on the bottles in front of her. "This will take some time, Polly. Go upstairs and sit with Mr. Randolph."

The patient was asleep. For several minutes Polly watched him. In the flickering light she could see him trying to shift his body into a more comfortable position. His breathing was more labored than before. She struggled to keep the thought out of her brain. She could not empty her mind. His death, she knew, meant freedom for two hundred slaves. Perhaps the conjure woman was right. Why should she care about the life of one white man? Appalled and terrified by her own thoughts, she ran into Nancy's room. With a violent motion she opened the window. She entered the closet and frantically grasped for her bag, which was buried among the clothes on the floor. She felt the vial in her fingers. For a moment she closed her eyes and pressed it into the flesh of her hand. Then she stood up and walked resolutely to the window. There was nothing below except mud. Without hesitation she opened the vial and poured its contents out the window. After carefully placing the vial back in her bag, she returned to Richard's room. Picking up a wet cloth, she gently wiped his face. She wondered if she could have acted the same way if she were one of the persons to be freed.

Nancy soon entered the room with the tartar emetic. Polly assisted her in turning the patient on his back. He awoke. While staring into Nancy's face, which was only inches from his own, Richard drank the medicine she poured into his mouth. He whispered something in her ear. She told Polly to leave the room and close the door behind her. Within a few minutes Polly was summoned back into the room. He was asleep again. Nancy sent Polly to fetch her sewing. Deep into the night they both sat beside the bed. Nancy spoke not a word.

It was after two A.M. when he awoke again. He moaned for water. Nancy held the glass while he drank. Immediately after drinking, he vomited. Polly lunged to hold the bowl below his mouth. He gasped desperately for breath. Until he was finished, Nancy gently held her hand on the back of his neck. Then he slumped backward onto the pillow. "Send Judy in," he whispered between deep breaths.

Judith hurriedly entered the room. When Polly had awakened her, she was in the bed, fully clothed. As soon as her sister appeared, Nancy went back to her own room. Polly finished cleaning the floor and remained to fulfill the commands of the mistress of the house.

"I'm dying, Judy."

"No. You will get better." Her voice was choked with emotion. "Dr. Smith said—"

"Promise me you'll follow the will . . . as I've written it."

"I promise."

"Take care of the children, especially St. George. His life will be difficult." Judith began to weep. He placed his hand on her arm. "When I'm gone, don't let me be buried the first day."

"Yes," she managed to respond through her sobs.

Exhausted by his effort, he fell back into a fitful sleep. Judith returned to her room. Without regaining consciousness, Richard Randolph expired within two hours. When he stopped breathing, Polly was alone in the room with him. She held her hand to his lips. She knew he was without life. At the same time she began to weep, she wondered whether she should be happy for all of the others. It was premature. The widow, she knew, might choose to hide or destroy the will. Nobody would know. She resolved to protect herself. No matter what happened, she would say nothing about the will to any person.

The next morning Sally draped the room in white. Every mirror and picture was covered. The silence of mourning filled the house. The slaves were grief-stricken and filled with apprehension. They all knew their chief benefactor was no more. Their fate was now in the hands of his wife, a woman embittered by four long years of suffering.

Except for the five people sitting in the closed study, the house was empty. To avoid any chance of being overheard, Judith had assigned tasks, which were to be performed outside of the house, to each of the household servants. Sally and Polly were with the children. Mrs. Dudley and her children had returned to North Carolina. Nancy was gone for the afternoon—riding up toward Horsdumonde, she said. In spite of the hot summer weather, Judith had even closed the windows of the room so the voices could not be heard from outside the house.

Creed Taylor, their neighbor, had been invited as a close family friend. Taylor came with Richard's cousin, Brett Randolph. Over the years, Richard had relied on Taylor, a lawyer, for advice on problems relating to his property. Once again Taylor offered his condolences to the widow. "I will not repine," she replied. "He has gone out of a world of trouble to a place where there is no parting." The words were not uncommon to those who had been recently bereaved. But Judith's next words startled Taylor. "If I had no children, I too would gladly leave this world." He could think of no appropriate reply. Without attempting to respond, he sat on the sofa next to Brett Randolph.

Lost in thought, John Randolph sat alone on a chair away from the rest of the group. There were dark circles under his eyes. When word arrived of his brother's death, he was still in Petersburg, not yet completely recovered from his own illness. He had been distraught. Sleep, which had always been a problem for him, abandoned him completely. He spent most nights pacing the floor of his bedroom on the first floor or riding aimlessly through the moonlit countryside. On one of the few occasions when she was able to engage him in conversation, Judith had told him about the will. He said he knew about it; but he refused to read it.

Not as grief-stricken as John, St. George Tucker was still overcome with sorrow by the latest untimely death in the family. This time it was the favorite of his three stepsons from his first marriage. Like Creed Taylor, Brett Randolph, and his stepson John, Judge Tucker was about to hear Richard Randolph's will for the first time. All knew about its general provisions. Except for Judith, none had actually read it.

On the occasion of Judge Tucker's visit, Judith had asked them to hear it read. She knew their advice would be forthcoming. "Allow me, again, to thank you all for coming here. Richard would have wanted his will read aloud. I think he wrote it for that purpose. Would you do the honors, Mr. Taylor?" Judith's voice did not quaver. She revealed no sign of emotion.

Creed Taylor unfolded the document, cleared his voice, and began to read.

"To All whom it may concern, I, RICHARD RANDOLPH Jr., of 'Bizarre' in the County of Cumberland, of sound mind and memory, do declare this writing, written with my own hand and subscribed with my name this 18th day of February in the 20th year of American Independence, to be my last will and testament, in form and substance as follows:

"In the first place—to make retribution, as far as I am able to, to an unfortunate race of bondsmen, over whom my ancestors have usurped and exercised the most lawless and monstrous tyranny, and in whom my countrymen—by their iniquitous laws, in contradiction of their own declaration of rights, and in violation of every sacred law of nature; of the inherent, inalienable and imprescriptible rights of man, and of every principle of moral and political honesty have vested me with absolute property:

"To express my abhorrence of the theory as well as the infamous practice of usurping the rights of our fellow creatures, equally constituted with ourselves to the enjoyment of liberty and happiness—

"To exculpate myself to those who may perchance to think or hear of me after death, from the black crime, which might otherwise be imputed to me, of voluntarily holding the above mentioned miserable beings in the same state of abject slavery in which I found them on receiving my patrimony at lawful age; to impress my children with a just horror at a crime so enormous and indelible; to conjure them in the last words of a fond father never to participate in it in any the remotest degree, however sanctioned by laws (formed by the tyrants themselves who oppress them) or supported by false reasoning, used always to soil the sordid views of avarice and the lust of power:

"To declare to them and to the world that nothing but uncontrollable necessity forced on me by my father (who wrongfully bound over them to satisfy the rapacious creditors of a brother—and who for this purpose, which he falsely believed to be generous—mortgaged all his slaves to British harpies for money to gratify pride and pamper sensuality; by which mortgage the said slaves being bound, I could not exercise the right of ownership necessary to their emancipation, and being obliged to keep them on my lands, and so driven reluctantly to violate them in a general degree (tho I trust far less than others have done) in order to maintain them—that nothing, I say, short of necessity, should have forced me to an act which my soul abhors.

"For the aforesaid purposes and with an indignation too great for utterance at the tyrants of the earth, from the throned despot of a whole nation to the most despicable but not less infamous petty tormentors of single wretched slaves, whose torture constitutes his wealth and enjoyment, I do hereby declare that it is my will and desire, nay most anxious wish, that my negroes—all of them—be liberated and I do declare them by this writing free and emancipated to all intents and purposes whatsoever, fully and freely exonerated from all future service to my heirs, executors and assigns as far as the illiberal laws will permit them to be. I mean therein to include all and every servant of which I die possessed or to which I have any claim by inheritance or otherwise.

"I thus yield them up their liberty basely wrested from them by my forefathers and beg, humbly beg, their forgiveness for the manifold injuries I have too often inhumanely, unjustly and mercilessly inflicted on them, and I do further declare, and it is my will that if I should be so unfortunate as to die possessed of a slave (which I will not do if I ever can be enabled to emancipate them legally) and the said slave shall be liable for my fathers debts and to be sold for them, that in that case £500 be raised from my other estate, real and personal, as my wife shall think best, and in any manner which she shall choose, and applied to the purchase at such sale of such of the miserable slaves. I do hereby declare them free as soon as they are purchased, to all intents and purposes whatsoever, and in case I emancipate the said slaves—which I shall surely do the first moment possible—I do devise and give and bequeath unto them the said slaves four hundred acres of my land, to be laid off as my wife shall direct, and to be given to the heads of families in proportion to the number of their children and the merits of the parties, as my said wife shall judge of for the best. The lands to be laid off where and how my said wife shall direct and to be held by the said slaves when allotted to them in fee. I do likewise conjure my said wife to lend every assistance to the said slaves thro life in her power, and to rear her children up to the same practices, and impress it on them as her last injunction to do everything directed above relative to the said slaves.

"I now proceed to direct the manner in which my property is to be disposed of—having fulfilled this first and greatest duty, a most anxious and zealous wish to befriend the miserable and persecuted of whatsoever nation, color or degree by my will, as is seen written on this and another sheet of paper, each signed by my own hand and with my own name and connected together by wafers.

"Rd. Randolph, Junior."

Before beginning to read the second part of the will, Taylor apologized for his slow recitation. The handwriting, he stated, was difficult to read in some places. St. George Tucker and Judith Randolph listened impassively to the reading. Brett Randolph fidgeted with his pipe. John Randolph wiped tears away from his eyes. Taylor continued.

"In the second place I give and bequeath to my said wife all my real estate whatsoever, of which I die possessed and also all to which I have any claim or title whatsoever, to her and her heirs forever, in full confidence that she will do the most ample justice to our children—by making them independent as soon as they come of age, if she remain single, or by securing a comfortable support by settlements on them before any marriage into which she may hereafter resolve to enter (which if she do, money will be the only certain mode of providing for them), and to educate them as well as her opportunity will enable her.

"The only anxiety I feel on their account arises from a fear of her maternal tenderness leading her to too great indulgence of them, against which I beg leave thus to caution her.

"I now consign them to her affectionate love—desiring that they be educated in some profession, or trade, if they be incapable of a liberal profession, and that they be instructed in virtue and in the most zealous principles of liberty and manly independence. I dedicate them to that virtue and that liberty which I trust will protect every unfortunate and of which I conjure them to be indefatigable and incorruptible supporters thro life. I request my wife to frequently read this my last will to my beloved children that they may know something of their father's heart when they have forgotten his presence. Let them be virtuous and free—the rest is vain.

"Finally, I entreat my wife to consider the above confidence as the strongest proof of the estimation and ardent love which I have always uniformly felt for her, and which must be the latest active impulse of my heart.

"I hereby appoint my said wife sole Executrix of this my last will and testament but in case I should be so unfortunate as to be left by her a widower and die without any other will than this executed by me, I appoint in that case as my executors—requesting their attention to every injunction on my wife above mentioned, and relying on them to execute them and the directions in my said will (as she would otherwise do), to-wit: the following named esteemed friends: My father in law, St. Geo. Tucker, my brother, John Randolph, my friends Ryland Randolph, Brett Randolph, Creed Taylor, John Thompson, Alex. Campbell, Daniel Call and the most virtuous and incorruptible of mankind and (next to my father in law) my greatest benefactor, George Wythe, Chancellor of Virginia, the brightest ornament of Nature, and I rely on the aforementioned virtuous friends for the punctual execution of my will, and to the care and guardianship of my children, in case of the death of my wife either before or after me (to whom if she live I have entrusted them solely) and to those of them most nearly connected with me by friendship I look for assistance to my family after my death. If any among them do not choose to undertake the task imposed on them by me, I beg them not to do so from motives of generosity or delicacy, and to excuse the liberty which (it may appear to them least intimately acquainted with me) I have taken in thus calling on them.

"In witness of all the above directions which I again declare to be my last will and testament drawn by me from calm reflection, I have hereunto subscribed my name and affixed my seal the day and year aforesaid.

"(signed) R'd. Randolph Jun'r."

"There is only one witness to the will—Ryland Randolph," Creed Taylor added. "I am told he plans to leave Virginia soon. If he is not available when the will is probated, additional witnesses will be required to identify Richard's handwriting."

After Taylor ceased speaking, it was completely silent for several moments. Finally, Brett Randolph shattered the stillness of the room. "Why did Richard decide to write this last February? Did he know he was ill four months ago?"

"He told me," Judith replied, "he wanted to write it before he received news of the decision in the British Debts case. He did not want an adverse decision by the court to weaken his resolve to free the slaves."

"I spoke to him about the will after *Ware versus Hylton* was decided," St. George Tucker interjected. "Although I think it should have, the case did not alter his mind on the subject of manumission. It will be difficult to free two hundred slaves without bringing this house into financial ruin. Not only the considerable value of the slaves will be lost. The crops will be left untended. Future profits will be lost. How will the debt be paid?"

"You speak as though I have some choice in the matter," Judith said. "The will is clear. It requires freeing his slaves."

"There is almost always flexibility in the law. The laws on manumission and inheritance of slaves are particularly ambiguous." Judge Tucker pulled a page of notes from his pocket. "Under amended Chapter 189, effective the first of this year, a widow has one year from the death of her husband to declare she will not accept the provisions made for her by the husband's will. According to the latest version of the statute, she can make the declaration and claim a one-third portion of the slaves possessed by her husband, including those freed under his will. She would hold the slaves during her lifetime. Unfortunately, the widow must renounce all benefit under the will to obtain the one-third share. It is something to consider. You have a year to think about it."

"What if I make no declaration within the year?"

Creed Taylor responded to Judith's inquiry. "In that case, you would be bound by the terms of this will."

"There is another statute giving you additional time," Tucker added. "An old 1730 act is designed to remove any doubts about slaves finishing work on crops growing between March first and December twenty-fifth. By law, the slaves of the deceased working on his plantation must continue to work until the following Christmas. The act itself is of little importance. It simply reflects the custom observed by executors and administrators of estates. I refer to it merely to show you that there is time to decide."

"There is another problem Mrs. Randolph should consider," Creed Taylor stated. "Some of the household servants are your own property, are they not?"

"Yes," she answered. "Why, are they a problem?"

"Under the present laws, the slaves are personal property. When a woman marries, her personal property, including the clothes on her back, belongs to her husband. Therefore, your own servants would be freed under the terms of your husband's will. Correct me if I am mistaken, Judge."

Judith looked stunned. "Richard's will frees my own servants? He did not intend to do that; I am sure of it."

"The law is not entirely clear on this point," Judge Tucker stated. "It all turns on whether slaves are real or personal property. We have had several cases touching on this issue recently. The original Act of 1705 declared slaves to be real estate. The law on this subject was formerly all statutory, as slaves were unknown to the common law. The purpose of the 1705 act was to protect owners and heirs in settling and preserving estates. It was especially important in protecting a widow's dower rights. In 1748 there was an attempt to revise these laws. One of the amendments, which attempted to treat slaves as chattels instead of real estate, was disallowed by the crown. Another part of the revision did receive the royal assent; it contained general rules on chattels which were intended to apply to slaves but did not because of the disallowance of the other acts. Since then, the law has been thoroughly confused, at least until four years ago. At that time, in 1792, slaves were again declared to be personal property. We, of course, no longer required the royal assent. Unfortunately, two years ago, a new statute muddied the waters again by treating slaves as a kind of special asset with characteristics of both personal and real estate."

Judith appeared to be both distressed and thoroughly confused. "What does all of this mean for my own servants?"

Tucker responded in his most professorial manner. "Permit me to attempt to clarify this matter. There has been no judicial interpretation of many of these laws, so what I say is not certain. However, I believe the law is this: For the most part, slaves are to be treated as personal property. As a result of marriage, a wife's personal property belongs to her husband. Therefore, your servants would appear to belong to Richard and be manumitted by his will. Also, for purposes of the one-third portion the wife receives if she renounces the will of the husband, the freed slaves would be treated as chattels. This means you would have for your use during your lifetime the one-third portion of the slaves, but you could be deprived of them by creditors."

Brett Randolph was horrified. "I am not well-acquainted with all of this legal jargon. But you seem to be saying no matter what Judy does, she will be destroyed by creditors. If she accepts the will, the slaves will go free, the plantation will fall into ruin, and the creditors will take everything to pay the debts. If she renounces the will, she gets one-third of the slaves during her lifetime, but the creditors can take them in any case. It all seems incredibly unfair. At least if the will is followed, Richard's last wishes are fulfilled by the freeing of the slaves."

"I do not wish to be the bearer of more grim tidings," said Judge Tucker, "but even emancipated slaves are not safe from creditors. Under the 1792 act, if other property of a debtor is not available, a creditor can seize emancipated slaves even if they were freed for many years. The purpose of the statute is obviously to discourage manumission designed to defeat the rights of creditors. But there is no need to be excessively gloomy. The law is inclined to assist a widow, especially one in debt. Courts often dismiss the deathbed wishes of a testator to free his slaves as the product of a confused mind."

The loud, indignant tone of John Randolph's shrill voice startled everyone. "My brother was not on his deathbed when he wrote that document and it is not the product of a confused mind!" Although Judge Tucker was angry at the disrespectful nature of the comment, he said nothing. The room was completely silent. John opened one of the windows to let air into the oppressively hot room. After a moment he closed the window with a loud bang. When all eyes were on him, he spoke. "It is not quite as hopeless as you all make it sound. My brother wanted to emancipate his slaves; he believed it could be done without blighting the future of his family. So do I. First, under that abomination, the Jay Treaty, the debt question is to be subject to arbitration. Before *Ware versus Hylton*, the provision was to the favor of the British. Now it is to our advantage, since it is likely the creditors will not be able to collect for years. We have more time. Perhaps, if the Federalists lose the election this year, a republican government will be wise enough to join the French in the war against Britain. That would postpone payment of the debts indefinitely. Second, Richard spoke to me in some detail about our debts. John Marshall and Alexander Campbell informed him that John Wickham could arrange a reasonable settlement with our creditors. Wickham, you remember, was one of the counsel for the creditors in the original debt arguments. Marshall is a close friend of Wickham; his advice should be reliable. Third, I have far too many slaves at Roanoke. I can move more than one hundred here. Added to my slaves already here and those who choose to stay, we will have enough to maintain Bizarre as a profitable enterprise. Essex, Hetty, Nan, and Polly, Nancy's servant, will provide the core of a fine household staff. If I purchase additional slaves, Roanoke can also remain solvent. It's time that some of the land be allowed to remain fallow. It will accrue to our benefit for future crops. Finally, selecting the four hundred acres to be given to the slaves under the will should present no serious problem. The financial health of this plantation would probably improve with the loss of some carefully selected plots. Those who cannot subsist on the land we give them may come back to work for us. It may even be cheaper to pay them a wage, or a share of the crop, than to maintain them as slaves. Some of our northern 'friends' have been telling us that for years. Let us put their theories to the test. Whatever may happen, it is my intention to assure that my brother's last wishes are respected. I'll be damned before I permit British creditors to steal back the freedom we won at such great cost in the late war."

Creed Taylor nodded his approval. "Jack, have you ever considered becoming a politician?"

The many words of praise spoken that day had failed to move him. It was the sound of dirt striking the coffin that finally caused tears to appear in John Marshall's eyes. Campbell had always said that at funerals the living mourned more for themselves than for the dead. On a number of occasions he had even denounced the rituals surrounding death as primitive and useless. Marshall did not agree. For generations men had found the ceremony of mourning to be an appropriate method for the purgation of the emotions after the passing of another human being. How could one person, whose experience was limited to a single lifetime, contend with the collective wisdom of mankind developed over countless generations?

Many prominent members of the Richmond bar stood in silence in the stifling July humidity. They watched the gravediggers cover over the final resting place of one of the best known of their fellowship.

Once again John Marshall found himself asking the unanswerable question: Why did Alexander Campbell kill himself? There were many possible answers. For some years, it was well-known, his health had been deteriorating. Both of his marriages had been unhappy. His daughter was troublesome in the extreme. But those problems afflicted him last year and the year before. Why now? Certainly he had been disturbed by the loss of the British Debts case four months earlier. He had resigned his position as United States Attorney for Virginia. Marshall's mind turned to his own possible contribution to Campbell's mounting miseries. In April they had been on opposite sides in the debate on the approval of the Jay Treaty.

The gathering in Richmond had been one of the largest of its kind Marshall had even seen—almost four hundred persons present. The debate had lasted all day. Campbell represented the popular Republican position in favor of the House of Representatives' opposition to the much hated Jay Treaty. He had attempted to heap ridicule on his opponent, John Marshall, for supporting a treaty so contrary to the interests of Virginians—debt questions to be arbitrated by a committee that could have a majority of British members on it, failure to obtain the return of slaves taken by the British during the war, the absence of provisions addressing the continuing impressment of American seamen. Marshall's argument had rested on legalistic grounds, the constitutional power of the Senate to ratify treaties. Nevertheless, representing the immensely unpopular Federalist position, Marshall somehow had managed to rally support for the Senate's and President Washington's approval of the treaty. In the end, the gathering adopted a resolution stating that the welfare and honor of the United States depended upon giving "full effect to the treaty lately negotiated with Great Britain." Crestfallen at failing to gain what appeared to be a certain victory, Campbell had left the meeting in a state of bitter disbelief. In the midst of his triumph, Marshall had felt sorry for his humiliated opponent.

Since the debate, three months had passed. In the interim, Marshall had seen Campbell in good spirits on several different occasions. Had some event in his private life intervened? Marshall knew that Campbell had been disturbed the previous month at the news of the unexpected death of Richard Randolph. Since Randolph's acquittal on the murder charge, Campbell and Randolph had become close friends; yet surely they were not so familiar with each other as to plunge Campbell into despair at young Randolph's demise. Marshall's mind was agitated. He attempted to recall his most recent meetings with Campbell. Did he reveal a clue? Marshall could not recall any signs of danger. There appeared to be no simple answer.

Marshall's thoughts turned to his own problems. The death of Campbell had impaired his own perilous financial condition. The cause was the Fairfax Land case. Marshall's client of many years, Robert Morris, had persuaded him and his brother James, who had since married Morris's daughter, to purchase the remainder of the Fairfax estate, over 160,000 acres of the most fertile land in Virginia. Morris was supposed to advance the money. As part of the arrangement, Morris sent James Marshall to Europe to negotiate loans. John feared the loans would not be forthcoming. As Morris's lawyer, he knew that the old speculator was in grave danger of sliding into financial ruin. Part of the problem in raising the money was the fact that the title to the Fairfax estate had been in litigation for years. The Marshall syndicate's title to the land was clouded by confiscatory laws passed during the war, which both the 1783 treaty of peace and the Jay Treaty had nullified. Marshall was relying on the United States Supreme Court to remove the cloud on the Fairfax title in the case of *Hunter v. Fairfax, Devisee*. Representing the defendant, Marshall was desperate to get the case advanced on the court calendar and decided in his favor. He had already failed once. Finally the case had been scheduled for the fall term of 1796. Unfortunately, Alexander Campbell was the attorney for the plaintiff. Unless Marshall could obtain a substitute attorney for the opposition, the case would undoubtedly be continued for another term, perhaps to the financial ruin of John Marshall and his brother.

Standing beside Marshall at the side of the grave was John Wickham, the most sought-after member of the Richmond bar, after Marshall himself. Eight years Marshall's junior, Wickham was a close friend, although they were often adversaries in the courtroom. Wickham had, in fact, been one of the chief attorneys for the creditors in the British debt cases.

While watching the dirt cover the coffin, he whispered to Marshall, "I hope there is no plan to place a grave stone."

"Why do you say that?"

"It's in his will. He wrote, 'I hope no tombstone will be raised over me, because it will merely hinder something from growing on the spot.' Then he declared, 'If all men had tombstones erected over their graves, the earth in a few centuries would be one entire pavement,' or words to that effect. I think he would have preferred never to have been born."

"Eccentric even in death," Marshall muttered.

Wickham blew his nose into his handkerchief. As if afraid of having his action mistaken for a sign of grief, he explained he had caught a cold from his wife Mary. "Sorry to have to tell you, John. I will not be able to go to Philadelphia on the Fairfax case. You'll have to find someone else to replace Campbell. The case is so complicated, I would expect any new attorney to request a postponement until next year. It can't be helped." The gravediggers smoothed the dirt over the grave. Wickham changed the subject. "The cares of the world must have accumulated for him until they were too heavy to bear. What was the last stone that made the burden intolerable? Who would have thought he would do such a thing? It is so unlike the man. I always considered him to be a stoic. I'd pay a considerable sum to learn what was in his mind when he drank that dose of laudanum."

The slaves of Bizarre knew that Richard Randolph was an unusually generous master. On none of the neighboring plantations did the slaves receive weekly rations, clothing, or other benefits comparable to those provided the bondsmen of Bizarre. Passes for visiting other plantations were generously granted.

When it was raining heavily, outdoor labor almost always ceased. Whipping had disappeared. Yet of all the favorable conditions on the plantation, one was more cherished than all the others. That was the custom of ceasing all work, except for essential tasks, for the entire period from Christmas through New Year's day. The harshest masters in the county allowed a two-day period of rest; the most generous gave six. For years Richard Randolph had permitted his slaves to rest for more than eight full days, a luxury previously unheard of on the large Cumberland County estates. It was a period of recreation that seemed almost to redeem the dreary toil of the year and make tolerable the thought of another long year of drudgery. The field hands did cease work each Saturday at noon and rest until Monday morning. They also received Easter, Whitsuntide, and the Fourth of July as special holidays, with extra food, drink, and privileges. But the eight full days beginning with Christmas, with half the day before, was the jewel of their existence.

At the end of 1796, as Christmas approached, there was increasing trepidation as to whether the treasured custom would be continued. No word had been received from the big house; and since Richard Randolph's death, there had been portents of danger. In the six months after the master's passing, Judith Randolph had proved to be much more demanding than her husband. On several Saturdays the field workers had been kept at their labors well past noon. Worse, the mistress had authorized the whipping of a boy, younger than eighteen years, who was caught in the act of stealing a pig. In the past the master had reprimanded those caught stealing. In one case he had even penalized the culprit by assigning him to unpleasant tasks for two weeks. But a whipping would never have been approved. Now, with the coming of the holiday season, there were serious doubts about whether the sacred Christmas holiday itself would be violated. Nevertheless, preparations continued in the customary manner. Party clothes were cleaned and set aside. Lace and beads were stolen from the big house. Food was saved. When the customary end-of-the-year supplies were delivered from the mistress of the house—extra flour for baking, ample supplies of beef, and barrels of hard cider—sighs of relief filled the quarter. It appeared that the Christmas celebrations would proceed in the usual manner.

As she always did, Nancy permitted Polly to select a party dress and beads for the Christmas-season dances in the barn. "I never use them anymore; take anything you want," her mistress told her. Polly needed no encouragement. She quickly grabbed the white gown that had been her mistress's favorite. Nancy frowned at her. When Polly withdrew her hand from the gown, Nancy smiled. "I ain't goin' to let my Polly be outshine by dem other ladies." As she always did when Nancy spoke in slave dialect, Polly laughed at her mistress's skill in mimicry, which could be used to imitate anyone from old Daddy Syphax to garrulous Mrs. Dudley. Nancy placed the white gown in Polly's arms. "Anythin' else you be needin', jus' aks me." Polly forced another smile. She thought her mistress was overdoing it. Beneath the mimicry, she began to sense a bitter mockery which she did not like.

When Sally saw what her friend would be wearing, she resolved to take Judith's red gown and wear it at the dances. "She ain't gonna see it," she assured Polly. "She don't never come to de dance." At the first opportunity, Sally tied the gown around her leg and slipped it out of the house underneath her skirt.

There were no signs of change from past years. Husbands and fathers who belonged to other plantations visited Bizarre for the length of time permitted by their passes. The tables were filled; but the usual bacon and cornmeal were not to be seen. In their place were roast pig, chicken, baked yams, plum pudding, cake, and many other delights. Dressed in their holiday best, the celebrants assembled in the candlelit barn to commence the festivities. The women each wore something red—a red handkerchief about the head, a ribbon or a string tied to the hair. As soon as Sally appeared in her red gown, she became the center of attention, at least until the dancing began. The banjoman and the fiddler provided the music. To the stamping of feet and clapping of hands, innumerable variations on the cakewalk were performed. The field hands acted out the motions of their work—hoeing corn, planting tobacco, swinging a scythe—with a joy they never experienced during the actual labor. Sally, Polly, and the other household servants present performed their own unique steps—washing the floor, dusting the furniture, making the soap. Within a short time the winter cold outside was forgotten. The mass and movement of bodies more effectively heated the barn than a large bonfire.

The children were permitted to join the early dances which were their favorites, especially "Cuttin' the Chicken Wings," in which they flapped their arms, held their necks stiff, and scratched the ground like chickens. For the more difficult dances, the little ones stood on the side watching their older brothers, sisters, and parents dance; they would be sent off to bed before the serious flirting began. When the singing commenced, the children joined their elders:

"All de ladies goin' to de ball?
Don't go Sadday night
You can't go at all
Hog eye, hum um
Hog eye, hum um.
All de gen'mens goin' to de ball?
Don't go Sadday night
You can't go at all
Hog eye, hum um.
All de steppers goin' to de ball?
Don't go Sadday night
You can't go at all
Hog eye, hum um
Hog eye hum um."

The mood and jubilee beating quickened as the evening continued. "Sugar in a Gourd" was danced repeatedly. As more cider and rum were consumed, the songs became more daring.

"We raise de wheat,
Dey gib us de corn;
We bake de bread,
Dey gib us de crust;
We sif' de meal,
Dey gib us de huss;
We peel de meat,
Dey gib us de skin;
And dat's de way
Dey take us in;
We skim de pot,
Dey gib us de likker;
And say dat's good enough for nigger.
Walk over! Walk over!
Your butter and de fat;
Poor nigger, you can't get over dat!
Walk over! Walk over!"

Forced into a small space in the center of the barn by the huge crowd which filled every available space on the floor, couples danced "Settin' de Flo." Each pair performed in turn. Sally faced her partner, one of many young men seeking her favors. He bowed and they scuffed their feet along the floor. Smoothly, they switched partners. All of the dancers strutted around in a circle, clapping and shouting exuberantly as they moved. Polly drank enough cider so that she was even able to dance with her old beau Cuffee without feeling the bitterness of the past. He showed no interest in resurrecting the passion of days long passed.

In the midst of the celebration an event without precedent occurred. The dance came to a sudden halt. John, Judith, and Nancy Randolph entered the barn. They were accompanied by those remaining household servants who had always refused to mingle with the field hands. Immediately, a mood of apprehension dampened the spirits of the throng. Many prepared for dreadful news—the sale of the plantation, the tearing asunder of families, travel in coffles, bound in chains, to distant cotton plantations with brutal overseers. The unspoken terrors of many sleepless nights hung over the evening like the sword of Damocles.

Sally attempted to step behind a group of tall men. It was too late. She saw the mistress of the house staring at the purloined red gown. To Sally's surprise, Mrs. Randolph did not appear to be angry. She seemed lost in thought.

The question had been discussed for months. Judge Tucker advised against it. But John Randolph wanted the last wishes of his brother fulfilled. To

Tucker's surprise, Judith took the side of her brother-in-law. A tentative agreement with the creditors who held the mortgages on the Randolph estates, negotiated by the creditors' attorney, John Wickham, had settled the matter. Under the new arrangement, less than the total debt would have to be paid, and the payment would extend over a period of decades. The burden was heavy but endurable. The threat of financial ruin had been removed.

The news that St. George Tucker's proposal for gradual emancipation had been rebuffed by the House of Delegates in early December only strengthened John Randolph's resolve. On November 30 the judge had written the Speaker of the House: "Surely, the representatives of a free people cannot disapprove an attempt to carry so incontestable a moral truth into practical effect." Copies of his complete plan were provided the legislature. Within less than one week the proposal was tabled. Many legislators were shocked at the effrontery of a judge who would make such a radical proposal. Few bothered to read it. John was intent on demonstrating how extreme his family could be.

It was Judith who decided to make the announcement at the beginning of the Christmas holidays. The servants, she told John, would be useless for days after they learned about their freedom. "If we tell them at Christmas, they can use their own eight days to celebrate and think about their choices. We cannot afford to lose too many days of labor after the first of the year."

John Randolph waited until there was complete silence. He had already informed his own slaves that what was going to be announced did not apply to them. Essex and Hetty had anticipated news of the sale of Bizarre and all of its slaves.

"You know my brother loved you." His voice was filled with emotion. "Before he died, he wrote a piece of paper, a last will and testament, declaring the disposition of all of his property including you." He waved the paper in his hand. "When this paper is approved by the District Court, probably some time in the spring, you will all be free."

A murmur of stunned disbelief ran through the assembled slaves. A few screamed with joy. The cautious majority was silent. They did not know what it all meant for their lives. There were some mumbles of concern. "Where will we live? How will we eat?" A confused buzz filled the barn. John Randolph raised his hand to call for silence.

"You all will be as free as white people. You will be able to go, if you want, or stay here. Whoever decides to stay will be paid for working. The position of servants who leave will be filled by others from my own Roanoke plantation. Bizarre will continue to prosper. Four hundred acres down by Israel Hill is to be given to the heads of families. Those with more mouths to feed will be given more land. The property will be yours to live on or sell, as you wish. You are to be your own masters."

The mention of land dispelled the fear of the assemblage. There were some excited shouts of jubilation. "Hallelujah!" Fearful of insulting their white masters, most showed no emotion. Some even wore masks of sorrow.

"Remember, you are not free until you receive your emancipation papers. That will not be until after spring planting. Think about your future. We will have to know who is leaving and who is staying on. And, remember my brother. It is to him you owe your freedom. Enjoy your holiday."

Judith then stepped into the center of the crowded barn. "Let us give thinks to God for all the bounties He has bestowed upon us." She bowed her head. Most of the slaves did the same. Without another word, she departed followed by John and Nancy. The household slaves remained.

As soon as the whites had gone, pandemonium erupted. People yelled, cried, and embraced. "Chain done broke at last!" was the triumphant shout of many. Men extended the right hand of fellowship. "Bless de Lord. De day of jubilee done come!"

Polly hugged Sally, who looked utterly bewildered. "You is free, Sally. You can go where you want, like a white woman."

"You is free too," she exclaimed.

"No, I ain't. I belong to Miss Nancy, not Marster Randolph." As she spoke, Polly saw the old conjure woman approaching her.

For weeks after Richard Randolph's death, Polly had stayed away from the field slaves. Finally, out of sheer boredom, she had attended the dance one Saturday night in August. Within minutes of her arrival, old Jinna had summoned her. "Your friend done used my mixture?" Polly did not deny it. "Yes," she said. "At de right time, she empty de vial." The old woman had stared into her eyes. "Why," she asked, "ain't de slaves free?" Polly had shrugged. "My friend don't know."

Once again the conjure woman was upon her. Polly said nothing. Jinna's eyes twinkled. There was a great smile on the crone's face. She squeezed Polly's hand. "You done a great blessin'! You done freed your people." Tears ran down the cheeks of the nineteen-year-old. She began to sob. Without speaking a word, she ran out of the barn.

The celebration intensified. The dancing recommenced. It was more frenzied than anyone had ever seen it. The dancers leaped and twisted themselves into every conceivable shape. Whiskey and rum were freely passed around. The fiddler sang jubilantly:

"Guinea Creek and roarin' ribber
Thar, my dear, we'll live forebber;
Den we'll go to de Injun nation,
All I want in dis creation,
Is pretty little wife and big plantation."

Everyone knew the song well. All joined in for the chorus.

"Up dat oak and down dat ribber,
Two overseers and one little nigger."

When the song was over, the banjoman began a juba beating, rhythmically striking a sheep's rib on a hollow gourd. The song he sang was not as familiar as the other:

"Oh freedom, Oh freedom;
Oh Lord, freedom over me,
And before I'd be a slave
I'll be buried in my grave
An' go home to my God and be free."

1799

In years of observing the performances of men in the legal and political arenas, John Randolph admired few more than John Marshall and Patrick Henry. They had been magnificent defenders of his own family against both creditors and slanderers. Now, John found it difficult to believe that he himself would be entering that public arena to oppose them. They had joined the ranks of the political enemy—the anti-French, national government party.

Only a few years earlier he had told Creed Taylor, "I exist in an obscurity from which I shall never emerge." Often, he had dreamed about joining the political fray, never thinking it would actually come to pass. It was a mere fancy, like Nancy Randolph, which he toyed with in his mind in the absence of any hope of the dream becoming reality. In the past year, however, events had taken a strange turn. The American supporters of the French Revolution were suddenly fighting for their political lives. The fever of war had descended upon the land. Those who favored the French were denounced as traitors, and "Jacobins." The French Revolution was no longer in fashion.

It had been Abraham Venable, a member of the House of Representatives for five years, and Creed Taylor, in his first year as a State Senator, who suggested John Randolph run for Congress. At first he resisted the idea. "I cannot rationally entertain the smallest pretensions to public office," he had replied. Taylor persisted, and even St. George Tucker wrote to encourage his candidacy. "Government," Tucker said, "is like a seedling oak that has just burst the acorn and appears above the surface of the earth with first leaves; it advances with civilization and puts forth innumerable branches until it covers the earth and is finally regarded as king of the forest." It was always difficult for John to resist his stepfather, particularly when they were in agreement. His financial position was sound. With the assistance of John Wickham, the agent for his British creditors, John had accepted a compromise arrangement providing for long-term payments on his own British debts. His estates were saved. John finally acquiesced. He was to be a Republican candidate for Congress for the district of Charlotte, Prince Edward, Buckingham, and Cumberland counties. Now, only weeks into the new year, Taylor presented an even more startling proposal. He advised that John Randolph be the one to answer the speech of Patrick Henry to be made at the Charlotte Court House on March county court day.

The bizarre turn of events, which drew Marshall, Henry, and finally John

Randolph into the campaign, had begun with John Marshall's involvement in the purchase of the Fairfax lands. Until his Fairfax debts had threatened to overwhelm him, Marshall had repeatedly declined low-paying posts in the Federalist-controlled national government. His debts, he thought, were to be paid and his fortune made in the private practice of law. Then, President John Adams, in only the third month of his new administration, had offered him a remunerative position which was difficult to refuse—one member of a three-man commission to obtain a revised treaty of friendship and commerce with France. With his client and benefactor Robert Morris personally bankrupt and facing debtors' prison, and his Fairfax debts suspended menacingly over his own head, John Marshall accepted the post. It was a lucrative position; in the end, he would receive $20,000 for one year of service plus $5000 for expenses. St. George Tucker himself had attended the farewell dinner for Marshall. Although he disapproved of Marshall's support for the Jay Treaty, Judge Tucker thought Marshall to be an excellent choice for the preservation of pacific relations with France, which, partly as a result of hostility to the treaty, had begun attacking American ships.

Marshall left his cases to be handled by John Wickham and set off for France in the summer of 1797. Within a year the events that followed in Paris would shake the foundations of American politics. These occurrences became known when President Adams released the infamous XYZ correspondence in the spring of 1798 to howls of national outrage. The story is too well-known to repeat in any detail. The three American envoys, Charles C. Pinckney, Elbridge Gerry, and John Marshall, were met in Paris by the alleged agents of Foreign Minister Talleyrand. Described in the American dispatches as X, Y, and Z, the agents demanded a substantial bribe of fifty thousand pounds, and a large loan to France, as a prerequisite to negotiations. The American envoys had refused the insulting conditions. Marshall, in particular, led the opposition to engaging in a corrupt bargain with Talleyrand and the Directory. When he returned home, Marshall was amazed to find that he had become a national hero. His reception in Philadelphia was tumultuous. In the midst of an un-declared naval war with France, he had become the symbol of American virtue and patriotism standing against old-world corruption and cynicism. The twenty-year alliance with France was terminated. In spite of the fact that the British continued to impress American seamen into their navy, the black cockade of Federalism replaced the formerly popular tricolor of the French Revolution on the streets of American cities and towns.

The Federalists took advantage of the anti-French hysteria by passing leg-islation that would be the focal point of the upcoming election. A series of Alien laws aimed at pro-French immigrants extended the waiting period for naturalization from five years to fourteen, authorized the detention of subjects of enemy nations, and permitted the President to expel any aliens he consid-ered to be "dangerous." Adopted shortly after publication of the XYZ dis-patches, the Alien Acts were followed by Sedition laws which made it a crime to write, print, publish, or utter falsely or maliciously against the government or to incite opposition to the President or any act of Congress. The penalties were harsh, a fine not to exceed $2000 and imprisonment not exceeding two years.

The Republicans were outraged at what they considered to be a blatant transgression of the limits of congressional authority and the rights of free speech and press. In November of 1798 the State of Kentucky adopted Republican-sponsored resolutions condemning the Alien and Sedition acts. The resolutions stated that the Constitution is merely a compact among the sovereign states and that every state has an equal right to judge for itself when the national government has exceeded its powers. The rumors were that Thomas Jefferson himself was the draftsman. Shortly thereafter, the Virginia legislature adopted resolutions that asserted the right of a state to interpose its authority for the protection of its citizens against unconstitutional actions by the national government. In short, Virginia and Kentucky claimed that they possessed the lawful authority to decide which federal laws could be enforced within their borders.

Only one month after his triumphant return to Richmond, John Marshall was asked by General Washington to stand for election to the Sixth Congress as the Federalist candidate opposing Congressman John Clopton, an ardent supporter of Thomas Jefferson. The Federalist strategy was to persuade the strongest possible candidates to run in order to assure a majority in both Congress and state government. Although the Federalists held only four of the nineteen congressional seats in Virginia, many believed that the anti-French reaction to the XYZ dispatches could bring in a Federalist majority in 1799.

John Marshall was the only Federalist candidate who refused to support the Alien and Sedition acts. If he had been a member of Congress, he stated, he would have opposed the acts, not for constitutional reasons but because they were "useless." Despite his opposition to the unpopular legislation, within days of the announcement of his candidacy, scurrilous rumors were being spread about him in Richmond. Marshall, it was said, had fathered an illegitimate child while in Paris; Patrick Henry, it was whispered, opposed him. To protect himself from altercations in the press, Marshall decided to avoid making statements to the newspapers. The rumors continued. They soon reached Patrick Henry.

The same tide that swept Marshall into politics in the fall of 1798 brought back the long-retired and infirm Patrick Henry in early 1799. Like Marshall, Henry had for many years refused invitations to return to politics. Elected Governor of Virginia in 1796, he had refused to serve. That same year he had rebuffed suggestions from John Marshall that he become the Federalist candidate to succeed George Washington as President of the United States. But three years later even Patrick Henry could not resist the political storm battering the nation.

Aware of the great weight Patrick Henry's opinions still carried, friends of Marshall's opponent, John Clopton, continued to spread the rumor that Henry favored Clopton over Marshall. According to the stories, Henry, the enemy of aristocracy, opposed Marshall because he was a Federalist, the party of the aristocrats. By letter, Archibald Blair, the Clerk of the Executive Council, informed Henry of the rumors and the recent resolutions of the Virginia legislature concerning the right of the state to interpose between its citizens and the unconstitutional actions of the national government.

On January 8, 1799, Henry penned a letter that would be frequently used during the upcoming election for Congress. The original was so widely passed from hand to hand, it would be in tatters before the election was over.

RED HILL, CHARLOTTE, 8 January, 1799.

Dear Sir: Your favor of the 28th of last month I have received. Its contents are a fresh proof that there is cause for lamentation over the present state of things in Virginia. It is possible that most of the individuals who compose the contending factions are sincere and act from honest motives. But it is more than probable that certain leaders meditate a change in government. To effect this, I see no way so practicable as dissolving the confederacy. And I am free to own, that in my judgment most of the measures, lately pursued by the opposition party, directly and certainly lead to that end. If this is not the system of the party they have none and act *ex tempore*.

I do acknowledge that I am not capable to form a correct judgment on the present politics of the world. The wide extent to which the present contentions have gone will scarcely permit any observer to see enough in detail, to enable him to form any thing like a tolerable judgment on the final result, as it may respect the nations in general. But, as to France, I have no doubt in saying, that to her it will be calamitous. Her conduct has made it the interest of the great family of mankind to wish the downfall of her present government, because its existence is incompatible with that of all others within its reach. And, whilst I see the dangers that threaten ours from her intrigues and her arms, I am not so much alarmed as at the apprehension of her destroying the great pillars of all government and of social life; I mean virtue, morality, and religion. This is the armor, my friend, and this alone, that renders us invincible. These are the tactics we should study. If we lose these, we are conquered, fallen indeed. In vain may France show and vaunt her diplomatic skill, and brave troops; so long as our manners and principles remain sound, there is no danger. But believing as I do that these are in danger, that infidelity in its broadest sense, under the name of philosophy, is fast spreading, and that under the patronage of French manners and principles, everything that ought to be dear to man is covertly but successfully assailed, I feel the value of those men amongst us who hold out to the world the idea that our continent is to exhibit an originality of character; and that instead of that imitation and inferiority, which the countries of the old world have been in the habit of exacting from the new, we shall maintain that high ground upon which nature has placed us, and that Europe will alike cease to rule us and give us modes of thinking.

But I must stop short, or else this letter will be all preface. These prefatory remarks, however, I thought proper to make, as they point out the kind of character amongst our country men most estimable in my eyes.

General Marshall and his colleagues exhibited the American character as respectable. France, in the period of her most triumphant fortune, beheld them as unappalled.

Her threats left them as she found them, mild, temperate, firm. Can it be thought that with these sentiments I should utter anything tending to prejudice General Marshall's election? Very far from it indeed. Independently of the high gratification I felt from his public ministry, he ever stood high in my esteem as a private citizen. His temper and disposition were always pleasant, his talents and integrity unquestioned. These things are sufficient to place that gentleman far above any competitor in the district for congress. But when you add the particular information and insight which he has gained, and is able to communicate to our public councils, it is really astonishing, that even blindness itself should hesitate in the choice. But it is to be observed, that the efforts of France are to loosen the confidence of the people everywhere in the public functionaries, and to blacken the characters most eminently distinguished for virtue, talents, and public confidence; thus smoothing the way to conquest, or those claims of superiority as abhorrent to my mind as conquest, from whatever quarter they may come.

Tell Marshall I love him, because he felt and acted as a republican, as an American. The story of the Scotch merchants and old torys voting for him is too stale, childish, and foolish, and is a French *finesse*; an appeal to prejudice, not reason and good sense. If they say in the daytime the sun shines, we must say it is the moon; if, again, we ought to eat our victuals. No, say we, unless it is ragout or fricassee; and so on to turn fools, in the same proportion as they grow wise. But enough of such nonsense.

As to the particular words stated by you, and said to come from me, I do not recollect saying them. But certain I am, I never said anything derogatory to General Marshall; but on the contrary, I really should give him my vote for Congress, preferably to any citizen in the state at this juncture, one only excepted, and that one is in another line.

I am too old and infirm ever again to undertake public concerns. I live much retired, amidst a multiplicity of blessings from that Gracious Ruler of all things, to whom I owe unceasing acknowledgments for His unmerited goodness to me; and if I was permitted to add to this catalogue one other blessing, it would be that my countrymen should learn wisdom and virtue, and in this day know the things that pertain to their peace.

Farewell. I am, dear Sir, yours,
PATRICK HENRY.

Henry expected his involvement in the election of 1799 would not extend much beyond writing letters of endorsement for Federalist candidates. He failed to anticipate the degree to which General Washington had been angered by the pro-French activities of the Jeffersonians and the threat to the union presented by the Kentucky and Virginia Resolutions. Washington was enraged at the friends of France, whom he called "partisans of war and confusion." He threw his great personal influence into the search for the strongest possible Federalist candidates. One week after Henry wrote his letter endorsing John Marshall's candidacy, General Washington, from Mount Vernon, wrote to Patrick Henry about the grave crisis that had befallen the nation. Without naming Jefferson, Madison, or Monroe, he stated his regret that Virginia was leading the opposition to the honest efforts of the Adams administration to resolve the dangerous situation. He questioned the reasons causing the majority of the citizens of Virginia, whom he thought favored both the general government and the union, to elect men from a party opposed to that government and to support measures that would destroy the union.

One of the reasons assigned is, that the most respectable and best qualified characters among us will not come forward. Easy and happy in their circumstances at home, and believing themselves secure in their liberties and property, they will not forsake them, or their occupations, and engage in the turmoil of public business, or expose themselves to the calumnies of their opponents, whose weapons are detraction.

But at such a crisis as this, when everything dear and valuable to us is assailed; when this party hang upon the wheels of government as a dead weight, opposing every measure that is calculated for defence and self-preservation, abetting the nefarious views of another nation upon our rights, preferring as long as they dare contend openly against the spirit and resentment of the people, the interest of France to the welfare of their own country—justifying the first at the expense of the latter;—When every act of their own government is tortured, by constructions they will not bear, into attempts to infringe and trample upon the constitution with a view to introduce monarchy.

When the most unceasing and purest exertions were making to maintain a neutrality which had been proclaimed by the executive, approved unequivocally by Congress—by the State legislatures—nay by the people themselves, in various meetings, and to preserve the country in Peace, are charged as a measure calculated to favor Great

Britain at the expense of France, and all those who had any agency in it are accused of being under the influence of the former, and her pensioners; when measures are systematically and pertinaciously persued, which must eventually dissolve the union or produce coercion; I say, when these things have become so obvious, ought characters who are best able to rescue their country from the pending evil to remain at home? Rather, ought they not to come forward, and by their talents and influence stand in the breach which such conduct has made on the peace and happiness of this country, and oppose the widening of it?

. . . .

I come now, my good sir, to the object of my letter, which is, to express a hope and an earnest wish, that you would come forward at the ensuing elections (if not for Congress, which you may think would take you too long from home), as a candidate for representative in the General Assembly of this commonwealth.

There are, I have no doubt, very many sensible men who oppose themselves to the torrent, that carries away others who had rather swim with, than stem it, without an able pilot to conduct them—but these are neither old in legislation, nor well known in the community. Your weight of character and influence in the House of Representatives would be a bulwark against such dangerous sentiments, as are delivered there at present. It would be a rallying point for the timid, and an attraction of the wavering.

In a word, I conceive it to be of immense importance at this crisis that you should be there; and I would fain hope that all minor considerations will be made to yield to the measure.

If I have erroneously supposed that your sentiments on these subjects are in union with mine, or if I have assumed a liberty which the occasion does not warrant, I must conclude as I began, with praying that my motive may be received as an apology. My fears that the tranquility of the Union, and of this state in particular, is hastening to an awful crisis, have extorted them from me.

With great, and very sincere regard and respect, I am, Dear Sir,
Your most Ob^t & Very Humble Servt.

GEO. WASHINGTON.

In spite of his poor health, Patrick Henry could not resist a call to action from the man he respected above all others. Shortly after receiving Washington's letter, he announced that he would be a candidate for the House of Delegates and that he would personally address the people of Charlotte on March county court day. The announcement caused a sensation. The old warrior was returning to Virginia politics. No Republican wanted to share a platform with the greatest orator of the age. Thus it came to pass that Creed Taylor proposed John Randolph represent the Republicans by speaking in opposition to the great man on the first Monday in March.

At first blush Randolph was shocked at the suggestion. "I should speak against Patrick Henry? You must be joking."

Creed Taylor shook his head. "I am completely serious about this."

"I am running for Congress, not the House of Delegates. Let the one who chooses to oppose Henry in the election speak in opposition to him."

Creed Taylor laughed. "Nobody of any importance will oppose Patrick Henry for a local office. He will win the election uncontested. Don't you see. This is a great opportunity for you to enhance your own stature. The man who spoke in opposition to Patrick Henry. With a single appearance, you can become a hero. It will be David against Goliath."

"But I've never spoken in a political contest. You can't expect me to compete with him. He won't be Goliath. He'll be Hyperion to a satyr."

"He may be Hyperion, but you will certainly not be a satyr."

John Randolph responded coldly. He was uncertain whether Taylor was praising him or insulting him. Taylor usually spoke in earnest. So despite the anger rising within his throat, Randolph decided to disregard the remark. He merely stared sullenly at his benefactor.

"Nobody will expect you to outshine Patrick Henry. All you have to do is state the case against the Federalists and for states' rights. I've heard you do it countless times with wonderful eloquence. The majority of freeholders will be yours. Just think, you could actually eclipse Patrick Henry himself. In this crisis you can't sit securely under your vine and fig tree. This is a great moment for you. Do not let it pass you by." Without responding, Randolph turned his face away. Taylor continued his assault. "With men like you in Congress, we can elect Jefferson next year. Do you want Adams for another four years?"

At last John Randolph's wrath was stirred. "You know I can't tolerate another month of the fantastic vanity of that political Malvolio. The high priest of monarchy must go. If necessary, I would resort to our armory in Richmond. This Federalist reign of terror must cease. Be warned. If I do it, I intend to speak my mind."

"That is exactly what I want you to do, Jack."

Randolph looked down at the copy of Patrick Henry's letter endorsing John Marshall. Taylor had brought it to arouse Randolph's fury against the man he admired. For the second time Randolph read the passage about France destroying the pillars of all government and social life. This was truly the opportunity he had been dreaming about for years. His words might actually affect the course of great events. The excitement within him struggled with the apprehension of his own inadequacy. It was one thing to dream behind closed curtains; it was quite another to enter the stage and stand before the gaping faces of the pitiless mob. "Citizen Taylor," he exclaimed, "I will think about it."

A long blast from the conch shell awakened John White. His muscles ached from the previous day's labor. With the first stab of pain, he swore to himself that he would never take another drink. As punishment, he would definitely have preferred a whipping to being sent back to the fields. Compared to his usual resting place in the quarters of the household servants, the bed was intolerably uncomfortable. It was one of those old mattresses Daddy Syphax talked about—the ones made out of moss, scalded and buried to prevent fleas and then stuffed into the ticking. When Syphax talked about those old mattresses, John always used to laugh. "Dem beds slept good," Syphax would say, "better 'n de ones nowadays." It was no longer amusing. Another night on this bed and, John thought, he would be totally unfit for a day of bending and stooping in the fields.

The other slaves in the cabin had already departed. John had a vague recollection of someone trying to wake him. In spite of the pain, he threw off the coarse blanket and forced himself out of bed. The room was bitterly cold. For a few moments he experienced great difficulty in straightening his back. Through the crevice between the logs he could see that there was a thin layer of snow on the ground. Some of it had entered the cabin through the holes in the roof. The stool in the corner was dusted white. At least he did not have to get dressed. His exhaustion was so complete the previous night, he had not even bothered to take off his shoes.

After urinating in the slop basin beside the door, he gulped down several mouthfuls of hominy. He reached for his gourd filled with water. It was partially frozen. "It'll melt in the noonday sun," he assured himself. He reached for his second gourd. In it he placed a stale piece of corn cake and a slice of bacon which was hanging from a nail on the wall. Maybe by noon he'd be hungry. His lack of appetite was so marked, he doubted it would return during the day. Without further delay he left the cabin.

Fearful of verbal abuse or worse from the overseer if he was late, John hobbled as quickly as possible toward the fields. In the distance the overseer could be seen on horseback screaming at the slaves as they hurried to their gathering spot. The riding crop in his hand was in use for those moving too slowly. Before John was halfway down the hill, he heard the sound of the horse behind him. The riding crop stung as it snapped across his back. "You're late, Johnny boy. Field work too hard for ye?"

"He never woulda done dat when Massa Randolph was 'live," one of the slaves mumbled to John. "Gonna be bad dis mornin' till dis snow melt. Sky must o' been packed tight wid it."

Even in warm weather John disliked field work. In the cold weather he detested it. The cold invaded his body until he could think of nothing else except his shivering torso. The bitterness of the chill became his entire existence. He tried to think of the work he was performing. This time of year it was always the same, preparing the beds, hoed, raked, and ready for the sowing of tobacco seeds. When the ground was so hard, the labor was twice as difficult. He was thankful he had only two more weeks in the fields for his month of punishment to be completed. It was a mystery to him how the field slaves tolerated it year after year, with no end in sight. He knew what it was like. As soon as a crop was completed, work began on the next year's crop. Next month, they would have to plow the fields for sowing the wheat. The fields would also have to be prepared for the corn and the transplanting of tobacco seedlings—covering and uncovering the plants with straw to protect them from frost and flies. Then, for the placement of the corn seed, the poking of holes in the tops of the little hills with fingers or sticks. His back ached just thinking of the thousands of times he would have to bend if they were doing that. Then, the cutting of the tobacco under the hot summer sun. The thought of the warmth of the sun's rays made him wish it was August. He could almost feel himself cutting the plants, rhythmically swinging the blade with the sweat running down his face—the plants left to wither in the sun until they were ready to be carried into the tobacco houses. Before that job was done, it was time to plant the barley and rye. Then, in late October, would begin the tedious work of stripping. Because it was done at night after a full day's work in the field, it was especially disagreeable. He wondered how he had once survived a full year in the field. That was the summer he got caught stealing pigs. On that occasion, John Randolph had sent him to the fields and threatened never to bring him back to the stables. His parents, Essex and Hetty, for whom John Randolph had a special fondness, had interceded for him. The master had finally relented. Although he admitted he had done wrong, the punishment had been too severe. After all, he had only taken some of the master's property and converted it into food for the benefit of other property. This time he thought the punishment was unjust. All he had done was to get drunk, but only after the horses had been cared for. Screaming that "Johnny" had not sufficiently curried, rubbed, and fed his favorite horse, John Randolph had angrily shaken his servant awake. Even in his drunken stupor, John had realized, with horror, the harshness of the sentence. "Four weeks in the fields for you," were the words that had awakened him. He pleaded and wept. But it was all to no avail. White man's justice. As he commenced the day's work, his thoughts were bitter. Then his mind ceased to function. All was numbness. For a time, the pain and cold ceased to bother him. The body continued to work; the spirit had departed.

At noon all work stopped for mealtime. The spell was broken. In great pain, John picked up his gourds and walked over to Sam, one of Master Randolph's longtime field hands. Sam was one of the few laborers John knew from his last stay in the fields. So many new ones had been brought in since Richard Randolph's slaves were freed. The fields were filled with strangers.

One of the new men sat beside Sam. He was a tall, powerful-looking mulatto with tan skin, much lighter than Sam's or John's deep sable. His hands were massive. At least a foot taller than either of them, he was, John suspected, what Toussaint L'Ouverture looked like. "What you say your name was?" There was no response. The big man stared down at the ground. He was obviously uneasy at being spoken to. John thought he might be surly. In his deep bass voice, John asked again. "Your name, boy, what is it?"

The big man looked up at him. His face was scarred. He appeared to have been the victim of a number of beatings. In his cheerful, friendly manner, Sam interjected himself. "Tell de man your name. He don't bite."

The big man tried to speak. As if to form a word, his lips began to move; but no sound came out. He tried again. "B-Billy E-E-Ellis." His eyes dropped back to the ground. Not only did he stutter, but he appeared to be painfully shy.

"Name's Ellis 'cause his mammy's massa was Judge Ellis from Buckingham," Sam said.

"How you today, Sam?"

"De white man try to ruin my day, but I pay it no mind." He took a mouthful of hominy with salt and washed it down with water.

John turned his attention to the new slave. "You must be stronger'n a horse. Bet he can hoist up on end a hogshead o'tobacco." Billy Ellis shook his head affirmatively. "Where you from and how old?"

Once again his mouth began to move, but it emitted no sound. His whole face twitched and his eyes blinked with the effort to respond. "I'se b-b-borned ov-v-er in F-F-Fluv-anna. D-Don't know z'act d-d-date."

"You been beaten, ain't you?"

Billy Ellis turned and pulled up his coarse "oznaberg" shirt. His back was covered with the scars of numerous whippings. Sam whistled in amazement. "Don't do much whippin' here. Before de old massa die, weren't none."

"De massa here now," John added, "is de strangest white man I ever seen. One day he mean as a trapped coon. De next, he de kindest massa you ever did see. Massa Randolph do 'bout anythin' fo' his niggers. But, you mess up an' he sell you south. Ever since dat cotton gin come in, dey sellin' off niggers down south fo' two-three times what dey paid. Lotta scared slaves 'round dese parts."

Sam looked into Billy Ellis's eyes. "You hate de white man?"

The big man pointed to his forehead. "D-De b-b-buckra c-can't h-h-hurt me here."

Sam smiled knowingly. "He can and he will."

In John's pain-wracked mind, the remainder of the day passed in a blur. When he finally got back to his cabin that evening, he was too tired to make himself a meal. It was not necessary. His mother, Hetty, sneaked a piece of pork with some hoecake and milk down from the big house. John's strength and appetite lasted only long enough for a few bites. Then he dropped fully dressed into the bed. Within moments he fell into a sleep of utter exhaustion.

The fact that Patrick Henry had not spoken in public since his retirement made his appearance at Charlotte even more of a great occasion than it otherwise would have been. As John Randolph knew from previous experience, his brother's case and the British Debts argument in Richmond, an appearance by Henry meant enormous crowds. At the previous events the interest in the cases themselves would have attracted numerous spectators. On this occasion it was solely Patrick Henry everyone had come to see, perhaps for the last time. There were few literate people in the region who did not mark their calendars as soon as Henry announced his candidacy for the General Assembly and his speech at the Charlotte Court House on court day, the first Monday in March.

In order to assure he would not be late, John Randolph departed at an early hour on a swift sorrel stallion. Liberated from his sentence of four weeks of hard labor in the fields, John White followed him, driving a carriage containing several of Randolph's Republican supporters with food and drink for the journey of more than twenty miles. Even at their early time of arrival, the Randolph party was repeatedly halted by streams of people, horses and gigs clogging the roads to the courthouse. In spite of the pain from his blistered hands holding the reins, John was grateful to be riding with his master once more. The thought of the alternative, repetitive days of back-breaking labor, made his heart soar with thanksgiving to be back on the road. Over and over he swore to himself he would never take another drink of whiskey.

Although John Randolph was not a heavy drinker, on this occasion he was swigging something that looked like whiskey. It was supposed to provide a remedy for his dreadful cold. For half the week Randolph had been cursing the fates that on this momentous day he was afflicted with a badly congested head and a hoarse voice. This event, he feared, might mark both the beginning and end of his political career. To speak in opposition to the Demosthenes of the age was, he knew, foolhardy in the extreme. To do it with an impaired voice was almost certain to assure a disaster. Having rejected the existence of a God in Heaven who intervenes in human affairs, Randolph prayed quietly to the deity of his own will in order to summon the powers of mind and speech he required on this day of days.

He took another drink from his flask. When he saw John White staring at him, he glared back at his servant. "Johnny, what is forbidden to you I don't do. This is Mrs. Randolph's cold remedy, not whiskey." The slave appeared to be skeptical. Randolph rode over to the wagon and handed the flask to his bondsman. "It's nothing but linseed, licorice, and sun raisins simmered in water with a little brown sugar candy, rum, and vinegar. It's supposed to cure a cold in three days. Unfortunately, I didn't start taking it until last night."

The black man handed the bottle back to his master. "It smell worse den whiskey to me." He smiled mischievously.

The throng at the courthouse was immense. Everyone in the county appeared to be present. Classes had even been suspended at Hampden-Sidney College in adjoining Prince Edward County to permit the teachers and students to witness this historic occasion. The many young men in the crowd indicated that the students were not using the holiday for other private pleasures. It was as Creed Taylor had promised—a wonderful opportunity for an unknown candidate for Congress to win the votes of many of the freeholders of Charlotte, Prince Edward, Cumberland, and Buckingham counties. The beauty of the situation was that Randolph was not running against Patrick Henry. Undoubtedly, most of the freeholders would vote for Henry no matter what he said. Only one man in the world could win more votes from this crowd, and he was safely ensconced at Mount Vernon. Yet the people of the district were strongly inclined toward Jefferson and the Republicans, or "Democratic-Republicans" as some called them. If Randolph could appeal to their natural sympathies, he could win his seat in Congress on this day.

Randolph's reception did not increase his confidence. Ignoring him, Colonel Read, the Clerk of the County, walked up to Creed Taylor. "Mr. Taylor, don't you mean to assist this young man by speaking on his behalf?"

"Never mind," replied Taylor. "This young man can speak for himself."

A great roar emanated from the crowd as Patrick Henry's carriage arrived. He was earlier than expected. In order to spare himself the rigors of the twenty-mile ride from his estate at Red Hill, Henry had departed the day before and spent the night as the guest of his friend, Colonel Joel Watkins, who lived only three miles from the county seat. The moment Henry stepped down from his carriage, he was mobbed by admirers. Some helped clear the way for him as he moved toward the local tavern to await his hour upon the stage. Suddenly the buzz of the crowd was interrupted by a booming voice. Barring the path to the tavern, a Baptist minister pointed his finger at Henry's retinue like some Old Testament prophet. "Why do you follow the man in this way? Patrick Henry is not a god!"

It was the kind of actor's scene Patrick Henry cherished. On a golden platter he had been presented an opportunity to deliver a memorable reply in the polished fustian so adored by his admirers. Halting his progress toward the tavern, the great orator assumed a dramatic pose in front of the minister. "No indeed, my friend. I am but a poor worm of the dust, as fleeting and insubstantial as the shadow of the cloud that flies over yon fields and is remembered no more." Henry's worshipers smiled knowingly at each other. Their trip had already proved to be worth the effort. The Baptist was rendered speechless. Incapable of surpassing such a rejoinder, he disappeared into the crowd.

Breathing heavily from the exertion of pushing through the multitudes, Henry took a seat on the platform that had been erected by the side of the tavern porch. He was surrounded by many of his old friends, who chatted excitedly with the great man. In awe of this unforeseen moment in his life, John Randolph warily watched his opponent from a distance. He, John Randolph, was about to speak in opposition to the greatest orator of the age, a man he himself often spoke of in reverential admiration.

After waiting for a full half hour, Henry arose with great difficulty. He looked much older than the man John Randolph remembered. The careworn old gentleman walked slowly to the front of the platform. From past experience, Randolph knew there would be a transformation when he began to speak. Consistent with his withered appearance, however, the metamorphosis was not as impressive as it had been six years earlier. Patrick Henry truly was a sick old man. Nevertheless, the voice was still clear and powerful. Only those who had heard him in earlier days would have been disappointed; and there were many in the audience, from Charlotte and adjoining counties, who had never before heard the great orator.

"I stand here before you today because the late proceedings of the Virginia Assembly have filled me with great apprehension and alarm. They have planted thorns upon my pillow. They have drawn me from the happy retirement which it had pleased a bountiful Providence to bestow upon me. I had hoped to pass the remainder of my days in pastoral tranquility. But it was not to be. Recent political events are too fraught with peril for any thoughtful citizen to remain silent.

"The Commonwealth of Virginia has declared that laws enacted by the federal government are unconstitutional, that the state can interpose between the federal government and her own people for the purpose of arresting the evil. In so doing, this Commonwealth has quitted the sphere in which she has been placed by the Constitution of the United States. For this Commonwealth to pronounce upon the validity of federal laws is to pass beyond her jurisdiction in a manner not warranted by any authority. It should be in the highest degree alarming to every considerate man.

"I know of no way of judging the future but by the past. And history informs us that when one portion of a state opposes the general government which represents the whole of that state, the result is civil war. Thus, we may conclude that opposition on the part of Virginia to the laws of the federal government must inevitably beget their enforcement by military power. The likely result of the application of force is opposition by this Commonwealth. Ruinous war with a more powerful force is the path down which the General Assembly leads us. The only alternative to defeat would be foreign alliances. These alliances must necessarily end in subjugation to the foreign powers called in by us. Shall we again become a British colony? Or would you prefer to be dominated by the godless French? Consider well before you rush into such a calamity. Once you embark upon this journey there is no retreat."

When Henry paused, the completeness of the silence was startling. Few who had heard the clamor produced by the immense throng could have believed it possible to reduce it to such utter quietude. Henry reminded the multitudes that their own beloved George Washington had emerged from retirement to be appointed Lieutenant General, Commander of the Army of the United States. "Where," he asked, "is the citizen of America who will dare to lift his hand against the father of his country, to point a weapon at the breast of the man who has so often led you to victory?"

The rhetorical question did not remain unanswered. A drunken Republican in the front of the crowd shouted, "I would do it."

Once again Henry was presented with a foil for a dramatic response. "No!" he cried in a booming voice. "You, sir, dare not do it; in such a parricidal attempt, the steel would drop from your nerveless arm!"

With his challenger reduced to a stony silence, Henry continued his speech. He contended that for Virginia to dispute the laws of the union would be akin to the County of Charlotte refusing to obey the laws of Virginia. After describing the nature of the United States Constitution, he turned his attention to the legislation that had caused the great controversy.

"The Alien and Sedition laws were passed by Congress; and Congress is a wise body. The laws might be right or they might be wrong. But, whatever may be their merit or demerit, the Congress represents the people of the United States. The members of Congress are as much our representatives as are the members of the Virginia Assembly. They surely have as much right to our confidence. Are we not the citizens who elected them? You who have followed my career over the years know that I opposed the unlimited power over purse and sword consigned to the general government. But I was defeated by democratic vote and submitted to the will of the majority. For the political system to work, the minority in a republic must submit to the constitutional exercise of power. Otherwise, there is no lawful authority in the land.

"If I am asked what is to be done when a people feel themselves intolerably oppressed, my answer is—overturn the government. But do not, I beseech you, carry matters to this length without provocation. Wait at least until some infringement is made upon your rights which cannot be otherwise redressed. For, if you lightly recur to revolution, you may bid adieu forever to representative government. Remember, you can never exchange the present government but for a monarchy. If the administration have done wrong, let us all go wrong together. Let us trust God and our better judgment to set us right hereafter. Let us not split into factions which must destroy that union upon which our existence hangs. Let us preserve our strength for the French, the British, the Germans or whoever else shall dare invade our territory. Let us not exhaust ourselves in civil commotions and intestine wars. United we stand; divided we fall.

"If elected to the Assembly, it is my solemn promise to you to attempt to allay the spirit of rebellion which has been fomented there. If I am deemed unworthy for this office, I pray to God the task might be reserved for some other, abler hands to extend the blessings of peace over this community."

As if the speaker had become exhausted, the speech abruptly ended. With only a moment's pause to listen to the thunderous applause, Henry stepped down from the platform and into the crowd. He quickly disappeared into the tavern.

For many minutes the people wildly demonstrated their approval of the withered old man's remarks. In profound meditation, John Randolph sat with his head in his hands. After waiting for a lengthy period of time until the tumult subsided, Creed Taylor introduced the young Republican candidate for Congress. Then Taylor whispered to his protégé, "The old man's in his dotage; you can outdo him."

John Randolph stepped to the front of the platform. With a deliberate motion, he removed his hat and made a slight bow to his audience. The contrast was complete. Wise old age followed by callow youth. Where Henry had been carelessly dressed, without any apparent concern for his appearance, the tall, slender youth was clothed impeccably in a blue frock, buff trousers, and a gentleman's fan-top boots. His apparel was arranged with the utmost care. Many of his spectators were already leaving. A few in front hurled insults at the effeminate-looking young man. "This beardless whelp is gonna speak against old Pat . . . Sit down, boy! This game is for men."

Randolph began to speak. His own voice was so hoarse, it sounded to him as though a stranger were talking through his lips. He was pleased by the fact that the tones echoing in his head sounded less shrill and deeper than his usual voice. The noise from the assemblage rendered his opening remarks barely audible. The insults from the front continued. "Is this the best they can do, a tin whistle after a church organ?"

Standing far to the side, John White impulsively yelled, "Let him speak!" Several white faces stared angrily at him. "Shut your mouth, nigger," one of them snarled. Other Republicans in the gathering were also calling for silence. Finally the noise subsided enough for Randolph to make himself heard.

> "It is a task most difficult to address you in opposition to the great man who has just spoken. I must light my feeble taper before the brightness of his noontide sun."

The speaker was amused to use words he had once heard from Henry himself. The crowd appeared to be listening.

> "No man admires Patrick Henry more than I do. But now I am constrained to differ from him. In these difficult times, there are honest differences abroad in the land. Many of you are in disagreement with your neighbors on the great issues of the day which agitate the people of this state. Let us examine our differences without malice and in a spirit of brotherhood. It is in that light I ask you to receive my words, in the same friendly spirit Colonel Henry would, if he were still on this platform."

In spite of a steady stream of heckling, Randolph continued to speak modestly. It was only, however, when he began to criticize Henry's own words that his speech captured the interest of the audience.

"Colonel Henry has told you that the late proceedings of the Virginia Assembly have filled him with alarm. I am truly sorry that he has been disturbed in his retirement. But many of us once cherished the belief that his own alarm would have been awakened if Virginia failed to struggle against the evils he so prophetically warned us of on other memorable occasions. Now that those awful squintings toward monarchy, so eloquently described by him in the past, are fast emerging as realities, I would have expected them to be the thorns in his pillow. I would have hoped that he would be the first to exert his powerful faculties in rousing the people out of their fatal lethargy.

"Has Colonel Henry forgotten that we owe to him those very principles which guided the legislature in its recent course? He is alarmed at the rapid growth of the seed he himself has sowed; he seems to be disappointed that they fell not by the wayside, but into vigorous and fruitful soil. He has conjured up spirits from the vast deep, and growing alarmed at the potency of his own magic wand, he would say to them, 'Down, wantons, down!' But like Banquo's ghost, I trust they will not down.

"In the Virginia Convention called to ratify the Constitution, he warned us of the consolidating tendency of the powers of the federal government. He prophesied that it would destroy the states and swallow the liberties of the people without further notice.

"But there are other powers, many and important ones that look to the states and recognize their existence as bodies politic, endowed with many of the most important attributes of sovereignty. These two opposing forces act as checks on each other and keep the complicated system in equilibrium. They are like the centrifugal and centripetal forces in the law of gravitation, that serve to keep the spheres in their harmonious courses through the universe.

"Should the federal government, therefore, attempt to exercise powers that do not belong to it—and those that do belong to it are few, specified and well-defined, all others being reserved to the people and to the states—it is the duty of the states to interpose. There is no other power that can interpose. The counterweight, the opposing force of the state, is the only check to the consolidating tendency of the federal government. For in the federal system, the states are the primary guardians of the liberties of the people. No government extending from Canada in the north to the Floridas in the south can be fit to protect your individual freedom. Such a government must lack the common feeling and interest with the governed which is indispensable to a sympathy for individual liberty."

In some detail Randolph reviewed Patrick Henry's former words in opposition to the Constitution of the United States. Then he proceeded to describe the Alien and Sedition Acts as the very kinds of tyrannical laws Henry
had prophesied.

"Yet now he tells you these laws may be right or they may be
wrong. And what is the nature of the Sedition Act which fails to stir
the opposition of the great defender of human liberty. It is a law that
makes it an act of sedition, punishable by fine and imprisonment, to
utter or write a sentiment that any prejudiced judge or juror may
think proper to construe into disrespect for the President of the
United States. Do you understand that? I dare proclaim to the people
of Charlotte my opinion to be that John Adams, our so-called President, is a weak-minded man, vain, jealous and vindictive; that, influenced by evil passions and prejudices and goaded on by wicked
counsel, he has been striving to force the country into war with
France, our best friend and ally. I dare to repeat this before the people
of Charlotte and avow it as a warning to my countrymen. What then?
I subject myself to an indictment for sedition! I make myself liable to
be dragged away from my home and friends, and to be put on trial
in some distant federal court before a judge who receives his appointment from the man who seeks my condemnation, and to be tried by
a prejudiced jury, who have been gathered from remote parts of the
country, strangers to me and anything but my peers. You may ask,
'Is this man dreaming? Is this a fancy picture he has drawn for our
amusement?' I am no fancy man, people of Charlotte. I speak the
truth. I deal only in stern realities. In spite of your Constitution, there
is such a law in effect. It is in open contempt of those solemn guarantees that insure the freedom of speech and of the press to every
American citizen. Not only does it exist, but at this hour is most
rigidly enforced against men who represent you, the people. Men, the
sanctity of whose persons cannot be reached by any law known to a
representative government, are hunted down, condemned, and incarcerated at this very moment by this odious, tyrannical, and unconstitutional enactment."

Having described several cases in which patriots had been thrown into
prison for daring to criticize the President, Randolph proceeded to question
the need of a large standing federal army and navy in time of peace.

"Not only do we have a large army threatening to invade our
sovereign territory, but Colonel Henry's vivid imagination has pictured General Washington at the head of it, coming to inflict military
chastisement on his native state. And who, exclaims he, would dare
to lift his hand against the father of his country? Sternly has he re-

buked one of you for venturing, in an outburst of patriotic feeling, to declare that he would do it. I bow with as much respect as any man at the name of Washington. But while I love Caesar, I love Rome more. Should he, forgetful of the past, grown ambitious for power, and, seduced by the artful machinations of those who seek to use his great name in the subjugation of his country, lift a parricidal hand against the bosom of the state that gave him birth and crowned him with his glory, because she has dared to assert those rights belonging to her, I trust there will be found many a Brutus to avenge her wrongs. I promise, for one—and it is in no boastful spirit I speak—that I will not be an idle spectator of the tyrannical and murderous tragedy, so long as I have an arm to wield a weapon, or a voice to cry shame. Shame on you, I would say, for inflicting this deadly blow on the bosom of the mother who gave you existence and cherished your fame as her own brightest jewel."

Randolph knew his words were provocative in the extreme. Even the Republicans would be shocked by any criticism of General Washington. The Federalists were probably delighted to hear such "treason" spoken by a political enemy. But Randolph did not care if they were all hostile. The important thing was they were listening to him. It was not their love he wanted, only their attention. The great principles involved, he hoped, would carry the day.

The power he felt emanating from his words healed old wounds deep within him. He spoke with renewed confidence and strength.

"Are the Federalists asking the states to yield a part of their sovereignty? Asking a state to relinquish a portion of her sovereignty is like asking a lady to surrender part of her chastity."

Many in the throng applauded. Randolph's supporters were increasingly boisterous.

"If this federal government, then, is to be the sole judge of its own usurpations, neither the people nor the states, in a short time, will have any rights. This creature of their making will become their sovereign, and the only results of the labors of our revolutionary heroes, in which patriotic band Colonel Henry was most conspicuous, will have been a change of our masters—New England for Old England. If that is to be the nature of the change, I cannot find it in my heart to thank them.

"But the gentleman has taught me a very different lesson from that he is now disposed to enjoin on us. I fear that time has wrought its influence on him, as on all other men, and that age makes him willing to endure what in former years he would have spurned with indignation. I have learned my first lesson in his school. He is the high-priest from whom I received the little wisdom my poor abilities were able to carry away from political discourse. He was the inspired states-man who taught me to be jealous of power, to watch its encroach-ments, and to sound the alarm on the first movement of usurpation. Inspired by his eloquent appeals, encouraged by his example, alarmed by the rapid strides of federal usurpation, of which he had warned them, the legislature of Virginia has nobly stepped forth in defense of the rights of the states and interposed to arrest that encroachment and usurpation of power that threatens the destruction of the Republic. It is precisely because I venerate that Patrick Henry who was the mentor of so many of us that I now urge you to vote the Federalists out of power. Protect your state, preserve your precious liberties and defend yourself. Vote Republican. . . ."

The enthusiastic roar of the Republicans drowned out his closing state-ment. Although the crowd was no more than one-half of the throng that had listened to Patrick Henry, John Randolph was satisfied. His first speech, he believed, had been a success.

Before Randolph departed, Creed Taylor led him into the tavern where Patrick Henry was resting. The great man arose to shake the hand of the young man who had dared to oppose him. The expression on his face was a grave one. "Young man," he said, "they have told me about your speech. My only advice to you is to keep truth, cherish justice, and you will live to think differently."

Having received the congratulations of his friends and many Republican sympathizers, Randolph returned to his manservant and his horses. He was exuberant. "Johnny," he exclaimed, "I expect we shall soon be going to Phil-adelphia."

John White smiled broadly. Wherever it was, he knew it was far from the fields of Bizarre.

After sprinkling the ashes from the fireplace on the floor, Polly, on her knees, began scouring with a hard bristle brush. There was a long way to go. Before it would be as clean as Judith demanded, she would have to sweep up the ashes and rinse two times. While she scrubbed, Polly could hear the two sisters in the next room screaming at each other. Disgusted at once again being an excuse for the continuation of their perpetual struggle, Polly was unusually angry. She had lost count of the number of times they had argued about her. In the end they always concluded by fighting about something else. As far as Polly was concerned, they could both go to the devil. She was tired of the continual chores. At times she felt she would suffocate at the mere thought of continuing this work until she was an old woman—endless repetitive days without any change in her life.

As usual, Nancy was defending her. "It's enough if she just cleans up. She didn't intentionally spill it. You don't have to make her do the whole floor."

"It doesn't matter if she intended it. I don't care what was on her mind.

She has to clean it now or the floor will stain." Judith was trying to sound reasonable. As always, the sharp edge in her voice defeated her attempts.

"If she wipes it up, it won't stain. You can't ask her to do the entire floor. It's Sunday. Remember the Lord's day." Nancy's voice dripped with sarcasm. "My servant does not work today. If you weren't such a hypocrite, you wouldn't allow it. You and your damned mummery about the sabbath."

"If you don't like living in this house, you and your servant are welcome to leave at any time."

Polly could hear the sounds of her mistress running up the stairs. Then, the inevitable slamming of the bedroom door. At the threat of homelessness, Nancy always retreated. Her mistress was terrified, she knew, at the thought of being turned out into the world, without money or a place to live. Polly could not understand why she always confronted her sister when she was powerless to bring her side of the argument to a successful conclusion. Perhaps it was habit. When they were children, if her older sister used her superior strength, Nancy could run to her father or brothers. Now she could only retreat in ignominious defeat to the silence of her bedroom.

If her mistress was afraid of going out into the world without money, Polly certainly was not. Since the manumission of Richard Randolph's slaves, she had several times gathered up the courage to request her freedom. She clung to the dream of a future that made tolerable the dreary present. It was all to no avail. Nancy would not hear of it. "You're all I have," she would say. "Maybe someday, but not now." If Polly tried to find out when "someday" would arrive, Nancy was always vague and evasive. But that could not stop the thoughts. Polly closed her eyes and imagined herself walking with that handsome new slave. His powerful arm was wrapped around her; she was dressed in white with a parasol, just like the one she saw Sally with the previous spring.

It did not matter to her that most of the freed slaves at Israel Hill were miserable. The land, they said, was not much good for farming; and they didn't have enough money for tools, feed, animals, and the rest. Some of those who had received good plots signed papers they couldn't even read. Next thing they knew, white men were driving them off the land. A few voluntarily left the land to look for jobs. But white men didn't like competing with freed slaves, so they had to steal or move north. Polly had heard numerous stories of the hardships of the freed slaves. Bad as it was, they still preferred to be free. "I done seen both sides," one of them had told her. "Freedom's better 'n slavery even if you starvin'." There was something magical about the word "freedom." No matter how many times she turned to the Bible, she was still thrilled to read about Moses freeing the Hebrew slaves. Someday, she was certain, she would cross that River Jordan into the promised land. But that was for another season. Now, for the first time in years, there was something to make her want to stay at Bizarre. Ever since she first saw him at the dance the previous month, that new slave was constantly on her mind. To her regret, he had departed before she could gather the courage to speak to him. In later weeks he had not appeared at the dance. Moving as fast as she could, she scrubbed the floor. As was done every other Sunday morning, they would soon be distributing the two-week rations to the field slaves. He would be there, and so would she.

When the floor was finished, Polly was hungry. She walked through the covered passage connecting the plantation house with the kitchen, which was set apart to keep the smoke and odors out of the big house. Hetty did not cook on Sunday. Nevertheless, she usually could not stay away from her pots and pans. As Polly expected, she was there. From beneath her bright red turban, Hetty's plump round face was beaming as she watched her son John devour "somethin' good." Her husband Essex was also present. He was not eating. As soon as Polly entered the room, the succulent smells increased her appetite. She was surprised to see a fire in the hearth. In an instant Hetty offered her "somethin' good." Polly eagerly accepted. Reaching into the hearth with her huge metal spatula, Hetty pulled out a piece of hoecake. After brushing the ashes off, she handed it to Polly, who quickly placed it on the table to allow it to cool. "Chile, it don't taste like nothin' if you lets it get cold," Hetty warned. Polly picked it up and took a bite. Politely, she refrained from revealing she had burned her tongue.

John was excited about going to Philadelphia with the master if he won the election; and he was still going on about Patrick Henry and the speech at Charlotte. For several minutes Polly waited politely until there was a lull in the conversation. "Dat new big slave . . ."

"Billy Ellis?"

"Yeah, dat's de one. You worked wid him when you was in de field. Why's he so unfriendly?" Polly asked eagerly.

John shrugged his shoulders. "He's not. He been beaten bad for a long time. You oughta see his back. Had one mean massa in Fluvanna. De job he gave de young'uns was to pick de worms off de 'bacco plants. First time Billy done it, he missed some o' dem. Dat massa done made him eat de worms still on de plant." At the thought of it, John grimaced in disgust. Hetty and Polly groaned in disbelief. John followed with a worse story. Billy's master had once tied him naked under scalding drops from fat pork being cooked above him. "Got dem small burn marks all over de back o' his legs. Can't see de ones on his back. Dey covered over wid whippin' scars."

"You done taken a fancy to dat boy?" Hetty asked.

"I like de way he look. Right handsome man. Every time I see him, he fill my eyes."

"You kin see him right now," Hetty replied. "Dey's givin' out de food."

"So soon!" Polly exclaimed. Without another word she was out the door and on her way to the barn. Fearful of missing Billy Ellis, she walked as quickly as she could. Upon approaching the barn, she could hear the call of the foreman. "Who take dis piece o' meat?" The overseer's black assistant was cutting and weighing pieces of pork. In order to avoid any claims of partiality in distribution, the ration to be taken could not be seen until it was actually in the hands of the one who stepped forward to claim it. Judith, who customarily supervised the entire procedure, checked off the name of the recipient from a long list in front of her.

Nobody complained about the distribution of rations at Bizarre. Under Judith Randolph's supervision, it had always been generous and fair. At each distribution, adult males received two pounds of pork, for one week, and two peck of unsifted cornmeal, for two weeks. The females received smaller portions with additions for each child. Depending on the time of the year, additional meat, corn, sugar, coffee, and whiskey were distributed. The slaves' diet was supplemented by hunting, fishing, raising poultry, and the tending of private vegetable gardens.

With the death of Richard Randolph and the institution of more stringent punishments, including occasional whippings for serious misdeeds, the general attitude in the quarter had deteriorated from one of quiet cooperation to a clandestine struggle of "us against them." Stealing food from the plantation larder had become common practice. Sam and a group of his friends were particularly adept at the theft, slaughter, and cooking of hogs without being detected. Sam claimed the secret of his success had always been sharing with others so that nobody was inclined to squeal. Stealing from fellow slaves was not tolerated and almost never happened.

Because it was the first distribution of spring, each slave was given a spoonful of castor oil to help "clean out the body." Later in the day, new clothes would be given out for the warm weather—cotton trousers, light shirts, dresses for the women, and new shoes. The children simply wore a sack with holes for the arms until they grew to adult size. No shoes were provided for the young children, who went barefoot, or with wrapped feet in cold weather.

Once a month the children were invited to the big house for breakfast. There Judith carefully observed them eating so she could determine which ones were sick and needed special treatment. When Richard was alive, the slaves generally perceived this ritual as an act of generosity. Under the new harsher regime, it was seen as merely the protection of property whose value was increasing constantly because of the expanding demand for cotton workers to the south. With the rising fear of being sold "down the river" to the dreaded cotton kingdom, there was increased talk in the quarter of escape. Now that the panic over St. Domingo had passed, there were no patrols and passes were not checked. Escape would be much easier than it had been for some time. To keep the slaves fearful of escape, the overseer repeatedly warned that those who attempted to flee would lose any future chance of being freed like their predecessors. At Bizarre it was a threat carrying a substantial amount of weight.

With the diminution of travel restrictions, many slaves visited other plantations on Sunday, leaving family or friends to receive their rations. When Polly did not see Billy Ellis, she assumed he had gone off to Horsdumonde where, she knew from talking to John, he had a brother. For several minutes Polly observed the field laborers. While they waited quietly to receive their portions, the children frolicked. Polly permitted St. George Randolph to hide behind her while he played tag with the slave children, who always treated him respectfully. "The Saint," as he was called, could not hear nor speak, but he was white, and the son of Mrs. Randolph. Three-year-old Tudor stood beside his mother, looking bewildered as the older children ran wildly around him.

An old black woman called to one of the children. "Gal, come here and give yo' gramma some sugar." Embracing the old woman, the child kissed her on the cheek. "Dat's de way you does it," she said as she lifted the little girl from the ground. Turning to watch, Polly noticed Billy Ellis out of the corner of her eye. He was standing alone in back of the crowd, waiting for his rations. Polly's breast filled with excitement. He was even more beautiful than she had remembered him. For a few minutes she watched him. Remaining apart from the crowd, he spoke to nobody. There was something melancholy about his isolation.

Polly boldly approached him. "You been here some time and we ain't talked. My name is Polly. I work up at de big house."

Nervously, Billy Ellis looked down at her. His nod acknowledged her presence but he said nothing.

"What's your name?"

Looking very uncomfortable at the question, he remained silent for several uneasy moments. Finally, seeing speech was unavoidable, he attempted to respond. His entire face twitched with the effort. "B-B-Billy E-Ellis."

Polly had heard about his stuttering; she had not imagined it was so bad. His effort had been so great and his discomfort so obvious, Polly was reluctant to ask another question. Instead she did all the talking—how long she had been at Bizarre, her desire to be free, and especially her friendship with Hetty the cook. "I kin get you extra food," she said. He listened with interest but said nothing more. She was afraid of scaring him off. "I hope to see you at de dance next Sadday. Bye." Nervously, she walked away. She liked him. His affliction made him even more desirable, like a wounded animal needing her help. It was clear, he was too shy to come after her. Polly's mind was set. No matter how difficult the task, she intended to befriend him. For the first time in many months she felt eager about life. There was something to want, something within her grasp. Once more, tomorrow had become worth dreaming about.

"Mr. Johnston, who do you vote for?" The sheriff appeared to be bored. He had already asked the question of well over one hundred freeholders.

"Colonel Carrington," was the spirited response from the periwigged gentleman. A small group of Federalists applauded loudly. A few began to chant. "Black cockade, black cockade!" From the other side of the courtroom the rumblings of discontent were distinctly audible.

Colonel Clem Carrington arose from the seat at the end of the long table and nodded toward the voter. "Your vote is greatly appreciated, Mr. Johnston. I shall treasure it in my heart." As he sat back down, a slight smile flickered across his face. Carrington's clerk entered the voter's name on his list of freeholders who had announced the name of the Federalist candidate for Congress. The list was disturbingly short.

Appearing to be substantially less prosperous than Mr. Johnston, the next voter in line stepped forward. "William P. Hill of Bear Creek."

"Mr. Hill, who do you vote for?"

"The one who ain't a damned Federalist." Immediately, the courtroom was filled with laughter. "Too many o' them a' ready." There was more laughter, mixed with jeers from the Federalist side.

"Mr. Hill, there are two candidates in this election who are not Federalists. Mr. Powhatan Bolling to my immediate right." Looking absurdly proud in his bright scarlet coat, Bolling stood up, revealing his great size. With aristocratic disdain, he did not condescend to nod his head at the freeholder. "Senator Creed Taylor, at the far end of the table on my right, is sitting in for the candidate, John Randolph." Taylor bowed in the direction of the voter. "Both of these gentlemen are Republicans."

Mr. Hill appeared to be confused. He had not anticipated having to choose between two different supporters of Thomas Jefferson. After hesitating for several seconds, he blurted out his response. "The one who spoke after Pat Henry."

Creed Taylor arose. "That would be John Randolph. I ask that the vote be so recorded."

"Granted," replied the sheriff. The Republicans cheered. "Good boy, Bill," several of them shouted. The Federalist side taunted the voter for his "Jacobin" stupidity. John Randolph's clerk wrote the name of William P. Hill on the line numbered 61 on his list of freeholders who had voted for Randolph.

"On behalf of Mr. Randolph, who could not be here today, I thank you for your vote in favor of freedom and the sovereign State of Virginia." The Republicans wildly cheered Taylor's response.

A passionate Republican and an ardent supporter of France, Creed Taylor was delighted at the voting prior to the break for the midday meal. Randolph, whose ardor for France matched his own, was receiving two votes for every one of Carrington's. Powhatan Bolling's support was smaller than expected. In spite of the pain in his back and legs from repeatedly standing up and sitting down, Taylor's anger at Randolph's refusal to appear was abating. His ability to bear his aches and pains, he knew, was a direct result of the success achieved up to this point. "It is an unwritten rule of politics that the candidate must be present for the polling," Taylor had warned his political protégé. "You could lose this election because of your absence."

"Nonsense!" was Randolph's response. "Most of the voters heard my speech. If they're against the Federalists, they will vote for me whether I'm present or not. Beyond speaking, I will not solicit votes, I will not thank voters for performing their civic duty, and I certainly will not swill the vulgar mob with rum punch."

"That's Judge Tucker speaking. It's fine to be so stiff-backed when you're sitting on the bench. But politicians cannot be detached from the real world. And don't let me hear you speak of the 'vulgar mob' that way. Powhatan Bolling openly refers to them as 'that rabble.' That's why, come election day, he'll get damned few votes." Creed Taylor's advice fell on deaf ears. Randolph refused to be present on election day. His only concessions were to permit Taylor to be at the polls as his agent, to pay for a clerk to record his votes, and to provide a hundred dollars for any "miscellaneous" expenses. Taylor used the money to purchase enormous amounts of cookies, rum punch, and whiskey in order to "swill" the voters on election day. To assist him in the transporting and dispensing of the refreshments, Taylor had also borrowed Essex, John, and a wagon.

"Mr. Heth, who do you vote for?"

"John Randolph is my choice."

As he arose, the twinge of pain in Taylor's back caused him quietly to curse his absent candidate. Carrington nodded to his clerk, who stood up at the same time as Taylor. "I challenge that vote." The Republicans hooted.

"Mr. Heth's vote is challenged," declared the sheriff. "What is the reason, sir?"

After exchanging whispers with Clem Carrington, the clerk responded. "No freehold!"

"Mr. Heth," the sheriff inquired, "how many acres do you own?"

"Thirty, sir, and my house is on the land."

"What is the size of the house, sir?"

"A log cabin with three rooms. You were there once when it was only one room."

The sheriff glanced at the county magistrates sitting at the middle of the table. Present to act as election judges, they all nodded affirmatively.

"This man is held to be a freeholder eligible to vote." To the loud cheers of the Republicans, the sheriff declared, "Record the vote for Mr. Randolph."

"Please note my objection," Carrington's clerk replied. "We shall examine the land tax list."

Taylor leaned over to his own clerk. "When there's any question, challenge the vote for Carrington." The wait was not long. Following five consecutive voters for Randolph, a young stranger proudly called out his vote for Colonel Carrington.

In response to a challenge from Randolph's clerk, the sheriff asked for the reason. "No freehold and under twenty-one."

"When were you born, sir?"

"April, 1778."

"Can you prove that by document, sir?" While waiting for a reply, the sheriff unobtrusively counted on his fingers.

"I can!"

"What day in April?" one of the magistrates inquired.

The sheriff stopped counting. "Yes, what is the day?"

"The thirtieth."

The sheriff glanced at the county magistrates. One of them put his thumb down. The sheriff smiled. "I'll have to ask you to stand aside. You have no vote until your twenty-first birthday, which has not yet arrived by my calculation. Sorry, Mr. Trott." The Republicans applauded enthusiastically.

After another hour of viva voce voting, the sheriff, who had almost complete control of the proceedings, including the hours of opening and closing the polls, called a one-hour halt for the midday meal.

Shaking hands and chatting as he departed the courthouse, Taylor walked out into the bright sunlight. Slowly he made his way across the crowded courthouse green. He was regularly stopped by well-wishers. Several referred to the widespread rumors that the Republican legislature had collected arms at the Richmond armory for the purpose of resisting federal enforcement of the Alien and Sedition Acts. All of them suggested that armed resistance was a good idea. State Senator Taylor did not disagree.

With some satisfaction, Taylor noted that the crowd around the Federalist table was sparse even though they were giving out whiskey, cider-royal, and ginger cakes in a shady spot under the trees. In contrast, the table on the Republican side was jammed with people waiting in the hot sun to receive rum punch and cookies. One of Taylor's own servants, assisted by Essex and John, was busily serving the punch from two immense bowls. Maneuvering his way over the trampled grass around drunken loungers and clusters of people eating on blankets, Taylor meandered toward the tavern. As usual, a portion of the crowd was rowdy in the extreme. Surrounded by cheering spectators, two staggering drunks were busily pummeling each other. Taylor walked quickly past the fracas. Suddenly he stopped. A young woman walking alone looked exactly like Nancy Randolph. He could not believe it was she. He knew that she regularly rode about the countryside. Yet, in the six years since her trial, he had never seen her in a crowded public place. It was daring enough for a woman to have ridden all the way to the courthouse without a male escort. But for an infamous fallen woman to appear at the courthouse on election day was astonishingly bold. The disgraced young lady appeared to have finally broken out of her cage.

"How in the world did you get here?" he asked in a good-natured tone of voice. Nancy smiled broadly at him. He was pleased to see her in such high spirits.

"Looking for someplace interesting to ride out to. This seemed as good a place as any. I need a little excitement. The trees do become tiresome company. I hear that Jack is winning easily."

"Up to now. But we have a whole afternoon ahead. I expect he'll win, though. Only way a Federalist could take the district is a split Republican vote. Powhatan Bolling is not the man to do it. He only attracts eccentric members of the ancien régime, and today most of them are voting for Carrington." He chuckled gleefully. "I never did hear of someone winning without showing up for the election. This may be a first in Virginia. It must have been the appearance with Patrick Henry. Just about every man here seems to know Jack is the Republican candidate."

Nancy listened politely. Taylor knew she was not very interested in politics, so he changed the subject. "Good news for you. A new shipment of books arrived from Richmond. More than two dozen. Ride out to Needham tomorrow and pick anything you want."

"I haven't even finished the last pile of books you gave me. Judy imposes so much drudgery on me, I barely have time to read." She frowned in her coquettish manner. "But thank you; they're all I have."

"Don't look so unhappy," Taylor said in a gently mocking way.

"You'd be unhappy if you were a woman. I have no prospects for the future and no freedom to change my situation. For the foreseeable future, I must live the life of an unpaid servant. Be thankful you're not a woman." A cloud had passed over Nancy's exuberance with the speed of a summer storm. Her voice was filled with self-pity.

In a fatherly manner Taylor placed his hand on her shoulder. "Remember that old saying, 'This too shall pass.' For a young woman like you, your situation is certain to improve." Nancy affectionately hugged her old friend. Then, as if she remembered the fact that he was a married man only eight years her senior, she pulled away.

Since Brett and Ryland Randolph had moved away three years earlier, Creed Taylor and Sally, his wife, had provided the only society near Bizarre. Because of the greater financial opportunities available outside Virginia, Taylor himself had almost moved in the same year as the others. At the last moment he had decided he could not leave his beloved home. "You don't know how thankful we all are that you didn't move to Tennessee."

"With the way the price of tobacco is falling, maybe I should have gone south."

"Oh please don't say that. We'd all be lost without your company." A mournful expression flashed across her face.

They walked for a short distance together in the direction of the tavern. A number of people they passed looked at her with recognition in their eyes. Attempting to get a better look at the face beneath the large sunbonnet, one man walked shamelessly close to her. Taylor glared at the man who, realizing he had been noticed, hurried away as quickly as his dignity would permit. "I should be returning home. You only have a short time to eat. Tomorrow, I'll be over to look at the books. Tell Sally I'm eager to see her." Nancy kissed his cheek and walked quickly away.

Taylor wondered about the effect of the election on Nancy. With John away in Philadelphia, he thought, she would be completely at the mercy of her harpy sister. Then with some guilt at his uncharitable thoughts, he felt sorry for Judith. He reminded himself that it may well have been Nancy herself who was responsible for ruining her sister's disposition. He thought about John and Nancy. John used to speak about her often and quite favorably. Since Richard's death, he had ceased mentioning her. What came between them? he wondered.

That afternoon, many more Federalists and supporters of Powhatan Bolling appeared than in the morning. There were not nearly enough to overcome the big lead John Randolph had established earlier in the day. Seeing that the election was not as close as expected, the sheriff decided to close the poll as soon as the men waiting in line had all cast their votes. When the last freeholder present declared his vote, the sheriff went outside to the steps of the courthouse and called out loudly three times. "Gentlemen freeholders, come into court and give your votes now or the poll will be closed!" At three-fifty P.M. the voting ceased. Creed Taylor did not even have to look at the tally to know that his man was elected to the Congress of the United States. The younger generation, he thought, had arrived at the gates of power.

1800

There is something magical about the entry into a new century. It is largely an illusion, a change on a calendar of one number that had been constant during the entire lifetimes of those in being at the moment of transition. A seven changes into an eight, and all say a new era is commencing. Yet when 1799 flowed into 1800, there was a genuine feeling based on real events that an epoch had indeed passed. Virginia's two great revolutionary leaders had not lived to enter the new century. Two months after he was elected, and before he could assume his seat in the Virginia General Assembly, Patrick Henry passed into history. John Randolph's first political appearance had proved to be Patrick Henry's last.

The doctors said it was an intestinal obstruction. On June 6, 1799, after all other remedies had failed, Henry's doctor gave him a dose of liquid mercury. "I suppose, Doctor, this is your last resort," Henry is said to have told his physician; the doctor replied that the medicine would give him "immediate relief or . . ." When the doctor could not finish the sentence, Henry completed it for him. "You mean, Doctor, that it will give relief or prove fatal immediately." The physician did not disagree. Drawing his silken cap over his eyes, Henry had recited a simple prayer for his family, his country, and his own soul. Then, sitting in a chair in complete tranquility, he drank the medicine like Socrates taking the hemlock. After saying farewell to the weeping members of his family gathered around him, he thanked God for blessing him all his life and for permitting him to die without pain. None of the members of his family told him about the death of his beloved daughter, Mrs. Anne Roane, wife of Judge Spencer Roane, the news of which arrived at his home only five days before his own passing. The inscription on his gravestone was simple and just. "His fame is his best epitaph."

Six months later the only Virginian more renowned than Patrick Henry departed this world. Taken ill suddenly with an inflammation of the throat, George Washington died unexpectedly after his doctors bled him white. At the receipt of the news, the House of Representatives, meeting in Philadelphia for the last time, adjourned. It was newly-elected Congressman John Marshall who offered the resolution that included the oft-quoted description of Washington as "first in war, first in peace, and first in the hearts of his countrymen." For years after, Marshall made a point of informing those who mentioned it that the authorship of the line belonged to Henry Lee and not to himself.

Even the heavily Republican Virginia General Assembly unanimously agreed to wear black armbands through the session in honor of Washington. As only a short time earlier a resolution honoring the late Patrick Henry lost in the House, 58 to 88, it was not a foregone conclusion that the Virginia legislators would vote to honor Washington. In the next year, one of presidential election, even St. George Tucker could not grant his former commander unlimited praise. Although proposing a memorial to the honor of the General and President, Judge Tucker wrote that his "former unbounded veneration" for the character of George Washington was somewhat reduced by a few "circumstances in his administration." The partisan hostilities of the period, which were already quite heated, would increase considerably as the presidential election approached.

In the election of the previous year, the Federalists had doubled the number of Congressmen from Virginia. Instead of only four seats in the House of Representatives, the Virginia Federalists controlled 8 of the 19 seats from the Commonwealth. Although still a minority within the Virginia House delegation, the Federalists held firm control of Congress by margins of 19 to 13 in the Senate and 64 to 42 in the House. Thus, it was as a Representative of the minority party that John Randolph took his seat in the House. At the time of his election, he had barely attained the minimum age for a member of the House. Because he looked much younger than his age, his youth was the subject of constant attention. To his great displeasure, he was frequently called a "puppy" or "stripling" by the opposition. When he appeared in order to take the oath of office for the Sixth Congress, the clerk asked him if he was old enough to be eligible. "Go ask my constituents," was his haughty response.

On the second day of the new century, John Randolph made his second appearance in debate. The issue was one that would not disappear. Absalom Jones and other free men of color from the city of Philadelphia, with the support of the Quakers, petitioned for the adoption of measures that would in due course emancipate their race from bondage. When John Randolph arose to speak on the issue, the members of the Virginia delegation, including John Marshall, listened with great interest. It was well-known that Randolph's late elder brother had freed all of his slaves by a will that contained one of the most fiery denunciations of slavery ever penned in the Old Dominion. There was some fear that the effeminate-looking youth would break ranks with his Virginia colleagues and follow his late brother down the road to apostasy. His fellow Virginians were generally relieved to hear his short speech. He hoped, he stated, that the House would prevent the filing of petitions of a similar nature in the future. The Constitution of the United States, he declared, had put it out of the power of the House to act on the petition before them, and he trusted the occasion would be the last on which the interest and feelings of the southern states would be put in jeopardy by such applications. Randolph's southern colleagues applauded appreciatively. Young Randolph was truly one of them.

Several days later John Randolph was involved in the first incident that was to establish his reputation as a formidable enemy of the Federalists. Speaking in opposition to increasing the size of the armed forces of the United States, he denounced standing armies as inconsistent with the spirit of the Constitution. In the course of his speech, he used the terms "ragamuffins" and "mercenary" with reference to federal soldiers. Shortly thereafter, a group of officers from the Marine Corps, led by a Captain McKnight and a Lieutenant Reynolds, accosted him during the performance of a play. After the performance, he was intentionally jostled outside the theatre. Immediately Congressman Randolph wrote a saucy letter complaining to President Adams, the commander of the military. Claiming that the independence of the legislative branch had been attacked, Randolph demanded that action be taken. The President referred the letter back to the House. It was sent to a House committee which concluded that sufficient cause did not appear for the interposition of the House of Representatives on ground of breach of its privilege. In spite of a substantial Federalist majority, the report of the committee was rejected by the House, which was always zealous in the protection of its own members. The Speaker ruled all further action on the matter out of order. The affair received a great deal of publicity. Within weeks of his arrival in Philadelphia, John Randolph had established himself as a bold opponent of military arrogance and Federalist power. A new "champion of the people," he was clearly a young man not to be taken lightly.

Randolph liked his sojourn in the North no more than his earlier visits when he was a college student. Always longing for the green rolling hills of Virginia, he was particularly uneasy about the danger of living in Philadelphia, where thousands had died of yellow fever in 1793, 1797, and again in 1798. During part of 1799, out of fear of the dreaded disease, the capital had been temporarily moved to Trenton, New Jersey. In any case, the reign of Philadelphia as capital city of the nation was about to end. With the coming of summer, the government of the United States would be moving to the new federal city near Alexandria, Virginia. Randolph would be much closer to his estates, his family, and to Maria Ward.

The Randolph family had known the Ward family for many years. John still remembered the flight from Matoax when the traitor Benedict Arnold invaded Virginia early in 1781. On a cold frosty morning in January, Syphax had driven off with John's mother and her five-day-old son, Henry St. George Tucker, and her two-year-old daughter, Fanny. Essex was in charge of Richard, Theodorick, and John, who was riding a horse of his own for the first time. On the way to Bizarre they stayed with Benjamin Ward of Wintopoke. They were, John fondly remembered, received with great warmth and hospitality. Before resuming the journey, his mother was given the sorely needed opportunity to rest for a few days. At the time, Maria had not yet been born. Although John later met Maria several times when she was a little girl, ten years his junior, it was only after he had been elected to Congress that she caught his eye. A fifteen-year-old of remarkable beauty, she strongly reminded him of his beloved mother.

Perhaps there was more to politics than mere political power. John was amazed to find a beautiful young woman actually flirting with him. She seemed to be in awe of the fact that he had debated Patrick Henry and been elected to the Congress of the United States. In the course of their conversations she admitted to having been in love with him years earlier when she was only ten years old. There is nothing so irresistible to a young man as one who worships him. For the first time in years John returned to his early dreams of domestic bliss. He knew it was impossible; but that did not stop the dreams. How could a man lacking in virility, but who was scrupulously honest, court and marry a young woman of birth and beauty? It was all a ridiculous delusion. It had taken years to accept; but he had finally buried his hopes of conjugal contentment. Now, suddenly they were revived; he could not let them go again. From Philadelphia he wrote romantic letters to Maria. She responded warmly. With pen in hand and his love hundreds of miles away, he could be the man he always wanted to be. From a distance he was able to respond to her letters with an ardor that would be impossible if she were in his bed. It was mad, but he could not stop. For the first time in his life he was able to pour out the passion imprisoned within his soul and share it with another human being.

In the winter cold of Philadelphia, John Randolph was miserable. He boarded at Mirache's on North Fourth Street. His only company was John White, who served as his valet; otherwise, he was quite alone. Nathaniel Macon and Willis Alston, both congressmen from North Carolina, were located in the same lodgings. Randolph liked Macon and loathed Alston. Outside the House of Representatives, neither provided regular companionship for him. In his private life he remained isolated and unhappy.

Maria Ward was not the only person with whom he corresponded regularly. In his absence from Bizarre, Randolph had persuaded his friend William Thompson to live there. Following the death of his brilliant brother the previous year, William had himself become a melancholy creature. Randolph hoped that proximity might create a romantic attachment between his unhappy friend and his despondent sister-in-law, Judith. From out of the misery of two people, he hoped to bring forth a successful union, two souls consolidated into one. He wrote letters to Thompson encouraging him to resume his study of law as the best medicine for a wounded mind. The letters frequently referred to Judith.

> An amiable woman, who regards you as a brother, who shares your griefs, and will administer as far as she can to your consolation, who unites to talents of the first order a degree of cultivation uncommon in any country, but especially in ours—such a woman is under the same roof with you. Cultivate a familiarity with her; each day will give you new and unexpected proof of the strength of her mind, and the extent of her information. Books you have at command; your retirement is unbroken. Such a situation is, in my opinion, the best calculated for a young man (under any circumstances) who will study;

or even for one who is determined to be indolent. Female society, in my eye, is an indispensable requisite in forming the manly character. That which is offered to you is not to be paralleled, perhaps in the world.

Thompson attempted to please his friend. "To your sister, your most amiable sister, I try to render myself agreeable. There is a gentleness of manners, an uniformity of conduct, and a majesty of virtue, which seem to render admiration presumptuous." In February, Thompson left Bizarre to return to Petersburg. There, he became entangled with a lusty and wealthy married woman who, lacking all of Judith's cultivation, industry, and propriety, could be admired without overstepping bounds. In April he returned to Bizarre and wrote to Randolph praising the diligence of Judith:

> Our sister is now asleep; she would have written but for her being busy in finishing the children's clothes, and being obliged to write Mrs. Harrison. When I came in last evening, I found her in the passage, a candle on the chair, sewing. I could hardly help exclaiming, what a pattern for her sex. The boys are well; they have both grown— the Saint particularly, whose activity will astonish you. Everybody is cheerful—your arrival in anticipation is the cause.

But Thompson did not linger at Bizarre. He would not pursue a woman who had to be approached like a goddess, in fear and trembling. He fled from the practical and chaste Judith to return to his married friend, who John Randolph described as a "silly and depraved" woman. As his reason for leaving Bizarre, he wrote Randolph that he wanted to end rumors that he was at Bizarre to solicit the affections of Judith Randolph. He never again returned to Bizarre. John wondered if Nancy had anything to do with the failed attempt at matchmaking. Upon his return, he found no evidence of it. If something untoward had occurred concerning Nancy, he was certain that Judith would have revealed it.

For one of the few times in his life, John Marshall was pleased to be leaving the city of Richmond. The force of the hated Sedition law had at last reached Virginia. With the completion of the trial of James T. Callender two days earlier, even a Federalist as popular as Marshall could not feel safe in the streets. Certainly the federal military units sent to Richmond to assure order were more likely to provoke hostility against Federalists than to prevent it. Now Marshall found himself sharing a coach with Justice Samuel Chase, the most hated man in the entire city. Turning away from the beefy face of Judge Chase, who was sitting directly opposite him, Marshall watched the buildings of Richmond fade into the distance. His anxiety decreased with each passing mile. A physical attack on the coach, the two prominent passengers knew, was not entirely out of the question. The closer to Alexandria they got, the safer they were.

John Marshall had not remained a Congressman for long. Near the end of the first session of the Sixth Congress, he had come back to Richmond with the hope of rebuilding his law practice during the long summer recess. Because it was well-known that Marshall would have to return to Congress in the winter, many clients needing legal services over an extended period of time were reluctant to retain him. Thus, when President Adams offered him the position of Secretary of State, following the firing of Timothy Pickering, Marshall was not as drawn to the prospect of remaining in Richmond as he otherwise might have been. He accepted. The appointment had been confirmed less than one month earlier. Before departing for the new federal city, Marshall had worked long hours to conclude his private business. Just before his departure for Washington, he took the opportunity to attend the Callender trial, the most important legal proceeding in Richmond since the British Debts case was argued there seven years earlier. This time he was a spectator instead of a participant. Samuel Chase, the same judge who wrote the leading opinion for the United States Supreme Court in the British Debts case four years earlier, was the presiding judge at the Callender trial. In Marshall's opinion, the trial had been a caricature of justice. Now, in the coach, the man who had made it a travesty sat directly across from him, speaking in his usual intemperate manner about the "accursed Republicans."

Fifty-nine years old, fourteen years Marshall's senior, Chase spoke to the younger man as he did to most others—in an acid-tongued monologue which rarely ceased, even when the younger man attempted to speak. Chase possessed a brilliant legal mind. Marshall agreed with his view that the judicial power is the only proper and competent authority to determine the constitutionality of laws made by Congress and the states. But in Marshall's opinion, Chase rendered himself unfit for the bench by his total inability to curb his partisan nature in the courtroom. His judicial excesses, Marshall believed, weakened the Federalist party in a foolish and unnecessary manner. During the course of the trial, Chase had been as forcefully opposed to the defendant as the prosecutor. Finally, in disgust, Callender's attorneys walked out of the courtroom, leaving their client to the tender mercies of the Judge.

Since being appointed to the United States Supreme Court in 1796, only days before Marshall and Alexander Campbell had argued the British Debts case before the court in Philadelphia, Chase had become known as the "hanging judge" by his Republican detractors. One year prior to the Callender trial, he had sentenced David Brown of Massachusetts to a fine of $480 and eighteen months in jail for sowing sedition by erecting a liberty pole and daring to criticize President Adams. Less than two months before the Callender trial, he had presided over the trial for sedition of Jeffersonian editor Thomas Cooper. Acting more like a prosecutor than a judge, Chase informed the jury that the defendant's publications had effectively sapped the foundations of government. When the jury returned with a guilty verdict, Chase sentenced

Cooper to a $400 fine and six months in jail. Ten days later the second treason trial of John Fries began before Justice Chase. Fries was charged with leading a mob that freed two tax dodgers from prison in Pennsylvania during a farmers' rebellion against taxes. The defendant's attorneys were so angered by Chase's rulings, they withdrew from the case. Although Fries was unrepresented, Chase permitted the case to be tried, and eventually sentenced the convicted defendant to death by hanging. In protest, attorneys from Philadelphia announced they would refuse to appear before Chase on his next circuit.

Moving to his southern circuit, Chase arrived in Richmond in May with the intention of proving that the Sedition law could be enforced in the South. He himself initiated proceedings by convincing the grand jury to indict ardent Jeffersonian James Callender for his pamphlet "The Prospect Before Us," which vituperatively attacked President Adams. Chase then presided over the trial of the man he had hauled into court. Judge Chase shared the bench with District Judge Cyrus Griffin, who deferred to Chase's judgment on all matters before the court. The trial was the culmination of Chase's sustained attempt to curb Republican attacks on the Federalist administration prior to the presidential election in the fall. It had been completed only two days earlier, on June 3, 1800.

Early in the trial the rumors were that the Judge had instructed Federal Marshal David M. Randolph, the husband of Judith's and Nancy's older sister Molly, to strike "creatures called democrats" from the jury list. Whatever Chase's instructions were, the jury for the Callender trial was composed entirely of Federalists. During the course of the trial Justice Chase continually interrupted Callender's counsel to deny that charges in the indictment related to the mere opinion of the defendant. The Judge informed the Federalist jury that Callender's pamphlet was filled with falsehood. After implying that the defendant could later be tried for statements in the pamphlet not included in the original indictment, he admitted the entire work into evidence. Chase constantly interrupted the statements of defendant's counsel. He prevented a key witness for the defense, former Senator John Taylor of Virginia, from testifying, on the ground that his testimony would tend to prove the truth of only part rather than the whole of one of Callender's statements against President Adams. For later witnesses the Judge demanded that the defense first submit in writing the questions they intended to ask. After defense attorneys Philip Nicholas and George Hay were effectively obstructed, the defendant's third counsel, William Wirt, attempted to speak to the jury on the constitutionality of the Sedition law. Chase interrupted him several times and then ordered him to take his seat. Having ruled that the jury could not consider the issue of constitutionality, the Judge invited the defense lawyers to advance arguments to demonstrate that his ruling was mistaken. When the Judge in open court attacked these arguments as non sequiturs, all three defense attorneys withdrew from the case in protest. For the second time in two months a defendant appeared before Justice Chase without defense counsel. After the jury found Callender guilty, Chase announced it was pleasing to him because it demonstrated that the laws of the United States could be enforced in the Old Dominion. The Judge sentenced Callender to a $200 fine, nine months in jail, and bound him over on a $1200 bond to good behavior for two years.

As the coach bounced along the heavily rutted road, John Marshall listened with a blank face as Chase harangued him on the importance of Callender's conviction. Chase did not appear to be deterred in his exuberance by the knowledge that Marshall was the only prominent Federalist who had publicly opposed the Alien and Sedition laws. During his congressional campaign the previous year, Marshall had argued that the laws were useless and calculated to create unnecessary problems. As a result, New England Federalist Fisher Ames had denounced him as a "one-half Federalist, the meanest of cowards and the falsest of hypocrites." Justice Chase acted as though he were blithely unaware of all this. Speaking not as one trying to persuade Marshall of the errors of his past ways, but as a man certain of his own rectitude, Chase proudly recounted his recent triumph in the struggle against evil.

"It's a pity I couldn't have hanged the rascal. Can you imagine calling John Adams a 'hoary-headed incendiary,' and one who 'affects a yelp against the corruption of the French Directory as if any corruption could be more venal than his own.' It is unforgivable. I tell you, a licentious press is the bane of freedom and a grave peril to our society. What man of honor will enter politics if he must submit to that sort of malignant defamation?"

Marshall had been thinking about his wife's illness. He was surprised by the sudden silence. Chase had stopped talking and was actually awaiting a reply from him. The younger man hesitated before answering the rhetorical question. His intention was to avoid a conflict with the red-faced Chase, who, he knew, was not a man to be engaged in a reasonable dialogue on such subjects. "None" should have been his answer. Instead he failed to acquiesce completely. "There will always be men of honor to enter the political arena in spite of the dangers. I myself was libeled pitilessly in the last election. Despite the defamation, I won."

Chase was taken aback by Marshall's slight challenge. Immediately he launched into a bombastic lecture about the attempt by Jefferson and the Jacobins to seize power in the next election on behalf of the godless French. Marshall groaned inwardly at his failure to humor his choleric companion. At the first opportunity, he attempted to undo the harm by changing the subject. "Did you know there is some talk of having our government pay a sum in gross to the British in satisfaction for the claims of British creditors?"

As the author of the British Debts opinion, Chase was interested in the continuing negotiations with the British on that subject. For the first time he began to listen to Marshall. After speaking briefly about the Supreme Court deliberations in the British Debts case and the handling of Marshall's own argument before the court, Chase abruptly asked Marshall if he might become involved in presidential appointments. "My son Thomas would be an excellent choice as federal marshal for Maryland. What do you think would be the best way to obtain the position for him?"

Not wanting to become involved in furthering Chase's personal interests, Marshall nimbly eluded the subject. "You're a close personal friend of the President. Why don't you write him a letter?" Chase did not pursue the subject. He appeared to be tiring. After speaking of his kidney illness and nearly drowning while crossing the Susquehanna River earlier in the year, the Judge dozed off.

Marshall wondered if the country might not have been in better condition if the old Judge had drowned. Few men, he knew, had done more to assure the election of Thomas Jefferson in the fall. There would come a time when John Marshall would again think wistfully about the fact that Justice Chase had survived the freezing waters of the Susquehanna.

It was Polly who got Billy Ellis moved from the fields into John White's old position in the stables. Shortly before John White left for Philadelphia with his master, the newly-elected Congressman from Cumberland, Polly asked Nancy if there were some way to move Billy Ellis into the vacant position. In response to Nancy's eager inquiries about Billy, Polly had admitted that she was in love with the new field slave. Without hesitation, Nancy agreed to help. "Say nothing about this to Judy," she warned. "If I ask her, she'll never agree to it. But if Essex and Hetty suggest it . . ."

That was the way it was accomplished. Nancy proposed it to Essex, who encouraged his son John to recommend Billy to fill the position in his absence. John enthusiastically praised Billy Ellis to his master. After describing his great strength and excellent disposition, he added the crucial sentence, "He be de one to take my job." John was both surprised and delighted when his master instantly acquiesced. Before John Randolph's departure for Philadelphia, the order was given. Billy Ellis became part of the small community of slaves assigned to the big house and its ancillary functions.

Although Billy spent most of the time in the stables or on the road with Quashia, the wagon driver, Polly did see him much more frequently than when he was in the fields. They spoke often, or at least she talked and he listened. Occasionally she obtained extra food for him. Despite her best efforts, however, she was unable to break through the wall of separation he had constructed between himself and the rest of the world. He remained solitary, taciturn, and hopelessly shy. Polly's passionate embraces of Billy Ellis continued to be nothing more than evanescent dreams. Often she tried to imagine someone else in his place holding her in his arms. It did not work. Even the fleeting images in her mind were unsatisfactory unless he was in them. She bided her time.

One day in midsummer Billy was informed by Quashia that he would be accompanying Quashia on the trip to Richmond. Billy's great strength in handling heavy loads, and the fact that his regular companion, Simon, was ill, had caused Quashia to ask to be allowed to take the big man with him. Before Quashia was ready to depart, Billy had loaded the wagon with hogsheads of produce which were to be exchanged in Richmond for farm implements, tools, saddles, and numerous goods imported from England. For the two men, Judith wrote the pass which, as usual, stated the day of departure, the destination, and their expected time of return to Bizarre.

For Quashia it was a routine trip. On other occasions he had been sent, without the supervision of a white man, on trips as far south as Savannah. His master knew him to be completely trustworthy. For Billy, however, it was one of the few times he had ever been allowed to travel in a vehicle several days' distance from the plantation without white superintendence.

It was during their approach to Richmond on the second day of travel that a strange incident occurred. The August day had dawned hot with a slight wind from the south. It was much more humid than the first day of the journey. The midsummer heat was inescapable. To breathe became an effort. Sweat ran down Quashia's face in streams. He complained constantly about the heat. As usual, Billy remained silent. In the distance the shimmering figure of a lone rider could be seen approaching along the dusty road. As he came nearer, Quashia realized it was a black man on horseback. When he was within shouting distance, Quashia called out a greeting. It was clear from his bags he was a post rider. "Good day, brothers," he responded. After carefully looking over the two men in the wagon, the rider added, "You interested to j'ine de masons?"

At the absurdity of the question, Quashia made a grimace. "We don't care 'bout no masons."

"You be true men?"

"What you talkin' 'bout?" Quashia's voice contained a definite hint of annoyance.

The post rider spoke more directly. "Can you keep a 'portant secret?" After quizzically looking at Billy Ellis, Quashia nodded to indicate he could. "Ever heard of Toussaint?" He did not wait for an answer. "Blacks gonna rise like him and fight de whites fo' our freedom. De whites gonna die like sheep. You trust me?"

"I don't trust nobody," was Quashia's response.

"Where you from?"

"We comin' from Bizarre in Cumberland County."

"Is dat a big plantation wid plenty o' men?"

"Couple o' hundred."

"You tell 'em to be ready to fight when de word come. After Richmond taken, we's comin' into de countryside."

Quashia smirked with a skeptical grin.

"Don't you wanna be free, nigger?" As if to indicate he did not know the answer to the question, Quashia shrugged. The post rider was becoming increasingly irritated. "You put me in mind of a story," the rider said. "One day, a fox meet a dog. Why is it, de fox say, you so fat and I'se so poor? We's both animals. De dog say, I lay 'round massa's house and lets him kick me whenever he want. Den he gimme food. De fox shake his head. Better I stays poor and free . . . I'm like dat fox. I believes in freedom. You's like dat dog, fat and dumb."

Quashia became angry. "Shut yo' mouf', nigger!"

Billy Ellis's arm shot out. As if to hold him back, Billy grasped Quashia's shoulder. "I'll f-f-fight," he said.

The post rider smiled. "De whites got a armory in Richmond wid weapons dey keepin' to fight de federals. Next month, we's gonna take it. Den we come out to de country fo' more men. You tell de slaves in Cumberland. Only de ones you trusts. Tell 'em to hide weapons. When de time come, you be ready." Without another word he continued down the road.

Quashia looked at Billy Ellis. "Don't say nothin' 'bout dis, you hear. De whites hear 'bout it, and you a dead man."

Billy Ellis shook his head in agreement. "If it c-come, I b-b-be ready."

One of the least important-looking of the seven riders dismounted to open the gate. The other six rode through the gate and up to the plantation house. They were all on lathered horses. With spurs banging noisily on the stairs, Colonel Mayo Carrington, dressed in his militia uniform, walked to the open door. Essex barred his way. The Colonel spoke brusquely. "I wish to speak to Mr. Randolph."

"De massa's not here today, but—"

Before the old black man could finish speaking, Carrington pushed him aside. Judith Randolph stood at the far side of the room, ready to receive her unexpected visitors. "May I help you, sir?"

Although Carrington had not seen Judith Randolph for years, he remembered her vividly from the trial. She appeared to have aged considerably more than the seven years since she had testified for her sister. He could see that she recognized him. "Colonel Mayo Carrington, ma'am. I would like to speak to you in private."

Judith led him into the study and closed the door. "What brings you all the way to Bizarre, Colonel Carrington?"

"Very bad news from Richmond. It seems hundreds of slaves have been engaged in a criminal conspiracy and rebellion. It was only the heavy rainstorm last Saturday prevented an attack on Richmond. Before they could come together for another attempt, some of them revealed the plot. A few hundred have been arrested. There's also some talk of French collusion. We have reason to believe the Negroes were recruiting in Cumberland and further west. A number of bateau men are believed to have been carrying messages along the rivers. There may be a danger in this neighborhood. Militia units throughout the country are now searching plantations for concealed weapons. We have placed patrols along the river. All Negro boatmen are being arrested. We would like you to assemble all of your slaves for questioning and conducting a search of their quarters."

Judith appeared to be stunned. After several uneasy moments of silence, she replied, "You may do whatever is necessary, Colonel. Has anybody been hurt?"

"No, ma'am. The plot was uncovered before they could do any damage. If it were not for the storm, it could have been a bloody catastrophe. Damned treacherous race. We care for them their whole lives and they deceive us behind their smiling black masks. They are guilty of the vilest ingratitude. You can't trust a one of them. Do you have records of those who have been off the plantation in the past month?"

"Yes. I keep a copy of every pass issued. I'll get them for you."

"Are there any who have made trouble or who you might suspect?"

"No. But you had better ask that of the overseer."

After several minutes Judith and Colonel Carrington emerged from the study. Nancy was in the room speaking to the servants. With an inquisitive expression she looked up at Judith. Her eyes opened wide when she saw Mayo Carrington. With a shudder of recognition, she departed the room. Judith motioned to Essex. "Tell all the servants to assemble at the barn immediately. Those in the field also. Everybody is to be there!"

As soon as Carrington walked out of the house, Nancy returned to the room. "What in the world is happening?" she asked her sister.

With a disdainful wave of the arm, Judith dismissed her. "You'll find out soon enough."

In less than thirty minutes all of the slaves were assembled. Most appeared to be deeply concerned. It was highly unusual for the conch horn to be blown in the middle of a workday. Quashia walked over to Billy Ellis. "Don't say nothin' 'bout dat post rider," he whispered. "You hid any weapons?"

Billy shook his head. "N-not in d-d-de c-c-cabin." His face twitched noticeably as he spoke. An expression of terror on his face, Quashia cautiously looked around him to determine whether they were as conspicuous as he feared.

One of the militiamen was looking directly at them. He carried a musket in his hand, with two pistols at his waist. "Shut your mouth, nigger. No talkin'."

Colonel Carrington stepped forward. As though he were searching for somebody, he surveyed the faces of the slaves. There was a fearful harshness in his own countenance. "We've received word that many slaves in the Richmond area have plotted to attack the city. They have not succeeded. All have been arrested. The plot is crushed. By the laws of Virginia, any slave who plots to rebel or make insurrection or to murder any person must suffer death by hanging without benefit of clergy."

Essex turned to Syphax. "What he mean 'bout clergy?"

Out of the corner of his mouth Daddy Syphax answered, "Preacher don't say no prayers 'fore dey hangs you."

Standing behind them, Polly overheard the conversation. She knew what it was from her reading. For certain crimes they branded the criminal's hand in place of the regular punishment. Once his hand was burned, the person suffered the full penalty of the law the next time he committed a crime. "You don't get no second chance is what it means."

Essex was puzzled. "What de clergy got to do wid it?" Before he could receive an answer, a militiaman walked in back of him and with an open palm slapped him across the back of his head.

Seeing this, Judith angrily interrupted Colonel Carrington. "That man struck one of my servants. Your men are not to abuse my people. Any more of that and I will refuse to cooperate!"

Carrington brusquely waved his man away from the slaves. "You have no choice, Mrs. Randolph. We must strictly carry out the militia law whether you like it or not." He turned back to the slaves. "You will all remain here until your cabins are searched. Many of you will be questioned, today or at a later date. I already have a list of names here." He held a piece of paper over his head. "No one is to leave this plantation. Patrols are everywhere. Passes will not be honored. You are not to gather except for work. Remember these warnings on pain of death!"

Upon Carrington's command, five militiamen set off to search the slave quarters. Cabins were ransacked, mattresses cut open, chairs and tables broken. Only after Judith complained about the wanton destruction did Colonel Carrington send one of his officers to curb the excesses.

Twelve male slaves were led to the rear of the barn for interrogation. Carrington addressed them. "Your names are all on my list of those who have been given passes in the last month. Each one of you will be questioned separately. God's vengeance on any of you who lies." Unfolding a sheet of paper, he read aloud. "You are brought here as a witness. By the direction of the law I am to tell you, before you give your evidence, that you must tell the truth, the whole truth, and nothing but the truth. If it be found hereafter that you tell a lie, and give false testimony in this matter, you must for so doing have both ears nailed to the pillory and then cut off. Then you will receive thirty-nine lashes on your bare back, well laid on, at the common whipping post."

Quashia and Billy Ellis were third and fourth in line to be interrogated. The first slave was in the barn for no longer than five minutes. Simon, Quashia's usual traveling companion, came out in a shorter time. Quashia whispered to Billy, "No matter what dey tells you, I don't say nothin'! I wouldn't give dis trash a whore's dog to eat."

After ten minutes Quashia emerged. As he walked by Billy, he shook his head slightly in an unperturbed fashion. An uncouth-looking militiaman with a three-day growth of beard grabbed Billy by the arm and led him inside the barn. Carrington stared coldly into his face. Billy's eyes immediately dropped to the ground. "You've been to Richmond recently, haven't you?" Billy nodded affirmatively. "Anyone give you three shillings to join them?" Billy shook his head from side to side. "Quashee informs me you spoke to some plotters there. What did they tell you?" Billy shook his head. "Speak up, boy. What did they say?" Billy's face twitched wildly. The words failed to emerge from his trembling lips. Carrington brought his face close to his victim's. "Speak now or I'll have your ears cut off!"

"W-w-we d-d-did n-not s-s-speak t-to no p-p-plotters."

Carrington shook his head impatiently at the militiamen standing beside him. "Bring in the next one. Get this idiot out of here."

Within three hours of their arrival, the militiamen were on their horses, ready to depart. Carrington's parting words to Judith were a warning. "You are isolated here. I advise you to hire more white servants capable of bearing arms. This could be the beginning of a servile war."

"Did you determine the innocence of our servants?"

Carrington smiled. "None of your servants, ma'am, is under suspicion. But the law is interested in more than mere guilt or innocence."

Judith turned away and walked directly into the house. With trembling hands she took ten drops of laudanum to calm her nerves.

By the time John Randolph returned from Richmond, after attending several of the slave trials, the Negro situation appeared to be under tight control. Hundreds of slaves had been arrested. Week after week the executions continued in Richmond. Dozens had been hanged. Many more were expected to follow. Because the charge was insurrection, the usual thirty-day period between judgment and execution was not applicable. Within days of the guilty verdicts, the convicted slaves were being hanged. The justices of Henrico County had been constituted as a court of oyer and terminer to hear the cases against the slaves without juries. Judge St. George Tucker claimed that the absence of juries was actually a benefit to the slaves. The justices had dismissed some cases against the blacks for lack of evidence; juries, he said, would have convicted all of them.

The militia was out in force. Thousands of armed whites patrolled every area of the state. For the first time in weeks doors and windows were unbarred. Gradually life was returning to the way it had been before September 1, 1800.

As a result of the trials, the details of the plot were widely known. The newspapers, however, were remaining discreetly restrained about publishing information on the insurrection. Even those who published the news for profit were fearful of planting ideas in the minds of slaves who had not participated. Several of the Negroes who had assisted in organizing the plot were now testifying as witnesses for the prosecution. John Randolph had heard the most important of these, Ben Woolfolk. In detail the witness had revealed the particulars of the great conspiracy.

The leader of the plot had been identified as a powerful young slave named "Gabriel." He was about twenty-five years old, with some eduction, which was said to include the tactics of war. A student of the Bible, he wore his hair long in imitation of his hero, Samson. Some claimed he was also an admirer of Toussaint L'Ouverture, the great leader of the blacks in St. Domingo.

Gabriel had been elected "general" by his fellow conspirators. His lieutenants included his brother Solomon, a blacksmith, and Martin, a preacher. All were the property of Thomas Prosser, who had recently inherited a large plantation a few miles north of Richmond. Among his neighbors, Prosser had the reputation of treating his slaves with great barbarity.

Slaves had been recruited from all of the plantations in the region, from the estates of the Williamsons, Sheppards, Youngs, Seldens, and Winstons. What was most disturbing about the testimony was the fact that recruiting had extended into numerous other counties in the Richmond-Petersburg area and as far west as Charlottesville, more than one hundred miles from Richmond. Black bateau men had carried word of the plot along the James and perhaps other rivers. Post riders had enlisted slaves along their routes. Every black in the region was suspect.

The plan had been an ambitious one. The goal was nothing less than revolution. It was developed by the slaves that summer during numerous meetings at barbecues, funerals, and religious gatherings. The slaves were told their cause was similar to that of the Israelites in servitude to Pharoah, for whom one hundred true believers could destroy one thousand of the enemy. The slaves knew that the soldiers had been discharged, that there were no patrols, and that arms were available in Richmond. Weapons had been fashioned during the summer. Cutlasses were made of scythes cut in two and fixed into handles. Pikes, spears, and knives had been collected. Muskets and powder were stolen. The first attacks were to have occurred on Saturday night, August 30. At a brook six miles north of Richmond, a rendezvous of the slaves was planned for that evening. Some testimony indicated that more than one thousand slaves were expected. The attackers were to be divided into three columns marching on Richmond under cover of darkness. Two of the columns would seize the old penitentiary, recently converted into an arsenal with several thousand stand of arms, the powder house, and several other important locations in the city. The wooden buildings along the Richmond waterfront at Rocketts were to be set afire. When the whites rushed down to the river, the central column, the most heavily armed, would attack. The inhabitants of the city were to be slaughtered. According to one witness, only Quakers, Methodists, and Frenchmen, all of whom were thought to be sympathetic to the slaves, and white women who possessed no slaves, were to be spared. Control of the bridge across the James River would prevent a counterstroke. The capitol and the Governor's House were also to be assaulted. Governor James Monroe was to be held captive by the rebels. After taking Richmond, they would issue a proclamation summoning to arms all fellow slaves, including those who had been recruited in the countryside. Fifty thousand men were expected to join the rebellion within one week. If the plot failed, the plan was for the forces to retreat into the mountains, where fighting would continue.

On Saturday, August 30, the day for the commencement of the attack, the slaves began to assemble. It started to rain early in the afternoon but the slaves continued to arrive. Those who usually left the plantations on Saturday night to go into Richmond went in the opposite direction to Gabriel's pre-arranged meeting place north of the brook. That night one of the worst thunderstorms in living memory struck. The roads were inundated. Bridges were swept away. Fords became impassable. The brook swamp area was entirely flooded. Richmond could no longer be reached from Prosser's plantation. The gathering of discouraged slaves dwindled into a small band. The stars, they said, were against them. Gabriel decided to postpone the attack until the next night. Before the slaves could reassemble, their plans became known. Two slaves of Mosby Sheppard, Pharoah and Tom, revealed the plot to their master. Sheppard informed Governor Monroe, who called out the militia to guard the roads leading into Richmond and all key points within the city. Hundreds of slaves were arrested. Under threat of death, some testified against their brethren. Gabriel and his second-in-command, Jack Bowler, alias "Ditcher," escaped. Bowler was the first of the two fugitives to be caught. Gabriel eluded his pursuers for weeks. A $300 reward for his capture was offered. While he was at large, no white man or woman felt safe. The whole of the region surrounding Richmond was in panic for weeks. Finally, on September 24, Gabriel was apprehended on the schooner *Mary* when it arrived in Norfolk. He refused to reveal the details of the plot. Within weeks of his capture he was tried and executed. In all, no more than forty-five slaves were hanged. It was said that many of the owners demanded an end to the executions because the government payments to the owners of the executed slaves were far below the actual market value of those hanged.

When John Randolph returned from Richmond, he showed no signs of concern about the reliability of his own slaves. Other than assuring Judith that order had been fully restored, he said little about what he had learned until he sat down for dinner. In honor of the return of their uncle, St. George and Tudor were permitted to sit at the table with the adults. Nancy sat at the far end of the table between the two boys. Her task was to help them to eat and keep them quiet while John and Judith conversed. Nancy was customarily not allowed to join in the conversation unless called upon to speak. Over the years, she had become almost as silent at table as St. George himself.

"It may sound incredible, but there was testimony that your sister Molly was among those to be spared by the slaves."

Nancy was so amazed by John's statement, she blurted out a response. "That can't be true."

Before she could continue, Judith interrupted. "Nobody asked for your opinion," she snarled.

Accustomed to the petulant altercations of the sisters, John continued as if nothing improper had occurred. "The story was that Molly's reputation as a cook was known to Gabriel. He was not such a barbarian as to destroy the finest cook in Richmond."

"You are joking, aren't you?" Judith asked incredulously.

"No. It's all quite true. He must have heard of her cookbook or her reputation as a hostess. In open court, she was quite clearly identified as Mrs. David Meade Randolph. The rebellion could not—" When Essex entered the room, Judith's piercing glance silenced her brother-in-law. She had made it very clear to the family. "It" was not to be spoken about in the presence of the servants. Except for the babbling of five-year-old Tudor, the room was strangely silent while Essex remained in the room performing his chores as a waiter. When he left, Judith told him to close the door.

"This is intolerable. I can abide it no longer. I can't even speak freely in my own home. There is no more peace. I'm afraid to eat anymore or to feed the children. Who knows what they may put in the food." With an expression of anxious interest on his face, Tudor looked up at his mother. The "Saint" was blissfully unaware of the conversation; the eight-year-old only read lips when he was directed by gesture to do so. Otherwise, he seemed to be content to remain in his silent world. "Richard was right to free them. The mistake was to bring more of them here. We should sell them all and hire poor whites. They simply cannot be trusted. They are lazy, disobedient creatures." She lowered her voice. "Someday, they may kill us all."

"Who's gonna kill us, mommy?" Always alert to the conversation of the adults, Tudor was keenly interested in his mother's remarks.

"Nancy, please remove the children from the room. This conversation is not fit for their innocent . . . for them." Tudor grabbed at St. George's plate. The tall eight-year-old seized his brother's arm and squeezed with his powerful hand. Tudor began to howl. As soon as he was released, he threw his spoon at his older brother. Judith screamed at her sister. "Oh, take them out! Take them out!"

Nancy gently took the Saint's chin in her hand and placed it so that he was looking directly into her face. Without uttering a sound, she moved her lips slowly so that the boy could understand her directions. Obediently he arose and began to leave the room. Tudor refused to move. "I won't go with you!" he screamed.

"Tudor, come with me," she said softly. When he turned his back on her, Nancy grabbed him firmly by the arm and dragged him bawling out of the room.

For a few moments neither John nor Judith spoke. It was Judith who finally broke the silence. "I'd like to be rid of her and the Negroes."

John did not respond to her remark. Instead he tried to calm her. "There's been no sign of danger in this area. I would be willing to wager two of my most promising nags that the plot didn't extend to Cumberland. The only place where apprehension was justified is in the neighborhood of Richmond; and all the troublesome slaves there have been hanged. There have been some idle rumors about our blacks. Seems apparent to me they were ignorant of the whole thing. You have, doubtless, had the story with every possible exaggeration. The Federalists are already trying to make an electioneering engine of it. They're attacking Jefferson for his writings against slavery. They say

Callender plotted the whole thing from his jail cell in Richmond to assist Jefferson and the Jacobins in overthrowing the government. The French aspect of all this could be harmful to the party. There was testimony that a Frenchman who served at Yorktown was supposed to assist Gabriel in the military action. There were no names. But if they transform this into a French plot, we will have serious political problems. This General Bonaparte is not helping; he has everybody worried. Even I don't trust him."

As she often did when John began one of his long monologues, Judith listened impassively. At his last remark, however, she appeared to be surprised. "Why John, I thought you worshiped the French Revolution," she said with a hint of mockery in her voice.

"The revolution is finished. Bonaparte is a military adventurer. He'll turn France into a dictatorship. 'First Consul' merely sounds republican; it isn't. The man is an abyss of ambition. I haven't trusted him since he abandoned his entire army in Egypt to seize power for himself. What is really frightening about him is he may be the greatest general since Hannibal. If they had not been confirmed, the stories from Europe would be incredible. This summer he actually crossed the Alps with his entire army and conquered Italy in a month. It's more like legend than history. Be assured, the Federalists will use it all against us. Gabriel may have stolen the election from our party. Even Judge Tucker is being attacked in Richmond for his old proposal to emancipate the slaves. They say he represents Jefferson and—"

"Speaking of Judge Tucker ... He sent a letter last week. You should read it. He blames this trouble on the advancement of knowledge among the Negroes. As they learn to read and write, he says, they spread information from one to the other. They can form plots in the same way. I think he's right. Our only security lies in their ignorance. We should prohibit reading and writing among the servants. It can only cause mischief."

John shook his head in reluctant agreement. "Perhaps you're right. We can't have them forging passes and sending messages."

"And I want more white Christian men here who can bear arms. The children and I need protection. You're never home."

"I will see to it," he replied.

"And we must be more restrictive in the issuance of passes. They can no longer be allowed to wander about without supervision."

"It will be done. But no flogging. Kindness is the only way to make them behave. If a slave causes trouble, it's better to sell him than to decrease his value by damaging his appearance."

Judith did not disagree. Having achieved her aims, she attempted to turn the conversation to a more cheerful subject. "Will you be visiting Maria Ward before you leave for Congress?"

The young Congressman's face turned pale. He stammered. The question clearly troubled him. "I will no longer be visiting Miss Ward."

"Did you quarrel?"

"No. Whatever friendship there was between us is finished for now. She is only sixteen years old. Maybe when she's older." He spoke with a note of relief in his voice, as if he were content that it had ended.

"You don't seem very upset."

The smile on his face was not consonant with his words. "I've learned to accept the fact that people live and die alone."

"Was this her idea or—" Judith's question was interrupted by a loud shriek followed by agonized screams. "Now what's happened?" Judith asked aloud, with visible disgust. She and John ran quickly into the next room.

Tudor was sitting at the bottom of the stairs, blood flowing from his mouth. To stop the bleeding, Essex held a cloth to the child's lips. Polly stood beside him. Nancy was at the top of the stairs looking down on the scene. Judith began yelling hysterically. "How did this happen?" Her shouting only agitated the child. He screamed more loudly.

"Please, mustn't excite de boy! He needs to be hushed." The calm voice of Essex silenced Judith for a moment. The child's sobs became sporadic. "Go to de ice house and bring me some ice," he directed Hetty.

"How did it happen?" Judith asked again in a calmer voice.

Polly was terrified but she responded. "He was pushin' de Saint on de stairs. He jus' fell down. It all happened so quick."

Judith slapped her across the face. "You worthless girl. You're supposed to be watching them."

"Leave her be!" Nancy yelled from the top of the stairs.

Judith glared at her. "I left the children in your care." Nancy did not answer her sister. After glaring back at Judith, she simply turned around and retired to her room.

"Hush, chile." Essex rocked the boy gently in his reassuring arms. "He jus' bit his tongue. It'll heal itself soon enough. You'll be jus' fine, jus' fine."

When Polly entered the room, Nancy was staring vacantly at the wall. "I don't wanna live here no more. I want my freedom now!"

With an expression of profound pain on her face, Nancy turned toward her servant. "I need more time. Just give me more time. I'll find a way out for both of us."

The slaves resented having to spend part of their precious Sunday afternoon listening to the harangue of a white preacher. Mrs. Randolph had ordered that every servant, whether from the field or the house, had to attend. There were no exceptions. Polly intently watched Billy Ellis's face as he listened. She thought she saw a flash of anger in his eyes; but she was uncertain. He never revealed his emotions. From the stories about him, she suspected there was a great deal of pain beneath his placid exterior.

With jowls shaking, the minister exhorted the slaves to be obedient to the will of God. "Your master and your mistress are God's overseers. You must serve them as you would God Himself. That is the way it is on earth. Through his Apostle Paul, God has told you, 'Servants obey in all things your masters according to the flesh.' When you are punished, whether you deserve it or not, you must bear it patiently. For if you deserve it, you must be thankful He has chosen to punish you in this life for your wickedness than to cast your soul in the eternal fires of Hell in the next life. And, if the punishment is unjust, God will reward you for it in Heaven. The punishment you suffer unjustly here shall be to your eternal benefit in the hereafter." He then read Paul's epistle to Philemon. Walking among them, he carefully explained its meaning as a confirmation of his previous words.

When he had completed his sermon, the preacher asked questions and pointed to the individual slave he expected to answer. "Who says you must obey your master?" His chubby finger nearly touched Sam, who was sitting in the first row of listeners.

"God."

"That's right. And if a slave suffers unjustly, what is he to do?" He looked directly at Quashia.

"Nothin'."

"Yes. You must bear it patiently, the Bible tells us. You will later be rewarded in Heaven."

"Is it right for a slave to run away or to help a slave escape?" He pointed at Billy Ellis, whose eyes were firmly fixed on the ground. "You, the big one." Billy did not look up at him. Rather than confront the big man, the preacher pointed at Syphax.

"God say it ain't right, and I ain't 'bout to argue wid him." Despite the preacher's angry glances, some of the slaves laughed aloud. Syphax smiled mischievously.

After several more minutes of the catechism, the speaker concluded, "Be obedient and work hard. He that is a bondsman in this life is the Lord's freeman in the next. Your reward for obedience will be eternal salvation and a place in the mansion of the Lord. That is all for today. Go in peace." The crowd dispersed as quickly as if it had suddenly begun to rain. Judith, who watched the proceedings, was warned by the preacher that he had been speaking to "a hostile and unreceptive audience."

The next week there was neither master nor mistress on the plantation. John Randolph had departed, with John White, for the second session of the Sixth Congress, the first to be held in the new capital city, Washington. Desperate for companionship, Judith took the children, her maid, and one of her new white bodyguards to visit Randolph and Mary Harrison. The overseer was left in charge of Bizarre. Two days after her departure, Quashia and Simon returned from Petersburg. Quashia immediately informed Billy Ellis that a slave from Horsdumonde had told him that Billy's brother was seriously ill. They also warned him that the roads were overrun with patrols stopping every slave in sight. Despite their warnings, Billy insisted that he must see his brother. When the overseer denied his request for a pass, he went to Polly. It was the first favor he had ever asked of her. She was doubly excited, both by the opportunity to assist him and the fact he had thought to come to her. "I can write you a pass; but it sho' is safer to get a real one. I'll ask Miss Nancy."

Polly was confident her mistress would help. As long as Nancy refused to free her, Polly knew she could request almost anything without fear of denial. On this matter, however, Nancy hesitated. She was troubled. "In all the years I've been here, I never wrote a pass. Judy would be furious." Polly pressed her mistress. It might be Billy's last chance to see his dying brother, she entreated. Nancy was still reluctant. "What if he runs away?"

Polly pleaded. "Do dis for me. I won't ask no more favors. Please!"

Nancy sat down at the table, took a piece of paper and wrote the date at the top.

> Billy Ellis of Bizarre has permission to go to Horsdumonde to visit his sick brother. He must return by Sunday night, three days from this date.
>
> Ann Cary Randolph

Polly kissed her mistress. "Tell him he can borrow the horse and wagon." Eager to bring the good news as quickly as possible, Polly ran out of the room and down the stairs. Billy was so pleased he actually hugged her.

Early the next morning Billy started out for Horsdumonde. Quashia and Simon were there to see him off. "Watch out fo' dem paterollers," Quashia warned. "Lowdown buckra never owned no niggers. Dey jus' loves to beat someone else's."

Simon reassured him. "A nigger can always outsmart dat dumb trash. If you acts real stupid, dey leaves you alone."

There was a fall chill in the air. The roads were muddy from recent rains. Drawn by a black gelding, the wagon moved slowly down the road. For the first half hour of the trip, Billy didn't see another soul. In the season after Gabriel, many slaves who traveled the roads were unnerved by the absence of other blacks. The long anxious time after the rebellion was just beginning.

Suddenly Billy saw them. Within moments twelve horsemen surrounded his carriage. The leader, who looked like a gentleman, wore a military uniform. He politely requested the traveler's pass. "It's proper," he declared, and handed it back to Billy. As quickly as they had appeared, the patrol was gone.

The miles passed quickly, without further incident. The road was again empty. From the lowing of cows in a distant meadow, it was apparent Billy would soon be passing another plantation. If he continued at the same rate of speed, he would be speaking to his brother not long after candlelight. The sound of horses to the rear aroused him from his reverie. Another patrol brought his journey to a halt. The appearance of the second patrol of five horsemen was much more frightening than the first. There were no gentlemen in this group. They looked poor, dirty, and cruel. The leader had several days' stubble on his face. Most of his teeth were gone. "Where you goin', nigger?"

Billy handed him the pass. The man looked at it disdainfully and threw it back at him. He appeared to be unable to read. "I said, where you goin'?"

Billy's face began to twitch. "H-H-Hors-d-d—"

They all began to laugh. "We got a right smart one here." His remark was followed by forced guaffaws. "You one o' Gabriel's boys?" Billy was silent. "I tell you, you give these niggers an inch an' they takes an ell. Whatsa matter, nigger, lose your tongue?" Billy did not respond. The white man's voice was becoming more menacing. "Who you belong to, boy?"

"M-M-Massa R-R-Randolph."

The leader mimicked his stutter. "M-Massa R-Randolph." They all laughed again. "You got a pass, boy?" Again Billy handed him the pass. Not bothering to look at it, he ripped it in half and threw it into the air. "This nigger don't have no pass. Get off'n that wagon right quick. Now!"

Billy slowly lowered himself to the ground. "Jimmy, take him over by that tree." A young man, almost as tall as Billy, approached him. There was no spark of intelligence or sympathy in his primitive visage. He shoved the muzzle of his musket into Billy's face. The cool metal touched the helpless slave's forehead. The big white man pushed him toward a tree by the side of the road. The other four dismounted. One held the horses while the others surrounded their prey. "Take them clothes off," the leader commanded. Billy looked down at the ground. The big man nudged his face with the muzzle of the gun.

"Do it fast, nigger," one of the others shouted. Billy slowly removed his shirt and pants. "The shoes too." Billy moved as though every second of delay meant an extra moment of life.

The leader pulled out a knife and placed the huge blade against Billy's testicles. The slave pulled back. In an instant two of the men held him by his arms. "Do what I say, nigger, or you'll lose 'em." There was an evil smile on his face. "Now, put your hands out like this." As soon as Billy's arms were extended, the leader tied them with a thick rope. The men holding him turned him violently around so he was facing the tree. One of the men threw the rope over a massive limb. Two others pulled it tightly until Billy's toes were barely touching the muddy ground.

"He's good 'n' stretched," a new voice croaked. "You'll git blood on every stroke."

The whip tore into his skin. Billy twisted in pain but did not utter a sound. The force of the first strokes raised the flesh on his back in ugly red ridges. The blows continued to rain on his back and buttocks until he could no longer remain silent. His groans turned into screams. The cries made no difference. The beating continued. The blood ran freely down his back and legs. It poured out of the open wounds which in some places exposed pink muscle and white rib. When they cut him down, he was still conscious, his face half submerged in the mud.

"Should we kill him, boys?" The leader put a pistol to his face and pulled the trigger. The only sound was the click of an empty gun. "You much too valuable to kill. Clean him up, Jimmy!" Like a child who has not yet learned to handle buttons, the big man pulled down his pants. Within seconds the stream of yellow urine poured over the helpless slave.

"That's it, Jimmy. Piss all over him. Don't miss the face." Billy started to get up. The butt of a musket smashed into his skull.

When he awoke, he was in his cabin. His face and torso were wrapped in bandages. The slightest movement caused him to cry out like a wounded animal. Polly tearfully wiped his forehead. Her mistress handed her a bowl of water. "It's my fault," Nancy said. "I never should have let him go."

Polly waited a week before she told him his brother had died of fever two days after he set out for Horsdumonde. Billy uttered a prolonged howl of the most profound anguish. For the next hour he wept like a child.

1805

To a great extent political power exists in the eyes of the beholders. It is a matter of appearances, seen through a glass darkly. When the outward aspects of strength and influence disintegrate, so too does the power itself. At the beginning of the year 1805, John Randolph was the most powerful politician in the Congress of the United States. Within two fateful months the appearances would alter, and with them, the reality. The second term of office of President Thomas Jefferson was about to begin. John Randolph's prestige would not survive the first term. As the year commenced, Representative Randolph was at the edge of a precipice and did not know it.

Randolph's rise to power began after Jefferson's election to his first term as President of the United States. In February 1801 the tie in electoral votes between Thomas Jefferson and Aaron Burr, the vice-presidential candidate of Jefferson's own party, was decided by the House. At the time of the voting, there were rumors that the Federalists in the House would block Jefferson's election by elevating John Marshall to the presidency. John Randolph sent daily bulletins to his stepfather on the results of each ballot. St. George Tucker had informed his stepson that the union would be dissolved if Jefferson were not elected. Finally, on the thirty-sixth ballot, the deadlock was broken. Jefferson was elected the third President of the nation.

John Randolph had no strong personal attachment to Thomas Jefferson. He supported the leader of his party as a means of reforming the national government by the enshrinement of the principles of states' rights and support for the agrarian way of life. "If our salvation depends on a single man, it is not worth our attention," he proclaimed. "If one man is unqualifiedly necessary to our political existence, what is to be done when he is dead?"

At the end of 1801 Randolph's genial friend Nathaniel Macon of North Carolina became Speaker of the House of Representatives. Thereafter, Randolph was appointed chairman of the important Committee of Ways and Means. All measures requiring financial support fell within his dominion. In a short time he was one of the most influential men in the House. When Sam Smith and William B. Giles, his chief competitors for the position of majority leader, were elected to the Senate, his power became unchecked.

As majority leader, John Randolph was not a popular man. It was by fear, not love, that he controlled his fellow Congressmen. Using flattery, bullying, and the ever-present threat of his vitriolic attacks on the floor of the House, he charged directly at his goals with undisguised contempt for those who disagreed with him. "Mr. Speaker," he would cry out in his high-pitched voice. Clad in his familiar riding coat, breeches, and top boots, a planter's hat covering his straight black hair, which was parted in the middle, he would rise to his feet. His riding whip, either in his hand or on his desk, where he had prominently placed it, was an ever-present symbol of the oratorical thrashing an opponent could receive at the caprice of the formidable House leader.

From a distance he still looked like a young boy. It was only on closer inspection that the gray in his hair and wrinkles in his face revealed him to be something other than a stripling. Those who dared to insult him, and many who did not, would be quickly put in their place by that irresistible sharp tongue. Numerous were the stories of insults received from the brilliant young Congressman. A Federalist representative refusing to move out of his way declares, "I don't get out of the way of puppies." With piercing eyes aimed at the face of another enemy who would not be forgotten, Randolph snarls, "I always do; pass on." Randolph shaking hands with his colleagues meets an old adversary who states he cannot find it in his heart to clasp hands with one who called him a "damned old rascal." When Randolph questions whether he ever said that, his adversary confirms it. "Then it cannot be helped and must be true," replies the majority leader as he turns away. Sometimes an insult was not even necessary to arouse Randolph's acid tongue. On one occasion a gentleman began a conversation by informing Randolph that he had passed the Congressman's house that morning. "I hope you will always continue to do so," the young man replied. Knowing Randolph's reputation for dueling, many avoided exchanging insults with him. It was not only his lean skeletal figure and long bony fingers that were suggestive of death.

Randolph proudly played an important part in the great triumphs of the first Jefferson administration. Various taxes were repealed, the national debt reduced, sinecures abolished, and the territory of the nation doubled by the purchase of the vast Louisiana territory. Even the matter of British debts was finally resolved. The United States agreed to a single payment of £600,000, as originally proposed by John Marshall when he was Secretary of State in the Adams administration. The money was to be distributed after claims were reviewed by a British commission that would sit until 1811.

In one particularly crucial area, the assault on the judicial branch of government which had become the last bastion of Federalist power, Randolph had been an important leader. The opening shot in this struggle had been fired when the Republicans attacked the Judiciary Act of 1801. The act had been designed to provide a refuge for the defeated Federalist party. It had increased the number of federal judgeships, relieved the Supreme Court justices of circuit duty, reduced the size of the Supreme Court to five justices so that Jefferson would get no immediate appointment, and established six new circuit courts with sixteen new judgeships. One year after its enactment, the Republicans repealed the act. Many Federalist judges lost their jobs. "The judiciary," John Randolph declared, "would no longer be a hospital for decayed politicians." The Federalists protested vehemently that the repeal cut the heart out of the Constitution by destroying the independence of the judiciary. The Republicans passed a new judiciary act which restored the obligation of Supreme Court justices to ride circuit and abolished the August and December terms of the Supreme Court, which, as a result, could not convene until February 1803.

The next attack on the courts, many predicted, would be aimed directly at the Federalist judges remaining on the bench. It was widely known that Thomas Jefferson wanted to appoint his close friend Spencer Roane as Chief Justice of the United States. This hope had been thwarted by John Adams's appointment of John Marshall only one month before the end of his presidency. It was also common knowledge that President Jefferson had, for many years, considered John Marshall to be one of his most dangerous political enemies. He had publicly impugned Marshall's integrity in connection with the XYZ Affair. Marshall liked to tell the story of how, on his return from France, Jefferson visited him in Philadelphia, leaving a note which stated, "I was so unlucky as to find you out on two occasions." Because the "un" before "lucky" had obviously been inserted as an afterthought, Marshall used to show the note and tell the reader that it was the one occasion when Thomas Jefferson came close to telling the truth.

The combat between the executive and legislative branches intensified in 1803. President Jefferson sent documents to the House of Representatives which were to be used in the impeachment of Federal District Court Judge John Pickering of New Hampshire on grounds that the judge was both a drunkard and insane. The charges were accurate. Only six days after the House, under the leadership of John Randolph, voted to impeach Judge Pickering, Chief Justice Marshall delivered his opinion in *Marbury v. Madison*. Although the result of the case was a narrow legal victory for the Republicans insofar as the court ruled that Secretary of State Madison could not be required to deliver a commission to one of John Adams's midnight appointments, Marshall reached his decision by ruling unconstitutional the law of Congress that granted the Supreme Court original jurisdiction to issue a writ of mandamus. Marshall had shrewdly sacrificed a pawn to put the king in check. The infamous case established the principle that the national judiciary could determine whether a federal law violates the Constitution. Jefferson was infuriated by the decision, which gave vast powers to a branch of government both immune from the popular will and filled with his political enemies. There followed a great deal of discussion among Republicans of impeaching John Marshall and the other Federalists on the Supreme Court, including the hated Samuel Chase. To the surprise of many in his party, John Randolph was not in the least interested in impeaching Chief Justice Marshall. In fact, Randolph was fond of pointing out that his own stepfather, the well-known Republican judge from Virginia, now called "the American Blackstone" as the result of publication of his five-volume annotated version of Blackstone's *Commentaries*, had himself written an opinion in 1793, *Kamper v. Hawkins*, which was similar to *Marbury v. Madison*. Judge Tucker had declared that the Virginia Constitution of 1776 was the sovereign act of the people of Virginia, and as such, the supreme law of the Commonwealth; any act of government in conflict with that supreme law, Tucker ruled, was null and void. The decision itself was based on an earlier opinion, *Commonwealth v. Caton*, by the distinguished Virginia jurist George Wythe, establishing the principle of judicial review in the Old Dominion.

In spite of Randolph's coolness toward the critics of Chief Justice Marshall, the persistent rumors of a Republican plot to impeach the entire Supreme Court gained credibility shortly after the publication of *Marbury v. Madison*. In May of 1803 Justice Samuel Chase, in a speech to a Baltimore grand jury, allegedly attacked universal suffrage, the dismissal of the sixteen new circuit judges through the repeal of the Judiciary Act of 1801, and the "pusillanimous" administration of President Jefferson. As soon as the President learned about the speech, he wrote to a Republican member of the House, Joseph H. Nicholson of Maryland, who was then, along with Representatives John Randolph and Caesar Rodney, in charge of the Pickering impeachment. Because Nicholson, like Chase, was from Maryland, he was likely to be appointed to the Supreme Court if Chase were removed. Accordingly, Nicholson and Speaker Macon decided to entrust the management of the Chase impeachment to John Randolph, the most experienced and competent debater in the House. Without advance notice, Randolph brought the matter before the House in January of 1804 by asking for the appointment of a committee of inquiry to report whether Justice Chase had committed judicial misconduct that justified his impeachment by the House. Objections were raised that the proposed inquiry was not supported by precedent. Randolph replied that it was barely possible for a government in its teens to find precedents. The motion to conduct an inquiry carried by a vote of 81 to 40. Many perceived the proceedings to be the first step of the grand plan to impeach all of the Federalists on the Supreme Court. Randolph denied it. In a letter to Justice Chase, however, John Marshall was alarmed enough to suggest that "the modern doctrine of impeachment should yield to an appellate jurisdiction in the legislature." To avoid impeachment, Marshall appeared ready to surrender the principle of judicial review, recently established in *Marbury v. Madison*, and perhaps the independence of the judiciary itself.

In March of 1804 Randolph presented a resolution to impeach Justice Chase. Six days later, within hours of the Senate conviction of Judge Pickering, at which proceeding John Randolph was a manager for the House, the committee report recommending that Justice Chase be impeached for high crimes and misdemeanors was approved by the House, sitting as a Committee of the Whole, by a vote of 73 to 32. Representatives Randolph and Early were instructed to designate a committee to prepare the articles of impeachment. John Randolph drafted seven articles in his own hand, which were reported on March 26, 1804. The matter was then held over to the next session of Congress; it was again brought up in the House in December of 1804. On

December 3 the House accepted eight revised articles of impeachment prepared by John Randolph. Randolph was to be one of the seven House managers of the case to be presented before the Senate. The trial of Justice Chase formally began on January 2, 1805; but Chase was given one month to prepare his answer. In the interim an entirely unrelated matter reached the floor of the House. Unfortunately for Randolph, it was a subject that concerned him as passionately as the Chase impeachment—the long-awaited issue of the Yazoo lands. As it had during his visit to Georgia in 1796, the Yazoo matter foreshadowed a tragic upheaval in the life of John Randolph.

With an appearance of complete confidence, the majority leader of the House leaned back in his chair. Dressed in his favorite blue riding coat, John Randolph stretched out his long pipe-stem legs. Their extreme thinness was accentuated by his tight-fitting leather breeches ending in long top boots. In his right hand, covered by a thick buckskin glove, he held his riding whip, which he nervously tapped on his knee. If it were not so important an occasion, he might have placed his feet upon the table in front of him. The voting in the House on the Yazoo lands was about to begin. It was Saturday, February 2, 1805. He had awaited this moment for many years. Yet there was no sense of exhilaration for him. He was exhausted. It was, he knew, a dreadful misfortune that the Yazoo issue had come to the floor only days before the commencement of the Chase impeachment trial in the Senate. More than any other man in the House, he was responsible for the conduct of that trial. Nevertheless, only days before it was to begin, in his sickly condition and almost unassisted, he had to lead the fight on the House floor against the Yazoo compromise which had been prepared by members of his own Republican administration. It was, he knew, bad politics and too much for one man. Yet it had to be done. For Randolph, there was no middle ground on the Yazoo issue; it was a simple matter of corruption versus honesty in government.

Even Macon and Nicholson, his good friends, warned him against opposing the administration, in spite of the fact that President Jefferson himself was remaining aloof. There was no leadership from the President on either Yazoo or the Chase impeachment. Jefferson seemed to be preoccupied with the Walker affair. The story had already appeared in the press that, at age twenty-five, Jefferson had made improper advances to the wife of an absent friend. The scandal had recently been reported at length in a Boston newspaper.

Despite the silence of the President on the Yazoo compromise, there was no doubt that it had the full support of the administration. Nicholson was not optimistic about the vote.

There was an unusual air of excitement in the House. In the most bitter congressional battle within memory, the matter had been hotly debated for the past week. The financial prosperity of thousands of citizens hung in the balance. The call of the roll began on the resolution of the Committee on

Claims in favor of the compromise. Willis Alston was the first to vote. Randolph detested Alston, who used to board with him at Mirache's in Philadelphia during Randolph's first term in Congress. Alston voted "aye." As though his low opinion of the man had been vindicated by his vote, Randolph smiled contemptuously. It soon appeared the vote was going to be close. After twelve votes, it was 6 to 6. As expected, Alston, Baldwin, Belton, Bishop, Boyd, and Boyle had voted in favor of the Yazoo compromise. Anderson, Bard, Bedinger, Blackledge, Bowie, and Brown were opposed. There were no surprises.

Randolph's old college friend from Georgia arose. Of course, he voted no. It was ironic, Randolph thought, that nine years after the trip to visit him in Georgia, Joseph Bryan was present to vote on the Yazoo matter. It was that lengthy journey so many years before that had brought John Randolph into the midst of the Yazoo maelstrom. Early in 1795 the corrupt Georgia legislature had voted in favor of selling the vast unsettled territory west of Georgia extending all the way to the Mississippi River. Thirty-five million acres of the most fertile land on the continent, an area as large as six states of the union, had been sold to speculators for approximately one and one-half cents per acre. When it became known that almost every member of the legislature had a corrupt interest in the sale, and that many had been bribed, the people of Georgia arose in fury. The old legislature was voted out of office and the 1795 act authorizing the sale was rescinded by the newly-elected legislature. In a public ceremony the 1795 act was symbolically burned with fire from heaven. A magnifying glass was used which concentrated the sun's rays so as to cause the repealed law to burst into flame. It was at the height of the furor against the Yazoo fraud that John Randolph had arrived in Georgia. His revulsion against widespread governmental corruption was an experience he never forgot. He swore to himself to oppose always such abuses of governmental power. It became his obsession to assure that justice was done on the particular issue that had inspired him.

Between the time of enactment of the 1795 legislation and its rescission the following year, the land companies involved in the transaction sold the land to thousands of investors throughout the United States. Many purchasers were unaware of the original fraud. As a result of the invention of the cotton gin, the value of the land was expected to increase many times over. A fever of land speculation swept the country. Many of the original purchasers sold to new land companies organized in other parts of the country, especially in New England. On the day the 1795 act was rescinded, the Georgia Mississippi Company sold eleven million acres at ten cents per acre. A large number of purchasers in New England formed the New England Mississippi Land Company to defend their interests and to serve as a vehicle for later sales.

President Washington and Congress were concerned over relations with the powerful Indian tribes—Cherokees, Choctaws, Chickasaws—who inhabited the Yazoo lands. Under the Constitution, the federal government was the only body entitled to deal with the Indians. After lengthy discussions, Congress passed an act to appoint commissioners to arrange for the United States to obtain title to the Yazoo lands. The commissioners appointed by President Adams were unsuccessful. President Jefferson appointed Secretary of State James Madison, Secretary of the Treasury Albert Gallatin, and Attorney General Levi Lincoln as commissioners. Agreement was reached with Georgia for the transfer to the federal government of the Yazoo lands and the claims on them in return for $1,250,000, with five million acres to be reserved for satisfying claims. The new territory was expected to be admitted as a slave state when its population reached sixty thousand. In February of 1803, as provided by the agreement, the federal commissioners reported to Congress. Although they admitted that the title of the Yazoo claimants was questionable, they concluded that equitable considerations, including the need to protect innocent purchasers and to preserve public tranquility, made a compromise appropriate. Therefore, the commissioners supported the allotment of five million acres for the satisfaction of legitimate claims resulting from the 1796 rescission by Georgia. The claimants would be permitted to choose between compensation in money or land.

When a bill to adopt the recommendations of the commissioners came before the House of Representatives, John Randolph offered a resolution in opposition. His resolution declared that when the governors of any people have betrayed their public trust for their own corrupt advantage, it is the inalienable right of the people to abrogate the act endeavoring to betray them. Because it was legal for Georgia, as a sovereign state, to repeal its own corrupt law of 1795, he contended that no part of the five million acres reserved for satisfying and quieting claims should be appropriated to compensate any claims derived under the corrupt Georgia legislation. Furthermore, Randolph, who was openly proud of the fact he was descended from Pocahontas, claimed that Georgia had no right to make the sale in the first place because the Indians had not yet yielded title to the lands in question. In 1804 a vote on the matter was postponed until the next session of Congress. It finally came up for consideration in the House in late January of 1805, the week before the Chase impeachment trial was scheduled to begin in the Senate.

In opposing the legislation, Randolph was acting against the three commissioners, all of whom were members of the President's cabinet. One of them, Albert Gallatin, Secretary of the Treasury, had been an intimate friend of Randolph's since they served together in Congress. He was also Randolph's most trusted friend within the administration. Nevertheless, when the matter came up for debate in January, Randolph's friendship for Gallatin and his position as majority leader in the Republican House did not matter a jot to him. He was furious about the conduct of another member of the administration, Gideon Granger of Connecticut, the Postmaster-General. Granger was the most influential agent for the New England Yazoo claimants. As leader of the lobby for the New England Mississippi Land Company, Granger was actively using the vast patronage of the postal department to attempt to secure passage of the bill proposed by the President's commissioners. When Granger appeared on the floor of the House soliciting votes for the Yazoo compromise,

John Randolph became enraged. He would not, Randolph declared, compare the vast sale with earlier land speculation; it was a sale "not of a few acres, but of millions, not sections and half-sections, but of thousands of square miles, not measured by chains and perches but by circles of latitude and longitude." In a state of uncontrolled fury, he was about to cross the Rubicon.

On Tuesday, January 29, four days before the Yazoo vote, John Randolph had taken the floor to speak against the Yazoo compromise. In spite of the fact that he admitted on the floor of the House to feeling unequal to a full discussion of the matter due to a personal indisposition and the time pressures of preparing for the Chase trial, he spoke for hours. The tone of the fire-and-brimstone speech stunned his Republican colleagues and infuriated his political enemies. The Yazoo transaction, he proclaimed, was one of those subjects that pollution had sanctified so that the mysteries of corruption were not to be viewed by the public eye.

> "No, sir, the orgies of Yazoo speculation are not to be laid open to the vulgar gaze. None but the initiated are permitted to behold the monstrous sacrifice of the best interests of the nation on the altars of corruption. . . . The advocates for the proposed measure feel that it will not bear a scrutiny. Hence this precipitancy. They wince from the touch of examination, and are willing to hurry through a painful and disgraceful discussion. But it may be asked why this tenacious adherence of certain gentlemen to each other on every other point connected with this subject. As if animated by one spirit, they perform all their evolutions with the most exact discipline, and march in a firm phalanx directly up to their object. Is it that men combined to effect some evil purpose, acting on previous pledge to each other, are ever more in unison than those who, seeking only to discover truth, obey the impulse of that conscience which God has placed in their bosoms?"

Having insulted all supporters of the compromise in the House, Randolph proceeded to inflame the sectional hostilities involved in the dispute, aiming his criticism at northern speculators.

The shock and dismay of the House at his attack on the hypocrisy of northerners gave way to murmurs of disbelief when Randolph turned his guns on the Postmaster-General, Gideon Granger, and his earlier involvement in a controversial land speculation on behalf of a great land company on Lake Erie. That the majority leader would personally attack a member of the administration of his own party was contrary to all rules of political leadership.

> "His gigantic grasp embraces with one hand the shores of Lake Erie, and stretches with the other to the Bay of Mobile. Millions of acres are easily digested by such stomachs. Goaded by avarice, they buy only to sell, and sell only to buy. The retail trade of fraud and

imposture yields too small and slow a profit to gratify their cupidity. They buy and sell corruption in the gross, and a few millions, more or less, is hardly felt in the account. The deeper the play, the greater their zest for the game, and the stake which is set upon their throw is nothing less than the patrimony of the people. Mr. Speaker, when I see the agency that has been employed on this occasion, I must own that it fills me with apprehension and alarm. This same agent is at the head of an Executive department of our Government, subordinate indeed in rank and dignity, and in the ability required for its super-intendence, but inferior to none of the influence attached to it . . . Sir, when I see this tremendous patronage brought to bear upon us, I do confess that it strikes me with consternation and dismay. Is it come to this? Are heads of Executive departments of the Government to be brought into the House, with all the influence and patronage attached to them, to extort from us, now, what was refused at the last session of Congress? I hope not, sir."

The unprecedented attack concluded in the same acrimonious manner it had begun. The words were directed at the members of his own party who dared to support the position of the administration that had brought that party to power:

"What is the spirit against which we now struggle, and which we have vainly endeavored to stifle? A monster generated by fraud, nursed in corruption, that in grim silence awaits his prey. It is the spirit of Federalism! That spirit which considers the many as made only for a few, which sees in Government nothing but a job, which is never so true to itself as when false to the nation! When I behold a certain party supporting and clinging to such a measure, almost to a man, I see only men faithful to their own principles; pursuing, with steady step and untired zeal, the uniform tenor of their political life. But when I see associated with them, in firm compact, others who once rallied under the standard of opposite principles, I am filled with apprehension and concern . . . If Congress shall determine to sanction this fraud upon the public, I trust in God we shall hear no more of the crimes and follies of the former administration. For one, I promise that my lips upon this subject shall be closed in eternal silence. I should disdain to prate about the petty larcenies of our predecessors, after having given my sanction to this atrocious public robbery. Their petty delinquencies will vanish before it, as the stars of the firmament fade at the effulgent approach of a summer's sun."

By the end of his speech, his voice was hoarse. He complained of extreme weakness and nausea. To return to his residence, he required the physical assistance of John White.

As a result of this belligerent oration, Randolph's colleagues openly criticized him. He was charged with following the most extraordinary course of denouncing every man who dared to favor the Yazoo compromise, of saying that those who disagreed with him had either been bribed or gone over to the Federalists.

Undaunted by the heated criticism from Federalists and members of his own party, Randolph again took the floor only two days after his previous lengthy speech. Once more he vilified the "vile panderers of speculation." The scheme of buying up the western territory of Georgia, he charged, originated in Philadelphia, New York, and probably Boston. Characterizing the matter as a sectional struggle between North and South, he questioned the good faith of the later purchasers of the land. Many claiming to be innocent purchasers, he charged, were active partners and prime movers of the scheme. To illustrate the true situation, he referred to an example in *Dilworth's Spelling Book*.

"In one of the chapters of that useful elementary work it is related, that two persons going into a shop on pretense of purchase, one of them stole a piece of goods and handed it to the other to conceal under his cloak. When challenged with the theft, he who stole it said he had it not, and he who had it said he did not take it. Gentlemen, replied the honest tradesman, what you say may all be very true, but, at the same time, I know that between you I am robbed. And such precisely is our case. But I hope, sir, we shall not permit the parties, whether original grantees who took it, or subsequent purchasers who have it, to make off with the public property."

He resumed his philippic directed at Gideon Granger by describing the methods of an agent of the Postmaster-General.

"You must know, sir, that the person so often alluded to maintains a jackal fed, not (as you would suppose) upon the offal of contract, but with the fairest pieces in shambles; and, at night, when honest men are in bed, does this obscene animal prowl through the streets of this vast and desolate city, seeking whom he may tamper with."

After likening to serpents the Postmaster-General and other supporters of the Yazoo plan, he predicted that the President would never tarnish the unsullied luster of his fame by signing an act that would place a libel on his whole political life and establish a doctrine that would give republicanism its death blow.

The day after John Randolph's second lengthy speech, a letter from the Postmaster-General to the Speaker of the House was read on the floor of the House. Granger protested the attacks on his public and private character and requested an investigation into his conduct. The criticism of the majority leader grew more harsh. One day before the Yazoo vote, the moderate wing of the Republican party and the Federalists were united in opposition to John Randolph.

When John Eppes, the President's son-in-law, arose, the vote was 21 to 16 in favor of the compromise. A prominent Richmond lawyer, Eppes had been elected as a Republican to the Eighth Congress. Less than a year earlier his wife, Maria Jefferson Eppes, had died. When he voted against the proposal, Randolph and the opponents of the Yazoo compromise were renewed in their hope for victory. A member of Thomas Jefferson's own family had voted no. Perhaps other loyal Jeffersonians would follow his lead. The next four votes went the other way. It was 25 to 17 against John Randolph. Joseph Nicholson shook his head in dismay. Randolph was still hopeful.

The voting continued. When Matthew Lyon's turn came, the count was 40 to 28 in favor. Randolph turned away in disgust. He did not want to look at Lyon, a member of his own party and his most relentless antagonist on the Yazoo issue. "Uncouth demagogue," Randolph muttered audibly.

Lyon was almost twenty-five years older than Randolph. Born in Ireland, he had emigrated to America. He became an officer during the revolution and a successful man of business. Originally a resident of Vermont, he was elected to Congress two years before Randolph's first term. Randolph always regretted the fact that he had missed the infamous incident in 1798 when Lyon had spat in the face of Roger Griswold following Griswold's insulting reference to his military record. Griswold had retaliated by attacking Lyon with his cane. Ironically, only moments before Lyon's vote seven years later, Griswold had voted for the Yazoo compromise. On this day the two enemies were in the same camp. Politics did indeed make strange bedfellows.

There could be no doubt that Lyon was a loyal Republican. After his conviction under the Sedition Act, he had spent four months in jail. He had also cast the decisive vote of Vermont for the election of Thomas Jefferson over Aaron Burr. Shortly after moving to Kentucky, he was elected in that state to another term in the House. Republican or not, in these past few days he had earned Randolph's eternal enmity.

After Gideon Granger's letter to the Speaker was read, he was among those who leaped to the defense of the Postmaster-General. Because Lyon had received numerous contracts to deliver mail, he considered himself to be among those accused by Randolph of receiving bribes from Granger. As a result of his accusation that Randolph had lied egregiously, Lyon was ruled out of order by the Speaker of the House. When he arose again and was recognized by the Speaker, Randolph's supporters attempted to have him ruled out of order again. In the midst of a tumultuous shouting match on the floor of the House, Lyon's colleagues voted overwhelmingly in favor of his right to be heard. His loud booming voice had resounded from the walls of the chamber. It was clear that he intended to inflict injury on his opponent. Those who wished for a reasonable compromise of the perplexing Yazoo business, he declared, were charged with an intention to commit robbery and were threatened with being branded in the future as Federalists. Gideon Granger, he said, was a man of integrity and great talent. After explaining the nature of his own contracts to carry mail in various parts of the country, he directly addressed the conduct of the majority leader. His words were more venomous than even those of John Randolph himself. The Postmaster-General's character, Lyon stated, could not be injured "by the braying of a jackal or the fulminations of a madman." Turning to look at John Randolph, he inquired about the kind of man who had made the charges of bribery and corruption.

"These charges have been fabricated in the disordered imagination of a young man whose pride has been provoked by my refusing to sing encore to all his political dogmas. I have had the impudence to differ from him in some few points, and some few times to neglect his fiat. It is long since I have observed that the very sight of my plebeian face has had an unpleasant effect on the gentleman's nose— for out of respect to this House and to the State he represents, I will yet occasionally call him gentleman. I say, sir, these charges have been brought against me by a person nursed in the bosom of opulence, inheriting the life services of a numerous train of the human species, and extensive fields, the original proprietors of which property, in all probability, came no honester by it than the purchasers of the Georgia lands did what they claim. Let that gentleman apply the fable of the thief and the receiver, in *Dilworth's Spelling Book*, so ingeniously quoted by himself, in his own case, and give up the stolen men in his possession.

"I say, sir, these charges have come from a person whose fortune, leisure, and genius, have enabled him to obtain a great share of the wisdom of the schools, but who in years, experience, and the knowledge of the world and the ways of man, is many, many years behind those he implicates—a person who, from his rant in this House, seems to have got his head as full of British contracts and British modes of corruption as ever Don Quixote's was supposed to have been of chivalry, enchantments, and knight errantry—a person who seems to think no man can be honest and independent unless he has inherited lands and Negroes, nor is he willing to allow a man to vote in the people's elections, unless he is a landholder."

Lyon concluded by proclaiming, "I thank my Creator that he gave me the face of a man, not that of an ape or a monkey," and warned that he would not be deterred by the threats of the member from Virginia.

John Randolph remained silent. However, the hatred in the glare directed at Lyon was sufficient to inform the members of the House that the majority leader would neither forget nor forgive the remarks of the member from Kentucky. Randolph would not stoop to issue a challenge to such a plebeian as Lyon, a man he did not consider worthy of an engagement on the field of honor. He had no doubt that Lyon knew he would not be challenged. As far as Randolph was concerned, this knowledge made Lyon all the more uncouth and contemptible.

By the time Randolph himself voted no, the count was 46 to 39 for the yeas. From long experience he knew his defeat was imminent. From the S's to the W's there were at least fifteen more yes votes. The day was lost. Nevertheless, there was some slight satisfaction when his own vote was followed by the no vote of Thomas Mann Randolph, the brother of Nancy and Judith, and Jefferson's other son-in-law. When he voted, Tom Randolph looked directly at the majority leader. It was not the hate-filled expression directed at Richard Randolph during the trial so many years earlier. Rather, it was as if Tom were saying, "You see, sir, in a crisis, I am capable of supporting a Randolph from Bizarre." Or perhaps he meant, "I can, on occasion, oppose my wife's father." Tom and John bore no love for each other. But on both Yazoo and the Chase impeachment, Tom had been a reliable ally. When it was an issue of states' rights, Thomas Mann Randolph was a true Republican and a loyal Virginian.

The vote was complete. The resolution of the Committee of Claims had been adopted, 63 yeas to 58 nays. The northern Republicans had joined the unanimous Federalists to give the administration its victory. The southern Republicans remained firmly opposed. Ten of the twelve Virginians had voted no. John Randolph had no intention of conceding defeat to the Yazoo speculators, hypocrites, and thieves. He would never surrender to a monster generated by fraud and nursed in corruption. The shrill voice pierced through the noise in the House chamber. "Mr. Speaker!" He slowly straightened the planter's hat on his head and waited for the noise to subside. He would show them all; the fight was not over. His voice was hoarse, but clearly audible.

> "On this question I have nothing more to say than to congratulate my friends on the vote just taken. We are strong in the cause of truth, and gentlemen will find that truth will ultimately prevail. When I compare the votes of this session with some of the votes of the last, my objections to refer this subject are almost done away. In whatever shape the subject may be again brought before the House, it will be my duty, and that of my friends, to manifest the same firm spirit of resistance, and to suffer no opportunity to pass of defeating a measure so fraught with mischief."

At the end of the day's business, John Randolph received the condolences of his friends. Joseph Bryan and Joseph Nicholson spoke at length with him. The week had ended disastrously. In two days Nicholson and Randolph would both be in the Senate chamber as managers of the Chase impeachment. "We've made a great many enemies this week," Nicholson said. "Let's hope it doesn't harm us in the Senate."

Randolph remained in his seat until the House was empty. Lost in thought, and in a state of complete exhaustion, he walked slowly out of the House chamber. John White was waiting for him. On this cold winter's day almost all of the congressmen had rushed home. Out of the corner of his eye he saw his formidable adversary, Matthew Lyon, staring triumphantly and scornfully at him. Lyon was almost twice his own age.

"It's the vindictive school boy," Lyon said to his companion.

Randolph glowered back at him. "Do you intend to spit on me, sir?" he muttered. "Beware, I am not Roger Griswold."

Lyon's face reddened. "I wouldn't waste the effort, you eunuch!"

Although he had received similar insults before, Randolph was stunned by the remark. His face turned a shade brighter red than Lyon's. If Lyon had been a gentleman, he would have challenged him on the spot. But a duel with such a vulgarian was an impossibility. Pausing to regain control of himself, he spat the words back at his enemy. There was a look of cold malice etched on his face as he spoke. "Why should a man take pride in a quality in which the Negro is his equal and a jackass is infinitely his superior. But, then you, sir, are a jackass, are you not?" Before Lyon could respond, Randolph turned and disappeared out the door. Rushing out into the midwinter cold, John White hurried after his master.

His huge hand reached under her nightclothes and moved timidly upward toward her breasts. Polly awakened instantly. It was still dark. She was as tired as if she had just fallen asleep. Pretending to be sleeping, she turned on her stomach to thwart the progress of his journey. He persisted. To protect herself from this unwanted intrusion, she tightly hugged her body. With one powerful movement of his arms, Billy Ellis turned her over. Before she could react, her legs were pried apart. He was between them pushing into her. She received each upward thrust as she would an unwelcome stab of uncertainty. She wished it would stop. His eyes had that look of frenzy. His immense weight was crushing her. Her mind remained coldly detached from the act. To end it as quickly as possible, she tried squeezing him between her legs. He continued to have his way with her until his eyes suddenly closed. His body went limp. He rolled back to his place beside her. With her back facing him, she turned onto her side.

He used her like the others did, she thought. It was better when she admired him from a distance. Then, he had provided hope for the future. Now the future had arrived; it was no better than the past. For more than three years they had been together. At first life was better. He was clumsy and anxious. But all those weeks of caring for him, when he was hurt, had created a bond between them. When he was back on his feet, she could approach him without causing an awkward withdrawal. That first time it was she who had come to him. She had placed that massive hand on her breast. Her nipples were erect. She was on fire with desire. It was over in minutes.

There was little pleasure and some pain. After that she wanted to be with him, but not in that way. He wanted more of the same and took it. The first year she became pregnant. She wanted to jump over the broom with him. He refused. No such thing as marriage for slaves, he said. It was only for freemen. Before it showed, she had miscarried. There was blood, a lot of blood. Hetty told her there would be no more babies. Billy was pleased. Nancy knew Polly had been pregnant, but they did not mention it. Nancy did not want to discuss the subject.

Although it was strictly forbidden on the plantation after the Gabriel rebellion, Polly had tried to teach him to read. The white folks were strict in those first few years. There was fear and suspicion of all the slaves. The year after Gabriel, a law was passed restricting the movements of slaves and free Negroes. The patrols were everywhere. For two years after the aborted rebellion, there was talk of slave plots all over Virginia. Polly stole newspapers after they were thrown out. At night, by candlelight, she read them in secret. They were filled with reports of conspiracies and hangings of slaves. Charges of attempted poisoning were common. One slave, she read, tried to poison his master by leaving snake heads mixed with leaves at his master's door. Poor fool, she thought, to be punished for such superstition. After 1802 it became quiet again. There were no more reports of insurrections. The patrols became less frequent. But every year, the legislature in Richmond debated limitations on freed slaves. They wanted to end manumission. When she read about it, Polly became frightened. Her last hope for freedom was slipping away.

With her desire to remain at Bizarre again on the wane, Polly recommenced pleading with Nancy to be freed. Her mistress refused. After the third request, Nancy stated she would no longer discuss the subject. Knowing Nancy would not deny a different kind of request, Polly asked her to teach Billy Ellis to read. In spite of Judith's orders strictly forbidding reading and writing by slaves, Nancy reluctantly agreed. At first she was very careful. Because Polly was no longer allowed to sleep in the house after Gabriel, she would frequently visit Polly and Billy's cabin in the evening. When they were certain no one was about, Nancy would read special children's books to him, while pointing out each letter and the sound that it made. He listened with a respect he never granted Polly when she attempted the same thing. Polly resented it.

Both women were surprised at how quickly he learned. After one year he could read Nancy's notes listing the chores to be done. He even began to write notes to himself and to others. It became his preferred method of communication. Writing allowed him to speak without stuttering.

Polly listened to the sound of snoring. Turning around, she faced her lover. There was a tranquil beauty in his face which was never visible when he was awake. Anxious thoughts filled her mind. Sleep would not return. For having awakened her, she cursed him. She dreaded another day in the big house. All week Judith had been in one of her rages. For a whole year the mistress of Bizarre had expected a shipment of clothing, dishes, toys, and other goods from London. The previous week she received word from Norfolk that the ship had arrived. Judith was as excited as a child. Unfortunately, the goods were listed on the captain's invoice but had not been embarked. Upon receiving the bad news, Judith threw a tantrum of unusual proportions even for her. There was broken crockery all over the house. The servants knew she was dropping laudanum in ever larger amounts—thirty, forty, fifty drops without effect. Her disposition was worse than ever. Nobody willingly went near the mistress of the house. Nancy, St. George, and Tudor made themselves scarce. The servants, however, could not partake of the luxury of a well-timed disappearance.

Polly watched Billy's slow breathing. The regular sound of inhaling and exhaling, she hoped, would cause her to fall back to sleep. It was no use. Her heavy-lidded eyes would not remain closed. Daylight had broken. She was both fatigued and wide awake. Another day of misery lay ahead.

"How long your daddy been dead?" As he spoke, the little six-year-old black boy looked up at Tudor, who was three years older and a head taller.

"He died less'n a year after I was born," Tudor replied with a touch of anger in his voice. He had been repeatedly ill and irritable all winter. With a sudden motion, he brought the riding whip in his hand across the face of the six-year-old, who screamed with pain.

Polly ran between the two boys and angrily pulled the crop out of Tudor's hand. Picking up the black child who was crying hysterically, she yelled, "What you do dat for?"

"He got no right to ask me questions. I'm the master; he's nothin' but a slave. And so are you!" As if to dare Polly to do something, Tudor stood his ground.

Not wanting to deal with the bad-tempered nine-year-old by herself, Polly called Nancy for assistance. St. George, who was with Nancy in the next room, entered with his aunt. Over the bawling of the child in her arms, Polly described what had happened.

"Tudor, go to your room now!" Nancy sternly ordered.

"I didn't do nothin' wrong." Tudor would not budge.

"You hit Jimmy across the face, didn't you?"

"A master got a right to hit his servant."

"Don't argue with me, Tudor. Just go to your bedroom!"

As Nancy reached out her hand to grab his shoulder, Tudor defiantly pushed her away. "You got no right to tell me what to do. You're not my mother!"

Thirteen-year-old St. George stepped between Tudor and his aunt. He was much taller than his younger brother. With a single motion he spun Tudor around and pushed him toward the stairs. Tudor took one step in the direction of his room, turned around and kicked his brother in the shin. The Saint howled with pain. Screaming "Idiot," Tudor ran up the stairs without looking back. St. George trembled with anger. Nancy took the older boy in her arms and gently stroked his hair. So that he could read her lips, she put her face directly in front of his eyes. Carefully sounding out each syllable, she whispered, "Do not hit Tudor; you are too strong. You could hurt him badly." Reluctantly, the Saint acquiesced.

Within minutes Judith came down the stairs with Tudor in tow. She held a piece of paper in her hand. Walking directly up to her sister, she shoved the paper in her face. "What is this?" She was clearly enraged. Before Nancy could look at it, Judith began to read it aloud. " 'Dear Billy Ellis—please brush down the horses as I told you. Then—' "

"Where did you get that?" Nancy asked angrily. "That was in my room."

"I'll ask the questions here!" Smiling maliciously, Tudor stood behind his mother. "Billy Ellis didn't know how to read. Against my orders, you taught that slave, didn't you?" Trying to appear reasonable, Judith lowered her voice and explained, "I've told you how dangerous it is to permit the servants to read and write."

"Polly could read and write long before your precious orders. What am I supposed to do, beat her knowledge out of her?"

"Polly did not write this note. You did. You're helping him to read. Admit it!" Judith's face was crimson with anger. Polly knew that she and her mistress were in serious trouble.

"So what if I did? I don't see anything wrong in it."

Judith was beside herself with rage. "You, miss, are not to eat at the table anymore. You can eat in the kitchen with the servants. And from now on, you can clean out the chamber pots. It will free Polly for other work."

"I will not!" Nancy responded indignantly. "I'm going riding until you come to your senses." She began to leave the room.

"There will be no more riding for you either. Walk out on me and you'll be very sorry, believe me!"

Within minutes Nancy was in her riding clothes. From the window of Nancy's bedroom Polly watched her mistress ride away. Judith had made no effort to stop her. Not daring to leave the room, Polly waited. When the house was quiet, she picked up one of the many books stored in Nancy's room. Polly had been reading it for the past several weeks. It was a novel by Fanny Burney. Nancy had told her the author was an Englishwoman who had to pretend her first book was written by a man in order to have it published. Nancy had also spoken wistfully to Polly about how she wished she could write novels like Fanny Burney. Her mistress's comments aroused her curiosity.

Polly was well into *Cecilia, Or Memoirs of an Heiress*. It was about an orphan girl who falls in love with a rich man named Delvile. The girl was to inherit a large amount of money, but only if the man she married agreed to take her name. Even if the heroine was white, Polly was fascinated by the problems of Cecilia. They seemed more interesting to her than her own dismal life. She was eager to see how it was resolved. Then she planned to read the other Fanny Burney books, *Evelina* and *Camilla*, which Nancy owned.

In an instant Polly was so deeply involved in the troubles of Cecilia, she forgot about the wrath of Judith Randolph. Reading the pages in the warm sunlight pouring through the window, she sprawled comfortably across Nancy's bed. She closed her eyes to imagine the distant world into which she had been transported. Her reverie was interrupted by the sound of footsteps approaching the room. Without hesitation she jumped up, smoothed out the bed, and placed the novel on top of the other books stacked on the floor. When Judith entered the room, Polly was busily engaged in pretending to neaten it.

"Bring the tub in here and fill it with water," Judith ordered.

"But Miss Nancy's not takin' a bath."

"Don't talk back to me! Just do as I say." Without another word she walked out of the room.

When the tub was half filled, Judith returned and ordered Polly to stop fetching water. Without another word the mistress of the house walked over to the books piled on the floor and began to throw them into the tub. *Cecilia* was one of the first to go. Polly watched in horror as it sank slowly to the bottom of the tub, covered by other books, many of which she knew to be Nancy's favorites. Without looking at Polly, Judith muttered, as if to herself. "These things only cause disgust for the real business of life."

One after another, books by authors Nancy had fondly spoken about disappeared into their watery grave—Fielding, Richardson, Defoe, Smollett, Sterne, Voltaire, Wollstonecraft, Burney, and many others. Within moments *Evelina* and *Camilla* followed *Cecilia* into the tub. When it was filled with soggy books, Judith called for Essex. "Take the books on the floor and burn them." Essex cast a horrified glance at Polly. Then he began to carry out his orders.

Only two volumes were saved from destruction. Judith reverently placed the Bible on her sister's dresser. The copy of *Tommy Prudent or Goody Two Shoes*, which Nancy used to read to the children, she retained in her hand. The chastisement complete, she abruptly departed from the room. In a moment she was back at the door. "Your Billy Ellis will not remain unpunished," she announced ominously.

Polly waited for several minutes. Then she dashed after Essex to attempt to save as many books as possible. It was Essex who told her that Billy Ellis had already been sent back to the fields.

Nervously awaiting his turn to testify for the defense, John Marshall, the Chief Justice of the United States, scanned the crowded Senate chamber. It had been impressively rearranged and decorated for the impeachment trial of his colleague on the Supreme Court, Associate Justice Samuel Chase. At the center of the front sat the presiding officer of the Senate, Vice-President Aaron Burr. Under indictment in two states for the shooting of Alexander Hamilton, he had two weeks left in his term of office. Only three days earlier Burr had declared Thomas Jefferson and George Clinton to be duly elected respectively as President and Vice-President of the United States. It was the first time that the election returns had been counted without clearing the galleries. But these were unusual days in Washington. Because of the trial of Justice Chase, for the first time the Federalists had canceled their annual celebration of the birthday of George Washington. "We are indeed fallen on evil times," said Senator Plumer. "The high office of President is filled by an infidel, that of Vice-President by a murderer."

To the right and left of Burr's chair were two rows of benches with desks covered in crimson cloth. There sat Samuel Chase's jurors, the thirty-four Senators of the United States, twenty-five Republicans and only nine Federalists. Because a two-thirds vote was required for the conviction of Justice Chase, all nine Federalists voting together would not be enough to acquit the defendant. In order to prevent Chase's removal, at least three Republicans would have to vote for him on each of the eight articles of impeachment.

There was no doubt that Burr had done a splendid job of rearranging the Senate chamber for dramatic effect. The transformation had occurred during the month the trial had been delayed to give the defendant an opportunity to prepare his answer. The original drawings had been made by the talented Surveyor of Public Buildings, Benjamin Latrobe. Due to the slowness of the mails, Latrobe's plans did not reach Burr in a timely fashion, so the Vice-President gave the commission to Samuel Blodgett of Massachusetts. While the chamber was fitted up in a style suitable for a historic trial, the Senate moved its proceedings to a committee room. In the short time available, Blodgett completed the magnificent, if expensive, metamorphosis. Beneath the permanent gallery a temporary gallery supported by pillars was added. At each end of it were ornate boxes covered with green cloth, which was also draped over the rails. The new gallery was originally designed for the exclusive use of the ladies. Because, at an early stage of the trial, it had been found impracticable to separate the sexes, the new gallery was presently filled with both men and women dressed in the height of fashion. John Randolph, chief manager for the House, did not approve of the large number of female spectators. "They had much better be at home attending to their knitting," he had been heard to remark at the beginning of the trial.

On the floor of the Senate a large portion of the space was devoted to accommodating the members of the House of Representatives who daily attended the proceedings in Committee of the Whole. They sat in three rows of benches covered in green cloth, arranged in tiers which extended from the walls into the center of the chamber. To the right of the visitors from the House, an enclosure had been constructed to provide seats for the members of President Jefferson's cabinet. On both sides of the aisle running from Burr's chair to the doorway were enclosures covered with blue cloth. On the right and in front of Burr's chair was a box seating the seven Representatives who were managers of the case for the House—John Randolph of Virginia, Joseph Nicholson of Maryland, Caesar Rodney of Delaware, John Boyle of

Kentucky, G. W. Campbell of Tennessee, Christopher Clark of Virginia, and Peter Early of Georgia. With the exception of their chief, John Randolph, all of the managers were lawyers.

To the left of the chair of the presiding officer was the box containing the defendant and his counsel. Justice Chase had a pained expression on his broad, red face. He had aged considerably in the past few years. Now sixty-four years old, the white hair that capped his ponderous body only served to emphasize the bright color of his visage. "Bacon Face," the nickname given to him by the members of the Maryland bar, was obviously appropriate. Marshall was uncertain whether the agonized look on Chase's face was caused by his gout or the testimony being given.

Chase was surrounded by his bodyguard of brilliant attorneys—Joseph Hopkinson, Philip Barton Key, Robert Goodloe Harper, and John Marshall's close friend, Charles Lee. Next to Chase sat the most brilliant of his counsel, Luther Martin of Maryland. Even when he was drunk, which was most of the time, Martin was more than the equal of all seven House managers.

Years had passed since Justice Chase had completed his reign of terror against Republicans. From April to June of 1800 he had tried Thomas Cooper, John Fries, and James Callender in three infamous trials. Immediately after the Callender trial, the Republican newspapers had intensified the campaign to rid the judiciary of the terrible "hanging" judge:

> Cursed of thy father, scum of all that's base
> Thy sight is odious and thy name is Chase.

It was, however, only at the end of the first term of President Jefferson, almost five years later, that the long-anticipated moment of revenge arrived. One month after the original opening of the trial on January 2, and only two days after the completion of the Yazoo debate in the House, the trial began in earnest on Monday, February 4, 1805. After completion of the preliminary proceedings on February 9, John Randolph opened for the House managers with a speech of almost two hours. Chief Justice Marshall had been both encouraged and discouraged by the opening. For months Federalists had been contending that the Chase impeachment was merely a step to achieving the Republican goal of removing Marshall and his Federalist colleagues from the Supreme Court. Thereafter, Jefferson would appoint Spencer Roane as Chief Justice; the remainder of the vacancies would be filled by loyal Jeffersonians. As he had on the Yazoo matter, however, Jefferson himself had remained silent on the matter of the impeachment. Not once had he appeared at the Chase trial. It appeared to be John Randolph who was in charge of the entire effort. Since the trial of his brother in 1793, Randolph had shown nothing but the greatest respect for John Marshall. In the hour of need for the Randolphs of Bizarre, Marshall had been present. Randolph had never hidden his gratitude. During the Chase trial he repeatedly stated his profound admiration for the Chief Justice. In his opening remarks to the Senate, he compared

Chase's prejudiced conduct, filled with the "spirit of party," to the impartiality of Chief Justice Marshall in the Logwood case, which Randolph himself had witnessed. The "enlightened man" who presided in Logwood's case knew that although the defendant was "the basest and vilest of criminals, he was entitled to justice equally with the most honorable members of society." John Marshall, Randolph stated to the Senate, gave the accused a fair trial, unlike Justice Chase, who shaped the rules of law according to the political result he wanted to achieve. "We shall bring forward in proof," Randolph had concluded, "such a specimen of judicial tyranny as, I trust in God, will never be again exhibited in our country."

The profuse praise of Chief Justice Marshall certainly did not indicate an intention to impeach him at a later date. Yet there were those who warned Marshall that Randolph was merely Jefferson's creature. Having deeply offended the administration on the Yazoo matter, he would soon be discarded. After Chase was removed, it was said, Jefferson would find others who were not sympathetic to the Chief Justice. In any case, Randolph himself was laying the foundation for future impeachments by denouncing "the monstrous pretension that an act to be impeachable must be indictable." If "high crimes and misdemeanors" need not be proved to remove a judge, and, it was said, none had been established in removing Judge Pickering for drunkenness and insanity, the conviction of Chase could indeed be the precursor of a general attack on all Federalist judges. The Jeffersonian leader on the Chase matter in the Senate, William B. Giles, had certainly made it clear he intended to establish that impeachment was not a criminal proceeding but a means for the legislative removal of judges for political reasons.

Randolph's opening speech had been only one week earlier. It was now February 16. The Senate had been listening to testimony for the entire week. The first witness of the day was David M. Randolph, who was present to testify about the Callender trial. The brother-in-law of Judith and Nancy Randolph denied that as former Marshal of the United States for the District of Virginia he had attempted, in collusion with Justice Chase, to form a jury consisting entirely of Federalists. According to David Randolph, Chase had never said a word to him about excluding democrats from the panel.

As the testimony droned on, John Marshall for the hundredth time attempted to anticipate the questions he would be asked. In all, there were eight articles of impeachment. The first was for Chase's "arbitrary, oppressive, and unjust" conduct during the treason trial of Jon Fries. In his opening speech, referring to this article, John Randolph had foolishly discussed the law of murder. All eyes had turned to Aaron Burr. No skilled lawyer, Marshall knew, would have so heedlessly and purposelessly offended the officer presiding over the trial. Randolph was not a lawyer. He was capable of asking anything, relevant or irrelevant. Marshall deeply feared being asked a totally unexpected question by the erratic young Congressman.

John Randolph made no secret of the fact that he had drafted the eight articles of impeachment. Articles 2, 3, 4, 5, and 6 all concerned Chase's conduct during the Callender case in Richmond, five years earlier. Marshall cursed the day he had decided to attend the trial. He had been a witness to many of the specific acts of misconduct charged to Justice Chase. He was also fearful that Randolph, or one of the other managers, might ask him about his coach ride with Chase only two days after the completion of the Callender trial. If he ever repeated Chase's remarks made to him in private, they would clearly prove the charge that Chase had intended to procure the conviction of Callender by oppressive means. Marshall knew that Chase's state of mind had been, as charged, "manifest injustice, partiality, and intemperance."

Although Articles 5 and 6 concerned the Callender trial, they were merely allegations of procedural error in not following the laws of Virginia in a federal court as to the issuance of a capias against the defendant and requiring the defendant to answer the presentment of the grand jury without waiting for the court next succeeding. At first Marshall thought these charges irrelevant and ill-advised. Randolph was trying to kill a bear with a scattering of buckshot, when what was needed was one powerful shot to the heart. On further consideration, however, Marshall became very concerned about these charges. These were the types of minor errors of law, if they were in fact errors, which could be used to attack any federal judge. If Chase were convicted on either Article 5 or 6, every Federalist judge was in imminent peril of removal.

Articles 7 and 8, the last two articles of impeachment, concerned Chase's questionable actions with regard to grand jurors in Newcastle, Delaware, and Baltimore, Maryland. The eighth article concerned the occurrence that had caused President Jefferson in 1803 to suggest action to Joseph Nicholson, thereby beginning the impeachment process. Chase had made an intemperate and inflammatory political speech to the grand jury. In part, he had denounced the principle of equality stated in the Declaration of Independence, a document that Samuel Chase himself had signed in 1776. Marshall did not anticipate any questions on these last two matters, of which he knew little.

At last the moment arrived. Chief Justice John Marshall was called to testify. Rarely in his life had the imperturbable jurist ever experienced such pangs of anxiety. Not only his own tenure as Chief Justice was in jeopardy. The principle of judicial independence under the United States Constitution was in fearful danger of being extinguished as a direct result of this trial. Worst of all, he knew that the charges against the defendant were essentially accurate. Chase's conduct as a judge had indeed been biased, oppressive, and guided by a spirit of party. Marshall was between Scylla and Charybdis. He had to chart a precise course. On the one side lurked the many-headed monster that would devour him and the entire judicial branch; on the other was the perilous whirlpool of perjury.

Robert Goodloe Harper began the direct examination by asking Marshall about his role in helping his intimate acquaintance, Colonel Harvie, to obtain a discharge from the jury in the Callender case. Marshall explained that Harvie had stated he thought the Sedition law to be unconstitutional and, regardless of the evidence, he would have found Calender not guilty. Marshall stated that, as Harvie's attorney, he moved discharge of the juror on the ground of his being the sheriff of Henrico County, where his attendance was necessary as court was then in session. As requested, the court had discharged Colonel Harvie.

After Marshall's testimony on this matter, John Randolph approached him for purposes of cross-examination. There were dark circles under Randolph's eyes. His skin color was ashen. His wretched appearance confirmed the repeated statements he had made during the trial of being "under severe pressure of disease" and "nearly exhausted." The high-pitched voice contained not a trace of its usual hostility. As always with Marshall, John Randolph was exceedingly respectful. He immediately focused his attention on the Callender trial. "Were you in court during a part of the trial or during the whole of the trial?"

"I think I was there only during a part of the time."

"Did you observe anything unusual in the conduct on the part of the counsel towards the court, or the court towards the counsel, and what?"

A trained lawyer, Marshall thought, would not ask such a vague question. "There were several circumstances that took place in that trial, on the part both of the bar and the bench, which do not always occur in trials. I would probably be better able to answer the question if it were made more determinate."

"Then I will make the question more particular by asking whether the interruptions of counsel were much more frequent than usual?"

Before replying, Marshall hesitated for several seconds. "The counsel appeared to me to wish to bring before the jury arguments to prove that the Sedition law was unconstitutional, and Mr. Chase said that that was not a proper question to go to the jury; and whenever any attempt was made to bring that point before the jury, the counsel for the traverser were stopped." Marshall provided examples of the kinds of arguments between Justice Chase and counsel. He admitted he did not recollect them positively. Marshall was troubled by a twinge of conscience. Although he was telling the truth, perhaps it was not the whole truth. He feared he was giving the impression of being less than candid and much too careful.

Randolph asked if the interruptions by the judge only occurred when counsel pressed the point of the unconstitutionality of the Sedition law. Once again Marshall was extremely cautious in his answer. "I believe that it was only at those times, but I do not recollect precisely." Repeatedly he warned that his memory on those matters was indistinct.

Randolph's questioning of the reluctant witness continued to be gentle. Respectfully, he asked about the practice in the federal courts with regard to the procedural point in impeachment Article 6. Marshall replied that he could only speak of the courts he had attended in which the business of one term is gone through as far as possible before any other court is held. He was pleased to be able to defend Justice Chase on this point without being embarrassed. His satisfaction quickly faded as Randolph followed with a more difficult question about one of Chase's inexcusably partisan actions during the Callender trial.

"Was it ever the practice of any court, in which you have practiced or presided, to compel counsel to reduce to writing the questions which they meant to propound to their witnesses?"

"It has not been usual; but in cases of the kind, the conduct of the court will depend upon circumstances. If a question relates to a point of the law, and is understood to be an important question, it might be proper to require that it be reduced to writing."

Marshall had avoided admitting the truly outrageous nature of Chase's requirement that the Callender defense reduce questions to writing before asking them. Randolph did not, however, permit the witness to wriggle free from this particular hook. He asked about questions having to be written before they can even be propounded.

Marshall could not escape. Fearful of appearing to be too calculating and misleading, he answered the question candidly. "I never knew it requested that a question should be reduced to writing in the first instance in the whole course of my practice."

Randolph smiled. He knew he had drawn blood. But instead of probing at the open wound, he moved on to a more general issue. "I am aware of the delicacy of the question I am about to put, and nothing but duty would induce me to propound it. Did it appear to you, sir, that during the course of the trial, the conduct of Judge Chase was mild and conciliatory?"

"Perhaps the question you propound to me would be more correct if I were asked what his conduct was during the course of the trial; for I feel some difficulty in stating in a manner satisfactory to my own mind any opinion which I might have formed; but the fact was—"

"Mr. President, this question appears to me to be improper." The protesting Senator Cocke nodded in the direction of Aaron Burr. Before Burr could respond, Randolph stated he would not press the question.

Mr. Harper, Chase's counsel, arose. "We, sir, have no objection; we are willing to abide in this trial by the opinion of the Chief Justice."

"Regardless of the statement of Mr. Harper, I withdraw the question." Randolph abruptly changed his questioning to the exclusion of the testimony for Callender by John Taylor which tended to prove the truth of part of Callender's statements. "Did you ever, sir, in a criminal prosecution, know a witness deemed inadmissible because he could not go to a particular length in his testimony—because he could not narrate all the circumstances of the crime charged in an indictment, or in the case of a libel; and could only prove a part of a particular charge, and not the whole of it?"

Once again Randolph drew blood, as the witness could not defend the indefensible. "I never did hear that objection made by the court except in that particular case."

After further questions by Randolph evoking vague responses with numerous limitations stated by the witness as to the accuracy of his recollections, Mr. Harper returned to interrogate the Chief Justice. Vice-President Burr interrupted the examination with his own question which cut to the heart of the matter. "Do you recollect whether the conduct of the judge on this trial was tyrannical, overbearing, and oppressive?"

Marshall leaned back in his chair and took a deep breath. "I will state the facts. The counsel for the traverser persisted in arguing the question of the constitutionality of the Sedition law, in which they were constantly repressed by Judge Chase. Judge Chase checked Mr. Hay whenever he came to that point; and, after having resisted repeated checks, Mr. Hay appeared to be determined to abandon the cause, when he was desired by the judge to proceed with his argument, and informed that he should not be interrupted thereafter. If this is not considered tyrannical, oppressive, and overbearing, I know nothing else that was so."

In response to Randolph's question about epithets being used to refer to counsel, Marshall stated he had heard them so frequently spoken of since the trial, he could not tell whether his recollection was derived from the Callender trial or from the frequent mention since made of them. He admitted, however, that he probably did hear them spoken by the judge.

John Randolph's questioning veered into irrelevancies. Marshall answered without any problem. After an objection to one of the questions, the examination was unexpectedly terminated. John Marshall was greatly relieved. He had not lied. On a few points he had even been cooperative. Randolph had failed to ask any fatal questions. The Chief Justice had cleared the dangerous straits. Soon, he hoped, he and the Supreme Court would again be sailing in open waters.

John White could barely keep pace with his master, who was getting far ahead of him. Because of the obstinacy of his horse, which was constantly threatening to run away from him, John had to use two hands to pull back on the reins with both legs thrust forward to fight the periodic pulling of his mount. There was a chill in the March evening. It was beginning to get dark. Early that morning they had left Washington. In one day they had nearly covered the entire distance to Fredericksburg—almost fifty miles. John was extremely tired. In the gloom of dusk he could no longer see nor hear his master riding ahead of him. It was a relief to be out of his sight. During the previous few days, Randolph had been in the worst temper John White had witnessed in six years of serving him. In the past there had been many times when Randolph was irritable and sick. John often felt sorry for him. Illness was not unusual for his master. He seemed to enjoy his miseries. But this time it was different. Randolph appeared to be truly sick; and, despite the malady, he was in a state of continual fury. When he was not abusing John with his poisonous tongue, he was beating him with a riding whip. The man appeared to be on the edge of madness.

John wished he could simply turn and ride in the opposite direction. Yet he plodded forward, pulled by the inescapable chain of servitude. Then he saw his master ahead. Randolph had dismounted from his horse. Pulling furiously on the reins, he was attempting to get the beast to cross a shallow stream. His horse would not budge. The rider was exasperated. From a distance Randolph's shrill voice could be heard cursing the animal. "Better de horse den me," John White mumbled. He got off his horse. "Massa, lemme try." With a motion of complete disgust, Randolph dropped the reins and walked away. John picked them up. Making soothing sounds, he stroked the area between the horse's eyes. When the animal was calm, John several times reached into the water of the stream and rubbed the cold liquid on its snout. Within minutes he was able to walk his master's steed across the stream. With the water over the ankles of his riding boots, Randolph sullenly followed his servant.

Once on the other side, Randolph jumped back on his horse in a single fluid motion. An excellent horseman, he leaped a fence without standing upon the stirrups. Having cleared the barrier, he brutally spurred his horse and swiftly galloped out of sight. A few miles down the road John White caught up with him. He had stopped at an inn. As usual, his master was displaying his lack of patience for inconvenience. He had just arrived and was already berating the landlord for some imaginary delay. In another moment, John knew from past experience, he would get back on his horse to continue the journey. John pleaded. "Please, massa. I'm too tired for more ridin'. It's gettin' dark. Let's sleep here." Randolph reluctantly yielded. He himself appeared too fatigued to continue. They were given the last available room in the place. In a few minutes the valet was snoring loudly, wrapped in his blanket on the floor.

Unable to sleep, John Randolph went downstairs and watched the gaming at the hazard and billiard tables. "What's your game, sir?" asked the innkeeper.

"Whist." Randolph answered without a trace of interest in his voice.

The innkeeper led him into a private room where a game was beginning. With neither the desire to stay nor the will to withdraw, Randolph found himself at the table paired with a feeble old planter. The cards were dealt according to Hoyle, four-four-five at a time. The other team gained the privilege of naming the trump. Spades it was.

"I'll bet five dollars I get two tricks," the younger man on the opposing team said directly to him. Randolph's response was only a blank stare. He had not even bothered to examine his thirteen cards. "I said, five dollars I get two tricks," the man shouted at him.

Randolph glared at him. "You, sir, are not a gentleman." Flinging his cards in the middle of the table, he arose from his chair with a rage that startled those engaged in the game.

"What is the problem?" his partner inquired. Without condescending to respond, John Randolph wandered back into the billiard room. The gamblers seemed to be completely unaware of his presence. The worst catastrophe conceivable had happened to him. Yet they were oblivious to his existence. He felt utterly alone. He could not remember the last time he had been contented. He ran his fingers along the edge of the billiard table. Even his sense of touch seemed deadened. The bitter thoughts streamed into his mind. It was almost a year since William Thompson had died. His friend had never returned to Bizarre. On Randolph's advice, he had studied law. Randolph got him an office in the new Louisiana territory. Thompson married and set out for the West. Except for himself, they all married. The word came. Like so many before him, Thompson had vanished into the maw of oblivion. He wished he could follow. He had no more strength for the journey.

Returning to his room, he climbed wearily onto the bed, trying not to think of the city of Washington. He was pleased to be away from Babel, that sink of corruption on the Potomac. Now he could return to the pure life of agriculture. The merchants in Richmond were offering no more than seven dollars per hundred weight for tobacco. The prices were certain to rise. Then he would be able to pay more on the British debt. Thomas Mann Randolph had spoken to him about improved systems of crop rotation—planting larger tracts of wheat, corn, rye, and potatoes, interrupted by periods of fallowing and pasturing. Small tracts of turnip, barley, and oats. Use white clover as a restorative. Tom's ideas on horizontal plowing were interesting. Pliny the Younger, he said, had advised that hilly ground be ploughed only across the slope of the hill. That was over seventeen hundred years ago. Tom tried it, and the rain ran off the hill as the book indicated it would. Tom also recommended reading Jethro Tull's *Horse-Hoeing Husbandry*. Judy's brother knew so much about agriculture. But he was a fool. He got fine crops and failed to rush them to market—said he was interested in farming, not money, as though they were unrelated pursuits. Every year he was mired deeper in debt.

Images of horizontal plowing could not keep the bitter thoughts out of John Randolph's head. Against his will they intruded into his brain. Judge Tucker was interested in money. They still could not resolve the terms of the bequest his real father had left him. Had not his grandfather given his mother slaves at the time of her first marriage? Those slaves should have been part of his father's estate. But Judge Tucker had mysteriously obtained a deed for them from the grandfather and sold them. Only now did he begin to question whether his stepfather had violated his trust as guardian for Richard, Theoderick, and himself. Like all the others, he thought, his own stepfather had betrayed him. Nobody could be trusted. People could only be controlled like sheep. For three years he had quietly controlled them in Congress. Suddenly, in less than two months, it had all collapsed. January—Yazoo. February—the Chase impeachment. He tried not to think about it, but the thoughts could no longer be held back. There were so many mistakes. They said the managers had presented a weak case. The witnesses had not been properly prepared, not ready at the proper time. They let Chase be portrayed as an infirm old man worn out in the service of the country that was now degrading him. The worst had been his own final speech. He tried not to think about it. Closing his eyes, he attempted to banish the fearful specter. The harder he tried, the more it returned to haunt him.

Randolph had been sick in bed. He had missed many days of the closing speeches. Although he was weak and ill-prepared, he had insisted on making the closing speech for the managers. Had not the prosecution been instituted at his own motion? The articles of impeachment had been drawn by his own hand. It was his responsibility. He could not shirk his duty. His critics claimed the prosecution theory of impeachment had not been clear. So he began the speech with it.

"It has been contended that an offense, to be impeachable, must be indictable. For what then I pray you was it that this provision of impeachment found its way into the Constitution? Could it not have said, at once, that any civil officer of the United States, convicted on an indictment, should (ipso facto) be removed from office? This would be coming at the thing by a short and obvious way. If the Constitution did not contemplate a distinction between an impeachable and indictable offense, whence this cumbrous and expensive process, which has cost us so much labor, and so much anxiety to the nation? Whence this idle parade, this wanton waste of time and treasure, when the ready intervention of a court and jury alone was wanting to rectify the evil?"

He had been pleased by the examples he gave. If the President indiscriminately vetoed every bill passed by both the House and Senate, it would not be an indictable offense. Yet it would surely be an abuse of his constitutional power richly deserving of impeachment. Chase's misdemeanor in office consisted of a similar abuse of power. He demeaned himself amiss by exercising his judicial authority partially, unfaithfully, unjustly, and corruptly. Had he not stated the theory in plain terms? Why did they say it was not clearly defined?

One by one he had gone through the articles. John Fries was convicted and sentenced to death. In consequence of the arbitrary conduct of the court, President Adams, the arch-Federalist himself, had been compelled to pardon him. That point was plainly stated. For the Callender articles, Randolph had relied heavily on the testimony of Chief Justice Marshall. The Chief Justice admitted he had never heard objections advanced in any court of law similar to those raised by Judge Chase concerning the evidence proposed on behalf of Callender. This "great man," Randolph had stated, "more illustrious for his abilities than the high station that he fills," never knew a similar requisition made by any court. "And this is the cautious and guarded language of a man placed in the delicate situation of being compelled to give testimony against a brother judge."

Randolph wanted the world to know, he had no intention of ever attacking John Marshall. Continually he had praised the Chief Justice, that "able and excellent judge whose worth was never fully known until he was raised to the bench." The impeachment was against Samuel Chase. It was not a means to the end of removing John Marshall, at least not as long as John Randolph was majority leader of the House.

> "Can any one doubt Mr. Marshall's thorough acquaintance with our laws? Can it be pretended that any man is better versed in their theory or practice? And yet in all his extensive reading, in his long and extensive practice, in the many trials of which he has been spectator, and the yet greater number at which he has assisted, he had never witnessed such a case. It was reserved for the respondent to exhibit, for the first, and I trust for the last time, this fatal novelty, this new and horrible doctrine that threatens at one blow all that is valuable in our criminal jurisprudence."

In retrospect, Randolph thought the speech had many good points about it. But he could not wash the shame from his mind, far worse than any physical pain he had previously known. It was when he began to speak of the English law of impeachment that the speech began to falter. The material was unfamiliar. The pauses between sentences became longer. The crowd in the Senate chamber was becoming noisy. The restlessness was palpable. He solicited the indulgence of the court for the desultory style of his address, painful to him as he felt it to be oppressive and irksome to them. He begged forgiveness for his incompetency. Admitting to having lost his voluminous notes, he pleaded that the court rely on the strength of the case and not the ability of the advocate. It was shortly after that he had lost command of himself. The tears welled up out of some hidden compartment of his inner being. Out of control, he wept before the unsympathetic mob in the Senate chamber, before his colleagues in the House, before Matthew Lyon, before the gallery packed with ladies. It was as if he stood naked before them all—his hideous body open to the prying eyes of his enemies. The weakness he had hidden for so long at last was revealed to all. He did not recall any laughter. But the sound of laughter now resounded in his head. The humiliation was too painful to recall. It was too injurious to forget.

The vote itself, on March 1, was the rubbing of salt into his open wounds. Samuel Chase acquitted on all eight of the articles. The Federalists and six Republicans had voted unanimously against him on each article. On only three of the Articles, 3, 4, and 8, misconduct in the Callender case and the charge to the Baltimore grand jury, was there a bare majority in favor of impeachment. On the fifth article the vote was unanimously in favor of acquittal. On the sixth article there were thirty not guilty votes to four in favor of removal. Senator Giles, the Jeffersonian leader in the Senate fight against Chase, had voted with the Federalists on four of the eight articles. His vote of not guilty on the first article was the signal. There was treachery afoot. The administration had abandoned him. The men of his own party were attacking his prestige. James Madison, they told him, was openly gloating over his defeat. An abyss had opened between John Randolph and President Jefferson which could never be closed. A paper constitution is not unlike a lady's fan, a thing that can be expanded or contracted at pleasure. Now that Jefferson was in power, he expanded it like a Federalist when it suited his purposes. But John Randolph would never compromise his principles. For purposes of political expediency, he would not affect a glorious neutrality. He would never swaddle himself in a garb of moderation. Even if the President had abandoned them, he would remain true to republican principles. But his control over the House, he knew, was finished.

That first night away from Washington, John Randolph did not sleep. In the morning he was completely exhausted. His only wish was to return to Bizarre as quickly as possible. When John White's horse was found to be lame that morning, Randolph put his servant on the mail stage by way of Richmond. He mounted his own horse for a dash across the country. Until his arrival at Bizarre, the centaur barely rested. Then he slept for a full day.

"Now you're back, you won't go away?" Tudor expectantly looked up at his uncle for reassurance. "Will you, Uncle Jack?"

"No, Buona. I'll be here for the next few months." John Randolph affectionately tousled the nine-year-old's silky hair. Tudor did not look well. Usually a bit stocky, the boy was now exceptionally thin. For weeks he had been abed. Dr. Robinson had bled the child.

"Did you study your Caesar while I was away?" Tudor answered affirmatively, but with a look of distaste on his face. "Was it interesting?"

"The part about Vercingetorix was good."

"Now that I'm back, I'd like you to start translating from Latin to English one day and then back into Latin the next. It's an excellent method for learning a foreign language." Tudor scowled at the suggestion. "There is some talk of the President sending me on a foreign mission. I would like to take the Saint to England for treatment."

"Would you take me too?"

"You have to remain at school. You know your brother has special problems." When Tudor began to whine and protest, John cut him off abruptly. "Quiet! It's all very uncertain now. Don't get excited about it!" Randolph's voice was angry. "I'm sorry, Tudor. Forgive me. You've been in bed too long. It's warm outside. Why don't you come out with me. We can fly a kite."

"If you play marbles with me first. On yesterday, I played with—"

" 'On yesterday' is not proper English. 'Yesterday' is an adverb. It is not governed by any preposition. And yes, we can play marbles."

Over his mother's objections, Tudor was carried outside by Essex and Simon. While his uncle, with the assistance of Essex, flew a kite, Tudor, covered with a blanket, sat quietly on a chair. After a few minutes of watching, the boy became bored. Spying a small shrub by the edge of the woods, Tudor walked over and uprooted it. With one of the broken branches as his sword, he parried and thrust toward an imaginary enemy.

As though some great crime had been committed, John Randolph stared ominously at his nephew. "Why did you do that, Tudor?"

"Do what?"

"Nature planted this living thing. You have killed it for no useful purpose. It may have grown to provide sustenance for animals and shade for man. I hope you will never do the like again.

"I would not enter on my list of friends,
Tho' graced with polished manners and fine sense
Yet wanting sensibility, the man
Who needlessly sets foot upon a worm.

That's Cowper."

Tudor looked completely bewildered while he promised he would never do it again. His uncle placed a comforting hand upon his shoulder.

Later that afternoon, Tudor and St. George attended their uncle's annual ceremony of distributing the new blankets to the slaves. The ritual was usually performed before the beginning of winter. Because Randolph had forgotten to do it the previous fall in his rush to be off to Congress, he decided to take care of it on his first full day back at Bizarre. The field slaves were assembled in the barn. Randolph stood beside the piles of coarse blankets imported from England, purchased there by his agent with part of the proceeds from the sale of plantation tobacco. Tudor sat on a chair. With a blank expression on his face, St. George Randolph observed the proceedings without any apparent comprehension. His uncle knew that the Saint understood far more than his face indicated.

Essex called the roll of field slaves. One at a time they stepped forward. Each one showed the blanket he, or she, possessed. Those with three blankets were given three new ones. Those with two received only two. "He that has," Randolph declared, "to him shall be given that he may have more abundance." A few slaves possessed no blankets. They were turned away without receiving anything. "You who were careless or foolish enough to lose or sell all your blankets," the master scolded, "must learn to be wiser in the future."

Tudor whispered to his uncle. "If they got none now, how they gonna get 'em in the future?"

"They will simply have to rely on the mercy of their fellow Negroes, won't they?"

When it was all over, Randolph called Billy Ellis to him. "Billy, why are you with the field slaves?"

Billy had a more difficult time than usual getting the words out. "I'se b-b-bein' p-p-punished."

"For what offense?"

"R-R-Readin'."

With a flick of his wrist Randolph dismissed the tall slave. Essex wrapped a blanket around Tudor and carried him back to the house.

The next morning Tudor was sent away to recuperate while receiving special tutoring and treatment. Before leaving, he hugged and kissed his mother, uncle, and brother. Although she had taken care of him during much of his recent prolonged period of illness, he conspicuously denied his aunt Nancy any sign of affection. His mother made no mention of the slight.

On his first full day back at Bizarre, John Randolph had suspected there was something wrong. For the most part, Nancy had kept to her room. Only once during the entire day did he see her. Other than a perfunctory greeting, she said very little. When he did not hear her playing the harpsichord and she did not join them for dinner, he knew the sisters had been fighting again. As soon as Judith recited her usual mealtime "God bless us what we are to receive," she whispered without pause, "I must speak to you about Nancy."

"Please," he said brusquely, "I'm too tired to deal with domestic problems today. Tomorrow, after Tudor leaves." Judith wore that insulted look she always managed when she was put off. But she did not pursue the matter.

Immediately after Tudor's departure the next morning, Judith said nothing more on the matter. He knew she would raise it again. Not eager to deal with one of her tantrums, he remained silent. It was after the midday meal when she again broached the subject. "I want Nancy out of this house," she declared. "I have tolerated her presence too long. I stay home. I spin and weave for days. I clean. To keep us out of debt, I spend nothing. But when I ask her to help, she refuses."

Staring at the ceiling, Randolph quietly smoked his cigar. "There is nothing new in that."

"There is more, much more! The rules of this household have been violated. She taught Billy Ellis to read."

Randolph was interested but not perturbed. He did not consider it a major infraction. The rule was Judith's, not his own. "How do you know?"

"She admitted it."

Judith waved a note in her hand. "You recall, I wrote you about the marriage proposal Nancy received when she visited Williamsburg. Her heart 'revolted at the thought' she said. But it doesn't revolt at intimacy with slaves. Tudor found this in her room and gave it to me."

Randolph held out his hand for the note. He quickly glanced at it. "It tells him to brush down the horses. Hardly a capital offense."

"Look at the salutation, 'Dear Billy Ellis.' "

"Has she written others?" Randolph was suddenly interested.

"She admits there were many of them. This is the only one we've found. But Tudor saw her meeting with him. Once they were in the woods together.

Another time, he saw her go into his cabin while Polly was busy in the house. These are only the rendezvous he actually saw. You can imagine how many other secret meetings they must have had."

With a stunned expression of pain on his face, Randolph put his head down. He wrapped his arms tightly about his body. "This is your sister we're talking about . . . Maybe she was only teaching him to read." For the first time, doubt appeared in his voice.

"Do you recall how Billy Ellis came to leave the fields?"

"I think Johnny suggested him to me, to fill his position in the stables."

"Yes. I inquired about that. It was Nancy who asked Essex to suggest him to Johnny. She was the one who had him brought in with the household servants. She was certainly not teaching him to read when he was in the fields." Judith took the note back from her brother-in-law. As though preserving it for some future use, she carefully folded the document. "And you remember when he was beaten on the way to visit his sick brother. She was the one who wrote the pass for him without any proper authority. She could have asked Knowles to sign it. It was she who nursed him back to health." There was a triumphant expression on her face. "You know as well as I do, there is only one thing a black man wants from a white woman. We should be rid of him before we have another scandal on our hands. I sent him back to the fields weeks ago. A strong buck like that will fetch an excellent price. After he goes, I want her out of this house. You can tell her."

As if he had been struck a glancing blow, John Randolph was stunned. "I need time to think. Please, leave me to myself." He closed his eyes. His head ached. After all she had done in the past, he could believe that accursed woman capable of committing such an unspeakable act. Had she not made him doubt his own brother and hate himself? His brother's shame still stood between him and the unspoiled remembrance of Richard. The events were long past, but they still throbbed with life. The image of Presque Isle came back to him. The unfeeling smile on her face when they talked at her sister Molly's house so many years ago. He would not be diverted into the past. It was only the business of the present that had to be considered. Had she spurned him and taken up with a black man? The fury within him was explosive.

When he stormed into her room, Nancy was in bed reading a book. Like a child caught in the act, she quickly placed the volume under her pillow. "Nancy, we want you out of this house! The sooner you leave the better!"

With frightened doe eyes, she looked up at him. "Why? What have I done?"

"You take as many liberties as if you were in a tavern."

"What has Judy told you? Did she tell you she destroyed my books?"

John sneered at her. "No, she did not tell me. But it's no great loss if true. Heaven defend us from an overeducated female. She is finished for all duties of wife and mother. I've seen some of the books you read. Mary Wollstonecraft. Remember, a woman who unsexes herself deserves to be treated as a man. You always did lack those virtues of the heart which are the best part of a lady."

Nancy's voice rose in anger. "Don't you speak that way to me. I don't—"

"Silence, woman!" he yelled. "There is nothing more disagreeable to me than an angry female. I want you out of this house!"

Nancy's voice softened. She began to plead tearfully. "Where will I go? How will I live? I don't have any money."

"You've lived here as though it were a brothel. You can do the same outside."

The tears began to roll down her cheeks. As she spoke she continuously wiped them away. "What of Polly? I can't take care of her."

"It's your problem, not mine. Sell her. Leave her here. It's of no interest to me."

"But, you must—"

"Silence! Not another word! You are unworthy of notice or a response. You've ruined too many lives already!"

With a sudden hint of resolve in her voice, Nancy responded. "I will go as soon as I can." She turned away from him.

John Randolph hurried out of the room. He slammed the door behind him. It had all happened so quickly. Like Alexander cutting the Gordian knot, he had severed the long-standing ties between them with a few swift strokes. What had been torn asunder, he knew, could never be rejoined.

As a result of the late winter rains, the road was heavily rutted. With every rotation of the wheels, the wagon jolted the driver and two passengers. Nancy stared straight ahead. Her left hand tightly clasped her right, which was resting in the blanket on her lap. She appeared to be oblivious to the chill in the air. Polly turned her head slightly to the right and stared at the profile of her mistress. There was no sign of emotion. In the past few days Nancy had shed all her tears. There were none left.

It was bound to have happened. Those endless arguments with her sister. The hatred in that house. Yet it was strange, Polly thought, that she herself had been the cause of her mistress's expulsion. It was all because she had asked Nancy to teach her man to read. That may have been a mistake. But no slave at Bizarre had ever been sold for the crime of reading and writing. Now it had happened. Judith was searching for an excuse to be rid of her sister; Polly had given it to her. That made some sense. Poor Billy was merely the innocent victim, or so it seemed. Although she was not certain, that was what Polly had concluded. Nancy had simply refused to talk about it.

Polly turned around for one last time. Bizarre was already out of sight. The moment she had dreamed of for so many years had come to pass. Yet instead of feeling the elation she had always anticipated, there was nothing except the dreary dead weight of sorrow. Since the week her mother had died, she could not recall feeling so miserable. That also had been the beginning of a new life.

Was it only two days earlier? She would never forget that dreadful scene.

The slave trader had come out of the big house with the deed of sale in his hand. His man unlocked the shed and disappeared inside. Billy staggered out with shackles on his wrists and ankles. So little slack in the ankle chains. Instead of walking, he dragged his feet along the ground. They helped him into the wagon. Just like Nancy on this day, he sat and stared straight ahead. As soon as he appeared, Polly knew she would never see him again. A few years earlier she would have been insane with grief at the mere thought of such an occurrence. When the actual event occurred, it had not been intolerable. The catastrophe as imagined was far worse than the reality. Time had not stopped. Life had not ceased. She continued to breathe in and out. The pain was there, but she knew it would pass. Perhaps it was because they had already parted in spirit. There was only the hollow shell of the feelings they had once shared. Nevertheless, when the trader's wagon began to move, a wave of emotion had suddenly swept over her. There had still been life in what was past. She ran to the wagon. For what she knew would be the last time, she touched his hand. With an expression on his face of sorrow and total defeat, Billy turned to look directly in her eyes. Something was there she had not seen for months. Maybe it was affection.

"Where dey takin' you, Billy?"

He shrugged his shoulders. This had happened to him before. It probably would again. "Don't know." The words came out easily. Strange, she thought, that the words flowed at such a time.

The slave trader paid her no mind. The wagon lurched forward. She ran alongside. "I loved you, Billy." As if to signify he knew, Billy nodded. There were no more words. No one else shed tears for him. He had no kin there. Neither did Polly. After fifteen years at Bizarre there were few tears for her departure either. In the end she and Billy were both strangers, far from home.

He had predicted it would end this way. "Don't love me too much," he warned. When she swore her eternal love, he was scornful. "Till buckra do us part," he had replied bitterly. She never believed such a thing could happen. But he did. Maybe it was for that reason he always maintained a citadel within himself which she, nor anybody else, could enter. He did not look back. From the moment the wagon began to move away from her, Polly saw only his back.

Through it all Nancy had remained in her room. She had not come out to bid farewell to Billy Ellis. When Polly returned to continue packing their own bags, her mistress tried to comfort her. "I'm going to free you, Polly. You can follow him if you want."

"Where? Dat trader could take him anywheres." There was bitterness in her voice. The only thing they could be certain about was he was being sold south. That was where all the slaves were being sold. A slave on a cotton plantation in Georgia was worth twice what he could fetch in Virginia.

"Is dey goin' to bring him back when dey's done sellin' him?" little Joseph had asked. The tears in the little slave's eyes indicated he already knew the answer to his question. Polly only hoped this slave trader was not like the ones she read about in the old newspapers she took from the trash. One of those who sold slaves and stole them back for reselling. They killed the slaves eventually. "Dead niggers don't tell tales," one had confessed at his trial. Or one of those who beat a slave to death periodically to make an example for the rest. Over the years, she had seen many such stories in the newspapers. It was too painful to consider. She had to think of Billy as though he was dead. That was the only way.

The second morning after Billy's departure, they too left Bizarre. The household slaves came out to say farewell—Essex, Hetty, Syphax, Simon, Mulatto Nan, and the rest. John Randolph and Judith remained inside the house. It was the Saint who came running out, bawling like a child. For all his thirteen years, he could have been a five-year-old, the way he carried on. Inconsolable, he hugged Nancy and Polly until Essex had to pull him away. The boy could not be comforted. Nancy came to him one last time. She gently held his head in her hands so he could read her lips. "Remember me," she had whispered. "I will always remember you." The dogs were barking loudly. Polly wondered if he knew they made sounds. Did he even know what a sound was?

Nobody said a word as the wagon plowed through the mud. Even Quashia, who was usually quite talkative, was completely silent except for urging on the horses. It was only as they approached Needham that Quashia announced their location.

Creed Taylor and his wife Sally came outside to greet their visitors. Taylor knew they were coming. Nancy had sent a message with one of the slaves. They both hugged Nancy sympathetically. Taylor greeted Polly with respect. After a few words of thanks, Nancy went into the study with Taylor. She was in there for some time. Polly waited in the next room. One of the household servants watched her closely.

Finally, after what seemed like an hour, Nancy summoned her inside the study. There was another man in the room with Creed Taylor. Nancy held a paper which she gave to Polly. With that eager voice she used whenever Polly received a gift from her, she said, "Polly, read it."

Polly scanned it. Although she knew what it was, she was excited at the sight of the actual words. "I, Ann Cary Randolph, do hereby emancipate Polly, a black woman conveyed to me by my father, Thomas Mann Randolph. . . ." After Polly read the document, it was signed by Nancy. Creed Taylor then introduced Mr. James Moore. Both he and Moore signed as witnesses.

"Polly, for this deed of emancipation to be legally binding, it has to be proved by two witnesses under oath in the County Court." Nancy placed her hand on Polly's arm. "I don't know where I'll be at the time of the next court session. So, you'll be staying here with Mr. and Mrs. Taylor. When the time comes, he and Mr. Moore will appear in court as witnesses to prove the deed. After that you will be free to go where you wish." Polly nodded to indicate her understanding and approval.

"Polly is a fortunate gal," Creed Taylor interjected. "This may be one of the last manumissions in Virginia. This session, the Assembly almost passed a law repealing the 1782 manumission statute. There is no doubt in my mind that within the next year, the repeal will either be approved or a compromise bill will be enacted requiring all freed slaves to leave Virginia within months of their emancipation. In either case, the spirit of the revolution will soon be dead in this commonwealth."

Mr. Moore shook his head with disgust. "Can you imagine we have come to that. A man cannot even decide what is to be done with his own property."

Polly knew that Creed Taylor was the President of the Virginia Senate. His information was extremely reliable. There could be no doubt about her plans now. She would leave the state as soon as the deed was proved in court. As a freed slave, she would no longer be welcome in the land of her birth. "I have kinfolk in Boston," Polly declared. "Slavery don't exist up dere, and dat's where I'm goin'."

"As soon as the deed is proved, Polly," Creed Taylor added, "I myself will put you on a Richmond coach to New England."

Nancy remained that day at Needham. Polly was disappointed that her mistress chose to spend their last hours together with the Taylors. When she was a child, her mother had warned her not to get too close to white folks. "Dem white gals," she had said, "ain't your sisters and never will be." Over the years, how many times had that lesson been proved to her? She had lost count. Yet it was still painful when Nancy acted like her mistress rather than her friend.

Early the next morning Quashia loaded the bags. Creed Taylor had his servants place piles of books inside the wagon. Many were replacements of those drowned in the tub. To protect the volumes from the elements, a tarpaulin was placed over them. Nancy walked over to Polly and threw her arms around her former servant. "Take this money, please."

Polly protested. "You'll be needin' it yourself."

"Don't you worry 'bout me. I'll be staying with family and friends. My brother Tom will help me, with money I mean. I can always earn more as a seamstress. I actually feel relieved. For the first time in years, there's hope for the future."

Polly smiled. "For de two of us."

"There may be some hard times. Whatever happens, I won't let suffering defeat me. Don't you either. We've survived so much together. Hard times, you know, are like laudanum; after a time sensibilities decline." Smiling at her own words, she hugged Polly again. "Remember, write me by way of Tom. He'll see I get your letters."

Polly grasped at the last hope of learning the fate of Billy Ellis. "Will you write Judy?"

"No. She hasn't a latent spark of affection for me. There will be no more words between us."

Creed Taylor assisted Nancy into the wagon. "You can stay with us if you wish. You don't have to leave."

"No. The arrangements have been made." Before revealing any sign of emotion, she quickly turned away.

Polly watched the wagon drive slowly down the muddy road. She wondered whether, like Billy Ellis, Nancy would refrain from turning around for a last glance. If she looks back, I'll never really be free, she told herself. It was, she knew, a bit of whimsy, a childish game. For the last time Nancy turned and gave one quick wave of the hand. Then she looked to the road ahead. Polly smiled. She had lost the game but was happy anyway. There could be no doubt; she was indeed free. The dread of starvation had now replaced the fear of punishment. Shuddering at the thought of the future, she recalled what Nancy had often said to her. "When the gods want to punish you, they fulfill your desires."

The wagon ascended a slight incline and vanished behind the crest of the hill. Now they were both on unfamiliar roads leading into an unknown country.

PART III

THE FUTURE

❦

Whatsoever thy hand findeth to do, do it with

thy might; for there is no work, no thought,

no knowledge nor wisdom in the grave,

whither thou goest.

ECCLESIASTES

PHILADELPHIA
May 20, 1833

No it cannot be stopped that endless sound goes on and on and on at once the
most valuable and perishable of our possessions the tomb of hope simultaneously
destroying both desire and suffering everything vanishing in its irresistible torrent
the subtle thief of youth the rescuer of ancient wretches from the agony that is old
age it flows relentlessly onward—the old patriarchs of my youth have all been
gathered to their fathers and I have become an old man to their grandchildren the
Tidewater now a desolate expanse of abandoned fields, ruined churches, the Temples of the living God deserted the glebe sold and the mansions spared by fire fast
falling into decay—if only we could change this world as it does so effortlessly—
Maximus innovator tempus, quidni igitur tempus imitemur?—The watch was
a gift from Taylor I think or was it ... which will was the last one it must be the
one that freed them when the chief justice came to assist me in drafting it for
which neglect I was strongly admonished in a dream—the past is not in our power
to recall and we can neither predict nor control the future, the present alone is at
our disposal but it is constantly becoming the past after being altered by harsh
fortune—

> Thou hast no youth, nor age;
> But as it were an after-dinner's sleep,
> Dreaming on both

is there any present at all even as I think it slides away from me into the
bottomless deep never a moment to possess or enjoy all ceaseless and senseless
change—so vivid then it seemed it would never pass but it did the moonlight
sparkling on the water a golden path to a shimmering future on the far shore
come in he said the water's warm beckoning me to follow to the island but the
other refused to join us it was pointless he said to try in the heaving waters he
would only plunge in if there was something squalid urging him forward and that
day was pure unsullied by base desire unlike that later time the swarthy bought
woman languidly resting her legs apart while waiting for the boy who was then
still a man to enter her embrace it was he who brought me there but why must
my mind dwell on such sordid things always coming back to it against my will
must think of something more pleasant—Sancho, Dido, and Echo beautiful faithful
creatures the major fault of dogs is they attach themselves to so base an animal as
man ... measuring the sorrel gelding fifteen hands high and that stallion sired by

561

Old Sir Archie out of Lady Bunbury a beautiful animal not as good for racing as for breeding—if only Sir Henry had beaten Eclipse, difficult to believe that race was ten years ago, the pride it would have created south of the Patapsco if our horse instead of theirs had won ... the beauty of riding in October through the pathless woods the trees half leafless reminding me of my own approaching destiny so often sitting on my horse wishing to go somewhere but not knowing where to ride for I would escape anywhere from the incubus which weighs me down but it always follows me ... the name of the horse was Wildfire alarmed at the tattered wagon cover blowing in the wind he reared and almost crushed me against the tree I wish my miserable existence had then terminated it would have been sudden and spared me so many years of pain—the language cannot express one-thousandth of the torment I have been forced to endure such long and severe suffering makes death a welcome guest to escape the vulture who daily whets his beak for repast on my swollen liver his talons fixed in my very innards while I struggle with the bitter harvest which is the end of life when as soon as one agony ends another is lurking close behind it—my whole nervous system shattered crippled with sciatica the very bones disjointed with rheumatism the pain never ending with another severe bilious attack in the bowels the food passing through me unchanged, incessant diarrhea, cramps, spasms, nausea high fever with sweats nearly impossible to sleep unless by opium, brandy, and calomel—doesn't help the sore throat turning putrid that is they say when it is mortal—liver and lungs diseased to the last extreme spitting up crimson blood from the lungs staining the purity of the white porcelain bowl and my clean clothing—the fear overtakes me of losing control of my body and mind as when that boy punched me in the stomach I writhed without breath while the older boys paid no heed forced to seize the inner calm to breathe by the power of the mind itself over the body's desperate need for air—for a long time taking five grains of hypercarbonated natron in a tablespoonful of new milk and endless doses of Cheltenham salts this extremity of suffering eventually plunged me into opium for which I had a horror all my life after watching its brutal effect on my brother's poor wife ... strange there should be found inducements strong enough to carry on the business of this world all the uses of which are truly stale, flat, and unprofitable—endless cups of tea and crackers without butter, rhubarb, ipecac, calomel, and castor oil—a place filled with Yahoos and Yazoo men in a howling wilderness of monsters tearing one another to pieces for money, power, and other vile lusts where everything sacred is trod under the hooves of the swinish multitude and backstairs influence is king—those men who bring messages to the House govern its decisions although they do not appear on its journals the Yazoo men who live for the tarnished honors of this abode of shabby splendor—but for a few souls who have transmigrated from the generous Houyhnhnms those few men who are not unhappy as they are believers in the Gospels with a sunshine of the soul I can never possess yet ambition, avarice, and pleasure have their temples crowded with votaries who obstinately turn away from the only waters that can slake their thirst in the vast madhouse they have lost the innocence of the first gloss of youth and hardened their hearts against their fellow men by yielding the illusions of an ideal world as the mature mind spurns the luminous notions which

*brutal experience explodes forever losing the foolish visionary plans of the young
who believe so beautifully but so wrongly—lost in a desert of mediocrity where
Caligula's horse could be named senator without anyone taking notice—robes and
furr'd gowns hide all* Quam parva sapienter regitur mundus—*so I have become
cold, suspicious, and dead to my better feelings dulled by this long tedious journey
through life along which every hope was disappointed—I would gladly dismiss from
my mind recollection of the past that bloody field where my family and friends
have perished and crawl into a cave like Timon feeling contempt for other poor
foolish mortals who deserve to be consigned to Bonaparte in this world and to
Satan his master in the next since I can no longer imagine any condition under
which I should not be wretched yet I've never lost my belief in truth though it
looks ridiculous the Golden Helmet of Mambrino on my vile deformed body—
now struggling against wasting the end of my life in bed like a breeding woman
instead of in harness with my spurs on—"vanity of vanities saith the preacher"—
if He truly exists why does He punish me so who is more sinned against than
sinning and permit the suffering of innocent children—poor St. George and
Tudor—giving me the soul of a hero trapped in the body of Caliban worshiping the
idea of a family living on from generation to generation so we are not as ephemeral as the flies of summer yet placing no sap in my loins—I have been filled with
uncontrolled passion causing me to suffer the torments of the damned my nerves
without protective skin this old body embattled in celibacy for over forty years
hated of men and scorned by women to die without children—the pain I have
been made to endure by female caprice and lack of sympathy—weariness and
lassitude my portion at the end to be mourned by no person yet I bless God even
if He is deaf or does not exist perhaps but an atom in the mind of man or is man
an atom in the mind of God—He has removed all cause for happiness never an
hour of good health and inflicting me with slaves . . . still humiliated after all
these years weeping before the entire Congress—some wounds never entirely heal
. . . Theo urges me into the room where that harlot is waiting the sap rising within
me—since the scarlet fever so many years without that hardness in the loins the
ridiculous swelling necessary for procreation the only way we live beyond our
short miserable existences there was a volcano once beneath my ice but it burned
out long before its proper time . . . the pain is returning if only Johnny would
remove that wretched watch its ticks never ceasing an endless pounding in my
brain—people care nothing about the miseries of an old man—I am more than
satiated with this world an eternity here would be punishment enough for the
worst offender yet I drag on like a captive at the end of a slave chain in an endless
African coffle—that old king learned that no man is happy who is alive—those
from whom I had a right to expect a different conduct have betrayed a shameless,
selfish, bare-faced disregard of my feelings and abandoned me—I have not loved
the world nor the world loved me—strange my legs seem unnaturally long and
heavy they cannot move must not panic, the mind must maintain control . . .*

"Mr. Randolph. Mr. Randolph. *Mr. Randolph!!*"

"Who in the deuce are you, sir? My pardon. Be so good, sir, as to give
me your name."

"Dr. Joseph Parrish. Mr. Badger sent for me. He said you needed my services."

"Who is Mr. Badger?"

"The proprietor of this hotel."

"Oh yes. You're the doctor who took care of Mr. Giles."

"Yes, that's correct."

"That is how I selected you—Giles."

"Tell me, Mr. Randolph, how long have you been sick?"

Now there is a damned fool inquiry. This one begins badly. "Don't ask me that question! I have been sick all my life."

"What is troubling you now?"

"This city, sir. I've never liked it. A day here is one too many. We came here this afternoon to board the packet for England. We seem to be too late. Johnny, take the doctor's coat. It's wet. This is my body-servant, Johnny. If you need anything, just ask him—"

"What are your symptoms? Are you presently experiencing pain?"

"I do hate to be interrupted! Yes. I've been afflicted with pain for years, without respite. Haven't known a day of perfect health in my entire life. Job could not have suffered more."

"You seem to be having some difficulty in breathing."

"I'm so weak; I'm unable to expectorate. Unless I can expel the purulent matter from the lungs, my life is at an end. You can see my flesh is reduced to nothing. For years I've had violent and copious discharges of blood from the lungs. Yesterday, my expectoration was quite bloody, but I am not certain it came from the lungs. These attacks exhaust me so, I am frequently unable to speak. This churchyard cough keeps me awake nights. Only strong doses of opium give me any rest. I take it like a Turk. I've been sinking for years into an opium-eating sot. I'm wracked by pain every night from a disordered stomach. My bowels are torn to pieces. My digestive facilities are worn out. Diarrhea is endless. Terminated the career of every member of my family. Most of the time I have a fever. All of these problems are killing me. But it's phthisis will finish me. I've been affected by it for years. It was greatly aggravated by my voyage to Russia. That mad journey almost killed my servant Juba and may yet kill me. It has been a Pultowa, a Beresina to me . . . I have, you know, attended lectures on anatomy. I've read Moreton on consumption. Oh yes, I know all about it. I've tried all the cures—digitalis and foxglove, resin and yellow beeswax dissolved over a fire, fumigation of the room, hot drinks, cold drinks, no drinks." *It's starting again. I can't breathe. One time this coughing and retching won't cease.*

"Stay calm. Try to breathe slowly. Good. Your pulse is strong. That's an excellent sign."

"You can form no judgment by my pulse. It's quite peculiar."

"There are idiosyncracies in every constitution. You've been ill so long you must have acquired knowledge of the best course of treatment for your own case."

"I have been an idiosyncracy all my life." *He does not disagree, I see.* "Preparations of camphor are harmful to me. Ether would blow me up. Laudanum works well; opium has been my savior for many years. Calomel, the Samson of medicines, has never given me any ill effects."

"You sound as though you are quite capable of serving as your own physician."

"There is an old Spanish adage—a man who practices on himself has a fool for a physician."

"Has your condition worsened recently?"

"Today's difficulties have surely not been harmless. I was obliged to go from one hotel to another in search of lodgings. Johnny could only find a wretched hack. The glass in the carriage was broken so I was exposed to the storm. Mr. Badger was the first to accommodate me, so here I find myself. . . . You're a Quaker, are you not?"

"Yes. How did you know?"

"Mr. Badger informed me. I like the Quakers. You are your own minister. No need for the intercession of a priest. I have as little faith in priests as any man alive. I've always detested ecclesiastical tyranny and prelatical pride. I myself am a member of the Church of England."

"You mean the Episcopal Church?"

"No. That's a disestablished church without glebe lands in Virginia. I was born in the Church of England and have remained faithful to it—a diocesan of the Bishop of London. Actually, in my youth I forgot the teachings of my dear mother and became an infidel. For a brief time I held an absurd prejudice in favor of Mohammedanism. I actually rejoiced at accounts of the triumphs of the crescent over the cross. Perhaps it was my youthful readings of the barbarous cruelty of the crusaders in Jerusalem compared to the merciful Saladin. And daily to observe the practitioners of Christianity. So many worshiping Mammon. Self-righteous people grinding the faces of the poor in the dust and then, after taking the sacrament, abusing their neighbors for lack of religion. For over two decades, my feet did not cross the threshold of a house of prayer. Like my stepfather, I became a deist, that is to say an atheist. I was an unhappy young man. Had I remained a successful political leader, I might never have returned to Christianity. But it pleased God to subdue my pride. In the depths of my misery, I studied the Bible very carefully. I read books for and against. When my studies were completed, I realized the Bible is God's truth. The sublime feeling it inspires is proof enough for me of its divine origins. It would have been as easy for a horse to write Newton's *Principia* as for men uninspired by God to have created the Bible. Seek and ye shall find. How true, how correct. The death of my nephew finished my humiliation. To the refuge of Christ I was driven. I became reconciled to God. Soon I shall have to submit to His mercy. If He deals with me according to my deserts, I could not abide it. I pray daily for His mercy."

"What is it you like about the Quakers?"

"I have always found them to be neat and orderly in everything, with a spirit of brotherhood and the fellowship of man. Right in everything except politics. In that, always a bit twistical." *He says nothing. Keeps to his business. A gentle touch and manner. Perhaps, at last, I have found a genuine physician.*

"I want you to continue to take laudanum in the amounts written here. You need your sleep. Try to rest. On one of my next visits, I'll bring tincture of columbo and hypercarbonate of soda. I would like you to try them in place of opium. Good night, Mr. Randolph."

He makes a rather abrupt departure. I wonder if I'll live to see the morrow. "Draw me close to Him without whose gracious mercy I am a lost, undone creature . . . Johnny, ask Mr. Badger to come in." *A rotund, jovial creature is this Badger fellow. He took me in though his hotel was filled. I am among friends.*

"Mr. Randolph, how are you laying tonight?"

"I lie as easily as a dying man can. Would you stay with me for a while tonight? I crave company."

"I'd be honored, Mr. Randolph. Any man who's taken a shot at Henry Clay is a most welcome guest in the City Hotel."

Seven years and this is what I'm known for. Is that to be my place in history? The man who shot at Henry Clay. "As for life, it is a battle and a sojourning in a strange land; but the fame that comes after it is oblivion."

"What's that, sir?"

"Marcus Aurelius."

"Who?"

"I assure you, Mr. Badger, I never intended to shoot at Clay. It was quite unnecessary. He's a man who will someday cut his throat with his own tongue."

"That's very good, very good indeed. Why did you duel with Henry Clay? I've forgotten what brought it about. Was it that business of 'the corrupt bargain'?"

"It's an old stale story. But if you are interested."

"Oh, I am indeed. It would be an honor to hear it from you, sir."

"It was a speech I gave in the Senate—started the business. My motto has always been *'Fari quae sentiat—* Say what you think.' Many years ago I played a humble part in bringing down the father, King John the First; and, I attempted to repeat the performance with his son and heir, John Quincy, King John the Second. In the speech, I referred to the bargain between Adams and Clay as 'the Coalition of Blifil and Black George—the combination, unheard of till then, of the Puritan with the blackleg.' "

"Who are those two gentlemen, Black George and the other?"

"Two names out of Fielding. Please do not interrupt me. That's not important. Johnny, bring me that laudanum." *The man is good-natured but an ill-educated oaf.* "Clay was insulted by the speech. He knew which epithet applied to him. He sent his second, General Jesup, to me with a challenge on April Fool's Day. An appropriate time, but I knew it was not a joke. Immediately, I went to see Thomas Hart Benton to inquire whether he would be my second. Because he is a blood relative of Mrs. Clay, he could not accept that role. Nevertheless, in confidence, I revealed to him my intention not to fire at Clay. You see, there was no proper cause for a duel. I accepted the challenge but protested against the right of a minister of the Executive branch to hold me responsible for words spoken in debate as a Senator criticizing that minister. If I fired at Clay, I would be conceding that he had a right to make me answer."

"Why then did you accept the challenge?"

"With me, matters of principle have always been subordinate to matters of passion. My own seconds were a Colonel Tatnall and General Hamilton of South Carolina."

"Isn't he the Governor of South Carolina, the one who threatened this past year to call out the state militia against old Andy Jackson?"

"Yes. Until a few months ago, he was the Governor of South Carolina. He was also the President of the Nullification Convention. Had the federals invaded South Carolina, I would have had this old carcass tied to my horse Radical to fight beside my old friend. Unlike Jimmy Hamilton, I am not a nullifier. I favored secession." *It was Clay who prevented an effusion of blood, perhaps civil war. Had I shot him seven years ago, perhaps the inevitable would not have been postponed. Had I only known the future, perhaps . . .* "We are drifting from the subject at hand. The duel was finally arranged for one week later, four or four-thirty on a Saturday afternoon. I requested it be on the Virginia side of the Potomac. If I fell, my blood would be received by the sacred soil of my own country. On the day of the duel, Benton came to see me. He told me he had visited Clay, and he described Clay's unsuspecting wife and sleeping son. Immediately, I assured Benton I would do nothing to disturb the sleep of the child or the repose of the mother." *Clay would have had them to mourn for him. When the sod of Virginia rests upon me, there will not be one person in this accursed world to grieve for me.* "In fact, the law of Virginia then prohibited dueling; I did not intend to violate that law by firing at my opponent." *While Benton was there I wrote several codicils to my will. What did they say? This failure of memory now, when it is so important, is troublesome. Was it then I freed Johnny? No. It could not have been. If only Leigh were here.* "Johnny, do you recall I changed my will on the day of the duel?"

"No, suh. But I remember you sent me to de bank to git some gold coins. You was real mad when dey wouldn't gimme none."

"Oh yes. I do recall that. I wanted to give Benton and my seconds gold coins, as souvenirs of the great occasion. When you came back empty-handed, I rode to the bank myself. I requested all the money in my account, four or five thousand dollars. When the teller tried to give me bank notes, I demanded gold. Do you remember? That insolent fellow asked me if I had a cart to put it in. They made it so difficult to get a few pieces of gold, I closed the entire account. Did get the gold, though. Nine pieces. I gave Benton a note to open in the event I was killed. Tatnall, Hamilton, and Benton were to receive three pieces each to make gold seals to wear in remembrance of me." *If it had only happened then. I would not have had to suffer seven more long years. For what purpose? Only to reach Calvary in this forsaken place.* "Johnny and I arrived at the place chosen for the duel. It was a forest above the Little Falls Bridge. We were to use pistols at ten paces. There was no practicing. After the word 'fire,' the words 'one, two, three, stop' were to be recited swiftly. When I was informed that Clay was fearful of not having enough time to take aim under these rules, I began to suspect that he intended to kill me. I told Tatnall that if I saw the devil in Clay's eyes, that he really meant to take my life, I might change my mind and fire at him. But only for the purpose of disabling him. To the last possible moment, I remained inside the carriage. General Hamilton was with me for a time." *Once again I was reading* Paradise Lost. *Clay, I knew, would be unnerved if he heard I was occupied with poetry.*

> *O! Why did God, Creator wise! that Peopl'd highest Heav'n With spirits masculine, create at last This Novelty on Earth, this fair Defect of Nature? And not fill the world at once with Men, as Angels, without feminine? Or find some other Way to generate Mankind?*

Even at that moment, Nancy intruded upon my solitude. Doom impending, and my brain spews forth that vile creature. Nothing so unfits a man for intercourse with life, or death, than the object of his infatuation. Is there anything more odious than a woman who barters herself away in marriage? Yes. Oh yes! One who submits to the lascivious embrace of a black, a slave ... Destructive, damnable, deceitful woman!

"Mr. Randolph, are you ill?"

"No. When you live too many years, your mind tends to wander ... Where was I? Oh yes. The ground was marked off. We won the choice of position. I stepped out of the carriage wearing a rather large morning gown of vast circumference. I was the only one there who knew it was a comedy. It was that costume saved my life. Johnny stood on a little hill next to Benton. I could see he was worried. It was a beautiful place. The sun was beginning to set. Despite my objections, Tatnall gave me the pistol with the hair trigger sprung. My thick buckskin glove set the pistol off into the ground. Jesup protested vigorously, but Clay said it was clearly an accident. After receiving a new pistol, I exchanged shots with my opponent. I aimed below Clay's knee to disable him. It's no mercy, you know, to shoot a man in the knee. The bullet hit the stump behind him. His shot kicked up the earth behind me at hip level. 'This is child's play,' he said. We both demanded another exchange of shots. Clay's second shot pierced my coat near the hip. I then raised my pistol, discharged it into the air, and said, 'I do not fire at you, Mr. Clay.' I advanced on him with my hand extended. Clay held out his hand in peace. 'You owe me a coat, Mr. Clay,' I said. With great emotion, he replied, 'I am glad the debt is no greater.' On Monday, social relations were restored by an exchange of cards. So you see, Mr. Badger, I never did try to kill Henry Clay."

"A wonderful story, Mr. Randolph. I'll always treasure it."

"Johnny, do you remember a few hours after it was over, a runner came from the bank to say they overpaid me by mistake that afternoon? 'I believe it is your rule not to correct mistakes except at the time and at your counter,' I said. The mistaken amount was paid back to the bank that Monday. People must be honest when banks are not. I've always paid my debts. My father left his sons burdened with an immense debt owed to British creditors. Spent most of my life paying it. The final payment was made only a few years ago. Pay as you go—that's the philosopher's stone. A President of the United States retiring from office who can say to those who elected him, 'I leave you without debt,' would occupy a prouder place in history than one who won as many battles as Caesar. . . . Hamilton, Tatnall, and Benton all got their gold coins. I had the seals made for them in London. Johnny, get me a glass of that old Madeira."

"Suh, you know you ain't supposed to drink."

"Do it! You see. I will not tolerate disobedience in a servant. Dueling is a necessary evil. It's like a private war—fought on the same basis as war. Both are permitted when there is no other redress for injury. The Yahoos and Yazoo men must be kept down. A man must be able to shoot at one who invades his character, as he can at one who breaks into his house."

"Have you been in other duels?"

"Only one other where I was almost shot. That must be . . . over forty years ago. A schoolboy adventure. We quarreled over the pronunciation of a word. We were members of a debating society. But that was only part of the argument. It was politics. I dissolved my connection with William and Mary College for it. We met in a field near town. The first fire was exchanged without effect. It was on the second shot I hit him in the hip. I saw Robert B. Taylor not long ago. He still carries the ball in his hip. A good man . . . Twice, I challenged Daniel Webster. He refused to duel. Webster is a coward and a Yazoo man. Both of Jeffersons' sons-in-law, John Eppes and Thomas Mann Randolph, challenged me for trifles. The seconds settled the disputes. Over the years there have been so many arguments. I threw wine in Willis Alston's face and broke the glass over his head. Years later he objected to the presence of my dogs on the floor of the House. He threw himself in my way on a staircase and insulted me. His head like a ripe pumpkin waiting to be smashed. Gave him a caning he'll never forget. They fined me for breach of the peace. The satisfaction was well worth the fine. It was only a few days later Eppes challenged me for delaying action on a bill. That was the year he lost the election to me. They imported him into my district like a racing stallion; but he lost. General Wilkinson was his instructor on shooting. That scoundrel Wilkinson once challenged me. Called me a prevaricating calumniating poltroon. It was at the time of the Burr treason trial. John Marshall, you know, appointed me the foreman of the grand jury in that case. I would not lower myself to fight a Yahoo like Wilkinson, nor a filthy plebeian like Matthew Lyon. You see, my life has been one long war." *Her brothers. Thomas Mann Randolph. No more self-command than a child. Threatened Dick but never did issue a challenge. That's why she wrote the letter. Dick burned it. He was too honorable to use her to protect himself.* "That other brother, with my name, 'possum' Randolph. I went to collect a debt from him. I didn't say anything to provoke him, and he attacked me with a knife. Cut my coat. I had to beat him off with my riding whip. It was after that I began to call myself John Randolph of Roanoke so nobody would mistake me for her dear brother Jack. That was the year I left Bizarre and went to live at Roanoke." *Judy was horrified. Said she hoped never to see her brother again. But she made her peace with him ... and with her. She never could finally break the bonds with her own family.* "Have I been an Ishmael, my hand raised against the world?"

"Mr. Randolph, you don't seem well. Perhaps you should try to sleep."

"No, I can't sleep. 'Macbeth hath murdered sleep.' "

"I once saw you speak. As fine an oration as ever I've heard."

"You never heard Patrick Henry. There was a speaker. Shakespeare and Garrick combined."

"The best you ever heard?"

"Oh no. The greatest orator I ever heard was a woman. She was a slave and a mother. Her rostrum was the auction block ... Do you play chess?"

"No."

"Do you have a wife?"

"Yes, I most certainly do."

"I'll not keep you from her. Go home!"

"But I'd be—"

"Go home to your wife!"

No home or wife for me to return to I'd rather die in this Yankee city than return to Roanoke lonely savage habitation for twenty-three years dreary beyond conception condemned there to solitude like Robinson Crusoe the wild man of the woods living a life of seclusion without a single ray of enjoyment forced into miserable celibacy by the betrayal of my own body no pleasure in that—a man needs friends and children around him to support the dreariness of old age—at first it was not all savage solitude Theodore Dudley living with me and Bev, if only we had not quarreled he may not have gone to Missouri my brother could have been nearby all these years; then there were John Randolph Clay, the Bryan boys, Tudor and poor St. George all educated by me, where is the gratitude of those still living—after the fire Judith said she would come to Roanoke to live but never did, she could not have tolerated those simple log cabins in the depths of the forest—too much of a taste for civilization—yet I might have remained at Bizarre if she had not made her peace with the betrayers of her own husband her dear sisters and brothers who never stood beside Dick when he needed them but instead spread the vile slander throughout the countryside (poisonous creatures) but then Bizarre was gone within three years of my departure almost exactly twenty years ago the same time I lost the election to Eppes imported into my district to defeat me and successful only on the second attempt—Eppes could not speak well in public at best a fair reader of documents—yet in spite of my opposition to the war I would have been victorious if not kept from attending the election at Cumberland Court by the fire that destroyed Bizarre my library reduced to ashes the Encyclo-

pedia of Diderot and D'Alembert, seventy volumes of Voltaire, Rousseau, Hume, infidels all, perhaps it was the will of God or merely a spark from the fireplace a careless servant or was there a young Gabriel or Nat Turner on the plantation who intentionally and maliciously applied flame to wood—poor St. George distraught to see his beloved home in ruins no doubt it was the beginning of the destruction of his mind although when he came to Roanoke he seemed himself reading and writing as well as he ever did Judith also defeated by that fire all of her precious possessions incinerated she had only laudanum and God left to her especially later after both her sons were lost forever—so little survived the conflagration I found that picture covered with ash of the gentleman leaning on the workbench and my own portrait next to the one of Nancy which was not damaged in the slightest how exquisitely characteristic that she stands unharmed while all about her collapse into the dust even now ensconced in her palace in New York with a strong healthy son though no doubt not a real Morris but the offspring of some vile coupling with a servant he must now be twenty years old and she indestructible in her wickedness while all the houses of my life have burned and vanished into dust—Cawsons, my birthplace, Matoax and Bizarre when it burned marked the beginning of this final third of my life—less than two more weeks and I'll be sixty, Richard would be sixty-three this year I cannot bear to think of it— the portion most filled with woe beginning the year of the fire that unusually cold winter and the heavy onslaught of Hessian flies during the spring of 1813 the floods and near failure of the wheat crop with falling tobacco prices then the loss of my seat in Congress so they could carry on their mad war and finally pass the Yazoo land bill during my two-year absence from the House (never with me there) four years after Marshall's decision in Fletcher and Peck, Jefferson's commissioners finally triumphant while I remained mired in my grim solitude insupportably cheerless and desolate days in the forest that isolation eventually becomes dangerous—a mirror that reflects the deformity of the human mind and heart to whomsoever will dare look into it—I have lived in dread of insanity and shrink at the idea of ever returning home except to be planted in the sod with a large unmarked stone over my final resting place none to pay homage to me while the world worships at the grave of St. Thomas of Cantingbury—Becket himself had no more pilgrims at his shrine than the unworthy saint of Monticello—until I return to the ground I am resolved to bear my suffering like a man condemned to the rack and submit without a murmur to living the rest of my life in lonely pain disappointed in every hope and looking forward to nothing better in the bitter days that remain—to win an exemption from the agony and other plagues of this wilderness I would gladly crawl into some hole where I might commune with myself and then be silent forever . . .

"Dr. Parrish, please accept my apologies for calling on you once again. You've been most generous to make so many visits."

"No need to thank me, Mr. Randolph. If you are feeling better, I am already rewarded. You do look much improved this evening."

"I am a little better. Johnny drove me and Badger about the city. We went down to Chestnut Street and the United States Bank. I needed to get out of this room."

"Try this medicine tonight. I mixed it especially for you. Tincture of columbo and hypercarbonate of soda, as promised. I would like to decrease the amount of opium you're taking."

"No! I shall soon die in any case. I don't want it. I will not take it."

"Why?"

"That is my affair, not yours."

"I'm afraid it must be my concern if I'm to continue as your physician. You called me here to assist you. I am trying to do my best. I've treated you with respect. I am not insensible as to what is owed to me."

"Yes, of course. I humbly beg your forgiveness. I promise I will try it . . . There. You see before you a pliant patient."

"I do not mean to alarm you, but your situation is serious. It would give me some comfort to call in a second physician for purposes of consultation. You, of course, would choose the consulting physician."

"No. That is quite unnecessary. I have complete confidence in you. In a multitude of counsel there is confusion. It leads to weakness and indecision. The patient may die while the doctors are staring at each other. I know. I've seen it many times."

"A second doctor might be able to anticipate complications which could arise from your present condition. Treatment now may prevent future problems."

" 'Sufficient unto the day is the evil thereof.' I have always preferred a doctor who relieves the patient of the existing malady without undertaking to prescribe for problems he might endure at a later time. Sit down and talk to me. That is your best course of treatment for tonight."

"I am happy to oblige you."

"Johnny, get me the wicker basket with the newspaper clippings, and my spectacles too. You see how efficient he is. He knows where everything is kept. On a trip to Europe, with all this baggage, he is quite indispensable. . . . This is the one, from January twenty-first. Read it aloud."

" 'If South Carolina listens to the siren song of peace, she will surrender her independence and that of the whole South. She must resist compromise on the Tariff of Abominations. If she retreats now, state sovereignty will be extinguished forever. If the national government possesses such power, it can accomplish anything. It can emancipate every slave in the United States. Omnipotence is not to—' "

"The word doctor is 'omni*po*tence.' The accent should be on the third syllable."

"I was taught to pronounce it the other way by—"

"Pass on."

"By my—"

"Pass on!"

"If you say so. I stand corrected."

"Do you know why I cut that out and preserved it?"

"No."

"That is the future in a nutshell. It was written a few months ago by my half brother, Beverley Tucker. Many years ago, Patrick Henry warned us that the powers in the proposed federal constitution would some day be used to destroy the sacred sovereignty of the states. He saw the secret sting lurking beneath the wings of the butterfly. This year, you saw, it almost happened. South Carolina had to assemble an army to protect herself. President Jackson threatened to march 200,000 federal troops in there to enforce the oppressive tariff laws of the national government, treating a sovereign state like a rebellious province. It was only Clay's compromise tariff bill that prevented civil war. South Carolina surrendered this time. But mark my word, in less than twenty years Congress will attempt to liberate every slave in this country. Then, no compromise will be possible. This nation will split along the line of Mason and Dixon, between the slaveholding and nonslaveholding states. The Union will be finished. We think we are living in the better days of the Republic, but we deceive ourselves. We are very near the time of Marius and Sulla."

"I am not a student of politics. But it did not appear to me that South Carolina surrendered. She claimed the tariff law was in violation of the Constitution and not in force within her boundaries. It was the national government which capitulated by eliminating the tariff over the next ten years. Isn't that correct?"

"No. Actually, most of the tariff reductions won't occur until the last six months of the ten-year period."

"If it is a question of slavery, as a Quaker I am in favor of the abolition of the vile institution, without, of course, the shedding of blood. You, no doubt, would favor nullification of an abolition law."

"You are wrong about that. I am no nullifier. The doctrine of nullification is sheer metaphysical nonsense. A state cannot both remain in the Union and refuse to obey the Union's laws. The only proper end to an unresolved dispute between the central government and a sovereign state is secession. When the states entered a league of amity for the common defense and welfare, they did not part with any portion of their sovereignty. They never surrendered their right to withdraw from the compact when the benefits of union are exceeded by its evils. There is no magic in the word 'Union.' It is merely a means of preserving the liberty and happiness of the people. When they are no longer happy, they are free to withdraw from this confederacy. The central government is merely a thought in the minds of the states. At any time as an act of will, they can extinguish that thought as they wish. Secession, you see, is an undeniable right, although I freely admit it is a desperate remedy. It will be used when the dispute is over something more important than tariffs. Our recent unpleasantness was merely a skirmish over an outpost. War will come when the citadel itself is attacked. In short, the problem of slavery must remain untouched by the national government. Upon that fact depends the life's blood of our little ones now bawling in their cradles."

"I must admit to not understanding what all the recent fuss was about. Is a dispute about tariffs worth destroying this Union?"

"You northerners wail about the hardships of slavery. It is the tariff which has imposed the most dreadful privations on slaves, all to the benefit of the plodding sons of industry and gain. On many plantations last year, the annual supply of blankets for slaves could not be purchased because of the excessive costs of manufactured goods from abroad—the result of protective tariffs. You see these books about you. I purchase all my books with the imprint of Cadell of the Strand, London. Because of your northern tariffs, the costs are infamously high."

"Why don't you have your books bound in New York or Boston? It would be much less expensive."

"Patronize our Yankee taskmasters who have caused such a heavy duty to be imposed on books from foreign shores? Never, sir, never! We must and shall defend ourselves! . . . That is not to say I proscribe northern literature. No matter from where it comes, I always admire talent, like William Cullen Bryant. That poem 'Thanatopsis' is a marvel. If General Wolfe would have preferred writing Grey's Elegy to the capture of Quebec, I would certainly have surrendered my seat in Congress to be the author of such a poem.

> "Yet not to thine eternal resting place
> Shalt thou retire alone, nor couldst thou wish
> Couch more magnificent. Thou shalt lie down
> With patriarchs of the infant world, with kings,
> The powerful of the earth, the wise, the good,
> Fair forms, and hoary seers of ages past,
> All in one mighty sepulchre."

"Your illness seems to have left your memory unimpaired."

"That is quite correct. Literature has been at least one-half my worldly enjoyment. I have stored vast treasures in my mind. To accumulate such stores of knowledge and then to die. A complete waste. The world left to the ignorance of youth. It renders life in this world utterly without meaning. How miserable is the state of our mortal existence. To end a wreck on some distant shore.

"In life's last scene, what prodigies surprise,
Fears of the brave, and follies of the wise!
From Marlb'rough's eyes the streams of dotage flow,
And Swift expires a driv'ler and a show."

"You are certainly the most entertaining of all my patients."

"My illnesses have destroyed all my taste for reading of every sort. Books, once a necessity of life, no longer hold any charm for me. Twenty years ago, if you had told me there would come a time when I no longer cared for Shakespeare or Milton, I would have laughed at such nonsense. Yet, it has come to pass. But that's an entirely different subject. Let us return to the one we were addressing. I know that as a Quaker you disapprove of slavery."

"As a human being, sir, I do indeed. It is a terrible reptile coiled within the bosom of this nation. It must be removed before it destroys our country."

"Like all northerners, you assume that because I am from Virginia I support slavery. Your assumption is wrong. The United States Constitution itself gives sanction to the holding of human beings as property. My actions over the years have protested efforts by the national government to attack an institution only the states can alter. That does not mean I support slavery. From early childhood, all my instincts have opposed it. I supported my older brother's efforts to free more than two hundred slaves by his will. After thirty-five years, what has become of them? They were given tools, assistance, and land near my own plantation. Now they have become almost extinct. The few who remain are degraded wanderers and drunken thieves. Oh no. The problem is not as simple as you suppose. As we become older, we wear out the fine feelings of our youth. We become hard-hearted, or perhaps wiser. We discover that our youthful beliefs were based on false impressions. You see, all of my misfortunes are slight when compared with that of having been born the master of slaves. I have often lamented this burden; but I bow with submission to Him who has called me to that state. We slaveowners are the ones who must deal with the real problem. Slaves are becoming so expensive to maintain that they will soon be advertising for runaway masters. I truly wish to free my slaves, as a matter of justice and humanity. From my experiences, however, I have found that great injustices cannot be cured in a fortnight. Time, the great innovator, must be allowed to take its course. Slavery will die a natural death when the cost of labor begins to consume all the profits. The cardinal principle governing the whole course of my political life is that it is unwise to disturb a thing at rest. Change is not reform. Most slaveholders are men of humane disposition. We will deal properly with this question. That is not to say the problem can be covered over with a carpet until the whole house tumbles about our ears. You may as well try to hide a volcano in full operation. . . . Time and understanding are necessary. But your Yankee abolitionists refuse to wait. Mr. Garrison's *Liberator* will emancipate nobody. His carping accusations without any real understanding of the problem have produced a revulsion in my own mind. They have almost reconciled me to Negro slavery. What then must be the effect on those in the South who have no scruples on the subject? The truth is since the institution of the passover, no two people of distinct races have been able to occupy the same territory under one government except in the relation of master and vassal. Every society must have its drudges. It is only our superiority in numbers and intelligence which has maintained us in the role of masters. Unless we keep it that way, we will deserve to become the servants of the blacks."

"You confuse me, Mr. Randolph. You say you oppose slavery but wish to maintain the white race in the position of power. We are all children of God. Why not permit each unique individual person to succeed as far as the limits of his own special talents? Forget about the color of a man's skin and treat each person as a fellow human being equal in the sight of God."

"This equality idea—all men are created equal—is the legacy of the unfortunate rant of St. Thomas of Cantingbury. I, sir, am an aristocrat; I love liberty and hate equality. Teaching slaves they are equal to their masters only encourages them to cut their masters' throats. I wish that every one of my slaves could be made white, but they cannot. They must remain black and bondsmen. I treat them like my horses and dogs, which is to say considerably better than my equals. This is a dangerous world. You, no doubt, heard about Nat Turner. There are many Gabriels, Denmark Veseys, and Nat Turners among the Negroes. After Nat Turner's rebellion, the Virginia General Assembly debated the question of abolishing slavery. You Quakers joined in the fray. Last year, the final result was enactment of a tighter system of slave control. To us it is a matter of self-defense. We slaveholders must protect family, wives, and children first. We will not permit our blacks to cut our throats in the night. This constant pushing from the North only puts back the cause of freedom for decades. Slavery will fall of its own weight, not from the demands of outsiders. The only solution is to let time have its way."

"If time has its way, most slaves now living, including your Johnny, will die in bondage."

Johnny will soon be free with his wife Betsey. I can't say that. I'm not certain it's true. When I punished all the slaves two years ago, sent them into exile at Judge Leigh's place, the will was changed. Those cornfield slaves were useless inside the house, except Mulatto Nan at the Lower Quarter, Archer's wife. If only I could recall which will was the last one. Before it is too late, this must all be reviewed by the lawyers. "Johnny, when were you born?"

" 'Deed, suh, I don't rightly know."

"How long have you been my body-servant?"

"Since you first run fo' Congress."

"That would be thirty-four years ago. Do you want your freedom after all these years?"

"Don't rightly know what dat means."

"It means I've decided not to take you to Europe. As soon as I get on that packet for England, you are going back to Roanoke alone. You need not if you choose not to do so. If you prefer, you can call on the manumission society in Philadelphia. They will take care of you and I shall never see you again. . . . Doctor, you see the tears in his eyes. Why do you weep? Don't you want your freedom?"

"Massa, I don't deserve dis kind o' joke. I got feelin's. You forget dat. You know I love you better den any man or woman in dis world. When you get back, you know I'll be back at Roanoke wid Betsey, not wid dem freedom people."

"Then you shall go to Europe with me. You see, Doctor, there are few situations in life where friendship is so strong and lasting as between master and slave. The slave knows he is tied to his master and must always remain under his control. The master knows he is bound to maintain his slave. They are like husband and wife, or parent and child. Our friendship will endure as long as there is a drop of my blood to which Johnny can cleave. He has always been treated well. In all the years we have been together, he has been whipped only a few times. On each occasion, the chastisement was just—for drunkenness, disobedience, stealing, and the like. When we sailed together to Russia three years ago, my three slaves were shocked at the constant beatings on the man-of-war. The *Concord* was the name of that ship. In a voyage of three weeks, we saw more whippings than during seven years on a plantation with hundreds of slaves. All three of my servants, Johnny, Juba, and Eboe, were seasick during most of the crossing. I myself took care of them, and my secretary, who was also ill. On an earlier trip abroad, Johnny observed with horror the hovels and miserable peasants between Limerick and Dublin. At the time, he told me he was proud to be a slave from Virginia. Isn't that true, Johnny?"

"Yassuh. I'm always proud to live de life God give me in dis world. If I was white and free, I be proud o' dat too."

"My Negroes possess a patience and serenity I covet." *Juba does always get uneasy when I call him Jupiter.* "They are able to live for the moment without concern for the phantoms of the past and the terrors of the future. Truly, I do envy them. Do not be so certain they want to be free. Freedom can be a heavy burden. . . . Be warned. This matter must be left to the South. If the North insists on interfering, the Union is finished."

"Surely as an American, you do not wish to see an end to the Union."

"I am not an American. I am a Virginian."

"This has been a very enlightening conversation. Although I fear we shall never agree on the question of slavery, I have understood what you said. Until tomorrow. Remember to take the medicine before going to sleep and again when you wake in the morning. You may eat meat once each day. Mutton would be acceptable. Crackers, coffee, and tea can be ingested as you wish. Try to stay away from alcohol and laudanum. Your disease is certainly pulmonary consumption. I need not tell you how serious that is. You must get plenty of rest."

"Do you think I'll be able to board the next packet for Europe?"

"Let us first observe the course of your illness. Good night, sir. I shall see you again tomorrow."

"I am feeling better. You are advised to leave a bill with Mr. Badger. I may decide to leave this place in the morning. God bless you, Doctor. God bless you, He does bless you, and He will bless you. . . . Johnny, did you stop the keyhole?"

"Yassuh."

"Good. You can go to sleep now." *The doctor is a good man but he doesn't understand. Only we comprehend the true difficulty of ending it. Beverley understands but he's of the younger generation who fail to see the evils of slavery as the doctor does, so unlike his father, all emotion with a scorn for pure reason he is the future and I trust nothing to the men of the future—Bev always was a saucy child constantly fighting with Henry during their visits to Bizarre—when Bev moved to Roanoke after I conveyed him that parcel of land we quarreled (I cannot even recall the cause) and Judy tried to poison my mind against him, if we hadn't fought he might not have gone to Missouri, his persistent melancholy always reminded me of my younger self, what a pleasant surprise this past year when at my call he returned to Virginia to assist me during the nullification crisis but not to support Calhoun's absurd metaphysical theories so foolishly conciliatory when it is now clear state sovereignty can only be preserved by the destruction of the Union at least according to Bev while Henry advises prudence to avoid a bloody rebellion—but a sovereign state has no authority superior to it and is therefore incapable of rebellion said Bev who wants disunion and an effusion of blood as though it were an adventurous escape from the mundane—we spoke for hours and the solitude at Roanoke for a time was no more my brother returned a true communion of minds we agreed secession was the only proper resolution of the crisis once the Force Bill threatened us so he became my amanuensis and together planned to fight the national government before it devoured its own creators who have it in their power to extinguish that government at a blow and how he flushed with excitement when the Charlotte Court House resolutions reciting the right of secession were adopted Bev smiled at me and said these people are finally ready to fight for their freedom (the day of reckoning has merely been delayed disunion will come) there is a difference between us I see secession by force as a terrible necessity for self-defense is the first law of nature but I would merely resist encroachments and attempt to keep on the windward side of treason while he delights in the idea of rebellion wanting the bright banners of war raised high even without cause praying for rivers of blood to water the tree of liberty fiat justitia ruat coelum . . . have I let justice be done if the most recent will revoked all predecessors and codicils that was last year when my thoughts were dark as blackest Hell the slaves to be sold not freed or was that an earlier testamentary provision—sell them and vest the proceeds in bank stock—I must ask Leigh to clarify this matter which so burdens my mind preventing the rest I need to recall it . . . Richard wading out into the sparkling moonlight path stark naked his back so muscular suddenly turns come with me Jack he says right hand extended there's nothing to fear on a night like this the water is warm and I'll watch you—don't be a fool says Theo we'll get a bottle and get drunk together interested always in his own pleasure he threw my books out the window come with me Jack he says and you won't be sorry his vulgar friends carry me out of the room there's pleasure to be found in this town and I reluctantly agree without any freedom to disagree if only he had not taken me to that whore . . . that's what St. George needed a harlot poor ill-starred unfortunate boy his destiny sealed before his birth to be the most pitiable stepson of nature deaf and dumb yet so intelligent a handsome boy black hair and dark piercing eyes he could have had any woman he wanted if only he could hear and speak but the curse cleaves to him as it does mercilessly to me it was his misfortune to fall in love with his cousin Jane Hackley an amiable girl utterly without charm according to Judy yet she refused him cruelly perhaps with the encouragement of her harpy mother—the bounties of God wasted by the ignorance of women—he became a frantic maniac when I could have given him a whore he at the age of illicit desire and prurient interest when he needed a woman above all things so hostile to his mother she never could love him and his home in ashes the room at Bizarre he adored so he might never have lost his reason with that familiar roof over his head then others spurned his attentions and the Saint begins to brood over the cause of his failures which he knows to be incurable tearing to tatters everything his hands can seize cut off from all that distinguishes man from brute beast he will not even look at his mother the once beautifully written letters unintelligible he takes no more joy in life not even the hunting he once loved—though he could not utter a command to the dogs on that day he killed one brace of partridge and one of woodcocks missing only three shots and two of those on horseback—raving in his letters about the devil and the terrors of future punishment from that insane asylum it was the spring of 1814 that dreadful year I received Judith's letter declaring his insanity and took pitiful St. George from Farmville to Roanoke poor unhappy boy just before the greatest flood of the Staunton River in two decades that summer destroyed the corn and tobacco crops the slaves without food in utter misery with British landing parties burning Hampton and Havre de Grace then marching on Washington I a vedette of all things ordered to proceed to the York road just below the confluence of the Pamunkey and Mattapony lost my horse and suffered violent bilious attacks leaving the military only to receive the worst blow of all Tudor seriously ill his mother already becoming a skeleton with disease and grief hastened to her sister at Morrisania where the family curse must have driven Tudor the last possibility of carrying the blood of my father into another age my own best hope my own creation everyone said he was one of the most promising students at Harvard wonderful in Greek and Latin tall swarthy and brilliant so much like Richard except in temperament which was more like my own—Josiah Quincy secured him quarters in the house of Harvard's President*

Kirkland but they failed to supervise the boy—then to hear he was ill the news arriving from Nancy of all the people in this world like a cat always landing on her feet from housekeeper to mistress of Morrisania the nearest relative with money Tudor did not hesitate to borrow from her his hemorrhages staining the fine carpets of her northern palace the heedless ingratitude of children that he should turn to her for help yet to the home of the destroyer of her marriage Judy rushed to his aid after obtaining a loan from Judge Tucker then I foolishly followed desperately worried about Tudor and strangely eager to see her again in her new lair it was a Monday at Port Conway 3 A.M. the call for the stage not a light in the place the steep stairs looked like a passage to step expecting a floor and nothing but a void falling down that endless staircase senseless on my face shot through with pain my left shoulder and elbow severely damaged ankle twisted head bruised but saved by my hat I boarded the stage each jolt an agony all the way to Baltimore when I rested then north again until at last I confronted her in her new home—she should never have been seen after her expulsion from Bizarre but the ripples of the past remain long after the stone has sunk to the bottom of the pond—triumphant in her Yankee riches and old one-legged Morris the soul of hospitality with his kindly blue eyes smiling at the child he believed to be his own Nancy talking incessantly of her good fortune filled with false friendly chatter as if the past had never happened,

> *A set of Phrases learn't by Rote;*
> *A passion for a Scarlet-Coat;*
> *When at a play to laugh, or cry,*
> *Yet cannot tell the Reason why;*
> *Never to hold her Tongue a Minute;*
> *While all she prates has nothing in it.*

pretending to have forgiven her years at Bizarre as though she were not the cause of everybody else's misery—oh the odor of insincerity—along with Tudor and me she speaks of her fear for the child's life because he is Morris's new heir threatening the fortunes of the nephews Ogden and Wilkins and the others her talk of fear for the murder of her child by poisoning makes me consider that other infant she bore and perhaps murdered at Glenlyvar and who might now carry the blood of my father into the future oh the way she flaunted her child as the embodiment of her triumph over the poor Randolphs of Virginia knowing my line was in danger of perishing while her blood flourished oh how it is an illusion to think that beauty is goodness.

> *And I find more bitter than death the woman*
> *whose heart is snares and nets, and her hands as bands*

Smiling at Morris with that cruel innocent face like an amorous spider before she devours her mate as incapable of goodness as St. George is of playing the flute her intended victim innocently turning to me and thanking me for offering pro-

tection to his beloved Nancy after the trial—you mean permitting her to remain at Bizarre that was my brother Richard not I but his meaning he says was my kind offer of marriage to a woman disgraced in the eyes of the world—that she would dare boast to Morris of rejecting an offer I never made roused me to cold fury—what words could then be spoken I held my tongue though I had said nothing of marriage but only of moving to Roanoke—that evening at last alone with Tudor who I had taught never to betray a secret now confirmed in pulmonary consumption the end of my family line he told me of her dalliance with servants revealed to him by David Ogden and how he saw her love letters to Billy Ellis her in the woods alone with that half-naked buck damned bitch making the two-backed beast with that black a son of Ham then Tudor following his stories with a tale I never before heard and could not have imagined—Uncle you heard her speak of poisoning (his mind as always following mine) it was after the burning of Bizarre, Joseph told me for years the slaves spoke in whispers of the death of my father and the emancipation of all his slaves an old conjure woman said it was Polly, Nancy's maid who freed them with a dose of poisonous medicine ... enraged, Uncle, I thrashed him for impertinence and never mentioned it until I found her mind running on poisonings and the murder of her precious child the key to the old man's fortune ... Uncle he said if ever Mr. Morris's eyes are opened it will be through this child despite all her smiles in his presence she cares nothing for the boy except as an instrument of power and when I asked my mother who gave my father the dose that finished him she said it was a tartar emetic mixed by Nancy which seemed to make him deathly ill

> Could I find out
> The woman's part in me! For there's no motion
> That tends to vice in man but I affirm
> It is the woman's part: be it lying, note it,
> The woman's; flattering, hers; deceiving, hers;
> Lust and rank thoughts, hers, hers; revenges, hers;
> Ambitions, covetings, changes of prides, disdain,
> Nice longings, slanders, mutability,
> All faults that may be named, nay, that hell knows,
> Why, hers, in part or all; but rather all;
> Nor even ...

immediately that morning I left Morrisania with but a short word to her to remember the past as if she could care about what cannot be grasped in those vile harpy claws but she had the temerity to write later I gave Morris a note of my permission for Tudor and his mother to pass the winter in his house—nothing but the lies of an evil woman she who made a great show of attachment to Theo then left his wasted remains unwatched—in the rush from Morrisania to New York misfortune struck again (troubles do come not as single spies but in battalions) the driver overturned my coach riding over a pile of stones in the street left from an unfinished house the ligaments badly wrenched the patella detached *from the joint muscles on each side ruptured the knee irreparably ruined so I could not walk and later only with cane and tight bandages forcing me to remain in the city five more long weeks then the nephews Ogden and Wilkins came to visit not difficult to discern their impressions of Nancy who they said had caused Morris to be estranged from all his relatives and who drove away his old domestics that there be no witnesses to his death and my own name had been used by her to produce a false impression as to her chastity as I had offered her marriage after the trial—the lie once again—the child is not my uncle's says Ogden but is the offspring of an illicit amour with . . . an Irish name it was who was formerly a domestic in Mr. Morris's service it was then I decided to inform the old man who treated Tudor with great kindness for if a person is deceived and I by my silence suffer him to remain in that error I am implicated in that deception unless he is one who has no right to rely on me for information but she not he wrote back that her husband and the child were too sick so applying the golden rule which has guided me through life I took pen in hand for a history of her crimes written to her but sent to the unfortunate husband to warn him of the danger to his life yet he takes no heed but sends his own emissary a man of no consequence who I find is certainly not in the camp of David Ogden—before I left for Philadelphia, Ogden obtained my deposition for use in court against the false heir apparent not because of my admiration for the greedy scheming nephews who were more interested in preserving their own fortunes than saving their uncle from the harlot's schemes but to let justice be done especially for Richard as to her who ruined my brothers and so cruelly treated me while wrecking her own sister's happiness a woman surely undeserving of good name or domestic contentment—then she who must have the last word shamelessly pens a long deceptive reply addressed though never sent to me but all over Virginia to provide a weapon to my political enemies like an avenging demon her wrath knows no bounds of decency or truth brutally attacking even helplessly ill Tudor . . . . one year to the month of my departure from New York Dr. Hoge preached poor Tudor's funeral sermon at Cumberland Court House without even the empty shell of his body to weep over better to have given up his life in the arms of his sick mother than to perish among strangers in a foreign land yet it matters not where we die only that spring he was sent to England in search of health scarcely had he reached Cheltenham when despite the springs he fell into the arms of death the news coming to me many weeks after the departure of his soul the letter from Dr. Brockenbrough dropped from my hand as if I had touched molten iron my heart as if it had suffocated the final humiliation to one who foolishly thought happiness could be found in this barren existence (I was driven finally into the refuge of Christ the Redeemer) Tudor's last hours under the care I later learned of Mrs. Marx of Croydon who years later informed me of his last pathetic words— Don't grieve for me I die happy—her own funeral I attended long after to fulfill the obligation of her generous attention at Tudor's deathbed yet where we die is only of interest to the survivors there at Cheltenham is lodged in the bosom of the earth the treasure of my heart the end of the Randolphs of Cawsons Matoax Bizarre and*

Roanoke made by me in my own image the last hope of a future for our family his only recognition in life a posthumous degree from Harvard unaware at graduation of the death of one of her own students better never to have children so one can feel detached from life without hostages to fortune the beautiful little boy with the shining eyes—everyone is going to die Uncle aren't they—yes—why do they die—old age accidents sickness—where do they go—nobody knows—but they can die at any time my birthday is in September could I die and miss my birthday—no you will have many birthdays and children—he smiles innocently unaware of the weight of what he has asked (youth is supposed to go to light not darkness) Reverend Rice hoped to make a clergyman of him as he had lured his mother away from the Church of England to the cold Presbyterian faith I expected Judy to give herself to some dour Calvinistic man—as soon as she heard Tudor was ill in New York she rushed to see her son and sister and at great sacrifice of my own time and health I followed after her to lend assistance only to find her so friendly again with Nancy as though they had never quarreled spitting venom at each other year after year . . . Judith angered at me for writing the letter to Nancy she would not even permit Tudor to sit for a portrait with Sully in Philadelphia on the feeble pretext the paint would be injurious to his lungs and when finally I requested she relate the circumstances of Richard's death she confirmed Tudor's story yet if it was Nancy who mixed the fatal dose of tartar emetic how could she remain so friendly with her sister who poisoned first her marriage and then her husband—women thou art strange creatures concerned with little more than the appearance of things without scruple in misrepresenting the truth (as weapons against a foe) deficient in reason without sense of justice Judy's indulgence of the propensity of her sex to use scorn and sarcasm may have been the engine that drove unfortunate Dick to stray on to that road to the dungeon and the cruel ordeal that rendered his untimely death a welcome release from his blighted reputation Judith's tantrums marred a woman with no shadow on her honor but whose ungovernable tongue made her so odious—how often have I seen it the most amiable of men received with cold looks from their wives their affection barely tolerated their friends slighted so that homes that should have been temples of hospitality are transformed into hostile territory repulsive to travelers who wish not to see a uxorious man rendered wretched by the intolerable caprice and ill-temper of his wife—yet her saving grace was that she devoted her entire existence to house, children and religion the chamber pots as sweet and clean as teacups constantly washed and sunned I attended the sacrament the year I left Bizarre when she made her profession of faith to the Presbyterian Church she said her feelings of desolation were replaced by joy and peace when she learned to accept her suffering as proof of God's love because (she said) she became innocent as a little child and could be born again how often I have looked for that peace and found only bitterness yet when Tudor died her joy of soul ended with him she was all tears and declining health a walking cadaver of disease and grief—there is no such thing as a happy ending only sad ones postponed—living with the Reverend Rice and his wife in Richmond she remained there a woman of migraines laudanum and fits of temper this earth no longer having any charm for her she longed for the peace of another world which she found within a year of Tudor's death—said Reverend Rice she died in a state of grace her last words "Christ is my only hope"—strange that day of her death I could not shake off the impression she had joined Tudor in the undiscovered country from whose bourn no traveler returns where soon I too must journey if God wills it to meet at last the grim King of Terrors ... the awful mystery that shrouds the future alone makes the present tolerable.

"Mr. Badger asked me to come immediately. Has your master's condition become worse?"

"Yes, Doctor. He say he's dyin'. Dis time it do look bad. But he been sayin' dat fo' de last twenty years."

"I heard that, Johnny. God punishes Negroes who aren't respectful to their masters."

"Massa, God don't aks 'bout your color. He aks 'bout your heart. A man's soul depend on de man's life, not his color. You know dat. I know you do."

"I do agree with you, Johnny. Your servant, Mr. Randolph, is a wise man. What is your condition this morning?"

"I am dying, sir, dying."

"Your breathing seems improved."

"Did you bring the instruments for a bronchotomy as I asked?"

"Yes, I did. But your breathing does not appear to require surgical assistance."

"Doctor, I am past surgery."

"I hope not, Mr. Randolph."

"I am past surgery! I am also past a voyage to Europe. My case is irremediably hopeless."

"I had the apothecary divide your sulfate of morphis into papers of one grain each."

"Bless you, Doctor. You always do what I ask. This past night has been a horror for me. I've been feverish with pains in every limb and joint. This churchyard cough has not permitted me one-half hour of undisturbed sleep. It gives me solemn warning. I haven't touched a drop of Madeira or laudanum. One can't rush into the presence of the Creator in a state of inebriation. . . . Johnny, get me the chamber pot. Life is a comedy, is it not? And a poor play too."

"That is a question I cannot answer. Breathe deeply. Good. Now exhale. Again . . . and again."

"Doctor, listen to me. Listen! I want you to be my witness. I confirm every disposition in my will, especially that respecting my slaves whom I have manumitted and for whom I have made full provision. Do you understand?"

"Yes. Believe me, Mr. Randolph, I rejoice to hear it."

"You must remember what I have said. You may be a witness."

"Of course, I shall remember. I cannot stay here now. I've had a message to see another patient. As soon as I'm finished, probably this afternoon, I'll return as quickly as possible."

"No! You must not go. You cannot. You shall not leave me now. Johnny, lock the door."

"Massa, I've locked it. De key is in my pocket. De doctor can't go now."

"I really must leave for a short time."

"If you go now, you need not return."

"Please, Mr. Randolph, be reasonable. I must see other patients. One is in worse condition than you. You have my solemn promise. I will come back in due time."

"Forgive me, Doctor. I retract that expression."

"On the subject of the will, I understand what you said. I assume your will fully explains itself."

"No! You don't understand. I know you don't. Our laws are extremely particular on the subject of slaves. A will may manumit them; but provision for their subsequent support requires that a declaration be made in the presence of a white witness. The law requires that the witness, after hearing the declaration, continue with the party and never lose sight of him until he is dead. You will be a good witness for Johnny. You see the propriety and importance of remaining with me. Your patients must make allowance for your situation."

"Yes, I do understand. It does seem to be a very peculiar law."

"Early this morning Johnny told me I was dying. He is correct, isn't he, Doctor?"

"I will not deny it. To be candid with you, I am surprised you have lasted so many days since my first visit."

"Ah. Finally the truth is out. I am relieved to hear it. I would as lief die here or in my carriage or at some wretched inn on the road to Washington. It matters not. We hold life not a moment longer than it pleases Him who gave it. . . . When I was young, I could not understand how people faced death with equanimity. Now that I have arrived at the sublime moment, I do understand it. 'Let there be light and there was light.' That is sublimity. It is vague, obscure, and magnificent. . . . I would not trade my miserable condition with another human being, no matter how fortunate he might appear. Do you know 'The Fountains,' Samuel Johnson's fairy tale?"

"No. I never heard of it."

"A girl—I can't remember her name—rescues a little bird who is really a fairy. For her kindness, the fairy reveals two fountains, one of joy and one of sorrow. A drink from the first fountain grants a wish, while a drink from the second removes the evil effect of the first. The girl drinks and wishes for beauty. She gets it, and the envy and hostility of others of her sex. She wishes for wealth. It quickly becomes tedious while leading to obsequious insincerity from her friends. Next she tries intelligence. It makes others uneasy; they shun her. At the same time, it makes her aware of the emptiness of life. You know, 'He that increaseth knowledge increaseth sorrow.' Turning to the second fountain, she renounces every wish except intelligence which she does not want to surrender despite the fact it has increased her misery. A final wish for long life brings decay, boredom, and the death of friends. Finally she renounces the last wish and accepts death. I too accept my fate with open arms. . . . Johnny, stop crying and help me. Bring me my father's golden breast button—yes, that's it; you see, he knows where everything is. Place it in the bosom of my shirt."

"Won't go on, suh. Needs a hole on de back side of de shirt."

"Then get a knife and cut one!"

"Here, Johnny, use my pen knife."

"Thank you, Doctor. Johnny, put a napkin on my bosom."

It is done. My father rests near my heart. One of the progenitors who passed the curse on to the present, to this doomed family, this House of Atreus brought into the world to be the engines of our own destruction. My whole name and race prostrate under this curse. I feel it cleaving to me, strangling me. Have we fared better than those in the endless African coffles they brought long years before to this distant shore piled on our backs until we stagger under the black weight of them? That father gone before his children could know him replaced by the good judge who could not even return to care for his dying wife. The first blow I ever received was from the hand of this man less than one week after his union with her. She suffered so terribly. Sweat covering her face she could still smile at me— Why doesn't he return home? Is the law so important superseding her and her flesh and blood— Nobody else has ever understood me. Only she who loved the dogwood open in the woods, the wild honeysuckle beginning to bloom. For so many years she has not seen it. Never will, never. Yet fortunate she has not seen what happened to the three sons of her first union. One dead of dissipation at an early age, forgotten by all but his own kin. The eldest son, the young prince, humiliated before the merciless mob. The best of us struck down by the hand of the wanton who first stole his good name which is better than precious stones carrying the putrid decaying flesh of him or the other in her womb—or was it born alive—the one who though illegitimate may have carried the family name and blood into the future to be passed from one generation to the next instead ending its brief life in darkness buried under a woodpile by the hands of its father or uncle its inno- cence destroyed by the sin passed from the first parents in an unbroken chain through the past and the present into the future which finishes here that except in the veins of a maniac possessed of a deaf and dumb spirit there should not run one drop of the father's blood in any living creature besides him whose organs of increase shriveled by disease bear no seed so he is the last of his family which will soon be utterly extinct except for that madman who will carry the blood for as many years as he clings to his sorrowful life his brother the last hope of the family putrefying in a foreign graveyard under the ground I purchased in Cheltenham as you go from town to spring he rests on the right hand of the path through that mournful cemetery where men lie like nations and empires which are founded and grow destined sooner or later to decay into dusty death and then oblivion yet having eaten fully of the poisonous fruit I have accepted my bitter heritage the burden of caring for dark men and women passed on to drag me into evil as unwanted as the debts that came with them not fully paid until three decades after that first election but the Negroes remain unlike the debt unredeemed by any such promise because I saw my brother's goodness and generosity did not and could not resolve the problem in this brutal world where the perverse depravity of mankind rules and where death—which is not as bitter as the woman who lures with smiles— at last releases me from the cruel dilemma I have not solved before arriving at that unknown land into which all roads relentlessly plunge through the dark dusty and silent grave and thus the curse is transmitted to a new generation . . .

"Johnny, he's asleep. Please open the door. I must visit my other patients. I'll probably return before he wakes."

"Sorry, Doctor. I can't do dat unless he tells me."

"Remorse. *Remorse!!* Let me see the word. Get a dictionary. Let me see the word!"

"Please, Mr. Randolph, calm yourself. There's none in this room."

"Write it down, then. Let me see the word!"

"May I write it on one of your cards?"

"Yes! Yes! There is nothing more proper."

"Here, I've written it above your name."

"Where? I don't see it."

"There, in pencil. Johnny, get him some laudanum."

"Write it on the back . . . Good. 'Remorse.' You have no idea what it is. You can form no notion of it whatever. It has contributed to bring me to my present situation, but I have looked to the Lord and hope I have obtained pardon. Now let Johnny take your pencil and draw a line under the word. Yes."

"What do you want done with the card?"

"Put it in your pocket. Take care of it. When I am dead, look at it. You see how all the precious things of this world vanish like a bubble on the water."

"Mr. Randolph, please listen to me. What you are doing here to free your slaves is very important. But your only witnesses are a self-interested slave and a member of the Religious Society of Friends. Let me call in other witnesses. Mr. Badger can be summoned from downstairs."

"I've already communicated this to him."

"Then let me call two young physicians, my son, Dr. Isaac Parrish, and my young friend and former pupil, Dr. Francis West."

"Dr. West from the packet, the brother of my friend Captain West?"

"Yes, that's the one."

"Send for him. He's the man. I will have him. Go see your other patients and come back. Johnny will unlock the door. But first go to the bureau and take the proper payment for your services."

"No, please, I cannot do that."

"In England it's the custom. Johnny, open the door."

"I'll return with the witnesses."

Strange that I was at Glenlyvar for my first visit that day but had to learn the story from Banister did Richard not trust me or nothing happened that night vitam continet una dies when I first heard and later copied Marshall's own notes of his closing argument it twice convinced me—in May, Carter Page and his gorgon wife thought Nancy pregnant so she must have been advanced three or four months yet she did not show it in September when I saw her many times how could this be and Nancy asking her maid if she looked smaller ... it was before the trial I showed Nancy at Matoax her brother Tom's letter to Richard defying him to transfer the stigma to his dead brother that must have caused her to write the letter for Richard admitting the child was Theo's but when she gave it to him he burned it in her room before he left for Cumberland Court she told me so many years later at Prior's but did he refuse to use it as a matter of honor or because it was a lie and then in despair she sent me proof of her guilt through Dr. Meade when she left Virginia claiming she had not told the truth earlier for fear of the wrath of her brothers but she never told Judith such a story or was she herself the one who decided to transfer the stigma to Theo who was safely silenced forever out of shame for the wrong she did her sister's own marriage when I informed Judith of her admission that Theo was the father Judith said that was what she always believed with a pained expression that belied her words perhaps it was how the two sisters lived with each other for twelve years after the trial but there is another explanation not inconsistent with Marshall's argument delivered with his usual unpretending grace—if she was pregnant in May with Theo's baby and then miscarried it would explain her question to her maid for then she would have expected to look smaller could she then have been impregnated again between May and September how many times I've asked that hypothetical question the doctors always telling me it is unlikely but a woman can sometimes conceive within months of a miscarriage ... Richard was unsatisfied with his sharp-tongued shrew why not turn to the beauty in the next bedroom alas the truth always hidden in the hearts of a few all of whom except her now lie buried under the sod and she incapable of telling the truth or of being believed if she did so Marshall's ingenious use of syllogistic reasoning his conclusions appearing to follow inevitably from the initial premises fails if there is another explanation consistent with those premises is not the pain in Richard's eyes when he looked at her admission enough yet I cannot believe he would do it refusing always to speak of it he never said a word implying personal guilt—did not that scoundrel Talleyrand or was it Voltaire say words were invented to conceal thoughts as though the world were an endless masquerade ball all the desperate participants dancing in disguise except she did not wear a mask after her father's death when I asked her to live with me at Roanoke she had begun to speak to me as she used to before Theo when her coquettish advances and retreats left me badly confused but still ardent so my hopes were rekindled—I will soon come into my majority and my own lands at Roanoke if you are unhappy at Bizarre you can live with me there but she said nothing looking at me as though I were a madman she turned around and walked out of the room my heart offered up with a devotion that knew no reserve only to find myself an object of utter indifference the pain the humiliation better not to feel love as a woman may torture at her will with me entirely at her mercy I shall never trust anybody else—why is it a fellow with no intelligence a male gossip with a full portion of admiration for his own personal charms should be more successful in a room full of women than a man of real merit it is all surface appeal only appearances matter nor is it just fine women who throw themselves away upon coxcombs for clever men often marry silly insipid women and propagate a race of simpletons there is no fairness in it only for us to play the parts which are given by Him who is the master of our fates mine to be a bishop who can never leave his own color entrapped for a lifetime on black when my heart yearns fervently for red I have had such a strong predisposition for this universal disease which everyone it seems must have at least once in a lifetime the noblest infirmity of our natures which I who have never forgotten the experience of my youth can still feel the hot tears wet on my cheeks . . . Maria Ward was only a faded memory of the genuine passion beautiful but of limited dimension serene and transparent unlike Nancy carved out of Burke's vision of the sublime vast dark mysterious awe-inspiring obscure tempestuous full of danger and pain that for which my soul has always longed . . . after she crushed me at Presque Isle I should have been on guard against that most wicked and deceitful of all things my own heart yearning for love without which there is no defense against filthy despair no need being more important to a young man yet my heart would not learn its bitter lesson I wrote all those letters to Maria and she responded from afar to the warmth still emanating from my long-dead desire but in her presence she seemed to know as if by female instinct I was only half a man as if her letters were written to another she was cool and distant and did not have to say it in my presence fleeing her home I could not untie the reins of my horse so cut them with a knife and rode off in great haste my last illusion of hope (in which I never truly believed) dashed to the ground so she married Peyton Randolph (Edmund's son) I did not really care for there was never real pain in it for me and now they are dead both husband and wife—is it a triumph for me that my miserable life continues beyond theirs— but Nancy still lives how real the pain with her a decade before Maria at her sister Molly's home at Presque Isle my back leaning against one of the pillars to give me strength I told her my surprise on learning from Richard that she was engaged to marry Theo he is unworthy of you I said believe me knowing Nancy's love of animals I told her how Theo thrashed me as a young boy when I tried to save the kitten he was torturing he is just as cruel now I told her indifferent to the feelings of others interested only in his own selfish pleasure weak and wicked believing happiness to consist of only money finery and sensual gratification never thinking of anyone but himself saying of women you must be brusque and brutal with them so they don't make you weak missing from school for days only returning when his money was exhausted then trying to borrow more for drinking gambling and prostitutes perhaps I should have told her of that night he and his friends dragged me away from my books to that dark whore but she would not have listened— you're all against him your entire family she said you can only say how wicked he is with nobody to give him the love he needs and wants so desperately don't ever speak of him to me again she said with that cruel wicked smile on her face the eyes told me that I was a vile repulsive creature you are nothing to me she said scornfully and walked out of my presence she who I loved better than my own soul or Him who created it she prostrated all my faculties rendering me hopelessly wounded at age eighteen—why has God tormented me with this false goddess who shines and stinks like rotten mackerel in the moonlight so hard and so untender without compassion she laughed at my suffering—I dreamed of her and tried to protect her but it was Theo she wanted my staged scene at the portico did not succeed telling her I have something personal to say to her I can contain no longer, then declaring I cannot reveal it for then I thought there was no risk of a direct rejection but she did not respond because she did not care about my pain I could have tolerated hatred even repulsion but not her indifference her lips parting in a smile without feeling looking through me as if I did not exist the face of an angel with a stone-cold heart she revealed so many years later in that letter addressed to me and sent to everyone but me—my mean selfishness and wretched appearance she wrote—why do my feelings flow to a creature such as this unless the gods toy with me—as flies to wanton boys—oh how I hated the gods I did not then believe in only out of desperation did I begin to tell her of Theo but the battle was already lost she waiting for the moment to be rid of my unwelcome presence an indescribable nausea pierced my brain the wound gushing with the life's blood of my vainly cherished hopes and dreams yet my mind remained strangely calm at the knowledge of complete failure as if time were standing still . . . the necessity of loving and being loved so strong within me that in all the long years that have followed more than four decades a day has not gone by when I did not think of her . . .

"Massa, dey's all here now."

Who's here? Oh yes, the slaves, the manumission of the slaves. "Johnny, stop blubbering and put the pillows behind my back so I can sit up and greet these gentlemen. I'm cold. Put that blanket over my head and shoulders. It's slipping. Place the hat on my head. There. You see it holds the blanket in place. Now, Mr. Badger, introduce these gentlemen to me."

"This is Dr. Parrish's son and Dr. Francis West. Of course you know Dr. Parrish. As you see, we have four witnesses."

"Gentlemen, gather 'round me. You see my strength has returned. . . . No punishment except remorse can exceed the misery I feel. My heart swells to bursting at past recollections. Now I mean to do as I would be done by. Every man who leaves the great high road of the Golden Rule will have the chalice which he himself has poisoned put to his lips by the God who rules us all. God does not require abolition societies to carry out His purposes. To each one of you standing before me, I confirm the provisions of my will respecting the manumission of my slaves and direct them to be enforced, particularly in regard to the provisions for their support. Especially for this man, my faithful body-servant John White, to whom I extend my blessing. *Hunc hominem liberem esse volo.* This man I wish to be free. Do each of you understand me? You?"

"Yes."

"And you, Dr. West?"

"I understand."

"Dr. Parrish?"

"Yes. Before your arrival, Mr. Randolph informed me Virginia law states that a will may emancipate slaves, but provision for their support requires a declaration in the presence of white witnesses who remain until the owner is gone. Is that a correct statement, Mr. Randolph?"

"Yes. You can visit your patients now. The young gentlemen will remain with me."

"As soon as I've seen my patients, I'll return. You have my solemn promise."

"Good-bye, Dr. Parrish ... Johnny, I'm cold. Get the fire up quickly. Oh God! Oh Christ! End my suffering quickly."

I hang suspended between two worlds never have I been so far from this one the sorrows and pains which now agitate me soon will seem distant perhaps I shall see Richard again except for our mother's death his sudden end was the worst blow of my life could it have been my illness if Richard contracted the fever sitting by my sickbed at the Thompson's—if only he had departed Petersburg as soon as I fell ill he might be here still ... at the time of his death I was too grief-stricken to do more than make a brief inquiry as to the cause Judy said it was an emetic that caused his final dissolution but he had been quite ill before that never was there talk of poison until Tudor mentioned it at Morrisania perhaps it was not Nancy but only her maid so many cases of poisoning by slaves over the years—George Wythe no that was his own nephew not his slave or those hundreds of people at the Fourth of July feast all poisoned by the black cook—could I have accused her unjustly or perhaps she poisoned him because only he knew her guilty secret ... so many are gone Joseph Bryan, the Thompson boys, Maria Ward, Peyton Randolph, my entire family except St. George, Judith, Patrick Henry

> *And millions in those solitudes, since first*
> *The flight of years began, have laid them down*
> *In their last sleep—the dead reign there alone.*
> *So shalt thou rest, and what if thou withdraw*
> *In silence from the living, and no friend*
> *Take note of thy departure? All that breathe*
> *Will share thy destiny. The gay will laugh*
> *When thou are gone, the solemn brood of care*
> *Plod on, and each one as before will chase*
> *His favorite phantom; yet all these shall leave*
> *Their mirth and their employments, and shall come*
> *And make their bed with thee. As the long train*
> *Of ages glide away, the sons of men,*
> *The youth in life's green spring, and he who goes*
> *In the full strength of years, matron and maid,*
> *The speechless babe, and the gray-headed man—*

Shall one by one be gathered to thy side,
By those, who in their turn shall follow them.

Judge Tucker gone six years did not approve of my attack on the law of descents— Why Jack he said you ought not be against that law for you know if you were to die without issue you would wish your half brothers to have your estate— the temerity to speak to me of having no children—I'll be damned sir if I do know it—he did not approve of my response and we never shared a friendly word again (I was then angry about his conniving as to my father's slaves) but maybe he was correct some day my estate will be in the hands of his children or their blood all of mine scattered in cemeteries as ephemeral as the flies of summer except for poor demented St. George—"Each revolving year, each hour that snatches the day, bids us not to hope for immortal life"— God tears us from this world gradually so we can leave it willingly and plunge with joyful heart into His infinite ocean of eternity . . .

"Dr. West, will you perform the tracheotomy and ease my breathing?"

"No. It will not help you now."

"Then give me the knife, sir. I will do it myself. You're all too timid. . . . Doctor, come closer. Put your ear to my lips. Can a woman be pregnant in May, miscarry in the spring, and be pregnant again in September, of the same year? Please answer my question!"

"It is unlikely to occur, but it is possible."

"So all you physicians say. Never a plain yes or no. Let some fresh air in this room. It is much too hot here."

Dear Mother you are the only person in this world who ever knew me taught me to read and love books to pray to God . . . that day we fled Matoax, Arnold and Tarleton so close, she left her bed Henry only one week old in her arms throwing father's most valuable papers into the pillowcase and his dagger into her stays—what is that for Mother I asked—John your mother shall never be insulted she said with that wonderful voice which could charm birds out of the trees so beautiful and amiable, sparkling eyes and dark hair but for her I might now be a French atheist holding my hand as together we said "Our Father who art in Heaven" on my knees beside her how she hated cruelty to animals perhaps that is why Theo loved to torture them but on that cold winter morning everyone hurried to pack the trunks Syphax drove the wagon—must have been over half a century old then now over one hundred years old he wrote to me for help last year—Essex with Richard and Theo and me riding my own horse for the first time Colonel Tucker leading our party on the road to Bizarre the British were coming everyone said burning houses and seizing slaves for sale in the West Indies it was Lafayette saved Richmond . . . she told us we were safe and we always believed her then later she promised she would not die and would soon be well yet I watched her prolonged agony and followed her body to the grave wondering that the sun continued to rise and set as if nothing of importance had happened her words lived on in us—it was at Roanoke when I was eight or nine she lifted me upon her horse saying John all this land belongs to you and your brother Theodorick it is your father's inheritance when you get to be a man you must not sell your land it is the first step to ruin for a boy to part with his father's home be sure to keep it as long as you live keep your land and your land will keep you and so I have kept it and added to it soon to become the property of strangers when I all but friendless am ushered out of this vale of tears . . . Without my dear stepfather's urging she never would have sent me to Walker Maury's school he assured her they were old schoolmates born the same year he was always Maury's fervent partisan I pleaded not to be sent away to Orange County two days away from my beloved mother but he would not hear my pleas and when coachman Toney left me there my heart died although I knew crying was something boys my age were not supposed to do not able to control it cast on the wide world without a parent Theo and Dick apart from me with the older boys the little brutes in my class immediately taunted me while I was shocked at their vulgar clothing and boorish manners only four or five sons of gentlemen in the school envied and hated by the others but worst of all Walker Maury himself that most peevish and ill-tempered of pedagogues that first day I coughed repeatedly—what was that asks Maury—nothing sir—not nothing boy with the first of many vicious blows to the back of my head believing knowledge should be beaten into boys' heads that cruel unforgiving face snarling as he threw books at us from the desk which was his throne in a fit of capricious temper beating one boy then another without reason every day his rattan flecked with innocent blood thin-skinned sensitive creature that I was vomiting every morning in terror of another day of humiliation and pain even lunch made disagreeable as the martinet insisted each bite be chewed twenty times tapping out the number with the dread switch requiring urination at exactly ten o'clock wielding the rod unmercifully a flogging for me every Monday morning and at least two times each week for idleness in refusing to accomplish the very learning I would have cherished with a proper teacher so when the school moved to Williamsburg I was older and more rebellious that one day I joined the other boys in copying from one student's lesson at last a part of the group—who is responsible for this outrage cried Maury—James the one I thought to be my friend pointing at me bringing down on my head an exceptionally savage beating and teaching me for all time never to place in another's hands something that can hurt you never trust other persons never Richard indignant at the unjust treatment determined to go home as we later did I because of my illness sent to Bermuda for more than a year finally with a good teacher his name (strange I can only remember the bad ones) Ewing it was Mr. Ewing with old Mr. Tucker that wretched return voyage the beginning of the illness costing my mother her life two years later Theo and I returned to Maury's untender hands Theo unlike Dick never attempting to protect his younger brother but in Tazewell at last a friend . . . they dangle those false awards in front of you all through school as though they were the chief purpose of life then distribute them unjustly on the basis of personal favorites and petty spite Maury talking and ad nauseam of his receipt in 1774 (to him the most important year in history) of the Botetourt gold medal for the enlargement of classical learning died of yellow fever the same year as my blessed mother angel and devil removed from my life simultaneously I hoped they buried his medal with him one less of the false glittering awards of life—at Princeton College the prize for elocution won by mere ranters knowing I was superior to my competitors with a sense of deep pride in that knowledge I finally learned to despise fraudulent accolades granted unfairly by the foul play of schoolmasters rather than on any system of true merit so many pedagogues with minds like poor parcels of land rendered more barren by intense cultivation yet having the power to dangle those spurious honors sought by those too foolish to perceive their utter worthlessness—even representative government as great a cheat as transubstantiation—looking back along that long road I would not accept all of those illusory baubles in exchange for one moment of pure happiness—hanging on the gate with little black Amos swinging me to and fro and the real prize love which is in everybody's mouth and in almost nobody's heart the grand prize in the lottery which falls to so few it can hardly enter into the calculation of life's probabilities its absence driving me frequently to the brink of despair that memory of its sweet softness the foulest of recollections no truth being more certain than the enjoyment of passion falls short of expectations but once tasted the desire cannot be extinguished Theo and I both at college he detesting books and his dissolute companions forcing open the door of my room where I studied they threw the books on the floor and out the windows dragging me off to join their revelry—what you need is to fuck the right woman Theo shouts exuberantly in his unending lust for pleasure his debauchery repelling all the virtuous emotions which render men superior to brutes at last I consent with fear in my heart to enter the brothel with him and he pushes me into the room where the whore sits on the edge of the sheetless bed her voice a passionate murmur of the promise of unlimited pleasure my heart pounding with fear and lascivious anticipation she stood and let the dress slip from her shoulders dropping in a disordered pile around her ankles her nakedness a blow to my fiercely aroused lust she waits for a moment as I stand paralyzed my shoes as if nailed to the floor then she floats back to the bed her legs open urging me with a hint of impatience in that soft voice to take off my clothes so I did as if in a dream without awareness of their removal her hand reached out grabbing my arm and pulling me down to her warm soft silky flesh quickly possessing my entire soul which for a few brief moments breaks the bounds of its earthly chains and soars freely above its unending loneliness joined finally to the throbbing core of another world becoming one with it something in the feel of flesh which joyfully breaks through the oppressive wall of separation created by society's rigid rules the touch of her warm hands moving luxuriously up my back the intoxication of my heated senses separating me forever from my long-despised innocence—better it had never happened to once taste that forbidden fruit thereafter spending a lifetime expelled from Eden always lusting after the succulent plant just out of reach of one doomed to suffer the endless torments of Tantalus the pleasure swiftly obliterated by Theo—you just fucked a quadroon he laughs (the one-quarter portion of blood all that matters to him) oran-goutans prefer nigger women why shouldn't you he laughs again playing with me as if torturing another one of his kittens and I hate him at that moment with all my heart for a few hours of evanescent pleasure paying the price to the winter of old age it is the Prince of Darkness who still tempts me with that mulatto whore—our debauchery cut short by the letter from Richard summoning us to our mother's deathbed as if in punishment of our dissipation . . . after she was gone Theo and I both sinking into gambling drinking and profligacy until he became a skeleton of himself drunkard and scoundrel ("Youth's a stuff will not endure") yet having Nancy though I warned him to respect her youth and innocence he said she only came like a cat when he didn't call her and once having had her so he no longer desired her his indifference seemed to attract her all the more until he died at Bizarre only months before scarlet fever removed me forever from the hope of love and a family to carry my seed into the future and decrease the pain of a miserable old age

> *Days of my youth! Ye have glided away;*
> *Locks of my youth! Ye are frosted and gray;*
> *Eyes of my youth! Your keen sight is no more;*
> *Cheeks of my youth! Ye are furrowed all o'er;*
> *Strength of my youth! All your vigor is gone;*
> *Thoughts of my youth! Your gay visions are flown.*

Judge Tucker's best poem yet I cannot even remember its title . . . Resurrection or Resignation it matters not

> *Day of my age! Ye will shortly be past;*
> *Pains of my age! But awhile can ye last;*
> *Joys of my age . . .*

I can think not of one . . . cannot even concentrate on my plans for the week . . . all is chaos beneath that false appearance of order in nature ending life on bloody sheets the crucifixion awaiting each mortal . . . all my years expecting to fear death but now there is no reason for fear as there is nothing to be done except lie down in the dust . . . perhaps the day of death is better than the day of birth.

"Tell me, Doctor, what will happen? I want to be conscious when it comes for me. To look at the face of my personal Prince of Terrors, or is he the same for all? To understand him as a mortal, if only for an instant before vanishing forever from this place. 'By thine agony and bloody sweat; by thy cross and passion; by thy precious death and burial; by this glorious resurrection and ascension; and by the Coming of the Holy Ghost, Good Lord deliver us.' "

Theo gave her flowers secretly thinking her foolish in her joy but using it for his own purposes only interested in the surfaces of life what people eat and wear while I refused to use such deception as a matter of personal integrity perhaps I was a fool . . . Theo's face was not then fixed in a mask of indifference smiling with pleasure as the three of us walked into the warm moonlit water the sparkling reflection beckoning in a golden path to the far shore let's swim out to the island Richard says but Theo turns back refusing to participate in an endeavor that

*appears to promise no immediate pleasure while I would follow Richard any-
where—and ever since have refused to swim with the popular current of the day
in ignoble security—without looking back he is already ten yards ahead so I follow
confidently along the glittering way to the island when after many minutes the
moonlight suddenly vanishes behind a cloud all darkness and terror the journey
hopelessly long I cannot complete the course in the black heaving waters my strength
disappearing in the absence of the shimmering brightness which had urged me
forward into what had become a dark abyss—years later I knew what it must
have been like for Billy Harrison in the moments before he drowned in the Ri-
vanna—the vague idea of death flashing through my mind Mother help me there
is nothing I cry out when Richard grabs my arm and pulls me back into the land
of the living he swims with me on my back in his powerful grasp returning to the
shore that night the three of us looking into the starry sky and I knew those timeless
minutes of tranquility would reside forever in my mind certain that nothing
would ever harm that perfect moment's promise of happiness which in my childish
mind was unlinked to the past or future no thought of life's dying taper and the
eternal silence of death's perpetual reign ... but it does not redeem all that suffering no I would not wish to repeat life's poor play my secret and solitary existence
never shared with another my labors all in vain guided by nothing but empty
dreams ... all that pain as trivial as the tears of infancy ... if only for one instant
to see the indifferent face of oblivion ... the great unknown ... all these people
shrouded in darkness ... it's moving ...*

EPILOGUE

*Thus the sum of things is perpetually
renewed, and mortals live dependent one
upon another. One race increases, another
diminishes and in swift succession the
generations of living creatures pass and
like runners hand on the torch of life.*

LUCRETIUS
ON THE NATURE OF THE UNIVERSE

‿ও

John Randolph died at 11:45 A.M. on May 24, 1833, in a room in the City Hotel, 41 North Third Street, Philadelphia. A postmortem examination verified what many of his contemporaries suspected. Randolph's withered testicles indicated that he had been impotent for many years, possibly during his entire life. Opinions differed as to the cause of this condition.

His body was brought to Norfolk on the steamboat *Pocahontas* and then up the James River to Richmond on the steamboat *Patrick Henry*. In conformity with his instructions, he was buried near his dwelling house at Roanoke under a large unshapely stone with no inscription. According to local lore, his body faced west instead of east, contrary to the burial custom of the time. It was said that he desired to look west so he could keep an eye on his old political adversary, Henry Clay.

After the death of John Randolph, his half brother, Nathaniel Beverley Tucker, commenced describing himself as Randolph's intellectual heir. He adopted all of Randolph's notions of state sovereignty and vowed he would never rest until the Union had been shattered. Unlike his half brother, however, Beverley Tucker began publicly to defend slavery. In 1836 he published an election-year book called *The Partisan Leader* with the subtitle *A Tale of the Future*. To accompany the subtitle, the book was given a false publication date of 1856. *The Partisan Leader* portrayed a country divided by sectional strife. The lower South had left the Union. Virginia was engaged in fighting a guerrilla war against the federal government in an attempt to join the prosperous Southern League. In the story, the older brother, Hugh Trevor, is presented as a misguided moderate who is unfavorably compared to his liberty-loving rebellious younger brother. Henry St. George Tucker, Beverley's older brother, took umbrage at the portrait of him as a contemptible dolt. Beverley denied that the fictional brothers were based on the author and his older brother. He did not deny, however, that his tale was intended to be both hortative and prophetic.

The year after John Randolph's death, litigation began concerning the disposition of his property. The legal proceedings would continue for more than a decade. Randolph left a substantial estate consisting of over eight thousand acres of land, almost four hundred slaves, a valuable collection of purebred horses and diverse personal property. He also left three wills with numerous conflicting codicils.

Written in 1819, the first will, in part, freed all of his slaves:

> I give my slaves their freedom to which my conscience tells me they are justly entitled. It has a long time been a matter of the deepest regret to me that the circumstances under which I inherited them, and the obstacles thrown in the way by the law of the land have prevented my emancipating them in my lifetime, which it is my full intention to do, in case I can accomplish it.

The executors, William Leigh, William Meade, and Francis Scott Key, were instructed to use proceeds of the estate to resettle the testator's slaves on a body of land within the United States not in excess of four thousand acres to be purchased for that purpose. The emancipated slaves were to be given cabins, clothes, and tools.

The will of 1821, which expressly revoked the will of 1819, stated in its first provision, "I give and bequeath all my slaves their freedom, heartily regretting that I have ever been the owner of one." His sole executor, William Leigh, was instructed to use a sum not exceeding $8000 to transport and settle his slaves in some other state or territory of the United States. Each slave older than forty was to be given not less than ten acres of land. Property was to be sold to provide additional funds to better the conditions of the manumitted slaves. Special provisions were included for Randolph's favorite slaves:

> To my old faithful servants, *Essex* and his wife *Hetty*, who, I trust may be suffered to remain in the State, I give and bequeath three-and-a-half barrels of corn, two hundred weight of pork, a pair of strong shoes, a suit of clothes, and a blanket each, to be paid them annually; also, an annual hat to Essex, and ten pounds of coffee, and twenty of brown sugar.

Johnny, his body-servant; Juba; Hetty's daughter, Nancy; and Queen were given the same annual allowance as Hetty.

Codicils to the will of 1821 were made in 1821, 1826, 1828, and 1831. The codicil of 1826 confirmed all bequests made for the benefit of the testator's slaves. His body-servant, John, was to be treated in the same manner as his father Essex was in the will of 1821. John's wife, Betsey, was to receive the same treatment as Essex's wife Hetty under the will of 1821. Randolph "humbly" requested that the General Assembly let the named slaves—Essex, Hetty, John, Betsey, Juba, Celia, and "mulatto Nancy"—and any others of his old and faithful slaves as desire it, "to remain in Virginia, recommending them, each and all, to the care of my said ex'or, who I know is too wise, just and humane, to send them to Liberia, or any other place in Africa, or the West Indies." He noted that this was the only request he had ever made to the General Assembly of Virginia. Additional amounts were bequeathed to his executor as a fund to be used at his discretion for the benefit of the slaves.

The residue of the estate was left to the executor, William Leigh. No security was to be required of the executor for faithful discharge of the trust reposed in him—"his own character being the best security, and where that is wanting, all other is unavailing."

The codicil of 1828 revoked testamentary dispositions or codicils made after the will of 1821. "As lawyers and courts of law are extremely addicted to making wills for dead men, which they never made when living, it is my will and desire that no person who shall set aside, or attempt to set aside, the will above referred to, shall ever inherit, possess, or enjoy any part of my estate, real or personal."

The codicil of 1831 left additional funds to William Leigh for carrying into execution his wishes concerning his slaves. His faithful servant John, "sometimes called John White," was given, in addition to previous bequests, an annuity during his life of fifty dollars. Randolph also entreated the General Assembly to permit John and his family to remain in Virginia.

After twelve years of consistent testamentary statements in favor of his slaves, John Randolph's intentions suddenly changed upon his return from his mission to Russia. For alleged misconduct, he temporarily banished many of his most faithful slaves, including John, to the plantation of his friend and neighbor, Judge William Leigh. In January of 1832 he executed an entirely new will which revoked all previous wills and codicils. Most of his estate was given to the heirs of his half sister Fanny. Henry St. George Tucker and William Leigh were appointed executors. They were directed to sell Randolph's slaves and other perishable property and to vest the proceeds in bank stock of the Bank of the United States, or in other investments if there were no U.S. Bank—"which may God grant for the safety of our liberties." The executors were authorized to select from among his slaves a number not exceeding one hundred for the use of his heir.

In 1834 the will of 1832 was presented for probate on behalf of the residuary legatee under that will—John Coalter Bryan. The application was opposed by the trustee for the slaves under the will of 1821 and by the legal representative of Randolph's insane nephew, John St. George Randolph, the son of Richard and Judith Randolph. Proving that John Randolph's faith in his good character was justified, William Leigh renounced all personal benefit in the various wills and codicils, which included a substantial estate for Leigh himself, so that he could qualify as a witness in favor of the emancipation of John Randolph's slaves, as provided in the will of 1821. Leigh testified that Randolph was insane for a time after his return from Russia, including the period when he executed the will of 1832, and did not regain his sanity until one year before his death. A Mr. Marshall's testimony was consistent with Judge Leigh's. After his return from Russia, Marshall testified, Randolph uncharacteristically began to use obscene language and became extremely harsh and abusive to his slaves. During this period, it was said, he drank spirits to excess. In support of the theory that when his mind was clear John Randolph intended to free his slaves, Dr. Joseph Parrish deposed that Randolph was of sound mind and memory when on his deathbed he declared his intention to free his slaves.

The opponents of the 1821 will challenged the document on various grounds, including the alleged insanity of John Randolph at the time of executing the earlier will and codicils. Randolph's half brothers, Henry St. George Tucker and Nathaniel Beverley Tucker, had personal reasons for opposing the will of 1821. That will included a provision insulting to their late father, St. George Tucker:

> I have not included my mother's descendants in my will, because her husband, besides the whole profits of my father's estate during the minority of my brother and myself, has contrived to get to himself the slaves given by my grandfather Bland, as her marriage portion when my father married her, which slaves were inventoried at my father's death as part of his estate, and were as much his as any that he had. One-half of them, now scattered from Maryland to Mississippi, were entitled to freedom at my brother Richard's death, as the others would have been at mine.

There is no evidence of improper conduct on the part of St. George Tucker with regard to this matter. Many gave little credence to the defamatory provision both because of the late Judge St. George Tucker's unblemished reputation for integrity and John Randolph's reputation for engaging in malicious invective. In order to attack the will of 1821, the lawyers for Beverley Tucker were prepared to assert that John Randolph was insane as early as 1811, and from 1814 to 1815, and 1818 to 1820.

After proceedings in numerous trial and appellate courts for almost twelve years, the case was submitted to a jury which found that the will and codicil of 1821 were the only true will and testament of John Randolph. This conclusion was consistent with the judgment the Court of Appeals of Virginia had rendered a decade earlier, when it declared the 1832 will to be null and void on grounds of the mental incapacity of the testator. A compromise was involved in the final resolution of the case recorded by the jury. The slaves were freed and given $30,000, while St. George Randolph received property valued at more than $50,000. Many of the records in the case were destroyed by the great fire in Richmond shortly after the triumphant Union army swept into the capital of the Confederacy. One piece of testimony that survived the Civil War is extremely interesting. During the course of the will litigation, William Leigh testified that in 1815 John Randolph read him some of the contents of a letter he had written to Mr. and Mrs. Gouverneur Morris. When Leigh asked why he had written such a letter, Randolph replied that he had been persuaded to write it by David Ogden; he had agreed to write it because of the great kindness Mr. Morris had shown to his nephew Tudor.

During the twelve years of litigation following the death of their master, John Randolph's slaves remained in bondage. Beyond the occasional passing reference to the name of a slave in a letter or legal document, little is known about the personal lives of the slaves of Bizarre and Roanoke. Even in death they are not equal to their white masters, at least as to the leaving of footprints in the dust heap of history. Yet, occasional prints do remain. For example, in 1837 Daddy Syphax, who assisted the flight of the Randolphs from the British invasion of Virginia in 1781, wrote the son of Henry St. George Tucker seeking assistance. He was then over one hundred years old. In 1844 the great-granddaughter of St. George Tucker described "Cyfax Brown" as having attained the age of 116 years. In 1839 John White conducted a tour for a group of students from Hampden-Sidney College through his former master's dwelling in Roanoke. John showed his master's rooms, furniture, and even a partially read book open facedown on the table, as it was left by Randolph when he ceased reading the night before he commenced his final trip to Philadelphia. The book was *McNish on Drunkenness*. According to the account left by one of the visiting students, John encouraged them to take cards and invitations sent to his late master as souvenirs of the visit.

The instructions in John Randolph's will to resettle his slaves in another state or territory in the United States were consistent with the growing movement for the colonization of freed slaves either in Africa or remote parts of America. John Randolph himself as well as many other prominent people, including John Marshall, Henry Clay, James Madison, Daniel Webster, John Tyler, Lafayette, and John H. B. Latrobe (son of Benjamin Latrobe) were active in the American Colonization Society. William Leigh, sole executor of the will of 1821, faithfully carried out John Randolph's direction to transport and settle his slaves outside of Virginia in a state or territory of the United States. In 1845 he purchased in trust 3200 acres of land, all in Mercer County, Ohio. The Randolph slaves were officially manumitted on May 4, 1846. On the list of slaves to be emancipated, John appears as number 285 and his wife Betsey as number 286. They are both described as being of dark complexion.

In June of 1846 the emancipated slaves commenced their journey from Virginia to Ohio. By July 1 they arrived in Cincinnati. On July 7, 1846, the boats carrying the blacks arrived in Dayton, Ohio. According to the *Dayton Journal and Advertiser* of that date, a Mr. Cardwell, who was in charge of the expedition, pointed out John Randolph's former body-servant. The newspaper states, "The boy highly flattered acknowledged the compliment by making three low bows to the persons on the shore, to whom the announcement was made." This may be the last print in the dust of time left by John White.

The Ohio newspapers closely followed the journey of the 385 former slaves of John Randolph. Many stories complained bitterly that a southerner on his deathbed should be able to clear his conscience, after a lifetime of living on the fruits of slave labor, by emancipating his slaves and sending them to Ohio. "We have nothing to do with slavery, and it is neither our interest, nor our duty, to add to the ignorance of our State in any way." What right, it was asked, does Virginia have to pour upon Ohio its newly-freed slaves? Many suggested that the slaves should have been sent to Liberia. The whites of

Mercer County and an adjoining county began to organize to halt the journey of the freed blacks. At New Bremen an angry mob of whites with muskets and shotguns, some of them members of "the Society of Precious Blood," assembled to prevent the landing of the blacks from Virginia. When Randolph's manumitted slaves, many of whom were children and old people, arrived at New Bremen early on a Sunday morning, the mob demanded that the contractor, Mr. Cardwell, remove them by ten A.M. the next day. The local white citizens surrounded the blacks with a large number of men armed with muskets and bayonets. Cardwell was taken into custody and forced to charter two boats for the blacks, who were brought to the Mercer County line under armed escort. According to the *Cincinnati Gazette*, "a number of those who were fiercest in their opposition to the blacks, loudest in their threats to shoot, were the very men who sold them land, received wages for constructing the buildings, and actually pocketed a large amount for provisions, not two weeks before the arrival of the poor creatures, whom they have so unjustly treated." This newspaper account indicates that $32,000 was paid for the land in Mercer County.

When William Leigh arrived, he concluded that the opposition of the whites made impossible a settlement in Mercer County. When he attempted to establish the black settlement in Shelby County, he was again met with threats of violence. By early August, Judge Leigh had returned to Virginia. The freed blacks were scattered from Piqua to Cincinnati. Many were turned over to farmers who, like their former white masters in the Old Dominion, gave the blacks food and clothing in return for their labor. Judge Leigh later arranged for the sale of the Mercer County lands he had purchased for the settlement. The manner in which the funds were used, including $15,000 given as surety that the blacks would not become a public charge to the people of Mercer County, remains uncertain.

In 1903 descendants of the emancipated slaves of John Randolph began to hold reunions in Miami County, Ohio. In 1907 some of them filed suit against fifty-four white residents living on the land once purchased by Judge Leigh. In 1917 the Supreme Court of Ohio (*Morton v. Kessens*) held in favor of the white residents by ruling that the executor William Leigh had the authority to sell the land as a result of the white opposition to the black settlement. The court also ruled that the action was barred by the statute of limitations. The court indicated that in the absence of proof to the contrary, the presumption obtains that the funds from the sale of the Mercer County lands were used for the benefit of the former slaves. The records of the proceedings of the executor and the settlements made by him, the court noted, were destroyed when the Richmond courthouse burned at the end of the Civil War.

The slaves liberated in New York by the Emancipation Act of 1817, effective in 1827, fared little better than the slaves manumitted by John Randolph. Blacks were systematically excluded from numerous occupations that used the skills they had learned as slaves. In 1821 the Republicans sponsored an amendment to the state constitution which increased property qualifications from $100 to $250 for blacks while abolishing it for whites. The effect of the amendment was to disenfranchise blacks for fifty years. Of 12,559 blacks in New York City in 1825, only 68 were qualified to vote. By 1855, only 100 of 11,840 blacks in the city could vote. Proposed amendments to grant equal suffrage to blacks were overwhelmingly rejected by the white electorate in 1846 and again in 1860. The discriminatory property qualification in New York was not eliminated until the ratification of the Fifteenth Amendment to the United States Constitution in 1870.

The surviving papers of the widow of Gouverneur Morris indicate that after the death of her husband much of her energy was devoted to defending her reputation against the scandal caused by the 1814 letter of John Randolph and the doubts cast on the legitimacy of her son by her husband's disappointed heirs. Due to the unsavory business transactions of David Ogden, who did not pay debts Gouverneur Morris had guaranteed for him, the Morris estate was in debt for over a decade. After years of great financial difficulty, in 1831 Mrs. Morris was finally able to free her late husband's estate from debt, thereby leaving her son's property unencumbered. As part of her effort to eliminate her debts, Mrs. Morris, using Dr. David Hosack as an intermediary, signed a contract with Jared Sparks to write a biography of Gouverneur Morris based on his diaries and letters. The papers were placed in Sparks's possession and the selection of materials to be used was left to his discretion. The following year Sparks published a life of Gouverneur Morris which contains little about the subject's private life or his years after leaving the Senate in 1803. Pursuant to their contract, the profits were shared equally between Sparks and Mrs. Morris. Later, Mrs. Morris and her son would complain that Sparks left the Morris papers in disarray and retained some items contrary to the agreement to return everything to the widow.

According to her own papers, Mrs. Morris was severely ill in 1829. Dr. Alexander Hosack, the son of David Hosack, came to Morrisania to bleed her. He gave her medicine which, she wrote, nearly killed her. Dr. David Hosack would die in December of 1835 of apoplexy; his son took eighteen ounces of blood from him before he expired. Dr. Hosack's Elgin Botanic Garden is now the area bounded by Forty-seventh and Fifty-first streets and Fourth and Sixth Avenues, as appearing on the old Street Commissioner's map. After Hosack's death, it would become one of the chief sources of revenue for Columbia College.

David Ogden became one of the most successful lawyers in New York. From 1820 to 1840 he would argue more important cases before the United States Supreme Court than any other lawyer from the state. One of these was the celebrated case of *Cohens v. Virginia* (1821) in which Chief Justice John Marshall's opinion stated the power of the federal courts to review a state court in a criminal case in which the state itself was a party. Alexander Smyth, former commander of the regulars on the Niagara frontier in 1812, appeared for Virginia. David Ogden died in 1849. His obituary stressed his kindness and benevolence of heart.

On May 28, 1837, Ann Cary Morris died. She was originally buried beside

Gouverneur Morris. Their son provided funds to build St. Ann's Church in the heart of Morrisania. Dedicated to Mrs. Morris, the church was consecrated in 1841. A vault was constructed under the church to hold the remains of Ann Cary Morris. Another vault, within the boundaries of the church property but not beneath the church, contained the remains of her husband. Inside the church a stone was placed with the following inscription:

AND HERE BY HER OWN REQUEST
REPOSE THE REMAINS
OF
THE WIFE AND MOTHER
IN MEMORY OF WHOM
THIS CHURCH
WAS CREATED
TO THE GOD SHE LOVED
BY FILIAL VENERATION

Gouverneur	Ann Cary
Morris	Morris
Nov. 6, 1816	May 28, 1837
in his 65th year	in her 63rd year

Morrisania would be destroyed by the coming of the railroads. Gouverneur Morris's great pastoral estate has vanished in the torrent of time, replaced by one of the most infamous slums in North America, the South Bronx.

The son of Gouverneur and Ann Cary Morris would travel to the state from whence his mother fled. He would meet and later marry his first cousin, Patsey Jefferson Cary, the daughter of his mother's youngest sister, Virginia, who at age seven had been with her sister Nancy in the room at Glenlyvar that fateful night in 1792. The son of Ann Cary Morris would become an early member of the new Republican party and an ardent supporter of the Union which his father had considered dismembering at the time of the Hartford Convention. The grandson of Ann Cary Morris would fight in the Union army against the Army of Northern Virginia led by his distant cousin, another illustrious son of the Randolph family, Robert E. Lee.

St. George Randolph, the last of the line of the Randolphs of Bizarre, died shortly before the commencement of the Civil War. Having spent much of his life in an insane asylum, the mute and deaf old man was free in his last years to walk or ride on his own horse about the familiar countryside near Charlotte Court House. It was said that the old man could read books in English, French, and Latin. A description of him from 1856 has been preserved for posterity. He possessed snow-white hair with a full white beard and was "erect as a Virginia pine." Like his uncle John Randolph, he had dark piercing eyes and walked with his feet straight forward "like an Indian," befitting a descendant of the great Pocahontas.

In December of 1879 the great-grandson of Frances Bland Tucker and St. George Tucker came to Roanoke to remove the remains of John Randolph to Hollywood Cemetery in Richmond. The grave was so deep that for a time the diggers feared they would not discover the remains. Finally the shovels struck the coffin. When the lid was removed, the outlines of the figure could be seen. Except for hair and bones, there remained only dust. Consistent with the local lore, the body was facing west instead of east. The roots of a tree had thrust into the interior of the skull.

And, lost each human trace, surrendering up
Thine individual being, shalt thou go
To mix forever with the elements,
To be a brother to the insensible rock
And to the sluggish clod, which the rude swain
Turns with his share, and treads upon. The oak
Shall send his roots abroad, and pierce thy mould.

Author's Note

A Generation of Leaves is a work of fiction that is partially based on fact. The factual material was gleaned from extensive primary and secondary sources examined over a period of five years. These sources include diaries, letters, newspapers, legal documents, and other materials from the period covered. Whenever a scene or portion of the novel was found to be inconsistent with these historical records, it was discarded or revised to remove the inconsistencies. The intention is to tell a story that could be an accurate representation of real events insofar as there are no contradictions of the imperfect fragments of fact in existence after the passage of almost two centuries. No doubt, documents will be uncovered at some future time that prove a fact in the novel to be inaccurate. That is the nature of history. Since the most important elements of the novel are fictional, they can never be disproved. That is the nature of fiction.

The great nineteenth-century poet and historical novelist Alessandro Manzoni, author of *I promessi sposi (The Bethrothed)*, wrote that there were two diametrically opposite major criticisms of the historical novel. First, the historical novel fails to instruct, while confusing and deceiving, because it leaves the reader wondering which events described are real and which are invented. Second, the historical novel distinguishes invention and history too clearly, thereby eliminating the possibility of a unified belief in the narrative or the aesthetic pleasure that belief produces.

To respond to the first criticism, I have added two appendices to the novel. The first appendix contains two complete letters and portions of two others. These actual letters were not included in the novel by choice of the author; but they do shed further light on the events in the story. The second appendix sets forth a chronology of real, as opposed to fictional, events. The chronology reveals the factual skeleton to which has been engrafted the flesh of fiction. With reference to the second criticism, the author declines to reveal, beyond the information contained in the chronology and letters, which events, characters, speeches, and the like are real and which are fiction, as such revelations may damage the possibility of a unified belief in the narrative. Because the events in the novel primarily concern the interstices of history rather than history itself, let the truth about these events be what the reader takes to be true.

For generously providing access to many rare books and manuscripts, I thank the following institutions: The Boston Athenaeum, the Lamont Library (Harvard University), the Boston Public Library, the Massachusetts Historical Society, the Social Law Library (Boston), the Harvard Law School Library, the New York Public Library, the New-York Historical Society, the New York State Archives, the Supreme Court of New York, the Virginia Historical Society, the Virginia State Library, the Earl Gregg Swem Library (College of William and Mary), and the Library of Congress.

APPENDIX ONE:
FOUR LETTERS

The first letter is from Thomas Jefferson, then Secretary of State. It was written to his daughter, Martha Jefferson Randolph, the day before the hearing at the Cumberland County Court on the infanticide charge against Richard Randolph.

The second letter contains a portion of Martha's reply written more than two weeks after she testified at the hearing. The references in the letter to "Mr. Randolph" are to Thomas Mann Randolph, Jr., Martha's husband and Nancy Randolph's brother. The "old gentleman" is Colonel Thomas Mann Randolph, Sr., of Tuckahoe, Martha's father-in-law.

The third letter was recently discovered among the Tucker-Coleman Papers at the Earl Gregg Swem Library of the College of William and Mary in Virginia. From Ann Cary Morris to St. George Tucker, it was written as a consequence of John Randolph's accusatory letter of October 31, 1814, addressed to Mrs. Morris but intended for the eyes of her husband. Only the first four pages of the eight-page letter are included in the appendix.

The fourth letter is Ann Cary Morris's response to John Randolph's letter of October 31, 1814. Although it was addressed to him, John Randolph claimed he never received it. Copies of the letter were sent to many of Nancy's friends and relatives in Virginia as well as to some of John Randolph's political foes.

1. To Martha Jefferson Randolph from Thomas Jefferson

Philadelphia Apr. 28. 1793.

MY DEAR MARTHA

I am now very long without a letter from Monticello, which is always a circumstance of anxiety to me. I wish I could say that Maria was quite well. I think her better for this week past, having for that time been free from the little fevers which had harrassed her nightly. A paper which I some time ago saw in the Richmond gazette under the signature R.R. proved to me the existence of a rumor, which I had otherwise heard of with less certainty. It has given me great uneasiness because I know it must have made so many others unhappy, and among these Mr. Randolph and yourself. Whatever the case may be, the world is become too rational to extend to one person the acts of another. Every one at present stands on the merit or demerit of their own conduct. I am in hopes therefore that neither of you feel any uneasiness but for the pitiable victim, whether it be of error or slander. In either case I see guilt but in one person, and not in her. For her it is the moment of trying the affection of her friends, when their commiseration and comfort become balm to her wounds. I hope you will deal them out to her in full measure, regardless of what the trifling or malignant may think or say. Never throw off the best affections of nature in the moment when they become most precious to their object; nor fear to extend your hand to save another, less you should sink yourself. You are on firm ground. Your kindnesses will help her and count in your own favor also. I shall be made very happy if you are the instruments not only of supporting the spirits of your afflicted friend under the weight bearing on them, but of preserving her in the peace, and love of her friends. I hope you have already taken this resolution if it were necessary; and I have no doubt you have: yet I wished it too much to omit mentioning it to you. I am with sincere love to Mr. Randolph and yourself, my dear Martha Your's affectionately,

TH: JEFFERSON

2. To Thomas Jefferson from Martha Jefferson Randolph

Monticello May 16 1793

DEAR PAPA

I recieved your kind letter of April the 28 a week ago and should have answered it imediately but that the house was full of company at the time. The subject of it has been one of infinite anxiety both to Mr. Randolph and my self for many months and tho I am too sensible of the iliberality of extending to one person the infamy of an other, to fear one moment that it can reflect any real disgrace upon me in the eyes of people of sense yet the generality of mankind are weak enough to think otherwise and it is painful to an excess to be obliged to blush for so near a connection. I know it by fatal experience. As for the poor deluded victim I believe all feel much more for her than she does for her self. The villain having been no less successful in corrupting her mind than he has in destroying her reputation. Amidst the distress of her family she alone is tranquil and seems proof against every other misfortune on earth but that of a separation from her vile seducer. They have been tried and acquited tho I am sorry to say his Lawers gained more honour by it than they did as but a small part of the world and those the most inconsiderable people in it were influenced in there opinion by the dicision of the court. In following the dictates of my own heart I was so happy as to stumble upon the very conduct you advised me to, before I knew your opinion. I have continued to behave with affection to her which her errors have not been able to eradicate from my heart and could I suppose her penitent I would redouble my attentions to her though I am one of the few who have all ways doubted the truth of the report. As the opinion I had of R.R. was most exalted would to heaven my hopes were equal to my fears but the latter often to often presides. The divisions of the family encrease daily. There is no knowing where they will end. The old gentleman has plunged into the thickest of them governed by the most childish passions. He lends the little weight his imprudence has left him to widen the breaches it should be his duty to close. Mr. R-s conduct has been such as to conciliate the affections of the whole family. He is the Link by which so many discordant parts join. Having made up his difference with David Randolph there is not one individual but what looks up to him as one, and the only one who has been uniform in his affection to them. My Little cherubs are both in perfect health . . .

3. To St. George Tucker from Ann Cary Morris

Morrisania March 2, 1815

Dear Sir

The report is wholly false of any personal differences having taken place here between myself and the parties who dared to slander with base calumny the dwelling sacred to conjugal Harmony, parental delight and Genuine Hospitality. There is no doubt that God, ever Just, will wring from Tudor in his last moment of expiring life an acknowledgement of his horrible Slanders.

Poor Dick possessed some noble qualities and had he not married so unhappily before he was old enough to have his principles fixed, he would have been an ornament to human nature. My discovery of his weaker side founded his Friendship for me who left Home to avoid a marriage hateful to me. Having visited my father's excellent sister and my brother at Monticello, I accepted an invitation to Bizarre. Dick entered my apartment one morning, threw himself on his knees, and begged that I would listen to him and not alarm any one. He declared his own unhappiness, that he knew his wife did not love him, that the first night of their marriage she made him sit up altogether in a corner of their apartment at Presqu isle (this she had boasted of) to shew her power. He endeavored to shake my principles. I said I would be silent because Polly, the woman who waited on me in 1791, would soon be up with water and she had better find him in the room than meet him coming out of it. He proceeded to tell me that he had once entered the chamber of Miss Betsey Talliaferro, afterwards Mrs. Call, at old Mr. Wyth's, the house now Mr. Skipwith's in Williamsburg, that she received him in her bed and that the same reception had been given him by a Miss Hetty Ludlow in New York. I burst into tears and exclaimed, "Oh my poor Father, what has your wretched marriage brought on your child. I will write and conjure him to send for me. I am engaged to your brother." The tears streamed from Dick's eyes. Mine fill with a recollection of the Heart-rending scene. Polly came with water. She had witnessed much anguish at Tuckahoe. She was daughter to the faithful creature who nursed all my mother's family. I made the best appearance that the case admitted by turning to her and saying Polly I wish my mother had lived. Dick left the room professing Friendship for me. I wrote to pray my father would send for me; his wife answered that the horses were too lame to travel but it was no secret that she [set] out with them to meet Frank Corbin and old Colonel Bassett. I had no home to receive me. It was a winter of extreme misery for me. I might in the spring have married Gen¹ Lee, Ben Harrison, or Archy Randolph. Two days before Dick's death [?] on his sending for me and giving the servant sent an errand out of the room that he reproached himself and seemed very unhappy. I tried to soothe him and promised as far as possible to protect his memory if I survived him and serve his children. I had then no idea of his danger (the day after Mrs. Dudley told me I had better prepare you to hear he was ill). He seemed comforted and spoke much of my affectionate and grateful disposition at the same time declaring that I was the only sincere Friend he ever had, except you my dear Sir. Ryland Randolph knows that I left in Jack's care a letter from Dick to me containing this very acknowledgement or declaration which ever it may be called. After the return from Bermuda, Dick repeated the frantic kind of scene already described and conjured me not to marry any one, that the idea distracted him. My only refuge was in his brother. He then came to his reason and I do think Nature made him of her best materials; but, he had one Fault of great magnitude. He was the victim of his marriage with a cold hearted malignant haughty woman. A proper match would have established his natural feelings of Honor. Indeed he was the only man I ever knew whose destiny seemed entirely to depend [on] his choice of a wife. To Judy I owe nothing but harsh, abusive language. When finally driven from Bizarre, I dreaded that my sufferings would drive me at last to destroy myself. I would then have made any possible sacrifice for Saint and Tudor such was my devotion to them. Saint George's misfortunes and his affectionate letters keep alive my feelings for him. No humane person can ever wound him. I trust the age of 19 never matured more baseness than Tudor possesses. I have a tender virtuous husband and a lovely promising child . . .

4. To John Randolph from Ann C. Morris

Morrisania, January 16th, 1815.

Sir:

My husband yesterday communicated to me for the first time your letter of the last of October, together with that which accompanied it, directed to him.

In your letter to my husband, you say, "I wish I could withhold the blow but I must in your case do what under a change of circumstances I would have you do unto me." This Sir, seems fair and friendly. It seems, Sir, as if you wished to apprize Mr. Morris and him only of circumstances important to his happiness and honor, though fatal to my reputation, leaving it in his power to cover them in oblivion or display them to the world as the means of freeing him from a monster unfit to live. But this was mere seeming. Your real object was widely different. Under the pretext of consulting Com. Decatur and Mr. Bleecker, you communicated your slanders to them, and then to Mr. Ogden. You afterwards displayed them to Mr. Wilkins, who, having heard them spoken of in the city, called on you to know on what foundation they stood. How many others you may have consulted, to how many others you may have published your malicious tale, I know not, but I venture to ask whether this be conduct under a change of circumstances you would have others pursue towards you? You have professed a sense of gratitude for obligations you suppose my husband to have laid you under. Was the attempt to blacken my character and destroy his peace of mind a fair return? There are many other questions which will occur to candid minds on the perusal of your letter. For instance, did *you* believe these slanders? If you did, why did you permit your nephew to be fed from my bounty and nursed by my care during nearly three months? Could you suppose him safe in the power of a wretch who had murdered his father? Does it consist with the dignified pride of family you affect to have him, whom you announce as your heir, and destined to support your name, dependent on the charity of a negro's concubine? You say I confine my husband a prisoner in his house that there may be no witnesses of my lewd amours, and have driven away his friends and old domestics that there may be no witnesses of his death. If I wished to indulge in amours, the natural course would be to mingle in the pleasures and amusements of the city, or at least to induce my husband to go abroad and leave me a clear stage for such misdeeds. Was it with a view to multiple witnesses of my ill conduct that you published tales tending as far as they are believed to make his house a solitude? It cannot escape your observation that you take on you to assert things which, had they existed, you could not know. Thus you say your brother "passed his word and the pledge was redeemed at the hazard of all that a man can hold dear!" Pray, Sir, admitting (tho it is not true) that I had exacted from your brother a promise of secrecy, how could you have known it unless he betrayed it? and, if he betrayed it, how was the pledge redeemed? Again you say that "I instigated Mr. Morris to write to the Chief Justice whom I knew to have been misled." Had the instigation been a fact, how could you come by the knowledge of it? Like many other things in your letter, it happens to be a downright falsehood, and is, therefore, a just standard for him to estimate the rest of your assertions. Permit me to observe also that it is an additional proof of your intention to spread your slander abroad!; for, had you meant to communicate information to Mr. Morris, you would not have hazarded such a charge. People of proper feelings require that the evidence of accusation be strong in proportion as the guilt is enormous; but those, who feel themselves capable of committing the blackest crimes, will readily suspect others, and condemn without proof on a mere hearsay, on the suggestion of a disturbed fancy or instigations of a malevolent heart. Those who possess a clear conscience and sound mind, will look through your letter for some proof of my guilt. They will look in vain. They will find, indeed, that you have thought proper to found suspicions on suspicions of your nephew, and, with no better evidence, you have the insolence to impute crime at which nature revolts. You will perhaps say that you mention a piece of evidence in your possession—a letter which I wrote on leaving Virginia. As far as that goes, it must be admitted, but permit me to tell you that the very mention of it destroys your credibility with honorable minds. To say, as you do, that I laid no injunction of secrecy will strike such minds as a pitiful evasion. If you had the feelings of a man of honor, you would have known that there are things the communication of which involves that injunction. You have heard of principle and pretend to justify the breach of confidence by my want of respect for your name. But you acknowledge that you communicated the information to my sister and her son Tudor (this is a boy of eleven years old) shortly after you became possessed of it. Thus was my reputation, as far as it lay in your power, committed to the discretion of a woman and a child many years before the imputed want of respect for your name! Formerly Jack Randolph—now, "John Randolph of Roanoke." It was then a want of respect to the great John Randolph of Roanoke to say he had done the honor of offering his hand to his poor cousin Nancy. I shall take more notice of this in its proper place, and only add here that among the respectable people of Virginia the affectation of greatness must cover you with ridicule.

But, to return to this breach of confidence, without which you have not the shadow of evidence to support your slanders. While on the chapter of self-contradictions (which, with all due respect to "John Randolph of Roanoke," make up the history of his life) I must notice a piece of evidence not indeed contained in your letter, but written by your hand. I have already hinted at the indelicacy of leaving your nephew so long in my care with the view of meeting observations which no person can fail to make on a conduct so extraordinary in itself and inconsistent with your charges against me. You pretend to have discovered, all at once in this house, the confirmation of your suspicions, but surely the suspicion was sufficient to prevent a person having a pretense to delicacy from subjecting himself to such obligations. One word, however, as to this sudden discovery made by your great sagacity. Recollect, Sir, when you rose from table to leave Morrisania, you put in my husband's hand a note to my sister expressing your willingness that she and her son should pass the winter in this house. Surely, the discovery must have been made at that time, if at all. You will recollect, too, some other marks of confidence and affection, let me add of respect also, which I forbear to mention because you would no doubt deny them, and it would be invidious to ask the testimony of those who were present. One act, however, must not be unnoticed. It speaks too plain a language to be misunderstood, and was too notorious to be denied. When you entered this house, and when you left it, you took me in your arms, you pressed me to your bosom, you impressed upon my lips a kiss which I received as a token of friendship from a near relation. Did you then believe that you held in your arms, that you pressed to your bosom, that you kissed the lips of, a common prostitute, the murderess of her own child and of your brother? Go, tell this to the world that scorn may be at no loss for an object. If you did not believe it, make out a certificate that "John Randolph of Roanoke" is a base calumniator. But no, you may spare yourself this trouble. It is already written. It lies before me, and I proceed to notice what it contains in a more particular manner.

And first, Sir, as to the fact communicated shortly before I left Virginia. That your brother Theodoric paid his addresses to me, you knew and attempted to supplant him by calumny. Be pleased to remember that, in my sister Mary's house, you led me to the portico, and, leaning against one of the pillars, expressed your surprise at having heard from your brother Richard that I was engaged to marry his brother, Theodoric. That you hoped it was not true, for he was unworthy of me. To establish this opinion, you made many assertions derogatory to his reputation—some of which I knew to be false. Recollect that, afterward, on one of those occasions (not infrequent), when your violence of temper had led you into an unpleasant situation, you, in a letter to your brother, Richard, declared you were unconscious of ever having done anything in all your life which could offend me, unless it was that conversation, excusing it as an act of heroism, like the sacrifice of his own son by Brutus, for which I ought to applaud you. The defamation of your brother whom I loved, your stormy passions, your mean selfishness, your wretched appearance, rendered your attentions disagreeable. Your brother, Richard, a model of truth and honor, knew how much I was annoyed by them. He knew of the letters with which you pestered me from Philadelphia till one of them was returned in a blank cover, when I was absent from home. By whom it was done, I knew not; for I never considered it of impor-

tance enough to inquire. It was your troublesome attentions which induced
Richard to inform you of my engagement. At that time, my father had other
views. Your property, as well as that of your brothers, was hampered by a
British debt. My father, therefore, preferred for my husband a person of clear
and considerable estate. The sentiment of my heart did not accord with his
intentions. Under these circumstances, I was left at Bizarre, a girl, not seventeen, with the man she loved. I was betrothed to him, and considered him as
my husband in the presence of that God whose name you presume to invoke
on occasions the most trivial and for purposes the most malevolent. We should
have been married, if Death had not snatched him away a few days after the
scene which began the history of my sorrows. Your brother, Richard, knew
every circumstance, but you are mistaken in supposing I exacted from him a
promise of secrecy. He was a man of honor. Neither the foul imputations
against us both, circulated by that kind of friendship which you have shown
to my husband, nor the awful scene, to which he was afterwards called as an
accomplice in the horrible crime, with which you attempt to blacken his
memory, could induce him to betray the sister of his wife, the wife of his
brother; I repeat it, Sir, the crime with which you now attempt to blacken
his memory. You say that, to screen the character of such a creature as I am,
the life and the fame of that most generous and gallant of men was put in
jeopardy. His life alas! is now beyond the reach of your malice, but his fame,
which should be dear to a brother's heart, is stabbed by the hand of his
brother. You not only charge me with the heinous crime of infanticide, placing him in the condition of an accomplice, but you proceed to say that "had
it not been for the prudence of Mr. Harrison, or the mismanagement of not
putting *me* first on my trial, we should both have swung on the same gibbet
and the foul stain of incest and murder been stamped on his memory and
associated with the idea of his offspring." This, Sir, is the language you presume to write and address to me, enclosed in a cover to my husband for his
inspection, after having been already communicated to other people. I will,
for a moment, put myself out of question, and suppose the charge to be true.
What must be the indignation of a feeling heart to behold a wretch rake up
the ashes of his deceased brother to blast his fame? Who is there of nerve so
strong as not to shudder at your savage regret that we did not swing on the
same gibbet? I well remember, and you cannot have forgotten that, when
sitting at the hospitable home of your venerable father-in-law, you threw a
knife at that brother's head, and, if passion had not diverted the aim, he would
much earlier have been consigned to the grave, and you much earlier have
met the doom which awaits your murderous disposition. It was, indeed, hoped
that age and reflection had subdued your native barbarity. But, setting aside
the evidence which your letter contains, the earnestness with which you disclosed in the presence of Col. Morris and his brother the Commodore [your
desire] to shoot a British soldier, to bear off his scalp and hang it up as an
ornament in your house at Roanoke, shows that you have still the heart of a
savage. I ask not of you but of a candid world whether a man like you is

worthy of belief. On the melancholy occasion you have thought proper to bring forward there was the strictest examination. Neither your brother or myself had done anything to excite enmity, yet we were subjected to an unpitying persecution. The severest scrutiny took place; you know it. He was acquitted to the joy of numerous spectators, expressed in shouts of exultation. This, Sir, passed in a remote county of Virginia more than twenty years ago. You have revived the slanderous tale in the most populous city in the United States. For what? To repay my kindness to your nephew by tearing me from the arms of my husband and blasting the prospects of my child! Poor innocent babe, now playing at my feet, unconscious of his mother's wrongs. But it seems that on my apprehensions for his life first flashed convictions on your mind that my own hand had deprived in October, 1792, that of which I was delivered. You ought to have said, the last of September.

You must, Mr. Randolph, have a most extraordinary kind of apprehension; for one child can induce you to believe in the destruction of another. But, waiving this absurdity, you acknowledge that every fact, which had come to your knowledge, every circumstance you had either heard or dreamt of in the long period of more than twenty years, had never imparted to you a belief, which nevertheless you expect to imprint on the minds of others. You thus pay to the rest of mankind the wretched compliment of supposing them more ready to believe the greatest crimes than "John Randolph of Roanoke." Doubtless there may be some, who are worthy of this odious distinction; I hope not many. I hope too that, in justice to the more rational part of the community, you will wait (before you require their faith) until some such flash shall have enlightened their minds. Mark here, for your future government, the absurdity to which falsehood and malice inevitably lead a calumniator. They have driven you, while you endeavored to palliate inconsistency of conduct, into palpable self contradiction. Sensible as you must be that no respectable person can overlook the baseness of leaving your nephew so long, or even permitting him to come, under the roof of the wretch you describe me to be, you are compelled to acknowledge that you did not believe in the enormities you charge, until yourself had paid a visit to Morrisania. Thus you not only invalidate every thing like evidence to support your criminations but found them on circumstances which produce an effect (if they operate at all) directly opposite to that for which they are cited.

You have, Sir, on this subject presumed to use my sister's name. Permit me to tell you, I do not believe one word of what you say. Were it true, it is wholly immaterial. But that it is not true, I have perfect conviction.

The assertion rests only on your testimony, the weight and value of which has been already examined. The contradiction is contained in her last letter to me, dated Dec. 17th, of which I enclose a copy. You will observe she cautions me against believing anything inconsistent with her gratitude for my kindness, and assures me that, altho' prevented from spending the winter with us, she is proud of the honor done her by the invitation. With this letter before me, I should feel it an insult to her as well as an indignity to myself if I made any observations on your conduct at Bizarre. No one can think so meanly of a woman who moves in the sphere of a lady as to suppose she could be proud of the honor of being invited to spend a winter with the concubine of one of her slaves. Nevertheless, tho I disdain an answer to such imputations, I am determined they shall appear in the neighborhood under your hand; so that your character may be fully known and your signature forever hereafter be not only what it has hitherto been, the appendage of vainglorious boasting, but the designation of malicious baseness. You say I drove Mrs. Dudley from my sister's house. A falsehood more absurd could hardly have been invented. She left the house the day before your brother was buried. I shall not enter into a detail of the circumstances, but this assertion also shall be communicated to the neighbourhood. It is well that your former constituents should know the creature in whom they put their trust. Virginians, in general, whatever may be their defects, have a high sense of honor. You speak with affected sensibility of my sister's domestic bliss, and you assume an air of indignation at the violence of my temper. Be pleased to recollect that, returning from a morning ride with your brother, you told me you found it would not do to interfere between man and wife; that you had recommended to him a journey to Connecticut to obtain a divorce; that he made no reply, nor spoke a single word afterwards. Recollect, too, how often, and before how many persons, and in how many ways, you have declared your detestation of her conduct as a wife and her angry passions. One form of expression occurs which is remarkable: "I have heard," said you, "that Mrs. Randolph was handsome, and, perhaps, had I ever seen her in a good humor, I might have thought so; but her features are so distorted by constant wrath that she has to me the air of a fury." And now, as to my disposition and conduct, be pleased not to forget (for people of a certain sort should have good memories) that, during full five years after your brother's death, and how much longer, I know not, I was the constant theme of your praise and, tho you wearied everyone else, you seemed on that subject to be yourself indefatigable. I should not say these things, if they rested merely on my own knowledge, for you would not hesitate to deny them, and I should be very sorry that my credibility were placed on the same level with yours. You have addressed me as a notorious liar, to which I make no other answer than that the answer, like your other charges, shall be communicated to those who know us both. You will easily anticipate their decision. In the meantime, it may not be amiss to refresh your memory with one sample of your veracity. There are many who remember, while your slaves were under mortgage for the British debt, your philanthropic assertion that you would make them free and provide tutors for them. With this project, you wearied all who would listen. When, by the sale of some of them, a part of the debt was discharged, and an agreement made to pay the rest by installments, you changed your mind. This was not inexcusable, but when you set up for representation in Congress, and the plan to liberate your slaves was objected to in your District, you published, to the astonishment of numbers, who had heard you descant on your liberal intentions, that you *never* had any such idea. Thus your first step in public life was marked with falsehood. On entering the door of Congress, you became an outrageous patriot. Nothing in the French Revolution was too immoral or too impious for your taste and applause. Washington and Britain were the objects of your obloquy. This patriotic fever lasted till the conclusion of Mr. Chase's trial, from which you returned, complaining of the fatigue of your public labors, but elated with the prospect of a foreign mission. As usual, you rode your new Hobby to the annoyance of all who like me were obliged to listen. Your expected voyage enchanted you so much that you could not help talking of it even to your deaf nephew: "Soon, my boy, we shall be sailing over the Atlantic." But, all at once, you became silent and seemed in deep melancholy. It appeared soon after that Mr. Jefferson and Mr. Madison, knowing your character, had prudently declined a compliance with your wishes. A new scene now opened; you became a patriot, double distilled, and founded your claim to the confidence of new friends on the breach of that which had been reposed by your old ones. I know not what others may think as to your treacherous disclosure of Mr. Madison's declaration, "that the French want money and must have it," but it is no slight evidence of his correct conduct, in general, that *you* had nothing else to betray.

With the same insensibility to shame, which marks your allegations, you have denied the fact of turning me out of doors. This also shall be made known in the neighbourhood where it must be well remembered. I take the liberty again to refresh your memory. Shortly after your nephew (whom I had nursed several weeks in a dangerous illness at the hazard of my life) had left home to take the benefit of a change of air, you came into the room one evening, after you had been a long time in your chamber with my sister, and said, addressing yourself to me, "Nancy, when do you leave this house? The sooner the better for you take as many liberties as if you were in a tavern." On this occasion, as on others, my course was silent submission. I was poor, I was dependent. I knew the house was kept in part at your expense. I could not therefore appeal to my sister. I replied with the humility, suitable to my forlorn condition, "I will go as soon as I can." You stalked haughtily about the room, and poor, unprotected "Nancy" retired to seek the relief of tears. Every assertion of yours respecting my visit to Grovebrook is false. Mr. Murray cannot but acknowledge that I went there with Judge Johnston in his carriage, on my way to Hanover, after repeated invitations from his family, conveyed in letters from his daughters; that I left there in the chariot of my friend, Mr. Swan; that they pressed me not only to prolong my stay but to repeat my visit. Of this, Mr. Curd, a gentleman sent by Mr. Swan to escort me, was a witness.

You are unfortunate in what passed two years after when I saw you at Richmond, but, before I refresh your memory on this subject, I must notice another malicious falsehood respecting my residence, while in Richmond. You say I took lodgings at Prior's, a public garden. It is true Mr. Prior owned a large lot in Richmond, and that there was a public building on it, in which public balls and entertainments were given, and this lot a public garden, but it is equally true that Mr. Prior's dwelling and the enclosure round it were wholly distinct from that garden. In that house, I lodged. My chamber was directly over Mrs. Prior's, a lady of as good birth as Mr. John Randolph and of far more correct principles. All this, Sir, you perfectly well know. From that chamber, I wrote you a note, complaining that your nephew, then a school boy in Richmond, was not permitted to see me. You sent [it] back, after writing on the same sheet, "I return your note that you may compare it with my answer, and ask yourself, if you are not unjust to one who through life has been your friend." This, with the recital of your professions of regard, made to my friend Lucy Randolph and her husband and her husband's brother Ryland, led me to suppose you had, in the last scene at Bizarre, acted only as my sister's agent. I therefore, wrote to you, remonstrating against the reason you assigned for turning me out of doors, which you yourself knew to be unfounded, for you had often observed that I was "Epicene, the Silent Woman." You knew that I was continually occupied at my needle or other work for the house, obeying, to the best of my knowledge, the orders I received, differing from any other servant only in this: I received no wages, but was permitted to sit at table, where I did not presume to enter into conversation or taste of wine, and very seldom of tea or coffee. I gave my letter open into the hands of Ryland Randolph, to be put by him into your hands. I pause here, Sir, to ask, whether, on the receipt of this letter, you pretended to deny having turned me out of doors? You dare not say so. You shortly after paid me a visit, the only one during your stay. You sat on my bedstead, I cannot say my bed, for I had none, I was too poor. When weary, my limbs were rested on a blanket, spread over the sacking. Your visit was long, and I never saw you from that day until we met in Washington. Some days after, you sent your nephew to offer me $100 on the part of his mother. I supposed this to be a turn of delicacy, for, had you been the bearer of money from her, you would have delivered it, when you were in my chamber, and given me every needful assurance of the quarter from which it came. But, let it have come from whom it might, my feelings were too indignant to receive a boon at the hands of those by whom I had been so grievously wounded. I readily conceive, Sir, that this must have appeared to you inexplicable, for it must be very difficult for you to conceive how a person in my condition would refuse money from any quarter. It is true that, afterwards, when in Newport, suffering from want, and borne down by a severe ague and fever, I was so far humbled as to request not the gift (I would sooner have perished) but the loan of half that sum. My petition struck on a cold heart that emitted no sound. You did not deign to reply. You even made a boast of your silence. I was then so far off my groans could not be heard in Virginia. You no longer apprehended the [reproaches] which prompted your ostentatious offer at Richmond. Yes, Sir, you were silent. You then possessed the letter on which you grounded your calumnies. You supposed me so much in your power that I should not dare to complain of your unkindness. Yes, Sir, you were silent, and you left your nephew nearly three months dependent on the charity of her, to whom in the extreme of wretchedness you had refused the loan of fifty dollars. Yes, Sir, you were silent. Perhaps, you hoped that the poor forlorn creature you had turned out of doors would, under the pressure of want, and far removed from every friend, be driven to a vicious course, and enable you to justify your barbarity by charges such as you have now invented.

You say you were informed of my associating with the players and my decline into a very drab by a friend in Richmond. Your letter shall be read in Richmond. You must produce that friend, unless you are willing yourself to father the falsehood which in Richmond will be notorious.

I defy you Mr. Randolph to substantiate by the testimony of any credible witness a single fact injurious to my reputation from the time you turned me out of doors until the present hour; and God knows that, if suffering could have driven me to vice, there was no want of suffering. My husband, in permitting me to write this letter, has enjoined me not to mention his kindness, otherwise I could give a detail of circumstances which, as they would not involve any pecuniary claim, might touch even *your* heart. You speak of him as an infirm old man, into whom I have struck the fangs of a harpy, after having acted in your family the part of a vampire. I pray you, Mr. "John Randolph of Roanoke," to be persuaded that such idle declamation, tho' it might become a school boy to his aunt and cousins, is misplaced on the present occasion. You know as little of the manner in which my present connection began as of other things with which you pretend to be acquainted. I loved my husband before he made me his wife. I love him still more now that he had made me mother of one of the finest boys I ever saw; now that his kindness soothes the anguish which I cannot but feel from your unmanly attack. I am very sorry I am obliged to speak of your nephew. I would fain impute to his youth, or to some other excusable cause, his unnatural, and I must say, criminal, conduct. I hope the strength of my constitution, the consolation I derive from the few friends who are left and the caresses of my beloved babe will enable me to resist the measures taken for my destruction by him and his uncle. Had his relations rested only on your testimony, I should not have hesitated to have acquitted him of the charge; but a part of them at least, not fully detailed in your letter, was made in Mr. Ogden's presence. This young man received several small sums of money which I sent him unasked, while he remained at Cambridge. Early in April, by a letter, which he addressed to me as his "Dear good Aunt," he requested the loan of thirty or forty dollars. I did not imitate the example you had set but immediately enclosed a check payable to his order for thirty dollars. I heard no more of him until the end of July, when a letter, dated in Providence, announced his intention of seeing me soon at Morrisania. At the same time, letters to my husband mentioned the dangerous condition of his health. On the 4th of August, a phaeton drove to the door with a led horse, and a person, appearing to be a servant, stepped out and enquired for Mr. Randolph. He was directed to the stable, and shortly after Mr. Randolph landed from the boat of a Packet. His appearance bespoke severe illness. I showed him to his chamber, and venture to say from that time to the moment of his departure he was treated by me with the tenderness and kindness of a mother. The injunction I have already mentioned restrains me from going into particulars. My health was injured by the fatigue to which I was exposed, the burthen of which I could not diminish without neglecting him; for I could not procure good nurses or servants. My husband's health, too, was, I believe, injured by the confinement which this youth occasioned; for he was prevented from taking a journey we were about to make for air and exercise among the mountains of New Jersey. We were also under the disagreeable necessity of keeping a servant whom our friends had denounced as a thief. By the bye, I have reason to believe he is one of those "ancient domestics" you have taken under your protection. If so, I must in justice to myself inform you that your friend, Geo. Bevens, dismissed only two days before your arrival, was shortly after admitted to a lodging in the Bridewell of New York for theft. I had an opportunity, indeed I was made by my laundress, to observe that your nephew (though driving his phaeton with a servant on horse back) had not a pair of stockings fit to wear; his man, Jonathan, dunning him in my presence for his wages. At one time, in particular, passing by his door, I heard Jonathan ask for money. My heart prompted me to offer relief. As I entered his room for that purpose (it was two days after a violent hemorrhage which threatened his life), he was rising feebly from his bed, and, when I mentioned my object, said in a tremulous voice, "My dear Aunt, I was coming to ask you." I bade his servant follow me and gave him $5.00. Tudor had returned the $30 first borrowed but, shortly afterwards, increased the debt $10 to furnish as I supposed, his travelling companion, Mr. Bruce, [of Rhode Island] with the means of returning home. A few days after that, I supplied him with an additional $20. I gave stockings and, before his departure, sent $30 to one of Mr. Morris' nieces to purchase handkerchiefs which he wanted and which his mother said he could not afford to buy. The evening you left Morrisania, I received a note from this lady excusing herself for not executing my commission by reason of the death of a cousin and returning the money because she understood that my sister was to go the next Tuesday. You witnessed my surprise at receiving such information in such a way. You will recollect what followed. After your departure, I communicated the note to your nephew, and told him, as he was going to town, he could purchase the handkerchiefs for himself. I gave him thirty dollars which he put in his pocket and thanked me. Two days after, when in town, he said to me, "Aunt I wish you would choose the handkerchiefs yourself; I should value them more." He forgot, however, to return the money. I purchased the Hdkffs, together with a merino tippet to protect his chest, and received again his thanks which were reiterated the same day by his mother at Mr. Ogden's. The debt, amounting to $65.00, she paid at Morrisania. The $30 were enclosed in her note, dated Saturday morning, of which I send you herewith a copy together with that of the 3rd November from Philadelphia.

And now, Sir, put the actual parties out of the question, and say what credit can be due to the calumnies of a person in your nephew's situation soliciting and receiving favors to the very last moment. Let me add, after he had poured his slanders into your ear or repeated them from your dictation, he left me to discharge one of his doctor's bills, which he said I offered to pay, and receive his thanks in advance. Is it proper, or is it decent to found such calumnies on the suspicions of such a creature?, even supposing them to have originated in his mind, and not been, as is too probable, instigated by you? Could anything but the most determined and inveterate malice induce any one above the level of an idiot to believe the only fact he pretended to articulate? Who can believe me cruel to my child? When it is notorious my fault is too great indulgence; that my weakness is too great solicitude, and that I have been laughed at for instances of maternal care by which my health was impaired. You cite as from him these words, "How shocking she looks. I have not met her eyes three times since I have been in the house." Can you believe this? Can you believe others to believe it? How happens it you did not cry out as anyone else would have done? "Why did you stay in that house? Why did you submit to her kindness? Why did you accept her presents? Why did you pocket her money?" To such an apostrophe he might have replied perhaps, "Uncle I could not help it. I was penniless, in daily expectation that you or my mother would bring relief. When at last she came, I found her almost as ill-off as myself. We were both detained till you arrived." To this excuse, which is a very lame one for a person who had a phaeton to sell or pledge, any one who feels a spark of generosity in his bosom would reply, "Why, then, wretch, having from necessity or choice laid yourself under such a load of obligations, do you become the calumniator of your benefactress? Are you yet to learn what is due to the rites of hospitality, or have you, at the early age of nineteen, been taught to combine profound hypocrisy with deadly hate and assume the mask of love that you may more surely plant the assassin's dagger? Where did you learn these horrible lessons?" This last, Sir, would have been a dangerous question on your part. He might have replied and may yet reply, "Uncle, I learned this from you."

But, to return to the wonderful circumstance that this young man had not met my eyes above once a month, though he saw me frequently every day. That he met them seldomer than I wished is true. I was sorry to observe what others had remarked, that he rarely looked any one in the face. I excused this sinister air to myself, and tried to excuse it to others as a proof of uncommon modesty, of which nevertheless he gave no other proof. I sometimes succeeded in my endeavours to make people believe that this gloomy, guilty look proceeded from bashfulness. I know not, and shall not pretend to guess, what heavy matter pressed on his conscience; perhaps it was only the disposition to be criminal. At present, [now] that he has an opportunity (with your assistance) to gratify that disposition, he will, I presume, be less capable of assuming the air of an honest man, and he will probably find himself frequently on leaving good company in condition to repeat the same sentence of self-condemnation: "Uncle, I have not met their eyes three times since I have been in the house."

You make him say, "my first impression as far back as I can remember is that she was an unchaste woman—my brother knew her better than I—she never could do anything with him"—This too is admirable testimony to support your filthy accusations.

Pray, Mr. John Randolph of Roanoke, why did you not inform your audience that, when you turned me out of doors, this Mr. Tudor Randolph was but nine years old, and his brother, poor deaf and dumb Saint George, just thirteen— Can it be necessary to add to your confusion by a single remark? It seems to me, if any one present at your wild declamation, had noticed this fact, you would have been hissed even by a sisterhood of old maids. Unluckily for you, I have letters from poor Saint George, one of which, written shortly before his late malady, is filled with assurances of attachment. In that which I received, while I was in Washington, he makes particular and affectionate inquiries respecting Col [Monroe's] family. These show that he does not participate in your ingratitude, but feels as he ought the kindness of that gentleman, who, at your instance, took him into his family in London and watched over him with paternal care. You repay this favor by slanders which I have the charity to believe you are too polite to pronounce in the Col's presence. I have a letter from my sister telling me the pleasure St. George manifested at the present of my portrait I made him. I have a letter also from her, shortly after her house was burnt, in which she tells me among the few things saved she was rejoiced to find my portrait which you brought out with your own. By this act, you have some right to it, and, should my present ill health lead me shortly to the grave, you may hang it up in your castle at Roanoke next to the Englishman's scalp—a trophy of the family prowess. I observe, Sir, in the course of your letter allusion to one of Shakespeare's best tragedies. I trust you are by this time convinced that you have clumsily performed the part of "honest Iago." Happily for my life, and for my husband's peace, you did not find in him a headlong, rash Othello. For a full and proper description of what you have written and spoken on this occasion, I refer you to the same admirable author. He will tell you it is a tale told by an idiot, full of sound and fury, signifying nothing.

ANN C. MORRIS

Appendix Two:
Chronology

1741   New York Conspiracy trials.

1744   Publication of Daniel Horsmanden book on New York Conspiracy.

1752   Gouverneur Morris and St. George Tucker born.

1755   John Marshall born.

1761   Adèle de Flahaut born.

1766   Creed Taylor born.

1769   David Hosack born.

1770   Richard Randolph born.

1771   Theodorick Randolph born.

1772   Judith Randolph born.

1773   John Randolph born.

1774   Ann Cary (Nancy) Randolph born.

1775   John Randolph, Sr. (father of Richard, Theodorick, and John) dies. David Ogden born.

1776   British invasion of New York City.

        Publication of first quarto of Gibbon's *Decline and Fall of The Roman Empire.*

1777   New York Constitutional Convention—G. Morris unsuccessfully attempts to abolish slavery in New York.

        G. Morris first publicly announces idea of a canal from the Great Lakes to the Hudson River.

1778   G. Morris a member of the Continental Congress—serves on committee to investigate state of the army at Valley Forge.

Frances Bland Randolph marries St. George Tucker.

1780   G. Morris becomes citizen of Pennsylvania—loses leg in an accident.

Henry St. George Tucker born.

1781   Family of St. George Tucker leaves Matoax in flight from British invasion—Syphax and Essex accompany the family.

G. Morris becomes assistant to Robert Morris, the Superintendent of Finances for U.S.

St. George Tucker at siege of Yorktown.

1782   G. Morris first proposes plan for decimal coinage.

Virginia law authorizes the private manumission of slaves.

1784   Nathaniel Beverley Tucker and Maria Ward born.

1785   Charles de Flahaut born.

Congress resolves to make the dollar the money unit of U.S. (G. Morris plan as revised by Thomas Jefferson).

1786   G. Morris purchases Morrisania from half brother and British General Staats Long Morris.

1787   G. Morris is a commissioner to Constitutional Convention from Pennsylvania—writes preamble to the U.S. Constitution and is responsible for final style and arrangement of the document.

1788   Virginia ratifies the U.S. Constitution—John Marshall and Patrick Henry on opposing sides of the debate; G. Morris present at debate; also in Virginia as agent for Robert Morris—G. Morris visits Tuckahoe, home of Nancy Randolph.

Frances Bland Tucker and Walker Maury (John Randolph's mother and old teacher) die.

1789   G. Morris arrives in France, begins to write diary, meets Adèle de Flahaut, witnesses convening of Estates General.

Fall of Bastille.

1789   Royal family forced to return to Paris from Versailles.

Ann Cary Randolph (mother of Judith and Nancy) dies.

Richard Randolph marries Judith Randolph.

1790   G. Morris on unofficial mission to London, discusses British debts, impressment, and treaty obligations with British government.

Martha Jefferson marries Thomas Mann Randolph, Jr.

Thomas Mann Randolph, Sr. marries Gabriella Harvie.

Randolph Harrison marries Mary Randolph.

1791   Fearing assassination, Talleyrand writes will making Adèle de Flahaut his heir.

King and Queen unsuccessfully attempt to flee France.

St. George Tucker marries Lelia Skipwith Carter.

Mass insurrection of slaves in St. Domingo.

1792   G. Morris confirmed as American minister to France.

Wars of the French Revolution begin in Europe (commencement of twenty-three years of war).

G. Morris plots to help royal family escape France; August revolution; republic established in France; massacres begin; Lafayette flees and is imprisoned by allies; Talleyrand, Adèle and Charles de Flahaut flee France; all ambassadors except G. Morris leave Paris.

Theodorick Randolph dies. (February 14).

St. George Randolph born.

John Randolph stricken with scarlet fever.

Richard, Judith, Nancy, and John Randolph visit Glenlyvar, home of Randolph and Mary Harrison—rumors begin (October 1) that baby born to Nancy Randolph.

As part of revision of Virginia laws, certain statutes are suspended for a nine-month period beginning at the end of 1792.

1793   G. Morris ceases making entries in his diary; Louis XVI executed; Reign of Terror begins; Marie Antoinette executed.

1793   Richard Randolph publishes letter stating he will appear in court to answer charges against him; Richard in jail; preliminary examination of Richard Randolph (April 29); Patrick Henry, John Marshall, and Alexander Campbell represent defendant; Richard and Nancy Randolph acquitted of charges against them.

British Debts case argued in Richmond—Patrick Henry, John Marshall, Alexander Campbell, and James Innes appear for debtors; John Randolph present at argument; Federal Circuit Court holds payment to state loan office under sequestration law of 1777 is a valid defense.

Colonel Thomas Mann Randolph, Sr., dies.

1794   Tom Paine imprisoned in France; the Convention abolishes slavery in the French colonies; Genêt removed as chargé d'affaires in U.S.; France demands removal of G. Morris as Minister to France; G. Morris leaves Paris and resumes writing diary.

1795   G. Morris and Adèle de Flahaut reunited at Altona. Tudor Randolph born.

1796   John Randolph visits friend Joseph Bryan in Georgia—arrives in midst of Yazoo land turmoil.

Richard Randolph executes will emancipating all of his slaves (February).

John Marshall and Alexander Campbell argue British Debts case before U.S. Supreme Court in Philadelphia. In *Ware v. Hylton*, Supreme Court rules that under Supremacy Clause of U.S. Constitution, peace treaty with Britain supersedes state law sequestering British debts. (Justice Samuel Chase writes lead opinion.)

On opposite sides in Richmond, John Marshall and Alexander Campbell debate approval of Jay Treaty.

John Randolph ill at Petersburg—sees brother Richard for last time

Richard Randolph dies at Bizarre—Benjamin Latrobe, present at time of his final illness, describes visit in his journal.

Alexander Campbell commits suicide by an overdose of laudanum—death of Campbell causes U.S. Supreme Court to delay hearing in *Hunter v. Fairfax, Devisee.*

Virginia General Assembly rejects Judge St. George Tucker's proposal for the gradual emancipation of slaves.

1797   G. Morris present as Lafayette, newly released from prison, is delivered to American consul at Hamburg.

John Marshall one of three American envoys to France—XYZ affair.

1798   President Adams releases XYZ correspondence; John Marshall returns from France as a national hero.

Alien and Sedition Acts passed; Virginia and Kentucky Resolutions adopted claiming right of states to decide which federal laws can be enforced within their borders.

George Washington persuades John Marshall to run for Congress.

1799   G. Morris returns to Morrisania after decade in Europe.

New York enacts law for gradual emancipation of slaves.

Patrick Henry writes letter endorsing John Marshall for Congress; letter from George Washington urges Patrick Henry to run for Congress or the Virginia General Assembly.

Patrick Henry and John Randolph address the people of Charlotte County on March county court day.

John Randolph and John Marshall win House seats in sixth Congress.

Elected to General Assembly, Patrick Henry dies before taking seat.

Fear of yellow fever causes capital in Philadelphia to be moved temporarily to Trenton, New Jersey.

George Washington dies.

1800   G. Morris appointed U.S. Senator.

Congressman John Randolph opposes petition calling for general emancipation of slaves.

William Thompson ends stay at Bizarre.

Washington becomes new capital of United States.

John Marshall appointed Secretary of State by President Adams.

Callender trial in Richmond; Justice Samuel Chase brings the Sedition law to Virginia; John Marshall attends part of the trial and leaves Richmond in a coach with Justice Chase.

Gabriel slave revolt fails.

Nat Turner and John Brown born.

1801   John Marshall appointed Chief Justice of United States Supreme
        Court.

        House breaks tie vote between Thomas Jefferson and Aaron Burr,
        electing Jefferson as President. John Randolph assumes leadership of
        majority in House of Representatives.

1802   Senator G. Morris unsuccessfully opposes repeal of Judiciary Act of
        1801.

        Problem of pre-revolutionary war debts settled when U.S. agrees to
        a single payment of £600,000. (Money distributed by commission
        which hears claims from 1803–1811.)

        Adèle de Flahaut marries and becomes Madame de Souza.

1803   G. Morris's term in Senate ends; he mentions idea of Erie Canal to
        Simeon De Witt.

        John Marshall's opinion in *Marbury v. Madison* establishes principle
        of judicial review of the constitutionality of federal legislation. (U.S.
        Supreme Court will not overturn another federal statute until Dred
        Scott decision of 1857 invalidates the Missouri Compromise of 1820.)

        Justice Samuel Chase's speech to a Baltimore grand jury causes im-
        peachment proceedings to be initiated against him.

1804   Dr. David Hosack present at Burr-Hamilton duel; G. Morris oration
        at funeral of Alexander Hamilton.

1805   House adopts Yazoo Compromise despite Majority Leader John Ran-
        dolph's bitter opposition.

        Impeachment trial of Samuel Chase in Senate—John Randolph one of
        seven managers for the House; John Marshall testifies for the de-
        fense—Chase acquitted on all eight articles of impeachment.

        Nancy Randolph leaves Bizarre.

        St. George Randolph sent to England.

1806   Virginia law enacted requiring that manumitted slaves leave Virginia
        within one year of emancipation.

        George Wythe dies of poisoning. (The law prohibiting the testimony
        of blacks against whites, incorporated into the revised Virginia laws
        by Thomas Jefferson with the concurrence of Wythe, prevents ad-
        mission of crucial testimony against Wythe's grandnephew, who is
        almost universally believed to be guilty.)

1806   Maria Ward marries Peyton Randolph.

John Randolph denounces Florida negotiations with Talleyrand and openly breaks with the Jeffersonians.

Christmas eve anti-Catholic riot at St. Peter's Church in New York City.

1807   G. Morris, Simeon De Witt, and John Rutherford appointed Commissioners of Streets and Roads for New York City.

Jesse Hawley articles on canals begin to appear in *Genessee Messenger*.

Aaron Burr treason trial before Chief Justice John Marshall; John Randolph foreman of grand jury.

1808   Abolition of African slave trade in United States.

G. Morris visits Nancy Randolph in New York City.

1809   Death of Tom Paine in New York City.

Nancy Randolph brought from Connecticut to be employed at Morrisania as a servant.

200th anniversary of Hudson's discovery of Manhattan.

G. Morris writes John Marshall before marrying—on Christmas day, surprise marriage of G. Morris and Nancy Randolph.

1810   Horsmanden book on New York Conspiracy is again published after sixty-six years.

Canal Commission established—G. Morris President of Canal Commissioners.

New York Legislature purchases Elgin Botanic Garden from Dr. David Hosack.

John Randolph moves from Bizarre to Roanoke—begins to call himself John Randolph of Roanoke.

Opinion of Chief Justice Marshall in *Fletcher v. Peck* upholds Yazoo land sale and overturns rescinding act of Georgia legislature on grounds that the Contract Clause of the U.S. Constitution has been violated.

1811   "Trinity Church Riot" trial—David Ogden one of counsel for defendants.

1811   Plan of New York Street Commissioners published.

First Erie Canal report recommends use of inclined plane.

John Randolph canes Willis Alston and is almost in duel with John W. Eppes.

1812   G. Morris and wife return from unsuccessful trip to Washington to obtain federal funding of Erie Canal.

New York Legislature authorizes borrowing five million dollars for construction of Erie Canal.

United States declares war on Great Britain.

American army under command of New York militia Major General Stephen Van Rensselaer is defeated at Queenston; militia refuses to cross Niagara River.

G. Morris delivers speech at New-York Historical Society.

1813   New York Common Council decides that John Randel's street survey is a public record and that William Bridges can be given exclusive rights.

Ann Cary Morris gives birth to Gouverneur Morris, Jr.

Armistice in Europe following Battle of Bautzen ends; Austria joins coalition against France; Battle of Leipsic ("The Battle of Nations"); Elster Bridge blows up.

Bizarre destroyed by fire.

John Randolph loses congressional election to John W. Eppes.

1814   Fall of Paris—abdication of Napoleon.

William Bridges–John Randel war of letters in New York newspaper.

New York Legislature repeals authorization to borrow five million dollars for Erie Canal.

G. Morris delivers speech celebrating Napoleon's downfall; anti-Federalist riot outside Washington Hall in New York City.

Death of William Bridges.

Yazoo compromise approved while John Randolph not a member of Congress.

Madness of St. George Randolph.

1814   Tudor Randolph ill at Morrisania.

Washington burned by British.

Benjamin Latrobe, living in Pittsburgh, is fired as agent of Robert Fulton's Ohio Steamboat Company.

British suffer triple defeat at Baltimore, Plattsburg, and Fort Erie.

Judith Randolph arrives at Morrisania. After fall down stairs at Port Conway, John Randolph arrives in New York City and writes accusatory letter (pp. 196–200) to Mrs. Morris, sending it to G. Morris.

Hartford Convention begins to meet.

1815   Ann C. Morris replies to John Randolph letter.

War of 1812 ends.

John Randolph regains seat in House of Representatives.

Napoleon escapes from Elba, decrees abolition of slave trade; Battle of Waterloo; Charles de Flahaut assists Emperor's departure from the battlefield.

Tudor Randolph dies in Cheltenham, England.

1816   Judith Randolph dies.

G. Morris does not participate in report of the Canal Commissioners—by statutory change, he is no longer a Commissioner.

The year without a summer.

G. Morris's inaugural speech as President of the New-York Historical Society.

G. Morris writes last will—dies eleven days later.

The American Colonization Society is formed to promote the colonization of free blacks in Africa.

1817   New York Legislature enacts law abolishing slavery in the state effective July 1, 1827.

Law passes to build Erie Canal—ground broken.

John Randel completes the placing of monuments for the streets and avenues of New York City.

Mrs. Morris commences litigation against David Ogden.

1819 First will by John Randolph.

Alabama becomes state (Mississippi in 1817); completes admission of the Yazoo lands into the Union.

1820 Dr. David Hosack becomes President of New-York Historical Society.

Benjamin Latrobe dies of yellow fever in New Orleans.

Governor of Virginia, Thomas Mann Randolph, proposes emancipation and deportation of slaves.

John Randolph opposes Missouri Compromise.

1821 Second John Randolph will.

1822 Yellow fever epidemic in New York City.

Denmark Vesey slave conspiracy fails in South Carolina.

1823 Sir Henry, champion of the North, defeats Eclipse, champion from the South, in horse race on Long Island; John Randolph present.

1824 Lafayette visits New York City and New-York Historical Society.

1825 Lafayette leaves United States for last time.

Celebration of completion of Erie Canal.

John Randel removed as contractor for Chesapeake and Delaware Canal as a result of earlier dispute with Judge Wright over Erie Canal.

1826 Thomas Jefferson and John Adams both die on the Fourth of July, the 50th anniversary of the signing of the Declaration of Independence.

John Randolph duel with Henry Clay.

Maria Ward dies.

1827 All slaves emancipated in New York pursuant to 1817 legislation.

St. George Tucker dies.

Publication of Walter Scott biography of Napoleon.

1829 John Randolph makes final payment on British debts.

1830 John Randolph mission to Russia accompanied by John Randolph Clay and slaves John, Juba, and Eboe.

1831 Jared Sparks, through Dr. David Hosack, receives G. Morris's diaries and letters from Mrs. Morris.

William Lloyd Garrison begins publication of the *Liberator*.

Nat Turner slave revolt in Virginia.

1832 Virginia debates on abolition of slavery lead to laws more tightly controlling slaves.

John Randolph's last will provides for sale, instead of emancipation, of slaves.

Nullification crisis begins in South Carolina; Beverley Tucker returns to Virginia to assist John Randolph.

1833 John Randolph and Beverley Tucker succeed in obtaining Charlotte Court House resolutions stating right of secession.

Nullification crisis resolved by Clay compromise tariff legislation.

John Randolph dies in Philadelphia hotel—on deathbed attempts oral manumission of John White and other slaves before several witnesses, including Dr. Joseph Parrish.

British Parliament liberates slaves in West Indies one month after death of William Wilberforce.

1834 Randolph will litigation begins.

Simeon De Witt dies.

1835 John Marshall, David Hosack, and Mary Harrison die.

1836 Beverley Tucker publishes *The Partisan Leader*.

Madame de Souza (Adèle de Flahaut) and Creed Taylor die.

1837 Ann Cary Morris dies.

1838 Talleyrand dies.

1839 Stephen Van Rensselaer and Randolph Harrison die.

1841　St. Ann's Church consecrated—Ann Cary Morris buried inside.

1842　Gouverneur Morris (son of Ann Cary Morris) marries first cousin Patsey Jefferson Cary.

1845　John Randolph will litigation ends—slaves to be freed under 1821 will.

1846　John Randolph's slaves emancipated—driven out of Mercer County, Ohio, by angry mob of whites. William Leigh arranges for sale of Mercer County lands.

1848　Last bottle of G. Morris's Tokay wine (wedding gift from Marie Louise to Marie Antoinette, purchased by Morris during French Revolution) is opened at a Morris family marriage.

　　　Henry St. George Tucker dies.

1849　David Ogden dies.

1851　Virginia Constitution prohibits the freeing of slaves.

　　　Nathaniel Beverley Tucker dies.

1859(?)　St. George Randolph dies.

1870　Charles de Flahaut dies on the morning of the Battle of Sedan, the beginning of the end of the last Bonaparte empire.

1879　Remains of John Randolph removed to Hollywood Cemetery in Richmond.

1891　John H. B. Latrobe, son of Benjamin Latrobe, dies in 38th year as President of American Colonization Society.

1900　Walter Reed made chairman of commission to investigate the causes of yellow fever. (Concludes it is transmitted by mosquitoes.)

1917　Supreme Court of Ohio holds in favor of white residents of Mercer County in lawsuit filed by the descendants of the emancipated slaves of John Randolph.

About the Author

Robert S. Bloom is the Deputy Administrative Assistant to the Supreme Judicial Court of Massachusetts. He has written numerous legal articles, legislation, and court rules. He is also a founder and supervisor of the first state court department for the preservation of historical court records in the U.S.

Robert S. Bloom lives in Newton, Massachusetts.